THE MAJOR BESTSELLING NOVEL BY SUSAN FROMBERG SCHAEFFER

The story of a woman's life-long odyssey of survival across the map of a shattered world.

"ANYA IS NOT ONLY FIRST RATE BUT OF THE FIRST RANK . . . Schaeffer's art has created a work which, like other great novels of our time, is about itself and its audience. ANYA, strong and beautiful, is an achievement of power and importance." *The New Republic*

"SCHAEFFER IS A DAZZLING WRITER . . . Her vacation spas and country houses are full of the rich smells of kitchens and gardens, the colors of wallpaper and flowers, the gleam of sun and silver. And then, suddenly, the colors dissolve, the smells rot, and every touch is painful and threatening . . . Susan Fromberg Schaeffer's kind of knowledge is rarely dared; when it is, it is rarely explored with anything like the necessary courage. This is a book as dense and vivid with human pain as anything I can remember." *Chicago Tribune*

(continued)

Anya

A Novel

SUSAN FROMBERG SCHAEFFER

AVON
PUBLISHERS OF BARD, CAMELOT, DISCUS, EQUINOX AND FLARE BOOKS

For Neil

Cover photo, detail of a photograph by Arnold Genthe, from the collection of Lida Moser.

"A Refusal to Mourn the Death by Fire of a Child in London" from THE POEMS OF DYLAN THOMAS. Copyright 1945 by The Trustees for the Copyrights of Dylan Thomas. Reprinted by permission of New Directions Publishing Corporation.

AVON BOOKS
A division of
The Hearst Corporation
959 Eighth Avenue
New York, New York 10019

First Avon Printing, January, 1976
Third Printing

Printed in the U.S.A.

CONTENTS

PROLOGUE

A man's dying is more the survivors' affair than his own.

Thomas Mann in *The Magic Mountain.*

THEY are two lights. My mother and father. Very often I dream about them. I dream about them all the time. And when I dream about them, I am completely happy, completely happy. I never dream about my sister. Verushka. You know, it is so hard to get people here to say her name properly: Verushka. I think I must be saying it in the back of my mind all of the time. The way people here say it, it sounds like "where is she?" And of course I wonder about that, too. I've told them, when I used to talk, say "Fairushka," and spend a long time on the *fair;* then you'll have something like it. But it isn't quite true; I do dream about her sometimes. She adored me so, and I loved her. But I didn't adore her. No. Sometimes I still feel guilty about that. I can remember only one dream in which Verushka came to me. She was so young when she died. I think she was pregnant. She knocked on my door and I said "Come in." It was all so ordinary. I was still in bed with a medical textbook propped up on my stomach. "Well, Anya," she asked, "how do I look?" She was holding a little white dog against her stomach. I didn't know why; I was afraid to answer. My parents never trusted her the way they trusted me. Suspicious, I was suspicious. She was up to something. It was a nice dog; I said so. Then she lowered it and put it under her shawl; it was right over her womb. "How do you like me like this?" she asked. She was smiling, but I think she was afraid. "All right, it's normal." "Is it all right, Anya?" she asked me. "Of course," I answered and she smiled, and turned away. Then I woke up. The little dog, the little dog. Verushka, my sister.

I am not a religious woman, no. How could I be, with a father a vegetarian and an atheist? But I am traditional in my own way. My family did not observe, but I light the candles, I always light the candles. My parents lit them, too. They said it gave a feeling. And I believe in Yom

3

Kippur. Then I think of everyone lighting the candles, the *yahrzeit* lights. I think how it must look from above. I think this is how heaven must look, and I think two of those lights are my Momma and Poppa. My dreams about them are not interesting, not interesting at all. They are always the same. Momma comes in. She wants to know how I am; have I been getting enough sleep, do I eat? She never forgot the time I was so sick in Warsaw and didn't tell her until later. I didn't want to worry her. Sometimes she comes with Poppa. They always ask the same thing: how am I, am I all right? When she is with my poppa, the dream is short. They ask how I am, then they move back into the room; they reach the door; they want me to come with them. They beckon to me; they smile. And always, always, when I try to follow them, I wake up. I can't follow them, and in the dream, I want to, so much. But they don't stay in the doorway too long. They go so fast, it's as if they don't want me to follow. I wake up crying, but then all day, I am happy. I am never so happy as when I dream about my parents.

It's different when I dream about Stajoe. When I dream about him the whole day is spoiled, ruined. And always, the same dreams. He wants to know where I've been, what I've been doing. He was a jealous man, very jealous. Usually, he asks me these questions and goes. But last night he came beautifully dressed. And he talked to me for a long time. He told me he had come to take me with him; he said I was his. I felt my wedding ring tighten on my finger like a snake. He had on his leather gloves, his best coat; he always had the best tailors. His hat. Always so elegant, so elegant. And he spoke to me in his way, calm and intelligent. He was very positive. "I came to take you," he said. "It is enough. He has had you all this time. You are my wife." I didn't answer. He went on, persuading me, as if I were a child who just needed to be reminded. "You remember the wedding," he coaxed, "the storm, the Café Europa? You know you never forgot." He smiled at me. Such a handsome man. Finally, I came to myself. "Stajoe," I told him (he was like a judge), "I lived with you only two years, and with Max for more than twenty-five; that is more than a quarter of a century, a very long time. How can you expect me to leave? You are strange to me. I love Max now. I can't say I always did, but I do now. Here in this country, any nice-looking woman would be happy to marry you. And your diplomas

4

would be good here, too." He was not interested. He was always a ladies' man, and he was not interested. "Listen, Anya," he urged, "I brought a lot of money with me; your life will be luxurious. It will make up for the past." Then I saw there was a long closet in back of him. "Yes, yes," he insisted, "money, it's full of money. And our rings, I found our rings. And your mother's big diamond ring you sold for the pig's head when Ninka was sick. I have that, too. Come with me; I am waiting for you." "But," I said, raising my voice (back in the old days I always spoke so softly, not the screaming hag I am now), "I am not the same. I don't want this; I don't want any money. The ring is gone. Ninushka is growing up. She's seen your pictures. She knows you are her father. You would only confuse her." Then he changed. He was wearing high tight leather boots, laborer's boots, and a worker's short jacket and a worker's cap that shaded part of one eye. "But I want only you," he insisted again. He was going to stay there, repeating that one sentence for the rest of my life. I was terrified.

I have all the bad dreams everyone has who went through it: the ghetto, the labor camp, the flight to America. There is a tremendous room, and people keep coming in and coming in; they are preparing themselves for war. It is obvious in what they do. Somehow, I have sneaked outside. I see another big group of men going into the room in German uniforms, and they begin fighting with the others. Then they are all screaming and yelling terribly. During the fight, music was playing, German songs, very loud, and suddenly, I saw the people were naked and streaked and smeared with blood. "Where are their clothes?" I thought to myself, and I came out from my corner where I was hidden, and start to help with the dead, putting them on the rough shelves like merchandise. On some of the shelves, we stack them like logs for a stove, one row this way, the next row at right angles to the first. At first, I cannot tell who the bodies are. Then I recognize many of them: One was my dead brother, but then it wasn't my dead brother, but my sister, and the music was so loud; that was why I was confused. It was a German melody, and when I woke up I could still hear it. I woke up trembling and sweating. But I have learned to look at the window in the bedroom, and as soon as I see it is empty and gray, or empty and blue, then I know it is a dream, and everything is all right. It is over, and the day begins like any day.

But it is not the same when I dream about Stajoe. Finally, I had to tell him to stop talking. "I am sorry," I scolded him. "If you had the smallest feeling for me, you would never bother me like this. Never. Never." I woke up screaming that word. When I woke up, the whole cushion was wet, and the day was spoiled, and I had one of those headaches.

The doctors say they come from an injury to the head. A woman in the camp hit me in the head when I was in the *appel*, the lineup. I was not standing up straight enough. They say the blow injured a nerve. And whenever I dream about Stajoe, I have one of those headaches; they are like nails being driven into the plates of the skull. I do not want to dream about him. There are times I think I would rather be shot. Tell me, do the dead hate the living so? I can understand it. I can understand coming back and watching and being just as you always were, and talking, and no one answering, and touching someone, and they do not feel. Such loneliness! Sometimes I think the dead must be very lonely. Terribly lonely. How could I ever be so lonely? And I am very lonely. Terribly lonely. How could I ever be so lonely? And I am very lonely. Let me tell you; I had a vision one day. It wasn't a dream. I know the difference between a dream and a vision. There was a dark room, and everyone was crying. I said to myself, "It's lonely to lie in this box not having my parents near me. What are everyone's tears to me? The only real tears are the parents'."

In the old country the family carried the coffin, the fathers and brothers, all the way to the cemetery. My mother and father were not there. And I kept crying that I didn't want to be buried this way. Where was my mother? Where was my father? No one. No one. So it would mean I could not be buried. I couldn't help it; I started telling Max, "Listen, Max, you have to be very careful. Not everyone is so good. Today money, only money; it's all anyone cares about. Promise me you'll be careful; the next one shouldn't waste everything we worked for. Believe me, we worked hard, and you need someone to take care of you." But of course no one listened to me; I was already dead. How could anyone listen? So I started running around the room. I wanted my

6

mother and father. And when I couldn't find them, I was so drained of everything, I felt like a thin pane of glass

I was with my Momma to the last. To tell the truth, I dream of her more often. My father was a saint, but my mother was human; she had her faults. And I was with her to the end. "Max," I said, "I want to be buried near my mother, near Momma, please, near Momma." But I don't even know where her grave is. You don't know how terrible that is, not even to have her grave. If I had it, I could pretend she was there; she *would* be there. So, there was no one to bury me, no one to lie down next to. I told Max not to try carrying the coffin himself—to be careful of his bad back. You see, even when I was dead I was a busy body. So I sat down next to him on the wooden bench, and I was so lonely I knew this was the worst thing. So many nice people. That was the terrible thing. So many nice people killed, no trace. No trace at all. As if they were less than leaves. Then the loneliness fell over me and covered my face like a sheet and I was too tired to pick it up, so I let it lie there.

IN HISTORY

※

May you live in interesting times.

Chinese Curse

1

My name is Anya Savikin, and I am going to take you into the apartment of my parents, the apartment where I was born, and where I lived until I was married, in Vilno, Poland. I want to be sure that you can see this apartment, that you can picture it so clearly you feel you are walking through it, because it is very far away in time, and it is so easy to think that you know what something looks like, what something was like, and really have no idea at all. This is even true for the people who lived in the apartment and its rooms, so it is much more difficult for people who have never been in the rooms at all. I want you to go through this apartment so you have a memory of it: my memory. My memory of it is almost twenty-five years old, and undoubtedly I have done some retouching, have repainted some of the walls and plastered some of the cracks, but memory is a form of reality after all. So I do not want to give you a photograph at which you can look and say, "Oh yes, this is what it looked like," and really have no idea at all. If you are going to learn a person's life, then, like learning a language, you must start with the little things, the little pictures, the tiny, square images, like rooms, that will grow into a film, but not like any film, one you have been in as an extra. You will have the feel of the polished wood table on your fingertips; you will have the smells of the kitchen in your nostrils. This is my ambition. Perhaps it is too much to ask.

This, then, is my home in Vilno. It is on a very quiet street, a very wide street, and it is lined on both sides by very elegant buildings. Ours is the highest, on the north side of the street, and it is five stories tall. We live on the first floor, but because the street is so high and runs over the crest of a hill, it is always very light in the apartment. On both sides of the street are oak trees; our house is on the left side, and on both sides are oak trees. In winter, they throw gigantic shadows, and cover the buildings with jagged lines like Egyptian letters, undeciphered. In the summer, they shadow the buildings with black lace and gray lace, though at times the sun is so intense the shadows themselves appear to be deep green. The sides of the streets, the sidewalks, are paved with asphalt, but in the center, the streets are made up of round heavy stones which are simply driven into the dirt beneath. Centuries of horses and *drozhkas,* horse carts, have smoothed them out slightly and driven them down farther, but not much. When the men come home for dinner, which takes place at two in the afternoon, leaving their banks, and their stocking factories, and their meat markets, and their furniture stores, the street comes alive as a tinsmith's; metal wheel after metal wheel on the stones, and hoof after hoof. By two-thirty, the street is completely silent. Not even a child can be seen playing. Everyone is inside eating his dinner. Then, at four, the men return in their carriages, and the clacking, the clip-clip-clop-clopping, begins again. Again there are the sounds of children, louder in the afternoon than in the morning; they are racing against the sun, they have just been called in from play to dinner and this is the last time they will go out for the day. So their voices sound louder and louder, and eventually, as the sun sets, the voices of birds, who always sing loudest at sunset, even if they have not sung all day, join them and it is a kind of concert.

Every day, at five o'clock, or four, depending on when she finishes her work, a Mrs. Bialy from the neighborhood, whose husband is paralyzed, appears in the courtyard of our building with a huge Russian basket filled with pretzels, and small cakes covered with poppy seeds, and bagels, and hot rolls with baked onions sprinkled on top. If the day has been very long for the children, my mother, and the mothers of the others, will send out the maid with a huge tray of chocolate milk. The chocolate milk is in a big pot, and the cups are tin cups. We are not too careful when we are playing. The children will eat as much as they want of the rolls and the cakes; Mrs. Bialy will be paid by the maids, and so she will earn her living, and the children will go on playing until they are called in for supper, which is not a very big meal. They will add to their cakes and their rolls a piece of pickled fish, some knockwurst, some eggs, some lox, nothing much. If it is still light, they may go out again, but not out of the court, or if they are still older, not further than they can be seen from the apartment windows. If they are in school, they may not go out at all, but up to their rooms to prepare their lessons. It is a very regular street, and the people on it live neat, regular lives. On the whole, they live neat, regular lives. But the lives of all the children are absolutely in order.

Our building was planned and built by my Uncle Pavel, my father's brother. It is made of brick, painted white, almost yellowish. He built it for the first private gymnasium for Jewish boys in Poland. At the time, Jewish boys had a very difficult time getting admitted to a gymnasium and the school naturally did very well. Boys came to it, not only from Poland, but also from Russia, which is where both of my parents, and each of their families, were born. The school was admired throughout the city because it was what was then called very "forward-looking." Its discipline was very great, and the students tended to rebel. Uncle Pavel, however, was innovative, and blamed himself for problems; he generally succeeded in solving them by giving students even harder assignments than they were required to do at the time their nonsense began. This technique would first stupefy the offender, and then induce in him a white-hot dedication to his project, so that the parents of the poor creature slaving away in his school uniform which he felt he had no time to remove considered Uncle Pavel something of a miracle worker. I believe his main weapon was shame.

Unfortunately, Uncle Pavel had his own ideas of miracles, and when he saw what was beginning in Russia he wanted to take part himself, somehow to help reorder the country, and so he returned. Just as he had bought and built the gymnasium in a fit of fever which had burned for fifteen years, so he dropped it and left for Russia with the same suddenness. My father heard from him occasionally, but although his handwriting was magnificent, he did not often make use of it, and then he was not heard from at all. I was not yet alive when my parents heard that Pavel had been shot by the Communists. My aunt remembered only a day when they were all sitting on the couch, a white couch, in the dining room, and there was a letter lying at their feet like a shot bird, and they were both crying. "It's Pavel, dear," my mother said, and she explained to my aunt. Evidently, no one was surprised.

But meanwhile, here was this huge building with an acre in back of it, entirely unoccupied. The government stepped in, prepared to turn it into an apartment house, the rent going to the government, since naturally Pavel had left no will. But my father had a certificate and some papers proving he was Pavel's brother, and also a diamond brooch he had brought with him from Bialistock, and so he was given the apartment on the first floor; nor did he have to pay rent. "Frankly, more than I expected," my mother said when he told her. And this is the apartment we lived in until I got marrried.

It is in a very long building, almost a block long, and it is built in the shape of a square U. In the center of the U in a huge cement court and in the court is a tiny building where all the wash for the tenants is done by the various maids. The little wash building is very small and made of bricks, which are almost entirely covered by ivy and grass. Inside is a huge stove to heat it, because the winters in Vilno are bitter, and from September on, everyone is prepared for winter and the days of thirty degrees below zero, and sometimes forty. There are giant pots inside this building, not tubs, but huge tin pots for the wash, and the water is heated for the laundry on the stove. Then the maids scrub the clothes on corrugated boards, also giant-sized and tin, and when they are through, take the clothes up to the attics to dry. They argue endlessly over who is doing the best job as they push their damp hair back from their wet foreheads with the backs of their hands. Here they scrub and talk, and talk and scrub, so that there is nothing going on in any of the families in the same court that cannot be discovered by speaking to one of the maids. A very loyal maid will know when to keep quiet, but she will have to be clever and invent stories or she will be expelled from the society of the washers. So the maids have many responsibilities to look after, too. And the children do not make their jobs any easier, because occasionally, when they are lonely (their parents are on holiday, or visiting, or their best friends are sick with a fever) they will steal in with the maids and sit under the work table listening. And the maids have to teach them never to contradict the stories they tell, and soon the children learn to sit under the work tables, absolutely silent. Our maid, Anzia, once carrried my small brother in with the laundry, not knowing he was there at all until she got to the bottom of the basket, and then he got a good beating, because she said he could have been smothered, and she would have been to blame.

14

In back of this court is the garden, the old gym grounds, almost an acre long. Here, flowers grow in the summer and every kind of vegetable and fruit tree: radishes and cabbages, and cauliflowers and cucumbers, and date trees, and in a corner, a beehive. There is one man who is hired by the court to take care of this garden, and this is all he does. The children are allowed to play in it, but only if they keep away from the vegetables and the flowers, and they have no dogs or cats to cause havoc in the garden, because the building does not permit the keeping of pets.

2

Now we are going to enter my parents' apartment. Like all the apartments in our building, it runs the length of the *U* it occupies. First, we go through a wrought-iron gate, and down two steps, and then we are facing the front entrance. The front doors are made of solid oak and are elaborately carved with leaves and animals. In the center of each door is a huge circle carved to look like braid, and in the center of the circle, an enormous ram's head, and each ram's head has twisted curving horns which almost reach its pointed chin; the horns look like shofars. Anzia, the maid, polishes these doors, and the brass knockers on each of them, every day. When the doors open, we go up two steps and then we are in the foyer, then in the long long hall. My parents' apartment has eight huge rooms, and straight ahead of the end of the corridor is my room, mine. It looks out over the garden, or that part of the garden you can see from any one place, the garden was so enormous.

The first room on the left side of the corridor is the kitchen; then comes the first dining room, and then the second. And on the opposite side of the corridor were the three bedrooms: the first, nearest mine, my sister's, Verushka's; the second, the bedroom of my two brothers, Emmanuel and Mischa; and the third, the bedroom of my parents. Emmanuel was the oldest; I was three years younger; Vera was three years younger than I was, and Mischa was the baby; he was ten years younger than I was. So between Emmanuel and Mischa were thirteen years, and we must have thought of him as a toy, almost a doll; he was terribly spoiled. None of us knew what to do for him first. My father used to laugh and say Mischa had seven parents, the three other children, the two of them, and the two maids, Zoshia and Anzia. Momma worried that Mischa would never learn to walk. "Pass the baby," Vera would say to Emmanuel, and he would be handed over. My brothers shared a room and the idea that it was silly to talk with girls; they left us pretty much alone, though if anyone had troubles, Vera would creep in and try to find out what was wrong, "and make it better." I worshiped Emmanuel and saw him at meals, but hardly spoke to him; I played with Mischa; he was too small to talk to.

All the floors of the rooms, except mine and my sister's, were made of the most beautiful parquet, but the floor of the hall was entirely carpeted with a deep red rug, because above all, my mother valued comfort, coziness, and so it was. When we came in from playing in the thirty degrees below zero weather, it was as if there was a fire already lit on the floor; it was like walking on warm coals which did not burn, but only heated.

Every day, Zoshia had to scrub the parquet. First she would get down on her knees and scrub the wood with a very fine steel wool; then she would take two brushes. They attached to her feet with leather straps, and she would dance back and forth over the floors until they were gleaming like gold. Little Mischa used to go dancing down the hall after her, and Zoshia, who was his special favorite, would take two huge pillows and tie them around him, one in front, one in back, and then tie newspapers around his feet with a rough cord, telling him they were brushes, and off he would go after her down the length of the hall, falling down, getting up, and then into each of the bedrooms, where she would fold back the rugs, and they would dance their way through the house. If one of us came out and tried joining the dancing in the hall, if I was tired of my lessons, if Vera was tired of her piano, Mischa would start screaming and try to push us away; this was his dance and Zoshia was his partner. On weekends, my father used to stand in the entrance to his study and watch, smile, and shake his head. I was teaching Zoshia how to read. She was a peasant girl who worked for us all year, and she had worked for us since she was eight; once a year her father would come to the house and my mother would pay him her wages for the year. Once a year we would hear him in the kitchen, loudly telling my mother how lucky his daughter was, how other employers were not good to their girls, but what astounded him most was that his daughter could read. She would write him a little list of things she needed from the country: eggs, a chicken, a goose, and of course, he could not read a word, and naturally, he was struck dumb with delight. When he got back to the village he would take it to every hut. I taught Zoshia fairy tales; I would read them to her and then point at each word and gradually, she learned. She was very quick. As soon as she learned one, she would go in to Mischa, or out she would go with Mischa, and read the fairy tale to him, "The Monkey with the Glasses," "The Man and the Bear," and come back to report how much he loved them, when the truth was, she loved them herself.

So the apartment floors gleamed like gold, and there were fairy tales in the cracks between the parquet.

Now I am taking out my room, and the rooms of my family, from where they have been stored in an old filthy trunk for fifty years, where they have lived inside one of those glass globes that turn upside down and set snow swirling over the scene, where this part of my past has been a country in a clear glass globe in which my mind has kept the snow swirling. Now it is settling, and now I am opening the door to my room, and I am going in. Straight ahead is the window, an enormous window, which goes from the ceiling to the floor, because these windows were originally intended for schoolrooms. Even then I was a great lover of color, brilliance, warmth, and the two main colors in my room were red and blue. My floor, which was only a cold gray concrete, was covered with a red and blue rug, not a patterned rug, but a rug made of red and blue threads. It was a very long, narrow room, only slightly wider than the corridor that led to it. The window had a small glass shelf built across it because I always loved plants; from the time I was old enough to go out with a spoon I had my own corner of the garden. How my father and mother used to laugh at my efforts! "She raises mud," my mother said laughing, and then Anzia said something, and then my father said something, and then they were *all* hysterical and *I* was very proud of myself, to be causing all this commotion.

And on the windows were curtains, in two layers. The bottom curtains were made of white tulle, and crisscrossed, tied with a ruffle made of the same material, and hanging on each side of the window was a panel of brightly colored cotton covered with tiny flowers. Then, on one side of the room was a bed, not an ordinary bed, but specially built. The bottom was a large box with a lid and the mattress rested on top, so when the mattress was lifted, there was space for storage and space for hiding

18

things from Mischa, or private things not yet ready for the glare of the family, dreams, glimpses of the future, veils, like undeveloped negatives. The dust ruffle was made of the same material as the curtains, and the pillows too were covered with it. They were huge down pillows, each as wide as the bed, and there were hundreds of little pillows, each in different materials, on the side of the wall, and they were all trimmed with ruffles. In the mornings, after the wash, Anzia came in with her curling iron, and crimped the curl back into the ruffles of the big white pillows, so it was all very feminine. Next to the bed was a little beige rug embroidered with red flowers. Comfort, always comfort; the feet should not be cold, although underneath the little rug with its hooked design of a troika in a circle of flowers, there was already a heavy rug covering every inch of the floor.

On the other side of the room was a little desk, and books all over it, and on the desk near the door a wide étagère filled with more books. Over the desk and over the whole length of the walll were pictures, all in the same gold frames; one was my diploma; there were pictures of composers, Beethoven and Mozart, and two pictures my father bought for me because he loved the writers so much: Baron and Lermontov. And in front of the windows, which shone on sunny days like great uncut diamonds, was a little table made of wicker, a little round table that I had bought myself, and on each side two big wicker armchairs, everything upholstered in the same material as the flowered curtains. The wicker set also had two little benches, and they sat on each side of the desk. There was no wicker anywhere else in the house; I bought this myself with money I saved from giving French lessons.

We had a governess to teach us French when we were young. She was a very funny woman; she always carried an enormous bag, and everything you wanted you could find in it: half an apple, a pair of scissors, a book of stories, a needle and thread; if you could name it, it was there. And one song she used to play over and over on the piano: "Give me a husband, a husband, give me a husband, a husband, a husband"; oh, she was so funny. But she was also very practical and she decided since I was so good at French, and I was so thin (I was only ten) I should give French lessons to the smallest child of a family she visited because the man had a store that served sodas, and I could have all the sodas I wanted. So I went. Even then I was very ambitious, maybe too ambitious, I don't know. So this was how I saved up for the wicker furniture, with the twenty zlotys a month for the lessons (but of course the main thing was the sodas), and when the set arrived my parents were so surprised. "Oh, I am on my own now," I told them, and they laughed and laughed. So that was my room. It was very cozy. The walls and the ceilings were painted blue, and when I went to bed at night I felt as if I were wrapped in the sky; it was my blanket and I fell asleep in it like a star.

Then came the next bedroom, the first on the side of the hall near my room, that of my sister, Vera, Verushka. It was not like mine at all, not at all. Verushka was very musical. We had an old gentleman come to the house; once he had been a distinguished pianist. Even with arthritis, he still played like the angels. He gave us both lessons at once, and after a year, he used to clap his hands over his ears when I played. Finally he called my father in; this was too serious to discuss with my mother. "As my name is Professor Bunet," he said, "she has no talent, no talent at all. It is a crime to be throwing out this money, and I," he said, drawing himself up to his full height, "I cannot stand it." My father bowed. "But this one," he pointed to Vera, "*she* has a talent; she is a genius. I will give lessons only to her." He stood still, waiting for the thunderclap, but inflexible. "Anyu?" said my father, looking at me. "Oh, fine," I said. And it was. I was really terrible, a horror, and it was only Vera's good nature that kept her from putting cotton in her ears after she saw me looking at them the first time she tried it. She would not hurt anyone, my sister, Vera, but my playing was killing her.

So most of Vera's room was taken up by the grand piano, and sheet music, millions of sheets, *all over*, all over. She had the same kind of bed I did, but she slept on the composers, the stories of their lives, their pictures; she didn't have enough space on her walls to take care of them. To the side of the grand piano was a huge window, but Vera did not like curtains; when she was playing and looked up, she liked to see out. And she had a huge shelf of books built into the wall on both sides of the bed. My mother used to come into Vera's room before Anzia got there and shake her head. "Vera," she said, "you are going to sink into the basement; Vera, I can see it now. You had better dress yourself warmly." The basement was very cold and ran the whole length of the apartment, and was, thanks to Uncle Pavel, for our use only. Vera's room was painted a light cream color and she had a green carpet. No, she was not like me at all. So romantic, so romantic! She lived in this world as if it were a book. If she wasn't home by dark, my parents were pacing up and down in front of the windows, looking. They did not trust her at all. She was always in love. Eight hours a day she played the piano, and while she played she dreamed, and when she stopped, she dreamed again; she was much more closed in than I was. Emmanuel was more like her. He would make an exception for her and take her out of the category of younger sisters, the afflictions, and they would talk, but none of us ever knew what they talked about. We would hear his door opening, his feet, her door closing, her door opening, her feet, his door closing.

I would come back from a date and tell my parents everything. Vera, nothing. She had a will beneath the dreaming, but they did not trust what it would make her do because they did not trust her head, her judgment. And of course it turned out they were right.

No, we were not like each other. We did not even look alike. Vera was very tiny, not even five feet; I was not so tall, five foot one, but she was like a tiny porcelain statue, skin like china, pure white, clear green eyes, and long black hair that fell below the piano bench when she practiced. And such tiny hands; it was hard for her to take the octave. She was so much more generous than I was. She would give away whatever she had. Sometimes she would get a present, a sweater, a necklace, and she would jump up and cry, "Oh, this is for Anya; she is blond; it would look so much better on her," and I would take it, I would actually take it. I was not so generous with my own things. She did not mind Mischa, either. She would let him pull her hair; she would let him sit on her lap and bang on the piano, and then my dear father would come in and say, "Please, Verushka, stop, the piano tuner will be living here tomorrow." But she did not care; Mischa was happy.

But I was another story. I was terrible, terrible. One day, I came into my bedroom, and Mischa had gotten one of the big down pillows out of its fabric cover and was lying on it. A child never looked so happy. But I, I was horrified. He lay down and slept there. I was so crazy about my skin, my beautiful skin, absolutely crazy, such a small child, there was no harm he could do, he was only six, but I was afraid: germs, dirt. I woke him up and took the pillow and put on a new cover, and after that my mother used to tell everyone about the cover and the pillow to show how terrible I was. No, I was not a child; I was sixteen. And Vera was shy, very shy and retiring.

When my father came to Poland from Russia, he brought with him a whole mattress of Karinsky money; it turned out to be absolutely useless, but he also had brought a huge pin in the shape of a gigantic star; it was made up of enormous diamonds and rubies, blue diamonds. No one would ever see anything like this anymore; it was worth a fortune. So he sold it, and with the money he and a partner bought a stocking factory, and immediately they were doing very well. They made wool stockings, and then the men in the factory soaked them and pressed them on forms where they were dried and blocked; they were of excellent quality. But my father was not really meant for business; he was a scholar, the son of a rabbi. He spent most of his time in his study, reading and translating and reading. This was the one thing that made my mother angry. She had to get up in the middle of the night, wake my father up and lead him back to bed. She was always worried that he would not get enough sleep, he would make himself sick; so she kept after him.

But she was worrying in the wrong direction. While my father had his eyes on his books, his partner had his eyes on the ledgers of the business. So when he saw my father coming in later and later and not really interested in the business, he got bold; and sure enough, everything he gave my father to sign, Poppa signed, and the next thing we knew, he had completely cheated my father, and run off to Brazil where he was never found, and the business was ruined. But no one seemed worried; my father went off one day and came back as the treasurer of a bank. At night, he worked at home as a correspondent for the bank; that way he made extra money, translating letters that came in to the bank from all the countries. He was a very educated man; he knew twelve languages. But one day the government sent someone, like an official from the Internal Revenue Service, to take an inventory of the house. The official went from room to room, very important, writing down everything valuable; if we didn't have the money to pay the business expenses, the bankruptcy, he would take these things away.

When he got to my sister's room, he wrote down, "one

piano," then crossed it out and wrote down "one baby grand piano," and then, when he got back to the *chornoi stolova*, the black dining room, where my mother and father and Verushka and I were sitting on the couch, he read the list. When he got to my sister's piano, it was too much for me. My sister without her piano. "Listen," I cried, jumping up, "we do not have to listen to you. Who are you? There are others higher than you, you know; you better watch out." And there he was, poor thing, cataracts on both eyes, a hunch-back, one arm crippled, and he was sitting in a chair. All of a sudden he turned bright purple and started stamping his feet up and down on the floor, almost as if *he* were pedaling the piano, and began screaming. "You keep that little girl quiet! That little girl shouldn't mix in!" My mother didn't say anything, my father didn't say anything, Verushka was sitting there with her eyes like empty plates, and I was standing in the middle of the room shouting, "There are other authorities, you know; who do you think you are. I suppose you want to carry the piano out now; go ahead, let's see you try it. Oh, you'll be sorry about this piano yet; go ahead, let me tell you, you'll be sorry if you take it or not." Then he jumped out of his chair, still purple, his eyes absolutely bulging out of his head like a frog's, and looked as if he was going to say something, but he changed his mind and ran out of the house. So we paid our expenses, and he never came back. And the only difference was that my father went to the bank and stayed up later, but otherwise, everything stayed in place, just as it was.

I can still see my father's study; wherever you went in it, books. He had a very impressive desk, carved, a huge flat top, and millions of drawers. Usually, in the space above the kneehole only one door was built, but my father had two, and there were four drawers on each side. He had a big red leather armchair that swiveled, and he used to take me in the room and teach me geography. I repeated the names of the cities like a monkey: Noygorod, Dnepepetrovsk. And he used to take me to museums, and read to me, and take me to movies. I don't know why he paid more attention to me than the others; perhaps it was because I was the first girl. The walls of his study were painted dark red, dark, like blood, and there was a dark green carpet on the floor; and his desk was the home of a magic lamp, the bronze figure of a sheik with one upraised arm holding three globes of glass. And this was the room at the end of the corridor, nearest the door.

My brothers' bedroom was very plain, two nickel beds, two little desks, white curtains, and a linoleum rug. The linoleum of those days was very beautiful and came in magnificent colors and patterns. In my brothers' room the linoleum was turquoise with a black design. Of course, Emmanuel, being so much older than Mischa, didn't have too much to do with him, and Emmanuel, being much older than Vera and I, had little to do with us either—except for the conferences he and Vera had, over romance, I am still sure. "It's too busy," Momma used to wail; "someone's always going out a door." And the truth was, if we didn't eat dinner together, some of us might not have seen each other for weeks at a time. Yet because Momma and Poppa were always telling anecdotes about all of us, and because of the house, to which we all belonged, there was a closeness which had nothing to do with how much of each other we saw. When Mischa was at home, Emmanuel was at school; when Mischa was at school, Emmanuel was working. But Mischa was a genius at making a mess of his room; it was impossible to forget he was there, and my mother used to come and stand in their doorway and shake her head: "Anzia, get a hose."

And then there was my parents' bedroom. It was not the common thing, but they had a double bed. And the furniture was all dark, dark mahogany, which was at that time the most fashionable and the most expensive. Their room had a parquet floor and a beautiful oriental rug, with pinks and purples. Whoever came to stay with us wanted to know where they had gotten it, because in those days it was very unusual, a pink oriental rug. And there was a pink chaise longue; if my father wasn't in his study reading, he was lying on the chaise longue reading. They had a pink bedspread and a pink cover for the chaise longue, and purple piping, and pink drapes. The room had huge windows, and when we were inside it, which wasn't often (only if we were allowed in to watch Momma getting dressed to go out, or if one of us was sick, or unhappy), it was like living in the center of a chocolate candy raspberry-filled. It was a wonderful room. I have a dim memory of a time when they had a big nickel bed, like the ones in my brothers' room; at its foot were little curtains hung between the pipes which formed the footboard. And like all of us, they had a small rug on each

24

side of the bed for comfort. Even my father's room, dark red, was bright because of the windows, although it was darker than the bedroom, really, the darkest room in the house.

So we each had our separate place. And my room was the only one that was locked, because of Mischa. You see, I didn't want him to get in. I kept the key over my door in case Momma needed anything, or Vera, or the maid. And when I close my eyes I can see Anzia making the beds in her special apron; it was a white apron with sleeves, a special uniform for making the beds. Everything was so clean, no germs could get from the kitchen to the beds, or in from the bathroom. So if she touched the beds, she had to put this on. And then later, when I got married it was the same thing with my maid. I didn't know any better.

In the meantime, we were growing. I was in the gymnasium, busy with my geometry and trigonometry and literature, getting A's in everything, except the Polish language, which was not as familiar to me as it was to the other students, since at home we spoke only Russian. Vera was constantly in her room, playing the piano. She did not want to go to the gymnasium at all. But my father's ideas were very advanced for his day, and he believed that everyone should have an occupation, and if not a profession, then a trade. "The world is a surprising place," he used to tell us; "everyone must know how to do something." One afternoon when we were all sitting at the table eating dinner, Verushka explained, as patiently as she could, tears streaming down her face, how geometry was no use to her, none of the subjects were any use to her, wasn't that true? "My dear daughter," said Poppa, "even Michelangelo knew medicine and carpentry and probably plumbing," and he cut a piece of beef from the bone on his plate. "So it is settled," he said, and we finished eating in silence, Vera eating too, her tears drowning the food.

Then one Saturday, father was not at home. He had gone to Warsaw on bank business and we did not expect him back until Wednesday. Emmanuel was out with Genya, his new girl friend, at a café. ("She'll get him; wait and see," Momma said, positively. "She knows how to do it.") Mischa was off to follow Zoshia, who now had to get dressed in a tiny dark corner of her room, since his interests had grown with his height and now included more than fairy tales. We ate our dinner in the black dining room, the *chornoi stolova,* the one for everyday use, for the children, or whoever came. This room also had the great, tall windows overlooking the court, and plain white drapes with a design woven into the fabric. The walls were painted pale cream. A man from one of the villages had made a cardboard stencil and stenciled on a border of turquoise flowers; they ran around the top of the room like a ribbon, just under the ceiling. It was not an elegant room, but very pretty, and when we were smaller, Poppa used to pick us up to see if we could touch the border yet. "Oh, she has gotten so large; she can almost touch it," he would say, putting Vera down, but I think even Emmanuel, who was over six feet tall, could not have touched it. Still, it was a game and it went on with every new child.

The black dining room had a huge oak table, a very long one, rectangular, and large, high oak chairs, and the whole family and guests could sit down at it very comfortably. Then on the wall in back of it was the infamous sideboard. You see, my parents were very strict, and they believed that we had to have a good base, a good *fundáment,* Momma called it, so after a certain hour there were no pastries and chocolates for anyone, and even if we were to have them, she would count out the portions as if they were dangerous drugs.

In the meantime, the pastries and chocolates lived their delicious lives behind the intricately carved panels of this huge buffet which rose three-quarters of the way up the wall, and it did not help our appetites, believe me, that the torturer who made it had carved it not with leaves, but with every imaginable kind of animal—a cat, a dog, a rabbit, bears, unicorns—and in the top doors was a tiny, perfectly carved procession of troikas. The doors were enough to inspire the imagination of any stomach. So when we heard Momma come into the room with her ring of tinkling keys, our pointed ears were up, like foxes. There was also a highboy, a tremendous one, carved out of the same wood. When Momma was out, Mischa and Vera and I were at them both with hairpins and pieces of hangers, trying to open the locks. But they were big brass locks and it was hopeless. Still, we never gave up, and in the end we usually wound up with our noses pressed to the places where the doors opened, trying to smell where the pastries were hidden, so if we tried again and succeeded, at least we would open the best chest. Because the children were always in there and spilling things, we had a linoleum rug which was very beautiful. In the center of the rug, which was the same color as the chairs, there was no pattern, but it had a tremendous border of bright red roses. It was really very pretty, and no one had to feel guilty about the endless glasses of milk and the plates of soup that were forever landing on it.

But today Poppa was not home, so it was not such a cheerful room, and then, it was a very strange thing for October, it was pouring. Usually, by this time of year there would be snow, or at least hail, hammering at the windows as if the house were being stoned. And whenever this happened, Momma would give a shudder, and look at the window and say, "The Jews are chosen, but they are very unlucky." So we finished eating in silence. Momma finished last and looked up at us. "Come," she said, "we'll go sit in the white dining room." This dining room was usually reserved for company, and we never ate dinner there when only the family was home unless it was the Sabbath. We must have looked frightened, because Momma smiled and said, "No, no bad news. Let's go sit on the couch." In the white room we all felt better immediately. It was such a colorful, such an elegant place. The walls were papered white, covered with a beige design like lace, but the first thing anyone noticed was the carpet, the deep red carpet, and then deep red velvet drapes which hung from the two huge windows which took up the facing wall, and under the red drapés, white ones, thin as webs, crisscrossed underneath. The furniture was all mahogany, and everyday, when Zoshia finished polishing the parquet, she would polish the furniture with a special wax my mother bought in the country, during the summers while we stayed at the *dacha,* the country house.

In the center of the rug was a huge round mahogany table; it must have been eight feet long, and had no leaves as modern tables do. The room was so huge, it always stayed as it was. And this table cost a fortune. Even today I am amazed, remembering the cost. It was what we called a *preference* table. *Preference* was a very elegant and very difficult card game, something like our Bridge, and this was our father's game, his special delight. There were slots for the chips cut into the wood, twelve of them, one slot for each player, but most of the time, unless he had guests, the table was covered with *another* piece of mahogany, and when there was company for dinner, or when Momma wanted to look at it, there was a beautiful ta-

27

blecloth made of the same red velvet the chair seats were made of, and embroidered all over with huge beige roses. Against the wall in back of this table was a huge mahogany breakfront. In this Momma kept all the silver pieces and her knickknacks, and all this was reflected in the mirror of the breakfront, and then again in the long mirror between the two windows on the opposite wall. And these mirrors also picked up the glitter and sparkle of the huge crystal chandelier that we had made especially for us; it is hard to describe, a shape something like a tear, or a cupola turned upside down. And then, on the other wall, in back of the table, was a huge couch covered in red velvet, very deep and very soft, and it covered almost the length of the wall. It was tufted, and once you sat down on it, you never wanted to get up again.

"Momma," Vera whispered, sinking in first, "tell us a story." I slid down, waiting for Momma. If she would tell us a story, we knew what it would be. It was a ritual. "I will tell you a story," Momma said, her back to us; we heard the tinkle of her keys. She opened the mahogany breakfront and took out the two huge silver candlesticks and set them in their place in the middle of the table. Then she went back and lifted down the huge silver basket which on special days sat between them. It was the most unusual thing, one of the wedding presents her father had made for her in Paltava. The basket itself was ordinary enough, silver made to look like wicker, and of course, the handle, as was the style, was twisted with vine leaves. But around the rim of the basket little animals were marching in pairs, and after looking at it for some time, everyone would suddenly realize: the animals from the ark! They were all there, the giraffes, the zebras, lions, tigers, ducks, swans, and finally, when one followed the row of animals long enough, a tiny Noah and his wife. "Now," Momma sighed, putting it down, "I will tell you a story; what story do you want to hear?" The rain kept streaming down the windows, but it was losing its gray battle with the red velvet. "Nu?" she asked, "what story?" The reflected light from the chandelier was shining between the vertical bars of the high-backed chairs and lighting the carved mahogany arches over them where we had rested our heads so many times; it was hard to believe our heads had not done the shining themselves.

28

VERA began the catechism. "Who was your father, Momma?" "My father," Momma began, and then interrupted herself, jumping up. "Are you sure," she asked, "I shouldn't get some fruit for the basket?" Vera grabbed for her skirt. "Momma," she said again, "who was your father?" Momma settled in, smiling. "My father," she began, "was a famous *antiquarish,* an antique dealer. He was so wealthy, the Russians gave him the title of 'Respectable Citizen.'" "What was a Respectable Citizen?" Vera asked. "A Respectable Citizen was someone who made so much money, and paid so many taxes, he was permitted, even if he was Jewish, to go to the capital." "And did he ever go to the capital?" "He did," Momma answered; "he did go to St. Petersburg, many times." Now it was my turn.

"And what did you do there, Momma?"

"I went to the Marinska Gymnasium."

"Did everyone go to the Gymnasium?"

"No, only myself, and my sisters and brothers, because even though we were Jewish, our father was very rich."

"Were things always happy there?"

"No, they were not; there were many troubles then, you know, especially during The Great War, in 1914."

"What happened to you then?"

"Then I slept in a coffin."

"In a coffin, Momma!" Vera exclaimed as if she had never heard this before. "In a coffin," Momma continued. "The Russian White Guards, the *Dinikins,* were conducting a pogrom, and raping the Jewish girls, so at the edge of our estate was an old man, a peasant really, but our Poppa had set him up in business and called the doctor for his children and taken them to school in our sleigh, and what business should this peasant be in but a coffin business. So the old man came to Poppa and told him what was going on, and he told Poppa to hide all the girls in the coffins, and all the children too, because there was a rumor a lot of children had been caught in Paltava and killed."

"And did they close the coffin on you, Momma?" I asked.

"They did."

"And were you afraid?"

"Only when I heard the metal gates rattling, and the sounds of boots stamping, and the hammering of the little man went on and on, and for one minute I thought, 'He is nailing us in!' But then I heard him shouting, 'What kind of men are you! I cannot even go to mass and now you have nothing to do but hit the tops of the coffins. I hope you wake up one of the dead and they sit up in there—it will serve you right. This is a sin, a sin!' Even in the dark I could see him, how the veins around his eyes must be standing out, blue. And *then* I heard him say slyly, 'Come here, come here, you.' I could see his expression, malevolent, so old he looked like a bald woman, a witch. 'Hit *this* one,' and he was so close to me, I knew he meant mine. But the Russians were very superstitious and they disappeared like bugs."

"Would you have jumped up if he had hit the coffin, Momma?" Vera asked.

"Oh, yes," Momma said. "I was not stupid, and Poppa was not stupid; neither was the coffin maker; that was why we were all still alive, and the coffin maker had us all dressed in shrouds, and I am so pale, I still am, you can see it, yes?" she asked, smiling. She had Vera's skin and the same long black hair; now she parted it in the middle and pulled it back in a chignon; that was the fashion of the day. But still, there were times, and today was one of them, when she looked more like a sister than a mother. And she loved compliments. "And my hair was all down, and stringy from the dampness in the box, and I would have frightened my own momma!" she finished. She thought a minute, as she did every time. "Yes, yes, I would have jumped up."

"And what did you do when you finished school?" Vera asked, going on to the second part of the story.

"Then I taught school for two years."

"Where did you teach school, Momma?"

"I taught in a little school your grandfather built for me; it was something like a long porch attached to the main house ('annex,' Verushka)"—she was very proud of any English words she picked up—"and it had long pine benches the coffin maker made for us, and the little children sat in rows like little birds, and I taught them for two years."

"And then what did you do, Momma?" The rain streamed.

"Then I married your father."

"But you were in Russia and Poppa was in Poland," we both cried out simultaneously; an eavesdropper would never have guessed that I was entering medical school in the fall, and Verushka had already given her first concert, last month in Symphony Hall, and the whole town was talking about her with such pride. Momma used to say she was afraid to feed Poppa anymore, because with my entering medical school, and Vera playing the piano, and his adoration of music, especially Mendelssohn and Mozart, he would take another bite and explode, and every time Momma said that, she would puff him up even more.

"Oh, I forgot," Momma said. "I meant to tell you; you will never guess how stupid I was. When I was little, my friend Rivka and I locked ourselves in an outhouse, and we decided, because our busts were so big, we were going to cut out little pieces. Did you ever hear of anything so stupid?" "Momma!" both of us screamed, "how did you meet Poppa?" "Oh, Poppa," Momma reminded herself, as if she were trying to remember who he could be, "Poppa is a long story. Are you sure you want to hear it?" "Momma!" we screamed again.

"First," Momma began, "you have to understand your grandfather's nature. He was a very religious man, a very good-looking one, but above all, very religious, and when it came to the Sabbath, he bordered on fanaticism. Momma used to say he wore the fanatic's coat. On Saturdays and holidays I did not go to school, even though, you know, I was the one Jewess in the Marinska Gymnasium, but I was still a very good student. And your grandfather was very devoted to his family. He came from Lithuania and was educated there, and he had a sister in Vilno who had three daughters, and his sister, Great Aunt Emma, had lost her husband, and all three of her daughters were the most beautiful girls. And when her husband died, the circumstances were not very good; a lot of money was lost, and one of the daughters didn't marry wisely, but she married a very wealthy man, who was probably not exactly a man, and the daughter got sick because of this and developed a cyst of the womb. She was a very strong

31

brunette and a very tempermental woman, and she needed a normal man, but he could not be one to her. She took sick; she had nurses; he supplied everything; he was very generous, but Great Aunt Emma wrote my grandmother, 'If someone would just come, someone from our own blood, we would not be so lonely.' So, who should be sent? Everyone was married. It had to be Rebecca, me. And I was very beautiful, and my poppa, may he rest in peace, was afraid that someone would annoy me, or God knows what to me (fanatics have vivid imaginations, let me tell you), and of course, he remembered the coffins and how they had saved us, so he decided to smear my face with black ash and dirt, and he personally messed up my hair. You know; he pulled a piece this way and that way, and finally, at least from the neck up, I looked like a monster.

"But was this enough? No, this was not enough. Poppa stood back and decided my body still looked good, too good, such a tempting morsel I was, and everyone in the village was always telling him what a beauty I was, and why should my father be any different from other fathers, and not believe them? So he had me put on a lambskin coat from one of the peasants on the estate, Luchia (she was very angry, but Poppa promised her a brand-new coat), but was this good enough? No. He had to cut some holes in the coat here and there and smear that coat with some ash from the stove, and Luchia was in a corner of the room crying, because she didn't have her new coat yet, and this was her best one, but Poppa was positively possessed; he was absolutely possessed. And was this enough? No. He had to have Luchia's shoes, made from straw, so there Luchia was in front of the stove, barefoot, and crying even harder, and there I was, turning into a frog, when suddenly a candle flickered on in Poppa's head and he thundered at me, 'Stay there!' and ran out of the room. Well, what should he come back with, but one of Luchia's shawls, and he put it around my neck and crossed it over my breasts, like those curtains over there"—and she pointed—"and he tied it in the back. Then he told me to stick out my hands, and put on her gloves, and he smeared *them* with charcoal, and for good measure cut the tip from one thumb and stuffed it with paper. Now Luchia was hysterical. But Poppa was beginning to be convinced. My features could not be seen: my beautiful nose, and my beautiful hair, a haystack, and my beautiful teeth, like pearls. So Poppa started coming toward my mouth, and I began screaming, 'What are you going to do to my mouth; you are going to pull out my teeth!' And then Momma said 'Enough, enough,' and Poppa stood back and he decided his work was well done.

"So then what happened? There was a twenty-four-hour trip on the train, all the way from Paltava to Vilno. If I had looked like myself, a lady, a proper man would have approached me in the proper way; he would have helped with the luggage, found me a seat, asked if I needed something to drink or to eat, but did this happen? Of course it did not happen. Who should come near me but a drunk with a big red nose full of beige scales, and all the way to Paltava he followed me; he followed me all night, and I was hopping out of one seat and into another but no one wanted to sit with me because of the way I looked; and who would? So they would hop up when I hopped in and then the drunk would hop into the seat next to me, and so it went for twenty-four hours. I have never had such a nightmare, never. But finally, we arrived, and he was right behind me, just where he had been all along. And there on the platform were my two aunts, not the sick one, but the other two daughters of Great Aunt Emma, and one of them was holding a picture of me, and they were looking *all over*, up and down, behind them, in front of them, on the tracks, between the tracks, every place; it was terrible. And there I was, two feet away, and of course, did they recognize me? No. They had one picture and I was another.

"And they started to scream, 'Rebecca! Rebecca!' and finally I couldn't stand it anymore and I said, loud as I could, because I was bent in half, laughing, 'Aunt Doba Aunt Doba, it's me, here I am, here I am.' They almost fainted when they saw me. 'Why did he do it?' they kept screaming; 'what's the matter with him? Did he lose his mind? What happened to him, what happened to him? How could he send a child . . .?' But they took me home, and started washing me and scrubbing me, until I felt like a parquet floor, and every time I opened my eyes, it was another embroidered towel coming at me. Such a scrubbing, but *finally* they saw the picture of my face coming out. 'Doba, it's the right one.' 'Thank God,' Doba said, pulling me out of the chair and hugging me. 'You go up with the maid and she will dress you and you will rest,' and all the way up the stairs I could hear them:

33

'What happened to him, what happened to him? Is he crazy? Maybe the wrong one really came, Doba, no? You should go see him. No, it is not funny; stop laughing, to send a child that way,' and then, poor man, he got letters from them every single day for a month. 'What was he thinking of, his own daughter, he should know better,' but you know, I had gotten there safely, and until the end of his days, who had been right? He was, he insisted, especially since it was only because I got there safely (because of his ridiculous costume) that I met your father." "But what did one have to do with the other, Momma?" cried Vera. Oh, we both knew our cues.

"Well," Momma continued, "I stayed there for long months taking care of my aunt and she did not let me go *anywhere*; she would not let me out of her sight. It was Rebecca who had to give her her medicine, otherwise she would not take it. And she was such a beautiful, beautiful woman, she died in such pain when it happened. But while I was there, she was jealous; sick people are very jealous, you know, jealousy is the most terrible thing; sometimes I think, the most terrible. And so she was selfish. And they put the most beautiful robes on Aunt Vanya. She had special cooks, special sheets, special quilts. One day she got the idea she would get better if only they would change the color of her room, and they changed it; it was white, they painted it yellow. She got quite an argument from her sister, Doba. Doba was very superstitious, and reminded her of how red roses meant love, but yellow roses meant betrayal, and she told her this story of a woman whose husband used to give her a red rose, one more for every anniversary, and then, when the wife's mother got sick, and she went back to Russia for some months, she got fewer and fewer letters. She didn't know how, but she knew something was up, and she wrote her husband she was coming back early for her anniversary; and sure enough, there was only one yellow rose in the vase, and one mistress on another street, and that was the end of the marriage. The wife was heartbroken. But Vanya kept insisting that yellow meant sunlight, and there was no talking to her. So all the servants carried her into the guest room, and when they took her back to her room, it was bright yellow. And believe me, every servant in the house was up all night embroidering new towels and new quilts to match the walls; that's how fussy they were. But occasionally, after an exhausting day and long nights in terrible

34

pains, Vanya would fall asleep and I could go downstairs to sit at the table, or in the dining room with the rest of the family. Then, it was completely an accident, there was a young man visiting with distant relatives of Vanya's, and he would often stop by. Then he began to stop by more and more. He was only twenty-two, and he always looked straight at me and smiled. I thought he was flirting, and of course, in Poppa's house, flirting was not allowed. So I used to drop my eyes, and afterward, Doba would tease me and say, 'Rebecca, why are you so red, Rebecca? You look like a tomato plant. Do you have a fever, Rebecca? Do you want to lie down?' Oh, they were never finished teasing, and even Vanya, when she felt well, was always teasing and telling jokes.

"One day, after she had me running up and down the stairs, getting cold towels and hot towels, and sending for the doctor, and telling the servant to go to the market for lemons, she said, 'We have been working very hard, Rebecca, no?' And I must have looked puzzled, because she was smiling, you know, when just a few minutes before she had been screaming. And she said, she couldn't believe it: 'You don't know the story about the man and the fly?' And when I said no, she made me sit down so she could tell it to me. 'Once there was a man who was laboring in the fields, and all day a fly sat on his nose. All day, he threw big clumps of hay into the wagon with his pitchfork, and finally, it was night time, and he lay down under a tree, and took out his bread and salt and cheese. The fly was still there, although, all day, the man had been trying to brush the fly from his nose. Then said the fly to the man, "We have been working *so* hard; *I* have never had such a hard day in my life," and right on the man's nose, he folded his wings and fell asleep. So it is with us, no, Rebecca?' Vanya did not often say much to me, you see, she was always so tired, or in such pain. Then she said, 'Rebecca, you are like a daughter to me, but I am not a good mother to you. I know it. But perhaps you will learn something from this. I have not learned anything.' And she took hold of my hand and started to cry, big gentle tears, and I started to cry, too. 'But I am not a good daughter,' I sobbed. 'I can't do anything for you.' 'Well, today, you can set the table for the Sabbath, and I will say my prayers, and Rebecca, I will pray for you first.' "
Momma had never told us this part of the story before, and Vera and I listened, transfixed. "Oh, I felt so terrible."

Momma said, crying. "I could not help her; there was nothing I could do, so how could I hate her for being selfish? But sometimes I did hate her, and I am ashamed to think of it." Momma stared ahead at the streaming window. "So then I helped Vanya get dressed in a special white gown, and we set the little table in the corner of her room with a special cloth, and she knelt there with her head between the candles, her forehead resting on the prayer book, and said a *Boruchu*. And of course, there was no morphine.

"Meanwhile, this young man kept coming. Finally he told Doba he could not stand his curiosity anymore, and asked her, 'Why is this girl, your relative, sitting so still all the time, and looking so different from the Polish girls; I don't understand it.' So Doba started to smile, and said I came specially from Russia to visit with them, and she kept on smiling, because your father was almost as shy as I was. Finally he found some nerve, and told *his* relatives, who told Doba that he would *love* to meet me, and, of course, it was arranged one, two, three. We began meeting in the dining room—with all the aunts watching, naturally—but Vanya, you know, she was so selfish, she would not let me go long, and when we went out in the garden, she did not want us further away than where she could see us from her chair, and not for more than an hour. She had a special chair, covered with a bright yellow-flowered pattern and stuffed so thick with down it took two of us to pull her out of it; anything to make her comfortable. But the young man, Boris, you know who that is, and I began to exchange books, and suddenly little pressed flowers began appearing in mine, and so things went on for eight months. Then one day, I was sitting in that chair, reading a letter from your father, and I heard a strange noise from her bed, and she died. And it was terrible. If it hadn't been for your father, I really don't know what would have happened to me. I had never seen anything like it before, and it was so awful, because in spite of everything, I loved her. Sometimes I think I loved her so much because it was so awful; we shared so much suffering together. Then, in her will, she left me a lot of money and jewelry, I don't remember what. I didn't need it; my father was so wealthy; and I had not helped her; she had died, but still, so it was. And Doba said, 'It will be part of your dowry; it will buy clothes for your children. Good always comes from bad in the end; you'll see.' So I was persuaded to take the things.

"Doba must have had her suspicions, and so did I, and we were both right, because, sure enough, this young Boris told Doba he wanted to marry me. She gave him permission to ask me. So I told him I would let him know, because where my father was concerned, there was no question at all: he would have to be consulted. Boris came from a small *shtetl*, a small village, in Russia. His father was a rabbi, and he knew five languages and he was a private lawyer, a profession that exists only in Russia. His father had an office where he translated all kinds of requests, petitions to the czars, letters to all countries in all kinds of languages, and the most beautiful, beautiful handwriting; it looked like a work of art. It was so beautiful, and your grandfather wrote all your *metricas*, your birth certificates. But Boris told his father that he was choking to death in the small town and he wanted to go to the big city. His father said that Boris was a grown man now, and if his son wanted his help, he would give it to him; so Boris went to Vilno. His father was an unusual man; there were not too many like him at the time. Most were fanatics. He did everything and he read everything. Your father's love of books comes from him, no? And his beautiful handwriting.

"So when Boris got to Vilno, someone gave him the address of a lawyer, and immediately he had a job, and then he moved in with Doba's distant relatives, and then he found this strange girl from Russia who was afraid to look at him. He came to the lawyer in Vilno when he was only thirteen and began making money the first week, and a few weeks later he was living in the same room he lived in when he met me. And the lawyer liked your father very much. So he asked your father what his real goal was, and what should your father say, but first of all (do you hear, Verushka?) that he wanted to finish gymnasium, but he did not want to burden his parents. The lawyer, Rosinski, told him not to worry; they would accomplish everything he desired. He introduced him to a young Doctor Gershovitz, who gave him a lot of work to do during the day, and your Poppa started studying at night. He finished the gymnasium at night in just three years—it was remarkable! He took the exams and he passed them; that was all. But he wanted to do still better; you know, go further up. But Doctor Gershovitz said he didn't think he could help him any longer because his field was medicine, and my Boris was interested in law and business, but Boris got better and better jobs, and by the time he was twenty-one he had a very high position. You see, everyone who saw him trusted him. And then it was time to enter the military, and of course your father, a vegetarian, he didn't want to go. But he did go. And got very sick. Typhus. And he was almost dead. Then your grandmother began praying and contributed enormous amounts of money to the *schul;* she prayed that she should go instead of him. And what do you think, all of a sudden, he started getting better and better, and she took sick. She was a young woman, and all of a sudden she didn't get up and he was well. There is this superstition—do you know it—among the Christians, that if you exchange crosses, you exchange fates. Well, maybe it is not true, but experience, horrible experience, sometimes ... do you believe it?" Neither of us said anything. "So then he returned to Vilno, and then we met, and my father came all the way to Vilno to look at this villain who wanted to marry his daughter, and the wedding was in Paltava, and it took ten days, everyone drinking and dancing and falling down, and money was never thought of. For four weeks they prepared food, baking and cooking, and getting out the cherry wine from the cellar, and no bottle was less than ten years old. And then it was The Great War. But that is another story—how they escaped to Poland with the mattress. You know it."

"It's stopped raining, Momma," Vera said, jumping up suddenly and facing out the window overlooking the court, so to us she was just a silhouette. I sat where I was, my arm around Momma. "The story has gotten longer, Momma." "Your lives have gotten longer my children," she said. Then she was quiet. "You know," she said, "this may be the last summer the whole family spends together at the *dacha.* After this, it is medical school for Anya, and the grand piano for Vera, and who knows, Emmanuel may marry that Genya. She's not a bad girl. It may be the last summer at the *dacha* after all." Vera turned around and sat down at my mother's feet, wrapping her arms around Momma's legs, pressing her face to Momma's knees, and we sat there in silence. Momma began stroking Verushka's head, and tracing the white part down the middle of her black hair. "If you are going out, Verushka, please put on a warm coat." "I'm not going anywhere,

Momma," Vera said and we sat there in perfect silence until Anzia came in and asked us if we were ready to eat, and if we were eating in the usual place, and we sat still until dinner was ready.

4

AND Momma was right. It was the last summer we spent
together at the *dacha,* but it was like all the other summers there, absolutely perfect. Every year, my parents
rented the same big house in the country. Momma was
determined we were going to be healthy, "even if she kills
us," Emmanuel used to say, gulping down the carrot juice
she made herself by grinding the carrots and then squeezing them through a muslin rag; and the air in the country
was so strong with the smell of pine and beech and birch,
when we first came it would make us dizzy. The house
was in the middle of a deep forest, and there were six or
seven others in a line, but the woods were so thick, and
they were so far apart, each house seemed the only one in
the world. All around the house grew mushrooms and berries and this was the time when Zoshia really took over.
She was a farm girl and she knew her way through the
woods, and we would all troop out with her, each with a
basket collecting mushrooms and berries, and Zoshia
would take them from us when we got home, throwing
out the poisonous ones, and we ate blackberries and rasp-
berries and strawberries with sour cream and sugar on top
for breakfast, lunch and dinner. And there were so many
mushrooms, Anzia used to cut and dry them for the winter, and the extra berries were preserved carefully in jam.
Other days, we went fishing. Mischa loved to watch the
fish jumping on the hooks; Verushka and I thought it was
terrible and would not look. We all ate them fried in butter. Poppa used to say he never recognized us in the summer unless we were half-purple; if we stuck out our
tongues and they were normal-colored, a dish of berries
immediately appeared. So we waited for the first of May,
when the big wagon came to the house on Zevrensky
Street, and half of the household—samovars, blankets, pillows, linens, shirts, the whole household really—was piled
on this wagon two poor brown horses would pull all the

way to the *dacha*. And we liked it there, the primitive feel of it, the comfort, and how clean it was, as if the air washed everything by just coming in the windows. It was as if the air poured in, and you caught hold of it, like a tulle, between your fingers. And it was only twenty miles from the city, which was why my mother liked it more than the elegant resorts, like Druzgeniekie; that was so far away.

Here Poppa could come three times a week and breathe the wonderful air. So when I think of the summers, first I see the wagon leaving, piled up with half the house, looking like an eviction on wheels, the two maids sitting on top, and by the time we arrived separately, by train, everything was in order: the samovar was panting with steam, everything was cozy and pleasant. There was no electricity, just a kerosene lamp hanging over the table; and in all the rooms, wood stoves, because even in summer, the nights were cold, very cold. I remember that, the maids sitting on top of everything like figures on a crazy wedding cake, and getting there, and the complete happiness and the dizzying air, and then Poppa's arrivals when the "*dacha* husbands," the brothers, and the guests came in by train, all of them loaded down with packages, cakes, candies, pastries, presents of all kinds, and how we all looked forward to those Friday nights, and how we got dressed up for them. So we were washed thoroughly, and combed, and our hair filled with little clips. Then grownups and children would dress up in peasant dresses made of brightly flowered material, the background always black, all of them had little aprons. Then we wore corals and all kinds of beads. And from the minute we saw Poppa, our eyes were already glued on his packages: what did he have for us? Poppa used to say it was a frightful thing, arriving in the middle of these four cannibals; he and Momma used to say how terrible we were, as bad as we were with our Aunt Rivka who always came to the house with a box of cheap marmalade candies, and the three of us, Mischa, Vera, and I used to sit on the couch like three vultures, our eyes glued to the box, not saying a thing. Aunt Rivka would not give us anything until Momma came, because she knew if we got hold of it, all Momma would find would be the wrappings and strings. "They are kissing and hugging, but they are snooping, Rebecca," Poppa used to say, his face so contented he hardly seemed human. Momma always seemed human;

41

she had a temper. But Poppa was a saint, an angel. He seemed that way to all of us, and a word from him hurt; he so rarely said anything to scold us; when he did, it was an arrow.

It was a strange summer. Zoshia was fully grown and now when Momma would send her to have the chickens slaughtered she would come home red and flushed and excitedly tell Momma she had been followed part way home, the men had talked to her and tried to stop her in the market. I thought she was imagining it, but Momma took it more seriously. She told Zoshia if it happened again, she must immediately call a policeman and tell him she was being bothered, and the young man would be arrested, because it was against the laws of our country to bother a girl. But then one day, Zoshia took her book of fairy tales to a bench in the park, and someone came up to her and talked to her, and Vera came home and said she saw them go off for a walk. Then none of us thought more about it. After all, Zoshia was growing up, and Mischa was growing up, and Vera and I used to pinch her, her body was so hard and strong we couldn't believe it.

But it was a dreamy time. Zoshia would be playing croquet with Mischa; Zoshia would be picking berries with Vera; I would wander off and find a field full of sun, and lie down just as I was, and remember. That was what I was doing, remembering. Momma had said it would be the last summer, and it was, and already, it was different. I found a special tree which dripped sap and which had caught three insects. I used to lie down in front of it and stare up into the sun, eyes open, or closed, watching the sun through my skin, tracing veins in the orange sky inside the lids like lightning. And I would remember. I remembered how I had gotten admitted to medical school. Momma had gotten a cyst and she had to go into a clinic for an operation. She didn't want Poppa to know so she waited until he was away on business, and then I went with her. The whole night my friends and I sat on the steps of the clinic waiting for the doctor to bring his report, and we all prayed. Life without Momma! Every time I thought of it I invented new prayers, and new prayers again. The cyst was not malignant. But the doctor stayed and talked to us; he said something to Momma about what a lovely daughter she had, and Momma told him her lovely daughter wanted to be a lovely doctor. The doctor looked grave. A woman and a Jewess. Finally, he said to

42

me, "I will tell you what to do. Go to the house of Professor Mishenska; he is the head of the school. Tell him you have something to speak to him about, and that it is very important. He is a very stiff man, very formal, but if you get him in his own home—you know, he is one of those men, if you get him in his own home . . ." and then he would not say any more. He said goodbye to Momma, congratulated her on her good luck, and left the room. The door was not even closed before Momma had my wrist clamped in her hand like a vise: "Do it, Anya!" she said, "do just as he says! And when you do it, don't tell anyone, not your best friend, not Vera, not even me. When you want to do something, you must do it, and you must not tell anyone." She was so intense, and her eyes burned so blackly, I was frightened. "Get dressed, Momma," I said, but already, I was planning.

As soon as Momma was better, I got dressed in my best suit, a navy-blue skirt, a navy-blue jacket with silver buttons, a white shirt with a ruche and a low neck, and ruffled white cuffs, white shoes and a white hat, and sneaked out of the house like a thief. I was going to the doctor's house. I got there in the *drozhka* and rang the bell. I will never forget that bell; you turned a little handle in the great door like a key, and inside, the tiny tinkle. A maid in a black uniform came to the door. "I want to speak to Professor Mishenska; I have something very important to talk to him about," but already I could see a bald head half-peeking from a door that had opened a crack on the side of the entrance hall. "This young girl says she has to talk to you," the maid repeated, addressing the onion-like head. The rest of the body materialized. He did not look very frightening; he was short, plump, still in dressing gown, a magnifying glass dangling around his neck from a shoelace. He looked me up and down, from head to toe. "What have we to talk about?" he asked in astonishment. "Professor, sir," I began, "I have heard you are a very hard man, but I must talk to you. Ever since I can remember, I have wanted to be a doctor. I even read the medical journals; since I've been thirteen, I've been reading them. I do volunteer work in hospitals, especially in the children's ward, and my marks in the gymnasium are very good. Except in Polish; we always talk Russian at home. But everyone tells me there is no hope. Tell me sir," I said, looking up at him, "can I have any hope?" His face collapsed; he suddenly looked young. He touched me on

43

the shoulder. "A person must never lose hope," he said, showing me to the door. I think I was still babbling, repeating my name over and over. "Good morning to you, young lady." So I went home, and I told no one.

But three months later, when the lists were to come out, I was back and forth to the university's medical building. The lists came out, nailed to the door, and there was my name: second on the list! A woman and a Jew! I didn't know what I was doing. I ran all the way to the bank to tell my father, and while I was running, it started to rain, but I didn't notice, and when Poppa saw me come into his office like a drowned cat, he started to cry. Momma knew even before I got home. Vilno was a small town really; everyone knew everyone else, and everyone was happy. Children ran to their mothers to tell them, and their mothers ran into my mother, and so it was done. And so the sun sailed down the sky, and I thought to myself, Zoshia is still playing croquet, and Anzia is still stringing mushrooms, and Momma is stirring the great kettle with jam, and then I heard my Poppa's voice saying "But my dear daughter, is this ethical?" and I burst out laughing. Because suddenly, in the middle of that meadow, I saw them, all the boys with newspapers in their hands. During the week, between twelve and two, my friends and I used to go into the city to trap boys for the weekend. One week I decided to trap them all, so I went to a café with Rachel, my best friend, who lived across the street, and at the café tables were telephones with huge numbers, so someone could see you and ring you for a date. To everyone who rang, I said, "I don't know; I don't know what you look like, but I will meet you across the street from my house Saturday night at seven, and so I will not forget you, it is such a long time, carry a newspaper with you." And that Saturday night, there they all were, peering up at our tall windows, me hidden behind the curtains, calling Verushka and then Momma, then Zoshia and then Anzia, and then Poppa. Oh, you should have seen their faces. It was a concert, a concert of laughter. But then Poppa said, "My dear daughter, is this ethical?" And I answered, "It is fun, Poppa." "It is fun for *you*, Anyu," he said, going into his study and closing the door. So, lying there in the meadow, in front of the tree with its three insects, I knew once and for all it was wrong, and I would never do anything like that again.

And of course, I became a terrible pest because my

brothers had not yet reformed. On the contrary, they loved the country and the country boys, and bets, they would do anything on a bet, and there was one country family they apprenticed themselves to, even Emmanuel, when he was there, and Poppa would hear of their doings on Fridays, saying only he was happy not to be there all week to see it himself. "But I suppose I am not too late to hear about it now," he commented one Friday, cutting a piece of herring so neatly it was as if he were cutting out a piece of wood for one of Mischa's endless model toy planes. "Not too late, Rebecca?" he repeated, questioning. "Oh, not too late at all; two more days, and I would come home by train myself. First, I should have you start with Mischa; while the others are out collecting mushrooms, and while Emmanuel tries to break his neck climbing trees and riding a wild horse, he collects stories." "Oh, yes, Poppa, lots of stories," Mischa said, excited and half-choking. "Swallow first," Poppa cautioned. "Well, Jakob, you know, from the village, he is so clever, his teacher, the rabbi, always falls asleep in the middle of lessons, and this winter when we weren't here, when the rabbi fell asleep, Jakob had some melted wax and he put it on the desk on the middle of the rabbi's beard, and then the class sneaked out on the porch, and then the rabbi, you know, he didn't hear any noise, so he woke up and was getting ready to shout, 'Nu, what are you doing?' but he jerked up his head and he left half his beard on the table, did you ever hear anything like that, Poppa?" "I can't say that I did," Poppa answered. "And then this winter," Mischa babbled on, "Jakob, oh, he is so clever, he and the other boys got together to help make a wedding for this man in the village; the man isn't right in the head, and he's very poor, and they wanted to do something nice, but then at the last minute, you know, they couldn't stand it, so they loosened up the wheels, and they hid in the bushes, they were all snowy anyway, they hid all around the square, and they kept calling to the horses, and by the time they had gone around the square seven times, all the wheels had fallen off." "They had to spoil it," Momma muttered to herself. "And what else?" Poppa asked. "And Jakob made a bet with his best friend, Irving, because Irving always wants to eat, he eats up everything in the house, so Jakob bet him he couldn't eat twenty-four eggs and a sausage, and Jakob cut the sausage up nicely with some onion, and cooked it all up, and Irving finally couldn't eat anymore; he said he was going to bust, but Jakob told him he would lose the bet, so he finished all of it, and he was sick all day and all the next day. Then Jakob and Irving decided to do the same thing to Jascha, and they bet him he couldn't eat two big sugar cakes covered with herrings and he ate them and he was sick for two days!" Mischa was hysterical, gasping for breath; his eyes were filling with tears. "Everything for bets," Momma grumbled; "I think you better tell him your best story, Mischa." Mischa turned his guilty purple color and began to take a sudden interest in his supper. "What story, Momma?" he asked, innocent as grass, but he was definitely turning his mottled, guilty color. "You know what story; the story about the bear." "About the bear?" asked Mischa, as if that animal had just that second been invented. "About the bear," Momma repeated, remorseless. "Now."

"Well, Poppa," Mischa said, "it was a good joke for fun. Anya says we should have fun," he said looking at me from under his lids: "remember about the newspapers?" "I think you had better tell me about the bear," Poppa said quietly, his hands folded in his lap. Mischa was studying the pattern on his plate. "He'll remember those roses forever," I thought to myself. "Well," Mischa began, "we thought it would be a good joke on Jakob's mother. You know how she is always worrried about him for nothing; you say so yourself." "Always worried about him!" Momma interrupted, furious. "I should think so! Jumping off the wagon like that because it didn't stop fast enough for him, and the iron wheel running over his ear, and then hiding for hours so they wouldn't see the blood; poor things, they thought he was dead." "Please, Rebecca, I want to hear about the bear," Poppa said, and we, *we did not breathe*, because Poppa never interrrupted Momma unless there was a fire. "So, the bear," Poppa reminded Mischa, inexorable.

"We told Jakob's mother he was caught by this bear," Mischa started sulkily, "and we told her the bear was going to get him because Jakob had climbed up a tree and the bear was going after him. I mean, Poppa, Irving told Jakobs's mother and I stayed behind with Jakob, because I was supposed to cut a branch off the beech tree and frighten off the bear by pretending I was an Indian and whooping and all that." "So you were supposed to be helping Jakob," Poppa commented. "You *could* say that, Poppa," Mischa said, draping himself over this straw of hope. "Anyway, Poppa," Mischa went on, carried away all over again, "you should have seen them! Jakob's mother came running and all the servants, and some more of the mothers from the village, and Irving's mother, and they came running right down the hill where Irving said we were; they even had their aprons on! And there he was, lying under a tree, and there I was with my branch. I had covered my face all up with mud, you know, so it would look like quite a battle, and Jakob had me hit him in the eye so he would have a good bruise, and they kissed me and hugged me, and Jakob's mother made the servants carry him all the way home, and they said they couldn't understand it, because all the *dachas* are in the valley, and the animals never came down from the forest into the valley until the middle of the winter, and Jakob's mother said she would be grateful to me always, and she gave me a big piece of poppy seed cake. It was such a *good* joke, Poppa, and everyone telling me how brave I was!" Mischa doubled over, banging his little fist on the table.

"So you saved Jakob from a bear?" Poppa asked slowly. Now even Momma was looking down at her plate. "Would you like to hear a story I know about a bear? It isn't a very long story. Once there was a bear and a man and they were very good friends. One hot day, the man fell asleep under a tree and a fly settled on his nose. The bear saw it, and because he liked the man (the man, you see, Mischa, was his friend), he decided he would get rid of the fly as a favor to him; then the man wouldn't have to wake up and swat it off. Since he was such a very good friend, he went over to the man, and took his great big paw, and swatted the fly, and while he was swatting the fly, he knocked off the man's head, and the man lay quietly under the tree for a very long time. The bear sat on a stone for some time and waited, but he got tired of it, and went back into the forest very sad, because he had lost his best friend. There is a moral to this story, Mischa, in Russian. It goes like this: 'This is what we call the service of a bear.' Do you understand what that means, Mischa? We leave the *dacha* in a week, but Jakob's mother is going to live here all winter, and in the winter, there will be real bears; there will be all kinds of animals. Jakob is already wild, you know that. How do you think his mother is going to feel every time he is out and comes late? How would your mother feel if her son had been rescued from a bear invading the valley, for the very first time, in the

47

middle of the summer, if it got dark in the winter, and you were not home? I think, Mischa, you were the bear in this story, and to tell you the truth, I don't want to hear any more of these stories, especially about how you helped people, but what I do want you to do is go to your room and think about my story, which *I* think is a very good story. Do you think it is a good story, Mischa?" "Yes, Poppa," Mischa answered, pushing back his chair so it scraped; "it is a good story," and he crawled off to his room.

"What is happening to them, Rebecca?" asked Poppa as if he had just seen the end of the world, "and Emmanuel, I know he's not here much but why doesn't he watch him?" "Oh, he has stories to tell, too," Momma answered. She was gloomy. Emmanuel was not there for the weekend; he had stayed in the city to take Genya to the Café Europa. "Do you think it is because it's their last summer?" asked Poppa. "I do think that's it, Boris," Momma said, considering. "You know, the girls are so good; I think they are *too* good. Verushka is at that keyboard you got her from some old piano day and night, practice, practice, without hearing a sound. And when he's here, Emmanuel acts as if he were younger than Mischa. If he doesn't get his mail, he has a horrible temper; I've never heard so many doors slam." "Well, we know what *that's* about, at least," Poppa sighed. "Then it probably is because it's the last summer," he decided. "Probably," Momma agreed, "probably." "You know, Borya," she went on, shaking herself out of some sleep, some pool of time, "next week Anzia will go back with you on Wednesday to prepare the house, and then she'll come back with you on Friday. How the days run away. They run away like that stupid bear," she grinned; "I'm sorry, Borya, I can't help smiling at Mischa sometimes; he's such an idiot," she said, indulgent after all. She was a Momma, our Momma. "Being an idiot will not help him if he is going to play with bears in the woods," Poppa retorted. Once his mind was fixed on something, he was not so easy to distract. "So," he said, his voice coming from a distance, as if he were swimming back from the future or the past, "when is the party for the summer's end?" "Next Sunday," Momma answered. "How is the house; is it all painted?" "All painted," Poppa reassured her. "And the bay windows, did you get the man with the scaffold?" "They are all washed." "Soon we will be going home," Momma sighed; "they are growing up."

"I don't like to change the subject, Rebecca, dear, but what is the matter with Zoshia?" To the end of his days Poppa always treated Momma with the exaggerated courtesy of a worried suitor. "She doesn't seem like the same girl, so pale, so sad, and she sits in corners with a book on her lap; she doesn't read it. It's Anya's book, *The Brothers Grimm;* you know how she loves it." Instantly, Momma was alarmed. When we were home, Zoshia was not allowed farther into the park than she could be seen from the white dining room windows. Momma's tongue was sometimes a snob, but her heart, never. She felt almost as responsible for Zoshia as if she had been her own child. "I haven't noticed anything, Boris, but, you know, I think I will talk to Anzia about it. They are always together in their room, and if anything is wrong, Anzia will know and tell us about it." "At least call a doctor," Poppa suggested. "Oh, Boris, she is not sick. She was out yesterday picking mushrooms." "And chasing bears," Poppa said, finally smiling again. Vera and I looked at each other. Poppa turned to us. "And what are your Momma and Anzia and the two of you doing about this party? What are you cooking up now?" We told him, and he listened to the recipes and the dress patterns and the fabric patterns as if they were the most fascinating poems from Lermontov he had ever heard.

And so we had the end of the summer party in a clearing in the woods, in the dizzying beeches and pines. All the maids had been cooking pastries for a week, and when the husbands and brothers came, they were loaded down with chocolates. We were all dressed in our peasant outfits. The families had their small orchestra and everyone danced on the lawn. It was so close, so close, and so happy, because during the summers all the families were like one family. There was so much forest, so many children, that keeping track of them—which ones were about to be eaten by bears, which girl had sprained an ankle and was sitting on a stump surrounded by toadstools three miles from the *dachas*—was a project for everyone; every mother was everyone else's mother. So the music went on, losing itself in the tops of the pines, while the little children played hide-and-seek, and the winner, who reached his tree and pounded on its bark three times, screamed with excitement. Vera and I and the other girls danced; Emmanuel sat quietly with Genya who had come with him just for the weekend's party; Momma and Poppa sat with the other parents, and by the end of the night, at the end of the cherry wine, they were dancing too. Fireflies were flickering under the beeches and pines and the smallest children ran around to everyone with jars covered with pieces of muslin showing everyone their "candles," their country candles; I will never forget them. And in the morning, we should be going home.

Then, all of a sudden, Momma started to sing an old Ukrainian song she remembered from her mother. She had this deep pure voice; all Ukrainian women had such beautiful voices. There was just the sound of my momma singing this song, the little shrieks of the children after the fireflies, still free, flickering in the air like notes. It is a long time ago now, but I hear it, I do hear it: "The boys don't go to the balls; the girls all bewitch them; they bewitch them all. They have Grigory, beautiful Grigory; he is sick with love; he calls on heaven, but no love comes. Then Grigory sings, he sings, 'It would be better, better, not to go to balls, not to love, not to know what it is, and now to forget.'" When her voice died out, another woman began singing far from the fire, too far for us to see who she was, and she sang about a very sick man. Her song was also a very old song: He lay on the grass covered with wounds; everyone passed him by; no one stopped to look, and he wondered, "Why? why? is it my wounds, my terrible wounds? Yes, it is my wounds from which blood pours like water; I feel death coming upon me; I feel cold sweat gathering like dew, but wait! Suddenly someone is coming! He is bending over me; he is wiping the dew from my forehead, the tears from my eyes; he has a holy hand, a saintly love. He does not mind my wounds; he is taking me with him on his back; he is pouring balsam on my wounds. He is God, he is God, and when no one would help me, then God would." For a moment there was stillness, the sound of crickets, little laughs coming from the trees like birds. A man began to sing an old song about a poor mother whose daughter was courted by a rich man. He sent the family embroidered towels; the mother accepted them. Then the daughter sang, "You have taken the towels; now I must marry, I must be married and miserable, but you, you will be happy." Now the mother sings, "My dear girl has gone to her room; she has taken sick and died." And then a stranger sings, "There is a huge cross in the middle of the road; the mother lies at its foot. She does not hear the *drozhkas* coming down the road, but she sings and sings, 'What have I done? I have buried my own daughter.' "

In the dark, Vera was pressed close to me; I could feel the whole outline of her body. She was not a little child anymore. "Such sad songs, Anya," she whispered, linking her five fingers through mine the way we used to when crossing streets. I snuggled closer to her. Then I was crying, Vera was, too. But the orchestra started playing again. Vera jumped up, bending over me, and said, "What are we crying about? Come, let's dance," and we did until Momma came over saying, "You're ready to drop and we have to get up early." We left, and in the morning, the whole procession to the *dacha* went on in reverse: the cart setting off for Vilno with the two maids on top, but this time burdened down with more, much more than they had before, jars of pickles and preserves, mushrooms, candied apples and strawberries that Anzia and Zoshia held between their legs, holding on to the wagon for their lives, and then we were at the station waiting with the others for the train.

No sooner were we home than Momma began preparations for winter. This year, Momma was demented with hurry. Everything had to be ready quick! Quick! Anya was going to medical school; Vera would be giving concerts; there was no time to waste! Anzia flew through the apartment like a bat, and Momma was after Zoshia like a cat after a mouse. "Who is coming with me to the store?" Momma demanded of us; "it's time to get the windows sealed." We had double windows, one pane inside another, but even with double windows the cold got in, so the stores sold colorful strips of puffy cotton wool in all colors, cut to the width of the window sills. Every winter, Momma and one of us would go to the store and buy new cotton linings in bright colors. "Anya will go," Vera answered, reading some sheet music; "she does it best. Remember how she used to give orders when she was eight? The poor saleswoman, she was probably transferred to the potato cellar for her health." "She did give orders," Momma grinned, remembering. And so we went.

We picked out navy-blue cotton for the white dining room, and yellow cotton for the black dining room, bright pink for Momma's room, red for mine, always red. "Get some orange for Verushka, just this once," I pleaded. I wanted to smuggle some color in there. "She won't like it," Momma warned. "She won't notice," I promised. We bought it, conspirators. The next stop was the store, a drugstore, that sold special paper flowers, only at this time of year, made with special wire stems to stick into the cotton. They were beautiful and looked so real, but they were fantastic, fairy flowers. We always took a big Russian basket with us, and Anzia to carry it. As soon as we filled it with flowers, she got on the bus with it and took it home. "Yellow and red ones for Verushka," I demanded. "Poor Verushka," Momma sighed; "next you will be rouging her cheeks while she sleeps." "And would it be such a bad idea?" I demanded. Oh, I was saucy. Momma giggled. She would get so excited by shopping, just like a girl. "Home, Anya!" she cried, right in the middle of the store. I was laughing. "They will think you are ordering a horse!" Momma was already buried in thought. "First, we have to get you ready for school; then we have to fill the house for the winter. Then we have to get Anna to come in for the month and make over all your dresses and make you some new ones. That medical school has costume balls, and you will want to go as a gypsy; you'll want fancy dresses; Verushka can't play on the stage in her nightgown, no matter what she thinks."

So it began. The cellar had to be full of everything. First, Momma would order nine square meters of logs. Then three men came to saw the logs so they were just the right length for the ovens. We never got tired of watching this; the two men sawing, the third splitting them with the ax. It was a guarantee of warm winters, songs on the white couch, the story of Momma smeared with dirt coming from Paltava, like a present, but one that had first fallen in the mud. Then the men started to fill the woodsheds. There was one shed for each apartment. They were like tiny barns really, and they were in the court, but crouching against the walls of the house as if they needed warmth. Momma could never believe we needed so much wood, but she would go into a panic if we had one log less than she ordered, for each room had to be heated, and each room had its own Russian stove, its bottom built of bricks, then above the bricks a little iron door, and when Momma wasn't home, we would roast a potato in there, or keep an old teapot hot, and then above the doors and the bricks came the tiles, and above the tiles, a circular brass grate. On the floor of all the rooms, in front of the stove, was a circular brass mat, like a rug, to catch any of the coals that fell out of the stove. Every day, Zoshia had to polish the mats, and the brass pots and pans, and the brass on the stove in the kitchen.

"The wood is taken care of, Momma," we reported. "The wood is taken care of, and you'll all starve to death in the warmth. Hurry up, Anya." And then we would go down to the kitchen to watch Anzia prepare the sauerkraut. From the way Momma carried on, no one would believe a family could survive the winter without it. "If you eat it for a hundred years, you will live forever," she would answer invariably when we teased her with her sauerkraut obsession. Poppa would join in, too. "It's a disease, Rebecca, a disease," he claimed, chomping on a cabbage stem. "Boris, are you going to read in this kitchen? We will have Lermontov in the sauerkraut," Momma said, losing her temper. She could not be teased in her kitchen. "Pushkin and I are going," Poppa said, leaving in exaggerated dignity. "Goodbye to Pushkin," Momma called after him. "She hates me," we heard him say, his feet in their slippers padding down the corridor to his study. "She hates me and I will stay up all night and lose my sorrows in Russian literature." "Don't think he won't," Momma glowered. Sauerkraut was no joking matter. This was the creation of the world going on here. There was no time to lose; she might forget a continent; she might leave out a sea. Such seriousness! For three days, Vera and I could stand it; then we retreated to our rooms, pawns taken off the board by the white queen. And our places in the kitchen were quickly taken by the children on the street, Mischa's friends mostly, who loved eating the stems of the cabbages. Then, when the one hundred and eighty pounds of flour arrived, the kitchen lost its mind. In the meantime, big sour yellow apples were put in to cook with the sauerkraut, and sour with it, and later, they were put in big barrels, and taken to the cellar, where their life was not long, believe me. Momma always believed in sharing things, and while we were cooking, or watching the maids cook, the poor neighbors were invited to come with their bowls and fill them with sauerkraut and potatoes, apples and meat. And there were a hundred and fifty pounds of potatoes on their way to the cellar while small watermelons were pickling, small pears and plums and apples packed all over the cellar in the straw. Anzia would be busy making the most wonderful preserves from rose leaves and apples, and these would be sealed in jars, and these too would go down to the cellar. They were joined by two hundred pounds of flour, two kinds, one flour for white bread, and one for dark bread; one hundred pounds of sugar; all kinds of cereals, kasha, everything. Then there were braids of onions; in the summer, one braid hung in the kitchen, but in the winter, everything was in the cellar, in the straw. The onions had a beautiful orange skin. There were two kinds of them, one very strong, one not. The house was full of everything.

Then, before the big holidays, before Passover, and eight weeks before Chanukah, something else started. The geese who were in cages in the woodshed were taken in and slaughtered and stuffed full of special balls of fat and flour, right through their beaks, and they were fattened up for the holidays. Then came Chanukah. The gribbonis was made, Momma's famous gribbonis for Chanukah. And when Momma saw it being made, she would always say, "If you eat this for a hundred years, you will live very long, not forever, the way you do when you eat the sauerkraut, but very long just the same." Then the honey wine was made. Making it was a very long procedure because Anzia and Zoshia had to boil the wine for a long time, and then sterilize it through a special filter paper, drop by drop. Then it was corked and filed away, because the longer it stood, the better it was, and every year, we would get out wine at least six years old. And if this were not enough, Momma would come in to watch the apple wine; first, grinding the apples in the nut-grinder, then for each glass of juice, Anzia would stir in one glass of sugar, and sometimes she and Momma would take turns, because Momma really loved this; this was her idea of cooking: pouring in some sugar, every now and then stirring it. Then Anzia and Zoshia would carry the jars into a corner of the kitchen behind the brass pot and the wine would ferment. Then it was sterilized through the special filter, and it would join the honey wine, and the cherry liquor made from enormous black cherries. And right before the holidays would come matzohs in a very big box, almost as tall as Vera, sixty pounds of them, for matzoh meal, matzoh farfel. Then Anzia would start to cut black radishes like macaroni, and boil them, and the smell, the smell was horrible. Then the maids had the kitchen to themselves. They would cook the radishes with a lot of honey and nuts, and this was called ingemachtz. And every year, we could never believe it, by some incredible miracle, this dreadfully smelly stuff, it was so delicious, we could not stop eating it. But while it was cooking, Poppa would pad through the house with a book in one hand, holding his nose with the other.

Everything was boiled or cooked in honey. In the country, Momma used to buy enormous amounts of honey right from the beehives. The whole family liked honey all year round. We ate it under the shining bay windows.

And then, when Momma was sure we would not starve, came the dresses for the children. Anna, the seamstress, was invited. She made all our school clothes, making over Momma's dresses for Vera and me, but that year something new happened. One day, while Anzia was cooking povidlo, made from Hungarian plums, in the courtyard, Momma sent us out to help her. This was a hard job and Zoshia was not feeling well again, so Momma had told her to stay in bed. To make this povidlo was no easy thing. A workman would build a little barbecue out of bricks and put wood crisscrossed on the bottom, and then over the wood went an iron grid, and on top of the grid, a huge pot with a hundred pounds of plums. There we would stand for the day, with the maids, and a huge wooden spoon, a ladle really, its handle almost two feet long, stirring and stirring, all day. We were not so happy to go out and do this now, Vera and I, because we were so busy with other things. We had not been stirring ten minutes when Momma came out to get us. "A visitor," she announced calmly. So naturally we thought it was Aunt Rivka with her box of marmalade candies. I looked at Vera, and Vera at me; we were ready to throw ourselves into the kettle. But it was not Aunt Rivka, it was Madame Kirilova, the most famous, the most expensive dressmaker in the city! And while we waited there like two door posts, Momma was saying that she wanted Madame Kirilova to make us each two outfits of our own choosing, to be *so good* as to make them! We could choose whatever we liked, but we were not to choose gowns, since we had been promised those already, nor costumes for the balls, since those too had been promised us.

So that was the end of medical school and the piano. Madame Anna Kirilova! This was not the Anna who came to the house in an old navy dress my mother gave her, the front of her flat chest covered with pins, constantly eating dried peas she kept in her pocket; she was so nervous, dreaming only of a husband, a husband, no! This was the woman who dressed the most elegant women in

55

Vilno and some of the most elegant women in Warsaw would come all the way to Vilno for an appointment with her, and they would have to be made months in advance. Momma must have been planning this a long time. We were out of our minds kissing her, and hugging her, until she had to scream, "Stop, stop! You will tear my clothes; I won't have anything to wear; we won't be able to afford new ones for you!" And Poppa smiling in the background saying, "Rebecca, you have bewitched them; Rebecca, they will never be the same again. Now they are only fit for husbands, rich husbands: you know some rich husbands, Rebecca?" And Vera and I were up all night in her room. She pushed all the sheet music right off the bed and I came in with a notebook, and told her, "I know just what I want!" But Verushka, you know, she was dreaming, and she said, "You know already?" in a dreamy voice. "I have to draw mine out first." And she did, dress after dress.

"I want," I told Verushka, "first of all a tuxedo, a green velvet tuxedo, just like a man's, with three buttons, and underneath, a white satin blouse with a big ruche and long sleeves and a ruffle at each wrist, coming down just to my rings." "What kind of skirt?" Vera asked absently, drawing some strange-looking thing; it looked like a Grecian gown. "A long plain skirt, also green velvet," I went on, "with two little pockets trimmed with grosgrain, and, yes, two little pockets on the jacket, on just one side, one above the other, also trimmed with grosgrain." "Where did you see anything like that?" Vera asked. "Oh, in a picture," I said, but really, I had seen a woman at the *dacha* wearing something like it, a very elegant lady from Warsaw, and I was already crazy about elegance. "And what else?" asked Verushka, drawing another fold on this strange thing. "Then a suit. Another elegant suit. You know, I will have to study a lot, so on Saturday nights, I will go to night-clubs, so I need a suit, a very elegant one, no? It will be navy-blue and sewn onto the collar will be two foxes to wrap around my neck and one end will hang over one shoulder, and there will be little pockets, of course, in the skirt and the jacket, and underneath, a blouse made of the same color, but silk, and a scarf attached at the collar, blue and white polka-dotted silk, lined in white, and white on the other side. "Oh, I am in it already!" I cried. "And you?" I asked, hopping with curiosity. "Something purple maybe," Verushka answered. "Purple what? A purple bathrobe?

56

Purple what?" "Purple with gold buttons," she answered dreamily. Then Momma knocked at the door. "Have you decided?" she asked, crinkling her nose. "*I* have decided; Verushka wants purple with gold buttons." "Then you will go see Madame Anna first, tomorrow morning, early please, and don't change your mind all the time, she's a busy woman." "Are you joking, Momma?" I asked. Momma peered at Verushka, and went out without saying anything.

So I went to Madame Anna's, and it was a new world. She showed me her fabrics, and then she pinned them to me, and cut the patterns on me; every day I came back, and there was the tuxedo, just as I had seen it, developing, like a picture out of a negative, a dream, a dream! Nothing could happen to me in medical school with a tuxedo like this! Then Verushka finally came, and they made her a purple suit with gold buttons, and everything was trimmed in gold braid; and a little suit with epaulettes made of red wool, with gold buttons again, and she had Madame Anna make it look like the uniform of a soldier; and everywhere we went, it was "Adorable, adorable!" Oh, we were so vain, it was disgusting. "Good morning, Princess Vera, good morning, Princess Anya," Mischa howled, banging on our doors to get us up. "What are you doing?" Momma demanded, after him fast. "And where is Zoshia; she should be up." "I'll see to *him*," Anzia promised, and there was only one more week until medical school began.

So Momma decided I had better have my ball dress made in advance, because the ball was only eight months away, and she had our old Anna make this dress, but, I don't know, maybe it was the circumstances, or her jealousy of Madame Anna, she was completely inspired. The gown was navy-blue chiffon to show off my long blond hair, wavy by nature. The back of the dress was open, slit from the neck to the waist. The front had the most unusual collar; it stood out on both sides of my face like little ears, little wings. And the material under the collar was gathered by tiny stitches into shapes like little tears. Then the skirt had three roses, huge roses, made from the same material, but of gold, halfway down the skirt, and from each of the roses hung a streamer of gold crepe de Chine which went right down to the hem; and the hem itself was gathered into huge scallops, and at the tip of each scallop was the golden streamer. Then I had golden shoes of my mother's, and her beautiful golden bag from Paltava; it was made from real gold, real gold, a metal bag, mesh, and the top, which snapped shut, was shaped like a tiara and covered all over with valuable stones. This came from my grandmother, and Vera and I used to share it. And my father used to laugh and say this was a new way for people to get ready for medical school and the concert hall.

But then Poppa decided we needed new coats to go over these things, so the next thing we knew, we were back at Madame Kirilova's, and she was trimming a black coat with ermine, and making a white ermine hat and black and white boots with white cuffs of the same fur, and a scarf, black on one side, and ermine on the other, with six ermine buttons down the front. And, when I put this coat over my tuxedo, I was impossible, impossible. I was a different person; I was so vain. I loved the feel of my body under my clothes. I spent hours looking at it without clothes, then with clothes; finally, I decided nothing was lost in putting on the new skins. And there was no doubt at all, my father was a nervous wreck; he was afraid the clothes were changing me, and the day I left for medical school in a plain skirt and blouse and my old blue coat, he was a resurrected man. And Vera, what kind of coat did she want? "A warm one." And when Poppa heard this, he asked Momma if she remembered how we had to build a special wooden platform for Vera's piano and piano stool, because when she first got it, her feet didn't reach the pedals, and she would not have blocks on the pedals or on her feet; Poppa was afraid she would be spoiled, willful. "But now," he said, "now, Rebecca, you see, she was a professional, even then." "Boris, you worry too much," Momma answered; "Anya will get over it too." So that was the first I knew I had something to get over. And I got over it right away—in the anatomy lab, with all the cadavers in formaldehyde and the terrible smell; immediately, my nose made me forget all about clothes.

5

Now things start moving faster, and I am always running instead of walking. It is very hard to describe, how there is a change, and there is no change. In one minute I am the little doll, the blond doll, five feet tall, with the thick blond braids, revolving like the figure on top of a music box on the bedroom chest of my parents, and the movement is slow, and the movement is determined by their hands, for they decide when to wind it, and my existence is determined by them, by my father, who gave the box to my mother, by my mother, who decides what jewels to take out, and when. And at other times the little figure is not on top of a music box, but something big, a barn or a church, and the night sky is torn with lightning and thunder, and the jagged lightning shows billowing black clouds traveling across the stars, clouds which otherwise you could not see.

In another minute, I see my life as two decks of cards; in one hand, I have the same deck I have always played with, but in the other hand is a new deck, all with different face cards, and I am sitting at the Preference table with my father. Nothing has changed, but still, I am very quickly shuffling the two decks together, and I always win; I always hold the winning hand. It is partly because I am young, but I always hold the winning hand. And there is a voice in the background asking if this is the best hand to hold. And in that hand of cards, the face cards are always the same: my mother, my father, my sister, Verushka, Anzia, Zoshia, my two brothers, Emmanuel and Mischa, but as I mix the two decks, there are new face cards: the face of Max who works with me in the Prosectorium, the Anatomy Room, the faces of the other boys—they change quickly; I never get to know them very well—the faces of the girls studying psychology at the university; and these cards stay for a while, and then are thrown down on the table, scooped up later, or forgotten. And it is hard to say at what moment the balance changes, and the faces change once and for all.

I remember the drawing master who used to come to us and have us draw railroad tracks in perspective. I see that drawing, the thin triangle, meeting at a vanishing point, and at that point, it is impossible to tell the train from the dot, but then there is a moment when the train appears, when there is no longer any question at all, and the closer it gets, the faster it moves; then it is rushing upon you, stopping in a scream of brakes and steam. So it was the day I went to the university and found my name on the first lists of those admitted to the medical school, the list like a giant white card of Preference, that the decks began shuffling together, that the music box began to revolve under a ceiling that was not the ceiling of the house, that the train in the picture began to move toward me, very fast.

And meanwhile, at home, what has changed? Zoshia is a little paler and sleeps more; the two maids who come once a month to do the laundry by hand and hang it to dry in our attic still arrive; the clothes still dry in perfect peace, free from their human bodies. I still wake up early and run out of the house, but now my blond braids are not flying, because I pin them up under my medical school cap to show my new position, and I still stand on the corner of Kransky Street to wait for the bus, but this bus goes to the medical school. Now my schedule is irregular; some days I am there at nine, some days I am not through until seven. When I run home from the bus, before going in, I still stop in front of my friend's house across the street and call her: "Rachel! Rachel!" and she gets up and comes out onto the balcony in her nightgown. She is always sleepy; she always wants to know what's going on. And I always ask her, what are you doing, still asleep at twelve? And we make some plans to trap some boys for Saturday nights, right there on the street. Or if there is a ball at the medical school, I tell her about the preparations going on, and that I will tell her the rest later; will she come with me downtown to sell tickets to the businessmen, who buy them to show their support of education, and hopping up and down, I tell her we will talk about the rest later. "Go back! Get dressed!" And she retreats from her balcony in her white gown, sleepy, and when I knock at her leaded glass door, the maid tells me she is asleep, but she will wake her up. We do not spend time dreaming in my room any more, about romance, about who we will marry, and how we will find him, or wonder what being married is like, telling each other our strangest ideas. And we never look for Emmanuel's collection of "bad cards," photographs in brown and white that cleared things up for us.

And some days, I do not run home quickly, but go slowly. I have chosen anatomy and chemistry for my first year; I have fallen in love with the university as if it were a person. I love the walk from the Prosectorium, a completely round building, to the Chemistry Building, three stories high and a fifteen-minute walk away, or, if I am late, a five-minute ride on the bus. It is like a great dear body with the arms here, and the legs there, and the head somewhere else, and we are the blood that moves through them all, keeping them whole and alive. But there are days when I cannot get used to the smell in the Anatomy Lab, when the formaldehyde makes me dizzy. Finally, I faint. Max, a student who works with me, has evidently picked me up. I hear the buzz of boys' voices all around me, and the voice of Professor Kobielski, angry. Then I understand they are telling him they were in such a hurry to look at something, they pushed me from my stool and I hit my head. "These are bodies, not rivers, please do not dive in like fish," he tells them severely, but he give me a suspicious look. I know I am as yellow as my hair.

Later we go to the candy store and have sodas, and Max talks to me earnestly: "Anya, you have to get tougher about it; you have to get tougher. It is a dead body, *dead*. It walked around; it was a person; it had a name; it is a dead person. You have to think about that and accept it. Someday you will be on a slab, I will be on a slab, we will all be on slabs." The faces of the other three boys stare at me like judges. "Maybe," one of them suggests weakly, "it's because our cadaver is a man? Maybe it's modesty?" I just shake my head no, hopelessly. I can't say anything, but the surface of my lemonade moves suddenly, like a disturbed sea; I realize I am crying. But I'm stubborn; I won't raise my hand to wipe away the tears. I didn't ask them into my eyes. So Max picks up his napkin. In the candy store there are real linen napkins, cross-stitched with flowers, red and green. He wipes my eyes for me. "We'll all be on slabs, won't we, and then there won't be exams. It won't be so terrible; think of all the sleep we'll get. Think of how long it will take. Think how many slabs will be empty if you stop diving into the

bodies." He is trying to make me smile, and he is succeed-
ing.

I have the lemonade glass with its iced rim pressed to
my gnawed lips; I keep staring at all of them over it.
"Drink something," Jakob says in a husky voice. "Drink it;
you'll feel better." And now I do drink from the glass, because they have not told me a girl who faints should study
psychology, not medicine, and because it was Jakob who
asked me to drink, and the whole school knows he is an
anti-Semite; and he is very upset. I drink the lemonade
with my eyes riveted on Jakob. He gets up from the table—he had been sitting at the edge, nearest the aisle, opposite me—and he rushes out. Max nervously tinkles the ice
in his glass. "He'll never finish," he says with authority.
"He'll finish up in law," Henryk says; "he's more frightened than you." We all sit there in silence, and the waiter
comes over in his white apron, rubbing his hands, asking,
"Anything else, young lady, young gentlemen?" We support this candy store, and he is very impressed by students
from the university. Who knows, we may grow up some
day and save him when he lies bleeding in his bed.

So on days like that I walk home. And when I get home,
I go into my father's study and sit down in the big armchair next to his desk. I do not even take off my coat, but
sit there with my books on my lap, a patient in a waiting
room. And Poppa puts down his pencil, raises his head,
pushes his glasses back on his nose. He has gotten balder,
and now, as he pushes back his glasses, he also raises his
eyebrows, and because he has gotten balder, he seems to
be pushing up his eyebrows. He doesn't say anything right
away; I drink in the red of his walls like a transfusion. He
just looks at me, and finally, I start to speak. "I don't
know what to do, Poppa. I can't stand the smell in the
Prosectorium; I can't stand it." Then I stop, shut off, a radio. He looks at me. "Anya," he says, and his voice is not
sympathetic at all, "a human being can get used to anything. A human being can get used to what he must.
Sometimes I think that is one of the most frightening
things in life." He still speaks Polish with a heavy Russian
accent. "You'll get used to it; you'll see. I remember your
first injection; do you remember it? You were supposed to
inject a grapefruit. You had your poor momma looking all
over the house for a grapefruit, a grapefruit in October, and
when she gave it to you, you took one look at it and burst
into tears. So you injected me, and here I am—I'm not

62

black and blue; I don't have any bubbles in my blood; I'm not dying of pain; and now you give injections as if you were sticking a pincushion. Believe me, you will get used to it; you will probably even forget there was a time you were not used to it. This is nothing." And the next thing I know, I am on the street, calling to Rachel. We sit on her bed making plans for the school ball, and soon I sit next to the dead body, eating a tuna sandwich.

Anatomy is becoming my favorite subject. I love the way people ask who my anatomy teacher is, and when they hear, pucker their skins, and say, "Ooooh, he is so hard, so modern; he doesn't teach like the others at all. How can you stand it?" Now Max and Henryk and Jakob have decided our body needs a name. We have decided to call him Alexander. We fight over him, oh, do we fight over him: who gets to take the arm home to study before the exam (the Prosectorium checked out parts of the body like medical books). I march off home triumphant—I have the arm. Professor Kobielski who is so hard stands in front of the room, beginning the course. "First, you will make an incision in the lower abdomen. Then you will observe all the organs. You will draw an exact diagram of what you find, and you will compare these diagrams with the diagrams in your book, noting any abnormality. Then, on the other side of your diagram, you will write what caused the abnormality. Is it congenital; is it pathological, functional, or structural, what is it? If you think it is pathological, you must make a tissue sample and prepare a slide; examine it under the microscope and draw a diagram of what you see and give an explanation of what you find." ("But this is *pathology*," whispers Jakob, indignant; "what do I know about microscopes yet?") And Jakob is in such a fury, he makes his first slide of the intestine and turns the knob of the microscope so violently, he cracks the slide in two. "Your hope is not to become a surgeon, I devoutly pray," Professor Kobielski comments. It is the mystery of our lives, how he always manages to materialize at the wrong moment.

"And please," he continues in his severe voice, "do not refer to the parts of your cadaver as if they belonged to you: *my* arm and *my* leg. It is a disgusting habit to get into, and the lady who complains that 'her' penis is diseased will not get the professional attention for her cadaver she wants." He seems to know everything we do. "Please, Mr. Ravinsky," he says to Jakob, "your Alexander is not a pig you have taken to the slaughter; be so good as not to slice through all his veins at once. You can't find the plexus because you have just cut it in half. The rest of you move over to the next table and observe." And then one day we were all doubled over in laughter. "May I know what is so funny?" he asks, inclining himself toward us from a great height. "Oh, just a joke," I say, bursting into hysterics again. "Do you want to hear it?" asks Max; he is the boldest of us all. "I think I had better not," the professor answers, disappearing like a mist, but with a hint of a smile. He must have been through this himself once. And still, we are cackling, because I had just been dissecting poor Alexander's penis, and suddenly I said, "Oh, I just found out Alexander is not dead!" Poor Max almost fell into the stomach cavity, and all afternoon it was, "Oh, I just discovered," and this horrible cackling from us, like chickens around chicken feed.

Then, one day, I came home from school and the whole house was in an uproar. In the kitchen, I could hear my mother screaming, her voice sharpened like a knife. "How dare you? How dare you?" and Mischa's protestations, almost inaudible. As I am taking off my coat to put it in the big wooden cabinet in the entrance hall, I can hear Anzia reading aloud in the black dining room; she is reading in an odd flat voice. So I went on into the kitchen. Momma had her key ring out and was shaking it in Mischa's face. Her face was blood-red and tears were streaming down and dripping from her chin. "How dare you take things without my permission? How dare you! How many times do I have to tell you to ask, and I'll give you what you want; I know what to give you. And now you have eaten it all up, and I have nothing for company, how dare you!" So Mischa had taken Momma's keys, which she sometimes hid under her pillow, and opened the oak credenza and eaten something, but still, this was incredible. Even Poppa was taking part. I couldn't understand it. What had Mischa swallowed? The crown jewels? Mischa stood there, white as the guilty flour he had swallowed. And Poppa! What did he have to do with stolen pastries, sweets before meals?

"Listen, Rebecca," he said, trying to calm her down (but even *his* voice is raised; his voice; when he always said, "Oh, you know that is a low person, listen to the way he speaks; he booms."), "listen, Rebecca, you are as bad as the cook in *The Cook and the Cat*." He meant a Russian story Momma always used to read to us, and then Anzia, and then Zoshia, about a conceited cook who thought he was brilliant because he could sign his name or something, and one day, he came home, and his cat was right in the middle of the kitchen, eating his prize squab, a delicacy, cooked specially in vinegar. The cook, so proud of his education, gave the cat a terrible lecture: "How can you do it? I am stunned." And the drunken cook went on with this lecture: "I have always considered you a very honest cat, a very nice one; how dare you disgrace yourself like this? I cannot believe my eyes." Instead of taking the squab away from the cat, the cook talked and talked and talked, and in the meantime, while he continued talking, the cat finished eating, and the narrator of this tale, who always carefully pointed out the moral, said that *he* would not have talked to the cat; he would have killed him. This must have been what Poppa meant to say; Momma was like the narrator, and she was killing the poor cat, Mischa, but really, she should just talk to him and take back the keys; enough was enough.

"Don't bother me with stories!" Momma screamed; "in the meantime, Vera is in her room reading *Resurrection* like a half-dead lily, and the rest of the time she sits at the piano playing that lullaby the mother sings to her illegitimate child, 'I will teach you to hate men from diapers,' and you want to tell me stories! I tell you, they know what's going on!" "They do not know, Rebecca," Poppa boomed, and I shrank against the tiles of the oven; "but they will know if you say another word. Mischa, please go to your room; your mother is not herself. No, Anzia, take Mischa to his room and read him a story there; you can listen, too. You'll live through it. Now, Rebecca, and Anya, too, we'll go to my office." From the time I was twelve, Poppa and Momma took me in as one of the council; the family called us the Triumvirate. Momma was sobbing and choking as if she couldn't breathe, and Poppa was marching in his slippers, stiff as a soldier. I followed them. I had no idea!

"So," said Poppa, as he closed the door, "it is all about Zoshia. She won't be here any more." No Zoshia! I was too stunned to speak. "Mischa will be especially upset," Poppa continued, "and he mustn't find out anything about it. Personally, I would prefer it if Vera didn't find out, either. She is crazy enough, but your mother thinks she knows. She may know; she's a snoop, your sister. So,

Anya, we told the children that Zoshia has to go to the country to take care of her father who is sick and has no one. But the truth is, she is four months pregnant, and your Momma thinks, and I think, she can't stay with us." Momma choked; I kept silent. "I know it's hard," he went on, "but it's because of Mischa. You know how he adores her, and how she influences him; who knows what would happen to him if he found out?" I was already counting back four months. So it was that last summer in the *dacha*. Poppa noticed how pale she was; he wanted to call a doctor. She complained to Momma about how the men followed her. "It was some Chasidic man who came over to her in the park with a bag of compliments, like the fox to the crow, and he took her home, gave her vodka, and the rest I don't have to explain to you, a medical student. So she got pregnant; so she's gone. She told Anzia and Anzia told your mother." Gone where? I was remembering teaching her to read; it was as if a sister were gone, a sister or a child. "Your Momma found a woman in the country, near the *dacha*. She's a poor woman and needs help. She promised to call a midwife for Zoshia when the time comes. Momma gave her some money. Zoshia, you know, she didn't seem too unhappy, not after she got there and saw the seven children and the country." "She was unhappy," I said. Momma sobbed louder. "Of course," Poppa said; "do you have a better idea?" I shook my head; no, I didn't. "We will have a new maid, Josefa, next week. It is better your brothers do not learn of this yet; it's better. She was like another mother to them. I know you'll be careful."

I wanted to cry with Momma. But Poppa trusted me, and he depended on me. "You will talk to Vera, please?" he asked, and I thought, for the first time, that it was painful sometimes, how he put all his hopes in me, and how he trusted me. "Are you sure she's all right there?" I asked; "the woman is a good one?" "Very good," Momma said, sounding as if she were saying "berry bood." "I asked everyone in the town about her." "How did you find out about her?" I asked. "I asked Mrs. Bialy." "Why couldn't she stay with Mrs. Bialy?" I asked. "Mrs. Bialy is too close; the boys would see her, Vera would see her, your momma would see her and walk around every day with this red nose thinking it is all her fault." "It is my fault!" Momma screamed; "I should have watched." She was sobbing again. "You watched her when she was young,"

Poppa said. "You couldn't follow her every time she took the chickens off to the slaughter." "I should have watched," Momma sobbed again. "Stop it, Rebecca!" Poppa ordered; "there is such a thing as the fate of a human being. You can't believe, after everything we've seen, that you are responsible for everything in the world. Can you believe it? Then I must give up my atheism and believe in God, because she lives in this house. It was Zoshia's fate."

"There is no such thing as fate," Momma cried; "there is only responsibility!" She ran out of the room; seconds later, the door to her pink bedroom slammed. Poppa took off his glasses and rubbed his eyes. "Poor Zoshia!" he said. Then, "I don't envy your Momma. I remember, when the Revolution began, she asked where we should go, and I had to decide. I got the uniform of a Red Guard and we fled to Minsk where I was not known, and a lot of us got together. I got hold of a train and so we came here. But if we had left sooner, or later, or on a different train, who knows what? I don't take any credit. I did the best I could, but the earth was moving. If anything had happened to her, I would not have lived; I would not have lived. How much can one person do? Your Momma wants to think there's a way of controlling everything; I can't believe it. Please talk to Vera." "What should I tell her? You said you didn't want her to know." "You decide, you decide," Poppa said. His hand was resting on the globe on his desk; he began spinning it slowly. "Fate," he murmured. "The globe is packed to the core with the dead; that's the fate of a human being. Responsibility is the road you choose to the pit. Well," he said, putting his glasses back on his nose and pushing them down hard, "I am going to translate from the *Tartar,* and then I'll talk to your Momma."

When I went into Vera's room, there was a copy of *Resurrection* flung on the floor, right near the door, and she was staring at a picture of Zoshia she had drawn in charcoal and singing this song about the woman who had been raped, and was rocking her child, promising her she would be taught to hate men from her days in diapers. She knew. I told her the whole story. "I would have kept her here!" she cried passionately. "What would you have told Mischa?" "I don't know, I would have kept her here!" "They couldn't," I said. "They didn't want to!" There was no talking to her. All night, I could hear her playing that horrible lullaby until I wanted a diaper to strangle her with, my own sister. In the morning she was tired, and there were big greenish circles under her eyes. "Will we visit her?" she finally asked. "Perhaps after she has the baby. By then, she can invent some excuse. Maybe by then we can also take Mischa." "That would be nice," she said dreamily; "the baby will be nice."

On Monday morning, Josefa, the new maid, came, and Momma welcomed her, showed her the room which she would share with Anzia, and the bed, which had been Zoshia's. Then Momma locked herself in her room crying. When I came home from medical school, I took off my coat, put it away, and went into Momma's room; she was still crying. I took off my dress and got into bed with her. I nuzzled into her side until I could feel her stomach against mine; it was so much rounder than mine. "Hug me," I asked, and we both fell asleep. I had never done it before: this was her bed, and Poppa's.

So things went on again as before. We had our first costume ball at the university, and naturally I wanted to go as a gypsy. Momma didn't even bother to ask me, but just told Anna when she came: a gypsy costume. And when I complained that she should have asked me first, I might have changed my mind, she said, "But you *always* want to go as a gypsy!" She was right. I loved pretending to tell fortunes, taking the hands of rich gentlemen, the soft pink hands, sometimes even powdered, and trying to read things in their rivers, things that had gone under; I could bring them up to the surface again. "Will you take Rachel?" Poppa asked. He knew the answer, but he was still curious; maybe I had changed more than he thought. All these years, I knew his opinion of her. He didn't like her. He would never forbid me to see her, but he used to ask, "What kind of a life is it? The life of a parasite. Life has to have a goal. Do you think she is the right friend for you if she isn't your equal?" But after he saw I had entered medical school and was fulfilling my duties, he never mentioned her again. And I did not accept all dates; I didn't want to disappoint my parents. As for myself, I could have kissed the stones of the school. For me, Professor Kobielski was a dark, mysterious personality, with secrets hidden in his past, all the years before I had met him, locked closets. Vera had her books; I had my professors. And sometimes, my whole body would flush hot, as if with a high fever, but I didn't know what it was, or if I did, I was frightened and ignored it. So when boys came to the house, Anzia would tell them I wasn't there. But some of them would go into the court and see the light in my room. And how I was teased! Henryk used to say, "At Anya's, you are thrown out with real elegance." But they were not angry; they understood I was a serious person, at least about school.

"Of course I am taking Rachel." Rachel and I had been friends since we were nine, and in the gymnasium I would refuse a date unless the boy could produce another for Rachel; I didn't enjoy myself if I was out and she was home. Other girls often hurt me, but Rachel, never; perhaps that was it. So I was always there, or she was always here, and our parents got to know each other. Rachel's mother understood her better than I did; Rachel had a passionate nature, and very early, her mother was trying to arrange a marriage for her. Rachel looked Emmanuel over, but he never looked back: his little sister and her friends. In the town, there was a young man who couldn't get a job, but was very good-looking; Rachel saw him one night at a café. Momma was persuaded to approach his mother and mention the possibility of arranging a wedding, but it didn't work; the other woman would not speak to her again. Now, though, the boy was twenty-one and he still had no job. His mother approached mine in the butcher shop where they were both waiting for their orders and asked Momma to bring the details of Rachel's dowry. They were very tempting: ninety thousand zlotys, half an apartment, and setting the young man up in a business. After the costume ball, and by the time of the medical ball, it was arranged. But I told Momma, "A wedding you arranged in a butcher shop is nothing to count on; I'll take her with me. Maybe she'll meet someone better." "She never does," Momma sighed.

But Rachel was filled with energy unusual for her now, and she went all over the city with me and we sold tickets and came home with big donations. And while we went to all the offices my father suggested on his list, Anna stitched my gypsy costume. It was a very exciting ball! All our parents came, of course, and the medical school had reserved the most splendid hall in the city. We had a big, big room with eight entrances, and at each was a table covered with a white cloth, holding fresh flowers, and we pinned one to each of the contributors, the older men, the philanthropes. And my table was doing the best. The dancing floor gleamed like egg yolk; the red velvet drapes reflected themselves in the yellow lake; the two orchestras played the "Polonaise," the exquisite dance where the boys and the girls do not touch. Momma and Poppa were dancing too. Then Professor Kobielski asked me to dance. It was such an honor! "Do I smell like formaldehyde?" he asked me smiling; "do I make you want to faint?" I blushed redder than the drapes on the wall. He had known what was wrong from the start. "Thank you," he said with a bow, and I was enchanted, I was a queen with a star tiara lighting another world.

Then we were on our own. Flirting. The huge buffet drew everyone, but I was so excited, I didn't want anything to eat. Just then someone tapped me on the shoulder; he looked twenty-seven or -eight, and I was seventeen. First I noticed his shoes, then his tie, then his tuxedo. He didn't look like anyone else there. He was German but he spoke French to me because my German was so bad, and he would not let me go! We danced all night; he would not leave. Even when he went for punch, he took me with him. "I'm afraid I'll never find you again," he said. Then he began to visit. Vera liked him right away; she studied German and she could talk to him. It was his summer vacation and we went out every night. We saw *Metropolis, The Blue Angel,* a Mendelssohn concert, plays and more plays, and when he had to leave, he wrote every day. Momma was wringing her hands: "Germany! Do you know where it is? It is not around the corner!" But this time, Poppa stopped it; if I went to Germany, he said, it would be the end of my education. If he had threatened me with death, he could not have frightened me more. I stopped writing; there were no more letters with foreign stamps.

When my winter vacation came, Momma decided I needed a rest. I looked green; I was working too hard. She was sending me to Zakopanie, she announced, the winter resort, and I was to stay in a suite with my Uncle Frederich, my father's brother. I hardly knew him—he had visited after each of our births—but Momma wouldn't trust me with anyone out of the family. "However," said my mother, watching me pull things out from underneath my mattress like a crazy person, "there is something you have to do there. You have to gain forty pounds." She took out a list with a diet. "I have already sent your Uncle Frederich a copy," she said severely. This

is what it was: two pints of sour cream, one loaf of bread
with butter in the morning, three eggs, eight glasses of
milk, as much ham as I could eat, because it would fatten
me up the fastest, and on no account was I to sleep
through breakfast.

They took me all packed up, with a special skirt divided
like pants in the middle. I was really wearing pants but
looked like I was wearing a skirt when I crossed my legs,
and I had enough warm woolen stockings for a centipede,
and woolen sweaters Anzia had knitted with little pictures
of people skiing. They put me on the *wagon-lit*, and I slept
most of the way. It took some time to get there because
the resort was in the middle of the high mountains, the
Karpats. Sleighs from the hotels met the trains and
brought us to them. There was my Uncle Frederich at the
station, waving the list: "I expected a skeleton," he said.
"We'd better hurry: I don't want the sour cream to spoil."

I had the most wonderful time. The hotel was high up
in the mountains; in the valleys were taverns. The first
night I was there, there was a knock at the door; I
thought it was the maid and told her to come in. But it
was not the maid at all. There stood two boys who had
lost their way to their rooms. I was already in bed with
my blond hair down, in the quilts and covers I had
brought with me specially, because Momma was sure that
in what the hotel gave you, you would freeze to death.
One of them saw me in this bed, under my enormous flowered quilt, made of the same material as the drapes in my
room, and I was wearing a nightgown to match. "Oh," he
said, "we didn't know a queen was staying here," and they
tried to persuade me to get up and come dancing. I told
them I was too tired. Would I promise for tomorrow,
then? I said I would. And the next day we went all over
the valleys in a sleigh, and no matter where we stopped I
ate as much as I could; it was a good thing they turned
out to be millionaire's sons! "Let's go to the tavern with
the gypsy," one of them suggested and we were off to it.
There was a five-year-old gypsy playing a violin.

The next day I found out about the sun baths higher up
in the mountains. You had to get up early and take a
sleigh a long way, almost straight up; then there was a
walled-in place in the middle of the glittering snow, high
up, high, as close as you could get to the sun by sleigh.
When you went into the enclosure, there were benches
and you sat in your blouse, unbuttoned, head tilted back,

and turned brown, as if it were summer. It was not cold at all. Every morning I used to get up and run after the sleigh and sit there sunning until noon, munching on my loaf of bread and butter, or finishing what sour cream I had left from breakfast. Then one day a new woman came, the daughter of a contessa, so the gossip went, who took off all her clothes and lay down on a bench. It was a little cloudy; we were the only ones there. At first, I didn't notice anything. It was usual for women to exercise and sun themselves naked at resorts; it wasn't so usual in the snow, but still, usual. Then, after I finished my bread, I saw it; she had plucked a question mark in her pubic hair. I couldn't wait to get out of there.

Then there was a mixup with rooms, and I was put in an annex, Uncle Frederich in the main building, and for one night, I shared a room with a seamstress. In the middle of the night, I heard someone come in. He was spending the night with her, while I lay facing the wall, consumed with curiosity heating up like an iron. And in the morning who should it be but Rachel's older sister's husband. I hadn't seen him for years, not since his wedding, when Marina, Rachel's sister, moved with him to Warsaw. When he saw me, he wanted to bury himself! "Anya," he pleaded, "I came to buy some silk for Marina; would you come to the shops and help me pick something out?" "Pick someone closer to you," I told him. Oh, I was mad. But I couldn't wait to get home and tell Momma. It was always like that; I knew she would be waiting for me. At home, when I had a date, she would wait up and I would have the boys find a piece of candy for Momma "so she could get to sleep." The boys had to go all over for it, all over. Then I would sit on the edge of the bed. "Tell me," she would insist, eyes flaming, propped by her pillow, while Poppa snored like a buzz saw, or else translated in his study.

So I came home all brown, absolutely like chocolate; nobody could call me green, but the guiltiest person, the guiltiest person alive. I had gained only twenty-seven pounds; the closer we got to the station, the guiltier I felt. I was so guilty, and the train was pulling into the station and there was Momma. I snuck up to her. She turned around to look, but didn't recognize me; I had gained so much weight. So she decided I had eaten enough. "Can I stop the sour cream?" I asked. "Please," she answered, eyeing me critically, and immediately in the *drozhka* on the way home it was, "tell me, tell me." "Fat!" Mischa screamed. "Juicy!" Momma contradicted. "What did she do? Eat all the snow on the mountains?" Emmanuel asked. "I don't like it," he judged, on his way out somewhere. "How much weight *did* you gain?" Momma asked. "Only twenty-seven pounds," I admitted guiltily. "Ah," Momma sighed with satisfaction. "I thought if I told you to gain forty, you would accomplish at least half of what I asked."

But, of course, then it was medical school and I began shrinking like an icicle in the sun, and no one would believe my tan was natural, but said it had come from a box. There I was, with my white teeth, big blue eyes, blond hair, and chocolate skin, and it was compliments and more compliments, jokes about my inconstancy, how my love affair with Alexander was ill-fated—how our relationship was dissolving under their very eyes; he was being eaten up with sorrow; he was not the same as he was, and on and on until I regretted ever having made that joke about how he was still alive. "What's the matter, now?" asked Professor Kobielski one day while we were trying to shelter Alexander from his sharklike eyes. Jakob, we feared, had just severed the carotid artery instead of the jugular vein and we were trying to shield the evidence with our own bodies. "Oh, Alexander here is being eaten up by love for Miss Anya," Max said. "Oral examinations on Friday," Professor Kobielski announced ominously. "Would that all of you last as long as Alexander." That shut us up.

So the tan faded; the usual ways burned themselves back. Again, I was running back and forth to the bus, calling for Rachel; if I called her on the way to the bus, she would stagger out onto the balcony and ask, "Off to Kafkaska Street?" which was her way of asking about the medical school. She had barely finished the gymnasium. I don't think she liked to think about my life at the university, especially since the costume ball, dancing only with my father, and her father, and with the German man, who was afraid to say no to me. One morning I was unusually tired; we had just finished a long series of exams. Anzia was brushing and braiding my hair; my clothes for the day were already laid out on the bed—navy-blue skirt, navy-blue blouse with polka dots, white collar and cuffs— when the phone rang and it was my father. "Your father wants to speak to you," Momma said, coming in, search-

73

ing my face. She seemed afraid I could read her mind. "To me?" I said, amazed. "At this hour? What can he want?" "Answer the phone and find out."

"Anya, listen to me," he was saying, relapsing into his early dialect, "nor you nor your sister are to go out today." "But why? You know I'm busy; I *have* to go; I have classes." "You will not go," he said, while I was bent over trying to tie a shoelace on my patent leather shoe; "some stupid boys have started a kind of pogrom of the Jewish students, the girl students." Right away, it was as if I were turned to ice. Our university had many beautiful Jewish girls, not in medicine. Jewish girls in the medical school could be counted on the fingers of one hand, but they were mostly in psychology, and in chemistry and biology. One girl was more beautiful than another. They came from all over Poland and were not real "Vilno" girls, who had a tendency to be heavy in the back, and stuck out below the waist, so that Max said he could always tell a Vilno student from behind. The girls were not thin, but magnificent; they were statues. "The Index, the fraternities, have iron nails attached to their hands, very pointy and sharp, and their goal is to go after the faces of the beautiful girls, and demolish them."

"Oh, Poppa, this can't be true," I wailed, but I knew, I knew it was. "True or not, you are not going out, nor is Vera." "Where did you hear it?" "From someone in the bank. It's a public place. News travels around fast here." And I already knew what he meant. Someone, a gentile for whom he had done a favor, had heard something, or seen something, maybe from one of his own children, and had told my father: "Keep your daughters in; they are going after the faces of the girls." So we stayed home. And as the girls came out of their classes, the boys went after the faces, only the faces; it was horrible.

Max came to the house late in the afternoon. One of the leaders of the Index had fallen in love with a beautiful girl, a Jewish girl; she had a magnificent face, olive skin, and hair down to her waist, and she was just nineteen. She fell in love with him, and lived with him. It was very unusual; no one did anything like that. But no matter what her parents tried, they couldn't stop her. And it was his idea, the boy she lived with, to demolish faces, or his parents' idea, because they didn't like what they saw him doing, but whatever the reason, he was the one who began it. And she was the first one they went after. Max told me down one side of her face were deep scratches like tracks, going right under her scalp to her chin, and she would not come out, even to go to the doctor. The next morning, we heard she had thrown herself under a train, but she was not killed; her arms and her legs were cut off, and this is how her parents got her back and took her in again, their beautiful daughter. I couldn't believe it. These were the same boys I had my *preparats* with; we sat on the same benches; we took the same courses with the same professors. Then I realized they very rarely came to the house, unless they wanted to borrow notes, or a piece of the cadaver. Only Max, who was also Jewish, and who somehow kept his distance too, came often. I was frightened and very much hurt, and for the first time, I began to think about God. Was there such a thing as God? Had he protected me from the iron nails? Was it just coincidence that my father heard the story when no one else's did? My mother had said there was no fate, only responsibility. But if my father had not been told, if it had not been his fate to hear, he would not have called me, and I would have been defaced, destroyed. He exercised his responsibility, but was it coincidence or fate that led him to do it, that made him able to do it? And then I began to believe, I don't know why, because no one in my house believed, that there was a kind of fate, but that it was not determined by accident. It was determined; the fate of a human being was determined by a superpower, perhaps not the God I always heard of, but a superpower nevertheless, and I began to believe in him, to talk to him.

And while I was thinking this out, my mother got the news that Zoshia had given birth to a baby girl; she was very excited. She bustled around, finding old baby clothes, packing up a huge wicker Russian basket, the same one we used for mushrooming at the *dacha,* and set off for the country lady's to congratulate Zoshia and, as father put in, to kiss the baby to death. But when she got there (I could not go because of school, nor could Vera, and Poppa had his work) she did not find the baby or Zoshia. Where was Zoshia? The woman only cried. Where was the baby? The woman cried again. Finally she told Momma that Zoshia had disappeared, and she had left the baby in a basket on the steps of the country church. "You know, Mrs. Savikin, this is everyday," the woman said, and she went on to say that she thought Zoshia had killed herself. For weeks they had seen her, when the woman's children were in bed, staring into the rapids under the little bridge. It was a spot forbidden to swimming because the water moved so fast; there was an undertow and it was dangerous. Boys from the school used to bet they could swim there. So many boys had drowned, the little village council had passed a law against entering the water for a half mile in either direction.

Mother came home like a corpse. The basket was forgotten; Momma had left it with the woman saying she should take what she needed for her children. Momma was cold as ice. She told me, and I told Poppa. And for weeks: "It is my fault," but this time her eyes were dry, no tears, no tears, until we began to worry about her. But then somehow Vera heard and became hysterical, and this brought Momma back. We could hear her in Vera's room talking, talking, and then one night I was standing in the hall, with my ear pressed to Vera's door and beckoned to Poppa. He tiptoed down the hall in his slippers. It was unmistakable. They were both sobbing.

Then there were exams, and the first year of medical school came to an end, and I was at the top of my class.

6

"So," Poppa said when the excitement over the grades finally burned down; "it's time to make plans for the summer." He and Momma and I were sitting in his office. I had a suspicion something was going on, since each time I had mentioned the *dacha*, or leaving for the *dacha*, Momma had changed the subject. She seemed particularly uncomfortable if I brought it up in front of the others. "Do you want to go to Druzgeniekie?" Poppa asked directly. "For a week?" I asked. We had a villa in Druzgeniekie, which we rented out every year. It was part of Poppa's inheritance, but the family had never spent the summer there because it was too far for Poppa's weekend visits. "No, alone," Poppa said, "for the whole summer. You're old enough, and your Momma and I have been talking: There will only be Mischa left at the *dacha* with us; Vera won't be there all summer; she has to give concerts. Emmanuel has his job. We think it's time; that is, if you want to go. There are many, many young people there; it's very pleasant. I think you would enjoy it."

Enjoy it! Except for visiting Warsaw, staying at Druzgeniekie had been my dream for years. Rachel and I used to sit up plotting: How much could it cost to go to Warsaw? How much? We would live in a little attic; we could live on bagels and herring; how much could *that* cost? "If you want to go," Poppa went on, as if trying to conceal his persuasions, "Anzia will of course go with you, and naturally we won't rent out the *dacha* there this year. Your Uncle Frederich will be nearby if there are any emergencies. He says he doesn't mind; he survived your visit to Zakopanie very nicely; and I don't have to ask Rebecca how often she will visit if she doesn't get a letter every twenty-four hours. But you want to think about it and let us know, I understand that; you've never been there, and the idea's something new to you." Poppa was flowing on, smoothly as a river, and I was a little pebble trying to make a ripple in the current.

"Poppa! When can I go!" I finally demanded, raising my voice. "She wants to go," he said to Rebecca, his eyebrows traveling halfway up his head in surprise. "I told you," Momma said. "Are you sure?" Poppa asked. "Poppa!" I screamed. He looked very disappointed. "Then go tell Verushka you're going, and that she can visit you if she can think of a way of packing her piano to get it on the train." But Momma got me first: I needed new clothes. "I have everything I need," I protested. I felt guilty; they would not have the income from the *dacha* now. It was a great deal of money lost because of me. "First of all," she said, "you need a new bathrobe. You can't run through the streets after the water baths in that thing you draggle around the house. I'm sorry to be so mundane. I will tell Anzia to make you a terry cloth bathrobe, a very long one, and some blouses, and embroider some towels, maybe a runner for the porch." She went on thinking out loud, but I didn't hear the rest of it, because she was drifting off to the kitchen, compiling a new list for me, clothes this time, not sour cream and ham.

I couldn't wait to tell Rachel. "Druzgeniekie!" she marveled; "can I come?" "Of course," I said, important as a landlord; "I have an extra room. Anzia's coming too. We won't have anything to do but enjoy ourselves." "Will you go by train?" she asked. "Of course, by *wagon-lit;* otherwise I would be sick to my stomach the whole time; you know how green I get even on a swing." "Will Anzia share the compartment with you?" "What a thing to ask!" I exclaimed; "where else should she sleep?" "Well, she's only a maid," Rachel considered. "And you're only a friend," I said, getting off the bed in a huff. "Sometimes I think you have common ideas," Rachel muttered from her bed. "I'm surprised you think at all, sitting there in your christening gown all day like a bisque doll." "Are you taking your doll collection?" Rachel asked; insults slid off her like a seal. "I am *not* taking my bisque dolls" (I had sixty of them, neatly lined up in front of the winter flowers on the windowsill); "but if I took them, they would go third class." "Hmmm," said Rachel, who didn't have the slightest idea of what I meant, "of course, I shall have to ask my fiancé what he thinks of the trip." "Oh, please do, please do," I told her; "I don't want to interfere with anything of real importance." "Oh, no that would not do," Rachel agreed solemnly. And, since it was Saturday, and only two in the afternoon, Rachel decided it was time to comb her hair. Her parents had built a special tiled and mirrored bathroom adjoining her room by a mirrored door. If Rachel was going in to comb her hair, I knew I would hear the key turn in the lock, and I would have at least an hour to lie on her bed and dream, staring at her crystal chandelier.

The lock turned in the door. I lay back on Rachel's bed, the bedclothes still tumbled. I hardly ever saw the bed made; as soon as one of the maids had straightened it, Rachel was back in. I lay back in the tangle of satin and pillows. "Hypnotic, like a watch," I thought watching the prisms of the chandelier cast shadows on the wall and the floor. The bed seemed to be moving under me. "I'm falling asleep," I thought to myself; then I began thinking about the girls whose faces had been ruined by the iron nails. What had it felt like? There was the sound of water in the bathroom, the clink of metallic objects on glass trays. Rachel might be brushing her hair with a silver brush. Slowly, as if someone were telling me what to do, I began raising my hands to my face. What had it felt like? I pressed my four fingers of each hand under my eyes, my thumbs against the angles of my jaw. "Pull down," I ordered myself; "pull down." I pressed in; it hurt. It hurt terribly. "Press harder," I ordered my hands, as if they were soldiers obeying commands. I pressed harder. I couldn't bear the idea of the scratches, the red stripes down my cheeks. But I had to know what it felt like.

"Am I going crazy?" I thought to myself; "I must be going crazy." Terrified of something squirming inside, I pressed my hands to my side; I prayed Rachel would come out. There was absolute silence on the other side of the door. "If I did it somewhere where no one could see it," I thought, "then I would know how it felt." But where? My mother had the eye of an X ray. I moved slightly; the inside of my thighs rubbed. "There!" I thought; "I'll do it there." It would be invisible; no one would know. I pulled the covers over me; my hand slid to just below my pants. I pressed down with one nail; I dug it in, and in. "I'm crazy, I'm crazy," I kept saying to myself, but I was drawing my nail down, almost two inches; it had gone through the skin. The dampness of blood was against my finger. The pain was blinding. So this is what it had been like, and forever, it had gone through the skin. The dampness of blood was against my finger. The pain was blinding. So this is what it had been like, and forever, the scars forever, on the face, and worse, it had been worse, they must have been beaten; some of them must have lost eyes: I pictured scars running through eyebrows and lips; jagged ones, straight ones. The pain in my thigh was screaming with its open mouth. I began crying, turning my head into Rachel's big pillow to muffle the sobs. It was a long time; I don't know how long. Rachel came out, looked at me; the sight of her satisfied face stopped my tears like sand. "Don't worry, Anya," she said, settling next to me, "it's not that long we'll be separated. I'll miss you, too." So I let myself pretend that's what it was; I put my head in her lap and sobbed.

At home, Momma spotted something right away. Every time my thighs rubbed it was agony, and as luck would have it, she was taking something from the cabinet near the door. "What's the matter with you?" she demanded. "You're walking like a duck!" "Oh, I twisted my ankle," I said in my most positive voice. "I've got to get some books," I went on casually, and walked down the long corridor, every step burning like iron, and my mother's eyes, Momma's eyes, entering the small of my back like two nails. "Am I crazy?" I kept asking myself; "am I crazy?" I wanted to talk to Poppa about it, but I couldn't. This was the first time I couldn't talk to Poppa. "I ate at Rachel's," I told Anzia, staying in my room. It darkened slowly and naturally. But when it was completely dark, I knew I wouldn't be able to sleep. There were hands sifting through the air like dust. I waited until I heard the music stop in Vera's room; I waited until the light went out under her door. Then I crept into her room, and stood with my back against her closed door, listening to the sound of her regular breathing. When I was sure she hadn't heard me, I stretched myself out on the floor along her bed, falling immediately asleep. In the morning, when the gray light began to enter the room, I woke up first and went back to my bed. A small bandage took care of the scratch on my thigh; it healed slowly, and so, I thought, did I.

The whole family and all the maids came to see us off at the train. I kept looking around for Anzia, who seemed to be constantly vanishing, but was really only being pulled aside by Momma for further instructions about what I should eat, how I should get plenty of air, how I should lie down in a hammock after meals so I would gain weight, how if I got sick, she was to get in touch with the family at the very first sign. And then there was a pale corkscrew of smoke opening the air, and the train was letting itself through the familiar streets, and, because it was going to a new place, looking entirely new.

And so we arrived in Druzgeniekie. Anzia celebrated her arrival with scrubbings: the porch, all the floors in the house, then the walls, the curtains. By the end of the week she had gotten a pail of whitewash from one of the workmen's wives she had spoken to in the village, and was painting the stones all around the villa a brilliant white. In back was a ruined foundation which Poppa had never removed. "It's a piece of history," he used to say, and Anzia got busy in it with flowers. "The piece of history is also a flower pot while you are here," she said, transplanting tulips and berry bushes donated by Uncle Frederich, and everywhere a blaze of color, hot pink rhododendron, roses, tulips; it was a botanical miracle. Poppa had instructed Anzia to have the village painter paint the villa "if it needed it," and Anzia took one look at its sparkling white front and decided it did. But meanwhile I was not there. I was all over the town, all over, while Anzia was embroidering the runners for the porch she had begun at home the minute she heard where we were going for the summer. Her fingers flew through the cloth with the needle, like sun on the water.

I had never seen such a pleasant town. And the people! There were people from all over: from America, from Germany, from France, from Russia! And all ages. People who came because of the mineral water treatments, the spring water, and young people, like me, for the dances every night at the villas and hotels, at the cafés, the nightclubs. In the summer the town opened like a Japanese flower: almost ten thousand people arriving with suitcases, and baskets of fruit, and maids, and elder sisters; invalids in cane wheelchairs, younger nieces pushing, running off after dinner, the young men right behind them. There were hotels all over Druzgeniekie, located not on the streets, but all set into the forests, so that their windows looked out into the thick trees. And there were two beautiful rivers: the big Nemen, and the small one, the Rotnichanka, with its beautiful cascades, and that was the first thing I saw, the cascades at night, with insects, not fireflies

81

exactly, because they were all colors, buzzing on and off like electric tubes.

The first night I was there, I heard some singing in an odd language. I asked an old woman I could barely see except as a shimmer of linen: "What is it? What is that?" "I am sorry, my dear," she answered me in French; "I do not speak Polish. What you hear are the peasants singing on the other side of the river. If you come down in the morning to take the waters, and walk farther down the bank, you will see all the way across the river to another country: Lithuania. At night the peasants come down to the bank and sing, and we old ones come down and listen to them. Of course," she finished, "we don't understand a word." Lithuania! And she was speaking French! Our governess had left us when I entered the university, and my French was very bad. Immediately, I saw a chance to improve myself, and, I don't know why, I always liked old people.

"May I ask what your name is?" I inquired shyly. "I am called the Madame Colonel here, but if you would be so good and call me by my first name, it is Tatania, but I prefer Tania. I would be grateful; it takes years from my life." "May I come speak to you tomorrow?" I asked; I was frightened at my own boldness. "By all means," she said; in the dark, she sounded as if she was mocking me. "And how will I know you?" I asked, because in the dark, listening to the peasants, she was only a moth-glow. "I am always dressed the same way," she said (surely I was imagining it; there was something frightening in her voice); "in white linen, like a corpse that has risen. My sister, who stays at the Lido, always dresses the same way too, but you will not confuse us, because she never goes out. There are people who wish I would not go out, too," she laughed, a high amused cackle. Nearby, some people murmured with annoyance. "May I ask why your sister never goes out?" I wanted to know about someone who never came out of her room to hear the peasants sing, to walk in the long neat alleys through the gigantic thick pines. "She is ninety-three, you see," the Madame Colonel explained, "so she does not often hop, like these grasshoppers," and out of nowhere, her hand moved suddenly, clawlike, a lobster at the bottom of this blueness. "Here, my dear; cup your hands. When I was your age I found them fun." I took them. I could feel the strange quicken-

82

ing leaps against my gently clenched fists; they were making my fingers sticky. They felt very odd; I let them go.

"Now," she said, "let me hear you call me Tania; it will help me sleep well; it will help me forget my age. It will erase the terrible picture in my mind. You want to know what that is too?" she asked in her sinister voice; "it's my face, my face. It cracks mirrors." "Tania," I said, almost choking on the name, as if I were pronouncing the forbidden name of God, "may I come and see you tomorrow?" "I shall be in the woods, my dear, with my linen umbrella. You will know me; I am the walking mushroom. The sun, the sun, it is so hot for one like me, you know. Very good, my dear," she said, getting up creakily. "Now, may I ask your name?" "I'm so sorry," I answered; in the dark, I blushed like a radish. "I am Anya Savikin." "Well, Miss Anya, tomorrow under the umbrella then," and she began moving away from me, slowly and jerkily like a retreating cloud on a string.

On my left, I could feel another presence. "It's beautiful here," I said aloud to the darkness. "Oh, yes," answered a voice with a thick English accent, and suddenly, I felt that Druzgeniekie was a kind of ark, two of every nationality, "and bathing in the falls is even nicer, don't you know?" "In the falls?" I asked. "Oh, yes," said the woman; "I come every morning, at seven, before breakfast. You go in quite nude, then run back and get dressed for breakfast; quite good for arthritis, you see. Very cold, very invigorating for the bones." "What do you wear to the falls?" I asked, completely agog. Not since my fifth birthday, when my mother had spent the night before braiding my hair in thousands of blond braids so that they stood up all over my head until it looked like a cake with candles, and she had dressed me in a costume with wings, so that when I stood on the table I looked like an angel, not since then had I felt so intensely that the world was a remarkable place. "A long bathrobe," the woman said, "and a towel for your hair, unless you like it to drip, which I do not. The young do not usually come that early; they are too lazy after all the dancing at night."

"Dances?" I asked in a whisper. I was worn out with all these surprises. "Every night, my dear, at every hotel—the Karinsky, the Lido, the Zimanska, the Adria—and every night they give prizes, you know, who has the nicest hands, the nicest eyes, the nicest legs, who is the most beautiful girl at the Lido; it never ends." She sighed. "So they don't get up so early. Still, I would not miss it," she went on. "Of course, you know, it is women bathing in one place, and men in the other. You're so young; I didn't mean to give you the wrong impression." "What else does one do?" I asked, afraid of trying the patience of this encyclopedia of delights. "You know, it's nice to have you ask me these things; it makes them seem new to me. The wife of a diplomat can come to feel that there is nothing new in the world, although my husband insists there is a great deal new, especially now, but he does not explain himself." I sat there like a nun who had taken the vow of silence. "Well," she went on, "there are exercises, every morning after breakfast. You go in your bathrobe deep into the forest, and there's a spot cleared away, one for men, and one for women, and each has an instructor for the exercises, and a shower when you're finished. You take your robe to these also, and the clearing permits you to burn all over; it's really very nice." I was already planning how early I would have to get up to do all these things; I was afraid to waste a minute sleeping.

"And then the young," she went on in a dreamy voice, "they dress to kill, and walk around the parks overlooking the Rotnichanka, where the two orchestras play until dinner, arm in arm, stopping at colorful kiosks for yogurt, arm in arm, always arm in arm (you call the yogurt *kafir*), and they buy chocolate waffles wrapped in silver paper. Ah," she said starting to laugh, "I am describing it to you as I saw it on my honeymoon. But it hasn't changed. And when you go to the edge of the park, near the bank, you can see the houses of the peasants Madame Colonel spoke of. You can't see many, you know, the forest is so thick, but you can see them coming down to fish, and getting in their boats, and of course their huts, their poor huts. From the park, however," she said, her voice changing tone, "they look very picturesque. And," she went on, pulling herself up and laughing as if telling a joke, "I forgot the beach, there is the beach! I think, Lady Anya, you will have a great deal to keep you occupied. You don't mind coming here alone?" "Oh, it's much better that way," I assured her; "this way, I can run all over; I can do whatever I want! It's much better, much!"

"What is your name?" I asked her. "I'm Mrs. Eliot. Mr. Eliot is with the diplomatic mission to Germany. Do come have a kafir with me tomorrow. We exiles tend to get lonely." I promised I would, and stumbled through the big dark field separating the falls from our villa, where Anzia was waiting for me. She took one look and decided to bathe me herself and put me to bed. The last thing I said to her was, "But wake me at six! Don't forget to wake me at six!" "Since when do I forget to wake you on time?" she demanded angrily, tucking me in; then I felt her rough hand on my forehead and I was sound asleep.

The next morning Anzia woke me at six, holding my robe. I hopped out of bed into it, and started running to the door. "Open it first," Anzia called after me, and, as I was already flying down the street and into the big field, she called, "When do you want breakfast?" "When I come back!" I called over my shoulder, and then I was running. It took ten minutes to get to the falls, running all the way, and when I got there, I flung off my robe, and myself into the water. From between the thick ropes of water, I looked around at the other women, wondering who was the English woman, who was Madame Colonel, but by then I had cooled off, and run out, flinging on my robe, wrapping it around me, and flew back the other way, through the streets, past the park with its iron tables and bright umbrellas poking through their centers, the stores, and the few people who were beginning to come sleepily out of the buildings. When I got back, Anzia had breakfast ready: two eggs, some ham, sour cream and berries, a glass of milk straight from the cow. "Where's the cow?" I asked, my mouth already full. "The farmer came by after you ran off; you nearly knocked over his cart." "You are trying to fatten me up again," I accused her. "No," Anzia said, "but if you are going to run like that I should be feeding you coal instead of food. Don't run so fast going downhill; you won't be able to stop yourself; you'll fall on what's left of your head."

"So," I said, jumping up, "I am off to the park." "Trapping them already?" she asked, with a grin. And when I got to the park, the two orchestras were already playing; I stood there a few minutes, then asked a maid where to find the sun baths and where the exercises were. I flew there and stayed until twelve. But dancing, dancing was my goal. After exercises, and after lunch, I used to take a blanket into the forest to read and rest for dinner, and then, the dancing. And so it went every day for the whole month of June. One night I won a prize for the most beautiful hair, another night for the most beautiful eyes, and then it was the waterfalls, and exercise, and sun baths, reading and flirting, dancing and staying up late writing to Momma, trying to coax her to come see for herself, and Poppa to come and look, or at least they could send Vera.

Then one day after dinner I ran into the Krinitza Hotel. "What's new in the evening here?" I cried out, and from the corner, a very tall man said, "Tonight they are picking the most beautiful girl in Druzgeniekie; you should come; I'm sure you'll win." "Oh, thank you very much for nothing," I said, looking him up and down. He was blond and pale, not Jewish at all. He looked Irish. After the episode with the iron nails, I had changed. "I'm sure I'll win, too," and I danced off to borrow the book I had come for from Mrs. Eliot. But when I came out of her room, he was waiting at the entrance to the hotel. He followed me as if he were trying to introduce himself. "I'm sorry; I'm busy," I called out, and ran off down the street thinking, "He's handsome; yes, he is handsome, but I have no use for him." The next day, there he was again. He had found out all about me. "You are Anya Savikin, and you are a freshman in medical school; you have a very good index and you're staying in your villa with a maid named Anzia." "You will make a very good detective," I said, and dashed off. Oh, I was mad.

And everywhere I went I looked for the Madame Colonel. But I never saw her, only this blond man with blue eyes, and finally, one morning I woke up and Anzia told me this blond man had been walking up and down in front of the house since six-thirty. "You go out and offer him some lemonade, and I'll go out the back door," I told her, and I did, into one of the alleys in the forest, and right ahead of me was a figure dressed entirely in linen. It was the old woman. She seemed to be walking along, hobbling on something like a stick. I ran faster so I would reach her before the road bent. "T-T-Tania," I called out as loud as I could, gasping for breath, and the figure stopped, but did not turn around.

"Oh, Miss Anya," I heard her voice say, but still, she did not turn around, and when she did, I was stunned. Her face was the face of a mummy, yellow as a lemon, wrinkled like the bark of the pine trees. She had said her sister was ninety-three, but she looked even older; her face was just like a monkey's. She looked as if she had grown from the floor of the forest; she looked like some kind of mushroom. I stood there speechless, taking it in. She was dressed entirely in linen, a whitish-gray linen, in several layers. Underneath the outer wrapping was a kind of loose white shroud with sleeves, and over it a kind of white linen shift; a big puffy linen turban covered her head. Attached to the turban's rim were some bright red curls. I stared harder; I could see the stitches holding them on. She must be bald! On one arm she carried a huge linen bag that closed with a drawstring of rope, and in the other, she held a huge white linen umbrella she kept over her head, even in the forest alleys, to protect it from the sun. On her feet were some kind of rope shoes, and linen stockings, too. All of this flashed into my eyes at once.

"I am not what you expected?" she asked, smiling, and now I was afraid to look, because I expected her teeth would all be gone, or eaten to dark stumps, but she had two rows of perfect brilliant teeth. "I have aged, no doubt; I have aged." She kept staring at me. I could see, there was a wickedness. "Take my arm," she said, offering a linen mass. I grasped her stick of an arm through it. "I know your Uncle Frederich. I buy some of his berries; they are the biggest berries I've ever seen, and I have seen many many berries, many, many, I have been all over the world. Come, we will talk." And we hobbled on until we came to a flat wooden bench with a wooden back; it was set into the trees. By this time, I had unglued my eyes from her face and was inspecting the great mass of coral ropes she wore about her neck. "Ah, my dear," she said in French, "you want to know about the corals. I bought the corals in the Polynesian Islands. They were a present to me from a diver." She looked at me as if I were a germ under glass. "Of course I was much younger then." I mumbled something about how they must be heavy to wear in the heat. "It is worth it, it is worth it," she insisted; "they take away headaches, and the evil eye. Do you know how you can tell if they are working? They change color." "Change color?" I echoed. "That is what I said; you are too young to be deaf, and too smart to be a parrot. You see how light they are, but they were not always this light. Once they were much darker. But I have had many headaches, and have known many evil eyes, and they have grown lighter. I have sucked the color out of them. It is because of them I look so well." "Of course," I said, remembering Momma: "Always be polite, polite, you'll never be sorry."

"Of course," she mimicked sourly. "Of course," she said again, positively, "it is true." Then she stared into the trees. Suddenly she started, as if someone had shaken her by the shoulder. "I must tell you; I almost forgot what it was I must tell you: Never refuse a husband, never, no, it is not good, not good, not gooooood." She stared at me maliciously, drawing the last word out and out. "Do you understand?" she asked, grabbing me by the hand. I nodded, yes, I did. "I have to show you something," she said, rummaging slowly but obsessively in her bag. She pulled out a picture of a beautiful woman with dark hair wearing a huge hat whose brim dropped over one eye, and ostrich feathers curling around it, curling right down to the point of her chin. "You see, Anya, it is frightening what can happen to a human being; it is frightening. There I am, right there. *Ah, bonjour, ma petite*," she said, getting up, fingering her corals with her free hand, holding her umbrella with another. "Never refuse a husband, never; bad, it is bad, isn't it bad? I've had so many. *Bonjour, bonjour,* we will talk again tomorrow. I can't concentrate at all in the sun; your Uncle Frederich says I am a vampire. I really think only at night, when the sun goes down, when the decay stops, can you understand?" And the next day was the same thing: the picture came out, never refuse a husband, and, with some variation, it is frightening what can happen to a human being. But if I met her at night, at the falls, she would talk intelligently about French literature and describe, as if she were still there, the Indian temples she had seen, the pyramids, the Russian steppes. And that night I saw the two of them, the Madame Colonel and her sister walking; I ran back into the hotel to the dance. "They can frighten you to death, you know, Anya," Uncle Frederich said when I asked about them, "when you see the two postuments walking around." "Oh, I am not frightened; I can get used to anything," I told my uncle, but I woke up in the middle of the night thinking two white things wrapped in linen were bending over my bed.

The next day I was beginning to get bored. I had gone to the falls; I had done my exercises; I had done my reading; and now I was walking to the beach along the river, kicking the ground. Then someone called to me. "Aren't you a student of mine?" he asked. It was Professor Singleyevich, my professor of biology. Everyone had been talking about him at the resort. They were saying his wife had just given birth to something half-dog, hald-child; it was horrible. "Oh, yes," I answered; "I just finished my freshman year." "And do you like it here?" he asked. "Oh, it's beautiful here," I said, and, I don't know why, I started to complain, "but I am restless; I can't always read and dance and dance and read." "Yes," he said. He looked lonely and unhappy. "Would you like to come work for me, a few hours in the morning and a few in the afternoon? I know you, and there's no one here; it's hard to get help in a place where everyone wants to lie down on the ground or sit up under the waterfall." "Oh, gladly, gladly!" I cried, jumping up into the air. I was red all over. "Come to the office tomorrow morning at nine-thirty," he said; "it's next to the Café Adria."

So I went, and gave injections, looked in the microscope, and sometimes, when I was all dressed up for a dance, a peasant would come in a wagon and say someone was sick and Doctor Singleyevich said I was to give the injection. Then I would get undressed again; Anzia would lay the gown out neatly on the bed; I would put on the white uniform and get into the cart with the peasant, sitting on some straw in the back. And it was horrible, because immediately I turned green—the stone roads, the metal wheels—but if the doctor wanted me to go, there was no question. Usually it was twelve miles one way and twelve back, and this was the first time I had seen people so poor. Sometimes their pillows were black as the earth packed tight in the cracks of the walls. Then I wouldn't take any money. And when I got back, I would lie down, eat something, because everything I had eaten had been thrown up in the cart, and get dressed to go to the dance. "That food you are eating must have a lot of sleep in it," Anzia commented; "you are never in that bed any more." "So long as I'm healthy you won't tell Momma?" I pleaded, and Anzia agreed.

Then Doctor Singleyevich told me Doctor Krinsky was complaining about how selfish he was; would I like to work for one of them in the morning and one of them in the afternoon? "Oh, gladly, gladly," I said, turning red all over again. Things could not happen fast enough for me. I was always very ambitious. Finally the two doctors put their heads together and decided I should open a little clinic of my own at my villa. But, they suggested, first I should get an "electrolization apparatus" so they could send me all of their mild cases. I wrote Poppa telling him, asking him what he thought, and, what do you think, three days later he arrived with the machine himself.

"So," he said, surveying the house like an engineer, "the verandah can be the waiting room, or this front room here can be the waiting room. Anzia, you will call a workman, and have big metal locks, with bars first, then locks, installed on the other doors so no one goes from one part to the next. But Anya," he asked, "do you really want to do this? It's a lot of work." "Oh, Poppa, it is so much fun!" I cried. "Do you believe in this machine?" he asked, inspecting the monster he had brought. It was a huge black thing standing there on the verandah like a domino, covered with dials and an electric outlet for a cord that plugged into the attachment which was a tube filled with many-colored filaments. The tube went into a long round rubber pad. When the electricity was on, it massaged the patient; they felt as if they were being pinched by needles. "Oh, I don't, Poppa," I answered, "but the doctors say it gives an effect and helps because the patients think they are going to get better, and they do get better; I've seen it." "What do they use it for?" he asked, peering at it again from a distance. "For impotence, headaches, nerves, things like that." "Things like that," he repeated, astounded. "And you give injections." "Of course," I said; "I even have a sterilizer from Doctor Krinsky." "A sterilizer," Poppa marveled. "I think I will stay until this office is opened."

Anzia and I got busy. Anzia attacked the house. "If that house were a person, it would be a skinless person," Poppa said comfortably from the wicker chair on the porch. Under Poppa's eyes, the office was set up. Every morning, Anzia scrubbed the wooden floors until their planks had turned golden; while the workman installed locks, she embroidered. The runner seemed long enough to go around the house. She embroidered it to go all around the square verandah. Then she repainted the stones in front of the house, and stood across the road and looked at it. Something was missing. So she got busy embroidering an awning, a thick strip of material which she attached to the verandah's roof, to protect the patients from the sun. Every night she took it down and worked next to the lamp, embroidering more and more flowers, and each morning, it rose more gloriously over the railing. A new wicker table covered with a cloth and a clean ashtray and fresh flowers appeared next to the armchair; then many, many, folding chairs we rented from the Adria.

Inside, the office was immaculate, absolutely immaculate. Anzia had the workman install a washstand; to it he added a back which stood against the wall and had two faucets. Above the faucets was a tin reservoir which Anzia filled with water every day so I could wash my hands, and underneath was a basin to catch the water, and it had rails on both sides covered with embroidered hand towels. Always steaming on the other wall was the hypodermic sterilizer which never showed a fingerprint. And there was I, in my braids and my white uniform, giving huge injections of thick yellow fluid to the young men, the impotent men, the rabbis with headaches, the priests with arthritis. Oh, it was very impressive, and so much fun, so much fun. My verandah was always crowded with patients, so I had a little bell I could ring and Anzia would come in and help me, and at the end of the day, if I was very tired, Anzia would wash and feed me first, and then get busy embroidering more and more for the office, cleaning it from the floor up. Poppa was very impressed. He went home, and gave his report, and all kinds of marveling letters arrived from Vilno, but always with the same motto from Momma, not to overdo, and to lie in the hammock after I finished eating. "So," Poppa said in his part of the letter, which was always at the bottom, "you can see you have impressed everyone here in this little town, and your Momma has had to turn away patient after patient looking for cures, but you may be sure we have told them where to find you in Druzgeniekie. Max was here yesterday to say hello to everyone. He said to tell you he would bring Alexander to you and see what you could do for him there. Do you have any idea what he was talking about?" Oh, he was very proud of me.

Then a young girl came for some hormones, and as she was getting off the little white couch, covered with a cloth, a tapestry hanging over it, she said, "Tell me, why do you treat Mr. Lavinsky so badly? He likes you very much." "Who is Mr. Lavinsky?" I asked. "I don't know any Mr. Lavinsky." "He's the man who has been following you around for six weeks!" she said, looking at me amazed. Mr. Lavinsky! Then he could not possibly be an Irishman! "I didn't know who he was," I answered, blushing. "Well, you do now," she said, rubbing her hip. 'Now I can tell him so he won't have to come in for his shot." And that night, when I went to the Adria to dance, there he was. And I was so embarrassed! "Tell me, why do you do it?" he asked me; oh, he was laughing. You know, I was so little, so young. "You're here to have fun," he said seriously; he was very impressed, very. "I'm from Warsaw," he said. "Oh," I cried. "I am going to Warsaw for a friend's wedding." After that we were always together.

Then Mother came to visit. "Where is Anya?" she would ask, and always the same answer: with Stajoe Lavinsky, the Irish engineer. "I have fun helping people," I used to say severely; he would look at me, bewildered. But Momma could not stand it. "Why Warsaw! Why Warsaw! Twelve hours away by train!" But mostly, she kept quiet. One day Stajoe and I went to the rock overlooking the Nemen and had our picture taken the way everyone did: I put on the photographer's kimono, and held a lacquered painted umbrella, and Stajoe wore a man's robe, also Chinese. We took the picture right away; I would not part with it. I kept it in the office while I worked, right under the towel the sterilized needles lay on. I sneaked looks at it between patients; I sneaked looks at it during patients. And everytime we went out, it was photographers and more photographers. They were all over, with their big cameras, and the second they saw us, they would throw their heads under their black cloths, and immediately offer dripping copies of the pictures they pulled from their pails, we could not get enough of them. One night, about a week after Momma left, we were sitting overlooking the Nemen, listening to the peasants. I thought I saw the gleam of the linen lady in the background. He said, "Anya, I want you to marry me. I know I haven't been myself this summer, I've made a bad impression, but I want you to marry me; I'll be very good to you. I'm an engineer; I have a good job. You won't be sorry, I promise."

But I could not answer him. My mother could not stand so much as the thought of Warsaw; my father had not even met him. "Stajoe," I answered, holding his hand tight, "I can't decide anything without asking my parents." "But can I have any hope?" he asked. "A human being must always have hope," I said, repeating the words of the medical school dean. "I have to leave tomorrow," Stajoe said hopelessly; "I'm very busy; I have business." He was not good at putting his feelings into words. "But I can't tell you anything else!" I insisted. "Will you write to me?" he asked, squeezing my hand so hard I cried out. "I'll write, I'll write," I promised fervently. The fireflies flashed in colors; the next morning, he was gone.

In the next few weeks the summer was gone. I was closing up my little practice, and getting ready for medical school, and already planning the trip to Warsaw for my friend's wedding. Then came the first letter from Stajoe: "You are the light of my life. I cannot see anything without you; I cannot live without you. Remember the tormentress in *The Blue Angel*? So you are to me." The letter practically glowed in the dark, like the fireflies. On and on they went that way; but I didn't appreciate it. So in my first letter, I wrote back; "I don't believe in words; I believe in actions," and good enough, the next letter was a request to come to Vilno for Christmas and meet my parents during my vacation from school. So I asked Poppa. "It is up to you," he said; and Stajoe came.

We went to shows, the movies, the opera; he bought four tickets and invited Momma and Poppa; he came to dinner at the house several times; then he had to go. I was going off with Vera to look at her dress for a concert when I saw him going into Poppa's room; I knew what was what. And what Poppa would tell him: "Ask my daughter." But when he came out, it was conversation and more conversation. Finally, he was waiting in the entrance hall. He was very nervous. I remember, he kept standing there, twisting his gray hat in his hands by its brim. Finally he did manage to speak. "Anya," he said, "I ask you again. Will you marry me?" I was bright red, staring at the floor. Verushka had already made her pronouncement on the subject: He was beautiful, he was tall, magnificent—as a rule, Polishmen were not tall, but shrimps, like Poppa—he was well educated, he was well read; what did I have to think about, exactly?

But it was not so simple for me. I had my medical school, and I could not forget it had seemed so funny to Stajoe, to see me working in my little office in Druzgeniekie. And I was very young; I knew I was very young. I was unusually mature and responsible in my career, but for the rest of me, it was somewhere behind, traveling in a peasant's wagon, trying to catch up. I was not ready to decide. But still, I felt sorry. His hat was circling and circling like a globe, and I felt guilty. "I can't answer you," I told him; "it's too soon. I'm only nineteen. I want to finish this year in school. Who knows how I will develop? Maybe you won't like me at all. This year we have rounds, we have to visit the insane asylum. It may change me. You don't know how, or if you will like me any more.

I can't decide." "Then I'll write," he said. "I'll continue to write," and he kissed my hand and went outside to wait for the *drozhka* alone. I stood in the white dining room watching his horse and buggy until it disappeared from sight.

Then I went into Poppa's office and closed the door. "You know I have never told you what to do," he said, "but you are opposites, real opposites. He is like a cold Englishman and you are not. I can't tell you anything; this is only my impression. You know me; I wouldn't direct your life; I wouldn't take that responsibility. I have to trust your judgment." But in the kitchen, Momma, the pot, was boiling. "Warsaw! Who needs Warsaw!" This was still her constant refrain. "What are you, a cripple, that I should have to come to you, twelve hours away? I do not want it, I do not want it." So there was Momma and medical school, and the two of them began to have an effect. I wrote fewer and fewer letters, longer and longer apart, describing the city, how much snow we had, more and more abstract, how much snow had melted, and so he knew. And I began to forget about him. But Momma was not finished. "Just in case," she said when I surprised her talking to Aunt Rivka who was leaving for Warsaw, "it cannot do any harm. She'll drop in on them and see what they're like; that's all. It won't hurt to know what they're like; they have nothing to hide, do they?" And thousands of investigators were dispatched, and dispatched again, and always, the good reports, which came back to Momma, not like doves, but locusts. The last one was from Rachel's mother, who told Rachel, who told me "that it should only happen to her daughter." "How can I forget him when you are so busy with your private detective agency?" I exploded one day, and that was the end of it. But Momma still cast an evil eye on the daily mail.

And so the second year at medical school came to an end. Again I went to Druzgeniekie; again I opened my little practice; again I came home and began school. There was no more talk of Stajoe. When we were on pediatrics, I was going to be a pediatrician; when I was on surgery, I was going to be a corpse. This Max said, looping his hand through my belt when I stood in front of him (he could see right over my head) as we observed the surgery; it was, according to him, anatomy and Alexander all over again. But I got used to it too. Then we were on the psychiatry service. Twice a week in the mornings we used to

94

take a bus on Kafkaska Street into the outskirts of the city to the asylum. And now it *was* anatomy all over again. I would come home on Wednesdays and Fridays like a zombie. All over the wards were women, unwashed women with hair hanging like cooked macaroni, hanging, and jealousy, endless jealousy, unwinding like thread, weaving webs around everyone's ankles. And fear; it thickened the air like gelatin. "Don't touch me!" one of them would keep crying, covering her face. I had never seen anything like this, this unending jealousy, this unending fear; the women constantly asking, "Am I crazy? Am I really crazy?" and then the hysterical, the horrible, laugh. And the woman with the scarred face who sat in the corner with her back to the room. The women walking around all day, all day, saying, "She took him away from me; I'll kill her, I'll kill her. What does he see in her? I will get her, I will scratch her eyes out." Were passions, human feelings, so unreliable, so dangerous? And I was terrified. The sight of the square gray building with its barred windows hung in my nights like a square, mutated moon. I even preferred the men's side, where they exposed themselves, saying terrible things, where my face was always red, but not this unending, unending jealousy, a terrible disease. But the fear hung in the air there, too. Then, one Friday, Max came to the house late at night.

"Doctor Gershonsky is dead," he said, and burst into tears. "He can't be dead; what are you talking about?" I grabbed his hand. "He took us around the asylum this morning!" "He's dead, he is dead!" Max insisted, his voice rising. "He's not only dead; he's cooked!" And! Max began to laugh like one of the patients, horribly. Poppa's door opened suddenly."Come in here," he said, putting his arm around Max's shoulders. Max was trembling from head to foot. "Come, sit down," Poppa said, putting Max in his chair, covering him coat and all with a blanket, and still, the whole chair shook. Max's hands were pressed to his eyes; he sobbed loud and raw. I started to say something, but Poppa looked at me and shook his head. Gradually, Max stopped crying, but he still shook. Then the shaking stopped.

"Now tell us what happened," Poppa said gently. "I stayed late, to help; there was supposed to be a special demonstration." Max began crying again. Poppa kept quiet. He got up and got another blanket from the chaise longue, tucking this one under Max's chin like a bib. "And then?"

he prodded. "Three patients grabbed him; they threw him in." "In what?" Poppa asked. "You have to tell us; you'll go crazy yourself." "Into the soup caldron. It was dinner time, it was boiling, it was all filled with grits, pieces of meat, cereal, it stuck to him, God, it stuck to him. We couldn't stop them, we couldn't, they threw him in, they had abnormal strength, abnormal." Max began to cry quietly. "Abnormal," he kept repeating, "abnormal. They didn't even know he was trying to help them." "Then what?" Poppa asked. "We got him out; he was screaming for three hours, and he died, he died." He turned to me. "He's dead, Anya, he is dead!" It was a long scream, like a dying scream. Then he cried; then he sat still.

"Where are your parents?" Poppa asked. "In Warsaw, visiting Grandma; she's sick." Poppa considered. "So you're left with the maid. Anya, tell Mischa he is to sleep on the soft in the black dining room; Max will sleep with Emmanuel. And if your Momma thinks it isn't proper, tell her I say it's unfortunate." When I came back, Poppa had Max drinking tea with honey wine. "So come," he said to him, "Anya and I will put you to bed." I expected resistance, but there was none. Max followed us down the hall like a baby. "In here," Poppa said. "Anya, turn around while he puts on his nightshirt." I turned and studied the door. "You can turn around now," he told me. Max was under the covers. Poppa tucked him in, bent over and kissed him. "Good night, Max. I'll be up very late, so don't worry about disturbing my sleep. Anya, kiss him goodnight." I did as I was told. Then Poppa closed the door, but only part way, leaving open a crack for the light.

"Now for you," he said turning to me; "how are you?" "I don't want to go back," I said, crying. "Doctor Gershonsky was such a good man; he was just trying to help." "Goodness is not its own reward in this world: it's about time you found that out. Those who help are sometimes destroyed first. As for you, you'll go back. You must learn to accept the fate of a human being. You will not live forever just by avoiding the insane asylum. Tomorrow the bus to Kafkaska Street could turn over and kill you like a fly. I'm surprised at you. People who go through disasters often end up superstitious, a little crazy, but I'm surprised at you. You've seen the illnesses, the sick children, what have they done? You've taken this place in medical school; someone else couldn't have it. Now you have to live up to your responsibility. And you have to go back because of

96

Max. He's protected you often enough. He'll be afraid; he won't be able to say so. He will know you're afraid, but that you'll reassure him anyway. You owe him that because you've called him your friend, and he *has* been your friend." "It's sad to grow up," I said in a funny voice. "Not so sad as to run around like a baby in the grown-up world, knocking down buildings as if they were blocks. You should read the papers more. I expect you know better than to mention this about Max to anyone?"

"Poppa, I'm not an idiot!" I cried, indignant. "I hoped not," he sighed. "Sometimes you have to lead others out of the woods, so it's good to have some practice. Tell me, do I have to tuck you in?" "Oh, Poppa!" I was indignant. But before I went to bed, I stole over to the boys' room and looked in. Max was sound asleep and Emmanuel was a laundry lump in the moonlight. And Doctor Gershonsky, who had tried to help, was dead.

Poppa was also in the hall. "Don't forget," he said smiling, "next month is the university ball." "Are you trying to be mean?" I cried. I could not believe it. "Another thing to get used to is how good and bad insist on sharing a room," Poppa said, going into his office and closing the door for the night. Max never mentioned the incident again, but near the end of the year, he told me he thought he was going to finish his work in psychology. "It's just now becoming a science," he said, his face open and beaming. "One more year, Anya, one more year, and we'll be through." "Are you going to marry Max?" Vera asked. "It would make preparing for lessons easier," I answered teasing, but I was thinking about it.

And then I was back at Druzgeniekie again. I was overjoyed to be there, because next year would be my fourth year in medical school, and it would not be long before I had a practice of my own. And it was not long after Anzia had finished starching and ironing the embroidered runners, every now and then adding a flower, and the awnings for the porch, scrubbing the floors, repainting the white stones, bringing new brushes from Uncle Frederich's, when a very elegant gentleman in a gray suit with a long jacked appeared in my office. "Please be so kind as to forgo the hypodermic," he said smiling. "I am Mr. Lavinsky, and I wanted to meet the girl my son is so crazy about. I can see," he said, looking around, "why he is so impressed. But really, Miss Savikin, you must understand that he has become impossible. He does not eat; we can't talk to him. The maids are entirely out of control. When a letter comes from you, they are without mercy, teasing, and then, when he reads it, they are positively impudent. All morning, it is, 'And how are you this morning, Mr. Stajoe? And how is your *mood* this morning, Mr. Stajoe?' And his sisters and brothers give him no peace either, I can assure you. My wife is quite distracted. She says this is worse than when he had the chicken pox and we had to put boxing gloves on his hands to keep him from scratching, but then, you must know, chicken pox is only a problem for ten days, and this has been going on for two years." I was blushing; I was speechless. "So, Miss Savikin, I see you're very busy, and this is no time to speak to you, but I had to satisfy my curiosity. I have a responsibility as a father, after all. I see you're not as heartless as my wife believes." "Oh, I am not heartless; it isn't that at all." I was close to tears. "Please, won't you and Mrs. Lavinsky come to tea tomorrow. I wish you could meet my parents, but they aren't here. My Momma is coming next week, but Poppa is busy at the bank. Stajoe told me you're kosher; I'll buy special cakes from the kosher store." "Delighted, my dear," he said, bowing from the waist and kissing my hand.

The next day after the office closed, they arrived. Anzia was dressed in a white apron and tea was served on the verandah. "So nice of you to think of food, so very nice," Mr. Lavinsky kept commenting and eating. "I'm afraid good appetites run in my family. Well, Regina," he said, pushing back his chair, "you've seen your Heartless Woman; now we must let Miss Savikin get ready for her dance. You see she is not the witch you believed." "Isaac, I never said anything of the sort!" she protested. "He is only teasing me; pay no attention to him. It's his idea of a joke." "That's what she says when I tell the truth." Mr. Lavinsky pretended to mope. "It's been wonderful to meet you at last. Please convey our regards to your parents, and all their wonderful friends, and, most especially, to Rachel's mother, a lovely woman." "Issac," Mrs. Lavinsky exclaimed, "don't tease her!" "A lovely woman," he repeated, irrepressible.

So they stayed for ten days. I would have them for tea, and see them in the parks. Mrs. Lavinsky once came to the air and sun baths. She had the body of a teen-ager, such firm breasts, skin like marble, hair down to her waist. Stajoe's face was her face, the fine-boned face of a cameo.

But his disposition seemed to resemble neither of them. Then they disappeared. "Business, business," Mr. Lavinsky moaned; "the word should be struck from the dictionary. And with all the work I have to do at home!" "With all the work he has to do crossing the streets so his tenants will not see him because they haven't paid the rent; with all the work he has to do going out of his way, driving around the blocks, so he will not embarrass them in their homes," Mrs. Lavinsky said, both sarcastic and affectionate, "it's a wonder I see him in the house at all." "It *is* a wonder, Regina, my dear, that *you* manage to drop in between the hairdresser and the dressmaker." "Oh, stop, Isaac, what will Anya think?" "I think she knows we are joking," he said grinning. "Goodbye again."

Then Momma arrived, and the next two weeks were spent showing her everything in Druzgeniekie, taking pictures together on the famous rock near the river, sun bathing in the forest, visiting the falls. "It *is* wonderful here," she called to me from her hammock, "and, you know, *Resurrection* is not so bad after all; I thought your dear sister had spoiled it for me forever. What have you got there?" *"Mein Kampf,"* I called back; "it's really a fairy tale." We both fell asleep in our hammocks, our books clutched in our hands like purses. "This is wonderful," Momma sighed, coming back from the park in time to meet me at the end of my office hours. "After the sun, I feel like a sheet of pastry dough, pounded flat, and halfcooked." "You look good enough to eat," I said, kissing and hugging her. "Do you want to get up for the baths with me tomorrow?" "No, let these old bones have a rest. I'll make do with Anzia; she isn't the cascades, but she's almost as nice." Anzia slunk off, smiling. She could never be complimented to her face.

The next morning I flung on my red terry cloth robe and ran across the field to the Rotnichanka Cascades. Oh, it *was* wonderful there! Everything troublesome was washed away by this water. I crept out more slowly than usual, put on my robe slowly, tied it slowly, and started lazily down the street, when suddenly something jerked me backward. It was a hand; it was Stajoe's hand. I got so frightened I had palpitations. "Hello," he said, smiling. "Hello," I said, grinning like an idiot. "Shall I walk you back?" he asked. "It's the least I can do after you survived my parents." "And you, I see, survived their reports." "I didn't care about their reports," he answered violently. "I tell you, Anya, I have made a vow to God that if you will only marry me, I will observe the religious customs. I'll keep kosher. I won't be what I was."

"Momma is here," I warned him, ignoring his vows, which sounded to me as if they had suspicious motives. "Then I'm glad I made the vow," he answered. But from then on he was always there, at seven o'clock, waiting to walk me to the cascades. His hotel was three miles away, and he walked over. Even Momma was beginning to understand how devoted he was. So I could relent; we were all older. Now that I didn't have to choose between them, I could choose to see him. And somehow he had sensed the change and come. But still she did not accept him. "I do not know which you see first in Druzgeniekie, Stajoe or the sun," she griped. But he was polite to her, very polite, and she was getting used to him a little.

Then it was Sunday, and I wanted to borrow a dress for the night's dance from a friend in the hotel. "It looks stormy," Anzia warned. "That field is famous for killing people; they're the highest things in it, not a tree on the grounds there." "Oh, it will take me only a minute," I said. There was the sound of the screen door slamming; I was out under the purplish-green sky, running toward the bank of black clouds on the horizon. The house was gone out of sight. I had not gotten halfway across the field when the sky was split by thick stripes of lightning and I stared, fascinated. It was as if I could see, if I stared hard enough, a world beyond this one. Then it began to rain, and such a rain! The sky turned darker purple, and then absolutely black. The clouds which had been rolling in like heavy cigar smoke now joined into one seamless mass. The rain came down in a flat sheet, like cascades, but gray and heavy, and the lightning was fantastic; it was like nothing on this earth. I didn't know what to do. My mind shut its windows and doors; it was an abandoned house without a vane. Somewhere was a ruined church, but I wasn't sure exactly where. It was too far to the hotel, too far to the house. I remembered Poppa telling me to stay away from high places and high things during a storm. I stood there, my head a weather vane, turning this way and that, my dress plastered to my body, looking completely naked, my hair soaked, the two braids trailing long streamers of water. I was a lightning rod; I was waiting for the white-hot strike. My bones turned to iron where I stood; I felt my whole life rusting. And it was the weather doing all this to me. If I had only listened to Anzia. Where was everything? It was too dark to tell.

Suddenly I saw the tall figure of a man making all kinds of signs to me. Maybe it was some kind of maniac. But then I could hear him calling: "Anya! Anya!" I ran toward him without thinking. It was Stajoe. He had gone to the house and when he found me missing, asked Momma which direction I had taken, and had grabbed a weatherproof coat, galoshes, an umbrella, everything. When I reached him I fell against him sobbing. He picked me up, covered me with the coat, and carried me home like a baby in his arms. "Here you are, Mrs. Savikin," he said; "she's a bit wet, I think, but that's all." Momma was hugging me, hugging him, alternately crying "Thank God," then "honey wine," directing Anzia to get out some of father's clothes for Stajoe; couldn't she see he was dying of the cold, what was wrong with her? So we spent a cozy evening in front of the stove, talking. "I suggest you climb up on it," Momma told him; "it's the warmest place." "I'm fine, Mrs. Savikin, believe me; but Anya perhaps." "Oh, I am even finer, please." "I am endlessly grateful, endlessly," Momma told him, bursting into tears.

Then came a knock at the back door. It was a friend of Anzia's from a nearby *dacha*. A group of people caught in the field had taken shelter in the ruined church. It had been struck by lightning and all of them except for one teacher, had been thrown to the ground and killed. Someone thought she had been saved by her new rubber shoes, or else she hadn't gone in yet. "All of them killed." "Except for the teacher," Anzia reminded her. "All killed," Momma moaned again. "How can I thank you?" she asked Stajoe again, but he said nothing.

Naturally, the storm helped. Momma got used to him, and more than used to him. Finally I decided to talk to her. "What's wrong with him? Please tell me: what in your opinion is really wrong with him? He is handsome; he is Jewish; he is nice; he is an engineer; he is making a very nice living; he is educated." "I don't know," Momma burst out, "you do what you want." And I did. But first I wrote to Poppa to tell him what I had decided, and as soon as he wrote back, giving me his blessing, I was ready to write to Stajoe, who had had to return to Warsaw. In the meantime I had gotten a letter from Mr. Lavinsky telling me how impossible Stajoe was, and good psychologist, using my own language, telling me I should "cut the abscess." So the storm helped; the letter helped. I felt guilty, and I said yes.

Momma asked only that I wait until the end of the university year, and in the meantime I would apply to the University of Warsaw and prepare my trousseau. "Rebecca, by now you see it's fate," Poppa told her, which only made her more furious. "She avoided him," Poppa expanded. "She saw Max, she worked, and if it is a human being's fate, it is a human being's fate. Don't poison things." "Poison my own daughter's wedding!" Momma huffed, indignant. She became so helpful I couldn't wait to leave for Warsaw and begin preparations.

But I was determined to arrive there more beautiful than I had ever been, and to me this meant getting a tan. It was too late to go to Zakopanie; I had no time but my vacation. Rachel told me about a clinic four blocks from our house with quartz lamps that turned women out like mulattoes. I had to go there! A month before I was to leave for Warsaw, I made an appointment and stretched out under the huge lamp. I had a vision of myself as I had returned from Zakopanie last, all chocolate skin and blond hair. I was in such a hurry that when the attendant wasn't looking, I pushed my face up closer and closer to the lamp. She had said five minutes, but she got talking to the other attendants; I stayed there fifteen. It felt warm and good. At the end of fifteen minutes, I took out my mirror; my face was one huge blister. I could hardly see out of my eyes, my lids were so swollen. I took off my slip and tore off a piece, tying it around my head like a veil, and holding it up, ran home as fast as I could, thinking, "I've disfigured myself. I've disfigured myself for life!" So I ran to Momma. When she saw me, she sank back against the wall. "This is going to be a married woman! Warsaw is not ready for you!" She hauled me out of the house to the doctor. "She'll have to wait for it to burst," he said, pressing on my swollen cheeks, forehead, and chin. "Why did you do it?" "Don't ask," my Momma said; "the neighbors already have plenty to say about the nun in the white gauze veil; she frightens the children on the block." "At least she's willing to go out," the doctor commiserated. "Not much," Momma said.

"We will have to use this," Momma ordered me, mixing up some rice powder and applying it to my skin. It dried there, cracking like white dusty mud, and then peeled off; the layers of the skin peeling off, too. Within ten days, I was back to normal, better than normal. I had the face of a newborn baby. "Does the poor man know what he is getting into?" Momma asked the air. "Go ahead, enjoy yourself." She was finally resigned.

The very first day of winter vacation I took the earliest train to Warsaw. Momma could not come with us because Mischa had the chicken pox. Verushka had never had it, and Momma seemed more worried about how they would get Vera to stop reading her sheet music long enough if she did get the disease than she did about Mischa, who mostly lay sleeping. So Anzia and Josefa and Poppa took me to the train. "I miss Momma," I said, standing on tiptoes to peer down the tracks. "Is that it? Is that?" I demanded, pointing here and there. It was still almost dark, but the night was lifting like a lid. "You'll hear it soon enough; I'll tell your Momma it's the safest train I've ever seen, with three hospital cars in the middle, and that at the station I heard a new rumor, that it's possible to get chicken pox twice. Then she'll probably write and insist you stay in Warsaw the full three-week incubation period." "I miss her," I said again, straining my neck.

"It's just as well," Poppa said. "At the last minute, she would decide you were leaving *much* too soon, and your trousseau would consist of fourteen embroidered towels made by Anzia and Josefa here, and I should be the disgrace of the bank. But," he went on seriously, "you do believe me? You are to buy the very best. We are not wealthy people, but you will get married only once and I want you to have it, and so does Rebecca." "I will, Poppa; I will," I said, hugging him as if he had just arrived for a Friday night at the *dacha* loaded down with presents, when the scream of a steam whistle pulled us apart. "Her bags!" he called sternly to the driver of the *drozhka*. "I hope this is what you want; if you are disappointed *in any way*, you are to tell me. You have no obligation to us to go through with these plans, only to yourself. I would not care if all Poland knew you changed your mind." I felt a stab of terror. Last year, a young girl's marriage had ended in six months, something unheard of, and in due course we found out it was her body smell. Her husband could not stand it; he had become impotent. And my friend, Irma, had been engaged to a wonderful man when they had gone to the opera for the first time; she had bent over to pick up her gloves, and because of her décol-

103

letage, he saw the hair between her breasts, and that was the end of that.

"There is no disgrace in not knowing everything about the whole world," Poppa went on, running his eyes over the cars: not the first, that was most likely to be dangerous in a collision; not the last, for the same reason; not the one right next to the dining car, people walked by all day and night, and if you insisted, as did his daughter, on sitting cross-legged, with an ankle in the aisle, she might come home in a cast; I saw his eyes settle on the car three before the end. "The only disgrace is not believing what you see and then acting with dignity." "I will write every day," I promised, my eyes turning salty. "Well, perhaps it might be all right if you skipped a day and even called us on the phone," Poppa said grinning, bending over to kiss my cheek. "You look very beautiful, my lobster, but please, if they call for a doctor on the train, don't answer. *This*, at least, is supposed to be a vacation." "Goodbye, Poppa," I said, ashamed of my hurry.

Anzia saw me on to the train; put down the hamper of food Momma had sent to the Lavinsky's ("she wants you to eat as much of it as you want if you get hungry; she said, 'What are they, just strangers?' "); took off my coat, lay it across my lap, and bent over to kiss me. I put up my arms as if I expected her to pick me up and pulled her down and kissed her hard. "I love you," I told her. I felt her nod violently; then she straightened up and rushed off the train. I sat with my face pressed to the glass as the train began moving first forward and then back, then shaking side to side, puffs of smoke obliterating the little family on the platform, clearing to show them again, tears running down my face when the train started moving through the familiar streets, into the houses with the big grounds, into the part of the city where farms were beginning to show up between the houses, into the forest. I wanted to memorize everything, but I kept crying and the train had not been moving for forty-five minutes when I fell sound asleep.

I woke to the sound of a taffeta slip rustling in the aisle. A very beautiful woman was passing me on her way to the dining car. Then came a young man. Then a beautifully dressed businessman. Then an old woman. I was beginning to get hungry, imagining them all eating happily. Momma had provided me with her special silver mirror from Paltava; I took it out of my bag, inspecting my face.

104

How white the skin was! The traces of tears were gone. I would go sit down at one of the tables with its white cloth, alone on a train to Warsaw for the first time, and see who came to join me. Momma had instructed me thoroughly in train etiquette. If I did not like the person, I was to say, "I am sorry, but the seat is already occupied." If I did, I was to say, "Oh, please do sit down."

My dinner companion was the wife of Colonel Zhurkov, of the Russian army. She was going to Warsaw, and then Berlin. "My husband tells me," she said, cutting her filet mignon, "these are disturbing times. I tell him all times are disturbing, and he tells me, 'Yes, but these times are more so.' There are, my dear," she said, changing the subject as she saw me staring at her, "disadvantages to being raised as a great beauty." She had evidently seen me staring at her gray suit with its gray fur trim, Russian-style, about the neck, going down the side of the jacket, her magnificent red silk scarf, heavily embroidered in solid gold thread. She felt my eyes on the scarf. "And one of the disadvantages," she continued, "is the weight of valuable objects hung about your neck." She took off her scarf smiling. "Feel it," she offered, smiling. "Oh, it must weigh pounds!" I exclaimed. It was a work of art—cupolas, the winter palace, the bear, the Russian bear, peasants, their huts—so closely embroidered it took study to see each object; the detail was amazing.

"And where are you going?" "I'm going to Warsaw to prepare for my trousseau." "Your trousseau!" she gasped; "then you must let me start you off by giving you the scarf." "I can't take it," I protested so loudly that others turned to look. "If you don't take it, you will insult me," she said severely. "But you must love it!" I burst out again. "I did, I did," she answered, smiling, "but now it's your turn. And my husband has a habit of saying we will soon have to give away everything, so I would like to give this away myself. It is nice to make your own decisions occasionally, you know," she said, sipping her brandy. "Do you really mean it?" "Certainly. Stop jumping in your seat; you'll overturn the whole train. You must consider it a gift from one great beauty to another, except," she said, eyeing me critically, "I never could blush. I was always disappointed about that." "I would like to see you again," I told her, fingering the scarf, pressing it close to my stomach for safety. "One never knows about that, does one? Come, we'll go back together. You may go first, so if I fall down, I'll have you to fall on."

From my seat I watched her back retreating, and then it was the landscape of the scarf, the scarf. The real world could not compete. Outside, it darkened again. I was asleep, waking to the pull and halt of the train screaming into the Warsaw Station.

7

STAJOE's whole family was waiting; there were enough of them to populate a small village. He had two other brothers, and two sisters, and all but the youngest sister had married. Each brother and sister had a husband or wife, children, nursemaids, maids, and, because there were so many of them, there was an incredible din. "They are very noisy!" I thought to myself, astonished, but then I realized it was just that there were so many of them; even if each one whispered, there would be a racket. Mr. Lavinsky stepped forward in his long gray suit. He took me by the arm, steering me over to Mrs. Lavinsky, who kissed me with ceremony. The two of them took me down the line introducing me to them all: Benjamin, Gucha, Lyuba, Joseph, and finally "Stajoe, who, of course, you know."

We went out to a caravan of *drozhkas*. Stajoe, insisted he and I sit alone in the last. "There are a lot of them," he said, searching my face; "they are full Chasidim. I hope you can get used to them." "I am used to *you*," I said. "They seem very nice." "How long are you staying with us?" he asked nervously. "Only two days. It will be easier for us to get used to everything if I'm not always around. After that, I'll stay with the Brauns, friends of my mother's; he's a furrier. And during the day," I said reddening, "I'll order pillows and quilts and nightgowns, and at night, if you have time for me, you can come to call." "Every night," he swore. "How many nights?" "Ten nights," I sighed. "You aren't sorry?" "Never."

So it went. The first two days I stayed with them and learned the meaning of full Chasidim. On Wednesday, Mrs. Lavinsky began preparing for Friday and Saturday nights when all Mr. Lavinsky's Chasidic friends came for dinner the night after the Sabbath. "On Sunday," she said with some bitterness, "the good days start. It is because of them he won't give up his caftan; he's afraid these old Chasidim would curse him to death." "Regina, my dear, you don't want to give Anya the idea that we can't afford our guests," Mr. Lavinsky interposed, an edge in his voice. "Affording has nothing to do with it. It's peace and quiet I'm talking about."

I couldn't help sympathizing with her. Our house was always quiet—Poppa in his study, Momma singing in the kitchen, Vera playing her piano behind closed doors, and children who ran sent straight out into the courtyard—but here, two of the married sons lived in the endless apartment with their wives and children and their special maids; little friends of the children came to visit. The street was busy; there was no court, so they stayed inside. For the whole first day, I had a horrible headache. Then I was distracted by an argument between Mrs. Lavinsky and Gucha, her daughter-in-law. "Tell me, Gucha," Mrs. Lavinsky was saying, "why must you buy exactly the same dresses I buy? We are a little old for mother and daughter costumes, are we not?" "But," Gucha steamed, "just last month I bought the new dress with the ruched skirt and sleeves, and you went right out and bought the same thing in green. Now *I* cannot wear it; I don't see why *you're* complaining." I was horrified.

"You will be glad to go to the Brauns," Stajoe said gloomily. "Only because you'll have your own room back," I said. But the truth was, I was glad to go. Especially after the Saturday night dinner when I heard all the Chasidim pray. "It sounds like an operation without ether," I whispered to Stajoe, and then covered my mouth. I was insulting his family. "I hate it," he said with violence; "let's go for a walk." "You don't observe?" I asked. "No, but I made a vow that if you married me, I would keep a kosher house. I should have asked you first," he said sheepish, "but I didn't think it would happen." "It's really all right, what difference does it make to me?" He stopped me and kissed me. When I closed my eyes, I could see the Russian scarf, the little gold buildings; at the end of the year, I would be moving into one of them. "Your scarf is so beautiful," he murmured, fingering it; "you are more so." "Stajoe, such nonsense. Come, tell me how you'll like having a doctor keeping your kosher house." And the vacation flew.

After I moved to the Braun's, a comfortable distance from the Lavinsky's, in a fashionable part of town near the shops, I spent the days on my trousseau, the nights at the cafés and shows with Stajoe. The days and nights grew little wings on their feet, like pictures of Mercury I had seen as a child. During the day, I ordered my twelve sets of quilts and matching pillows; six turquoise quilts and twelve turquoise pillows; six gowns of peach and turquoise, and Mr. Lavinsky, who heard part of the discussion, remarked, "Whenever we discuss which pot we will use to boil fish for your wedding, you blush." He was right. I spent the twelve days in Warsaw in all shades of red; it was as if the sunlamp were getting its revenge. The quilts were great down quilts, stitched into diamond-shaped patterns, so the feathers would not slide from one end to the other; the pillows were covered in the same material. Then came supervising the lace envelopes they were to fit into. The lace envelope covered the quilt entirely, except for an empty oval shape in the center, and the rest was open work, through which the color gleamed. I decided I wanted the newest style covers, made like envelopes, with a lip folding over the top; the design of the lace was to be roses, great big roses near the center, then getting tinier and tinier as they moved out to the edges. The whole back was to be covered in the same tiny lace roses. I was to have six peach quilts and twelve peach pillows; six turquoise quilts and twelve turquoise pillows; six gowns of peach silk and lace to match the quilts, and six gowns each of turquoise and peach lace. I was in a dream! What was a kosher house compared to these quilts! I could not wait to make my home in them, and at night when I fell asleep tried to imagine a room made up of quilted floors, quilted walls, lace curtains, the great soft bed, the furniture all around.

The first night Stajoe took me to the Café Europa. It was the most elegant place in Warsaw, more like a night club; even during the day, women wore long dresses. The first time we went, I thought the big square entrance foyer was the café; then I saw the checkroom. It was big enough to hold a Vilno café. I was lost in the sparkle of the huge chandeliers, the red carpets, the surrender of my coat, the enormous tables without telephones. "Where are the telephones?" I asked when I caught my breath; I was wearing my green velvet tuxedo. "This café doesn't have telephones," Stajoe answered, amused. "What will you have with your coffee? Drink it down fast," he said, as if I were a child, "because we are going to the Warsaw Adria next." And there, for the first time, I saw colored people. They danced and played guitars; then came acrobats, dancing, gypsy musicians strolling, more dancing, the orchestra playing . . . it was almost light.

During the days, I watched the roses growing their petals. "No thorns," I told the seamstress, suddenly superstitious. I didn't want to sleep on thorns. I sent presents back to my parents: chocolate halvah. My mother could never get enough of it, so every day more halvah departed by the kilogram. I left in the same commotion, following the halvah by only a few days, but this time only Stajoe put me on the train. "You won't forget me?" he asked, gone white as a shroud. "Never, never, how can you think such things?" I cried, half-flattered, half-insulted. "And you," I teased, "there was something I wanted to ask *you:* Who was that woman with the big dark eyes and dark hair in the yellow dress? She stared at you all night in the Adria." "I didn't see anyone," he said, honestly puzzled. But I wondered. She had stared and stared at me, as if she were memorizing me, feature by feature, as if there were a purpose in it; I didn't like her. But there was the steam whistle. I forgot everything; I was going back, and how would I stand it? "You don't have to go," Stajoe pleaded. "I do, I do, I have to finish the year; it won't be so long. And the quilts," I flirted, "they take a long time."

Momma was standing on the platform. "Your father and his nonsense about the chicken pox!" she exclaimed. "I was afraid you would get it there, with no one to take care of you." She didn't know what to do first, kiss, or hug, or squeeze. And then Vera, and Anzia, Poppa and Josefa, Emmanuel and Mischa, even Aunt Rivka. The procession, smaller than the last one, returned to our apartment. In the hall, stacked like bricks, was package after package of chocolate halvah. "I'm going to have to live a long time," Momma burst out laughing; "oh, a long time, oh, Anya, so much chocolate. What is that scarf?" she yelped, spying it suddenly. "School tomorrow," Poppa ordered us all sternly. "First, Boris, Anya must tell me everything." "Then she better start now," he said; "why not in my office?" Struck dumb we all went in, and I babbled for hours.

The next Sunday I was up very early. I had made a new plan and called Mr. Krilova who had a farm and horses on the outskirts of Vilno and made arrangements to take lessons in riding. If I spent another summer at Druzgeniekie, I didn't want to have to take horse carts to peasants, so what could be more sensible than learning to

110

ride a horse? I knew without asking that Stajoe would worry and object, and I didn't want him to see me riding up to houses hanging onto the mane, half upside-down, so why wait I asked myself? This was my usual philosophy, and so far I saw no reason to change it. "What now?" Anzia asked when I came into the kitchen. I wanted her to help me lift the mattress of my bed so I could get at the divided skirt Anna had made for Zakopanie. "I'm going to learn to ride a horse; no more of those wagons." "The second part is good," Anzia agreed; "I'm not so sure about the first. You will be careful?" I solemnly promised. "Where are you going to find a horse in Vilno?" "The Krilova's, fifteen minutes by bus; it's all arranged." "Listen, Anya, those are wagon horses; they are not people horses. You can't ride them; they are dangerous. Make sure they give you a people horse." "A people horse, yes," I repeated. "And don't make fun of me," Anzia scolded; "sometimes you don't have so much sense." "I will find a horse that looks like a person before I even get on." "I should ask your mother," she fussed. "Please, don't worry her." "I won't worry her if you don't." "I'll be good," I promised, struggling into my coat. "Never mind the good, the careful," she answered, letting me out and closing the door.

The sky was just pinking when the bus let me off in front of the Krilova's. In front was a normal-looking house; in back, a line of pines, and behind them, the corral of horses. About time! I could see myself coming to the patients with my needles on a black horse in white snow, a white horse through the green spring forest, the branches shaking down dew, cooling me. "Here I am, Mr. Krilova," I called, catching sight of him just as he was about to round the house. I sloshed over through the mud; it was a good thing Anzia had seen to it that I took my heavy boots. "Are you ready, Scarlet Pimpernel?" he asked. "Of course," I answered, insulted; he had heard about the sunlamp episode from someone; "is the horse?" "The horse is always ready," he said, climbing over the corral. "Well, which one?" "The tall black one," I answered promptly. "Pick again," he ordered me. "I won't take the responsibility for him; he sees a mouse, he climbs a tree." "The big white one, then." "Let me think about it while I get the saddle," he said, leading the horse out and fastening the gate behind them. "Stand there," he ordered the horse, and to my amazement, it stood still, like a dog.

"Oh, this is not so hard," I thought to myself, but still, the animal was so big. They looked much smaller, even from a small distance. And what did he mean he was going to think about it? If I was going to ride, I wanted a good horse, not one of those skinny half-dead ponies he had. He would be sure to change his mind by the time he got back with the saddle.

"Nice horse, nice horse," I said, creeping over to the animal, "nice horse." He looked at me out of one eye. Why were their eyes stuck on each side of their heads that way? "Stand there, horse," I ordered, and he dipped his neck as if to say yes. It was just very big; that was all it was. Excitement was flushing my body from my toes up. I would ride *this* horse! But how was I going to get on top of him? If I climbed up on the fence, I could jump from it to his back. He had long hair on his neck; I could hold onto that. I climbed up. "Stand still, horse," I ordered again for good measure, and jumped on him. I could feel his body stiffen under me. "Walk along, horse," I ordered him in Polish; then in Russian: "Walk along, horse." But suddenly he didn't understand me. He was moving from side to side, back and forth; he was lowering his head, pawing with a front leg at the mud.

"Get off there," I heard Mr. Krilova shouting, and out of the corner of my eye I saw him running toward me in his red sweater, no jacket even, in this cold, and then I saw the horse's neck getting closer and closer; we were going up higher. "It's like an amusement park ride!" I thought, and then we were going up still higher, and the horse reared forward as if he were going to throw himself on the ground. The neck was coming at me again, and I saw the mud getting farther and farther away; he was jumping up; no, he was standing up! I tried holding onto his mane, but my gloves were wet, and the horse's mane was wet from dew, it was so early. I felt myself losing my grip and I was sliding. The neck was getting farther and farther away; I was sliding right back over his tail. The beginning of his tail was the last thing I saw of the horse. There was a flash of pink and turquoise sky and I was on my side in the mud. Mr. Krilova was shouting; Mrs. Krilova was running to the house; she was screaming, "Her knee, her knee!" and I passed out.

I woke up in a hammock in the Krilova kitchen. Mrs. Krilova had undressed me and washed off the mud and Mr. Krilova had gone down the road to call my parents.

112

They were bending over me; in back of them, Anzia was standing, shaking her head. "They put you in here because it's warmest," Momma said; "there's nothing wrong with you, just a swollen knee. The doctor said not to let you walk for twenty-four hours. Anzia will dress you; Emmanuel will carry you to the *drozhka;* you're very lucky. Mrs. Krilova, Mr. Krilova," she said turning to them, "I cannot thank you enough for taking care of my daughter. I didn't know about any of this. She had no right to disobey you, with your horse, and to worry you like this; God knows what could have happened." "She had no right," Poppa repeated, staring at me oddly. "Anya, this is not like you at all," he said. "Lately I thing she is under an evil eye," Momma said. "Don't start such nonsense," Poppa scolded; "the only two evil eyes are lying in that hammock. Emmanuel, pick up your sister; we have troubled these people enough." Emmanuel picked me up, looking disgusted. "I am so sorry," Poppa said, turning to them again; "please accept this," and he pressed something into Mr. Krilova's hand. "For almost killing your daughter!" he cried. "Believe me, you had nothing to do with it," Poppa said sadly.

"Put her on the couch in the black dining room and go out," Poppa ordered when we got home. "Anya," he said, closing the door, "what is the matter with you? First the sunlamp; now the horse. This is not a joke anymore. I want to know if you have any doubts about Stajoe Lavinsky." "What does one have to do with the other?" I asked him, sleepy with honey wine. "First you practically destroy your face; now you practically destroy yourself. If you're crippled, you won't be able to go off so fast, no? I want to know: Do you have any doubts? What were you doing on that horse without a saddle?" "I was just in a hurry, Poppa." "Those horses also pull coffins. This isn't like you; and why," he continued, stubborn, "were you learning to ride a horse in the middle of the winter? What was the hurry?" I admitted that Stajoe wouldn't have liked the idea. "Do you think he would like this better?" Poppa asked, raising his voice. "You have to decide. Either you can work out what you want with him, or you cannot. Getting your way by falling into the mud and breaking your neck is not my idea of avoiding an argument." I said he was only exaggerating because he was worried. Poppa said I sounded guilty to him; he wanted me to think about what he said.

"When did you decide about Stajoe?" he asked. I was

groggy and comfortable; I didn't want to think, but Poppa never asked questions just because he was curious. "Well," I began dreamily, picking my words like an exile who had stumbled into a foreign language, "you know how it is in a storm? You know where the church is, and the house, but your mind, it doesn't work; your body gives you orders. And then sometimes you can use your mind to tell you what to do with your whole life. But then there are the big things, and thoughts come up. It's as if there are animal burrows under what you *think* you think, you know? And the thoughts run along those and come up like animals through the holes in the field. Do you know what I mean? I mean, I didn't decide, not at any time, but everything scurried around, and that's what it was." Poppa sat there, thinking. "Then you probably made the right decision," he said slowly. "I told you, I don't know if I even made one!" "That's what I mean," he said. "At your age, maybe at any age, when it comes to people reasons are something to be suspicious of. But I wish you weren't having such a hard time fighting with your mind." He thought some more. I didn't want to think. Sometime later I heard Momma whisper, "Let her stay there for the night," Vera's voice sounding frightened; then the sound of a closing door, one ribbon of light, then nothing at all.

In the morning, I woke up, ready to go to school. I bent my right leg, then my left. I couldn't. It was swollen to three times its normal size. "Momma!" I began screaming, "Momma!" She took one look, and held on to the edge of the couch. "Emmanuel," I heard her calling, "we're going to take Anya to the doctor; carry her, please." They took me off down the block. "Oh, it is nothing," said Doctor Levin, "just fluid on the knee from the swelling. I'll puncture it; it will go away." He got out a huge syringe and got to work. "See all that?" he asked, proudly holding up the syringe; "now it will go down." It did. Tuesday morning I woke up and the knee was only twice as big as it had been before, but now the whole leg beneath it was swollen down to the ankle. This time Momma called for Poppa. From where I lay in a strange calm, I could hear him sending a message to the bank, then to the dean of Orthopedics at the Medical University; I knew they were both afraid I would lose my leg.

"Rebecca, this time we're going to the dean of the Medical School," Poppa said. Dean Kieliwicz took one look. "I will not even ask who did it," he said disgusted. "It should

114

not have been drained." "What then?" Momma was wringing her hands. "We put on a cast," he said, busily inspecting a porcelain bowl with iron chips showing through, "as soon as this thickens. And then she does not walk *at all* for a week. Is such a thing possible?" "It is more than possible," Poppa said grimly. So for a week the cast stayed. Max came with notes and diagrams, recitations of lectures; he had that kind of memory. When he repeated what he had heard, his voice had a mechanical sound, like a needle scratching in the grooves of a gramophone record. We went back the next Tuesday. Doctor Kieliwicz drew a neat line on the cast, took a small saw, and began sawing through it. "Now we stop here," he said, instructing me out of habit, "so as not to cut the skin." He tapped it gently with a small hammer. Nothing. He sawed again, and tapped again. Again, nothing. Finally, it fell off. The knee was now swollen three times its size, but below the knee was nothing, only wrinkled skin lying over bone. The whole leg looked atrophied, the knee of a mummy. Doctor Kieliwicz stared at it. "Give it time," he suggested, "and come back on Wednesday."

I was put back on the couch. Rachel came over. "My God!" she gasped taking a look; "I'm getting *my* mother!" Ten minutes later Rachel's mother arrived. "Listen, Mrs. Savikin," she said, "I would do anything for you, anything, after what you did for Rachel. This dean is no good; he is *no good.* We've got a very good doctor. He's not a dean, just an ordinary doctor, but he's very good. What, you can't spare the ten zlotys? What have you got to lose? Take her there." "Will you come?" Momma pleaded. "Of course, of course, Rachel, too; let's go."

So we drove to the outskirts of the city and into a very poor street. Mother looked frightened. "I told you he wasn't a dean," Rachel's mother reminded her, aggravated. "So," said Doctor Bloom, "you have a hatbox?" Momma looked at him as if he were crazy. "They do," Rachel's mother answered. "You have electricity?" Momma nodded, dumb. "Then you'll be all right," he told me. "First, no cast. Second, you slit the hatbox—it's balsa wood underneath—someone in the family can do that. Then you cut off the two ends. Then you get someone to fasten three blue heat bulbs to the top rim of this hatbox, which is now like a tunnel; you understand?" he asked me. I nodded. "Then, twice a day you put your foot through and lie there for twenty minutes with the heat bulbs shin-

ing on your knee. You won't like it because it's very hot."
"Will I be able to go back to school?" I said, speaking for
the first time. "In two weeks," he said. "You start, then in
two days I'll send a feldsher. He will tie a tourniquet
around the leg, right above the knee; this will force the
blood to circulate through the rest of your leg. Then he'll
come take it off; then you finish treatment. He will come
in the afternoon, and again. You understand?" I nodded.
It was as if I were waking up. Fear, there was fear.

The hatbox was stripped down to the balsa-wood frame;
Momma's biggest, most beautiful hat was evicted, ostrich
feathers and all. Emmanuel busied himself with the bulbs,
muttering about how far behind he was getting with his
own work. The first treatment began at nine at night.
Poppa came to sit with me. "How is it?" he asked. "Terrible," I complained; "I'm all wet." "That's because you
have water on the brain," he teased. If Poppa was teasing,
I was getting better. I lay back, roasting. Verushka came
in. "How do you feel?" she asked with the same frightened
look. "Like a pastry," I answered. She grinned. "Shall I
read to you?" "What, *Resurrection?*" "Oh, Anya," she
cried, "anything you want, anatomy, anything!" Anatomy
frightened her to death. Then I realized how frightened *I*
was. What was wrong with me, that I never realized how
frightened I was until afterward? But now I knew, so I
started crying.

"Everything back to normal," Poppa sighed, poking in
his head. Every day my knee got better. As for Rachel's
mother, she was an angel; who would have thought of
going to her little Doctor Bloom after the dean? Twice a
day the feldsher came with his tourniquet; soon I would
be back at school. "Sing me a song," I asked Vera. "What
song?" "The song about loneliness." She began. Vera always sat up straight in her chair when she sang, folding
her hands in her lap, like a good child, such a good child,
one of God's angels had she been a Catholic; she
would have been picked for his choir. She looked like
those pictures. Then her voice began coiling around the
room: "Sadness, leave me, leave me; the heart sweeps its
sad tune, such a sad tune, and no one can understand the
deep sadness in my heart, the deep sadness like a well. Oh,
my heart, my heart is a tree, a tree in a terrible storm; the
gale hurls me to the ground; so is my heart, my heart,
tossed, tossed. Oh, come, oh, dearest one, with a soft touch,
melt the ice, warm me up, heal the hurts of my heart, oh,

116

come, quickly come." And again, "My heart, so like a tree in a terrible storm, the wind is pushing, pushing to the ground, so my heart is thrown down, it is thrown down. Oh, come, come, come." It was a beautiful melody; the lyrics never sound right in any language but Russian. "What a beautiful voice," I said out loud. Everything was making such an impression on me; everything was eating in like acid now I was getting well. "I would give it to you if I could," Vera cried. We all knew I had the voice of a frog.

The next thing I knew, Momushka was disrupting the house with preparations for the wedding and preparations for the *dacha*. "One bottle for the *dacha*, ten for the wedding," I would hear her instructing Anzia. And then, "Why Warsaw, *why* Warsaw?" but as soon as I came into the kitchen, it was a kiss and a hug from a bear. She didn't speak to me of Warsaw; Poppa didn't speak to me of doubts. Soon even the wedding preparations fell into a normal pattern. "You will have to wear something," Momma said, coming into my room, wiping the perspiration from her forehead. "Anzia and her rum puddings," she sighed. "The house is like an oven; it's good she's starting early." "I thought the caterers were doing everything," I commented. "Anzia says the Lavinskys are leaving that night, and we will still have guests who want *real* food, not everything with swirls. I don't mix in when she gets started. Josefa is falling against the wall from the fumes; you can get drunk breathing in there. So," she went on, settling in my wicker chair, panting, "what do you want to wear? There's still my dress. It's only two inches shorter than you; we could let it down. But it is very fancy. You know, the old style; do you want it?" "No, but Verushka does." "Don't talk to me about Verushka," Momma said, brushing some crumbs from her apron. "This whole place is turning into a cake," she complained. "If pianos could gallop, she would ride off into the sunset with someone on one and they would get married by the piano stool standing up on its hind legs." "Oh, Momma!" I protested, but only out of automatic loyalty. "So stop grinning like a monkey," she grinned, "and tell me what you want to wear. I'm not insulted about my dress, believe me. If I know you you will want something from Madame Anna Kirilova, very elegant and plain, very up to date; am I wrong?" "Not about the dress," I answered. She looked at me, but let it pass. "So, then, tomorrow she expects you at nine o'clock. I am to tell you," she said, mimicking Kirilova's finicky talk, "that you will have the salon entirely to yourself; 'I will spare nothing,' that's what she said. I hope you're ready; I hope you're feeling good and strong. You can lose a lot of blood at Kirilova's with her pins. So," she went on, "don't worry about price. We've already settled it. As much as you want. And when you come back, we should have more news. Your father got a letter today from the Lavinskys saying they would call tomorrow, so we'll go down to the post office and take the call at ten."

After his business went bankrupt, Poppa had fits of economizing. In a recent one he decided to economize by getting rid of the phone; now the family was notified in advance, and would go down to the post office. "We should know when they are coming, for how long, when they are leaving; that's the most important part—Anya, you know I want you to stay longer. I know you're not saying anything, so we'll discuss it more later—and what they want specially during the wedding; I'm not used to all these Chasidic things," she complained. "The rabbi will know what to do." "Good for him," she answered sourly. "And," she went on, energetic again. "the synagogue is picked, all red velvet like your café, and the rabbi Mr. Lavinsky heard about all the way in Warsaw is all prepared to bore us to death; we have the cantor because of Vera and her professor. Believe me, it will sound like an opera. Maybe I will pretend it is an opera." "But I will not be taking off the costume," I warned her; I did not trust this teasing. "You'll look odd on the train in a veil," she said, getting up, puffing. "I have to go back to the kitchen; it's settled then?" "What have we been talking about?" I cried out. "It's settled then," she repeated, resigned. "All right, Anya," she said, turning around to me; "you've always been right about the big things; you've done what you wanted. I told you myself, when you want something, do it; don't tell anyone, not even me. Now I see at least you're listening to your mother about something or other, and I do trust you. I want you to know I trust you; you'll do the right thing. So, I'm going back to the kitchen," she said for the hundredth time. "Please remember I trust you," she scolded, her voice trailing off.

The next morning, I was at Kirilova's. The dress was selected, Belgian silk, extremely plain, but very well cut, with one odd touch, an old-fashioned high collar, like my mother's, with little silk-covered buttons fastening in silk hoops down each side of the neck. The veil was also to be plain: the best material, a broad silk band going over my head covered with tiny silk roses, and over each ear, like earmuffs, one giant rose with a nest of tiny little roses in the center of the petals. It was so beautiful, so pure. "You like it?" Madame Kirilova asked. I nodded, speechless. My blue eyes burned like lanterns; my blond hair fell, straight gold thread. "Almost like a nun," she mused to herself. "A nun! Just the opposite!" I cried. "Almost like a nun," she marveled again from some dream of her own. "A step forward please; there is something in that waist I don't like. Take a deep breath; do not move, please," and the experienced hands slipping in pin after pin like a faultless machine.

"They will be coming in two weeks, on Wednesday," Momma fussed; "hardly any time at all. You and Vera decide where to put your bed. The two sisters are coming too; they can take your room. The parents in the black dining room, but then we will have to wake them up before it's even light; maybe the other way around then. I don't know *what* to do," she wailed. "It seems to me it is already solved, Rebecca," Poppa said; "switch the rooms." "Switch the rooms, switch the rooms," she barked, flying down the hall like a crazy woman. "Her first wedding," Poppa sighed. "I've been warning her about this for twenty years, but no one is ever prepared for true catastrophe. I hope Verushka will give her a chance to recover; ten years, conservatively, I think it will take. Is that your diagnosis too, Anya?"

The Lavinskys arrived. "Where is their house?" Momma hissed to me, watching the caravan of trunks entering the house. The white dining room was lit up like the inside of a prism. All of the chandeliers were gleaming. Everything was polished. Anzia had candles burning in their silver holders all over the room. The best silver was out, the silver basket in the center filled with chocolate halvah ("What else?" Momma asked; "Vera ate so much of it she can't look at it anymore"). As soon as the trunks were put away, and the maids set to unpacking and hanging and pressing, the dinner, bought specially from a kosher caterer, began its procession to the table: all the traditional food—the challah, the wine, the fish—and for the main course, squab cooked in vinegar, Russian-style. The Lavinskys had good appetites and their forks went down only when they wanted to compliment the food. Momma was beaming.

"And such a beautiful house, Mrs. Savikin," Mrs. Lavinsky said, turning to Momma. "I don't know how you do it; such order, and *such quiet*," she marveled, "even with a baby grand piano and two boys. We expected to hear you all the way to the station. When we have time, I want to know how you do it." "Oh, I don't do anything," Momma cried, blushing down to the neck of her dress; "they have been such good children." "Not always, Rebecca," Poppa called from his end of the table; "we should tell them about Anya and the photographer so they know what to expect from her at the wedding." "Boris!" Momma exclaimed. "Poppa!" I protested. "I'll never forget it," Poppa went on. "Let people eat," Momma tried to interrupt, but it was no use. "We went out to take pictures when we were visiting in Paltava, and Miss Anya here was three, not quite so big as she is now since Rebecca started feeding her sour cream at breakfast; do you know about that?"

"Boris!" Momma cried again. "Rebecca, if you want them to think this is a quiet house . . ." Poppa interrupted. "The photographer had two beautiful tall chairs, the tops carved to look like palaces with spires, you know, photographer's chairs, one for each of us, and Anya was to stand in the middle. But she didn't want to. She saw a little chair somewhere in the corner, a three-cornered one, wasn't it, Rebecca?" "Boris!" she pleaded; she was beginning to smile. "Then it was, 'I want to sit on this; it's a small chair; it's not too big for me.' Oh, she was mad at the photographer. 'I am mad on him'; that's what she told us. Poor man. He was perspiring; Anya was sitting in the little chair staring at him. 'Perhaps you can make a bargain with her, Mr. Photographer?' I asked. 'Anything, anything,' he promised; he was distracted, I tell you. So they finally agreed she could sit on the chair as long as she wanted, even press the button to the camera and take pictures of him, if only she would stand there for two minutes without moving and just look right up at him, but she was not supposed to smile. So," Poppa finished up, taking his fork, "we have her picture in the album there. We're sitting in the chairs; she's standing in the middle, grinning like a golem. You see what you're getting into?" he asked Stajoe.

"But," Mr. Lavinsky interrupted, serious, "you said photographers at the wedding; is that proper?" Momma looked annoyed; she didn't like it, all this religion. "I spoke to the rabbi myself," Poppa said. "He assured me it's proper if we don't take pictures during the ceremony, but only during the dancing." Mr. Lavinsky looked relieved and helped himself to some plum sauce. "Remarkable plums," he murmured. Anzia, standing behind his chair, lit up like a candle.

As for me, I was sitting there next to Momma and next to Stajoe, but really, I was sitting with Momma on the white sofa, leafing through the blue family album. It had a blue velvet cover with a mother of pearl design in the center, and gutta-percha triangles on each corner. Inside were pictures of the whole family, back to her great-great grandfather, the first ones daguerreotypes, then later, the sepia cardboard ones, some in round cardboard frames, some in square ones. I was hearing Momma say, "This is your grandfather, the artist who was so good with the charcoal, and here is your Aunt Doba, who met me at the station, and here is your aunt, who died. This is my sister, Zunia, and this is Sofia, who fell in love with a married man and tried to poison herself, but she survived, paralyzed. She was the end of my Poppa, though. He was ninety, strong as a horse, but he never got over it. Look at that hair, down to her knees and so curly, it stands out like a tent. And after, she could not move her hands and Poppa used to come in and feed her! And how he used to cry when he came out of her room and saw the piano. 'I see her face in it!' he used to cry. And here is Momma, before the typhoid, such a beautiful woman. The last thing she said to Poppa before she died was, 'You will not miss me; you have so many children.' She had five, all of them finished the conservatorium. 'They will look after you. I've done a good job, Ivan?' 'You have, you have,' he sobbed. 'So there is nothing to cry about, and I am going with a smile. Because of you, I never had anything to do in life but smile, and I don't see,' she said, 'why in the next world I should do anything else but smile; especially when *you* come; then I will laugh.' Oh, he pleaded with her not to talk, to get better, but she said no, she wouldn't get better. She wanted to say goodbye to us; then she wanted him to sit with her, and they could finish as they began, looking at each other, 'It is good to die a normal death! This was the last thing she said. And do you know, it made him bitter for months, that she was not more unhappy to die;

121

then he understood, and was happy. 'I will never feel guilt,' he marveled; 'never.' And of course, she missed the pogrom that took my brother Mischa (we named your brother for him); she missed Sofia in her wheelchair; dear Momma! But she missed so many weddings! Who can say what was the best balance? I cannot. But she didn't complain."

"'A normal death, a normal death.' I think about that a lot, all the time when things are bad, how it is something to look forward to. I can't believe it, but it was, for her. And this is my friend, Tania, and Elena, and Anna," the edges of the album darkening with the endless turnings of her ringed beautiful hands, the rings changing with her birthdays and anniversaries and the small high boxes Poppa brought her from the city. "So," she said, picking it up one day, noticing the darkening, "you see, you can't live without leaving your mark." And I was thinking, in the old album there was only one, and sometimes two, pictures of each person—they were so expensive—a birth picture and a wedding picture, a picture after graduation from conservatorium. And in the album life was not continuous; it hopped from one perfect and important moment to another. They were only born, only reached their moment of perfection. The album kept them alive in a kind of heaven; they could not die And now, I was standing at the point of perfection, the bridal picture. If I was blessed, the continuity of life would take me over; if I was blessed I would see the whole circle. I would say it is good to die a normal death. But first would come the children, and the deaths, the children dying before me perhaps, hiding in coffins, watching aunts die, and still, if I were blessed, I would end saying, "Because of you, I never had anything to do but smile." How the memory worked! Like this album, cutting out, framing, somehow pushing the deaths to black borders in condolence cards while the rest of life went on and on, unpredictable and endless.

"What are you thinking about?" Stajoe whispered to me. "My wedding dress." But I wasn't, I was thinking about the little table with the album, pushed all the way into a corner to make way for the extra tables of food and pastries and wine. It was such a habit; anyone who sat on the sofa automatically began looking through it, each picture like a train station, at some point, the train crossing the border, the captions changing from Cyrillic letters spelling Paltava to Polish names of studios. "Your

122

Anya blushes a great deal," Mr. Lavinsky teased; "I wonder what he said to her?" And so the evening finished in a clatter of silverware, a tinkle of crystal, conversation subdued, everyone tired, at the same time avoiding sleep because of the suspense of tomorrow, what we had all come together for: the wedding. And I was afraid.

Momma came into my room late; Verushka was asleep, exhausted. "Did she cry herself to sleep?" Momma asked. I nodded yes. Momma shook her head. "You're afraid"; I shook my head. "You're afraid," Momma repeated again. "That's good; it means you're serious." She sat down on the edge of the bed and put her arm around me. Suddenly I flung myself against her, burrowing my head in her lap, crying as if my heart would break, my whole body jerking in convulsions. "Cry," Momma said; "nothing wakes her when she falls asleep, not even an explosion." And I did cry. I don't even know how long. But Momma never moved; her hand was stroking my head. "Little Anyu, little Anyushka who sat on the chair." "Sing me a song," I asked; "we can go out." "We won't wake her," Momma promised, looking at Vera where she glimmered in the moonlight; "nothing will wake her. Put your face close." And she sang me the same song she had sung the night the girls were attacked by the boys with the iron nails; it was a very short little song, but I loved it almost the best.

"Tell me, butterfly," she began, in a voice so low, it was almost tuneless, but it brought back all the other times, "what do you eat, how do you live? 'Oh,' said the butterfly, 'I live among the fields, the flowers of spring; their smell is my food, but my life is very quick, very short, not more than one day. Be so kind and don't touch me.' " I cuddled up. I could feel Momma smiling in the dark. "One more," I whispered. "One more," she whispered back. We were conspirators again; there was no one else. And she sang me the song about an old man who wanted to marry a young girl. He promised her a garden with cherries, a house to go with the garden, a man to cut the grass. But she sings to him that she doesn't want the house, or the garden, the grass, she doesn't want him; he is older than his stones, and he hobbles away. "These offers are more appealing in old age," Momma laughed. "Your Stajoe is a good young man," Momma said into the darkness, but a hint of a question in her voice. "Yes, Momma," I said. "They tell me your apartment is all prepared; you only have to buy some furniture." "Yes,

Momma." "Then I must tuck you in," she told me. "You have a life of your own now, and if he will be good to you, I will be glad to see this wedding. What does an engineer do?" she asked, puzzled, straightening up. I didn't know, either; I knew it was a good profession and that was important, but I didn't want details. She bent over to kiss me again, and as if her lips were drugged, she put me to sleep.

I woke up wondering what I was doing in Vera's room. The first thing I saw was the baby grand piano; then, turning over on my side and looking through the feet and the wires to the pedals, I could see her asleep in her bed. There was still very little light coming through the window. I crept out of bed and into the hall. It was silent as a tomb. I tiptoed down the hall and knocked on Poppa and Momma's door: no answer. I went on to the white dining room. Momma and Poppa were sitting on the sofa, the photograph album open on their lap. "We're trying to find a place for your wedding pictures," Poppa said. "Rebecca says we'll have to put them between the pages; it's almost full. For some reason unknown to me, she refused to start a new one. But *you'll* have plenty of room in yours," Poppa said, fishing for something under the folds of his dressing gown. "Oh, I'm sitting on it," he said pulling it out with relief; "it was the nearest we could find to ours." It was a red velvet album with mother of pearl inlay all around the sides like a border. "Sit down here," Poppa said, sliding over. I sat in between them.

"I hear Anzia," Poppa said finally. "I hear Mischa," Momma added. "Come, we'd better get dressed; the caterers will be repossessing this room soon enough." "I thought, Anya, you would want to get dressed with your mother, so I'm getting dressed with your brothers. This morning, the whole house will be like a Chasidic synagogue." He padded off, grinning. Momma watched while Anzia washed me; then she dressed me, arranging me, sitting up, on their bed like a doll. Anzia came in to dress Momma. She still looked like a young woman. "I'm wearing the blue hat you bought me, Anya," she said, lifting down the huge hat box from the top of the closet, taking out the navy-blue straw hat with its curled-up brim, its pointy top, its little ribbon over the brim covered with tiny gold roses. "Sometimes," she said, leaning into the triptych mirror, examing the hat, "I think you and Verushka are more alike than we say; you're always giving everything away. Do you realize," she asked, pinning the hat onto her heavy black hair with a magnificent diamond hatpin in the shape of a rose, "how many sodas and French lessons I am wearing on my head," "You *are* funny, Momma," I said, suddenly seeing her head as a sundae, sticky with lemonade and ice cream and chocolate. "I'm stupid," she answered, "to let you go all the way to Warsaw, but what will be, will be."

Soon we were all ready. There was a line of *drozhkas* halfway down the block. "Anzia comes to supervise," Momma announced to Mrs. Lavinsky's astonishment. "To supervise what?" she asked. "You never know; just in case, just in case," Momma answered nervously, brushing an imaginary fleck from her skirt; "is that a feather on your shoulder?" she asked solicitiously, lunging toward her, violently rubbing something off. "Oh, thank you," Mrs. Lavinsky said, nervously backing away; "don't you think it's time to get started?" "It is, it is," Momma jabbered, "the *drozhkas* have been waiting outside for almost an hour."

The Lavinsky family left first. We stood in the white dining room watching them drive off, listening to the sound of the horses' hooves, the metal wheels on the white stones. "What a racket," I whispered to Vera. I could see Stajoe's head in the last carriage, inches higher than others. "Now it is our turn," Poppa said. "Come Vera; help Anya with her dress." We went down the stairs slowly. "Don't trip," Vera warned me. "Don't step on it," I warned her. "Anya and I will go in the last carriage," Momma said. We got in; the others began to leave, Poppa and Mischa, Anzia and Emmanuel, then our *drozhka* was moving, too. "Don't study me like that, Momma," I complained edgily; "you make me think something's wrong." "I'm only taking my own wedding pictures now," she said sadly. "Paper has a way of disappearing; I will never lose these." She looked down at her skirt; the gold roses on her hat gleamed in my eye. I bent forward and held her hand. "I love you, Momushka," I whispered; "you know that. I'd never go away for good." "I know, I know," she whispered, smiling through her tears. "Look, Kafkaska Street, Anya, the Prosectorium, we're passing it." I jerked forward. "Now you're taking your own pictures," Momma sighed.

The carriage rolled on. "Anya?" Momma asked tentatively. "If you get pregnant, you know it happens, what about medical school? You lost so much time because of your leg." "I'll go back as soon as I have the baby; we discussed it." "You won't let anyone change your mind?" she asked shyly. "How could I?" I asked; "it's been my life; I would never stop." "But if someone wanted you to?" "They'd have to tie me to the bed, Momma, I mean it." She sank back, sighing. "I don't know where you came from," she wondered. "You were always there with your stories." "No," she said; "Vera heard them too; character's a mystery, at least, to me." We rolled on. "It's been a long way, Momma." "Your Poppa wanted the best synagogue; there it is," she said, pointing. I saw it as if I had never seen it before; it had sprung from the earth that minute. It was a huge red brick building taking up almost the length of the block, three stories high; the upper floors for the rabbi's offices and the tutors and the Hebrew classes; and downstairs, the most luxurious in all Vilno, a red carpet, red velvet drapes, cream-patterned walls, crystal chandeliers. But it was not just a building: I would come out of here in the same dress, but given away into a strange family, a strange religion, a strange city, Warsaw. For the first time, I understood something of Momma's fear.

"Not through those door," she said, motioning me away from the heavy mahogany doors at the center of the building; the brass knockers gleamed like King Solomon's mines. "There's a small entrance around the corner; we'll go in there and you can surprise everyone. Wait," she said, bending over and picking up the long hem of my skirt, "I'll help you; put your veil over your arm." So we went into the side door, two invalids supporting each other, two women grown old together. Vera was waiting. "Let me fix your hair," she whispered; "and I have something special. Momma, turn your back," and she pulled out of her bag a little white disk; the top unscrewed and there was a little circle of red. "Rouge, Vera!" I exclaimed. "Why not?" she asked, indignant. "He should know he is marrying the most beautiful sister in the world." "Listen," she said suddenly, "I think I hear the cantor singing. Are you ready?" she asked anxiously. "Yes," I answered, hoarse.

I came down the aisle on Poppa's arm. They were all seated in mahogany pews: Momma, Vera, Emmanuel, Mischa, Gucha, Anzia, Max, Professor Kobielski, their faces were running together, then rising like bubbles from a soap pipe; the faces were like circles of time, moths of time; they had no bodies; they were from every time of my life; every bit of my life had been gathered together in that room. And there was Stajoe waiting under the canopy. From the minute I saw him, there was not a sound in the synagogue for me. Everything took place in perfect silence. When we stood together under the red velvet canopy, embroidered with its gold threads, hung with its fringes and tassels, I didn't hear a word of the sermon. I saw myself walking down the red carpet, my friends divided by the carpet like the Red Sea. It was a miracle, cutting a path for us.

I could see myself only, myself from a great distance, dressed in my wedding dress, and Stajoe, dressed in his wedding clothes, which were strange to me, the Chasidic dress, a prayer shawl under his tuxedo, its white fringe showing, and over the tuxedo he wore an overcoat, a beautiful coat, fur-lined, with a fur collar and a hard hat, like a derby, the prayer shawl's fringes showing even under the overcoat. "What it is?" I had asked Momma. "They're supposed to wear it at all sacred occasions; it's supposed to be a shroud or something." "Not a shroud," Poppa corrected in passing, but I never found out exactly what it meant, not then. I saw Stajoe raising his foot to crush the glass; I saw him lowering his shoe; it was all in slow motion. I did not even hear the glass break. It wasn't until he gripped my arm to lead me away that sounds returned, that faces came into focus. I saw Rachel sitting next to Max. He looked happy for me, but no matter how hard she tried, she could not look happy. Her own marriage to Jakob Katzenellenbogen had not yet taken place. Then there were the voices of the family, everyone complimenting the rabbi and the cantor; we thanked them, Momma sighing, "It's over, it's over," as if she had just been through an operation, a thinning number of people to hug as everyone left the building to get into the waiting *drozhkas,* returning to our house.

At home, the two dining rooms were set with fancy foods and wines of all kinds. There was a small orchestra playing in the court and singing, Vera singing, then Momma, and some wild dancing of Stajoe's family. Momma lifted up her eyes to some heaven of her own. I began dancing with Stajoe, somewhere in this silent dream without a map, the noise only now and then flickering on, as if I were a radio being interfered with. Mr. Lavinsky materialized at my elbow. "Anya," he said, "at your own wedding, sit. It is bad luck to dance at your own wedding"; instantly, I sat down, frightened. Momma asked what happened; I told her. She was furious. "Nonsense, it's just nonsense, do you hear me? You'll be all right; what did I tell you, these Chasidim!" She bent over and whispered to Poppa. He shook his head, whispering back. She leaned over to me. "Poppa says pay no attention." But something was spoiled. So it went on, getting later and later. Finally, we were standing in the entrance hall, saying, good night, good night, like mechanical dolls. "Ach," Momma said, sinking into a chair, "go to bed, children; we'll take care of this."

In the morning Mr. Lavinsky came in before we had time to dress. He was still in his nightgown. "I came to say," he said smiling, "now when you stay with us, Stajoe won't have to sleep on the couch." Still smiling, he pushed back the covers and sat down on the edge of the bed. "Poppa," Stajoe said roughly, "hurry up and get dressed; you are going to miss that train." It seemed strange to me. While Stajoe was getting dressed, I ran out and told Momma. Oh, she knew right away. "He was looking for blood. I am disgusted, disgusted," she said; "to come all the way down the hall to tell you Stajoe would not have to sleep on the couch! He never slept on the couch! But what can you expect?" "You really think that's what he wanted?" I couldn't believe it. "What else?" Momma asked, her voice crawling with suspicion. "You watch out for him, Anya; although," she went on, she couldn't help it; basically she was so generous, "now he is satisfied his dear son married a virgin, he won't make any more trouble. So I would guess."

We saw the Lavinskys off at the train station. We waved at the train until it was a puff of smoke and a noise. Stajoe and I were not to leave for three days. As soon as we got home, there was Momma, crying. Nothing I said to her stopped it. It was like a hemorrhage. Vera tried, too. Nothing worked. It was heartbreaking to see her. Her eyes were red and sore. She walked through the apartment without making a sound, tears falling out of her eyes like rain. "I knew it, I knew it, the minute the wedding was over, so would be the good behavior," Poppa said, following her, saying the same thing over and over again: "What is it, Rebecca? It is just overnight, stop it, Rebecca, it is just overnight." But still it went on. "Momma," I pleaded, "I'm barely ever at home anyway; you've spent my whole life lecturing me about how I don't see my brothers unless we're eating. Vera is in the house more, with her piano, and you'll come to us anyway. What's there to cry about?"

But it turned out there was enough to cry about for three days, and for three days we stayed there. Poppa was sad, too, but he was busy, and not so much with me as with Momma. "We will visit, Rebecca; we *will* visit," I heard him saying the second night, and then, "All right, if I'm so busy, *you* will visit; then you'll have her all to yourself." Then came the third day. "So," Poppa asked, "are you coming with me to the station, Rebecca?" "I'm already dressed," I heard her answer, haughty, indignant, as if he were her enemy. Nothing could keep her away. We got on the train, Stajoe putting me next to the window so I could see them until the last second. I was waving and crying and waving. Vera was standing still as stone, but Momma was not crying; Poppa was standing with his sweet smile, waving, although I knew we were just a puff of smoke and a bit of noise to them. In a few minutes, I was lost in the sensation of leaning silently on Stajoe's shoulder, feeling his arm around me, and when I got tired of looking up at his face, of looking at my own, broadened in my wedding band.

It was still early June when we got to Warsaw, and very hot. My medical school records had been transferred to the university. There was not much left for me to do: a few courses and a thesis. But for the first week I didn't even have time to think about that with the seven days of feasts, the shevabrojas, the blessings. For seven nights, we came to the Lavinskys for a new party, celebration, a feast. Everything looked strange to me. I felt like a Christian woman, an Irishwoman. I wasn't used to their praying, so loud, their dancing; the women who had had to shave their heads after marriage and then keep them covered seemed to me monsters. But I had Stajoe; I was the center of attention. Nothing was too strange for me. The strange customs, the strange clothes, the strange blessings, none of it sunk in. It was like a foreign film; it was over when we went back to our apartment. We were preparing a nest. Within a week we had a normal life.

And we had our apartment, our perfect apartment, in the fashionable section of Warsaw, near the gardens, on Marsalskowska Street. It was in a new building, on the second floor. It had three big rooms and a huge kitchen. The floors were parquet, like the ones at home, but new, and we fell in love with it at three in the afternoon; the sun was pouring in from three sides like money. It was the corner apartment in an L-shaped building; the dining room looked out on the court, the bedroom on the gardens. The windows, too, were unusually big for a new house. We had everything ready: our maid, Stashka, was already living in the little room that opened off the kitchen, like Anzia's room at home. She had polished and waxed the black stones of the kitchen floor so they gleamed like marble. An old oak table took up the center of the kitchen, red and white checked curtains fluttered from the windows. It was a beautiful room: the warmth, the sun coming in was like coming into an egg. And the bedroom had been freshly painted light green. The superintendent thought the walls were too new for wallpaper, but we wanted something fancier than plain paint. "We can paint the moldings gold!" I suggested and Stajoe beamed. "I got those moldings from an old building they tore down," the superintendent swelled, proud to see them so valued; "only two apartments have them." So the moldings ran around the bedroom and the dining room walls like gold threaded ribbon. The bedroom had only two old beds while we looked for our bedroom set, but it had beautiful parquet floors. I had already taught Stashka how to take care of them: first, to scrub them with steel wool, following the grain, and then to strap on the foot brushes and polish and polish until they gleamed like melting butter. It was so brilliant; the floor reflected the crystal chandelier that sparkled under the green sky. Already there were two small oriental rugs on each side of the nickel beds. This was my Momma's teaching: curtains and rugs first; they were the base of all elegance. And white curtains crisscrossed the window, making the light grainy and snowy, and across the bottom half was a heavy shade, made of thick green material, the same color as the walls. The dining room made me most secure; it was as much like Momma's as I could make it. Red velvet curtains against the walls, mahogany furniture, the round mahogany table; it shone like a lake, reflecting the crystal chandelier, and on the floor, a huge Oriental rug in shades of green and pink, a gift from the Lavinskys. The extra pieces were French, in the very latest style, all inlaid and veneered; all we had to do was find a bedroom set. We looked for it like Columbus planning the discovery of a continent; it was to be the Lavinsky's main present to us. Off we would go in the *drozhka,* but not a store in the city

130

had anything we wanted. We would come back at night to the noises of a city street; I was sure I had never been so happy.

Then one night, we were sitting in the Café Adria, which had its tables out in front with their colorful umbrellas and tablecloths, but we were in the basement, the section for the nightclub, when another couple joined us. The woman seemed nice, but familiar. Her husband was a technical engineer, like Stajoe, even resembling him slightly. His wife began to tell me about new cosmetics courses; how cosmetics could be made from cucumbers and almonds, and of course, I was interested in anything new and fashionable. "It is good for times when you can't do much else," she said slyly, dropping her eyes. "Oh, I have plenty of time for that," I cried, and began complaining about how even in Warsaw, a second Paris, everyone called it that, there was not a decent bedroom set to be found. There we were, in our beautiful brick building, with more sun than Egypt, and no beds at all.

"Oh, I tell you what," the redhead bubbled, blushing so her freckles went under; "I have a friend, Lena, she lives on Manushkin Street, and she had a set specially made from special wood to order for her. Why don't you call her. But of course you shouldn't tell her what you want; just be mysterious, and say you want to talk to her, and then when you get there, you should try and find out. She wouldn't tell *me* where it came from," finished the plump little girl, whose name was Frieda Vronsky. "Would you be so good as to give me the address?" I asked poking Stajoe in the side. "A piece of paper and a pencil, quick, paper and pencil." Absently, he handed me his little book and the little gold pencil I gave him; he always carried it. I would have liked to know this Frieda better; she seemed to know her way about the city so well. But Stajoe, I don't know, he was very jealous. And he was in no hurry to continue with them. We went out a lot, but the only person's company he wanted was mine. Even when we went to his parents for Friday nights he couldn't wait to leave; his mother was very much hurt. He seemed to mind when his brother kissed me goodbye at the door; even his father. But I didn't pay much attention. I didn't like to fight. But the visit of my Momma kept coming up, and kept getting delayed. Finally at lunch I said, "Stajoe, please explain this to me. I don't understand. What is this, a monastery? Your parents send us full dinners every single

131

night. All we have to do is heat them up. Why must we rush off like that?" "It's too noisy there." "It was noisy when you lived there." "We'll stay longer next time." "What about friends?" "I don't make friends easily." "But it's lonesome for me," I cried. Then he looked frightened. "I think you should call your mother about her visit," he said.

So when we left the Adria and said good night, I told Stajoe that Frieda Vronsky had told me about a woman who had a beautiful bedroom set, specially made, but she wouldn't tell anyone where she got it. "I'm sure you can find out," he said, smiling and hugging me. So why should I have minded the jealousy? When he was at work, I would visit friends at cafés; other afternoons I went to his mother's and she taught me embroidery and cooking. She taught me to make beautiful shawls. One was gray silk, with a long black fringe, but covered all over with black open work that looked like fine lace; then, separately, she taught me to make the thin, crocheted three-dimensional roses, to be appliquéd separately. We sat there on her couch, each making roses. But Stajoe didn't like it; he did not like it. And the sisters and sisters-in-law were jealous, and of course, the *only* place his parents would come and eat was our apartment; because of Stajoe's vow it was kosher. And I began to worry about how unselfish the vow had really been.

Still, it was cozy. Every day Stajoe was home at eleven for lunch. He would eat a huge bowl of soup, full of mushrooms, beef, and vegetables; a loaf of bread with butter, some sour cream, and milk. Stashka would run out when she saw him coming to bring something fresh from the bakery. But the jealousy began to poison things. I didn't know what to make of it. Every afternoon I had to be home at five, no matter what. If Stajoe got home early, I would find him asking the maid where I had gone, whom I had seen, when I came back, when did I say I would come back, and on and on. The day I had set off on a trip across town to Lena Olensky's, whose house I couldn't find, I came home and found him cross-examining poor Stashka. "Stajoe," I said, "I want to talk to you." As soon as we got in the bedroom, I asked why he did it. "Why do you make me so small in front of the maid? What kind of woman will she think I am?" "I'm sorry," he apologized; "I can't help it; I won't do it again, I promise," but the next time I came home late, it was the same thing. "It is a

132

poison," I insisted, "it is a poison," but still I adored him, and again he promised he would not ask Stashka. "What is it? Did something happen with a woman? It has to come from somewhere." He began fiddling with his short-wave radio, pretending not to hear me. And that was the only black mark in the first weeks of our marriage.

Saturday we walked together through the Saxon Gardens; I had called Lena Olensky. "Listen," I told her, "I have to talk to you; I can't talk on the phone." Then I didn't say anything. "All right," she said finally; curiosity was getting the best of her. "Come over this afternoon." Stajoe left me at the door. "I'll wait by the tulip bed," he told me, grinning. Lena let me in; instantly, I looked all over for the bedroom. As soon as I saw it, I flew over. "Oh, Mrs. Olensky, what a beautiful bedroom. I have never seen anything like it; this set, it belongs in a museum. I have never never never seen anything like it, so magnificent, so beautiful, you must have inherited it." I always remembered Momma's advice: if you're going to use flattery, lay it on with a trowel. "No, I didn't inherit it," she said, starting to soften, but still suspicious. "What did you want to talk to me about?" "To speak frankly," I said, "someone told me you had the most beautiful bedroom set in all Warsaw, but I never believed it could be like this! My husband and I, we're just married; we can't find anything at all. This woman, I don't even know her, told me you had the best taste in the whole city; I should come to you. Oh, please," I pleaded as if for my life, "can't you tell me where it came from?" "Oh, I don't really know," Mrs. Olensky evaded; "my husband knows; he bought it for me." "Listen, Mrs. Olensky," I begged her, "we live in different parts of the city; we move in different crowds. No one would ever see yours and then see mine. I'd never get just the same thing anyway; we could never afford anything like *that*. You can tell me, don't worry. It is so beautiful; I don't know how you found it; you must be a genius." "Well," she said slowly, as if balancing a ledger, "I *think*, I'm not sure, it was made by a carpenter named Frumkin in Prague. I think so. I'm not at all sure. I'm sure I have it wrong; I have a terrible memory." She already regretted having opened her mouth, her precious set spawning identical twins in every apartment in the city. "You have to write him; maybe he might come. He only takes orders. It's very expensive, very expensive." "Oh, I am sure!" I cried; "I'm sure I can't afford it at all. But

133

you said Mr. Frumkin? What a funny name." "I really don't know. I told you," she said irritated; "I told you; it was my husband who bought it. He doesn't consult me about these things."

I was hopping up and down when I met Stajoe in the gardens. "Mr. Frumkin in Prague!" I shouted. "My father will find out the address." He jumped up, as excited as I was. Sure enough, we got the address, and in due time, Mr. Frumkin arrived in a shiny black suit with a big square pad of paper. "This will take a long time," Mr. Frumkin mourned, inspecting the bedroom; "I'm not sure you want it." "We want it," Stajoe said; "we don't want anything else." "I warned you," Mr. Frumkin told us, rubbing his hands, cleaning them of responsibility. "How long?" Stajoe asked. "At *least* six months," Mr. Frumkin answered indignant; "for hurries, you should go to the stores here; they have everything horrible ready-made." "We're not in a hurry," Stajoe said. "Good thing. And," he gloomed on; "it will have to be shipped. The closet doors are glass; that doesn't make it easier." "Fine, fine," I said, getting impatient. So we ordered it. It was the most unusual, the most remarkable thing. All the furniture was rounded, the footboard, the headboard. The big chest took up one wall; it was also rounded. It had four doors; inside each was a mirror, and on the front of each door, inside the inlaid wood which gleamed like glass, were two huge frogs, legs sprawled out as if they were swimming, nose to nose. The first door opened to hold coats. The second door was the man's section, with special drawers that pulled out for shirts and cuff links, and on top, a small section of tiny drawers, like cubby holes in a desk. The third door was for my good dresses, and the fourth was for storage. Mr. Frumkin had also made a manicurist table shaped like an *S:* a manicurist used to come to our house once a week and she and I sat at the table facing each other, each on an inlaid chair matching the beds and the wardrobe. The beds had tiny flowers inlaid in a garland in the centers of the headboard and footboard. I had never seen anything like it, and all day, I made trips from the kitchen and dining room, just to be sure it was still there.

One day at the Lavinsky's, I said something about the money, how much it must have cost. "Never tell your husband what you need money for," Stajoe's father instructed me; "just ask." "That's right," Mrs. Lavinsky chimed in; "yesterday I heard her asking Stajoe for thread money.

Never say what for." When Stajoe came in, Mr. Lavinsky blandly announced that he thought Anya needed a new fur coat; then he thought I needed a new dress, until they had Stajoe dizzy. He told me to let him know how much money I needed. At our home, too, it had been like that. "Rebecca," Poppa used to say, "I need some money for tobacco,"and Momma would give it to him.

Things went along in the dream seen through the white veil, and if there were little spikes, what then? They made the rest of the dream better. Even Mr. Frumkin had outdone himself; the furniture arrived in three months, and the next day, my mother came from Vilno. "I don't know which makes you happiest," Stajoe complained. "Pooh!" I told him, "the furniture didn't raise me; this nonsense is beginning to get on my nerves." But every time he saw Momma with her arm around me he would make an excuse; he had forgotten something; he had to get something at the store. He would disappear for several hours. She sensed it; she cut her visit from two weeks to eight days. "Poppa misses me, and the children," she told us over breakfast. But that wasn't it. Anzia had been there so long she could have run the house forever. If she saw Stajoe coming, Momma would take her arm from my waist and clasp her hands primly in her lap. One morning, after Stajoe left we were eating breakfast. "I don't know, Momma," I told her; "I don't feel well lately. I throw up." "Go to the doctor, Anya," she said, no alarm at all. I was astounded. A cough was occasion for a trip to the hospital in Vilno. "It's probably perfectly normal." The next day she went back; that night I called her. I was two months pregnant.

8

NORMAL or not. I did not want it. I thought of Frieda Vronsky and her tales of cosmetics courses until they seemed like a ghastly parody of medical school courses and until I was convinced it was talking to her that had done it. And I *had* signed up for the cosmetics courses; they were supposed to begin next week. Stajoe would be overjoyed. Whenever I asked him, he informed me he wanted twelve children. I decided to wait before telling him. I remembered, after Zoshia had left, Anzia telling me if only she had found out sooner, if only she had known before, until I demanded to know what she could have done if she had. "Well," Anzia said, "then the onions might have done some good." "What are you talking about?" I thought she had lost her mind. "Oh, Anya, it's an old medicine. You peel twenty orange onions and boil the peels for hours, and then drink it. It makes the baby go out." "That can't work," I told her positive. "It can't work, but it does," she said, turning her back to the stove. "I hope you don't have to find out; it's very bitter." I spent three days thinking, seeing medical school rolling off on wheels into another city, and sent Stashka on a long errand to the Lavinsky's; I suddenly needed some red thread and thin needles. Then I ran down and got some orange onions, and began boiling the peel. It tasted like acid. Nothing happened.

Jumping! I thought, remembering another one of Anzia's stories, and went into the enchanted bedroom, climbed on the enchanted bed, and began jumping off. After twenty jumps, I lay down and waited. Nothing. The soles of my feet hurt; I felt fine. In the morning, I told Stajoe. "I'll take the day off!" he threatened, beaming. "Please, please don't. I have to get special clothes, you know. These won't fit for so long." "I can't wait to see you a whole barrel," he said, hugging and kissing, half lifting me up, he was so tall. "Wait until you see what it looks like first," I cautioned grimly. "So," I asked, squeezing some orange juice, feeling as if I were wringing a neck, "what do you want, a boy or a girl?" "A boy," he answered promptly. Oh, he had no doubts. "Suppose I have a girl?" "You have plenty of time." Every time I turned around, I bumped into him. "Should you carry that?" he asked me. "What, an orange?" I snapped. As soon as he left, I planned on picking up beds and dropping them onto the floor; I did not want this. "No," Stajoe said, "the pot; it has hot water in it." "Well, since I'm not going to pour it on my stomach, I don't see what difference it makes." "Why don't *you* come downtown and have lunch with *me* at the Adria," he demanded. "I know it's not as much fun as chocolate waffles and gossip with your friends, but I would love it." He was as shy and unsure as a suitor all over again. "Good idea," I agreed, considering how many tramways and trolleys I would have a chance to jump off on my way. "At eleven," he said, "I'm stopping at Poppa's." "Please thank your mother for the red thread," I asked wearily. "What thread?" Automatically suspicious, "The red thread, the red thread, she'll know what thread." "At eleven," he sang out, running down the stairs and all the way down the street.

I went in and flung myself down on the bed, stomach first. Nothing. At least it was fun. I tried it again and again. Still nothing. But there was hope in jumping from a moving tram. But at eleven, I met Stajoe at the Adria, and to my disgust I never felt better. "What would you like? Not coffee?" he asked worriedly. "A waffle," I answered forlornly, hoping chocolate was bad for pregnancies; I had heard that too somewhere. "*Two* waffles for the lady," he instructed; then turning to me; "perhaps it will be twins." That was it. "I'm not a cat; I don't have litters. I expect to have one at a time. And if I have eighteen, I'm still starting medical school as soon as they're born." "I think you're in a bad mood," he said, looking more closely at me; "are you frightened?" I was guilty. I was imagining how hard I could jump from the café table to the floor. "Yes, frightened." "Don't be frightened," he said, eyes glued to my face; "don't be frightened; I'll take care of you."

For three weeks, I jumped off trolleys onto cement; for three weeks, I pushed the big cabinet back and forth; then the bell rang. "Police," said one of the two men; they were wearing army uniforms. "Yes?" I asked. I thought they wanted directions to someone else's apartment. "Stajoe Lavinsky, please," one of the men said; "he's under arrest." "Under arrest?" I demanded; "for what?" "He is charged with not having served his proper time in the military service." "Please," I begged; "this isn't true; where did you hear such a thing!" "We have a signed statement," said the second man, ignoring the first one who was glaring at him, "from one Frieda Vronsky to that effect." Freida Vronsky! "Oh, it's definitely a mistake," I said, relieved. "My husband doesn't even know her; we just met her one night in a café. She told me about a bedroom set and a cosmetics course." "Nevertheless," said the second man. "Nevertheless what? It *must* be a mistake; she doesn't know him." "Mrs. Lavinsky," said the second man, starting to cough, "she does know him. Her brother is one of his best friends."

"What are you talking about, have you gone crazy?" I cried, pressing my hands over my ears. "I think you had better sit down," he said, taking my elbow, "sit down. We have to wait here with you; there's no reason we all have to stand up." If there was only some way to warn him, some way! But there wasn't. I heard his steps on the stairs, his voice calling, "Anya, Anya" before he even got to the door. The two men got up. "Stajoe Lavinsky," said the first, who up to now had not spoken, "you are under arrest. You are charged by Frieda Vronsky with evading military service. This is a serious crime. You are aware of that? You must come with us." Stajoe towered over them. "Anya, call my parents. May I get my coat?" he asked. "And a blanket?" A blanket! Had he lost his mind too? "Go get them," the second man said. He came back with his blanket and coat. "Don't forget to call my parents," he reminded me; "and take care of yourself." "But you'll be right back?" I called down the stairwell. "I'm not sure, but I'll be back." A blanket! And Frieda Vronsky.

I was dialing, or misdialing, the Lavinsky's before he turned the corner. I kept getting it wrong, and finally I slammed the receiver against the wall, chipping the paint and sobbing. All Mrs. Lavinsky could hear when she finally picked up the phone was gasping and more gasping. "Anya? Is it Anya?" she kept asking. Finally I managed to say, "Stajoe was arrested"; the sentence sounded like a collection of nonsense syllables; and then I was crying again. "Calm down, calm down," she repeated; "calm down and talk; arrested for what?" "Freida Vronsky." I heard her gasp. "Oh, no!" she said; "I knew it! What did she do?" So Mrs. Lavinsky knew something about it. My curiosity stopped the tears.

"She said he didn't serve his time in the army, but she doesn't know him; does she know him?" I was crying again. "She knows him." Mrs. Lavinsky's voice was grim and metallic over the phone. "We tried to warn him. She was in love with him from the start; he never paid her any attention. Are you listening to me?" she asked sharply. I gurgled. "She's very jealous," Mrs. Lavinsky said, "very jealous; we don't like her at all. She came over when she heard about the engagement and told us he was getting married because you were pregnant. We didn't even tell him about it; just to keep away from her. Tell me," she asked, "you remember when you came for your trousseau? Stajoe said you saw a woman staring at you. What did she look like?" "She was plump, with dark red hair, or brown, I don't remember." It was, it was the same woman. "Well, Anya, we are in trouble, but it will be all right. I'm going to talk to Isaac; you get in a *drozhka* and come right over here. We have to get a good lawyer and find out what's a good prison; then Isaac and Stajoe's brothers will arrange things at the jail." "What's a good prison?" I wailed in amazement. "Oh, it's a matter of smearing; you find one where everyone wants a bribe. He'll be allowed to take his books; we'll send him his own food, even his own pajamas; his own blankets and sheets. You'll see, he'll come out of prison as if he had spent the time in a rest home. So please stop crying. Have you stopped crying? Are you getting your coat?" "Yes," I sobbed; "yes."

The Lavinskys got busy. Within a few days, there were convoys of food and books going to Stajoe, and under his plate coming out, every day, a letter for me. Books and food could enter the prison, but not visitors. But Stajoe found a way around this, too. He wrote me a letter telling me he had spoken to the other prisoners and found out there was a building facing the prison's courtyard where they were taken for exercise. He insisted (Momma was right: Sick people and people locked up are very selfish; they're like the old) that every day I climb the five rickety flights of stairs in a deserted building to the room where he could look at me. Every day I went. Max was in Warsaw, doing research, and found out what was going on.

"You stop, or I'll tell your mother," he threatened. "I have to, I have to," I pleaded; "believe me, it would be

139

worse if I didn't go; I have to go. Everywhere, I have nightmares of phones ringing, saying he's dead, he's murdered, I don't know what." "He is *selfish*," Max insisted; "why are you so blind to it? Those stairs are dangerous; you could fall." "I have to go," I repeated like a brainless parrot. "What are you, a stupid peasant?" he demanded furious. "Is this what you went to medical school for, so you could climb up and down five flights of stairs to see a man who just finished eating a home-cooked meal?" "Please," I pleaded, "I can't help it; you're just making it worse." We were standing in front of the old condemned building; Max was gray as the sky. "I'll wait for you here, and if anyone doesn't like it; too bad," he said surly. "Anya, you are an idiot. You can cry from today until tomorrow; you're still an idiot." I climbed up, following my stomach. There was Stajoe, the tallest, his bright blond hair; even from where I was, I could see his blue blue eyes. "Are you going to tell my mother?" I asked Max when I came down. "I think she'll need her strength for later," he prophesied, "but I can't promise for next time." "Please," I pleaded again, crying. He wouldn't even answer me.

Then the Lavinskys found out the name and address of Stajoe's judge. The arrest had been made by the Polish government. He would have a military trial; he had to wait in prison until the trial date. "That could take years!" I exploded, remembering my father's tales of Polish justice. Five o'clock the next morning I was waiting in front of the judge's house. I rang the bell again and again. The door didn't open, but I had my ear pressed to the wood and heard a man saying, "Who is there?" The front door opened a crack. "A woman is there," I heard someone reporting. "Tell her to go away," the man said. "I will not go away," I shouted at the top of my lungs; "baby killer!" "She has a stomach out to here," the woman inside hissed. The door opened. "What do you want?" the judge demanded, outraged. "I am a busy man; what are you doing waking up the neighborhood calling names at this hour?"

"This baby is yours!" I shouted; "you are responsible!" "What?" he gasped, astonished. "Close the door!" he ordered the woman in a panic. "This baby is yours; you're taking it!" I screamed. "You arrested my husband without any reason, just because some girl was jealous. I wouldn't even have married him if I'd known about it." My words were tumbling out and tripping over each other like mice.

"You're killing this baby!" I screamed again. "You're mad," he mumbled, backing away in horror. "Everyone knows you're the most severe, the most unjust judge in Warsaw; the whole city knows it. A judge without justice; how can you hold up your head? It's no wonder the country has a reputation like this." His professional pride was finally wounded. "I am not like that; I judge by the laws of the court. I have built up a reputation over a lifetime; I'm not going to throw it away over your husband!" "You're proud of being severe! You're proud of your power!" I shouted. "Change your opinion," he answered haughtily; "I am not like that. I will give a fair verdict." "But I know," I insisted; "you are very cruel. Where there's smoke, there's fire; everyone says so," I babbled. "And I am asking you, if you have any honesty left, please think twice before giving your verdict because he is innocent. A judge is supposed to think things out, weigh them out, that's what the scales mean!" "I don't need you to instruct me, young lady!" he said huffily.

"Can you imagine," I interrupted him, "you marry someone and a girl is in love with him whom you don't even know; and you're almost finished with medical school yourself, and then you're pregnant, and the girl is the sister of a best friend; can you imagine." He was still shaken from the shock of having my swelling stomach blamed on him; he was softening a little. "I am having trouble imagining all that," he said, "but change your opinion; I'm not like that." "I hope not," I said again; "Poland is famous for its injustice. "Don't try to make me feel guilty for the sins of a whole country," he said severely. "Go home and rest. I always think cases over. If it makes you feel better, I promise to think this one over, although I always think them over," he added grudgingly. The maid slammed the door behind me. I went home. But I couldn't eat; I couldn't sleep. And Max must have told my mother something; immediately came a call. "We're sending Vera," Momma said; "and what is wrong with you? Do you think there will be anything wrong with his eyesight, he won't notice what you look like, no matter what he's been through, when he gets out? What is the matter with you? For this you need an education?" "Send Vera," I sighed. "What do I hear about stairs, climbing stairs for three months?" "Nothing." "Vera will find out," Momma said with a note of triumph. "You're sending Vera to watch me?" I asked incredulous. "I would send Mischa if he didn't have to go to school. I don't know what has become of you; you're bewitched, completely bewitched."

So Vera came. Of course, I heard nothing from her about the stairs. She insisted on walking behind me on the way up, in front of me on the way down so I couldn't fall. I began to feel better. "You think this is romantic?" I asked, observing her at dinner. She blushed. "I tell you," I said, hitting the table, "I have never been so miserable in my life. Drama is good only in books, like your *Resurrection*. Very romantic, married six months, my husband in jail for three, climbing stairs day and night." "Don't exaggerate," Vera said absently. "And what have you got on *your* mind?" I asked. I had a nervous feeling *I* should be watching *her*. "Nothing much," she said poking her meat around on her plate like a satiated cat. "I'm going with the Lavinskys to the suburbs this weekend, to a hotel; come with us." "No, I don't want to," Vera said; "I'll look around here. Stashka will be here. You go." I didn't think about it. But when I got back, Vera had a young man for me to meet. "Isaac Abramson," she announced proudly; "an accountant. And he loves music." She couldn't stop staring at him. Right away, I forgot about prisons and stairs. "He seems nice," I answered Vera later; "exactly what do you know about him?" "Not much. A friend introduced me to him at a café." "Don't you think you should find out a little more?" "Why?" Vera cried. "Come, it's time to climb your mountain."

Still, something was making me nervous. "Where do you live, Mister Abramson?" I asked, flirting over my stomach. I had a vivid picture of my parents waiting up for Vera at night, each in a corner. As soon as they saw her, they ran into their room. She very seldom saw them. But they were always suspicious. And now I was suspicious. So the next day before two o'clock, I went to Mr. Abramson's address, and gave the janitor a zloty: "I'm curious about Mister Abramson; is he married?" I asked. "Oh, yes," said the janitor, "and a small child, a little girl." "Vera, I want to talk to you," I said as soon as I got in. "Yes, what is it?" she asked in her sweet chirping voice. "Is Mister Abramson, do you know, married?" "Oh, Anya!" she exclaimed, disgusted. "He is. He is married, and he has a child." Tears and more tears. Finally she stopped crying and began glaring at me.

"Why did you have to dig? Why?" she kept asking me. "I didn't think you, with your remarkable character, could be happy by making someone else very unhappy. Do you want him to be a bigamist?" She shook her head no. "I tell you, Vera, if you do not take yourself in hand, if you do not stop this, I'll tell his wife." "Oh, Anya," she cried, "why should you do that? Why should she be hurt?" "Why should *you* be hurt?" I demanded; "don't you think I see how you're suffering? It's painful. I tell you, I don't want his toe in this apartment again. He doesn't deserve your company. Don't you think I know what goes on with you? You know how I feel. If you are married, you have to stick with it; never mind his flowers and compliments and good impressions. How long have you been seeing him?" "The two months I've been here." "And what kind of future would it be?" I demanded; "he would be a bigamist, he would be; *could* you do it?" Her shoulders were shaking. "I have to send you home. You know that?" She nodded her head yes. "I am so sorry," I told her, "for both of us. I don't want you to go, but I have to do it, you understand?" More nodding. "Will you be careful on the stairs?" she sobbed. I promised. That night I put her on the train. And the letters from my mother did not cheer me up: "She looks terrible; she hasn't touched the piano for six weeks; she won't even go near it. I just thank God you were so alert. Your Poppa says the only medicine for this is time, which we must give her in big doses. Also, if you do not behave, he comes next week to bring you back here." Max arrived the following week. "You don't look good," he said; "but I won't say anything." Every week, I wrote home half a book, but now I was careful not to mention stairs or anything about the prison; I knew Vera wouldn't do it, either.

But exactly two weeks after Vera left, I did fall down a flight of stairs. "I couldn't find these stairs in the beginning; no, then I had onions," I thought, picking myself up and dusting myself off, but nothing happened. Then, ten days later, I was on the trolley going to the Lavinskys when suddenly there were terrible pains in my stomach. I got there soaking with blood. Gucha grabbed me and put me on the couch; Mrs. Lavinsky called the doctor. "Immediately to the hospital," he said, "immediately." When they carried me down, I thought it was my last minute. I had never been in an ambulance before, and the people in it looked like white ghosts, and then it was terrible. "Right into the operating room," the doctor ordered; "no anesthetic; she's too young to cut."

"I'm going to take the baby out," he told me; "it's dead." I could feel the hand going in, and then my voice, this terrible strong voice that belonged to an animal, screaming and screaming, and somewhere on the edge of my sight, people running in because of the screaming, and the child coming out in pieces, in pieces! There was no time for my mind to get ready. Everything rubbed against it, into it, as if it were a raw cut. Seeing it was worse than the pain. "You're lucky you don't have gangrene," I heard the doctor saying through the net of screams. "We're almost through now," and still I was screaming and screaming. "Where are the antibiotics?" I heard him roaring at a nurse; "do you want her to get peritonitis after all this. Get the medicine, run!" "Now put her out," I heard him telling someone. I was burning like an oven.

"Fever," the doctor said through a tunnel; "you're getting all kinds of antibiotics. You won't be the same person in the morning." "Did the baby come out in pieces?" I asked him weakly. My mind had hands; it kept pushing the baby back in, whole. "Yes, I had to put my arm in up to the elbow to get it out; you're very lucky to be here. Go to sleep." "Was it because of my fall?" "Probably; go to sleep." The next day I was cooler, but more dead than alive. I didn't want to sit up; I didn't want to eat. Then I woke up and Momma was there. My whole gown was soaking wet, and my hair. "Open your mouth, Anyushka," she ordered, and took a huge jar out of her bag; "soup. Anzia's soup." "I cannot," I pleaded. "Don't talk to me about cannot; swallow. Now for the strawberry jam," she continued, immovable. "Your Poppa wouldn't let me back in unless you finished everything." "Aren't you going to scold me?" I asked. "Not for staying alive; please, no nonsense, open your mouth." "It was very painful, even before, Momushka," I said. "The baby was pressed against the bladder. When Vera was there, I used to go into the bedroom and hit my head on the wall. I thought I would go off my head." "Stop talking and eat," Momma instructed. "You should have told someone. What is wrong with you lately? I'm afraid to go home." But within a week I was better; Momma took me back to the apartment.

The trial had been held while Vera was still there. Stajoe had been sentenced to eight months; since he had already served five months he had three more to go. They subtracted. "Are you going to tell him?" Momma asked. "When he comes out, not now, I can't stand it." "Please," she said, "go to sleep. Are you too old for stories?" I begged for one. "The snake and the lamb," Momma started, reciting from memory; I used to love this one. I memorized it for school. "Beneath a log, a snake lay low; he hated all the green earth so. All he ever did was hate; that was what made him a snake. A lamb came by one blue day; he liked to run, to jump, to play. He didn't think about the snake when he could jump about the lake. But the snake sneaked up and stung him good; the blues skies turned a hard dark wood. The poison burned in veins and blood; the little lamb claimed he was good. Who knows? hissed the evil snake, you may have come my back to break. I killed you so I could be safe. Oh, no, said the lamb, that is not true; you do just what you want to do. You can't help being so bad, and now the sky is growing sad; I cannot see a single thing just because of your bad sting. I would not hurt you with my toe; you killed me just to see me go. It is your nature, that I know. And then he saw the sky grow dark; the little lamb died in the park." I wanted to ask Momma how she remembered all that, how much of it had changed, or been changed for her by time, when she repeated it to herself because things were bad, but my eyes and lips were heavy and I gave up and slept a real sleep, a deep sleep, sure I would wake again.

9

Soon, I was myself again. "Strong as a horse," the doctor assured Momma as I climbed off the examining table. "It is the *fundament*, the base, you gave her, Mrs. Savikin; you did a good job on her." "So now I must see you off," I said buttoning my coat; it was April, but there was still a chill in the air. "There will be flowers in the Saxon Gardens soon," Momma said; "I remember them from an old trip. Now it is Vera!" she sighed, "but I don't think it will be so bad; she forgot about her *Francesca de Rimini* while you were sick. Poppa said he threatened to sit on her to keep her from leaving to come here; that's all we needed. Now, with such a good beginning, it will be only good from now on. You'll see; it's only just." "Here comes the train," I said, my arm around her tight. "The little clouds it makes," Momma whispered, "like little lambs. I wish I could draw pictures. Promise me, you'll take care of yourself?" I promised, and there was a chill in my stomach and she was on the train. "We will call you," she said, her head hanging out the window. "Put your head in," I called back; "the train is moving!" She was gone.

One of Stajoe's letters, leaving the prison under a plate, had arranged for me to meet him at the prison alone the day he was released. The rest of the family, he informed them in another letter, could come to the apartment after he had seen his wife. So I walked through the Saxon Gardens, then took a *drozhka* to the prison. Had either of us changed? We should have changed. He was waiting, tall and blond, not Jewish at all, even faintly tanned, just as I first saw him. I saw him first. "Don't ask, don't ask," I said, seeing his eyes traveling over my figure; "I'll tell you all about it when we get home." "Tell me now," he said the minute the clop of the hooves began against the stones. "I fell; the baby died; the doctor took it out, in pieces." "How could it happen?" he cried; "you were feeling so well!" There were tears in his eyes. "I thought I'd come home, you'd be there, in a few days, the other prisoner would make his escape," he was crying. "It could have been worse. It could have been the baby and *me*; believe me, I was very close to it. We could both be gone."

"Tell me, tell me," he insisted. I told the story again. It was someone else telling it, a mechanical doll. "Where did you fall?" "I don't remember." "On the steps of the building?" "It's possible; I fell several times, I really don't know. What difference does it make, forget about it, it happened, that's all." "It was on those steps," he said firmly, then nothing. "It was my fault." "It was not your fault, please; don't upset me with such nonsense. I'm so happy to see you again. Let's see, I'll tell you what else is interesting. First, there is a crack in the top of the kitchen stove. Second, Stashka's clothing hook fell from the wall and we had to plaster it in again. Third, Vera has stopped playing *Francesca de Rimini* in honor of my trials and tribulations. Fourth, Momma says drinking her orange juice and carrot juice is why I'm still here, and fifth, your parents say it has nothing to do with juices, but instead with the whole Chasidic population near the Krasinky Gardens whose prayers and fasts kept me alive to take me home in this buggy." I had forced my voice into its old gay way. Stajoe was taken in; he started to laugh.

"Did they drive you crazy?" he asked sympathetically. "Not at all. Your mother, especially, she was very good. Gucha wanted to come with me in the ambulance; they finally let her. You know, she's very good in emergencies." "You had to go in an ambulance?" he asked, horrified. "Please, I'm sorry I mentioned it; let's change the subject. Are you happy to come home?" "I cannot wait to get in that bed," he said. "I'm going to get in that bed, fully dressed, and I'm going to pull you in, all dressed, and we're going to lie there and look at the frogs on the cabinet, and think about how fast they multiply, and I'm going to think about how we can make up for this. Also, I'm going to tell you every day how sorry I am about Frieda Vronsky. All my parents ever told me," he continued slowly, "was that she was dangerous and I should stay away from her; I thought they really meant she was insane. I never really thought about it. That night we met her at the café, I didn't want to worry you—I didn't even know what about—so I didn't say anything. God knows what you must have thought."

"Frankly," I said, "I thought she wasn't right. I thought

you didn't know her. I thought she picked out your name for no reason. I didn't even believe you knew her; I told the policeman that." "I know; he told me." His face was dark. "Look, the gardens; we're almost there." As soon as we got home, I made the bed and put him in it. At five, Stashka answered the door; it was the Lavinsky's maid with baskets of food and an announcement that the family would be following at seven. "So now," I thought, "we'll have a normal life, and next year, medical school." "So now," Stajoe said out loud, "we can have that boy." I didn't answer him.

Momma wrote she would like to come from the *dacha* to visit in July; Stajoe seemed not to mind. But when I wrote my long letters home, I always wrote them when he wasn't there; or if he came into the room, I hid them under some books. He didn't like to see it. And he was back at work, eating his huge dinners at home at eleven. I was taking my cosmetics courses, and we were back at the cafés, eating the chocolate waffles, drinking the little demi-tasses. The first time I lifted the small cup, I had the strangest sensation, as if a dead person were doing this; then I realized for the first time how much I had expected to die in the hospital. I couldn't finish it. "You finish it," I said, pushing it over to Stajoe, and then, after he had, I said, "I think I'd like another cup, but with cinnamon." The second was no trouble to drink down. "Another waffle?" I asked, and he nodded to the waiter.

So things went on as before. One night, we were in the Nightclub Dymanska when Stajoe took my coat and I turned around and saw this bizarre man, gigantic, with a head like a cylinder, a monster. I was all dressed up, elegant again, in my banana-colored dress with the navy-colored macaroni pattern, my white panama hat, gloves and bag, and smiling, joking and smiling, but here was this strange man. He reminded me of someone. He was dressed in a tuxedo and a cape lined with white satin. Who was he? Then I saw the woman he was with: It was the Polish countess I had seen at Zakopanie, the woman whose daughter had plucked the question mark in the hairs of her body. I had asked Uncle Frederich who she was. "Oh," he said, "she's part of the Polish tragedy. You know, one of those young girls who married an old man. He died last month, and now it's life, she wants life, and believe me, she does not care where she gets it." But who was the man? Then I had it: It was our old tailor, from

Vilno, old tailor Frost. "Get lost, get lost. Old Tailor Frost," Momma used to chant every time she saw one of the suits he altered for the boys. "Your Momma's song is very funny," Poppa used to say, "but don't sing it in front of the tailor. He may be a bad tailor, but his feelings are good."

Momma had written me about him in one of her mammoth letters. "He's still sitting, Anya, stitching, all hunched up, a hunchback almost, but there's a rumor he's going to become a dance master. He's going to Zakopanie to open a dancing school where his pupils should give the ladies' shoemakers a lot of business." And then, "His dancing school is for the lowest boys, the lowest, gigolos practically, from the worst Jewish families, but he is doing very well, and they say there is a rich woman who came to his classes and is dressing him in her husband's clothes, and soon he may be able to retire altogether. Of course, there's the matter of his wife and children, but Anzia comes back from the market and tells me they have never been so fat or gotten so much attention. The children are clean as new coins, and the lady goes into the mud for her baths and her waters; a strange balance among things, I say. Your Poppa says not to tell you about this, but I know about the sun baths, and I thought you should know about the next chapter." Frost in the clothes of the late count! In a cape and white scarf, flinging it over his shoulder like the king! I couldn't stop looking. Finally he saw me.

"Shhhhhhhhhhhh!" he said, putting his big finger to one side of his nose and looking up to the ceiling; I was almost in pieces, laughing. Stajoe came back. "What are you laughing at? What's so funny?" he asked, smiling himself. I wouldn't tell him. Every time we turned I saw Frost turning to the music with the countess, and then my eyes would play tricks, and I would see him sitting and stitching, and sitting and stitching; I was laughing the whole evening. The countess was the picture of bliss; she was very happy. She must be giving him plenty of money. *What* is so funny?" Stajoe demanded. I finally told him. but I was still laughing so hard my stomach hurt. Stajoe sat back and smiled. He liked me like this. I remembered the first summer at my little office; he asked me why I did it. I said I had a good time helping people, and how impressed he was. But this impressed him more, this laughing and laughing until I was so helpless I hiccupped or cried.

"Get lost, get lost, Old Tailor Frost," I chanted beneath my breath; then I was off again. "She's not a bad-looking woman, either," Stajoe said, studying them, puzzled; "I don't understand it." But I couldn't explain; I was too busy laughing. Such a bad tailor! "I bet he can't even mend his own clothes," I gasped, and then collapsed. So it was nice, it was very nice.

It was July and Momma came again. Once more, Stajoe forgot things and had to go out, but this time Momma had company; another woman from Vilno had come to visit her daughter in Warsaw, and Momma was not so much with us. One Saturday night she wanted to stay up and read. Stajoe said he was very tired. "Come to bed, Momma," I pleaded. "Oh, no Anyushka," she told me; "I have to find out what happens to this count riding his white horse across the mountains. You see, the people in the village have just told him the mountains are full of vicious wolves that attack horses, but if he doesn't get to the baronial mansion on time, his betrothed will be married to this evil man, so it is very serious; I cannot be expected to sleep." "Where did you get such a book?" I asked from the doorway. "From Verushka of course, who else? Who needs the movies with her around? Go to bed children," she said without looking up. "In the morning I will be able to tell you whether the wolves got the count or the count got the girl. I should have not said that, Anya? You will not be able to sleep?" "We'll be able to sleep," Stajoe said irritable; "good night." "Good night, dear," she said turning a page without looking up. "Aha!" we heard as we went down the hall. "Dear Momma," I sighed, getting into bed; "I don't know whether she really thinks those books are so silly." "They are silly," Stajoe said; "very silly. I don't know why your sister reads them." "The artistic temperament," I told him; "you're lucky you don't have it." "Don't I?" he asked sadly. "Maybe it's something worse. You turn out your lamp; I'll turn out mine."

Six weeks after Momma left, I began to feel sick. The worry was a stone in my stomach. Soon I was vomiting, and when I went to the doctor, he said it: I was pregnant again. But this time, I don't know why, I didn't intend to do anything about it. "Let things take their course," I thought, going home in the *drozhka*. "Funny," I thought to myself, "it must have been the night Momma stayed up reading. Just before Stajoe, had been on a trip, and after, he had come home so late, he would fall right into bed, and that was that. She should have kept us for the end of the story." I was defeated. I told Stajoe immediately. "Oh, this time Anya," he cried, "nothing will go wrong; I won't let you out of my sight." "The doctor didn't suggest that," I said; "just long walks and plenty of milk." "And no falling downstairs," Stajoe warned me. "I want Stashka to go up and down with you." "Please don't bother me with Stashka and stairs; are you crazy? I knew you'd want to anesthetize me in the third month for safety. You'll just frighten me to death." "I'm sorry, I'm really sorry," he pleaded; "are you frightened?" "Not this time," I answered. What was the use? The sentence had been passed.

But this time things went slightly differently. I didn't look pregnant at all. I had a white raglan jacket, and a skirt made to get bigger and bigger, but it did not, because I did not, and everywhere I went, men flirted and flirted. It was dancing every night, or shows, dinners at the Lavinsky's on Fridays, dinners delivered to the apartment by the family, everyone watching over me, telling Stajoe I needed a coat; shoes; I needed more help; it was never too soon to hire a nurse; good ones weren't easy to find, especially in Warsaw; Mrs. Lavinsky and my mother in constant conference over the date; when Momma should come. But there I was. I didn't look pregnant; I managed to forget about it. Then it began again; the baby pressing on the bladder. I couldn't stand it. "Perfectly normal," the doctor said, examining me. "It will stay this way until the baby turns." "How long is that?" I ask dully. "About three weeks."

When Stajoe was home, I would go into the bathroom and repeat the ritual I followed when Verushka stayed, banging my head on the wall. Then I discovered biting my arm. "I'm turning into a vampire," I thought, looking at the toothmarks in my wrist after one very bad episode; "only a few more days." And we were walking more and more. There was not a baby carriage we passed in the Saxon Gardens that Stajoe didn't stick his head into. I wasn't so interested. "We'll have one to look at soon enough," I said; this was the thirty-eighth blond boy he had pointed out under a thin crocheted blanket. "At least let's decide what kind of carriage to get," he pleaded, excited as a child. "Something smaller than a train," I suggested; "I have to push it." "I can hardly wait," he kept saying. "Neither can I." Now it was the eighth month, and

151

suddenly I was bigger than a barrel, my legs all swollen with water. It wasn't easy to walk but the doctor had said ten blocks a day. I marched off like a soldier. Momma came at the end of the ninth month. Nothing happened. "Boris," I heard her telling Poppa, "I am going to be here a lot longer; Anya has decided to give birth to an elephant."

This time Stajoe was glad to see her. "Is this normal?" he kept asking her, looking over at me, the size of a pickle barrel on the couch. "It is normal for Anya," Momma said. "She's very original, you know; she's probably decided the baby should come out talking. Don't worry about it," Momma said, inventing a whole family history on the spot. "The women in our family have always taken a long time to produce their babies. My Poppa used to say it was worth the wait because of the finishing touches. You wouldn't want a rush job, would you?" And he would go to work calm. Then I would sit there and worry, and Momma would sit there and worry. "Let's read a book out loud," Momma suggested finally. "I can't keep looking at you like this; I'll scare the baby into looking like me, and then what will your Stajoe say?" "What should we read, the encyclopedia?" I asked. Oh, I was discouraged. "How about Lermontov, or *Eugene Onegin,* in honor of your father?" "Whichever is longest," I agreed; "maybe it will look like him." So we sat there and read *A Hero of Our Time* out loud, and we were half finished with *Eugene Onegin* when the doctor decided that if something didn't happen by Monday, I was to come down to the clinic and they would do something.

On Monday, Momma, Stajoe, and I were walking through the Saxon Gardens. "We will finish *Eugene Onegin* yet," Momma predicted. "Go home and polish the parquet," the doctor suggested. I strapped on the brushes. "Don't fall," Momma cautioned. I didn't fall, but neither did the baby. We went back. "Try scrubbing clothes on a heavy washboard," the doctor instructed; "it will make the baby move." The clothes were clean, Stashka was laughing, the baby was sound asleep. "Come in Wednesday," the doctor told me, resigned; "bring your nightgowns and bathrobe." "This is it," I told Momma; "tomorrow we go again. Tomorrow, Stajoe," I told him when he got in. Nine o'clock we were off. "I'm a monster," I wailed, clutching my stomach; "we should have left in the dark." Stajoe left me in the hospital. "We'll call you the minute anything happens," the doctor promised, "but, frankly, I'm not counting by minutes."

He came into my room where I was propped up in bed wearing one of my peach and lace nightgowns. "A shot," he said; "it will start things off." Sure enough, I felt some pains. They put me on the table. Nothing. They took me off. Pains. They put me back. Nothing. They took me off. "I am sick of hearing, 'Slide this way, Mrs. Lavinsky; slide that way, Mrs. Lavinsky.' The baby isn't coming today, Doctor; take me back." The next morning he was back. "Another shot," he said, not looking at me. "A horse shot, I hope." "Almost." This one worked. Immediately, terrible pains. "To the operating room, immediately! Excuse me, Mrs. Savikin," he told Momma; "don't worry." Momma was nervously stabbing her hatpin back and forth through the skirt of her dress. "Don't scream," the doctor told me, bending down; "wait until we get downstairs. Your mother's very nervous. I'll give you a shot as soon as we get there, right away." I bit my arm.

But it didn't take too long. I was on the table; I could feel the baby moving, and there were these terrible pains, the doctor telling me to push down, and then, this baby who did not want to come out coming out in a great whoosh! And the whole operating room smelled like oranges; everyone was saying it; I had eaten so many of them while I was pregnant. But then I heard the doctor. "The cord is around her neck; she's not breathing. Leave her; bring the baby!" I turned my head. I could see the baby. It was blue, and the cord was wrapped around her neck, choking her. "She is not alive, Doctor!" I heard the nurse say. "Into the hot water!" he commanded and they plunged the baby into steaming hot water, then very cold water, then hot water, then cold water, and I could feel myself bleeding like a faucet, but I couldn't stop watching the baby, into the fire, into the ice, in and out, in and out, and finally there was a cry, a little cry. "All right," the doctor said; "enough. Let's get this membrane off." I could see her little head covered with a membrane, a thin tissue. When I was born, Momma told me I was covered with a membrane from head to toe; "a shirt" they called it. "It means that's a lucky person," Momma told me with satisfaction. "Put her out," the doctor ordered, and again, a shot; I was asleep.

The next morning they brought me the baby. I was terrified! A thousand-year-old face. All wrinkled up. A monster. I counted: ten fingers, ten toes, no tail. No fur. Still, she was the ugliest baby I had ever seen. I began crying. "You will see," Momma said, laughing, "in three days she will be the most beautiful baby in the city," and in three days her eyes opened, the whole face smoothed out, the two eyes became big blue lanterns. I came home in the *drozhka*. I couldn't take my eyes off her. I forgot how they left me bleeding, how all the attention went to her. Her fingers were winding around mine; she did not want to come out into the air. I kept thinking: Now what will things be like? What will they be like? Momma left five days later, and this baby I didn't want became everything. The change was terrible; that's what it was like. Mrs. Lavinsky told me casually white walls were good for babies, and two days after we brought her home Stajoe had the janitor fastening sheets to all four walls; the green paint had to be covered. Fortunately for the window, it had white curtains. Then I got a letter from Momma. "Those letters should have a train to themselves," Stajoe muttered, going out on an errand while I read and pondered on the shortlived reform of selfishness. "Dear Anyushka," she began, "how is the baby? Still no tail? I don't know how I raised such an idiot. I have been thinking, and have decided it's all Anzia's fault for telling you those horror stories when I went out, but really, dear Anya, I don't believe a word of it. When you were born, I was looking all over Vilno for wigs. 'Why wigs, Rebecca?' your Poppa asked me; 'you have such beautiful hair; what are we, Chasids?' And then he realized I was trying to find a *tiny* wig for *your* head; I was sure you were going to be bald. I walked around the house with you for weeks, comparing your head to the mahogany table, and decided yours was shinier. Your Poppa always said I got my punishment combing out your hair with those endless knots and those thick gigantic braids.

"But I trust you're doing all right. It is your sister I'm worried about; she is moping around the house trying to see the baby from the windows of the white dining room, all the way to Warsaw, and Anzia has told me there is something new called a Jakob in the house who brings her flowers. I think she means to tell me we are not paying enough attention to something Verushka's up to; she's been right before, so I'm nervous. Would you do your aged mother a great service and write Vera what it's like to be a mother? Just tell her the truth. I'm sure she won't believe anything from us; she thinks she grew up like a tulip in a pot. Just tell her the truth, that's all; don't bother to exaggerate. I think we'll have less trouble. But really, I'm worried about her.

"So it will be medical school soon for you. It's getting hotter here. Some green buds are showing on that large tree in front of the house. I've only looked at it for twenty-five years, but I still don't know its name. But it is not a pine; I say that with great confidence. Your Poppa wants to know when you're coming to visit. We've had more and more refugees from Germany; the pogroms there are terrible, the people coming with all their furniture, even their chamber pots! It's a good thing we have such a big cellar. We're perpetually sleeping on couches so they can have our beds. But they expect to return to their homes soon—the precious Fatherland. So the house is full, but it's not like having you here. Come home soon. Love from," and the signatures, "your Momma, your Poppa, Vera, Emmanuel, Mischa, Anzia Josefa, Rachel," like a little passage out of the book of Genesis.

The baby was sleeping. When she screamed, she didn't scream like a normal baby, but like something choking for breath; she would turn pure blue. By now I knew how to stop it: A good smack on the diaper and she would turn pink and come back to life. The first time I smacked her, I turned blue myself; I didn't expect her to live through it. Now it was a matter of routine. "Dear Vera," I began, looking at the clock. Stajoe would not be home for hours. "Life here has changed terribly, terribly. First, we had to hang sheets all around Ninushka's room; white is supposed to be good for her. The doorbell is strangled. I fly to it a hundred times a day thinking I hear it; she mustn't be woken up. Also, the telephone. Finding it takes half an hour. Stajoe has it covered with so many covers and cushions, and he's turned something in it, so it hardly rings even without the pillows. When I'm not answering the door and finding no one there, I'm answering the telephone and hearing silence. Also, our baby turns blue when she cries, trying to match her eyes. Yesterday, I went to the market with Stashka, and when I came back, Stajoe was half out of his mind. His eyes were more red than a sunset from rubbing at them. He had been on the phone for forty minutes trying to call a doctor, and while he waited for the nurse's answer, he prayed. And what was the catastrophe? Ninka had turned blue for a change and he couldn't bear to hit her. So we tried to go to a hotel for a rest with a nanny who comes every day at eight, because we have no room for her in the apartment. I go all dressed up, elegant, you know, in my green suit with the three foxes, and the fox hat, and gloves and bag. They give us a wonderful room, and then, aha, Ninka begins her concerts, and we're transferred to the annex. Stajoe comes just for weekends. I go down to dinner alone. I eat in the nightclubs because they have phones at the tables. The minute the food comes, the phone rings: Ninka has come alive, and is up there screaming herself blue. The whole time I eat, I choke.

"At home, we have a special table for Ninushka, for her pots and pans, and God forbid that anyone should touch anything of hers; I tell you, I have become completely crazy. Then the nanny comes to take her for a walk. I spend most of my time hanging out the window, watching. The next time you see me, I'll be shaped like a V, my bottom pointing up to the sun, my head two inches from the ground. Stajoe wants to know what's the matter with me; there's the Nana, his mother, Stashka, and still, I can't leave her alone. Why not? Good question. Anyway, Ninka is now pink and going for a walk with poor Stajoe when he comes in. So I will write more later."

"I have some time off," Stajoe said, triumphant; "are we taking her out?" "Of course," I said severely; "she has to have two hours of air." "It is a nice carriage, isn't it?" Stajoe asked, putting her in it. It was beautiful, white in the very latest style, called an "auto" because it looked just like a little car. Its front was pointy; the sides looked like two little doors; the front had a windshield that rolled down so the baby could be lifted in and out, with little side windows for ventilation. "We had better dress her up warm," I said with authority. It *was* warm; in fact, it was hot, but here Stajoe always listened to me. "Put on two blankets," I ordered like a general. "Is her hat tied on tight?" I worried. "Good," I sighed with relief, standing back; "now close the windshield, and let's go." I was surprised there were so few mothers in the garden. It was a very hot day, and even in my white lace dress with its big floppy hat the heat was flattening. "Come sit down on a bench, Anya," Stajoe said, pulling me over with a worried look; "you look exhausted." "First let me look at the baby." I peered through the windshield.

She was absolutely purple, purple! "Stajoe!" I screamed,

"look at her!" "My God," he gasped, going white as my dress; "get her out of there!" He started cranking down the windshield. What had I done wrong? The windshield was there; it was meant to be used. And breezes, I was afraid of breezes, and bugs, bees, stings; they could kill adults! "She's all swollen!" Stajoe shouted, crying. Now I began to calm down and look at her. "She looks burned, Stajoe," I said, controlling my voice. Inside, I could hear my voice screaming again in the hospital when the doctor first pulled the baby out. "She has sunstroke. We have got to get her home. Take off her suit." While he was taking it off, I was pouring orange juice onto an extra diaper. "What are you doing?" he cried. "I'll put it on her; it'll evaporate and cool the skin down." That was technical enough for him. I dabbed the orange juice all over her. "Anya, she has a rash; she's all swollen up," he cried in anguish. "It's only sunstroke," I told him. Only! I didn't think she would live. She was screaming like a siren.

"Please," I begged, "run home with her. Tell Stashka to put alcohol all over her, not in her eyes I'll come as fast I can; you have longer legs." I ran after him, pushing the empty carriage. They had her on the kitchen table; she was screaming and gasping. What was the matter with me? Had I lost my mind? To wrap her up like a mummy in this heat? I took over the alcohol. Stajoe was calling a doctor; Stashka was just staring. But Ninka was screaming and screaming; she was not about to die any minute. Slowly, my mind began working again. "Stashka," I told her, "get the lilac pills from the chest. Bring me a pot of water." I dissolved three in the water; they turned it a light purple. "Genetian violet," I said; "we put it all over her. We'll take turns." "You can see the rash through the purple," Stashka moaned. "Please, I can see. Don't get it in her hair; all we need is purple hair, too." It was some weekend—Ninka screaming, the three of us up all night taking turns with the gentian violet; then, when it dried, covering her with talcum powder, tears running down our faces splashing onto the talcum powder, hardening like little cement birthmarks. While I put on the lotion, Stajoe fanned her with my white panama hat, getting purple fingerprints all over its rim. But Monday, she was all right, just a little of the rash left, but it took a long time to go away. It was some weekend.

Before he left for work, Stajoe asked me if Ninka was well enough to go to the doctor. "For what?" I practically shouted, taking hold of the hair on both sides of my head. "Her constipation," he said, "she was supposed to go today." "Oh, my God, Stashka; did you hear that? The doctor, the constipation; we were supposed to bring a specimen." "Anya, go to bed," Stajoe ordered; "the mother comes first now. Stashka will take the specimen, but you're going to bed. When she's finished, she'll put Ninka in the carriage, and you will see that she keeps it open, that's all. There's nothing to worry about." "But she's screaming!" I protested. "She's screaming because she's constipated; she can't move her bowels; that's why she's going to the doctor. Get into this bed." I got in. "Lie down," he ordered, I did, but I was going to get up the minute he closed the door. "Now," Stajoe said, taking off my shoes; "I see what you're up to. The dress, please; the slip please; I'm going to give these to Stashka and you can ask her for them when you want to go out, but she's going to call me if you come out of your room even *one minute earlier* than eleven." In the kitchen, Ninka was having one of her concerts. "Don't hit her too hard on the bottom; she has a rash on it," I said. "I was planning on dropping her on her head," he answered, pressing my shoulder back against the pillow. "Please, you're already half asleep."

"Whomever takes care of this child deserves a medal," the doctor told us when we got there. "I've never seen a specimen like this. You say she didn't want to get born either? I'll tell you what to do: Take four tablespoons of carrot juice, four of orange, and two spoons of honey. Mix everything together and give it to her. She'll be fine. Really, Mrs. Lavinsky, she's a very healthy child, except, of course, for her color." "Her color?" I asked in alarm. "It's not often I see a purple child, but for that I prescribe only soap and water. You must have had quite a time." "We did," Stashka piped up. "I bet everyone stops you with that carriage," he said bending over Ninka. "Look at those eyes, two blue plates; of course, now they clash a little with her skin. So, goodbye. Don't worry," he said, standing up. "Don't tell Stajoe I went," I warned Stashka. As soon as we got home and gave her a quarter of the mixture, our troubles were over; she was a purple child, but not a constipated child. "I'm taking a nap, Stashka," I said; "please put the phone to bed."

"Mrs. Lavinsky, Mrs. Lavinsky." Stashka was shaking me in a panic. "Come and look at Ninka; she has a white throat." "Naturally," I answered turning over. "No, inside," she said raising her voice, "inside; it's like a rash inside." "Wrap her in a blanket," I said, jumping out of bed and throwing on my clothes. I could hear the voices of children in the courtyard. "Should I get the carriage ready?" Stashka asked, but I was already halfway down the steps. "No, no, I'm going to run across the gardens to Doctor Oberzherzky; it's faster." I ran past the mothers and their carriages, the nannies, the children jumping rope. The huge medal Mr. Lavinsky had given me when Ninka was born—an enormous gold medallion, the face of Moses in the center, in such detail you could see the veining in each cheek, and around the edge of the coin the Ten Commandments, the Hebrew letters, each Commandment in precious stones—was clanking against the button of my blouse, and I could see the circle of tulips, red and yellow, the openings to the formal alleys among the bushes, but I would not stop to look. Were the centers of the tulips red, were they purple, were they black? I wouldn't find out now. I was running like crazy. "Le fleur?" I asked the doctor in terror. "Not diphtheria; please relax. The child will start screaming. It's only tonsils; I'll take a culture, In the meantime, grind these into her food, one every four hours," and he handed me a square box of pills.

Out in the park, in the sunlight, I sat down with Ninka on my lap and looked at the tulips. No wonder Momma didn't know the name of the tree in front of the house. "I'll get up in a minute and see what color their centers are," I promised myself; "in a minute," but I was beginning to watch her breath. From the beginning, her breathing had the strangest effect on me: I would start to breathe with her, and if she fell asleep, as she was asleep now, her little breath coming out noisily from between tiny parted lips, I would begin to breathe in and out with her. Stajoe wouldn't let me sit with her when we had company. Slowly my eyes would start getting heavy; inevitably, they would begin closing, opening less and less frequently. The first time it happened I remembered thinking, this is going to happen to me as long as I live; her breathing is always going to do this to me. Stajoe was fascinated by it. I meant to ask Momma whether this had happened to her. I had to go home and nurse Ninushka. But I fell asleep in the sun, bending over her. Her crying woke me up with a jerk. Streaky clouds were thinning out to thread over us. My hand flew to my throat; my medal was gone;

it was gone. I would tell Stajoe, but not Mr. Lavinsky. "The child, of course, comes first," he would say, "but still, it is bad luck."

"How is the purple child?" Stashka asked. "The purple child is fine," I said, thumping her into her crib. "The purple child has tonsils and gets these pills ground into her food every four hours. Call me if anything happens." I woke up at nine o'clock. The day had skidded off somewhere while I slept. "What did you eat, Stajoe?" I demanded. "Stashka warmed us part of Mother's dinner; your part is keeping warm in the stove. Are you still tired?" "Oh, no," I cried; "I want to go dancing." "You won't mind leaving Ninka?" Stajoe asked, incredulous. "Not tonight," I said with authority. "Eat first, then get dressed," he commanded, inspecting me. I got dressed slowly and lazily, etherized. I remembered Momma telling me about Verushka's scarlet fever; the skin had peeled from her hands like complete gloves. She would have felt those hands on her for the rest of her life if Vera hadn't lived. I fastened a strand of pearls around my neck.

"Dear Verushka," I began the next morning; "let me tell you why this letter has skipped the last four days. First, as you remember, we were taking Ninka out for a walk, and you remember the gold medallion? Gone. So let me describe my exciting life," and I wrote on and on and still I wasn't up to the tonsils.

"We're all going to Zakopanie for two weeks," Stajoe announced Thursday, "get ready." I looked dubious, such a long trip, a little child, the cold, the snow, the strange food. . . . "Think of the Viennese cooking, the Gurales, your favorite peasants, the embroidery, the carving, the nightclubs, the prizes and contests; are we going?" "Oh, we are going!" I shouted. I was overjoyed. Ninka had the good grace to rest herself and us. But after ten days there, in the beautiful snow peaks like the castle of the Snow Queen, the rumors began to thicken like a terrible blizzard: The war was settling on our noses like a fly.

BIBLICAL TIMES

In the summer, there's a grasshopper who hops about,
Not thinking what is waiting.
In the summer, there's an ant who spends her long day
Slaving.
Then winter comes with all its snow:
The grasshopper needs food and shelter so!
And so she asks the ant for help;
The ant is sleeping on her shelf.
The ant woke up and asked her this:
"What did you do in summer mist?"
"Oh," says grasshopper, with little hiss,
"I hopped and hopped and sang and kissed."
"Oh," says ant, on hearing this,
"You have sung and sung, and kissed and kissed,
Now listen to ant who tells you this:
You have been singing, now go dance."

Russian fable, as told by Mrs. Savikin

10

Before we left Zakopanie two days early, I insisted on calling Vilno. "Anya, there is no time," Stajoe insisted. "If there's no time for this, there's no time for anything: help Stashka," I ordered, turning my back to him and to the switchboard. "Your call, Mrs. Lavinsky," the operator said. "Hello, Momma; this is Anya." I could hear my voice, sounding as if I were asking for permission to stay at Rachel's for dinner, or for the night. "I wanted to tell you we're leaving for Warsaw right now; we're not taking any chances. . . . Poppa thinks so, too?" I asked. "I'll tell Stajoe. Listen, Momma," I said urgently, "you mustn't worry. I know if there are bombings—there are all kinds of rumors here—there won't be any letters and no phones. But it may not happen; it's never happened before. We'll be all right, and we'll come and see you. Do you understand?" Momma was crying. "Momushka, I have to go. Please tell Vera I miss her, and Ninka's eyes are just like hers; please tell Poppa not to worry. We'll come see you as soon as we can. And nothing may happen." "Something will happen," Momma said. "I don't want you lying to yourself; it's all right to lie to me, but you have to take all steps there." "I promise," I said, rushing over every word: Stajoe and Stashka and the baby were sitting in the *drozhka* outside the window. "Momma, I'm hanging up now. Please pay the charges—we have to catch the train—we'll send you the money." I hung up in the middle of a protest.

We took the sleeper back to Warsaw. The trip was very quiet. Stashka had the baby; Stajoe and I slept as if we would never wake up. Then the outskirts of the city began, the first houses, thickening and thickening, swallowing space. It was hard to breathe. "Will there be war?" I asked him. "What did your father say?" He respected Poppa's judgment absolutely. "He would be one of the first to hear at the bank, because of the bank." I had never heard him talk in such a disorganized way. "He says it's war. We're almost back," I said looking out. "We might have been safer at Zakopanie," I wondered out loud, but nothing could have stopped us; we were two homing pigeons. "Thank God," he said. "Are you frightened?" I asked him, shocked. "Aren't you?" he asked. He was staring straight ahead. The straightness of his stare brought back Momma's voice; she must have looked like that when she said something would happen, don't lie to yourself. "Something will happen." The words kept screaming in my ear like a muffled siren. It was the end of August; the air was very heavy. The heat was not just normal heat; it seemed purposeful, evil. It was thick, waiting. I couldn't imagine planes cutting through that thick air, laying those incredible eggs.

And then the *drozhka* turned the corner; our building was standing just as it stood before. The Hotel Roma was still across the street. The park was still peaceful and green. But everything was trapped in the hot, hot air; the sunlight affected everyone. It was abnormal, as if it were composed of thick gold motes, like pure gold bees. People spoke in hushed voices. Our friends didn't want to go to cafés; as for us, we didn't want to leave the apartment at all. When Stajoe came home, we pulled the curtains and sat inside, sealed off. "It's colorful this way," we apologized to each other. The air had turned against us. We were waiting; all Warsaw was waiting. At night we lay awake, staring at the ceiling. There were announcements on the radio: "In the event of an offensive, go to the basements." But there was no sound of a motor bringing something that might shell the city, no sound of the great buzzing of planes.

"No matter how hard we stare, we can't see through the ceiling," Stajoe whispered. "Why are you whispering?" I whispered back. I could feel him shake his head. "What are you thinking of?" "I'm thinking of how many people are waiting in every town," I answered; "in Vilno, they are waiting, they are waiting at your parents', we are waiting, they are waiting at Druzgeniekie. I wonder," I went on, I couldn't stop, "who will go out when it starts? Will the doctors go out? I remember one of the doctors told me, in the country a good horse is worth more than any one man; their horses could be shot. Who will shop? How will food come in? Will my Poppa go to work? He's not afraid of anything. During the last pogrom, he got in the *drozhka* and drove straight to the bank and walked in the front door. He'll go out. Momma will stay in to watch the children. 'Anzia,' she'll say, 'don't go out.' So how will the food come in?"

"They say," Stajoe told me, "that our President is fleeing the country with gold. A lot of the others moved their gold to England and are joining some kind of army there in England, for an African division." "Do you believe it?" "What else is there to believe?" We lay there in silence, staring at the ceiling. "I'm sorry I said that," he whispered to me, lying on his side, and covering me with his arm; "I'm sorry I said that. Please go to sleep. Tomorrow is a long day. They are teaching you mud packs in your cosmetics course." "I'm not going near the mud packs," I answered, thinking, that is the truth, that is the truth, he believes it; what else is there to believe but the worst. The war was peeling layers from our masks already; it had not even begun. "Don't be sorry," I said finally, turning back to him; "you're just the most sensible." I could feel him crying in the dark.

Three hours later there was a horrible clap, like thunder, caught on our building. Stajoe was already sitting up. "What in God's name is that?" "The bombs," he said, "the bombs. Listen, you'll hear the planes." And there it was, the steady drone. "But if there are planes—" And then there was another explosion; the whole building shook. Something was lighting the window shades from behind. Ninka was screaming. "The baby!" I shrieked. "She's here, Mrs. Lavinsky," came Stashka's voice; she was a tiny glimmer of white in the door. "Come in here," Stajoe told her, and the three of us sat on the edge of the bed that way, like birds on a twig, until the gray light began drawing itself on the wall like a chalk line around the window. "They'll go away with the light," Stajoe said for the thousandth time. And they did go. It was September first.

"Anya! Anya!" Stashka was screaming insanely from the kitchen; she had never called me that in my life. I threw Ninka at Stajoe and ran in. "The hotel, the hotel, oh, Anya." She was crying hysterically. "The hotel, the hotel, oh, Anya!" she kept screaming; her face was blotched red and white. "What about the hotel?" I demanded, grabbing her by the shoulders. "What about it?" I shouted shaking her. "Look at it!" she screamed in an accusing voice; "look at it!" She was beating the top of her head with her fist. The Hotel Roma was gone. There was an empty piece, a big jagged piece of blue sky; there were bricks all over the street. Men were scurrying back and forth trying to move the stones. There were no carriages; nothing could pass.

"Stashka, what?" I pleaded, grabbing her hands and holding them like a vise; "what is it?" "Anya, Anya, Anya," she kept sobbing, "Anya, my sister." It was her sister she was calling, not me. Anya was such a common name. Her sister worked at the hotel as a chambermaid. *"Bozhe moi,"* I heard myself saying, pulling her against me, going back into Russian, "my God." When Stajoe came in, we were both sobbing. "I have to go home, Mister Lavinsky, Mrs. Lavinsky, I'm sorry, I have to go home," she kept repeating. "Yes, yes," I said, "yes." I was looking for some money for her, some food, some jewelry, anything. "Yes, you have to go home. Go get your clothes; we'll help you." "No, I don't want them," she said dully, her head swiveling and swiveling, like a dog looking for its owner lost in a crowd. "No, I'm going home now." She went out of the kitchen. We walked to its entrance and watched her go slowly down the long hall, open the door, and close it behind her. Then there was the sound of her steps. She was gone.

"Stajoe, I won't stay here," I told him. "We will be more protected at your parents'; we've got to go there." Even as I was speaking, I knew we wouldn't be any better off there, but I wanted another kind of shelter: protection, to be together. "We've got to go there; I won't stay here." I knew I was repeating myself mechanically as Stashka. "But the bombs," he protested; "they might come back. It's not safe; this is our house." "I won't stay here." "Then get your things," he said, giving in; "I'll get mine." "How will we go?" "By foot," he answered; "unless you can fly. If we're going, we go now. It's safest when it's light." So we started out, our little bundles tied to our backs, Stajoe holding Ninka. "I don't want you to mention the name of every building that's gone," he warned me cruelly. "Save your breath; it's a long way across the city." "The park is a short cut." "The park is a short cut for the bombers, too." No sooner did he finish his sentence than it was bombing and more bombing. Through an open window we could hear a radio: "Go to the cellars; go to the cellars, air attack, air attack."

"Can you run?" Stajoe asked. I was wearing my high heels; even my slippers at home had them. We would run ten steps, then the boom of an explosion. "In here." Stajoe pulled me as soon as he heard it, and then there was silence and we began running again. In an archway we met a woman we had seen once at the Adria. "I have to get home, I have to get home!" she kept crying, and as soon as the noise stopped, she ran out. Then there was a terrible ripping sound; it pulled my eardrums in and out. I felt Stajoe's hand clamp over the back of my neck like a steel band. "Let's go; don't look back," he said, dragging me after him. In back of us I could hear screaming and screaming. I tried twisting my head; he would not let me do it. "Don't look back," he ordered; "look at Ninka." Then a volcano, the earth shaking under our feet, and we were in the courtyard of another building. "That woman didn't get home," Stajoe said. I didn't ask any more questions. I watched one building; for a moment it stood intact, then slid to the ground like a mud pack leaving a face. Only the wood bones, the supports, remained. When the noise stopped, we ran; when it began, we hid in doorways, under arches, down steps to cellars, anything. And finally we could see the Krasinsky Gardens, and in the middle of the block, the Lavinsky's house, the big red brick building with its five floors, its iron terraces facing out from each window onto the street. "What an old house," I sighed with relief; Stajoe was pounding on the door like a maniac and we were in.

"Regina," Mr. Lavinsky was saying, "get the rooms in the left hall ready; Gucha, take Ninushka, and see to her. So," he said, sinking into a couch, his eyes on his son, "tell me about it. Is it very bad out there?" "It's terrifying, terrifying," Stajoe answered. There were red flickers in my eyes as if I had stared too long at the sun. They were memories, after-images of flames, and dust in my eyes; I was afraid to rub them. "How did you get here?" Stajoe described our trip across the city. "I don't want to frighten you, and I only thank God you're here, but if it should happen again don't hide *after* the noises, because then they're usually done bombing for a while. That's the time to run. But," Mr. Lavinsky said, trying to change the subject, "that's not important; what's important is that you're here." "But there will be more bombs," Stajoe reminded him. No one answered. "Now," said Mr. Lavinsky, "when there's an air attack, we are going down in the basement; and, Stajoe, the Chasidim will also come, the ones who have no place to go; we'll pray there." Stajoe's face flushed. "Anya and I should go back to the old place," he answered; "there are all kinds of things we need." "We're not going anywhere until the bombing is over," I said flatly. Mr. Lavinsky watched us both. "Regina, supper, please. Where on earth is the maid?"

That night was another attack; we went down in the cellar. All Mr. Lavinsky's Chasidic friends who came for Friday nights were there, and such praying, I had never heard such praying, so loud, so desperate, such throwing back and forth of the bodies! Then, suddenly, a shrapnel sound was above us, but the praying never stopped. Later, we went upstairs; the shrapnel had gone through the first apartment of the house and come out the back; it had kept going until it killed a horse. "Where do you find a horse in Warsaw?" Mr. Lavinsky kept asking in amazement. "They pull the *drozhkas*," Stajoe said roughly; "it must have gone a long way from here." "So the prayers didn't hurt, Regina?" Mr. Lavinsky asked. She didn't answer him.

But it went on, day after day, hour after hour in the cellar, and the more time we spent in it, the more it began to smell, the faster the dampness caught us by the throat when we came in. In the meantime, I was trying to learn Warsaw Yiddish. I knew a little from home, but we had spoken in Russian mainly, and the two dialects weren't the same. For kitchen, I said "*kich*," but to them, it was "*kach*"; "*ich*," "*yach*"; it was impossible. "I don't understand, I don't understand," I said over and over again in Polish, and always, no matter what the bombing was like, Mr. Lavinsky patted me on the hand, saying, "Don't worry, don't worry; you'll learn, you'll learn." Mrs. Lavinsky came into my room one morning when I was nursing Ninka. "Don't cover up," she told me smiling; "I'm used to it." "I thought this was better," I answered blushing. "It's hard to know what will happen next, if there'll be any food." "You're a good girl, Anya," she said; "please, would you call me Momma. I can't stand it, this Mrs. Lavinsky. We don't fight over clothes. We don't fight at all. Yours is the only house we can visit and eat a dinner. I would like it very much." "It will be hard for me," I said smiling. "But you will try?" "I'll try." "And you're worried," she said, watching me, "about what?" "Oh, the city; it's all in flames; it's so hard to go out." I didn't want to answer her.

"But still you go out." She sat quietly, watching. "I'm

168

worried about my Momma and Poppa and Vera." "And Mischa and Emmanuel," she finished for me seeing me start to cry. "Go ahead and cry; Stajoe tells me when you try not to cry, you get a sore throat." "I don't want to bother you," I apologized, bending my head over the baby. "Please bother me; I haven't been bothered enough in the last years. I think that's been my trouble; what do you think?" She smiled and waited. "You wouldn't say, not yet," she sighed. "Listen, Anya, all these Chasidim, and their big families; I will talk to them. They'll know someone who's going to Vilno and you can send a letter. I'm sure of it, I'm really sure of it." I was staring at her as if she had just been transformed into a pure beam of light. "With your eyes open like that, you look just like Ninka, and Ninka looks just like Stajoe. Strange," she mused, "you're beginning to look like each other, a regular assortment. Come, it's getting dark. We'll go down in the basement and make another shawl, a more colorful one this time." "Oh, no," I protested; "it's dark down there, and your eyes, they're bad." "I refuse," said Mrs. Lavinsky, "to worry about my eyes while they are busy bombing the city. How long can we sit down there doing nothing without turning into potatoes? I have everything here," she said, picking up the big bag she had put down when she came in. "We'll make a three-cornered one, a long one; you can wear it over your best dresses when this ends. A long fringe, yes, like the last, gray silk with a black frame, a black fringe, and then we'll embroider it all over and make all the roses separately, but mostly bright ones, red and yellow and white; it's dark. I'm happy to teach you, believe me; I have too many maids. So," she said pausing before the cellar door, "how is Stajoe?" "He wants to go back to the apartment." "I knew it,'" Mrs. Lavinsky said. "Make him wait until this bad part is over. You can do it; I can't. I wonder what it's like out there. All we ever see is smoke and flames; it *must* look worse than it sounds." A perfect picture of the building that killed the woman flew into my eyes. I hadn't seen it, but I had seen the hotel blown up. It was there, then it wasn't; there was a spar, or several spars, and flames, then licking the charred wood. "Yes." "Yes, what?" "Yes, I promise."

Then for a while, the bombing stopped. "I'm going back to the apartment," Stajoe told me; "you should stay here with Ninka." "I'm coming with you," I insisted. There was something in me; it opened the wound I scratched into my thigh after the Vilno girls were attacked by the boys in iron nails. I had to see it, I had to know what it was like. But there was also something in me already closing, a door, a window, then all the windows and doors, that wouldn't let my eyes out with the rest of me; I would walk through the streets seeing and blind. So we went. The streets were quiet; they were emptied of people and filled with rubble; the whole city was a giant charred waste-paper basket. "It is terrible, terrible," I kept saying, but this was not Warsaw. Stajoe walked mechanically and fast. I knew he was walking through Warsaw streets; I was not. A thousand times I had to ask him to slow down. "I can't take such big steps," I pleaded. "It's not far," he answered; "it's not far."

The building was completely intact. Inside everything was covered with a thick thick dust, as if the city had been deserted for centuries. We climbed up to the fifth floor. Everything was exactly as it was the day Stashka left. I wondered what had happend to her, how many of her family were left. The windows on the left side of the apartment were smashed. Glass lay in icicles all over the polished parquet as if winter had packed up in a hurry and had to leave them behind. "It's good to be in our own place," Stajoe exhaled; his voice had gone dead. I didn't like it. "I'm going to lie down." He got into the bed, between the sheets, under the peach lace-covered quilt. "Come in with me," he begged. "Stajoe, please," I pleaded; "we can't stay here. Your own father said the worst bombing is in the center of the city, where the offices and the government are. We absolutely can't stay. This is the busy part; this is where they'll bomb first." He murmured something. "What did you say?" I was getting frightened. "It is our nest," he repeated more loudly. "Stajoe, what is it?" I shouted. "It's only satin and wood, furniture; when this is over, we'll do it all again. It's only cloth; these things aren't alive. Please, get up; I won't stay here."

"It is our nest," he whispered again. It took me a half hour to persuade him. We had gone too long without bombs; I was terrified. And we hadn't gone more than half a block when we heard the noise of a plane and the horrible thud and crash of a bomb. It was our building, what was left of it, lighting the clear blue sky like a giant candle. He began pulling me back. "What are you doing?" I screamed at him, frantic. "I want to look; it's lucky we

170

left when we did," he said, as if he were talking about someone else. He began poking among the rubble. "There has to be something. Look, here's a piece of plate; here's Ninka's white dog, here's a prism from the chandelier." "Have you lost your mind?" I whispered like a snake; "how can you be so sentimental?" The building was still burning in back of him; only the front half had been destroyed. I was afraid the rest would collapse and slide down, burying us. "They will be back, they will be back, we will be killed," and while I was pleading, I could see the bomb coming toward the apartment like an intelligent cloud, like an enormous germ, like a capsule of poison, killing everything at once—the crockery splintering like stars, the toys flying with wings, the bed ripped through its belly, the quilts in a flurry of feathers turning to embers in the high heat. "How can you be so sentimental? We will be killed," I kept crying, and finally he came with me.

"The building is gone, Momma," he said when we came in, and went into our room closing the door. "Tell me," Mrs. Lavinsky begged. "Later, later. We were lucky; there'll be plenty of time in the cellar." I followed him into the bedroom; he was sobbing and holding a chip of a dish. I should have known, I should have known after the ride home from the prison when he realized the child was gone, but even to me he sometimes seemed cold. I lay down on the bed and stared at the ceiling like a corpse; then I rolled over and bit into the pillow. If I started crying now, I would never stop. The burning feathers from the quilt, the charred bedroom set.

The Germans invaded. There was no resistance at all. They arrived, shaved and peaceful, driving through the passable streets in their trucks. Then the new horror began. They were snatching Jewish men young enough to work right out of their houses and taking them off to hard labor. Few of them, we heard from the Chasidim who came to the cellar, came back alive. No one thought Mr. Lavinsky was in danger—he had a long white beard and looked much older than he was—but Stajoe, Stajoe, they would swat like a fly. "Make the bed," Mrs. Lavinsky ordered. There was a crazy streak in the whole family! "Why, why?" I kept crying; "they're coming to take him away and you're making beds!" "No, no, Anya, you will make him up in your bed; we'll fix it so he can breathe under the covers and then you can sit by the bed." "But he can't stay there all the time!" I cried out. Stajoe wasn't

171

saying anything. "No, he can come out to go down to the cellar. No one will bother us during the bombing raids."

And so we made the bed, Stajoe underneath three quilts, coming out half-dead with heat. "I can't stand it in the cellar; it's one thing, then the next, damp, cold, hot, damp, damp, cold, it's enough to make you lose your mind." "I can't stand the praying; it's driving me crazy; let's go out," I pleaded. "It's not safe," he warned me; we didn't care. "We'll go stand in the hallway on the first floor; I'll carry Ninka." Every moment was a new danger, shrapnel, bombs, the Germans. Standing in the hall, it was an innocent thing; there would be silence, at least between the bombs. So we stood in the hall, the three of us, leaning against the wall. I was tired, and Stajoe's arm was around my shoulders; it was as if it was pressing me down into deep water. I began to fall asleep. "Sleep, sleep, both my girls," he whispered, and I did sleep. Then there was a loud explosion, and I woke with a jerk. Stajoe's arm was across my chest like a bolt. A breeze was blowing against our faces and I could see the house across the street. What was it doing there? Where was the rest of the hall? I looked down; there was only the ledge, one inch wider than our feet. "Close your eyes," Stajoe told me, and I did. And then I had a dream: My mother was lying on the couch in the white dining room in Vilno; she was covered by the same coat I had covered her with when she came back from the clinic after her operation. *"Borya,"* she was saying, her pet name for my father, "I know"— but what she knew she couldn't say immediately because she was interrupted by a fit of coughing—"I know they're not alive; I know they're not alive." Where were the others? The apartment was empty. Just my mother and father. "They are alive, Rebecca; they're alive. There's just no mail; remember, Anya herself said there wouldn't be any mail if there was a war." "They're not alive," Momma said choking, coughing, coughing so hard her eyes bulged, "and I don't want to live."

"Anya," Stajoe said, "this rope, they're throwing it up to us. I'll catch it, and then you lift up your arms, and they'll take you and the baby down first. Are you sure you can hold her?" I nodded; all I could see was Momma, and then I was moving through the air; how was it happening? I was moving through the air, holding Ninka, attached to the rope. "Take her into the cellar," someone was saying, but I pushed them back. "Never mind; let's get him down

172

first," the voice said. I saw them throw a rope up to Stajoe who threw it up to a man on the second floor; the man began lowering Stajoe. He was moving through the air toward me.

"This can't go on," I told him the next afternoon. "How long can you stay made in a bed? Things can't be as bad in Vilno. We have to go to Vilno; tell your parents we're going to Vilno. We have to do it." Mrs. Lavinsky knocked on the door. "I have found a Mister Rudaminsky who will take a letter to Vilno for you," she said. "We're going to Vilno when this bombing lets up," Stajoe was saying to her, but I wasn't listening. "Where is this Mister Rudaminsky?" I demanded instantly. Confused Mrs. Lavinsky gave me his address. "I have to go," I said, running out. I could hear Stajoe shouting after me: "Anya, the military curfew, seven o'clock, Anya, they shoot on sight, Anya, please," but I was already turning the corner. There were no trolley cars, no *drozhkas*, nothing. I ran as if my life depended on it. My mother was sick; I knew it.

"Mr. Rudaminsky," I choked, falling to his front door, "please, the curfew, you'll take a letter to my mother, you know my father from the bank, Mister Savikin, you've been to our house so many times, please, the letter, she's very sick; let me write something down, otherwise she won't believe it." "Oh, yes, Anyushka," he said, "I'll do it; I promise I'll do it." "Dear Momushka," I was scribbling and drinking the glass of water Mr. Rudaminsky thrust at me, "we are alive and well; we are coming to Vilno, don't worry about us." "I have to go," I said, jumping up, still panting; "the curfew, I have to go." "Anuyshka, I'll do it." He was frightened. I ran faster and faster. Why had the whole city turned gray? The sky was slate gray. It must be almost seven. If I was not in at seven, I'd be shot. I didn't have my papers, and with my blond hair, if I wasn't shot, they'd take me to the houses for the soldiers. The blocks went by like sets from an insane movie. I was the only character alive. "*This* is the dream," I thought, running, "this is the dream," and then there was the Lavinsky house, the door open, Stajoe a death mask, waiting. "Get in," I tried to say, "you're not safe," but I couldn't say anything; my lungs hurt. Everything I saw was contracting like a picture burning, the black edges getting larger and larger, leaving just one white thing in the center. Stajoe's dead face. I saw his two white hands reaching out for me; I fell into them.

When I woke up, I was made into the bed with Stajoe. Mr. and Mrs. Lavinsky were discussing how to get us to Vilno. "They'll have to rent a car." "And get a driver they can trust," Mrs. Lavinsky added. "I think it can be arranged," a third voice said. "How long?" the old man asked. "Two weeks, maybe three." "It had better be two," Mr. Lavinsky's voice said. "Anya! Anya!" It was Mrs. Lavinsky's voice calling to me. "It's settled; the car will be ready in ten days." "Thank God," I sighed; light collapsed again like a tunnel. But when I woke up, there was a point of light, a destination. I began to feel better, and watching me, Stajoe did, too. Ninka was still screaming herself blue, but, so it seemed to us, less often.

Finally, came the Wednesday morning we were to leave. By this time the bombing had stopped. "Not before light, just in case," Mr. Lavinsky instructed; "and you're going with a couple called the Kaplans. You don't have to get friendly with them, just share expenses. They're second cousins of Mister Kaplan's, a business friend," he said reassuring Stajoe; we had become suspicious of everyone.

At dawn, the car pulled up in front of the house. There was a ragged gray line surrounding the houses across the street, making them look as if they had been cut from a sheet of tin and were about to be pushed out by a hand. Some thin dirty clouds, like strips of blackened cotton, were traveling quickly across the sky like a fleeing army. "A beautiful day," I said, meaning it. The weather was threatening with its whole bag of tricks; there would be no planes. No matter how many times everyone told me, I would not believe the bombing had stopped. "Where is the horse?" I asked, taking a good look at the car. The thought of Vilno, my parents' apartment in Vilno, was acting on me like a poultice for a snake bite; I was becoming myself. "It's better you don't look too prosperous," Mr. Lavinsky said as if he were defending himself. "This way it won't be so likely anyone will stop you." "No one but the car," I quipped. He smiled. He hadn't heard me laugh in a long time. "It will be good to remember you this way," he said grinning. "Now if you only had your braids, you'd be the same girl we interviewed in Druzgeniekie." "That car must have cost a fortune," Stajoe accused him. "Of course," Mr. Lavinsky said; "what is money for?" "It should be used for something else," Stajoe said bitterly. "Thinking like that won't do you any good," Mr. Lavinsky said severely; "when have we not had wars?

You will just have to live through. Now you have something new to use your head about. You were beginning to give me the shivers, such a big man made in the bed that way. Every time the janitor went away without seeing you, I went down to the cellar and said a prayer."

"It's unusually cold," Stajoe said, looking across the street. Buildings were gone here and there, as if the city were a checkerboard and the pieces had been taken off, as if the game were suddenly to be played without rules. "Look how it blows Anya's hair." He placed his hand on top of my head and ran it down my hair to the base of my neck; he let it rest there, fastening my hair against the wind. "No point in bringing the baby out yet," he said; "no point. She'll turn blue in this wind." Mr. Lavinsky was staring at us as if we were creatures from another planet. Suddenly his eyes slid to the side, then back to the buildings Stajoe had been looking at. "And your money?" he asked; "where is it?" "Except for a little, sewn into my belt; here, look," Stajoe said, unfastening it. "In here, between the leather outside and the backing; the rest is in Anya's muff." Mr. Lavinsky looked at it. "Very good," he said with real satisfaction; "it looks like a cat that's got the mange; only another cat would want it. And the Kaplans, I don't know what they're doing, they have their money packed in the wheel, near the brake. I told them to watch out, because this way the driver has to know, but they think it's best." "There's no way of knowing," Stajoe said. I shook my head loose from his hand; I wanted to feel the wind in my hair. So free, it felt so free.

"Where's Mother?" he asked. "She's looking in the closet for words to say to you, also for extra jewelry, money; she would try fastening part of the house to the car, but she knows the streets are too narrow." "It's sad to go," Stajoe said. I was astounded to hear him actually say the words. To me, but not to others. Then Mrs. Lavinsky came to the door; she wasn't dressed. She was wrapped in her terry cloth robe, and she stared at us. "Just like when Zoya died," Mr. Lavinsky whispered in astonishment. We saw her moving her lips, trying to speak. Tears fell from her eyes, one after another, one at a time, like an army; there was no stopping them. "Goodbye, Momma," I said; "we'll see you again soon." Her lips formed the word "Momma." She stood as still as the two cement lions on either side of the door. She might have been made of stone. Her whole face seemed covered with a powder of plaster, as if she had just stepped out of a building that had just collapsed around her. She moved her lips again. Her eyes were narrow too, as if she couldn't open them. But her lips, they were covered with a thick white coating; she kept biting them, and little drops of blood began forming on them like red pearls. She couldn't say anything, and she couldn't move. "Please, Regina, say goodbye to them," Mr. Lavinsky begged, but she couldn't do it. "Kiss them goodbye," he begged. A tremor went through her whole body; her beautiful hair, so elegant, even during the bombing, hung straight down to the backs of her knees. She couldn't move her arms.

"She's paralyzed," I thought to myself in terror; "she can't move her arms," but her tears were moving like little cascades, sad cascades, leaving streaks in the white powder covering her face. "She cannot do it, Poppa," Stajoe said in a low voice, "she cannot; we'll kiss her goodbye. It's the same thing that happened with Zoya," and he moved forward and put his arms around her; he was so tall she disappeared from our sight. There was only his broad back, his broad shoulders, his head bending down; I could see his muscles tighten under his jacket. He was gripping her as if he wanted to crush her, and then I heard him whisper, "Momma, Momma, please, not like this; we'll be back; this time no one's leaving in a box, we'll be back," and he let her go. When he moved away, she was just the same, the steady stream of tears, her eyes did not even seem blank, the white powdery face. "Kiss her, Anya," he asked me, but I was afraid; she seemed dead, like the walking dead. I hadn't thought they were so close. Instead of moving forward, I raised my arms to her, as if she was a baby I was going to pick up. As if she were hypnotized, hers moved up from her sides and stretched toward me; I rushed into them, but they did not close around me. I felt them fall to her sides. I stood there holding her; she hardly seemed to breathe. "Goodbye, Momma," I whispered; "this can't last forever." "Anya says the Russians will take care of them, Momma," Stajoe said; he was desperate. "She says they almost took care of her whole family, and there are so many of them, it can't last forever."

"It can," she said in a tiny whisper. For a minute we weren't sure she had spoken. We stood still, stunned. "Regina," Mr. Lavinsky said, "the children have got to get in the car. I'm going to call for Ninka." The maid brought

176

the baby and handed her to me. We started down the steps. "Momma," Stajoe pleaded once again, his foot still on the last step, but she stood there, white, caked lips, her hair beginning to whip wildly in the rising wind. "Get into the car; I'll take care of her," Mr. Lavinsky said urgently; "take care of yourselves, and above all, keep your heads, and you must hope, you must, you see what it's like when someone stops. She will be all right, I promise, she'll be all right, but you have to go now. There will be too many Germans on the streets soon. Go now; we will see you again soon." The last thing we saw as we drove away was Mrs. Lavinsky, standing still as stone, and Mr. Lavinsky, climbing the ten steps toward her, ten steps which suddenly seemed to stretch and stretch with every movement he made, as if he could never reach the top.

"I'll always remember that," Stajoe murmured. "Isn't it odd, how even when some things are happening, small things, even then, like sitting on the grass and looking for the little balls of earth underneath, you know right then and there you'll never forget them. It is odd," he said, bending to kiss Ninka's forehead. "Who's Zoya?" I whispered. "Zoya was the third baby, the first girl; she died of scarlet fever. She came home from the gymnasium saying she didn't feel well and Mother thought she didn't want to take a test, and sent her back. When they brought her home, she was delirious and it was too late for anything." His voice was stiff. "Poppa thought Momma would die, too, but then she stopped it. It took a long time." He sounded as if he were talking about strangers.

The Kaplans were waiting at the window when the car pulled up, and then we were on our way to Vilno. "Your Lyuba," I said to Mrs. Kaplan, watching her with her baby, "she's very good; she doesn't cry at all." "She never cries in cars or trains," Mrs. Kaplan said and then our eyes met and we were quiet. What was the point of polite conversation? "Nothing is in flames," I whispered to Stajoe. "Then they've thought of something else," Mr. Kaplan said, overhearing me. But the beginning of the trip wasn't bad. None of us wanted to drive through the familiar streets; we only wanted to get out of the city as soon as possible. I pressed against Stajoe, one eye on Ninka, one eye on the sky. "There are *no* planes," he whispered into my ear for the ten thousandth time; "no planes." "Are you going to get carsick?" he asked me suddenly. The little car bumped and swayed in the high wind; its tires were not the best. I shook my head no. "No," Stajoe whispered; "you're too tired, and you were up all night with that screaming, and," he said slowly, "you're going home." I nodded, yes, I was.

When I woke up again, there were trees, no houses; we kept going. Each turn of the wheel unwound a tight spring in my heart; even my spine was softening, seeming to melt. But then we came to a small town the Germans occupied, and suddenly, there was a roadblock and soldiers and screaming. "Out!" ordered one of them, holding a rifle; "checkpoint." There was a blur of uniforms. Stajoe was staring at the driver. It was always possible the drivers were paid to deliver victims; we didn't know. But the driver looked as terrified as we did. "In here!" they commanded, pushing us into a tiny building; it was made of wood, and dark, dark. Little chinks of light crawled on the floor. "Your packages!" a soldier shouted. They took everything away from us, everything. "Nothing else?" he boomed, leering at Mrs. Kaplan, then at me. I was holding on to Ninka as if she were a piece of jewelry; they wouldn't want her. She started to scream. Disgusted, the man turned away from us and motioned to the two men. "You two will come with me," he ordered. "You will stay here." He pointed at Mrs. Kaplan and me. We looked at each other; I didn't expect to see Stajoe again. "My name is Anya," I said; "what's yours?" "Cassia," she said dully. "Can we sit on anything?" I asked her. "Just the floor," she answered without any expression at all. "Then it would be better to sit on it; we may be here a long time, and the children will want us." We had no food. Suppose he didn't come back? My breasts had gone dry. I had nursed Ninka until it felt as if she were pulling the veins, like strings out of my breasts. I had nothing at all.

And so we waited. I marked time, watching the worms of light move across the floor. "When they reach the third plank, he will come back." I told myself; they still had far to go. When they had almost reached it, he and Mr. Kaplan did come back. He was covered with mud, and his face, it had gone completely white; he looked like Mrs. Lavinsky on the steps. "Stajoe," I said instantly, "Ninka has nothing to eat." His pupils seemed to surface in his eyes like deepwater fish. "We still have some money; we'll find something." "You can go now," the officer said, appearing in the doorway; "have a good trip." They had flung everything of ours they didn't want into a big field.

"Let me look," I whispered to Stajoe. I saw where my muff went; it was near the edge of the fence. "It's dangerous." "We need it," I answered. That settled it. We walked around in the direction of the muff. It was resting against the barbed wire; I pulled it out. "That muff has nine lives," Stajoe said weakly. "Look, Anya, we have to find a place to stay overnight and rest; Henyk and I have been digging graves." "Did you think they were yours?" "Of course," he said, "of course." Again he looked like Mrs. Lavinsky. "Well, they were not," I said grumpily "we have to find a place to stay." "And a wagon to get us to the train station; there's a train station not too far away. One of the guards wasn't too bad; he told me. It leaves early; it can get us to Vilno." "Where is the driver?" I asked. "Gone," he said. But then he seemed to wake up. "There's a peasant's house down the road somewhere, behind a tree, behind two birches or something. He has a wagon and takes people in, and he sells some bread—if you have the money." "Let's go," I said, full of hope again; "let's go," I urged the Kaplans, and we walked off; the only packages we were carrying were our babies.

"This is the wagon, it's a big wagon, and a big horse," the peasant told us. "If you want, you can sleep in the barn." "What's in the barn?" Stajoe asked. "Just two cows," the peasant said. "They are quiet cows." "Quiet cows," I muttered. "At least if Ninka screams they won't put us in an annex." "You want bread?" the peasant asked slyly; "it's a lot of money." "How much?" I demanded. He looked me over. "Twelve zlotys." "Twelve zlotys for what?" "For a loaf." "Ten zlotys," I said, "and fifty for the wagon." "The horse eats, too," he said, crabby. "The horse eats better than us, and cheaper." I remembered the peasants at Druzgeniekie. "So we look like the king and queen to you? Fifty zlotys, and a good Christian like you are, I see your cross, you should not ask for a penny." He looked down at his feet; his shoes were made of layers of paper tied over with rope. "God sees what you do," I threatened. "We have some soup," he shuffled. "And how much is that?" I demanded; "we don't want to sell our children." "Sometimes it comes with the bread," he mumbled. "Sometimes?" I cross-examined. "I will bring it," he said, sulky. "Hmmmmph," I told him; "I'll believe it when I see it. God already knows what you will do." "Eh," he said, backing off, his eyes on me, then turning around and running to the house.

"Don't do that," Mr. Kaplan pleaded with me; "he might decide not to help us at all." "Offer him one penny more," I told him, "and he'll cut our throats in our sleep. Please, I know, I know." And sure enough, the peasant appeared with bread and soup. "Some soup," I told him, entirely ungrateful; "don't you have a garden in back of the house? What kind of peasant are you, can't you spare an onion? I'm not even asking about the chickens you're hiding in a coop." He slunk off and came back with an onion. "One onion," I said in disgust. "My wife says no more," he said shiny-eyed. "God sees her, too," I told him, starting to peel it. "Now it will make us cry, an evil omen for you; it's too bad. Will you get us up for the train in time? We can't walk all the way to Vilno on one onion and some watery soup." "Yes, Miss," he said. "Is the train safe?" I asked, staring at him. I had heard rumors of mines; somehow the peasants always knew. "Yes, Miss," he answered, blushing. "You will not lie to us; you would not want your soup and one onion blown up all over Poland?" "As God is my shepherd," he cried, banging his breast. "You are a good man," I said, crunching the onion; "God will reward you." He marched off, pleased as a pickle. Stajoe was amazed. "It wasn't easy getting the male peasants to pull down their pants for injections, either," I told him, and we laughed, we laughed, while we soaked the bread in the soup, feeding Ninka and Lyuba, the Kaplan's baby. "And now for the two quiet cows," Stajoe said, giggling like a boy. "Two quiet cows." The other couple looked at us as if we had gone crazy.

"See this good sun?" I told the peasant when he woke us up; "God is rewarding you already." The cart started jolting along. I rode up on the plank with the driver; his seat was just one piece of wood placed from one side of the cart to the other; Stajoe held the baby. "I have some bread for your journey," the peasant said slyly. "Did you tell your wife?" I asked, mischievous. He said no. "You are a good man," I said again; this time I meant it. "The train," the peasant said, gloomy as a cloud. It was packed full of people; they were hanging on to the little steps that protruded from the sides. "Go to the other side and hang on," he told us. "Your husband will push you on, you get in when it moves." "Thank you," I said, giving him the fifty zlotys Stajoe had taken from his belt; "we will not forget you." "Buy the tickets on the train, in case you fall off." "I will. Tell your wife a dog ate the bread." "She will know what dog," he said, sadly, looking down at his shoes. I didn't want to leave him. And who was he? I didn't even know him. There was no one I wanted to leave, no one. I was glad the Kaplans were coming; we wouldn't have to leave them right away. And I didn't even like them.

We ran around to the other side of the train; Stajoe held Ninka and pushed me as hard as he could, then hung on in back of us; the Kaplans were on the next set of steps. "We're going to break our necks!" I cried. "Just hold the baby," he gasped, and the train started moving. I couldn't even reach the bit of bread the peasant had given us, and we were so hungry, it was as if there was a hand in our stomachs, like purses, rifling through them, and when it couldn't find anything, it tore with its nails at the walls. But gradually, as the train picked up speed, we began to creep in. I went up a step; Stajoe went up a step; and then we were inside. But of course there were no such things as seats, and the train, stopping every ten miles, jolted and crawled. Finally, it took us to Bialistock. Now it was easier to buy something to eat. At the station, men were selling *kvas* and unbaked or half-baked bread; but it was something to give the baby, something for her to drink. We bought as much as we could. The next train, we heard, was going to Vilno. Stajoe paid; they let us in. The countryside began to look familiar. I recognized the hotel on the outskirts of the city, the insane asylum, the thick trees thinning out, then the train station faced by its familiar hotel. "Goodbye," Stajoe said to the Kaplans. I didn't look at them.

"It is Vilno, it is Vilno," I kept saying, and crying, sobbing; I couldn't stop. "Anya, your parents don't know we're here, they don't live at the station. Please, let's go." So we started to walk, and we came to the house. Not even a window was broken. Across the street, Rachel's house was entirely untouched. It seemed like a miracle. I twisted the little bell; it *was* a miracle. Anzia opened the door, and when she saw me, she let out such a scream, I thought she would shatter the windows herself. My mother came running to the door; she looked half dead. Then she began screaming: "Anya! Anya! Anya!" She sounded as if she were thoroughly mad, and she was grabbing me, and kissing me, and pulling me in. I could see my father; he was coming out of his office. Oh, I was home!

"Come in the dining room," Poppa said; "I'm sorry we

don't have much to give you to eat." Then I saw Stajoe watching me; I began to look around. The dining room was completely empty except for two chairs. Poppa saw my eyes resting on them. "We sleep there," he said gently. Where was the furniture, where was everything? Where was a bed? Where were my brothers? Where was my sister? "Where is everything?" I heard myself screaming. "Where is Vera?" and then their faces sped away like the last leaves on a tree; I felt myself floating down.

When I woke up, I was resting on a blanket spread out on the parquet; Momma was sitting on a folded one next to me, a handkerchief pressed to her mouth, coughing. "Momma, what is it; you're sick; what is it?" "Stajoe and your Poppa are feeding Ninka," she said, answering my next question before I had a chance to ask it; "and me, I had pneumonia. Your poor Poppa thought it was the end of me, then I got your letter, and I got better and better every day, and so you see." She was coughing again. "If you're better, what's that cough?" I asked weakly. "Nervous asthma, that's what the doctor says." She sounded beaten. "Vera is married," she went on, "to a Belgian engineer. She came home from the court and showed us the papers. He's very nice, her husband, but your Poppa is disgusted. 'If only I knew he wasn't married somewhere else,' that's all he keeps saying. There have been warnings of pogroms here, so Mischa and Emmanuel ran away to Russia. Emmanuel won't go far because of Genya; Mischa is trying to get to our cousins in Moscow. Vera will be here for dinner; we eat dinner and supper together." I lay still, drinking her in as if she were milk. "We were packed up to go, too," Momma said between coughs; they were getting less strong. "Then came Mister Rudaminsky with your letter. Your Poppa said, 'Rebecca, is a pogrom here worse than a pogrom in Russia?' so we stayed, waiting for you. I just cannot believe it; I couldn't believe it when I saw your letter." She wasn't coughing anymore. "I asked Mister Rudaminsky a million questions; your Poppa took pity on him. Now," she said, smiling, "where is our furniture? The Russians are here; they've occupied Vilno. They send soldiers and come in and take whatever they want. Last week they wanted drapes. Two weeks before they wanted beds. There was a nice one who must have had a short mother like me; he left us the two chairs. The rugs are gone, except in the dining room; I think it was too big for the offices. We have no heat and no light; we have no water. We go to the corner for water, or pump it at the fish market and carry it back. The little store in the basement across the street sometimes sells Vera some food if she pleads for a good long time. The fat old Polish lady still runs it. We'll keep you busy, we'll keep you busy." "Oh, Momma, how could it happen?" I cried. "It happened; there's no point in asking how. We do our best. And now I will be all right, too; your letter was the best prescription in the city." So she rocked me back and forth and I sobbed and sobbed.

I heard someone open the door and go away. I saw the Lavinsky house as if it were standing in the middle of our dining room. Who would go out for them now if they needed food? Stajoe and I were the only blond ones in the family; the Germans would pick up everyone else. What would they do? There were less people to go for water. Who could they send out for doctors? Stajoe didn't look Jewish; I didn't look Jewish; but we were gone. I could see myself standing in line at Gayavsky's Pastry. It had managed to stay open, taking a chance, a terrible chance, thinking something had to come back, almost like a dove to their ark. Something had to be done; we were rotting like damp bulbs in the cellar. I got some chocolates and cakes, I got them. And then I was running home and a German jumped out of the car with a huge pair of scissors and grabbed an old Chasidic man with a white beard and a *tallis*, and cut his beard off, pulling his head back and forth as if it were a radish stuck in the earth, cutting his beard off in jagged junks. Then he grabbed the ends of the *tallis* and cut them off. Mr. Lavinsky had told me a very religious man would have to find his beard and bury it; and the man might try, and he would probably be killed. He didn't even look at me running by with my blond hair and fancy box of cakes and chocolate. But the others? They all had dark hair. Dark-haired girls were being dragged to the Praga Gardens, gardens like a forest, and raped, all day, all day. What would they do? Momma was rocking me against her breast.

Feet tiptoed through the halls. I thought I heard Vera. I will not think about it, I commanded myself, and I did not; I will forget them, I said to myself, and I did forget them. And then something was crawling all over me, and pinching and screaming and hugging, and it was Verushka, four feet nine of her exploding in a fit of joy. A slate-gray door swung in front of Warsaw with a metal clang, and there was Verushka, tickling me under the arms, yelping her nursery rhyme about the bird who didn't do anything and had to go drink. There were the two of us, writhing on the floor, giggling and shrieking, the whole family bending over us like tulips bowing in a new breeze. "Verushka, up," Momma was laughing, "up. Stajoe, pull that married woman off your wife." Stajoe grabbed Vera and threw her up into the air. "You'll be next," he threatened Momma, catching Vera, who was screaming with joy. "Stajoe! Stajoe!" Vera began shouting, as if it had just dawned on her; "come on, come on!" Momma stood there, thunderstruck and grinning, while Stajoe bent over and Verushka threw herself on his back; she looped her arms around his neck and he began to lope around the room. "Boris, they are *all* out of their minds," Momma laughed; "Borya, how would you like to carry me?" "Oh, I'll try it, Rebecca," he threatened, moving toward her, "but it's a sad way to end so many happy years of marriage." "Get away!" Momma gasped at him. "Have you gone crazy, too, have you all lost your minds?" "You've lost your cough," Poppa said; he was actually laughing, advancing on her. "At least, Rebecca," he said, sitting down in a chair, catching hold of her arm, "I can hold you on my lap. So where is your cough?" Poppa asked, kissing her up and down the part in her hair. Momma tried to say something, then burst into tears. "Borya, they are here," she sobbed. "I thought that's what all this noise was about." Poppa's old smile had settled on his face like permanent sunshine that would never wear off.

"Where is Ninka?" Vera cried. "We threw her away," I cried like a maniac. "No, where is she?" Vera asked, starting to pout; "I want her, come on Anya, where is she?" "If she starts to scream, you do the walking," I warned her. "Where is she?" Vera persisted. Ninka was produced. "Eyes and hair," Vera whispered in astonishment. "And feet and toes," I added, "even elbows and knees." "Aha, Momma," Verushka said, "already we're in for it. Next Anya will be saying 'We must stabilize our lives.'" Stajoe was grinning at her as if she were a puppet from Punch and Judy. "Go ahead, Anya, say it: We must stabilize our lives." "You just said it," I told her crossly. "We have a dog, a little white spitz," Vera babbled; "Jakob's bringing her; I can't wait till you see her." "Is that dog in diapers yet?" Momma mocked. "She's only a puppy," Vera answered with some temper. "Well, I'm going to say it,"

Stajoe announced. "We must stabilize our lives. What is everyone to do for food and money?" "I have two pupils," Vera volunteered, her face buried in Ninka's stomach, "but Poppa says that won't last long if the Russians leave. The Germans might get here from Warsaw, then, Poppa says, no one will want to play the piano. But still, I do have them." "Don't eat her," I demanded. "Why not!" Verushka asked; "why not? She's delicious, she tastes just like bread. What have you been feeding her?" "Bread," I answered, a shadow falling over my sight, then crumbling like a wall when I looked at Vera and Ninka.

"Vera!" I remembered. "Momma says you're married." "I am married," she answered without emerging from Ninka. "Are you going to tell us about it, or do I have to come over and tickle you," I threatened. "Oh," Vera said very casually, "he's an engineer, too, but just between us, I don't want him to find this out, you know, he is very *short*, almost as short as Poppa." Poppa was grinning at her. "And he is twelve years older than she is," Momma put in, giving me a worried look. I knew what she was thinking. Most men were married by the time they were twenty-five; he was in his thirties. "Where is he from?" I asked. "Oh, that's one of the questions they're always asking. From Belgium. Really, he is very nice; you'll like him. But," Vera said in a voice unusually hard, "if you don't, you don't. Listen," she picked up steam, stroking each of Ninka's fingers separately, without looking, as delicately as if she were crocheting, "one of my pupils is the daughter of a Russian colonel. He says he can get us some jobs. There's a job for someone directing all trains at the Vilno station and taking care of the radios there, too. There's even a room on the station, because sometimes it's for a mother and child. He took one look at me and decided no use. And there might be a job for Poppa in an office, at Panari, because of all his languages. He wasn't too definite, though." "Anya will see what she can do about that," Stajoe put in; "she doesn't like wishy-washy people." "Oh, Stajoe, please, he's not wishy-washy; you mustn't think that. He may even be dangerous," she told him, her eyes opening like coffers. "Imagination," Stajoe said automatically. "I'm not so sure," Momma considered; "but Anya's back, and Stajoe and Ninka, and between us, we'll get it straight." "We'll all ask Ninka," Poppa said seriously.

The Russian man came to the house, and from the beginning, I didn't like him. He looked at me in the hall from

185

every possible angle, then went straight into Poppa's office and offered him a job. "Rebecca!" Poppa called out beaming. "So, Colonel Dovsky," I said, "there's also my husband. Vera tells me," I said, ignoring his eyes, "there may be a job for him at the railway station." "There's a job," he said with meaning, "but we would have to send him to Moscow for three weeks' training." "I'm sure he can find his way to the train," I answered. "And find his way back?" the colonel asked; "he's such a handsome man." "I'll worry about my husband's rails if you can take care of all Vilno." He bowed with a surprised but pleased look. So when Jakob came to the apartment for dinner that night, two more members of the family were employed.

"This is my husband, Jakob Kornfeld," Vera said shyly. "You might as well forget about her now, Anya," Momma said, "she breathes with him. I don't know why she lets him go out to shop alone except she is afraid of the soldiers." "I have the money," Jakob told us, putting fifty zlotys on the table. "I hope you won't have to do this much longer," Poppa told him; "it's very dangerous." "What is he doing?" I asked. "Every day he stands on line in front of the bank to withdraw fifty zlotys; that's how we got this table. Wasn't it the same in Warsaw? Didn't they set a limit on withdrawals?" I didn't remember; the Lavinskys had taken care of money. "You can withdraw only fifty zlotys a day," Vera explained; "our money's no good to us." "Soon the peasants will start with their black market," Poppa predicted. "Watch, in two weeks they'll be here with their wagons, selling everything under the sun, the sun, too; it's not impossible. Those people are like mushrooms," he said, shaking his head; "they can bury all of us, and it will only make the soil richer for them." "Boris!" Momma cautioned from the head of the table. "More cold cuts, Anya?" Poppa asked; "more bread?"

"I tell you what," Vera exclaimed, "let's just take most of this money; we can't do too much with it anyway—the fat lady won't sell us much; yesterday, she said to Jakob, what was money to her, mostly paper—and let's go to the club. Anya, Mrs. Ludovkin, the doctor's wife, opened a club for people who come to Vilno. She even invites people from little towns like Warsaw. There's tea there, and sometimes little cakes ("Or things that look like little cakes," Jakob interrupted), and people give talks sometimes, and there is even *jour fixe* before dinner, just like when we were in school. Even Rachel is there sometimes, and Max, you remember Max from medical school, he goes all the time." I looked at Stajoe. "Let's go," he said with more energy than I had seen since I saw him pick up the splinter of the shattered dish in Warsaw. "Let's *all* go," Momma said, jumping up. "Anzia, Anzia," she called out, "we're going to the café; you'll take care of Ninka?" "I'll take her into the kitchen with me," Anzia beamed from the door. "We'll bring you back something," Poppa promised; already we were scurrying for our coats.

"Look, Anya," Vera whispered when we came in. Mrs. Ludovkin kept the rooms deliberately dark. There were designs painted on the walls and on the floor in bright colors; it didn't look barren at all. "Rachel, *there,* and Max, *there.*" I couldn't move. There was Rachel and her husband; there was Max and the daughter of the textile company's owner, the biggest one in Vilno. "I think he's going to marry the boss's daughter," Vera whispered; "it's your fault if he winds up cutting coats instead of bodies." "Let's go sit with them," I whispered. We went over to their table; Max and Stajoe pulled up chairs from empty tables.

"It will be the Lithuanians next," Max was saying with authority. "Will that be bad?" Vera asked, anxious. "I don't think so," Max said; "some pogroms, maybe, but otherwise it'll be more or less like it is now." "No, it will be the Germans first," Henyk, Rachel's husband insisted, vehement. "How do you know?" I asked him. "The radio station," Vera whispered to me; "he works there." "They can say anything they want to on the radio," I said, tilting my head to her ear; "don't worry." We talked ourselves out, the same questions again and again, the answers always the same. "Ninka," I reminded Stajoe; we all got up, taking our coats.

"So, children," Poppa asked, "where does everyone sleep? Jakob and Vera have a new apartment, you know." "Oh, tonight we will sleep on our coats in my old room," Vera bubbled. "On yours, under mine," Jakob said. "We have blankets; don't be so silly." Momma explained to me, "Anzia, she's been getting wool; we can't find out where she gets it, and knitting afghans." "Maybe she's unraveling our old sweaters," I suggested. "No, they took them," Momma said, "for their families. Some of them even brought their children. They think they're here for a long time." "I hope so," I sighed, remembering the bombing. "But the refugees say the Germans aren't so bad," Momma told us as we walked slowly. "They all want to go back; it's their homeland too; that's what they all say. *Mein Kampf* is only a fairy tale, that's what the last one said, just like you did, Anya, that time in Druzgeniekie." Momma's memory cut into the light at the most amazing times.

"I'd rather have the Russians," Jakob said. "Me, too," said Stajoe. "If the two engineers agree, we had better hope the Russians stay," Poppa concluded, trying to cut it off. "What do you think, Boris?" Momma asked. "I think," he said, "we had better pray for anything but the Germans." We walked in silence. Poppa read all the communications in all the languages; his word was final. In the dark, Stajoe nodded his head. "They are good at their work," he answered in a tired voice. "So long as they're not here, let's forget it," Poppa ordered; "so everyone will be sleeping on the floor; it will be like an old party of your school friends." "We've slept on floors before," Vera said proudly. "And will again," Jakob added; "I wonder how the dog is getting along with Ninka?" "How much farther is it?" Vera asked automatically. "You're already there, you just don't know it," Momma answered, playful; "take one hundred more steps in your sleep." And so we came back to the house. "How was Ninka?" I demanded, rushing into the kitchen. The dog, Snowbell, began jumping and yelping down the hall for Vera. Anzia woke up with a jerk. "Very good." "No screaming?" "Why should she scream?" Anzia asked, annoyed. "Do you think she's gotten over it?" "Oh, they outgrow everything; she's grown into sleeping like a person, that's all. And look how warm it is near the stove; I opened the grate so she could see the coals."

Stajoe fell asleep on his coat under an afghan; I listened until I was sure of the rhythm of his breathing, then stole down the hall toward Momma's room. Verushka and Poppa both slept as if they had been hit on the head by stones. "We will be the good mothers," Momma used to say, looking enviously at Verushka and Poppa, "and also the nervous ones." In the dark, she was sitting up in her chair waiting for me. I slid down on the floor next to it. "Your Stajoe's changed," she whispered, resting her hand on my head; "he's so good with Vera." "Who wouldn't be? He was always good with Vera." "It's not just Vera," Momma mused; "he seems different. The things he says are more bitter, but he isn't; how can that be?" "I don't know, I didn't notice it." "You're too close, but I tell you,

188

he's changed. You have, too," she said, worry entering her voice; "you're more nervous. What is it?" I told her about the bombing, how we had stood against the wall when the whole corridor collapsed, leaving us on the ledge. "I can't stop seeing it, I can't, and what I see isn't the ropes coming up to us and then lowering us down, but I see us falling; I see Ninka falling; I see her head all broken and Stajoe all twisted. I can't stop seeing it. And it's funny, Momma, at the time I wasn't frightened at all; it's just since we got here. The walls keep crumbling and crumbling. We're sitting with Max, and the wall grows right up in the middle of the room and crumbles; then I feel like I'm still standing on the ledge and it's crumbling, too."

Momma was thinking. "You know what your Poppa will tell you, Anya? That you need to keep busy. He'll get up tomorrow and write to his brother's son in Kaunas and ask if you can work in his little Hospital for Special Diseases; and I, yes, I think you should keep busy, too. Sometimes, you know, I think we're living through biblical times, or we're starting to live through them; visions, dreams. I remember, my grandpoppa used to say, when you are living through biblical times, the living will come to envy the dead. Anya?" she whispered, "are you listening?" "Yes." "You and I are very strong, and so is your Poppa; but you're not so strong as a brick. When things happen you will have to feel them. You can't try to avoid that; if it's your nature, go along with it. You could have fallen from the ledge. I'm not happy to hear about it. Now you know there are other ledges, and you can fall from them, too. I think those are the ledges you keep seeing. But you can't just stand there, seeing the ledge and the empty space, because the wall will crumble; you have to move away when things crumble. And then you were holding Ninka. She would have fallen with you, and the two of you decided to go out and take her, so you must feel guilty; you almost killed her. Am I right?" She was. "Anya," she said more distinctly, "you can never keep track of all the bombs and guns and trains in this world, never. Don't take that on yourself. You won't be strong enough if you keep thinking that way." She was quiet a long time. "My brother, Mischa, he was killed in the pogrom. He wouldn't come into the coffin; he said he was afraid of them. And I didn't want him in it with me; it was crowded enough. And he was bad, you know, I thought he would make a noise. So he hid in the greenhouse, and they found him. Do you know, I still wake up at night seeing the greenhouse and all the flowers bent over him with mouths, chewing. It's as if they're chewing. Thirty years, I still see it. Your father says it's fate. I've never been able to believe it. Mischa comes up, my brother Mischa, and says, 'No, it was not fate; it was you.' But Anya, he was a child. Now that I'm so old, I'm beginning to think he's wrong, and maybe," she went on talking in the dark, "it's good I've been guilty all these years. There are times when the dead walk only in guilt, I think. What do you think? You don't know how many times I prayed for my Momma and Poppa to come to me in dreams, but they don't come. I haven't been lucky in my dreams. Only in Mischa. I'm lucky he comes, even that way." "I would like to go to the clinic," I said, holding her hand. "We'll take care of it tomorrow then. Go to bed; I'm falling asleep sitting here." "Happy sleeps, Momma," I murmured, bending over her; "good dreams." She was asleep, her breathing regular and deep. Stajoe was asleep, too. Tomorrow he would leave for three weeks in Moscow; Poppa would write to his nephew.

"How can I go to the clinic?" I asked Poppa in the morning; "it's in Lithuania." "With my papers," Poppa said. "We can arrange it by saying you're really Lithuanian. We'll get you Lithuanian papers." "But I can't even speak a word!" "That doesn't make any difference in these things," Poppa said. "The main thing is if dear nephew Savikin will take you." So Momma and Vera and I sat around in the kitchen with Ninka and Anzia, knitting blankets and more blankets, and crocheting squares. "We can make these into squares for the baby," Anzia said with satisfaction. "And we can go out to the greenhouses in the back now, Anya. You haven't seen them. They went up when you were in Warsaw. They are let out to a gardener; he will let us go in them and buy whatever we want; radishes, cucumbers, all year long." Anzia spoke in an awed, religious voice. "How did you manage that?" Momma asked, curious. "I have my ways," Anzia answered, her gray head bent over her knitting. "How old is the man, Anzia?" Momma asked. "How should I know?" Anzia answered. "I know how old his radishes are; they are two days old, and his cucumbers are one, and too hard to buy yet." "Is it safe to go out there? It's a glass building." "Oh, yes, yes, there's nothing around, nothing, you know, not even in the forests." "Between the servants and

190

the peasants we don't need the radio," Momma sighed. "Nothing in the forests?" Momma asked again. "Not for miles," Anzia said positively. "Then it's safe to send Anya to Kaunas?" Momma asked. "No doubt about it; there will be no trouble with the trains." "But they were mining them last month," Momma reminded her. "They are not now," Anzia answered, her needles clicking. "So we wait for the letter," Momma said. "How long is the trip?" I asked. "By *matritza,* an hour and a half," Anzia volunteered.

The letter came. Janek Savikin would be more than happy to have me; he would be honored. "Flowery creature," Poppa said. "You wanted me to go," I reminded him. "What had that to do with anything?" he asked. "They say," he went on reading, "you are to stay with them. They have," he said, looking up, "a whole house in the middle of the city. But I'm not sure. His wife, Katerina, she's an ex-patient, you know; tuberculosis. She still isn't so strong. I don't like having that disease around. Please come home if you think it's not safe. So, do you want to go?" "Of course, of course." "Then here are your papers," he said, handing them to me, and sure enough, there it all was: *Name*: Anya Savikin. *Nationality*: Lithuanian. "You'll leave on Sunday night and come back on Friday night, just like a *dacha* husband, my Anya." It was arranged. "You'll write to Stajoe, of course," Poppa warned me. "He'll be glad to hear it," I said. I was thinking of Colonel Dovsky and his dog-pack eyes.

The little hospital was a marvelous place. It was like the best of hotels, the food was wonderful; there was nothing anyone could want. And it was expensive, very very expensive; ridiculous. I did not dream that the doctors would give me such responsibility, checking blood pressure, taking temperatures, removing casts, letting me sit in on diagnostic conferences, admitting and treating emergency cases. There was one, a little boy with a stiff neck. I turned his head gently from side to side. "Doctor Savikin," I said (that is what I always called Janek at work), "I don't like it; I think it's meningitis." And the next day, it was the talk of the hospital, what a wonderful diagnostician I was going to be. But after a week, I couldn't live with them. It wasn't just that Mrs. Savikin coughed, and for a minute I thought, "That's what's wrong with Momma!" but she was sickly, and she was jealous. I was uncomfortable, and didn't know what to do about it. Someone had cut jealousy out of me. "Doesn't it bother you?" Stajoe used to ask after Vera had climbed all over him, always hanging on his back, "No, why should it?" I was surprised at him. "It's strange," he said. "No, you're strange," I insisted. I wrote Poppa telling him I would have to come home, but then, right before I left, I remembered a neighbor had told me that her second cousin had a very nice apartment and was almost my age, and would probably share; she would like the company. So I called her. Julia Doroshnik. "Oh," she said, all excited, "come right over; I would love to meet you."

I took the tram to Julia's house; it was a half-hour drive. All of Kaunas seemed brand-new; it was so clean, and like a little Paris. "That's what they call it," Mrs. Savikin had told me proudly, *"le petit Paris."* Julia lived in a white brick house, very narrow and tall, the shutters painted gold. When I got to the door, the sun was setting, striking it so its facade trembled with shades of red, as if I were seeing it through layers of petals, and the shutters and door glistened and glittered like doors to a fairy tale. Then the sun moved down as I crossed the street and the shutters and door turned red-gold, like metal heated up. "I'm Anya Savikin," I said, coming into the second-floor apartment; the same colors were trembling all over the inside walls like butterfly wings. "It's very pretty here," I said shyly. Julia Doroshnik was much richer than I was, that was clear, and, it was odd, she had an Oriental look. "My Mongol blood," Julia laughed, watching me; "my distant cousin has no Mongol blood, so he doesn't resemble me too much. It was nice of him to tell you about me. Come, sit down and talk." She rang a little bell. A maid in a white uniform came in with a tray of cakes and tea. "You're a doctor?" she asked, curious. "Oh, no," I said blushing. "Well, I want to hear all about you," she said, leaning back, and I began to tell her. "It was really like that with the Germans!" she exclaimed; "horrible! I can't believe it."

So I went on, Julia eating cake after cake. "Have more, have more," she said, "unless you get fat. I'm always losing weight, like some people lose needles in a rug." "Will you tell me about you?" I asked, shy again. I liked it here; the crumbling wall had not built itself once. Inside Julia's apartment was like the inside of a Chinese robe. "Well," Julia considering, "first, I'm a widow. Really, I'm divorced; my husband was impotent." She announced it as if she were stating the weather. "So now I'm making up for lost time. I have parties three times a week, just to keep the maids busy, and two nights a week, I go out to the nightclubs or a show. But still, you know how it is, I get lonely. My sister, Elena, I will never forgive her, got married and went off to live in France. For a while I had hopes, but her husband is the next best thing to a goat, so she won't come back." I told her about my cousin, how he was the perfect picture of a professor, spectacles, pointed beard and all, and his wife, Katerina, who looked like a vampire out of *Dracula*. "I have to look for a place; perhaps you know one." "Oh, you'll stay here; that's all settled." Julia pushed herself farther back onto the couch. "And please call me Julka, everyone does; everyone I let in, that is." She considered me with amusement. "I think I know someone you know: Max Ellenbogen, the young man you met at a resort, which was it, Zakopanie? 'A queen is here,' I think it was? Hmmmm," she considered, staring through a beam of sunlight into the sun, a huge red coin, "do they have night shifts at your hospital?" "Of course," I said, "the patients don't get well for the night." Julka laughed, then choked on a crumb. "I tell you what, see if you can get the night shift, because we will stay up late, and in the morning you'll be too tired to get up. This way you can stay out until it is time to go to work and then come home and sleep all day. What do you say?" "To tell you the truth," I cried, "I would love to; I really forget my troubles here." "There are no such things as troubles," Julka said definitely. "Fridays I go home," I reminded her, "to see my little girl, and Stajoe, my husband; he'll be home in two weeks." "Do you love him?" she asked absent-mindedly. "Of course!" "It's not always of course," Julka said, almost bored.

So I explained to cousin Savikin that I couldn't stay with him; I didn't want to inconvenience him. But he couldn't understand it. How could I inconvenience him when he had a whole house and all his maids. "Oh, it's just better that I'm with someone my own age," I answered. "Katerina will be disappointed," he said severely. "I will miss you both," I said dutifully, "but cousin, there's a favor I want to ask: Could I be on the night shift for a while?" "Strange child," he said to himself. "If you want it," he said dubious, "but why? No one else does." "Just to see what it's like," I assured him.

And at Julka's I did forget my troubles. I was again

193

working with medicine; I had a chance to acquire more knowledge, and I was making so much money, every Friday I came home with a package of money, tips from the rich patients, my salary; it was a fortune. Thursdays at the clinics they usually served pigeon in wine; it was delicacy after delicacy. Then, Julka would have her parties, pastry and brandy and tea, and we saw every show; we saw *Metropolis* five times in one week. "They say that's what it will be like soon," Frederick, Julia's friend, whom I had also met with Max at Zakopanie, whispered, watching the uniformed soldiers marching off like automatons to work. "Please!" Julia silenced him; "I won't hear it." So I would come home with money and every kind of cookie and candy, silk pajamas, clothes for the baby, sheets, linens, anything I could carry, and the family was always waiting for me at the station. Then we would sit in the kitchen, or in the dining room, talking, or Momma would sing, or Vera would play the piano, while I held Ninka, and on Monday I would return again.

After about six weeks, I came home from the shift exhausted and fell asleep on the couch; something woke me. "I think she's awake," I could hear Julia whispering. "No, she's not," Frederick whispered. The door to her bedroom was open. Neither of them had any clothes on. Naturally, Julka had the light on; I could see everything. I watched in shock, pretending to sleep. When they were finished, I pretended to get up slowly. Julka's face was smooth as a new-made bed. I thought it was a terrible disgrace. But still, it was the most wonderful time. And at night I would lie awake wondering how I got used to many things, if this was just part of being grown up, and other times, I wondered if I was used to anything, except pretending there was nothing to get used to. Of course, I never mentioned anything but the work to Stajoe about my life there; he was very proud, his little Anya, a doctor again. And Ninka was fattening up with Anzia; she wasn't screaming. We had to peel Vera from her like tape.

So it went on, on weekends Stajoe and Jakob discussing their enginerering. One weekend Vera pulled me over: "Anya," she said, "I've been to the doctor. He says I can't have children; something is closed." "What is closed?" I asked her. "I didn't want to ask," Vera whispered, her thin shoulders slumping like little wings; she was holding Snowbell, who was licking her chin. "Maybe he's wrong; there are plenty of terrible doctors in Vilno. We can go to Warsaw when it's over, and if something's wrong, maybe they can even fix it." "He isn't wrong," she said. "What does Jakob say?" I asked; I was trying to imagine Stajoe in his place. I shuddered. "Something about how it would be an obstacle to our endless love, having children, I mean. I think he means it, I do; I want to think so." "You shouldn't give up hope," I pleaded with her. "It's best that I do," she said. "We'll share Ninka," I promised her. "That's already wonderful," Vera said, straightening up, beaming.

Four weeks later, the doorbell rang at Julka's; it was one in the afternoon. I answered the door; Julka was still sleeping. "Cousin!" I exclaimed. "Your mother is very sick," he was saying without even coming in; "pneumonia. Your father thought you might want to come home." "Immediately!" I cried; "how long has she been sick?" "A week; they didn't want to worry you." "I want to take the train right away; will you call Julka later and explain to her?" "You have time for a note," he said, sitting down on a chair; "you have time; please write it."

Momma couldn't stop coughing. Vera and I took turns with her, then Anzia. Slowly, she started getting better but she was left with the bad cough. "I'm not going back," I told her. "We have enough money; Stajoe's working; Poppa's making money. Colonel Dovsky even picks him up every day and brings him home from Panari. There's no reason for me to go; I want to stay here." She didn't argue with me. The Russians had been driven out by the Lithuanians a short time after we came, but then the Russians came back. Still, while the Lithuanians were there, Jakob had managed to buy some beds and a little furniture, and a small store of food. Now the Russians were back; Poppa was also back at work. "I do not think, Borya," I heard Momma saying, "Colonel Dovsky comes to see you; I think he comes to see Anya." "Momma, what are you talking about!" I cried, rushing into the room. "I'm a married woman with a child. Where do you get such ideas?" "Ask your husband where I get such ideas," Momma answered, staring at me. "He's only jealous," Poppa said, dismissing it. But Poppa had the job back, and it was paying very well.

Then Stajoe was sent to Kharkov for some radio parts. Colonel Dovsky called. I had gone through so much because of the Germans in Warsaw, he was giving a special party for me, why wouldn't I come, I was being unreasonable. "Oh, I'm tired," I pleaded. "This will take your tiredness away; I'll come get you." I went with him. I couldn't believe what I saw. The table in his apartment was set for two; there were two candles. "Are you a villain from a movie?" I demanded, outraged. "Where are the guests?" "I have all the guests I want," he said, moving toward me. I hadn't realized how big he was. His black hair seemed to be darkening with every step. I ran out of the door, yanking it open so hard I almost tore it loose; then I was flying across the city. I was back at the apartment a half hour after I left. I hid in the entrance to the courtyard, waiting for my breathing to become normal; I was panting. Then I rang the bell; Momma let me in. "Now am I right?" she asked, looking me over. "No, no, I don't know, it was only very boring, that's all. I didn't want to stay. I'm going to bed, where's Ninka?" "In the trunk with Anzia." "Would you ask Anzia to bring her to my room? I'll keep her myself." Ninka was sleeping in an old blanket trunk Anzia had lined with cloth after Stajoe and Jakob pried off the lid. "I don't like it, Anya," Momma warned me.

Poppa sent a message to say he was staying overnight at Panari to catch up on some work. "I thought we had finished with that when the bank finished," Momma complained. "At least he'll probably go to bed early there." So we went to bed. In the middle of the night there were horrible noises. "Bombs!" I woke up screaming, running to the window. But I could see nothing, no flames, nothing. "Get away from the window," Jakob shouted, grabbing me and dragging me back into the center of the room. "Into the hall, fast." He went through the house like an inspector, waking up Anzia, Josefa. "Into the hall, into the hall," he kept repeating. "Until we know what it is these big windows are dangerous if there are bombs or shelling." "Turn on some lights," Momma suggested. "No lights," Jakob insisted. "Where's the noise from, Anzia?" Momma asked, confused. "It sounds far away," Anzia guessed. "Boris is far away," Momma said in a dead voice. "Mrs. Savikin, they are not bombing your husband," Anzia told her. "No," Momma answered. So we sat there in the dark hall all night. "Here we go again," Anzia said, resigned. I sat between Momma and Vera. They finally fell asleep, and watching Ninka, I finally did too.

"I want everyone to stay in the hall, except for emergencies," Momma ordered as we began winking on, one by one, like candles. We were sitting in the long dark hall when there was a knock at the door. "And no one's going out," Momma added before we had a chance to get up to answer it; "it's the old story. If there's trouble, there are riots in the street, robbings, rape; it will be just like a pogrom. Maybe that's what it is." Vera looked at Jakob; he got up. It was an old peasant. "Pardon, pardon," he kept saying, "I have Mister Savikin." "What is it?" Momma began shouting. "The Germans in Panari, pardon, pardon, but the Russians runned, Mister Savikin, he sleeped, so they beat him. I have Mister Savikin," he recited again. "We will bring him in, Momushka," Jakob assured her. Then they carried in my father. His whole head was beaten and swollen. One eye was almost unrecognizable, purple and blue and swollen shut; the lid seemed like a seam or a scar. He was completely unconscious. "Momma, he's not dead; he's not dead," I kept telling her, and in the background were these noises, the booms of explosions, muted. Why were they bombing if there was no one to fight? "Just to frighten," Anzia answered, reading my mind; "they think there might be someone hidden in the woods."

"We can't go out to get a doctor." Momma started crying now there would be nothing we could do with her. She herself had passed the interdiction against going out on the streets. No one could leave the apartment; she wouldn't permit it. "Jakob," I said getting up, giving Vera the baby, "we have to put him on the couch in the dining room; we can't move him anymore." Jakob and the peasant carried him in. Mother was just walking and crying and walking. "Anzia," I whispered, "please take her away until I wash him. This isn't good for her." I washed off the blood, but still he looked like a monster. "I'll do the best I can," I told Jakob, bending over, "but it's dangerous, a little knowledge, and this isn't the proper care." Every two minutes for four days it was jumping up from the hall to look in on Poppa through the glass doors. I would go in and talk to him, to see if he would answer, try to give him something to eat. Every two minutes, it was jumping up for cold cloths and injections from the medical supplies I had brought back from Kaunas, and still it was not the proper care. For four days, he stayed totally unconscious. Then he began to wake up, but it was two weeks before he was out of the mist. Before that happened, all he asked was, "What was it? What was it? What happened? What are the noises?" and whoever was there would explain over and over.

Momma walked through the house crying. Vera tried; then I tried; Stajoe; nothing. "Momma, he's getting better; he is!" I pleaded. "I know he'll get over this," Momma wept, "but I don't see anything good coming; I do not see it." She would stare straight ahead as if she were staring through time. "Do you know," she asked, calling her eyes back like a pack of wild hounds, "they are teaching little boys in special schools that Jews have telephones in their beards, that they use the telephone to call the devil, and the devil will do terrible things to little boys? I can't see anything good coming; I do not see it. You cannot even go out for food." "I can go; I'm going now," I said, starting for the door. But the woman would have nothing to sell us, or only a half-rotted potato. Our greenhouse had been looted and smashed. I would have to plead for a little grain, some sugar, anything. It was a good thing she was a religious woman. The whole store, tiny as a picture in a frame, was hung with dozens of prints of the Virgin Mary and hundreds of saints. "If not for me, at least for my father," I pleaded. I didn't know what to say; I was desperate. "He is so sick, at least for him; God will help you." "Some oats, you take it from my children's mouths." "How much?" "Ten zlotys," she said. I pressed it in her hand, and flew back across the street. Vera was heating up some sticks of wood to make Poppa a little tea. Momma was standing by the door trembling until I got in; who knew what maniac might be out with a gun, waiting. "See, Momma," I said in the corridor, "he's all right." "This time it's different," Momma answered; "it's different. I do not see anything good ahead; I don't see *anything* ahead."

Then Poppa was himself again, and there was a new horror for us. The German soldiers began beating on the door. "Where is the daughter, the daughter?" They meant me; I was the one always out on the street. Vera didn't go out; she was, I don't know, a little afraid. And I was still dressed very well, always very simply, but very well. "Behind the credenza," Poppa ordered in a whisper. I ran into the black dining room and slipped behind the oak credenza. There was just enough room for me when I sucked in my stomach, and no one could move the credenza, it was so heavy, but of course, if they really looked, they would find me. One day, I was hiding behind it, terrified, completely terrified; Stajoe was crying in the hall, and I remembered the days when the Russians were there. They sent a soldier in for curtains; sun struck his red epaulettes. "I am sorry," he said, taking down the drapes; "orders." I was sitting in the white dining room, in a chair, reading something or other. "Are you a movie star?" he asked in a small voice. "No," I answered. "A Jewess?" he asked. "Yes." "Oh," he said slowly, "you are born under an evil star, an evil star." Later, he sent us a big pot of soup, but would we eat it? We wouldn't touch it. We thought it was poisoned.

"Where is the daughter, the daughter, the daughter?" and the sound of fists. They took the place of the crumbling brick wall. "We have to do something," Stajoe said. "But what?" I asked. He didn't answer me. The next day it was Poppa. "You know influential people in Kaunas, Anya. Maybe you could get visas to Curaçao; they're still available. Try." And I did try. But I could only get two. No matter how much money I promised, I could not get more than two. "Will you come?" Stajoe asked me. "I can't leave my family." "What about mine?" he cried; "I left mine." "You wouldn't enjoy me. You go; I can't." And my answer lay between us like the rubble of a bombed building. Finally, he was resigned. "At least," said Poppa, when he couldn't convince me either, "at least we're all together."

"No one goes without crosses," Anzia said severely; "I have a friend who makes them." She produced eight crosses, enough for the entire household. "I am endlessly amazed at your friends," Momma said with the memory of a smile, slipping it over her neck, then one over Poppa's. I saw his hand go up as if to swat it off, but he lowered his hand gently to Momma's knee, and there it rested. "Your Poppa was right," Momma cried steadily; "we should have prayed for anyone but the Germans."

11

EVEN now things were settling into a pattern. Poppa brought his books into the hall, where we were away from the windows, and read, tilting the books to whatever light there was; when a door opened, he lifted up the whole book. "It is bad for your eyes," Momma scolded, but he just looked at her, tilted the book, and kept on reading. Momma sat next to him, silently crying. She was happy when she was lost in taking care of Ninka. "Such hair!" she would murmur, each time perpetually surprised. "Stajoe, blonds usually don't have such thick hair." "The eyes are not bad, either," Poppa added, without looking up. But we were afraid to leave the hall. It had been a week since the Germans arrived with their bombs; now it was quiet. I still ran across the street for food. "I need some brassieres," I said suddenly one day, startling myself; "I'm bigger since Ninka," but naturally, I didn't expect any. Brassieres seemed as far away as pigeons in wine.

Jakob had begun slipping in and out through the back door when Vera fell asleep; he didn't want to upset her. The dog slept on her lap. When she wasn't holding Ninka, or playing with her or Snowbell, she drew her knees up to her chin, wrapped her arms around them, and rested her head on the little bony platform they made. "Some brassieres, Anya," Jakob announced; "also some bread, a little milk, two radishes, and one onion." He was grinning from ear to ear. "How did you do it?" I whispered overjoyed; I didn't want to wake up Vera. "Never mind how," he laughed; "I run very fast."

I was getting stiff. Some of the doors had been opened a crack to let some light into the hall; the long corridor looked like a thin piece of striped material, white and black, white and black. "I'm going into the kitchen to talk to Anzia," I told Momma. Anzia had started off, a light in her eyes, the second she saw the radishes. I leaned against the tiles of the stove; they were cold, even though outside it was very hot. I thought about all the times we had come into the kitchen and warmed our backs against the tiles in the winter. I remembered the mattresses Poppa had put on the big rectangular tile tunnel that grew out of the stove and burrowed into the wall, and how each of us had slept there in turn when it was cold, or when Momma went out and it felt cold.

"Will they go back, Anzia?" I asked her. "Not this time," she answered sadly; "not for a long time." What was the point of asking her how she knew? She knew. "What do you think will happen?" I asked her again. "You can see for yourself this afternoon," Anzia said, slicing the onion so thin you could see through it. "Let me play the old onion game," I begged her. I didn't want to know what I'd see, not just yet. "Take it," she said. She had such a sweet smile. Why was I seeing her in the past tense, dissolving in a mist like the one that used to rise from her soup pots; nothing was on the stove. I took the onion slice and held it up to my eye. "I see Anzia," I said, "and she's very old, and a *little* green, not very green, just around the edges"—Anzia was grinning, slicing the radishes and the potato—"and she has the funniest wrinkles, not like the other old ladies'; they're round wrinkles, and in the middle," I said, adjusting my onion monocle, "is the mouth." "Enough, you'll hurt your eyes," Anzia cautioned me; tears were beginning to well. "Don't rub them. Zoshia used to think of such games!" She rubbed her hands on her apron, standing still, thinking; "such games. Remember the game about the carrot?" I said no. "I think that was with Mischa; I'll tell you later." My eyes were still tearing from the onion. "What's going to happen this afternoon?" "This afternoon, they will be coming through the city, no shooting, but you will see how it is." "Should everyone see how it is?" I asked her. "They better," she said, dicing the potato piece left; "finished."

That afternoon, there was a sudden commotion in the street. I had told Stajoe. We woke everyone up. All of us pressed against the walls of the black dining room, peering into the street, hiding our bodies from sight. The Germans came through like a parade, like a caravan on its way to a fancy dress ball. Their hair was combed and shiny, their faces shaven, their uniforms immaculate. Even the trucks shown like glass. "No one fought them," Stajoe whispered. "You see how it is, Boris?" Momma whispered; "they are here for good. I do not see anything good after this; they will not leave this time." Poppa was holding to both sides of Momma's waist; he said nothing. The trucks, big and small, rolled by, an endless black border on a mourning card. "It would be nice to think," Vera whispered to Jakob, "that it was only ten big trucks and ten little ones that kept circling the blocks, like in that funny movie we saw." "It would be nice to think it," Jakob whispered back. Momma was crying steadily. "They may go away," I whispered to her. "Not this time," she said again, "not this time."

The trucks rumbled by, one and one and one. I had lost count over an hour ago. "Where are the tanks?" I asked with sudden hope; they were less frightening, less formidable, without tanks. "They wouldn't bring tanks into the city; they must be outside, near the forest." "That's where they are," Anzia whispered from the doorway. They rolled by; they rolled by. "I do not believe it," I said. Stajoe's arms circled my breastbone and locked over me. He bent down and kissed my head, then Ninka's. "Look," he said softly, pointing, "see the mirrors fastened to the sun shields, there on the trucks, the shaving kits on the seats? It's the Germans now, for good." The last truck passed. Although it was still light, it felt as if the sun had set. Automatically we went back into the hall and sat in our usual places. Anzia came out of the kitchen. "It's no use to go out now," she told us. "I can get the food, but they're collecting Jews." "Collecting Jews?" I echoed, astonished. "Yes," Anzia told me, "a little boy from the forest was talking to one of them. The little children will point out who are the Jews on the street, and they will grab them." "Put them in prison?" "No, not all," Anzia said slowly; "the little boy said they wanted to kill. The soldier said he would teach him to shoot squirrels so later he could shoot Jews. The little boy told the soldier *he* had killed a squirrel with a rock on the head. So I think that is what it is. They will probably start in a week. So there is no use, going out. I can get some food, don't ask how." Vera folded her hands over her drawn-up knees, lowering her head. Jakob's arm went around her; Stajoe's went around me. I knew I would go out, too. Poppa was holding Momma. None of us could say anything. Anzia stood there staring at us, started to say something, changed her mind, went into the kitchen. There was the terrific clanging of pots, but it was sealed off from the terrible, terrible silence in the hall.

The week passed. There were no bombs. We were in and out of the other rooms more and more, but mostly, we wandered through them like ghosts. Everyone played with Ninka like a kitten; the minute they put her down, they froze in their places. Everyone wandered aimlessly in and out of the kitchen, watched Anzia, settled on a piece of furniture again like a misplaced fly sealed in by a hard pane of air. But still, the soldiers would come, shouting for me, "the daughter, the daughter," and then I was squeezed behind the credenza in the hall. Momma was forever fingering the little iron cross around her neck. "Where did you get these?" she asked Anzia. "You are missing eight of your worst iron spoons, that's all," Anzia said.

"We are living in biblical times," Momma said in a monotone. She looked more dead than alive, a hundred years old. "I don't want to hear that again, Rebecca," Poppa warned her; "not one more time. This is a sin; what you are doing. We are still alive. This is *zindig*; you are sinning against life. Let go of that cross and take Ninka from Vera; how long can she hold her before her arm gets paralyzed?" Ninka. Momma's face changed immediately. "I do not like it," Poppa said in my ear; "we have to watch her. Things have been happening too fast for her. But she's used to these things, they *shouldn't* be happening too fast." "Sometimes," I whispered to him, "it seems to me that she sees things." "*That* is something I do not want to hear again!" Poppa turned on me, gripping my wrist. "What, are you all to be deprived of reason, seeing everything but the Germans standing in front of you on the street? Don't encourage her; don't do it; and not yourself, not yourself," Poppa begged; "no one sees things." Poppa stared straight ahead at the wall. "It would be nice to read through the nights," he said aloud. "We can only go to bed, Boris," Momma answered, automatically comforting him. "There's no light once the sun goes; we can't get a thing for the lamps. If we go to bed early, you can get up while it's still dark and get that book you want from the neighbor." "What book?" Poppa asked, brightening. "How should I know, Boris? I can't even pronounce it." Vera was looking at both of them and smiling; Stajoe was smiling at me. "I never thought I would live to see another man buy my wife brassieres," he said. "I never thought we would live to hear it discussed in the hall," Momma chimed in, grinning. "Come, let's see what birdseed Anzia has for us, and then we'll go to bed so your father can get up to get his precious book." We followed her down the hall like ants after a piece of candy. None of us slept much now. I would lay awake thinking, "What is coming; what is coming?" Stajoe lay with his own thoughts. None of us spoke much. Vera was absolutely quiet. We were all thinking the same thing; What is coming? Except Poppa. He still had his books. Vera would not play her piano. "It would do you good," I pleaded. "It would attract attention," she answered. She was so good.

In the morning, Poppa was paddling about in his slippers and worst bathrobe. "Rebecca, Anya, Anzia," he notified us (none of us took a step now without telling the others), "I'm going to Mister Karlovsky's for the book." It was still dark out. Across the street, we could make out the outline of houses, some spiked, like old helmets. "Why does he use the front door?" Momma sighed; "there's the back." "He would still have to go around to get into the other house," Anzia reminded her. "That man would go into hell for books," Momma fussed. We smiled; we had heard all this before. "Anya, look out the window," she cried suddenly. "Oh, Momma stop it," I scolded; "you will drive us all crazy." "Look out the window," she ordered again. "So, there is Poppa," I called back, "about the same height. Aha, Momma, it is scandalous, I don't think he has any clothes; not that he doesn't have any at all, just a bathrobe and slippers. Oh, he's putting one foot in front of the other again. He's going to the neighbor's; he's closing the door; he's in." "Very funny," Momma said; "stay there." "Also, Momma, across the street is a shadow." "What shadow?" Momma shrieked in panic. "A shadow cast by a building, very remarkable." But was it? It seemed to be moving. Light was crawling up the sky; I thought I saw a small truck across the street. "A very uninteresting shadow," I said, but I was watching it; it seemed to be moving. Then it split in two. One shadow was taller than the other. "So, Anya, where is Poppa?" Momma asked anxiously. "He hasn't come out yet; he's probably reading their dictionary to see if it has any new words." "Probably," Momma sighed, sliding down against the wall to the floor.

All of a sudden I heard the sound of a heavy door closing. Then I caught sight of my father. The two shadows moved forward. I began fingering the yellow star on my blouse; we had been ordered to make them; the Germans knew the neighbors would report any Jews who didn't wear one. Afterward we never mentioned them, but someone was always twisting his neck, pulling down his head, to stare at it where it fastened to the clothes. And under our clothes the iron crosses were cold against our skin. "Nothing," I thought, seeing the first shadow, a little blond boy, maybe ten years old. *"Jude,"* he shouted; "Jew," and the man, the large shadow, came clear, ran across the street, grabbed Poppa and disappeared with him into the truck. I felt Anzia watching over the top of my head. "I'm going to find him," I screamed, twisting out of her grasp, running for the door; "I'm going to find him." Momma sat as still as if she had been shot. "Wait!" Anzia shouted at me; "take some food; take something." She ran back with an old jar of strawberry preserves. "Don't go,'" she pleaded. I snatched off my yellow star and threw it down. "Don't go; they will catch you and put you in one of the houses for soldiers."

But there was no one for her to talk to. I was already out on the street. Where had they gone? I had heard a truck while I took the jar; where had they gone? If they had started collecting Jews, they must take them to a big place. But what place? I decided to look. I could hear the neighbors at Momma: "Mrs. Savikin, what is your Anya doing? What is your daughter doing? You know where she'll wind up; she'll wind up in the whore house." Without my star, they would take me there if they caught me; Jews were not good enough for the German soldiers. But I was running as if I had never heard of feet, of exhaustion, of a beating heart. I was at the medical school, all over the grounds; no one, no one. I ran into the center of town; no one. How was I getting from one place to another? I had no idea. It was as if I appeared here, then there, then there; there were no steps in between. I was a firefly, winking on at the medical school, off, on again in the center of the town. It was getting gray; already it was getting gray. I could smell the strawberries; they were sour from the heat. Streets were running by like fleeing people, but I was not moving. I didn't realize it right away, that I had stopped. But then the tall man across the street was there over again and over again. I closed my eyes; he was there again. So I had come to rest. "Please," I said, coming up to him. It was as if he were the first person I had seen on the streets all day. My hair was in braids, I looked twelve years old. "Please," I said to him.

205

He was wearing some kind of uniform, but not a German army one. "Please, it is getting dark, I don't know how it happened, and my mother will kill me if I'm not home, but I want to see the Jews; they are killing them, aren't they?" I asked with enormous excitement. "Oh, yes Miss," he said proudly. "But *where* are they doing it?" I panted in excitement; "I want to see." "In the Botanical Gardens," he laughed; "where else, fertilizer right away." "Oh, thank you," I cried, and I was off.

The Botanical Gardens were surrounded with barbed wire. Inside were hundreds and hundreds of bodies, some twisted over each other; in one place, there were three men in layers, like anchovies. But Poppa, I had to find Poppa. And I did find him. He was beaten so badly he was barely recognizable. He was not recognizable; I recognized the bathrobe and the slippers first. His face was swollen like a moon; he was purple, covered with blood. But this time his eyes were not swollen shut; they stared straight ahead like fish eyes, huge fish eyes without pupils. "Poppa," I cried to him, "Poppa," but I couldn't reach him, the wire fence had such sharp edges. "Poppa," I cried, desperate, "take the strawberries, eat the strawberries, they will make you strong; you will be able to get up." The soldiers had done their job and gone home, there were no guards. My voice was the only sound in the world. The world had gone quiet, like the silence before a pianist begins to play. "Poppa," I cried into this silence, "take the strawberries, they will make you better. They are from the *dacha*." His arm moved for them. I lay down flat on the ground and stretched myself like rubber; he took the jar. I did not know if he recognized me. His lips did not move; his eyes did not move, only his hand. If only I could reach him, I could pull him out. But I couldn't; there were the sharp wires with their thorns. His hand closed around the jar; his eyes closed; they opened again. "Poppa, it is Anya!" I cried again and again, insisting, insisting, he had to wake up. "Poppa!" Not even his eyes turned toward me. "Poppa!" I cried one last time. It was getting dark.

"Get up," I heard a voice saying in my ear; "get up and go home; you have your Momma and your sister, your husband and Ninka." I looked at Poppa. It wasn't him; his lips had not moved. "I have to go now, Poppa," I said; "I have to go now." I walked off without looking back. *Bozhe pomogi,* I whispered; "God help me, *bozhe po-*

mogi," thinking, "How many more times will I say this, how many more times will I see this." Stajoe had said it was funny how you remembered some things, how when they happened you knew you would not forget them. He was not yet dead, but they would shoot him, perhaps, the final touch.

I walked home slowly. I would not have been surprised to find the Atlantic Ocean waiting at one corner, the China Sea at the other. It was as if a tuck had been taken in the whole world. It was a long way home, a very long way. It was dark now, but I could see every building as if the moon were a huge mean bulb screwed in the sky. It was full sun, cruel light, white light, and silent. My mind was developing the negative as I walked. I knocked at the front door. Momma came to it like a ghost. "Don't say it," she told me. "Mischa is home; he's come home to die. I'm going into him. Anzia will tell you, I can't," and she turned her back on me and walked into her room. She was not shedding a tear.

Anzia was in the kitchen cooking something. We stared at each other for a long time. "Did they get him?" she asked; her voice was dead. "Yes," I answered, the word sounding like a spoon banging on a pot. "They will not let him go?" she asked, her knife poised in the air. "They can't, even if they want to," I said flatly; "where is Stajoe?" "They are all with Mischa and your Momma." "Momma said to ask you about Mischa." "I cannot believe it," Anzia cried out; "what is there to believe? It is like a bad story. It isn't fair, just because you are Jewish, all this should happen to you." "Poppa always said there was no such thing as justice in the world," I repeated mechanically, impersonally. How could he have become a voice, a memory, so fast. Already I was quoting him; there would be no new words to repeat. "Climb up on the stove," Anzia pleaded. I climbed onto its rectangular tile tunnel.

"Is Mischa dying?" I asked her. "Who said he's dying?" she asked, indignant; "he just needs a good rest." "So what happened?" I asked again. "He got to Moscow—I don't know how that little boy got to Moscow—and he found your cousins, remember, the ones your Poppa talked about, but they didn't want him; they were afraid to attract attention to themselves; things are not so good there either. So when he got there, it was already cold—he left last summer, before you came back, and it took him a long time, getting rides on horses and wagons—and they gave him

some food and clothes, that's all. Your mother was shrieking that Boris would have fixed them, ach." So she went
on. "He went in deeper, to hide better, and came to this
little village, only women. All the men were at war, and,
you know, he was only twelve. He thought, all women,
what could be better, a whole village of mothers. But they
were peasants and they hadn't even seen a shadow of a
man; they had their own ideas. So they wouldn't give him
anything to eat unless he traded with his body, you know,
learning their games. So he got to eat potato whiskey and
a little oats, and they raped him." "Raped him?" I repeated in disbelief. "Raped him. Either he did what they
needed, or they killed him, and after he did his best, they
just kept after him, you know, playing around with him as
if he were a doll. He was all raw. When they didn't want
him for a while, they got him drunker. Then he started to
miss your Momma, and he got bloody diarrhea, so he
couldn't even walk, they gave up on him, but they fed him
a little, and when he could walk, they let him go in a
wagon. The last thing they asked was, did he have any
bigger brothers. He's been coming back for three months,
one wagon to another wagon, and your mother is sorry, she
says he would have been better off there. So that," Anya
said, chopping something, "is what it was."

The walls of the kitchen seemed to be moving in and
out, like lungs. "You are swaying, Anya," Anzia warned
me, lifting me down; "sit in the chair. He told us about
the mud huts, and the lice, some of them as big as a finger, Moscow's streets, how wide they were, but it's the
huts, the huts and the lice, over and over. Can you believe
it? He is only twelve."

"I am going in to Momma." The walls were still breathing in and out. "Go out," I told Vera and Stajoe.
"Momma, do you want him to sleep here?" "No," she
said, "in the kitchen with Anzia; it's better. This way, he
will know on what he is sleeping." She was staring at
Poppa's side of the bed as if it were a dead body; she was
relapsing into her Russian dialect. "He says Emmanuel is
coming back, too. We were wrong," she cried out suddenly,
"to be so close, so ridiculously close, to have them come
home for this!" "You were not wrong, Momma; never."
"Let me get Anzia to take him, and we can talk," she told
me. Her voice came and went in spurts as if a cat were
fastened to her throat, toying with her, then letting her go,
then grabbing her breathless again. So we were left alone.

"Come into bed with me," she asked; "no, I stay on Poppa's side. You see how it is," she went on; "you see how it will be. Soon we will have no time for grief, one will come so fast after another. That will be the most terrible thing. Do we have time to think about your father? No time. Now it is Emmanuel, and food for Ninka, and keeping Jakob in the house, and Emmanuel when he gets back, maybe married Mischa thinks, maybe even with a baby. There will not even be time for the dead, what can be more terrible for the living?" "Nothing at all," I said into the dark, "except to stop living." "How can we stop when one more of us is alive?" she cried out; "don't you think I would like to stop? I can't stop; I want to live, to be alive. Just while any of you are alive, that's all." There was nothing to say. "Please tell me exactly how it was," Momma was asking. "I don't want to think I may turn a corner and find him coming. I don't want to think if we look in just one more town, we shall find him." "We will not find him, Momma," I said, and I told her about the day. We fell asleep crying in each other's arms, with sounds of the door opening a bit and closing a bit; the rest of them were watching.

Emmanuel came back with his wife, Genya, and a baby named Lyuba tied to his back by a cloth. There was a flurry of excitement. Then it was as if each of us just moved down a step in a line waiting for something to happen. Stajoe began going out with Anzia; none of us paid much attention. Momma was right. Now it was how to feed Ninka, how to get a doctor for Lyuba who was always crying and bloated. Anzia was making Mischa soups with one potato and heaps of salt she got somewhere; he was getting better and better. But he did not look twelve, almost thirteen; he looked twenty. The fat little boy with the brown curls and red cheeks had gone on in a wagon, leaving this. It was odd how much he looked like Poppa; before, it was always, "He's the image of you, Momma." "Anya," Stajoe called me over, coming home, "I met a Christian woman; she knows about things before they happen; she's German. They probably planted her here. She can get us out with visas. She gave me a whole basket of food, eggs, bread, some butter, cheese, everything. She can get us out with the visas." "I told you," I said wearily, "either all of us or none of us. Or not me," I added; "I wouldn't stop you." "Listen, she says we're in terrible danger. There is something doing about the children, or there

209

will be something, and she knows a good farmer and his wife who would take care of Ninka until this is over. Please, for Ninka's sake, what do you say?" If he had plunged a fork into my heart, I could have stood it better. "It's for her sake," he insisted; "this woman says she'll be killed if we keep her. You don't want that." "I'll think it over and tell you tonight," I answered. Stajoe looked at me oddly, but he didn't say anything.

I already had a plan, but I wouldn't tell Stajoe about it; he would laugh at me. "Everything for safety," he said, coming into our room. I went into the kitchen, picked up a couple of eggs and a few slices of bread, some of whatever we had. In Vilno, there was a Yeshiva student who read Cabala. The whole city talked about him. He was marvelous; he knew all the mysteries; everyone said he could look at your hand and tell your future. When I was working for Doctor Gershovitz, I met a Hungarian diplomat who wanted to marry me, but, I don't know why, I was suspicious. "Write me a letter some time," I asked flirting. When I got it, I took it to the Cabalist. He took it. As if he were reading, he said, "This man is under the influence of dope; he's gone through a big sickness. It's not his fault, but because of it, he's addicted." Then I found out the diplomat had an abscess in his rectum, and Doctor Gershovitz had given him morphine for the awful pains; he was addicted to it. I remembered going through the files, and finding his. It was frightening. So now I would go again.

I walked all the way. I didn't see anything but Ninka's face, floating in front of me like a cloud my hand would go through if I reached out for it. I came to the worst section of the city—narrow dirty streets, crumbling houses, windows smashed, paper dipped in fat covering the windows. He was in the basement of the fourth house on the block. There were several bleached-out children in the basement apartment with him. "Do you remember me?" I asked. He shook his head yes. "I have something of terrible importance to ask you," I blurted out. "Sit down, dear," he said from his bed, his hand playing on his blanket, so dirty it was black, a black claw. "Tell me," he whispered to save breath; "what is it?" "My husband," I said, "knows a German woman living in Vilno who says the children will be killed. He says we should give Ninka to a farmer. I don't want to give her away, but I don't know what's right." "I will tell you," he said, "but first, some questions. I have to ask the questions, and then I answer them myself. If I don't give the right answers, I have no right to give you advice. Which child are you?" he asked, staring at me. "The second; is that right?" he asked. I nodded. "How many sisters do you have? One," he answered; "is that right?" I nodded again. "How old are you? Twenty-three. Is that right?" I nodded, amazed. "Then," he said, "you must not give her away. It would be different if there was an order, like in the time of Moses, but there is no such order. If there is no order that the children be killed, the child should stay with its mother." "I'm so relieved," I told him, grasping his hand; "you have no idea. I've had needles and pins in my head all day." "Oh," he said, "I won't survive what's coming, not for long. But you will survive all the troubles, you and your child."

I floated home. "Stajoe," I told him, "I've decided. Ninka is coming with me." He was furious. "But *I* am going to be saved," he retorted, turning red. "Then go to the woman," I told him. She was in love with him all right. The next morning, the neighbors began coming in: "They are building something; they are building something." "What, what?" Momma kept asking. "Oh, I don't know, a big fence." "I'm going to find out," Stajoe said. "Anya," he said when he came back, "they're building a ghetto. They're putting us all in it, in not more than a week. Please, think again. Take Ninka and come with me to the woman's." "I cannot," I said, crying; "I cannot." "*Leave* her and come with me," he begged; "we'll come back for her when it's over. They'll come and take you and put you in the ghetto. That's what it is. They are fencing off the worst streets in the city. There isn't enough room for all of us; they'll have to kill and kill. Please, think again, come." "I cannot," I cried; "I cannot." "Do you know what you are doing?" he demanded. "You are sentencing us all to the ghetto. I *have* to stay out. I have to do something for you; I can only do it from outside." "Then go stay with the woman," I told him. I was calm. "I am going now," he said; "if you change your mind, Anzia can bring you." "I will not change it," I told him and he left.

So we waited. "Now it comes," Momma said. "It's almost a relief; at last it comes." But nothing happened. Then, Wednesday morning, we were up after another sleepless night, dressed, wandering through the rooms, when the peasants fell in like a swarm of black bees filling

211

the house. The apartment filled with their sharp acrid odor like a cloud. "The kitchen, the kitchen!" they kept crying. Most of all they wanted the pots, then the towels. We were pressed against walls watching. We might not have been there, not people at all, just spirits. One huge dirty hand ripped the curtains from the glass door to the dining room. "I am keeping these towels," Anzia was shouting; "you can kill me first, I am a Catholic woman, idiots!" "She can have her share," a heavy voice called out. An elbow went through the mahogany credenza in the white dining room. "Silver! Silver!" the shout went up. The women were in the bedrooms, swarming, blankets, blankets, blankets. Anzia was all over, getting what she could. Then they were gone.

"Listen, Mrs. Savikin," Anzia said urgently, "the peasants always know first. Today they are coming to get you. One of them told me, if they find you with any jewelry, they'll kill you." Momma looked down at her rings, her wedding ring, Russian gold, reddish. "So," Momma said, "so, keep everyone out of the kitchen. Anya, come on." Momma was only four foot eight, Vera, four foot nine; I was the tall one, five foot one. "I'm going to climb up on top of the stove and pull out some of those tiles. Look under the sink. I mixed up some cement; it's in a bowl covered with a towel, all the way in the back, behind the brick part that sticks out. I'm putting in all my rings, and this picture of you; see I have it." She fished it out of her pocket. It was me at my fifth birthday party, my hair all in little braids like a cake, in my dress with the little wings. "Do you want to put anything in?" "My diploma, and my index from the university; I'll get them." I ran out. "Anything else?" Momma asked. "Are you putting in your wedding ring?" I asked her. "Yes," Momma said, "it's only jewelry, and the big diamond, and Poppa's rings." "Then I'll put mine in, too." I could see Momma hesitate; she was standing on a tower of things, the kitchen table, a little chest, then a chair. "All right," she said finally. She stuffed the things behind the three green tiles, then plastered them up. "That's good," I told her. "It's stupid, isn't it," she asked, climbing down, "how even in this bitterness there's this thread of hope, the idea that someone will come back." "Jakob is burying things in the yard." "They'll find them," Momma said; "they always found things in Russia. Dogs like to dig."

And late in the afternoon they came for us. "Out," a

soldier ordered. By now, the streets were lined on both sides with men holding machine guns. "In the middle of the street, walk," they ordered, and we walked, me and Momma and Ninka, then Vera and Jakob and Mischa, Genya and Emmanuel and Lyuba. There was only the sound of our feet, no *drozhkas,* no iron wheels on stones, nothing, only our feet; suddenly we were walking in a picture without sound. "Stajoe will help us," Momma promised. "Maybe he'll be the one who is saved," I said, "but I'm going with my family." Momma shook her head again. "We are too close," she said again and again, "too close."

And Stajoe was with the German woman. He had been with her for two days. We walked on and on, in the middle of the street like cattle. And then came the worst section of the city, and there was the fence. "In," the soldier ordered. We found some steps in an old building, and sitting in tiers fell asleep. And as I fell asleep the picture of the streets packed with people, bobbing and jostling, melted together, grafted together, all shades of black and gray and blue, over again and over again. "We have a room," Jakob said, coming back, and I will never forget it, the sight that filled the room. We were replacing other people; we were like pieces in a machine. On the table of the room were unfinished bits of bread; there were diapers hanging from ropes in the corners; some of the bunk beds were still warm. I walked around like a zombie in a trance. Sounds from the walk to the room were beginning to come back to me, as if it were a whole life flashing before a drowning man who had somehow reached the wrong shore. I could hear the marching, see the little packages everyone carried. The babies were crying; the Gestapo were shooting into the air; there were no noises, just the silence of the world ending. And no sooner did we look around, and no sooner did it begin to get dark, and the room to fill with cold, than the Gestapo ordered us to obey the Committee of Jews. Gestapo orders would be given to us through them. "So," Momma kept saying, rocking Ninka, "so." And we were all afraid to sleep. It was very late when the door opened. "They have come for us," Momma whispered, but it was Stajoe. All day he had watched from a window while we walked down the middle of the street, the packages, the crying babies. "I had to come," he said coming to me, crying. He and Momma and I formed a closed circle, with Ninka somewhere in between. "The people who were just here before went to Panari," he said. "The canister the Russians used there to hold gasoline is very good for blood. The German woman will try to bring us food, and Anzia will, too. They'll come to the fence." He was still crying. What had I done?

12

STAJOE and Momma had fallen asleep on the floor exhausted, with Ninka between them. I knew there were many more people in the room, and it seemed to me I could hear all their breathing, as if the room were a gigantic heart, holding us all in like a dangerous clot. I went to the window and stood there. Momma and Stajoe and Ninka were sleeping on their cots not more than three feet from the window. I could make out the shapes of the other bodies sleeping on the floor. "Those are the only bodies I care about," I said to myself; "and Verushka and Mischa and Emmanuel. The only ones." Through the window I could see the little gate in the wooden fence that surrounded the ghetto. The moon was hanging like a brilliant cold coin worth nothing at all. I kept watching the gate, expecting it to open. Outside, nothing moved, not even the shadows. The day had smashed in front of me like a broken dish; the world had smashed in front of me like a broken dish, the scenes of our lives painted on its rim. The longer I looked at the gate, the colder I got. Pieces, splinters, kept returning to me. Now I could see Verushka backing away from the peasants toward the wall, backwards, like a crab; when her back touched the wall, her face was absolutely without expression. And the cheese Momma had wrapped in her scarf, where had she gotten it? I could see the dirtiest, loudest peasant looking at me holding my child; "Here," he barked. He threw me a piece of bread. Another man saw him; he threw a piece of bread. So we got our crumbs.

How did I know Anzia would come to the wall? She had whispered it to me before we left; "Don't carry too much, Anya; you have the baby. I have all your dresses under the straw in the goose pen." "Ach, Anzia," I said to myself. She had always worried more than Momma, but her worries were like horses; they pulled actions behind them. So I looked at the fence. She would not come tonight. She would wait and see what happened. Veruska was not with us. Even coming here, she and Jakob had walked behind us, holding to every private minute. I had not carried Ninka all the way. A young man had taken her from me to carry; he said his name was Arthur. Arthur. He had made a chocolate paste of sugar and butter; he gave it all to Ninka. But when he got to our room, I didn't want him to come in with us. He understood. He would be a friend. Verushka was somewhere in another room. I had asked Momma something about it. "It is understood," she said; "we would embarrass them, such a crazy love," and she went on rocking Ninka back and forth, and rocking herself like the old men in the Chasidic houses, bending from the waist, her back straight.

And again and again the vision of the peasants in the apartment: like vultures, like vultures. They were robbing our house as if they were plundering our graves; we all stood there watching. It made no difference to them. According to the peasants, we were already dead. We were only spirits. Logically, we were already dead. "It is no small thing," I thought to myself, "the intuition of peasants." I felt my arm; it was there. I felt my pulse. It beat. Stajoe's arm went around my shoulder; his voice slid into my ear. "Come to bed," he said. I went and lay down on the floor. I pushed my head into his chest; eyes open or shut, I could see only the gate in the wooden fence. "There will come a time when the living will envy the dead." "No," I said to myself, "no," as if it were up to me to decide. Stajoe's breathing had become regular; I felt it and listened to it until I was asleep.

And then there was a thundering sound of static that exploded into a voice; we all woke up. Outside, it was pitch dark. "Come and register; come to the Judenrat and register," the loudspeaker voice commanded with enthusiasm; "we have jobs, we need people, come and register." "Let's go," Stajoe urged me, reaching across for Ninka. "No, children," Momma said; "not the first time. Go to sleep. Wait. Maybe the jobs are too hard for you. There'll be plenty of time for jobs." All around us we could hear the rustling sound of people getting up, muttering excuses as one blundered into another, and then the thunder of shoes on the stairs; they were going to the Judenrat for jobs. "Stay, sleep, wait," Momma said; "they'll find us jobs." Stajoe started to say something, then changed his mind. We all lay down. Then Momma's voice came again.

216

"If everyone is looking for jobs, maybe there's a better room. We should go see." "I'll go," Stajoe said, and went to look. "Just down the hall," he told us when he came back all excited, "is a room with a sink and bathroom and a hotplate that looks good." "Let's go," Momma agreed.

Immediately, that was our home. Again, we were asleep on the floor. In the morning when we woke up, the room was not nearly as crowded as the one we had been in first. "Something happened," Momma whispered; "something happened." "Maybe they just sent them to work outside," Stajoe suggested. "The jobs outside the ghetto are better; there are more contacts, more chances." "God forbid you should have such contacts," Momma murmured, getting up. "Oh," she complained, "I am sore." I was amazed; Momma never complained. "It's very quiet," I wondered. An old woman and her two daughters sat on the floor across the room; they kept to themselves. "We shouldn't go out until we hear something," Momma said; "too quiet; we have to wait; steps, something." She seemed to be listening. We sat still for hours. Ninka began to cry from hunger. I gave her a bit of bread smeared with chocolate. I told Stajoe about Arthur, and how he had helped me carry her. "Was he in that room?" he asked me. "No, somewhere in the building." More silence. Finally, we heard voices on the steps, women's voices; one was laughing. "I'll go," Momma said. She shut the door behind her. When she came in, she had aged twenty years. "They were all killed," she told us, crying; "five thousand killed. Everyone who went last night went straight to Panari; they killed them there."

An hour later, Verushka knocked at the door; Jakob followed her in. "You didn't go?" Momma asked numbly. "Oh, no," Vera said. "Jakob wants a job with the Gestapo, an engineer, he says we'll have better conditions, and I would like to try the piano, teaching it." "Who has a piano?" I practically screamed at her. "Who wants to play? You are crazy." Then, because I couldn't believe it, how I had screamed, I started to cry. "Don't worry, Anya, don't worry," Vera said coming over and putting her arms around me from behind; "I don't really want to work yet; you don't want to work yet, with Ninka; look she's starting to walk." Ninka had spotted her and was clambering up Momma like a plant up a trellis, stopping to wave an arm in Vera's direction and give a high-pitched shriek. "You will have plenty to do, cooking, all that." "What cooking?" I asked her sadly. "Anzia will come; you'll see," she told me. She had the faith of a child. "And Jakob found out there is a ration for us, every three days, but someone has to stand on line, so it's better we don't work for a while. Look," she said, running to it, "your room has a little balcony; Ninka can play on it. Ours has one, too," she said, pleased. "Where is your room?" I asked. "Two floors up," she said, looking up at Jakob and beaming as if she were talking about a marriage *dacha*. Momma couldn't help smiling. "If you have time between lessons, Vera dear, maybe you will visit us?" "I am already here," Vera pouted, "and besides, who knows, the soldiers will want lessons, maybe their children." "You stay away from the soldiers, I warn you," Momma told her loudly. "Jakob, you hear me, keep her away from them; nothing is more dangerous." "Yes, Momushka," he answered; he looked bewildered. "There will be forty in a room," Vera reported, triumphant to have found something out. "Forty!" I repeated in horror. "Yes, forty," Vera said, positive, "and no beds. Jakob has been to the Judenrat and they told him we will have to build our own beds, out of boards: we will have to sleep on our coats and clothes." "Vera," Momma said severely, "this is no picnic, why have you been to the Judenrat already? Did you hear what happened last night? Wait, they will send you an engraved invitation to Panari; there's no need to walk into the lion's teeth like a steak." Jakob was embarrassed. "Nevertheless," he said, "I'm glad we went. I think I'll get a Gestapo job, and we'll be safer. They have a special section for Gestapo workers, better quarters. After I start, you can come live with us." "We will see," Momma said. Stajoe said nothing, watching everything.

"I want to look around for myself," Momma told Vera; "this dove would come back to the ark with a cookie. Jakob," she scolded, "please. She has no sense at all; she is all love. I hope you won't listen to any of her advice." She said it playfully, but she was serious. "Anya," she said, turning on me, "what is the matter with your hair? A woman must always look her best, especially in the worst circumstances. Vera, what happened to your skirt? It's twisted halfway around your body." Vera began tugging at her skirt with both hands; I began combing my hair with my fingers. Both Stajoe and Jakob were smiling. "Look at that unfortunate stove," Momma commented, her eyes on the little electric hotplate in the middle of the big wooden kitchen table sitting in the center of the room. "It is supposed to cook for forty people; I don't envy it at all." "But you have a big Russian stove in the wall," Vera cried. "And what are we to heat it with, Verushka? Air?" Vera fell silent. "Look at that paint," Momma went on. The walls were painted white, but the paint was chipping; little pieces lay all over the floor. Dirt streaked the walls unevenly like mud deposited by a receding tide. "So this is it," Momma sighed; "at least we have a sink and a bathroom." "The pipes will freeze in the winter," Stajoe predicted; "I'll talk to the Judenrat about that. I know what to do about it." "I wish you would all leave the Judenrat alone," Momma worried; "first, let's go out and look." She started down the stairs. We followed her like ducks. "Such stairs," Momma called back to Stajoe. "As long as you're risking your life, tell the Judenrat about lighting the stairs. Also Ninka mustn't eat the paint chips; we will have to get it off the walls where it's loose." "Why?" I demanded. "Poison," Stajoe answered for her; "lead, no one can eat the paint. No matter how hungry they get." "But we will get food; Vera said so," I protested. "You should know in case; it doesn't hurt to know." "I don't want to know anything else," Vera complained. "Neither do I," I chimed in; "not for four more hours." "Like medicine, Anya?" Vera asked. "Like medicine," I answered.

"Well, these houses are something," Momma said, looking around. They were tiny and dark and seemed to tilt in all directions, holding on to each other for support. "How far do you think we are from home, Momma?" "About ten blocks," she said. "This is the poor section, the old Jewish section. It looks like it's been buried for a long time," she finished. "Where is the Judenrat Committee Office?" she asked. "Two blocks back, near the café," Jakob told her. "Café?" Momma asked, surprised. "Yes, nothing but tea; people go out at night and talk." "I can imagine what about," Momma said. "Are we allowed to look through the fence?" "Oh, yes," Vera said; "I already did." "She already did," Momma murmured in despair. "What did you see?" "A lot of Christian people looking in. A woman told us," she said, beaming at Jakob, "that if you have friends outside, they come to the wall and call whoever is near, and that person comes and gets you. That's how Anzia will get us." "Fine," Momma said; "fine." "These are very twisty streets," Vera went on, "dangerous at night. Jakob and I went out for a walk last night and could hardly find our way back." Momma was beyond saying anything; she was glaring at Jakob. He would hear from her later. We walked all over; three little streets in all, fenced off; there was not much. "A new transport is coming today, from the suburbs," Vera volunteered. "Listen, children," Momma said, "this place is very small and there are a lot of people. They will kill off the extras and the idiots. We aren't carpenters or furriers; they won't care about us. The last thing they want around are intellectuals. We will have to be very careful. There will be more tricks," she was thinking out loud, "a lot of tricks; don't do anything right away." Now Vera was listening. It was occurring to her: They might kill Jakob! Jakob! "And Vera," Momma ordered, *fix your skirt!*"

"What about Emmanuel and Mischa?" Vera finally asked; we were still looking around. "What about them?" Momma asked absently. She knew they wouldn't have been in a hurry to find work until they found her. "Mischa said he would be back to stay with us when we came in last night. He wouldn't go off; neither would Emmanuel. They're all right. We'll find them somewhere sooner or later. Mischa is probably resting." "He knows where we are," Vera said; "I told him to go to sleep near the balcony, for air, when he came in." "And where did you put yourselves?" Momma asked, laughing at her. "On the other side," Vera answered, innocent.

"Listen," Momma told us when we got back to the room, "as long as that new transport isn't here yet, we might as well try to get as many of us in the room as we can. Vera doesn't want to come, but we should get Mischa and Emmanuel. You can share taking care of the babies," she told me. "You can get to know Genya, your brother's a stranger to you by now. I wish I knew where Rachel was," she sighed. "We could get Rachel or Max. The more of us there are, the less fighting—strangers fight more." "If we went to the cafe," I said, thinking, "we might see her, or find out about her; Emmanuel, too." Momma nodded. "What do you think?" she asked Stajoe. "We won't be able to fill the room, but we should do the best we can. I'll get Mischa," he said, leaving. "If you can hold Ninka, I can hold you both," Momma said to Mischa when he came down. "Oh, Momma, I'm too big for that," Mischa complained gruffly. "Let me try anyhow," Momma insisted.

"What have you got to eat?" he asked. "We have some farmer cheese and bread; what do you have?" Momma asked. "Four hard-boiled eggs," he announced, a conquering hero. Later in the afternoon we heard the rumble of trucks coming up to the gate. Our room was right over the *torovaje*, the military checkpoint for the whole ghetto. "There's a church ten feet on the other side of that gate," Momma murmured to herself. "Don't torture yourself," I begged her. "Oh, I'm not doing that. It's just that it might be useful; you never know. But still, it seems cruel. Stajoe," she went on, "am I wrong, or did I last hear your voice sometime during the winter?" "I'm thinking about my family," he answered her. "They are all together; it will be easier for them," I said. "The five thousand people were all together last night," he said bitterly. "Leave him alone," Momma whispered to me.

That was the end of whispering. We stood on the balcony and watched the gate open. Thousands and thousands of people were pouring in, shoving and pushing, shouting, babies screaming. So this is what we had looked like last night, coming in. Then there was the noise on the stairs. "In!" a soldier boomed. Ten people came in; then two more flew into the room, stumbling into the others. The soldier had pushed them from behind. Everyone stared at every else suspiciously. The old woman and her two daughters had not moved once since we arrived. "How long do you think we'll be here?" I whispered to Stajoe. "With the devil's luck, until the war ends." "That could be years!" I moaned. "I would say three," he estimated; his blue eyes shone cold. "Three years here!" I gasped. None of the new ones looked at me; only one man turned his head a little. "Come," Momma said; "let's go out on the balcony; we should get all the air and sun we can. Such a sad child," she said, looking at Ninka; "she hardly ever smiles anymore." "Vera will come and play with her," I promised. "Vera," Momma sighed.

The day went on. We could see the roof of the church over the wooden fence. "I think," Momma said, "I'm going to go down and look for Anzia. She would probably come around dinner time; she's so used to feeding us." "I think I'll go to the Judenrat," Stajoe said. I was left with the baby and Mischa. I felt complete panic. I hugged Ninka to me so hard she screamed. I let her go and looked at her; she looked just like Stajoe. "There will be classes for the little ones," Mischa said; "as soon as she

221

gets old enough she can go." Almost thirteen years old. I looked at him; I didn't know what to say.

"What did I tell you?" Momma said, coming back in, panting and panting from the climb. "Here is your blue dress, and some lipstick and brassieres, some dresses for Vera and me, and a pound of cottage cheese and bacon. We'd better hide the food, or keep it with us," she told me, looking around. "Anzia says she will come whenever she can, but to the side, not right in front. Right now, she says, there are so many people who want to see what's going on, no one notices anything, but they will later. Also, she's getting married." Momma was bubbling with gossip as if she had just come back from a café. Married! "Anzia always used to say what for," I objected. "What for? Because she had us," Momma answered; "she doesn't have us now. She's marrying the cucumber man. Remember, you wanted to know how she got everything from the greenhouses in the back? That's how." Married! "What next?" I asked her. "Oh, you will see," Momma told me; "people will get married in here, in these houses made of coal; life goes on." "We are animals; we're all animals," Mischa said. Momma considered him. "Eat some of the bacon," she said finally; "eat and try to sleep." "Who can sleep in here?" he asked her. "Listen to the noise; no one is even shouting yet." "Why should they shout?" Momma asked him, watching. "Wait until morning when everyone has to use that hotplate and that bathroom," he predicted darkly. "And then?" Momma asked. "And then," Mischa said, "because there's only one of each, we will all rip ourselves to pieces trying to get it; we may even break the hotplate trying to get it." "Is that how it will be?" Momma asked. "Yes you'll see," he answered with absolute certainty. *"Bozhe moy,"* Momma murmured under her breath. She had never asked him much about his life in Russia; he never wanted to talk about it.

Stajoe came back. The door kept opening and closing like an open barn door in a gale. One person or another was going out or coming in, looking for someone, for a job, getting air, just standing on the steps. The door that had opened so many times finally opened to Stajoe's hand. "There are forty of us here," I thought again, in disbelief. "I have the job," he said, "an engineer at the radio station in the city. Oh, it's very good," he went on. "I will have news of the war, we couldn't get it otherwise, and outside contacts. I'll have a pass to go out. The woman will help us, you'll see. And," he turned to Momma, "Emmanuel is here somewhere; and another little lady named Lyuba and Lyubashka, both, and Genya. I'll go out to look for him again." "I will come too," Momma cried. "No, you stay here," Stajoe ordered her. "It will be better for you if you can go to the café tonight and listen and ask questions and maybe find Rachel for Anya." He went out again.

"That door is driving me crazy; it's like watching a piece of paper caught in a wind and any minute it's going to blow away." "You had better start thinking a new way," she said, "or you *will* go crazy. Think instead that it's not locked." "The people from the other rooms don't come in here," I wondered out loud; "there are five rooms in this apartment." "Like five countries," Mischa said; "no one will open another door. Why should they? Are things any better on the other side of the door? This way it's your home; at least you know who's a stranger." I stared at him. I almost wished he wouldn't say a word; his every sentence made me want to pull clumps of hair from my head.

Stajoe came back with Emmanuel and Genya and their little baby, Lyuba. She was a tall striking brunette. She adored Emmanuel. She wasn't very intelligent, but she adored Emmanuel and the baby; that was enough for him. And she was always very neat, dressed in her pride as his wife. It was impossible not to like her and impossible to be interested in her. But now we had the two babies as a common cause; we would be allies.

"Momushka, come on the balcony a minute," Stajoe called. Momma went after him with Ninka. "Just a piece of candy," he said shyly; "it fell down on the rug in the Committee's Office, so I pretended to drop something myself, and got it." "So it begins," Momma said sadly, taking it. "Please eat it," he begged her. "Sto, Sto," Ninka said suddenly. It was the very first time she'd really tried to speak. Vera thought she might start with her first word when she was ready; "Maybe when she's eight," she had said. Oh, I had worried! Everyone turned to me, amazed. We knew she was precocious. "Sto, Sto," she said again, then, more loudly, "food." Everyone turned in her direction. "Don't give it to her," Stajoe whispered to Momma. "It's too hard; she'll choke on it." "Sto, sto, food, food," Ninka kept repeating with something like triumph, and louder and louder, her little face turning red, "food, food, food!" There were angry mutters in the room. "I'll give

223

her some cheese," Momma said in a hurry, popping the candy into her own mouth slyly; "food, Ninka," she whispered, and Ninka shut off like a machine.

"Tomorrow there'll be a ration line," Stajoe promised me; "there'll be something to eat. And I can get something outside now. Anzia will bring things, and I can exchange them when I go out." "I have some underwear," I was thinking; I didn't need all of it. "The peasants will want that," he said with satisfaction; "do you think Anzia could get me a worker's outfit? It's safer that way." He meant he wanted a worker's cap, a short jacket, and high boots. "Oh, yes, she can." I knew about Anzia and her ways. "As soon as it gets dark, we'll go to the café. I hope Rachel has no children. It's been so long since I've seen her, not since our wedding. It's not so bad for us, but the children, I don't like it; it's the worst part."

"I don't like the others in here," I worried; "a very low class of people. I don't even know if we can trust them. Mischa says there'll be a lot of fighting." "There is already," Stajoe told me; "listen." Inside, a man was screaming at a woman. "You'll sleep under your own coat! I told you to take something warmer. It's your fault. Get away from me!" Stajoe pointed again. It was a man screaming at his wife; their two children just stared. "We can eat on our beds when we build them," Stajoe said; "then we can stay out of their way. Also, I heard some gossip at the Committee. They have what they call *actions*. They get orders from the Gestapo to eliminate so many people. They come for the old ones, or the sick ones, expecially the ones who don't work. We have to find a place to hide your mother until they're over.'" "How do we know when?" I asked, terrified. "They don't have any schedule; sometimes every two weeks, sometimes every day, sometimes, if they don't get enough one day, they finish the next. So if we hear anything strange, or that something is starting in another street, that's enough."

"In the oven," I said; "we can hide her in the oven." "Where?" he asked me. "Where they put the wood." I was thinking about Anzia hiding our dresses in the goose pen. "We'll be getting some wood to build beds, and now I'm commandant of the building; that might give us some co-operation from the others." "Commandant?" I asked in disbelief. "Fuses. From the minute Ganz found out I knew about pipes and fuses; they're blowing all the time, no one knows how to change them. I'll teach you, just in case. I think we can save some of the wood to put in front of your mother." "But Ninka will run to the stove," I cried out. "Those days you'll have to stay home and stop her. It's getting dark; let's leave the babies with Genya and go to the café. Maybe we'll find out something." Genya was not very adventurous; she preferred to stay where she was. "Where is it?" "Near the Judenrat; just a big room, a samovar, some weak tea, not much." Momma went with us. There were no lights on the street; voices poured out of windows like garbage. I tried imagining how many people were in each building and gave up. "How many people are here?" "Let's put it this way," Stajoe said; "in the winter it won't be very cold, there will be so many bodies heating the room. And no other heat."

The café was on the street level, one big dirty room, a lot of rickety wooden chairs and tables. In the middle of it was the samovar, a beautiful brass samovar that looked as if it came from Tulla in Russia. "Why didn't they take that?" I whispered to Stajoe. I was remembering Jakob packing the silver from the house into shopping bags, the candelabra, knives, forks. The little basket with the animals was about to go in. "No," Momma said, "this is for Anzia." She gave it to her. "It's for you, unless we come back." Anzia took it. "It will be safe with her," Momma said sadly. Then Jakob stood on line, just as he had waited at the bank, to turn in the silver and jewels. But Stajoe had managed to get some to the German woman. He would be able to have her exchange them for food. "What time is it?" I asked. He looked at his watch. It was a pocket watch. He had wound the gold chain around his wrist; it was the only watch he had left. "Seven." "Why didn't they take that?" I repeated again. "They do what they want; they don't have any principles, just rules. When there's an action, the Jewish police have to select the victims; that's a rule." "The Jews have to do it?" "The Jews." "I can't stand it!" I cried. "That's what the café is here for; they still need us for some things." He was bitter. But he was not blaming me by even one syllable.

Inside, the room was heaving like the deck of a ship packed solid with people. Even if Rachel was here, how would I find her? "Anya! Anya!" I heard a hysterical voice calling. It was Rachel. How she had changed! She had moved away from Vilno after her marriage. Her figure was gone entirely. On top she was flat as a board, and thin, but from beneath her tiny waist she looked like an onion; then came two thin legs. We fell on each other like two cut trees. "I'm pregnant," she sobbed, "pregnant; did you ever hear anything so stupid?" She was starting to laugh uncontrollably. "Stop, Rachel, stop," I begged her; she always listened to me. "Where's your husband?" "They're all dead," she wailed; "all except me, all. They sent them into the little ghetto for the sick and the old ones. The Cabalist, you remember him; he went too. They wouldn't let me go, just for spite. I wanted to go with them; they wouldn't let me." "You are the only one left?" I couldn't believe it. "The only one," she said, "and this baby." "Rachel," I promised her, "I'll get a job in the Jewish Hospital. We want you to come live with us. Will you come?" "Thank you, thank you, thank you," she kept sobbing.

"We'd better go," Momma murmured. "What's this about a hospital job?" Stajoe asked me; "you didn't say anything about it." "It's the first time *I've* heard about it; come, let's take her home." "You go," he said, hugging me, then Momma. "Maybe I can find something out." Momma was doing her best to comfort Rachel. "Tomorrow we'll have it, Mischa's morning," she whispered to me. I felt a real chill; my nipples swelled against my blouse. I felt everyone's fingers and eyes on me; how would we get dressed? "We sleep in our clothes," Momma said; "it won't be so bad." "Sometimes I think there's a glass window in my head you look through," I told her. "Sometimes you do. I thank God everyone doesn't." So we went back.

In the morning, whoever went to work had to be up at four-thirty. It was amazing how quickly we were organized. The patrols were waiting downstairs at six to escort the groups to their different places of work. But we were all up at four-thirty, whether we were working or not. Once people began getting up, it was impossible to sleep. "Now watch," Mischa said; "everyone will want something hot to drink." "Hurry up," Mr. Grimonsky was screaming at his wife. "What's the matter with you; you're so slow. Did you have to use such a big pot, what are you going to do, give some to everyone?" Mrs. Grimonsky looked desperate and turned up the dial. The pot began to boil faster; then it boiled over. Immediately, the little hotplate stopped working. "Why did you do that?" someone else started screaming; "what are the rest of us supposed to do now? You better give us that pot." Someone was grabbing at it. "Don't touch it," Mr. Grimonsky threatened. Someone's hand came out for the pot. Mrs. Grimonsky pushed it away; she hit the handle with her hand. The water spilled, half into the coils, half on the table, spilling in little waterfalls onto the floor. "Clean it up, you rat!" she started screaming. "You clean it!" another woman screamed; "you're hogging the whole stove!"

Outside it was still dark; one naked light bulb was hanging over the round table like a dead embryo. Rachel was sitting on the floor wrapped in her coat, shuddering. Suddenly, the light went out. "Look what you did!" Mrs. Grimonsky screamed like a crazy woman. "You made the fuse blow out; now we don't even have light!" We heard the sound of someone retching. Then Mr. Grimonsky was screaming. "Clean it up, you pig; it's all over the floor!" "You clean it up," a thin old voice screamed back; "you make me sick!" "I'm taking Ninka out on the balcony," Momushka said. I sat on the floor with my arm around Rachel; she was trembling all over. "Never mind," I told her; "they'll be gone to work soon; they'll be gone; it's almost time. Come out on the balcony," I coaxed her; "come on." "I don't know," Momma was saying; "I don't know. Where is Mischa?" "He went over to Jakob to see if he could get him a job." "Go and see Vera," Momma asked me.

I climbed up the two flights. There was the same din, the same fighting over the fuses, the bathroom, the hotplate. "But I'm bursting; what do you want me to do, do my business all over the floor?" a man was shouting. Vera was sitting on her coat next to Jakob, watching him drink some tea. "I got up at three-thirty," she said proudly, but I could tell she wasn't glad to see me, not until Jakob was gone. "I'm sorry for interrupting, Vera," I said, "but Momma was worried about Mischa." "Oh, she doesn't have to worry," Vera cried; "Jakob is an engineer for the Gestapo. He'll be going outside and get some more food, you know, all that, and," she said proudly, "he's going to tell them he needs Mischa and Emmanuel to help him. He's doing very valuable work." "Not too valuable, I hope." "Oh, Anya, he's a good man; what's wrong with you?" "I'll be right down," Vera promised fervently. "Today is the ration day; I want to get on the line early." "We'll go together, and Rachel," I promised. "You found Rachel?" Vera thrilled; "how's her husband; how's her mother?" "We'll talk about it later; you drink your tea with Jakob."

"Gestapo," I told Momma when I came down; "Jakob has a Gestapo job." "I don't like it," Momma said; "the further we stay away from them the better." "They will have more advantages," Stajoe said. "But they're right under Gestapo's noses; it's better sometimes to stay away and do without the extra potato." "We can't do anything about it," I said. There were more horrible screams from the corner; the daughters were fighting with Mr. Grimonsky. "It hasn't stopped yet?" I asked. "The fuse blew twice more when you were gone," Stajoe told me; "it's gotten worse. Well," he bent over to kiss me, "I have to leave. Have a good day on the line." "Be careful," I pleaded with him. "What can I do to get into trouble?" "Don't try exchanging things, not for a few weeks." He promised. "At least not until Anzia gets the workman's clothes." "Understood," he said, turning to leave.

"Thank God they are going," Momma muttered as the men began to leave. Mr. Grimonsky tried to slam the door, but someone grabbed it before it closed. The room emptied like a crazy train station. The old woman sat across the room, a pool of vomit in front of her. "You clean it," one daughter was screaming at the other. "I do everything; you do it!" the other yelled back. The old woman began retching again. "Look what you are doing to Momma!" the first one screamed. "They are disgusting," Momma said. "No one bothers to flush the toilet," she sighed. "It's a good thing we're the ones who got here first, near the windows; I don't think your sensitive nose would be able to breathe."

Rachel was stretched out on her cot, sobbing quietly. "It hurts all the time," she complained. "What does?" Momma asked her. "My stomach; should it hurt all the time?" Momma looked at me. "Sometimes; it's natural," I lied; "the position of the baby, it turns after a while, you know; then you feel better. Do you want to come with us for food?" "No, I'd rather stay here and sleep." Momma raised her eyebrows. "Go with Vera," she whispered; "I'll stay with her." "Where is Genya?" I asked, "and Lyubushka?" "Already on line. She'll try to save you a place, but the others won't let you in. Go get your sister; Jakob must have gone. And first bring her here; I want to see what the two of you look like." "What should we look like?" I cried; "this isn't exactly normal; I can't even

228

wash." "You can comb your hair, and you can wash. I have a little water—we can all use it—and this rag and a piece of soap; I got it from Anzia. What's this about working at the hospital?" "I was thinking about it," I answered guiltily. "But that would leave you and Genya with the babies." "It will be better for you," Momma said quietly. "You can wash there, and if anyone here gets sick, it will be better for us if you're there. Try and get the job. I just don't know what to do with Rachel." "Who will get the food?" "Genya and I will get the food."

Vera came down. "What are you trying to do, Vera?" Momma demanded; "be a hotel for bedbugs? Comb your hair. I don't know what's wrong with the two of you." "You're not making Rachel dress up," Vera sulked. "Never mind Rachel," Momma said; Momma's face had gotten so yellow; "I'll wash Rachel myself. Do I have to take a rag to you?" "Why should I look like nothing's happened, Momma?" I shouted; "it's a curse!" All of a sudden I was furious at her and Vera together. Momma just stared at me. But I didn't want to add to her troubles; she looked so old all at once. I would do what she said. "Here," Momma said, inspecting me; "put on this gold watch, rub your shoes with this rag before you go to the hospital. You want them to know you're coming for a job, not an injection. Go on, go on."

Near the café was a long line. Genya waved to us, but when we tried to get near her, everyone began shouting and pushing us. We went to the back. "Genya looks so pretty sometimes," I said, "and so tall." "Just look at *her* hair," Vera grumped; "it looks like she poured gasoline all over it." "You could use some on yours." In the hot wind, Vera's hair was flying all over. "You'd better start pinning it up; we won't get to wash it often." "I can't see anything," Vera complained; "I wonder what we're going to get." She kept dancing out to the very edge of the line. "We're almost there; you can't see because your hair is in your eyes." "I can't see because I'm so short."

"Name, please," the man at the table said. "Vera Kornfeld," she said proudly. "Here you are. Name, please." "Anya Lavinsky." "Here you are." He handed me a huge package. "What have you got?" I asked Vera, enjoying the suspense. "Some bones, a little meat, a few pieces of bread, and a carrot. Yours is so big!" she wailed; "open it up." Inside the white paper was a horse's head. Vera grabbed my arm; I was swaying. "I think we had better see

229

Momma about how to cook this," she was saying through a tunnel; "Momma will know how."

"It could be worse, it could be worse," Momma judged. "We just have to skin it, take out the eyes, so the men don't see them; it will give us plenty to eat." "Who will skin it?" I asked weakly. "I will," Rachel answered unexpectedly from the floor; "I will." "Anya," Momma said, "when it's two o'clock, tell me; I want to look for Anzia. We need sugar and bread and some onions, mostly onions." Momma came back at three. "She wasn't there, but she'll be there tomorrow. Stop it, Vera; it's no tragedy, nothing to carry on about. You'll see, she'll come tomorrow. Look, the others have fallen asleep," she said gleefully. "Let's get started with all this. We can boil it into a stew; you'll forget what it was, I promise you. Anya, think of it as your revenge on the white horse." "Oh, Momma," I moaned, clutching my stomach. "My apologies," she grinned, advancing on the table.

Genya burst in. "Some meat and bread," she called to us; "and two potatoes." "See," Momma told us, "it's not so bad." "Momma," Vera asked suddenly, "who's that man in the corner?" In the corner of the room was a small man with a dark, pointed beard, bent over something. "I don't know," Momma said. "He doesn't go to work; he wants to write." "Where does he get the paper?" Genya asked. "Someone said it was stolen from the Judenrat," Rachel said weakly. "Interesting," Momma said. "I wonder what he writes? We'll asked him when we finish with all this food." So we got busy. Stajoe came home at six with some sugar and flour. "I'll make that into some pretzels for the babies in the morning," Momma crowed; "oh, that is *very* good." Jakob had some bacon. "I told you," Momma said; "it will not be so bad." And really, we were not living in the narrow, filthy dangerous houses, but in the houses of each other.

The next morning Stajoe woke me up. I could tell it was very early; there wasn't a sound in the room. "I heard something," he said; "and last night in the café, too. We'd better hide your mother." "Momma," I whispered, shaking her, "an action." Stajoe carried a chair over to the Russian stove. "Can you get in without help?" "I can," her voice came back muffled; "I'll get in the back." "What can we put in front of her?" I asked Stajoe. "Bring the pot," he ordered. We put the stew pot in the oven, slightly to the side, as if we were hiding it from the others. "That's it, then," Stajoe said, putting the chair back. We sat down on our coats. "Lie down and pretend to sleep," he ordered me.

In a half hour there were soldiers at the door. "This one!" one pointed at the old woman. "No!" one of the daughters began screaming. "And this one," he said, pointing at the daughter. "All right, two from one room, that's enough!" Ninka was screaming, "Momma! Momma!" She meant my Momma, but the soldiers couldn't know that. Now everyone was up. "Don't let her go out all day," Stajoe warned me. "If you go to the hospital make sure Genya checks her, or Rachel. Put some water in there with her." This was our conversation now, perpetually giving each other instructions. I tried to get up, to go to the balcony to watch him leave, but my legs wouldn't move. He picked me up. "She'll be all right," he said; "she'll be all right. I think you should go to the hospital about that job. Who knows, you might think of some way of letting her in there. They say no one goes too often; they're afraid of the diphtheria patients. You could hide her there when it gets too bad for the stove." I held onto him until I could stand. The others promised they would check on Momma, and I left for the hospital.

The hospital gobbled me up as if I were food. It was inside the ghetto, so I didn't have to worry about getting there on time, or worry about the patrols unless they came at night; I didn't have to leave for work at six with the soldiers patrolling the sidewalk, carrying their guns, while the workers walked in the middle of the street. It was run by a Doctor Yurbo, a famous friend of my father's, and I was busy from the first minute, giving injections, taking blood pressures, even helping with operations. While I was there, I forgot about everything, but as soon as it wasn't busy, it was Momma, Momma, and the child, and then Rachel; what was happening to them?

"I want you to learn surgical massages," Doctor Yurbo said "that way you can get a Gestapo pass and go out by yourself. One of the Gestapo wives always thinks she needs a massage. The pass is a wonderful thing to have; believe me, I know." So I learned. And then a Gestapo wife wanted massages. The first few days, a soldier took me to Mrs. Cibiki's; after that, they let me go alone. I had the pass. "Aren't they afraid you'll run away?" Vera wondered. "Where would I run?" I asked her; "they know about the child." "The child," she repeated. "Ninka is so

231

sad; I think I'll go play with her." "I don't know what you'll do; she has no toys." "Oh," Vera said, "I saved four lima beans, and we found a little cardboard box in the street; it's not a bad rattle." She came down later, and in five minutes, she had Ninka laughing at the sounds. It was a miracle; she never laughed anymore. At night, we had built our bunks; we were finished in three days.

Meanwhile, Rachel was swelling up like a balloon; she was having trouble getting on her shoes. Momma stayed with her. Every night, I went out to the café. Sometimes Stajoe would go, especially if he thought there might be trouble; other times, he stayed inside, sitting under the light bulb reading, reading, whatever he could get his hands on. Then later he would go to the café. "I heard something about the children," he said one night; "they may not be safe very long." "Should I give Lyuba to the nuns?" Genya cried out; "Jakob could still smuggle her out." She had asked me this a hundred times, and a hundred times, I couldn't help it, my face would pucker up as if I were going to cry. She saw it, and she could never make up her mind. "Should I give her to the nuns?" she said again. I didn't say anything. I wouldn't give Ninka to them. I felt guilty enough; I didn't want to make decisions for Genya. We were supposed to share the food for the children, and I didn't always share; sometimes I gave all of it to Ninka. No one answered her. "I don't want to," she cried out, "but she'd be safe. What did you hear?" she asked Stajoe desperately. "Nothing definite," he answered; "it may be one of their long-range things. If it were definite, I wouldn't let Anya keep Ninka, not this time."

Six months here, getting up every morning to the fighting and screaming and the terrible smells, couples on the stairs tearing at each other like hyenas, and now they were threatening the children. A cold wind was working its way through the window. "I think something is coming loose," I said, getting up and jabbing a rag back into place. "Still," Stajoe said, "we should be careful and keep our eyes open." I looked at Momma; she was crying.

The next morning, we were up at four. Momma was out on the balcony with Ninka. If people stayed in the room and there was fighting, she would give Ninka the box with the lima beans and stand on the landing, or leave her with Rachel and walk down the stairs and stand in the little court. If that was too dangerous, she stood just inside the door. Then she would go up to look at the child, then go down again, every ten minutes. This morning she came up with news: "There's some kind of crew on the streets, not Germans, Jews. They're painting the streets near the outhouses white. Is it some kind of plague?" We were all so cramped. There was no such thing as sanitation; the conditions were terrible. Momma would go to the outhouse when the bathroom overflowed and stank. Whenever Genya was there with the babies, she would go rather than fight over the bathroom in the apartment.

"Diphtheria," Stajoe answered; "also, they're afraid of typhoid. They're painting with lime." Then I remembered that last night he had gone to a meeting of the building commandants with the head of the Judenrat Committee, Ganz. "Are there many cases?" I asked him. "You went to medical school; how many do you need?" "Diphtheria!" Momma gasped, sinking down on the board automatically in the middle, so the board would not tilt up and throw her off. "Should we stay in?" "No difference," Stajoe said; "they don't know where it's coming from. It could be the food, it could be anything. Just go on and don't worry." So there was something new not to worry about. I was brushing my hair. Last night at the hospital I had washed it for the first time in three weeks; I had to stay in to let it dry. I stopped dressing and sat down next to Momma. "Don't cry, Momma," Stajoe said, sitting down on the other side of me, bending rhythmically to lace his boots; "it'll be over soon. We'll forget all about this; we'll have a son." I looked at him; I didn't think he believed what he was saying. "It can't last forever; you'll see. When it's over, we'll forget." "And how will I forget my father?" I cried out bitterly. "If you're thinking about your father, what about my whole family?" There was not a sound from Momma. "Are we going to start competing over tragedies?" she asked finally. She wasn't looking at either of us.

"Here I am." Verushka cried, running in the front door. "I have some good news. They're putting aside a special building for the Gestapo workers, much bigger rooms, the pipes work, it's even heated, and not so much crowding. We can all stay together." "I can't go," Stajoe said; "I have to sleep here, because of being the commandant." "But you could stay part of the night," Vera insisted; "it will be so much better! You can come and eat with us." "I insist on it," Jakob said in back of her; "I absolutely insist. Then we will all be together, and Mischa and Emmanuel, too. It will be a little home again. What about it, Momushka?" "You know I don't like the Gestapo," she answered. But she did not want to make decisions for us; things were too dangerous. We had to make our own fates. She had said that more than once. She would not tell Genya what to do with Lyuba, whether or not to give her to the nuns, no matter how many times she was asked. "I will not mix in on such things," she said. "Oh, come on," Vera insisted. "Ninka is almost talking like a grownup; where can she play here, that parrot? I don't know what kind of stories that man tells her," she said accusingly, looking at the writer in the corner. "He thinks she's too little to understand." She was jealous; she always told Ninka stories. "Story! Story! Story!" Ninka piped up. "Take her away," Momma ordered. "What story?" Vera was asking, grabbing and hugging her. "Egg story," Ninka said. "Don't you ever want to hear anything else?" Vera asked mischievously, tickling her. "It's like talking to a foreigner who understands the language and can't speak it," she giggled aside to us. "Egg story," Ninka repeated, the edges of her serious mouth turning up into the shade of a smile.

"Once upon a time," Vera began, poking Ninka in the stomach, "there was a little chicken who laid an egg. You know what a chicken is? What an egg is?" "Big egg?" Ninka asked. "No, a very small egg," Vera answered her. "How small?" "Smaller than your lima beans," Vera said; "maybe much smaller. And then," she went on, "Grandpa tried to break the egg," and she banged on Ninka's knee so it jumped; "and Grandma tried to break the egg," and she pretended to hit Ninka on the head; "and they couldn't break it. They hit it and hit it but it would not break." "Why?" Ninka said. "It was very hard, dunce," Vera told her. "Hard?" Ninka asked. Momma was smiling, smiling and thinking; we were all watching and thinking: The Gestapo block or stay here? "Then along came a little animal, I think it was an elephant—" "Not elephant!" Ninka screamed. We were all smiling. "What then?" Vera asked; "I can't remember." "Mouse," Ninka shrieked indignant. "Oh, yes, a mouse. So along came this mouse, and it touched the egg with its—was it nose Ninka?" "Not nose!" Ninka shrieked again. "Maybe its tail?" Vera wondered. "Tail!" Ninka shouted, pulling Vera's hair. "It touched the egg with its little tail and the egg opened right away, and you know what, it was a golden egg, not a regular egg." "Why?" Ninka asked; "how mouse eats?" "I don't know," Vera answered; "that's just what happened." "Want to eat," Ninka considered. "Naturally you would, but when you get older, you might like golden eggs." "To eat," Ninka announced positively. "Well, if you can't have an egg, what would you say to a doll?" "No dolls," Ninka answered, sulky, turning her face away. "Are you sure?" Vera asked her. The back of Ninka's head nodded yes. "Then what is this?" Vera yelped, pulling a huge doll with blond curls out from under her skirt. "Doll! Doll!" Ninka screamed, beside herself. "Me?" she asked in a small voice. "It is for you," Vera told her. "Jakob gave two eggs for it, and he even has a real egg left for you. Will you feed the doll some of your food?" "No food," Ninka told her; "play with her, put her sleep, not feed doll, Ninka not feed doll." "Very good," Vera said; "here is your doll. Will you give her a name?" Ninka thought. "Vera Mouse," she said suddenly. We all started laughing.

"It might be better if we were all together," Momma considered. "Please finish getting dressed, everyone. Look, Vera," she said, taking Ninka from her, "I'll take her over and take a look. Where is the building?" "The one they're painting white, farther down this street." "I pass it on the way to the hospital," I told Momma; "I'll look too." So I walked by. It was a very big building. It reminded me of our old apartment, and here, painted white, it looked like a prince's palace. All over were beautiful Jewish girls, the most beautiful in the ghetto, in black uniforms with little white aprons; they did the sewing and cleaning. I had seen them for several mornings now, the beautiful dark-haired girls with their olive skin and their thick black hair, the beautiful bodies; all of them so clean, their hair so clean, and some of them even had stockings. I wanted to go there.

When I got home, Momma asked what I thought. "It looks very nice," I said cautiously. "Looks aren't everything," she said; "Stajoe can't sleep there at night." "He can come for most of it, and come to eat." "I don't think," Momma said, "we should give up this place. I'll go if we don't give up this place. I will go then." "Then let's wait for Stajoe," I agreed. He wanted us to go. "But your Momma's right; we'll keep this place. No one will know anything; there are some advantages to being the commandant." "Still," Momma said, "I would feel better if we
235

waited a week, just to see how things go, and," she went on, "it will give Vera and Jakob some time alone." "Rachel will come, too, of course," Jakob pronounced the next morning. But at ten o'clock Genya came running to the hospital; I was on the night shift. "Doctor Yurbo," I heard her saying, "where is Anya? Her friend Rachel is screaming and bleeding." "Anya," he said, turning around, "take two men and this stretcher here and bring her over. I'll tell the Judenrat we need her here as a worker. Go on, get her."

"Thank God it happened during the night," Genya panted as we ran back; if the committee had heard her, I don't know." Rachel was writhing on the floor. "All right, Rachel," I told her; "I'm going to give you a shot." "It's a death shot!" Rachel cried out in terror. "More good conversation from the café," I said bitterly to the men, rubbing her arm with some alcohol. "No, it is not; would I do it?" I injected her. "I am dying, I am dying," she kept screaming. "If you keep screaming that, someone will see to it," I scolded her. "Keep quiet; we're taking you to the hospital. In a minute, it won't hurt so much." She was covered with sweat. Momma was standing with Ninka on the balcony, keeping her hand over the baby's eyes. "It still hurts," Rachel whimpered as they lifted her onto the stretcher. "But not much," I whispered; "not much." "Not much," she whispered back like a little child. They were tying ropes over her feet and chest to keep her from falling off the planks covered with a sheet; this was the hospital's stretcher. "And when you get better," I told her as we came out on the street, "we will live in that new building, and you will forget all about it." Her eyes clouded over and she gave me a piercing scream.

"How far is it?" I asked, my head swiveling like a top. "A hundred feet more," the man said. Genya was on the other side. She looked at me, terrified. "Where does the doctor get the drugs for the shots?" she asked. "We don't know; we don't ask. He gets them, I think at night. Listen," I said, "you go back when we get to the hospital. I don't want too much commotion, and also, in case anything happens, and Momma has to hide." Genya ran back the instant we went through the hospital doors.

Doctor Yurbo took one look at Rachel and gave her another shot. "Not good, Anya," he muttered from the side of the room; "the baby's dead. We have to take it out." "An operation?" I asked. "Of course. She's down now as a nurse. We'll have to keep her here until she's better, at least two weeks. Then you'll have to watch out for her like your mother; she won't be able to do much for a while." "You have an anesthetic?" "Yes, I have it. Don't ask what kind; it works." "Can I go in with her?" "No, stay out; there are too many germs as it is. She'll be all right. Go back to the wards; if anyone comes, we don't want them to find an empty hospital." Doctor Yurbo came out an hour later. "The baby was dead; she's fine. She's not very strong. You'd better sit with her tonight; I'll send a message to your mother. Rachel won't be getting any more shots." "She doesn't need them?" I asked, cheered up. "She needs them; we don't have them," he said.

Momma came to the hospital at two in the morning. Rachel was finally asleep. "How is she?" Momma asked bending over to kiss her forehead. "A lot of pain, a lot, she says it hurts; she cries, just cries." "It was the last family she had. Well, now it is definite; we can't stay in the room. She's not strong enough anymore for it. When she comes out, we go to the Gestapo block." "Stajoe?" "Stajoe decided," Momma said, pulling up a steel stool; "he has changed so much." "Do you think it's because he thinks nothing matters anymore; he doesn't think we'll live, any of us?" They were still seizing people from rooms; we had been very lucky. "No," Momma said; "we're getting older. The way we live here, the Germans leave us all selfishness, or no selfishness. He's not selfish, not really, and he's older; I think that's what it is." "I wouldn't have believed it," I said, my eyes still on Rachel.

"It hurts," she whispered, moving in her sleep. Momma lifted her hands and dropped them in her lap. "It's a miracle she's alive, a miracle." "Please go back, Momma; you're exhausted. We never know about tomorrow; it's hard to rest in that stove." "Very true," Momma sighed, "very true. Look," she said, holding out a hand, "see this swollen finger. Arthritis. Just like my Momma. And at just the same age." "I'll be home for dinner tomorrow. How is Ninka?" "Oh, Ninka's happy; she's playing with her doll. It hops all over the bed; it jumps rope with a string Jakob got it, and it hears story after illiterate story about chickens and eggs. Also some bits about a man who murders his wives, and a boy who was eaten by wolves because he didn't listen to his mother. Ninka plays all the parts, or I'd have a hard time figuring it all out. I think Vera was right about our little writer after all." "He still has paper?" I asked, astonished. "A tower," Momma sighed. "You know what Ninka said to him today? It's eerie the way she's beginning to talk. 'Grandpa,' (I was beginning to giggle; she called anyone bald grandpa), 'top of your head nude like my knee.'" "What did he say?" "He said she was an extraordinarily intelligent child, and slammed his papers around." Momma was grinning. "Good night, Anyushka," she said straightening up. "Let Ninka sleep with Stajoe. She hardly knows him; he leaves so early, and comes back so late." "We don't dare keep her up, you know that it's not easy to fall asleep there." Ninka would get into bed at six and start playing; if she was asleep at eight we were lucky, the noise was so terrible. "I'll put her up with him," Momma promised; "she won't wake up. Once she sleeps, she sleeps." "Just like Vera," I thought. "Good night, Momma," I said.

Rachel slept and slept. It is good for her, I thought. What would I think about, I wondered? I had watched Stajoe, time after time, huddled around the others under the one light bulb, reading, or, if he was not reading, sitting on the bed, staring straight ahead, trying to decide what to do next. Sometimes it was food; sometimes escape, sometimes Ninka, sometimes Momma, sometimes me. I didn't want to think about any of those things. "Anzia will be back here soon," I thought to myself, and that reminded me of the Russian stove in our old apartment at home. "How can it be only ten blocks from here?" I wondered in amazement. It was almost as if the streets were separated by huge deep cliffs filled with violent water. It was a little cold. I checked Rachel's blanket; her head was cool. How many times did we sit on the stove with Anzia? Then I started to picture the stove. It seemed very important that I remember every detail, as if all our lives depended on it. The top of the stove, above the boilers for the pots, was a huge cavern built into the wall. It was rounded, like a cave, with a big carved brass border running around it. Into this cave, Anzia put the wood the man sawed in the fall; one layer facing straight out, the other on top of it, facing sideways, layer after layer. When she lit the logs, the flames shot up to the ceilings; it was as if the whole sky was in flames. They flickered in all the tiles, in the linoleum squares on the floor, in the polished pots. Then, when the logs burned down to ash, Anzia would sweep them out, and begin testing the heat of the huge cavern; this is where she baked the bread and the pastries. She knew from the way drops of water spluttered and danced when she sprinkled them on if it was too hot. Then she would take a special wet broom made of straw and stroke the floor of the oven, sprinkling again and again. When it was the right temperature, she put in the trays of pastries and bread, and closed the door which covered the huge opening. It was brass with a handle like an S, but in the shape of a dolphin. Then the smell would begin filling the house.

Underneath the huge cavern were two rows of bricks held in place with clay, and then the heavy iron stove which stuck out into the room for cooking meals. It had three boilers for pots, and a separate one, which stuck off to the side, just for water. Momma kept the water in a huge brass pot she brought with her from Paltava. It had a little faucet. On top of it was a huge brass ladle which was never used; it was just for decoration. It also came from Paltava. There was a little door underneath the burners to heat them. It opened for the small pieces of wood. It didn't take much wood to heat the burners, and then when we were through using them, a dinner could be kept warm in the little opening behind the door, after the logs had burned down. All around the little door were the big green tiles; and growing out from one side of the huge cavern above the burners was a gigantic rectangular tunnel made of these same tiles. It went into the wall, and on the other side of the wall, in the hall, there were the same green bricks, pouring out their heat from the kitchen. Beneath the tunnel was empty space, above it, nothing. We all climbed up onto this tunnel and sat on the mattresses Poppa put there.

"Now we hide Momma in it," I thought sleepily, but warm as a child, and I saw myself walking to the oven door and opening it, and there was a beautiful brand-new child and it was talking! "What do you want to say to me?" I asked it. "Aren't you too young to talk?" "Oh," said the child, "there are no children anymore." Then Rachel was moaning: "It hurts; it hurts." "In five days, Rachel," I told her, "you won't even know it happened." I was talking in my sleep; I was asleep again. People from our room were coming out of the stove; they were all sitting down at the round wooden table. We had to eat with them because Ninka was sick on one bed and Momma on the other. We had no knives and forks and had to use our hands. "Soon," I said, joking, "we won't know how to eat like people." "Look at the countess," one of them sneered; "she thinks we will survive. Look at her; there's hardly any food anymore, and she thinks we'll survive. She worries about forks; look at her!" I got up from the table and started walking away. "Look at her; she thinks she'll survive!" they kept screaming. I woke up to see Rachel sound asleep.

"Anya." Rachel's voice was calling me weakly. "Anya, was it a boy or a girl?" "A boy." "Did you see him?" "No, they wouldn't let me come in." "What did they do with him?" "I don't know, Rachel." "Did the nurse see him?" "Yes, she did; do you want to see her?" To my surprise, she said yes. I called the nurse. "Did you see the baby?" Rachel asked her. "Oh, yes," said the nurse, looking at me uncomfortably. "It was a boy?" Rachel asked; "there was nothing wrong with him?" "No, nothing," said the nurse; "it was just bad luck, Mrs. Ellenbogen, just bad luck." "But you saw him," Rachel insisted. "Yes, I did," she answered with a touch of annoyance. "So that is over too," Rachel sighed when the nurse went out. "Anya, I heard rumors too, about the children; that sooner or later they'll be taking them. Maybe it was just as well." One round tear after another spilled out of her eyes. "What will you do about Ninka? You must not let them get her." "They won't get her," I promised Rachel; "they'll never get her." "They got my son," she said crying; "they did."

Ten days later we moved into the Gestapo block, but Momma wouldn't let us bring too much with us. Oh, it was nicer! There was only the family in the room, and the inside of the room had been painted white. Jakob had even managed to paint the bunk beds white. Sun shone in the bare window and splashed on the floor; we all took turns scrubbing it. "I want to see my face in it," Momma said happily, busy with a brush. "I'm getting a job," Vera announced in the corner. "Now that we're all together, it's so nice, and if I work, there'll be more money for food." "Where will you work?" I called out from under the table where I was busy polishing. "In the Judenrat Office as a secretary; it's all arranged. I already have some pencils with red lead and some paper for Ninka; look at her." Ninka was sitting on the bottom bunk scribbling on a piece of paper. "What are *you* doing?" I called to her. "Writing story," Ninka announced importantly, "for Aunt Rachel; mouse and egg, but mouse not mouse, mouse Ninka with yellow hair, braid." "I wonder who that is?"

240

Vera called from her corner. "Momma!" Ninka shrieked, laughing.

"Already she has your habits," Momma laughed at me. "Look how good the place is," she gloated; she was attacking the table in the middle of the room. "I think I can get some more paint for it tonight," Jakob said. "Oh, that *would* be wonderful," Momma sang out. "Who's watching the pretzels on the hotplate?" Genya called from polishing the window. "You do it," Vera told her; "you'll break that window anyway if you keep at it; Jakob will get off the paint chips with a knife." "Isn't it nice?" I kept asking. "Look," Momma called to us, "from the balcony you can see all the way into the city; you can see everyone coming back from work."

We fed the children early and then waited until Stajoe could come over at ten to eat our dinner; we hadn't been to the café for the last few days. "Rachel, come out in the sun; Genya, bring a chair." Momma helped Rachel up. "Better and better," Momma pronounced, looking at her with satisfaction; "she's practically tan." "I feel much stronger," Rachel said. "Arthur was here before; you remember, Momushka"—she called her that now—"the man who gave Ninka the chocolate; he lives upstairs." "Oh, it is very nice here," Momma sighed again. "I think it's even getting warmer." "It just feels that way," Rachel purred. "You look much better," Vera said, hugging her. "Don't pull out her stiches," Momma warned, laughing. "When do they come out?" Vera asked, curious. "Two more days; that will make it two weeks. Half of them are already out; she's doing better than any of us thought." "I feel better now than I did before," Rachel agreed; "maybe I should get a job." "You'll do nothing at all until you look strong as a horse. We're not taking any chances," Momma warned. "But there won't be any actions *here*," Vera protested. "You are always so sure of things!" Momma answered, exasperated. "Well, there aren't; there haven't been any for two days. *Your* color is better, too." "I'm not yellow anymore?" Momma asked. "Not so very yellow," Vera answered. "You stay out on the balcony with Rachel."

"Would you sing a song?" I asked Momma. She had not sung one since we got into the ghetto; once in a while, she hummed to Ninka, that was all. "Which?" she asked. "About the butterfly." So she sang it: "My life is short, only one day, be so kind and don't touch me." Her rich voice warmed the walls. "It sounds sadder here, I think," she said. "I don't like singing here; no, I don't." "*We* liked it!" Vera exlaimed. "And if you had brought your piano, you could have played for me," Momma said, grinning at her.

So ten days passed in the beautiful white room. There was perfect peace, because in the ghetto, our life was unimaginable perfection: The gold air fell in; the brilliant sun struck the walls like silver; the floor gleamed. "No Mister Grimonsky to fight over the water," Mother repeated hundreds and hundreds of times. And Anzia came to the side fence twice, so there was plenty to eat, and no crying from Ninka or Lyubushka; even the rest of us were not hungry. Rachel was getting stronger and stronger; even her figure seemed to be returning to normal.

Then, suddenly, the building was swarming with Gestapo officers. Several of them were carrying notepads and pencils. They looked around the building, making notes. "See this," we heard one of them say. Then we could see him pointing to a room across the hall where the brassieres and underwear of the girls who cleaned were hung to dry. "Where else could they hang it?" Vera whispered, annoyed. "Bunch of old maids, checking up on the house cleaning." My mind had suddenly started up its old catechism of names of those taken in the actions. It was endless by now. At night, I repeated them to myself the way Momma counted apples falling from trees to put her to sleep; I fell asleep before I was a quarter through the list. "Keep quiet," I ordered Vera; it was starting again. They went into all the rooms and offices. "I don't like it; I don't like it," Momma kept repeating. "Look," Jakob said, when he came home, "I'll get Stajoe, and before we come for dinner, he'll go see Ganz; maybe we can find out what this is."

They were back in an hour. "Someone denounced the German officers for having affairs with the Jewish girls here, the maids. That's what the inspection was, to get evidence. It was probably someone jealous, or rejected, I don't think it's important, that part." "I don't know," Momma said, "before the ghetto, they sent soldiers to the front lines for having anything to do with Jewish girls." "But it's only the maids who are in trouble," Jakob argued; "*if* they are." He didn't want to break the family up. "What do you think?" I asked Stajoe. "I wish I knew," he said. "If you go back, then there's the problem of hiding your mother and Rachel. Here everyone is safe, unless this inspection means something." He was thinking. "I think it's safe to wait another week," he said; "we should find out something by then."

So things went on. Rachel was getting stronger and stronger; she let Ninka sit on her lap and tell her stories. "Why are you telling your Aunt Rachel stories?" I asked this child, who every day was beginning to talk more and more like an adult. The shortness of life was speeding her up, too. "Because Rachel sick," Ninka said; "she play with Ninka's doll, too." "Does Aunt Rachel like it?" "Oh, yes," Ninka assured me; "Rachel do; plays with doll all day." "I'm glad you two found each other," I told Rachel.

Five days later, all of us woke up to the sound of guns firing. Then there were soldiers on the stairs. Vera ran to the balcony. "The whole building is surrounded by Gestapo with machine guns," she screamed; "what is it?" "Whatever it is, I don't want any part of it," I said, dressing Ninka as fast as I could, then myself; Rachel was throwing on her clothes in layers. "Good idea," I said, doing the same thing. Then all of us did it. Before we had a chance to look around, a soldier with a machine gun was in the room. "Out!" he ordered; "to the front of the building; no one stays behind." "What is it?" Arthur asked sleepily; he had come down from upstairs. "You, too; out!" the soldier ordered. Arthur stuck to us; we all went down. Jakob had already gone down, to find something out. "Stick close to me," I called back to the others, going down first. "Stick close to Anya," I heard Momma call in a low voice.

Then we were out on the street. Jakob was already surrounded by soldiers, their guns leveled at him. They lined both sides of the street. Next to our building was an alley we could walk through to get to our own building; a line of soldiers blocked it. "Listen," I said to everybody, "when we get down, I think we can get through; just follow me." "Oh, no," Vera protested, horrified; "my place is with Jakob; I don't want to live without Jakob." "You can join Jakob later!" I argued as fast as I could. "We don't have time for discussions!" "I would rather not live than leave him!" she insisted, her little chest heaving. "Please, Vera, Verushka, come with me." "I will not," she said; "I will not. I won't move." "Verushka, please!" "No," she said. "We'll leave you alone," I warned her. "I won't be alone; I'll be with Jakob; I will not leave Jakob," she swore. Her lower lip protruded, her teeth biting into it. "Let's go," I said to the others.

The soldiers were looking in all directions, making sure no one would escape. One was staring straight ahead, looking bored. I walked straight up to him. "Oh," I said, "I think you're a father, too? What do you have, a boy or a girl?" "Two boys," he answered. "Do you have pictures?" I asked. I kept on talking. "Here they are," he said, pulling some out. "Oh, such beautiful children!" I said, forcing myself not to hurry. "Ours are hungry. We don't know how to get to Polanska Street; we don't live here. Can you tell me how to get to Polanska Street?" "Just go straight through behind me," he said; "then turn right for two blocks. It's not a good street," he said, looking at Ninka, legs dangling from my body, clutching her doll. "Oh, what is?" I cried; "I would be so grateful to know." "None of them are very good," he said, "but go through here; you won't have any trouble finding Polanska," and he stood aside. I went through first, then Momma, then Rachel. "You! Stop!" I heard someone say. We kept walking, but before we turned the corner the soldier had stopped Arthur. Emmanuel and Genya were not with us; Lyuba was with them. Jakob and Vera were left behind us. Mischa was gone. We walked to our old room on Polanska Street. Momma was coughing.

"What happened?" Stajoe asked, opening the door. The others were staring at us. "The Gestapo surrounded the building and took everyone out." It was so sudden I still couldn't believe it; I could not believe it at all. It was as if a fuse had blown in the beautiful white room, turning off all the lights there forever. "Where are the others?" "They must have stopped Emmanuel and Genya; she had Lyuba; Vera wouldn't come. Jakob went down to ask questions; they stopped him right away, Mischa, too." "We don't know what it means yet," Stajoe said tentatively. "Whatever it is, it's not good," Momma predicted; "it's not good if the Gestapo has anything to do with it." I told Stajoe the story: "Vera wouldn't leave Jakob; she wanted to stay with him." "But when they make arrests, they always separate men and women!" he cried out; he sounded totally defeated. "Can you find anything out from Ganz?" Momma begged. "Tonight there's a meeting; I'll ask then. If I go now, the others may want to know why I'm so interested. You weren't supposed to be there. Let me go to work as if nothing had happened. I'll find out more in the end. Send Rachel over to Doctor Yurbo, that's all. Then you can stay here, too."

We sat on our beds. The writer was scribbling in his corner. Mr. Grimonsky left quietly. Apparently he wasn't talking to his wife. "There is something!" someone cried coming in from the lower floor. "Momma, get in the oven, hurry up!" "I don't want to," she said dully. "I don't care; get in," I ordered her, furious; "how much do you think *I* can stand?" "Not talk to Momma like that," Ninka said. "Listen, Ninka," I told her, shutting the door, "if anyone comes, don't even look at the stove; *don't look* at the stove, you hear me? Don't go near it. Make believe Momushka isn't here. If anyone asks you, say 'Ninka don't know.'" She nodded her little head solemnly. I thought about a four-year-old child on another block who had lost his parents in an action and hidden himself in a stove when he heard the soldiers were coming. They were not really children. The soldiers came. "You!" they said to the writer; "and you!" The last daughter of the old woman got up. "Please, please, please," she kept sobbing; we could hear her all the way down the stairs. We kept staring at the tower of paper where the writer had been sitting. "I'll use that paper in the stove," Mrs. Grimonsky said. None of us could look at her.

It got dark. We hardly noticed. Finally Stajoe came in. He looked at Momma and shook his head. "All dead. They separated the men and women, no food, no water; then they took them out to Panari and shot them. One, two, three; not even to the prisons first." "I won't hear it!" I screamed, smashing my hands over my ears. "I'll be your sister now," Rachel said, coming over and hugging me. For a minute I wanted to push her away, push her down, hit her, call the police for her, anything, kill her. My bones turned to water. "Oh, please, please, please," I cried, burying my face in her breast. "Momushka?" I heard Stajoe asking gently. "I expected it." She wasn't crying. "I don't know how we'll explain to Ninka where the storyteller has gone, that's all." "She knows, she knows," I cried. Stajoe stared at me, horrified. "She's too young!" he shouted at me. "She knows," I repeated again, and then I was gasping for breath as if a hand was pushing me under wave after wave. "At least we had a place to come back to," Momma said, coughing. Her voice was dry as burned paper.

13

IT was sometime in the middle of the night. The moon was lighting up the room, the vicious moon, cutting through the morning, the black night. "Anya, are you awake?" It was Momma. "Come out on the balcony and talk." I put on my coat and climbed down; she climbed out of the bed she shared with Rachel. Rachel was sleeping sitting against the wall. "Remember," she asked me, "the old church in Warsaw? We used to visit it when you were pregnant?" "Which church?" "The church that struck the hours, and when it struck, a group of figures would come out, almost life-size, or bigger, it was hard to tell from down below and march around from one side of the clock face to the other." I remembered. "There was one like it near Paltava," Momma whispered. "Poppa used to take me to see it. He used to take me with a basket of food because I had to sit there all afternoon waiting for the people to walk in front of the clock and go back in. I remember, when I got older, I used to think about that clock a lot. I still think about it, how nice it was, all the time passing, and the people marching in front of the clock. No matter what time it was, no matter what time of the year it was, they never changed. Now," Momma said, looking at the moon, the blank face of a clock, "it seems we have all the time, and each time we strike an hour, there is someone gone. Soon there will be no one to walk in front of the clock." "That won't happen, Momma," I said with my arm around her; "it will not. You will be all right, you'll see." "No, I don't think so," she said sadly; "but you will, you will be, you and Ninka." A shiver went down my spine. "Stop," I pleaded; "you are giving me gooseflesh."

"You know," Momma said, "I was falling asleep, counting apples again, and then they turned into faces, and then it all turned into a dream about Vera; can you believe it? Already I'm dreaming about her. I went into her room and she had a white nightgown on, and her hair was combed for a change, and everything in her room was white; the sheets, and the covers, and she was waiting for Jakob. 'Do you want me to go?' I asked her, and she smiled. She did. So I left. They were so crazy about each other," Momma sighed; "so crazy in love. I still see her coming down the stairs holding onto the white dog, such an innocent, such an innocent; I've never seen anything like it. Your father was so disgusted with her too, the way she got married. But it would have been all right." She had not mentioned Poppa since his death. "What does it mean that I'm already dreaming about her? I never dream about your Poppa. Every night I pray I'll dream about him, so he will come back to me, I don't care how, but I don't dream it." "Poppa would say dreams are not fair anymore than life is." "Yes, your Poppa would have said that." We stood with our arms around each other on the balcony.

"You know," Momma said, "it is hard to know how to manage without her. She was such an idiot, you know; it was like having a baby around always, and so good, such a good one." "I don't know, either, I don't know, and it's terrible, but I'm so mad at her"—we were both crying silently through our talking—"so mad at her for not coming. I could pull her apart; she could be here now. It's terrible to be angry at the dead." "I can't believe Vera is dead," Momma said sadly; "maybe that's why I'm dreaming about her. I cannot believe it. I sometimes thought she would live forever, like a doll, a precious precious doll." "Come to bed, Momma." "Let me watch the clouds thin out across the moon; they're such sharp stripes, they look like they're cutting into it." "It's gone now, come to bed," I begged, tugging on her arm. "And I spend more time in the stove than I ever did at it," Momma thought out loud. "Please," I tugged at her sleeve again; "you'll be alone with Ninka and Rachel now." "And Mischa; we didn't even see him on the street," Momma murmured; "how are we to believe he's gone?" "Momma!" "I'm coming," she shuddered; "it's cold. How long have we been here?" "We can tell time by Rachel's pregnancy; over nine months, maybe ten. I don't count anymore." "Nine months, maybe ten; we are oldtimers already." "Momma, are you coming?" Yes, yes. I meant to tell you, I heard they didn't get enough of us today; so I'll have to stay in the stove tomorrow, and Rachel will have to watch Ninka." "No," I said, "you stay in the stove, and I'll take them both to the hospital. Things don't feel right; they'll be out for everyone after this Gestapo business." "Will Doctor Yurbo let you?" Momma asked. "Oh, Rachel is strong enough to work, and we can put Ninka in a bed and say she's sick. I don't want to take any more chances, not for a while." "I wonder who you will dream about?" Momma wondered. I didn't answer her; she was meandering. I dreamed about Poppa all the time, but not as he had always been, as I had last seen him. It was not such a blessing.

"Are you awake?" Stajoe whispered when I settled in. "Of course," I whispered back. "I am, too," Rachel whispered to us. "Me, too," Ninka announced from Stajoe's other side. "Quiet!" he ordered her in a low voice. "Your mother told you about tomorrow? She found out from Mister Grimonsky. I think he's attached to us in his strange way, or else all the empty beds are frightening him. He's not so bad. He told me he buried all the family wealth right in the middle of a busy street, under the cobblestones." "He has a peasant's mind," I answered bitterly. "No, he's not so bad." "I can't sleep tonight; it's too bright in here," I told him, staring straight into the moon. "Ninka," Stajoe whispered, "I'm putting you next to Mommy. Breathe in and out as hard as you can so you can put her to sleep." "Oh, Stajoe!" I exclaimed; "it won't work anymore." But Ninka was huffing and puffing like a little train; finally she must have worn herself out and fallen asleep. I listened to her breathing in and out, in and out, and the next thing I knew, Stajoe was getting me up for breakfast, and I was waking the others, pushing Momma into the stove, watching everyone get dressed, getting ready to leave. Just as I was near the door, the oven door swung open and out popped Momma's head. "Anya, comb your hair and put on some lipstick. If you're going to walk around looking like that, I have no reason to live." She meant it. "Close that door!" I hissed. "Let me see you comb your hair first," she insisted. "Are you satisfied now?" I demanded at the top of my lungs. "A little rouge wouldn't hurt," she said, pulling the door shut after her.

"Why do I have to walk around as if nothing has happened?" I demanded of Stajoe. "I've never pretended to know why our mother thinks things, but by now I believe she thinks the right ones. And," he added, "you *do* look good. Now." "That is not how I feel," I complained bitterly. "The Germans don't care how you feel; they care how you look. You never know when it helps, like with the Polish soldier yesterday." "What are you talking about?" I demanded; "my hair had nothing to do with it." "But it is beautiful hair," Stajoe coaxed, stroking it. "My hair beautiful?" Ninka asked. "Gorgeous," he complimented her. "Gorgeous," Ninka repeated again and again; "what gorgeous?" "It means even more beautiful than your doll." "Thank you," Ninka said solemnly, hopping up to him. Stajoe left with the patrol. Rachel and I left with Ninka for the hospital. And Rachel did begin working there; it was incredible to see Rachel working. "You know," Doctor Yurbo said, "you can bring Ninka every day." "No, she has to stay with Momma; she can't be alone." "I understand," he said sadly.

So nine more months passed. Anzia heard about Vera and Emmanuel and Mischa much later; she wanted to bring us the silver basket. Momma wouldn't hear of it. "They would take it right away from us. I want you to have it; the little ark is safer with you." Two days later, Anzia was back with a basket and ten kilos of meat; a little peasant boy helped her carry it. "Can you trust him?" Momma worried. "Oh, he's my stepson," Anzia answered, blushing. It was a feast. Stajoe managed to get some wood and we heated up the Russian stove Friday night. There had been an action that day and later on the Gestapo was insisting over loudspeakers that everyone left "enjoy themselves" at a concert. "It's always possible to find an orchestra among Jews," Stajoe said bitterly. We even invited Mr. and Mrs. Grimonsky to join us. "What was that grunt?" I asked Stajoe after Mr. Grimonsky left. "I think he was trying to say thank you," Stajoe laughed. But we were all demoralized, death-shocked. We had been there more than a year and a half. And a new transport would be coming in soon.

Then Mrs. Cibiki wanted me to come again to give her massages. I took some of my slips with me, and my Gestapo pass, and when I came home, I had fresh fish. It was a real holiday, fresh fish for the first time we'd been in the ghetto; we were all excited. Ninka was playing with the scales, the iridescent ones, Momma warning her not to swallow them or cut herself on them, and Ninka holding them up to the light like smelly jewels. "When did we last have fish?" Momma kept saying; "it must be forever. Oh, this will be good," she went on, stirring the pot; we still had plenty of onions and cucumbers left from Anzia's last visit. It was always feast or famine; we kept reminding each other of the feasts, as if there would always be another one to look forward to. Stajoe came in in his workman's clothes. "Well," he said, "I finally have some good news. It can't be too much longer. They've committed a real fiasco this time—Leningrad. They can't take it; the Russians will beat them. They'll be out of here soon, you'll see. We'll forget about everything, we'll have that boy yet." "Dear God, Russia!" Momma murmured, starting to cry. "Russia," she repeated again, the name of a savior. "Momushka will be a grandma again, and then she'll have to be bald; Ninka says so." Oh, he was trying to cheer us up. "Please don't talk about it like that," Momma said, her eyes clearing; "anyone might hear, you could get into a lot of trouble." "We can trust everyone here," Stajoe said, looking around the table. Two nights later, we were eating a real dinner, a beef stew, when there was a knock at the door. It was the head of the Jewish Police. "Stajoe Lavinsky," he said, "you are to come with me to the *torovaje*." "Please let him finish," I asked, infuriated; we did not often get to eat meals like these. "I cannot," he answered me; "he has to come now." I followed them downstairs. Four other men were waiting at the bottom; they were all from the Gestapo, and the head of the Gestapo was leaning against the wall of the building, smoking a cigarette. "Anya, the pictures!" Stajoe cried out. "Let me have them!" I shouted, but the Jewish policeman who had come into the room took his stick and hit me on the head. I saw the wood coming at me with disbelief; it was the last thing I saw. When I came around, Momma and Rachel were picking up the pictures of us as fast as they could; Stajoe was nowhere in sight. I ran upstairs, and out on the balcony. The Gestapo men were walking on the sidewalk talking, and down the middle of the street went a carpenter from our building, and Stajoe, down the center, between the thin dark buildings of the narrow crumbling street, like a tall, tall tree.

"Oh," I heard Rachel saying from far away, "you have a lump on your head the size of an egg." Momma was standing with her arm around me. It was some time in February or March; with its hands, the cold wind was pulling pieces of my hair loose and they kept coming back at my eyes like whips. I began to realize the balcony door was open. "Close the door, Momma," I whispered; "the others, they'll get cold." "Excuse, Mrs. Savikin, please," a voice behind her rumbled; I felt Mother jolt slightly to the left. Mr. Grimonsky was pulling insistently at her skirt like a child. "Excuse, please. They are not taking him to shoot, excuse, Mrs. Lavinsky, they are not taking him to shoot, no, no, they are taking him to prison," he insisted in his growly rumble. "How do you know?" I asked him; my lips were turning to iron, ice; a strand of hair lashed across one eye, closing it. It began tearing. I could feel Momma against me, shuddering from the cold. "He went with the carpenter; you saw? So," Mr. Grimonsky went on with difficulty, only God knew when he had spoken so many sentences together; all he did was shout and complain and insult; "they need the carpenter, the shoemaker more than anything, except maybe," he stopped to think, "furriers. They never shoot furriers. They arrested a furrier; they didn't shoot him." "What has that got to do with Stajoe?" Rachel cried impatiently. "Oh," Mr. Grimonsky growled on, stumbling; "they got them together, so they are going to the same place; you see it? So, if they will not be shooting the shoemaker, a shoemaker he was, not a carpenter like you told your Momma, they will not be shooting Mister Lavinsky," he finished triumphantly. Next to him, little Mrs. Grimonsky was nodding her head violently. "You think he won't be shot?" I asked in a small voice. "Not unless they shoot shoemakers; they don't shoot shoemakers, no, never, never, I know; or carpenters, either; I'm a carpenter." Mrs. Grimonsky was nodding so violently I feared for her head. "We will go back to our beds now," Mr. Grimonsky said with dignity; "but they did not take him to shoot, not with the shoemaker." "Thank you, Mister Grimonsky," Momma said feverishly. He hesitated for a long time, puckering his forehead. "A pleasure!" he said finally with glee, "a pleasure! And the little girl, she is very pretty." He bowed in an odd way and backed away from us; Mrs. Grimonsky imitated him, tilting herself forward stiffly and disappeared back into the room.

"What do you think, Momma?"

"Don't hope too much; but still," she thought, "there's sense in what he says. They must have been going to the same place."

"So what can we do?"

"Nothing, we just have to wait."

So we waited. We went to work, because now there

were fewer of us than ever, and less food than ever, and no one on the outside to exchange things for us. I was no longer giving surgical massages; Anzia hardly ever came to the fence. Mr. Grimonsky gave Ninka a potato, "for a toy," he told Momma, and Momma took it away from her to cook. "This way you can have the potato to eat and the potato soup to drink," Momma promised her; we even drank the water the vegetables were boiled in. Five days later, there was another knock at the door. No one in the room moved. The door opened an inch, then two inches. "Can I come in?" asked a frightened voice. "Come in already," boomed Mr. Grimonsky; "idiot, scare us all to death," he went on complaining in his bear's rumble. "I am looking for Mrs. Lavinsky," the voice trembled in from the hall. "She's in here, come in already," Mr. Grimonsky shouted. The door opened a little more and the man slid in sideways. It was the shoemaker who left with Stajoe. Everyone went back to their business; no one watched us. "I have a message for Mrs. Lavinsky," he said. "I am Mrs. Lavinsky," I heard myself saying; my hands and my nose had turned to ice. "Oh," he said with relief; "it's from your husband, in the prison." "He's alive!" I gasped. "Yes, yes," he said, opening his eyes wide to show he was telling the truth. "Here, somewhere," he began rifling his pockets, "is the message. I found it!" He handed over a tiny filthy sheet of paper. I unfolded it. In rusty red letters were two words only: "Save me." "How did he write this?" I asked the shoemaker. A muscle in my stomach was leaping in and out like a fish. "He took a piece of straw," the shoemaker said, warming up; "we had only straw to sleep on, so he took a piece and cut his arm, here," he pointed to his wrist; "then the straw was a pen and he wrote that. I don't know what it says because I can't read," he said shyly. "It says 'Save me,'" Momma said gently, putting him out of his misery; "will you tell us what it was like?"

"Oh, yes, grandma lady," he promised; "it was very dark and no food, no water. Then they did give us some, but not much. And Stajoe, he said I could call him that," he apologized, looking down at his shoes, "he can't get off his boots. I don't know why he has such boots, but his feet got swollen up, and we pulled and pulled, they won't come off. They hurt a lot, you know. So today, when they took me out, I said I would come with the note. For him, the boots are the worst, worse than the food. I think that is

252

what he said, exactly." "We cannot thank you enough," Momma said; "did you happen to hear what they took him in for?" "Something, treason, I think," he muttered, embarrassed. "But they let you go?" I asked. "Oh, yes, I said I would not steal any more sugar from the Judenrat." Momma and I just looked at each other. "Thank you," Momma said again. "Oh, yes," he answered; "oh yes," and he left the room walking almost backwards.

"I'm going out," I told Momma. "Where are you going?" "To Poppa's lawyer, Mister Lermonsky; maybe he can do something." "But that's in the city!" Momma protested in a panic. "I have a Gestapo pass; I'm going." I ran down the stairs and hid inside the door. A group of people were coming to the gate. I ran over to them and followed them out. I was dressed perfectly and my blond hair was combed; no one paid any attention. My yellow star was in my pocket; I remembered making it when the Germans had given the orders. Now I had taken it off after five blocks. Then I started running.

"Mister Lermonsky," I burst into his office, "please, you have to do something to help my husband; he's in prison with the Germans; please help me." "What, have you lost your mind?" he shouted at me, getting up from behind his desk as if he were on a spring. "*I* should go into the fire to help a Jew? What are you doing here?" He was running back and forth behind his desk like a trapped rat. "Go back, you have to go back." "You do something!" I insisted hysterically. "I should do something for a Jew?" he repeated in amazement; "get out of here, please. I will call the police!" I stared at him; I couldn't believe it. "I will call the police!" he shrieked again in terror. "Go to court for a Jew! She is crazy! They are all crazy! Get out of here!" I turned and walked down the stairs. Poppa had helped him all his life; he had called Poppa his *Judek*, his little Jew. All the rich Christians had one, one Jew they trusted to do anything for them and whom they protected in turn. He would not do anything for us. I began walking back slowly. So what if they caught me? Where was the prison? I could try going to it; maybe I could see him from the window. But I couldn't go. There was Momma and Ninka and Rachel. It was getting darker; was it going to rain? No, I had walked farther than I thought. I was no more than three blocks from our old apartment. "What am I doing here?" I thought in a panic; "someone will recognize me." And I began to run back to the ghetto. It was dark when I got near it; people were coming back from work. I slipped in with one group coming home and went through. Momma and Rachel were sitting, white as corpses; Ninka was sleeping on top of her doll.

"No use," Momma said, looking at me, not expecting an answer. We thought they got you!" Rachel protested with a sob. "No, they didn't get me, but it's no use, no use." "They may let him out yet," Rachel comforted; "they let out the shoemaker." I could see Stajoe trapped in his boots, his feet swollen, his stomach empty. I would have given anything to get him out; there was nothing I could do, nothing. For the second time, nothing. "The shoemaker only stole sugar"—I bent over to take off my shoes—"only sugar." Ten days later, an electrician came to our apartment before worktime. "Let me check the wires near your bed," he told me. I didn't bother to ask what wires he was checking. "Your husband was shot this morning. Here," he said, thrusting something at me. There were two pictures of our wedding, one of me in a black evening dress when I was pregnant, and another time of me, standing with Stajoe, both of us dressed as Orientals, standing against the rock in Druzgeniekie. The room began circling and circling like a carousel, or a figure on a music box. "Anya," Momma was calling. "Anya, you fainted; wake up." "Did I see his watch?" "Yes, yes, here it is," Momma said, handing it to me; the chain swung it back and forth. I felt faint again. "I'm getting better at this fainting," I said weakly. "Do you want to go to work?" Momma asked. What choice did I have? Only the workers were given rations.

But now, I decided, with Stajoe gone, I couldn't afford to work in the Jewish Hospital; there was no chance to steal any food there; the ration lines were more and more irregular; we got practically nothing. I went to the Judenrat and asked for Ganz. He had gotten to know Stajoe quite well; he liked him, and came to talk to him sometimes at night. "I want a job outside," I told him, "in the mill. Can you do it?" "Tomorrow," he promised, avoiding my eyes. "They will come for you at six." The first job they gave me was sawing wood. It was March; there was snow all over the ground. None of us had gloves. Another woman and I shared one long saw; I had one end, she had the other; we sawed back and forth until the log split. Meanwhile, my hair was combed, my dress was clean. "They can't eat wood," I said out loud bitterly; the woman

254

did not even look up. People talked to themselves all over the ghetto.

"Coffee!" the officers announced. "I want to talk to the head of this patrol," I said. "Come with me," the soldier ordered. I took off my coat "Listen," I told him, "I'm a hard worker, but I'm too small. I can't stand the work, or do it right. You need someone bigger. I want to work inside where I can really accomplish something." He looked me up and down. I stared straight into his eyes. "Well," he said, with surprise, "all right, inside; you can work with the grains, and grinding the flour." Then I could steal something. It was the biggest comfort to be able to steal two glasses full of flour, or some cereal. Momma sewed little bags; I filled them up, and walked out with them under my armpits. They may have known what we were up to. No one ever checked. Momma would make a paste of the flour with some water, and make little loaves for us. But I didn't like the way she looked; I didn't like the way Ninka looked; there was nothing I could do about it. Only Rachel looked good because of the food she got in the hospital where she worked, and she managed to skimp on meals, and bring something back to the room. She had even learned to give injections. "Now she gets more blood into the needle," Doctor Yurbo grinned at me when I came at night. "We used to transfuse them afterward."

Rachel was happy there; for the first time in her life, she was useful. And it was the place that had saved her life. "If she lives," I thought to myself, "she will have some happy memories from here." I could hear Poppa: "There is no justice, no justice at all." There was not. And Momma predicting the most terrible thing was that we would have no time for the dead. When did I have time to mourn for Stajoe or for Poppa or for Vera? I thought about them, but feelings never had time to attach themselves to thoughts; feelings were like threads of a web forever looking for rafters, pathetic threads hanging dustily in an old barn. Still, I was glad for Rachel. So six weeks went by. It was April. It was our second spring in the ghetto. There were strangers in almost all of the beds; Mr. Grimonsky and his wife still screamed over the water, but the newcomers fought louder. Momma still went down the stairs every ten minutes to find some peace; then she would run up to look at Ninka. Now Momma took Ninka to classes for the children, but she was the smallest there, and always hungry. "Force her to go," I told Momma;

"she has to learn something." "I can't do it," Momma said that night; "she gets hysterical; she turns blue again." "I'll stay home tomorrow and see to it." "You are staying in this school," I told Ninka, taking her to another dirty room, "it is *necessary*." The word "necessary" hypnotized her; somehow she had learned what it meant, but still, when I left her, she cried. "She'll get used to it," I told Momma, ignoring my quivering insides. "Pick her up at three, but if you hear anything get in the stove and leave her there. She'll have to find her way back with the other children or wait for me." Momma shook her head. "If I would only *brown* in the stove," she sighed; "what kind of stove is it that turns you yellow?" "A good stove; thank God for it." Last week the Gestapo had found two old men hiding in the double wall between our apartment and the hall. We all had our places and kept to them; there was no fighting over them. Besides, everyone thought the stove was too obvious, and maybe it was; maybe that was why no one had looked. "Strange there's no fighting over the places," I thought.

"What's the matter with Ninka?" I asked Rachel when I came home from work a few days later. Momma had gone down into the court, to stand. "She went to school today," Rachel said. "Ninka, turn your head up to me." Her little body turned over; she craned up her neck. Her forehead was feverish. "Come here," I said, picking her up; "come out on the balcony; I want to see something." "Can I take Vera Mouse?" she asked. "No, this will just take a minute; here we are. Open your mouth." The last rays of the April sun fell into her mouth. There were white spots all over the inside of her throat; her tonsils were covered with them. "Don't fall in," Ninka said, laughing. "Open again," I told her; I was filled with horror. The spots were there. "Rachel, I'm going to see Doctor Yurbo," I said, running to the door; "don't eat from the same things as Ninka." "I'm going to the hospital," I called to Momma; she nodded, looking up at the puffing clouds. "It is *le fleur* I'm sure," I insisted to Doctor Yurbo, hysterical; "please, a smear of her throat right away." "But the epidemic is over," he assured me. "Still, we don't take any chances; we'll send a man. Tadislaw! Go with this lady and take a smear for diptheria." He was back in an hour with another man. "Diphtheria. Doctor Yurbo says it's good you were so fast. We'll carry her over right away." "Where?" "Isolation." "I'm coming, too," I cried, throwing on my coat. Everyone in the room was staring, speechless. "Not good," Doctor Yurbo said again; "but don't worry, you'll see. She'll have the vaccine in a few hours; she'll start getting better right away." "What vaccine?" I practically howled. We all knew there was none; everyone who got diphtheria died. "Come into my office," he said roughly, pulling me after him. "When I say I'll get it, I'll get it," he said, angry. "But it's the middle of the night!" I wept. "So it is the middle of the night. There are lights in the hospital; I can see enough to give her the vaccine." "How will you get it?" "Never mind how; you're always asking questions. I'll get it; we got your Rachel anesthesia." I began to calm down. "Are you going to set foot outside this hospital while she's in isolation?" I shook my head, no, no, no. "Then we'll get *you* on the list here as a worker; you can go back to the mill when she's better." "How long will she be here?" "Let's just wait and see; you don't want her out before she's better. No more than two weeks. Probably. Remember, I said probably," he said, shaking me. "Two weeks," I repeated. "Probably," he reminded me.

At five in the morning, he came out. "She has the vaccine; it's already working. You'll see, in two days she'll stop getting worse and get better." "But she can hardly breathe!" I cried out. "Well," Doctor Yurbo said, "usually it is in the nose or the throat. Your Ninka is lucky and has it in the nose and the throat; it will take a few days longer, that's all. The nurse won't let her suffocate; stop carrying on like a maniac." "I want to go into her." "I don't have vaccine for you," Doctor Yurbo said, impatient. "Do you know what the mortality rate is for adults? It's ninety percent. But there's a window you can look in from outside; she's in the basement. Come on, I'll show you." He took me out. There was a little trench around the building. "For the lime," he explained. "If you put some flat stones down there," he pointed, "you can see her through the little window. Here." He handed me a piece of slate. "Go try." I crouched on the stone. There she was, inside on a little cot, choking, half-sitting and falling back, twisting and writhing. "Thank you." I didn't even hear him go.

There were stars out, cold and hard. The moon was glaring at me like one eye; someone had put out the other. Ninka was writhing on her cot, pushing herself up, choking; when she coughed, she turned purple. A nurse stayed next to her, mopping her face, patting her shoulder, helping to prop her up when she wanted to sit up and cough. I thought about the moon and Momma's clock. It was strange, but I never believed anything would happen to me, I still didn't. I didn't believe anything would happen to Ninka, either. And now this. I was glad Stajoe wasn't here to see it; he couldn't stand it when she cried from hunger. I had his watch wound around my wrist, but I didn't look at it; I didn't move. "I should be in the café," I thought to myself; "I should be hearing what to look out for."

An arm slid around my shoulders; from the fragrance, I knew it was Momma. Even now she smelled like oranges. "Anya, you can't stay here all night. Please, you were exposed, too; come home and go to sleep." "I can't, I can't," I told her; "you go back. I don't want to worry about you, too." She crouched next to me. "She looks terrible," she murmured. "She got the vaccine; she got it four hours ago." "What did Doctor Yurbo say?" "He said she'd be all right." "Then she will be all right," Momma said; "come home. You can't do any good here." "Did Rachel go to the café?" I asked, not taking my eyes from the window. Ninka seemed to be falling asleep. "Maybe she's dying!" I said out loud. "No, no, look at the blanket; it's going up and down." "Yes, yes, it is," I said, jubilant. "Did Rachel go to the café?" Momma hesitated. "Yes," she said in an odd voice. "One of the doctors told her they have already started giving death injections to the old and the sick. He thinks"—she stopped, looking away from my face—"that next there'll be an order to kill the children." "Why?" I screamed, beside myself; "why? Why can't we have them; what difference does it make?" "The doctor thought it was because they'll be liquidating the ghetto soon. They don't want children on their hands; they want workers." "We should get her well to get her killed!" I cried. "Nothing will happen to her; I know it. Nothing will happen to you. You'll figure out something; we'll do it together." "If she lives so I have something to figure out about," I said, pressing my nose to the window. Was the blanket moving up and down? It was. "I'm going back," Momma said; "I don't like leaving Rachel." "Please go back; if she's better in the morning, I'm going back to work at the mill. We'll need food for her when she gets out." "All right," Momma said, getting up. "Listen to me creak; I'm an old woman already." "Don't say that, Momma!" I cried out. "All right then, I'm a young woman with old bones."

"Her fever is dropping," Doctor Yurbo told me in the

morning; "go back to work; don't attract attention. We don't want all kinds of questions about her miraculous recovery." "Momma, I'm going to work," I said, dragging myself to the bunk where Momma kept her little pot of water, a comb, and a splinter of a mirror. "I'll go back to the hospital tonight." "Rachel will be able to tell you plenty about Ninka tonight. Go down with her; you look ready to fall down the steps again." "I told Momma what the doctor said," I told Rachel; "do you believe it?" "Why not?" "Why not?" I repeated.

I went straight to the hospital from work. From the window, I could see the nurse feeding Ninka something that looked like soup. She was still coughing, coughing and choking, but she looked better. "It's only a matter of time. She's better every day. Leave her here two weeks; she'll have more to eat, she needs the rest. When she leaves the hospital, she won't be able to get up for a while." "How long?" "Two or three more weeks." I thought about Rachel's new information. If she was right, then they would take Ninka—if they came for the children in less than five weeks. But the five weeks passed. Ninka was home on her bunk, playing with Vera Mouse and her box of lima beans, eating the pretzels soaked in water, "so she doesn't scratch her throat," Momma kept saying. "But it's all right now," I assured her. "Still," Momma said, counting to ten after dipping the pretzel in.

Rachel went out to the café. "Momma." I called her out onto the balcony. "I've decided to give Ninka away; I have to do it. One mistake with Lyubushka was enough." "Do you have a plan?" "Yes, I'll tell you when I'm ready to do something." "Is it all right?" I asked her, worried. "This is up to you, absolutely up to you." The next morning, I went to Ganz's office at the Judenrat. "I want to leave my child on the steps of the church," I told him. "I don't care about my own life, I just want her saved." He knew Stajoe very well. He sat there, watching me. "I made one mistake with Genya's Lyuba; she could have been given to the nuns. Believe me, I want to do this; I won't change my mind. I want you to do this; the only problem is getting her out." "Well," he said, slowly, "you can have my policeman. Get her ready, and whenever you want, he'll take her." "No one will find out?" I asked him. "No one will." "Then I want the policeman tomorrow morning at nine." "He'll be there."

"Momma." I shook her awake. "Tomorrow Ganz's policeman will take Ninka to the steps of the church; at nine o'clock; we'll dress her up. Do you still have her hair ribbons?" "Of course," Momma said. "I washed them last week." "What about her little blue and white striped dress?" "Rachel washed it yesterday at the hospital." "How's her hair?" "I've been dry washing it with alcohol from the hospital. I can't see any reason why we can't get her ready. I just washed her stockings and polished her shoes. But don't tell her about it until the morning," Momma pleaded. "No, but we have to get up very early." At four, we got up and began dressing her; Momma scoured every inch of her like a potato. "Listen, Ninka," I told her, looking into those big wise eyes; she was not a child at all; "we are going to take you for a walk, and then a policeman is going to take you for a walk and have you wait for me on the steps of the church until I come back from work. You will wait for me there? Quietly? Looking as nice and cheerful as you can?" She nodded, staring at me with her lantern eyes. "But listen," I told her, "a man, or woman, I'm not sure which, will come over to you, and give you something to eat. If he wants you to go with him, or with her, whoever it is, you go with him. I'll come later to get you." "What will they give me to eat?" "Oh, I don't know; an apple, maybe, or even a toy, a red ball. But you have to wait there and not tell anyone you come from inside the fence, you understand." "The *ghetto*, Momma." "Do you understand?" I asked, holding onto her shoulders. "Yes, Momma." So she answered me.

We had her dressed up like a doll, her blue and white striped dress, her long blue stockings, her heavy leather shoes with their knotted shoe laces. "Now for her hair," Momma said beginning on it, parting it in the middle. Ninka sat still as her doll. "Look how well it braids," Momma beamed, "and how it shines; the alcohol took away all that dirt and oil." Then she tied the two braids with string, rolling each one into a "basket" over each ear. In the middle of the braid coil, she pinned a long pink ribbon tied into a bow. "She looks marvelous," Momma said, "marvelous." "You would never know how hungry she was," I whispered. "Can I take Vera Mouse?" Ninka asked suddenly. "Of course," Momma answered. My throat swelled shut.

At nine o'clock, we went down to the front of the building; a Jewish policeman came up to us. "I'm looking for a Mrs. Lavinsky," he said nervously. "Here I am," I said like one of the dead. "Do you have a little girl who is supposed to meet her uncle at the church?" So that was what Ganz had told him. "Here she is," I said, pushing Ninka forward from behind my skirts; she seemed to be hiding herself. "Go on, Ninka, and go with the man or lady who comes to the steps. They will give you something to eat. Wait quietly, and later, I'll come and get you from them." I bent down to kiss her goodbye. She caught my neck in a vise. "Kiss Momushka, too." She grabbed Momma. "We have to go," the policeman mumbled, uncomfortable. "Wait quietly," I told Ninka again.

We watched her, holding his hand, four of her steps to his one, as they went out through the gate. Momma and I ran around to the slit in the gate facing the church. It was a few minutes after nine; I had wound Stajoe's watch around my wrist so hard it hurt. I loosened it. Ninka went up the steps of the church with the policeman; he bent over to say something to her, and turned around and came down. She stood there, good and obedient, as if she were waiting for me or for Momma. The two of us held onto the fence watching. Then the sun was right over our heads; it was almost the end of May. Time froze in the sky for us, but not enough to slow the sun. Then the sun began sliding down the sky. Still, Ninka did not move or cry. She bent down to say something to her doll; she turned around to look at the doors of the church, then back at the fence. She couldn't see us. It was beginning to get gray and drizzle. I finally looked at the watch. "I'm going to take her back," I told Momma. "No, wait," Momma said, "the church doors are opening." A mass was over; people began coming out. None of them looked at her. Then a tall man and his wife came out. The man, holding an opened umbrella, bent over Ninka, and said something to her. We saw him take something red out of his pocket and hand it to her; then he took her by the hand and she went off with him. When they got out of sight, I screamed and fell. "What is the matter with you, Anya, what is the matter with you, Anya? I am disgusted," Momma kept scolding; "she is the only one who will survive. Get up from the ground; you're getting dirty. You'll see; she'll survive. How can you carry on like this? Would it be better if she had a death injection?" "But we don't know for sure," I wailed. "When would we have known anything for sure," Momma asked; "after it happened?" Holding hands, the two of us walked back to the building on Polanska Street. It was still packed, but it seemed empty. I could still feel Ninka's little hand in mine. Now Momma and I were the only ones left.

Five days later, the electrician was back. "I want to check the wires near your bed. Listen, Ganz says that your little girl is with a good family. The man is named Rutkauskus. He's a good friend to the Jews, a Lithuanian. He lives on Forty-five Shaska Street." He talked as he pretended to work. "How is she?" "She's all right," he said. "Rutkauskus came to the Judenrat. He said he wondered if anyone had lost a baby; he had one, he said, but she was used to everything and ate all the time. But for three days, she screamed until he thought the neighbors were coming to look." "Thank God," I sighed, collapsing on the bunk. "Please thank Mister Ganz," Momma told him. He nodded. "While I'm here, I'll change the bulb; good to look real, you know," he smiled, climbing up on the table. "See, Anya! See!" Momma was beaming. "I'm going to the hospital to tell Rachel," I yelped, running out of the house. But at night, I wasn't so happy; Ninka still wasn't with me. The electrician was back a week later. "Fuses," he said solemnly. "They have false papers for her; they're calling her Luisa Vishinskaya so people will think she was left behind by the army when they ran away." "It is a problem for them," I considered; "Lithuanians are exceptionally ugly people, and she is so beautiful." "Yes, miss," he said, grinning; "*that* is a problem."

14

TIME passed. It passed much more slowly now that Ninka was gone, as if she had been the key to wind Stajoe's gold pocket watch, and the big gold watch through the sky we tracked on our jobs. It was almost September. At first I had told Momma, "Now I'll sleep, now my mind won't be a machine all night, thinking what to do with her," but she wasn't in the bunk breathing with me; I didn't fall asleep right away, and I would lie awake wondering: How is she? Were they kind to her? Did they feed her enough? Was she really strong enough after the diphtheria? And then it began. "I was wrong," I began telling Momma in a panic; "the rumors were wrong, we should have kept her. I have to pretend I hear her breathing at night to fall asleep." But then the rumors returned like a cloud of locusts that had missed their field. Now everyone was saying it: the children, they want the children.

A few days after the rumors returned, the soldiers came; they began lining everyone up on the streets. "Give the children!" they commanded all the women. It was pathetic to watch, pathetic, everyone standing in their poor clothes, half of them were yellow and coughing, holding onto the children as hard as they could. Most of the mothers handed the children over. It was a steely gray day. The soldiers were dressed in their long chenille coats; they blew open to show the black uniforms underneath. Gestapo work. "Oh, Momma, oh, Momma!" I cried; I couldn't stop crying. "Give the child!" a soldier ordered a woman near me. She shook her head no; she was too frightened to talk. The Gestapo man made a sign to his dog; the huge black and tan dog flew threw the air, overturning the mother and the baby. Terrified, she let go of the child. "Get it!" ordered the soldier. The child was added, shrieking, to the little group. Up and down the line were the sounds of sobs. "The child!" we heard again, and again the dog flew into the air. Another child was added to the group. The sobs were getting louder and louder; the dog flew into the air, a child crossed over to the other side, then in back of the line of soldiers. I was crying so I couldn't catch my breath. Momma's hand was tight on my waist. "We are living through biblical times," she said for the thousandth time, her lips a thin white scar in her face.

The dog flew through the air; another dog flew through the air. "Look how they pat the dog," she said to me; "look how they say it's a good dog, the innocent animals, the innocent animals, to turn them on the children. *Sabiki!*" she said loudly. "What did you say?" a soldier said in Russian, thrusting a gun muzzle into her face. "I said dogs," Momma said; "there are dogs all over; don't you see them?" "Why is your daughter crying like that?" he demanded; "has she someone to hide?" "Why don't you look in our room?" Momma suggested. "Soldiers are doing that now; everywhere, in the stoves, in the walls; we will get her," he leered, thrusting his face close to mine. "Please be careful, Momma," I sobbed. "It doesn't matter," she sighed; "it doesn't matter. After this, we know what to expect." For the next few days a thick silence fell over the ghetto. Rachel and I took turns going to the café. It was Rachel who came back like a sleepwalker. "They say Ganz told the Germans they can do what they want, no more orders; he will not do anything, no matter what." In the morning, we heard he had been arrested; by nightfall, everyone knew he had been shot. "This is the end, then," Momma said "probably tomorrow they liquidate the place. Let's start dividing things up. You take the pictures, this ring." "You have to keep the watch!" She still had the watch Poppa gave her, and a few plain rings Anzia had brought to the fence. "We have nothing to give you, Rachel," Momma said sadly. "As long as I can go with you, I don't want anything." "I know it's tomorrow," Momma said again from her darkness in the bunk; the three of us had crowded in together like fish.

Early in the morning we were all in the street. And then came the announcement: Everyone out on the street; take what you can carry on your backs. "Into the house," Momma said, chasing me as if I were a chicken. "Go comb your hair and put on some lipstick. It wouldn't hurt to wash that face again. And don't forget to bring that piece of mirrow down with you." "Please, Momma," I begged her, crying. "No crying; your eyes will get red. I'll wait down here." I combed my hair savagely and smeared on the lipstick. "Don't forget the comb and lipstick, either," Momma called up from the court. When I came back down, the whole picture had changed. People were in line, holding little packages; there were no little babies crying, no children at all. The ghetto gate was open; we could see the whole street. By now we all knew it was two miles to Rosa Field, our destination. We went along a long narrow street, lined on both sides with soldiers, and machine guns; they filled the whole horizon as far as the eye could see. There were two lines in a perspective drawing converging into infinity, forever and forever beyond sight. One of the soldiers seemed to be giving the orders. On an impulse, I ran over to him. "Listen," I said, "I know you need people for all kinds of orthopedic things for your hospital. My mother and I are experts, real experts; you wouldn't be sorry; we do good work." He looked me up and down. "I bet you do," he said crudely; "all right, you and your mother, go get her, wait for my orders in the *torovaje*." I motioned to her and to Rachel. "Not you." he said, barring Rachel from us. If his arms had been a roadblock, it could not have been more effective. He nodded to a soldier who pulled her away by the arm. How could I have forgotten Rachel! I pulled Momma into the *torovaje*. "We're experts on medical corsets and orthopedic things, *orthopedic things*," I repeated. She nodded. We sat there from ten in the morning until five-thirty; naturally, there was no food or water. The man never came for us. "He forgot," I whispered to Momma. "Or he had orders," she whispered back. "Maybe we can hide in here?" The loudspeakers came on. "Anyone caught hiding in this ghetto will be hung; anyone caught hiding in this ghetto will be hung."

"Let's go, Anya," Momma said, getting up. We went out. There were not many others, the administrators of the camp and the two of us. We started to walk, soldiers on both sides of the street, and a clump of them behind. We could hear them talking. "Oh, most of them have been shot by now; they're just dumped in the field," one was saying casually. "I guess they'll leave these, they did so much work for us." So while we had sat there, forgotten, the others had been killed. The sky was filling with misshapen black clouds like round rotten fruit. And then we saw Rosa Field. It was filled with people, thousands and thousands of people, surrounded by wire. "In!" the soldier ordered and we went through the little opening in the

265

wire. In a few minutes, we heard the gate clang behind us. And then transport after transport began arriving, mothers with children, most of the people more than half dead. "In! In! In!" the soldiers kept saying; "in, in, in."

And God was so good to us, it began to rain; the whole field was turning to mud between our bodies. It was cold and nasty; rain kept falling in tarnished silver lines. Momma and I huddled together. Soldiers moved around, bending over babies. "Death shots!" Momma gasped. I didn't answer. It was obvious some of the old and the young had already had them in the trucks; they were dying all around us. Where we were, we could see some people had managed to build little fires, shielding them with their bodies, to warm themselves. "The courage of some of them!" Momma murmured; "the courage!" "Do you want a fire?" "Anya, what for?" "Please, sleep," I begged her. We knew what was coming. They would not take the old and the sick to work. She looked terrible, yellow. "Please, sleep," I pleaded; "you look terrible. A woman has to look her best," I tried to tease her. "It's no use with me," she said in a tone I had never heard from her. "Try!" I begged. "I'll try," she said, leaning against me; but she didn't sleep. She was an intelligent woman; she knew what was coming. Lightning was forking all over the sky like electrified veins. "Rachel must be in here somewhere," I murmured, silently praying she wasn't one of the stiff bodies I saw in the lightning flashes. "You will find her," Momma promised me. "*We* will find her," I insisted, but she didn't make a sound. In the morning, they lined us up. The women had heard there was a new order. All women with children were to be killed; they could not stay on the worklines.

Some of the women heard it and ran away with their children. "How could they do it?" I asked Momma. "Everything for life," she answered dully; "everything to live." "What are the soldiers doing to the children?" she asked me suddenly. Soldiers were carrying little children up and down the lines of women. One passed us. We heard him cooing, as if he were talking to his own child, "Where is Mommy? Where is Mommy? Show us where is Mommy." "*Bozhe moy!*" Momma exclaimed. Then the little child lunged forward; we could see a woman move and cower back. The soldier with the child pointed at her; another pulled her out. The first handed her the child. "Both, to the death lines!" he ordered, bored. "No," I kept shaking

266

my head; "no." I had come so close; Ninka had come so close. One woman in our line was crouched down in back of us. "She must have left a child," Momma whispered after it was over; "see how she hid herself? So she is saved, and this is how it is." "Momma," I cried, looking at her; "please do something about yourself." Frantically I began combing her hair; she was yellow as skin painted with iodine. "Momma," I kept crying; "Momma." I had my lipstick out, I painted her lips, I smeared her cheeks, I rubbed the lipstick into her skin, I turned her head this way and that way. She stood still, like a good child. It did no good. She still looked a thousand years old. I was desperate. I couldn't think of anything more to do with her. "How do I look?" Momma smiled at me ironically; "am I all beautiful?" "Oh, yes," I said, sobbing, "yes, if you could only look happier." "I cannot look twenty-three," Momma answered; "don't torture yourself; we'll see what happens."

Then they began marching us through the streets toward the ramps outside of Rosa Field and the city. The trains were there, waiting. We could see more coming, first as little puffs of smoke, then as great noises, then huge closed cars, dirty and dull, rolling up. Suddenly I let go of Momma's hand and began walking like a robot in the opposite direction. I was going back to the city. I walked about two blocks. "Oh," a soldier said. He was looking at my shoes. They were covered with mud from the field; it was the only place so muddy. "Back," he ordered me, holding out his arm; he didn't beat me. I ran, catching up with Momma. She looked up at me. "He didn't let you, eh?" she asked, taking my hand. She would have been glad if I had gone.

At the train section they checked us again. There were two little gates, one to the trains, one to somewhere else. I remembered a story I heard about another camp that was liquidated before ours; how they had put everyone in graves and machine-gunned them; whoever was alive was alive, and then lorry-trucks began dumping dirt in, burying them all. I held on to Momma's hand. We were getting near the segregation point. "You," he said to me; "here!" "You," he said to Momma, "there." He pointed to the left. "Momma!" I screamed, running over to her side. I didn't think about the danger, that once you were there, you were there. I wanted to be with Momma. "Here," she said, taking off her watch, "take it; maybe we can still do something." She wanted to live, to be alive, to be with me. "Take the rings, too," she ordered me. "Please," I said, running up to the soldier, "take them." I was holding Momma by the wrist. I pulled her into the right line. Then, near the entrance to the trains, they checked us again. "You!" a soldier shouted at Momma, "to the left!" "Momma!" I shrieked, "Momma," and again, I ran over. I could hear her screaming, "You will live! You have someone for whom to live!" "Momma!" I kept screaming; "Momma" I was running up and down the line like a poisoned rat. She had hidden herself. "Momma!" "Enough, back!" A soldier grabbed me and pushed me to the right. I did not see her again. "March!" Our line began to move toward a little iron gate. It was about half a block to the ramps. My head kept turning like a pinwheel. Momma was gone. I looked for an hour; we stood there for an hour. "In, in," the soldiers ordered; "in, in!" They packed us in the train so tight we could not fall down. I heard the door clang shut; I didn't feel anything, not even sorrow. I was completely numb.

THE LION'S JAWS

The mouse came running in to the rat;
Good news, he mewed, good news!
The cat is caught; what do you think of that?
The cat has walked into the lion's jaws.
Now we will have bread and fat.
Oh, said the rat,
I don't know about that.
The strongest animal in the kingdom is the cat.

Russian fable, as told by Mrs. Savikin

15

THE train jerked forward, then stopped. It jerked forward
again and began to move; it stopped again suddenly,
throwing us against each other. "The color of the train is
dark red," I thought; "there must be a hundred and fifty
of us here." The train began picking up speed, throwing us
against each other again. "It must still be raining," I
thought, hearing the little metallic pings coming from all
ends of the car, as if hundreds and hundreds of dwarfs
were sealing us in with tiny gray silver hammers. But it
was as if someone else were noting these things, and telling them to someone else too bored or stupid or tired to
pay attention. "If they are taking us like this," a woman in
back of me whispered, "they must be taking us to a death
camp." At the field, we had heard the first rumors of
them. What did she mean? I wondered to myself passively.
"They wouldn't put animals in here like this unless they
were taking us to a glue factory," she answered someone
near her. Then for a while there was silence. It was a
wooden train with no windows. I don't know how long it
was moving. I leaned back in my corner, against the
boards in the car, my arms folded across my breasts as if
to protect them. I was leaning against the two other
women pressing on me. Outside it must be cold, I thought
automatically, but in here, there were so many of us, we
were warming each other up. "I have to go to the
bathroom," someone whimpered; no one answered her.

The train ran forward and forward. There was nothing
to see. Occasionally, if I opened my eyes, they would play
tricks on me, and I could see the mountains of Zakopanie
coming into view, or the little houses before Druzgeniekie,
but when I closed my eyes, I didn't see anything. Then I
opened my eyes and saw the Warsaw Station and Stajoe's
family lined up like an unending train. How long had we
been traveling? It was impossible to tell. But then the car
began to have a familiar smell. "Ignore it," I heard me

telling myself, but the smell was getting thicker and thicker. I was abnormally sensitive to smells; my stomach was beginning to heave, my legs were beginning to get numb, my lips were numb, too. If we were going north, it was getting colder inside. I opened my eyes and saw the family waving to me as I got on the train with Stajoe; I saw Momma painted with lipstick. "It's been a long time," I thought. "I wish I had gone with her; it would have been easier on her, not being alone; who knows how long she'll have to wait, and in the rain." But the smells were getting worse. The woman had been right to ask about bathrooms; there were none. I could feel my own body letting go; it was as shocking as if I had been holding on to a raft in a cold sea and had seen one wave too many and decided to let my fingers loose. And my stomach was rebelling; it was rising. Every time I breathed in the odor, I felt my stomach heaving. I tried focusing on the seams of planks, but I couldn't really see them; I tried focusing on a light head three rows in front of me; it was no use. I was vomiting violently; no one said anything. "If I only had Vera's piano!" I thought to myself, and then, "what did I want it for, a potty?"

So the train went on and on. The wheels of the train turned, the wheels of the body turned, the wheels of hunger spun, the mind jammed and played the same scenes over and over again, or none at all. "I should have stayed with Momma," I thought to myself again, but who knew where they had taken her? She might be on a train like this herself; we might all meet in the same place when the wheels came to a rest. It did not stop. Finally, there was a slight tremor and a slight hiss of brakes; we were still going very fast. Then the brakes hissed again. We were slowing down. "Bathrooms!" whispered a familiar voice. Who was she? We were all from Vilno in this train. If the voice was that familiar, I probably knew her. But my eyes were closed. When they were closed, their lids were shades pulled down on this world. It did not exist; it was a black place with white streaks that sometimes looked like clouds, sometimes like mountains, sometimes like fireworks. It was the world forming. Nothing had happened yet, nothing was going to happen; one white shape was the shape of an anvil, pulled out of proportion; nothing had taken its definite form. The most frequent shapes were the fireworks and the shooting stars, the streaks that traveled fast from left to right, always from left to right. One last braking, and the train came to a full stop. Outside there were some voices, a commotion in German; someone outside said something about water. The train started up again. The woman who had mentioned the bathrooms was crying softly. I closed my eyes; it was getting colder in the train. If it stopped, I would clean off my dress with the handkerchiefs Momma gave me. In a few minutes it did stop. Then came the banging and clanking of the door drawing back.

Outside, it was brilliant white; the sun was not at the top of the sky. "It must be ten o'clock, or ten-thirty." That was the time we had left. "It must be twenty-four hours," I thought. But I was staring into the forest. The forest was like the world behind my lids; some vertical stripes, light ones for the birch trunks, dark green for the pines, but dark, dark inside. "Peasants live in that forest," I thought to myself with joy, "peasants like the people Anzia and Zoshia knew. They are going on with their lives." I wanted so much to go into the woods and find the peasants' huts, the thatched huts, to feed the pigs and the cows and the chickens, the little things that never hurt anyone and who were killed for a reason, or who killed like the bears, without pretending to have a higher nature. "I would be good there," I thought, as if I were actually promising someone. The train was resting on a kind of red mud embankment; I could see myself jumping down from the train, scrambling down the embankment, and running across the field into the forest; there would be flowers and flowers. Then I saw the patches of snow lying on the ground like torn pieces of clothes. No, it was September 7; it was getting colder. At the foot of the embankment, soldiers were clumped together in their uniforms and chenille-lined coats, rifles over their shoulders, talking as if they were just meeting at a café. What were they telling each other? It must be so nice to talk that way, about anything; one lit a cigarette, puffed at it twice, then threw it on the ground and stubbed it out.

The sun had gone behind a sheet of ice, but it was casting a brilliant light. The inside of the car was unpainted, rough brown boards, some of them almost gray from the weather, like driftwood. "From the leaking water," I thought, looking up for the first time, seeing the cracks in the roof. It was so quiet here and nice. The peasants' huts were only just beyond the thick fringe of the forest. The soldiers' breath came on the air, puff, puff, puff, as if they were little steam engines themselves. I shivered in the cold, but with the door open, I could see the trees. And the smell was not so bad; the wind was taking it out like a good white nurse. The little group of soldiers began breaking up. Four men marched through them with an iron pail of water. It was huge; patches of metal or dark paint had flaked from its side. They began their climb with it toward the train. Instinctively, everyone moved back, clearing a place. They slammed the kettle down, spilling the water. "Anyone dead?" asked one of the soldiers, looking at us, sniffing. "No one? Then drink the water." We must have been traveling for more than a day if they were asking about the dead. "There will come a time when the living will come to envy the dead." No, that was wrong; I was already one of the dead, with the ghosts and splinters of my life on earth. The splinters cut into my skin; it didn't bleed. Now and then there was a drop of blood, mocking life, but it was not real. I was embalmed by Momma's death; they had embalmed the wrong people. Why didn't they know we were dead? And why wasn't I sure? My mind was rattling the door of insanity; it moved back into the safe house of the moving corpse of Anya Lavinsky; it shut the doors; it sat on bare planks in an empty corner, knees drawn up, shattered glass spattering the whole floor. There was no ladle, no cup, but we drank.

I had out my handkerchief first; I drank a little, then dipped it in. I used half of it to clean the front of my dress, the other half for my face. "Look at her," someone in the car jeered, "trying to wash!" "If they're talking more, they must be thinking we're getting out," I told myself, but now I knew I was still talking to Momma. I didn't think we were getting out. There were no other trains, no wagons, not enough soldiers, just this little group that had re-formed at the bottom of the embankment, puffing out their little white clouds of breath.

As soon as we finished drinking, the men took the kettle. Two of them held it; the other two slammed the door into place. "No!" the woman in back of me howled like a wolf. Who was she? She was on my left, pressed against the boards of the side of the train. "Liska!" I thought; "Liska!" remembering the story of her broken marriage, her terrible smelling body. "No," she kept screaming, but the train was picking up speed, and it was definitely colder. "Liska!" I said out loud, trying to call her. But she didn't hear me, and I didn't call her again. I went back behind my lids counting the shooting stars, the anvil shape and the straight white line beneath, the white shapes moving from right to left, like amoebas. A cold wind yanked them open. There was a hole in the train! Liska was beating on the boards like a madwoman. "Stop it!" I called to her, automatically; "you will hurt yourself; stop it!" But she was banging and kicking with all her strength, and it wasn't her strength, it was the strength of ten men. The board was giving way against her; I could see one jagged edge tilt out into the air, and another edge jut in, splintery and rough. "Liska, stop it!" I called again, but she was hammering at the cross-bar as if her arms and hands were made of iron. There was blood running down her arms; they were dead white. The board came loose and flew out. Systematically, Liska began on the one next to it. "Stop it," I kept saying, "stop it," but the smells were disappearing for me, my stomach was settling. The second board was splintering like the first, and then it was gone. I could see the rails behind us, receding into the distance into the neat tall triangle, the vanishing point, the witch's cap. On one side of the track was the forest, so near I could hear it breathing; on the other was a great rough field, overgrown with huge weeds, turning dry and brown and crackling in the wind. When Liska turned to look in the train, her eyes seemed to have fallen from her head; they stared, wide, without pupils. Her face was carved out of stone. Then she turned back to her own little door and walked through it.

I was sobbing hysterically, but I felt only the jerks of my body, not what was causing them. What would happen to her? There was the sound of a bullet, but the train was moving on; it was impossible to see anything. She must have broken her arms and legs; perhaps she was already dead. Then the same noise started from the other side of the door. My eyes would not move from the place of the sound. A new window appeared; light fell in like stones. There was a scream from a woman inside the train; there was the sound of a shot outside. The noise began in the back of the car, in the front. I could hear Momma's voice saying: "They are all going crazy now, Anya; you don't have to go with them." And the car was getting colder and colder, catching all the cross winds. The trees looked so tempting, like peasants, old old peasants, with skin so old it was elephant skin. "A person can get used to anything," Poppa was telling me and Max was holding my belt in the Prosectorium. I closed my eyes and began tracking the shooting stars; they were brighter now that there was more light in the car.

It couldn't have been much longer, or it was very much longer, before the train stopped again. There was a little building of old wood built up on a platform. A man came out of it with a big hammer; two more men came out with planks of wood already cut to size. I heard them at our car, nailing each board back in place, Liska's board, the other woman's board, four boards all together. From the other cars came the sound of more hammering, but dimmer. It was almost dark outside; inside it was all dark again. The train started up. "In the morning, it will be forty-eight hours," I thought to myself remotely; it was as if I would tell myself about this some time later, when I had time to hear. "It's as quiet as an ear," I thought to myself, remembering Momma's favorite Russian expression when all but the two of us were asleep in the apartment; I almost started to laugh. "Soon you will be crazy, too," I thought to myself, but the amoebas were moving through the shooting stars and though I was standing, I was falling asleep.

When the train stopped again, it was for good. This was a place; it was pitch dark, but there were sounds of activity; all around you could feel it. People were coming and going, giving orders, asking questions. A wooden ramp was wheeled against both sides of the train; a man's voice kept shouting "Down, down," and we went. Then there was the dim shape of an arched building with an open door, the dim shape of men with rifles against it. "So the building must be white," I thought, and we walked on. There was no light at all, but the thin straw mattresses on the floor were bright enough to see. There was a scramble for them. Then the men came in with kettles of coffee and pieces of stale bread and we were left alone.

On the mattress next to me, someone was crying. In the faint light I could see her; she couldn't be more than seventeen or eighteen, and she had thick dark hair like Vera's, twisted in braids on the top of her head, and big eyes; even in the dark I could see her dark eyes. "What am I going to do?" she kept asking me. "You're asking me?" I said in a tired voice; "I wish I knew myself." "But I just got engaged," she protested, as if that should have protected her against everything, that should have made her safe. She reminded me of Vera. "Who knows what

276

will happen when this is over?" I told her; "you may find each other again. The important thing is to get some sleep," I instructed selfishly; it wasn't my voice. I was exhausted. "Yes, sleep," she echoed like a child. "What's your name?" she asked in a little voice. "Anya Lavinsky. What's yours?" "Sonya Reibman." "I will see you in the morning, Sonya," I said, falling asleep on my back, something I had never done before, even when I was pregnant. I was reminded suddenly: Stajoe using his engineering skills to arrange hundreds and hundreds of pillows around the stomach of this blond whale trying to sleep on its side in his beautiful bed. "Good night, Sonya," I said again, more softly.

16

A STRANGE screaming woke me up. "What is it?" Sonya asked, grabbing my wrist. I started to shake her hand loose, then stopped. "It sounds like a siren," I answered; "maybe that's how they wake us up here." "Maybe we're going to be bombed!" she whispered dramatically, trembling with terror. "Stop inventing tragedies for yourself; the Germans are not going to waste bombs, flying over their own camp, dropping bombs and probably missing, and the gasoline for the planes, and the fliers who fall into the trees; what are you thinking about?" Sonya subsided. "They'll probably tell us what it is," she whispered. "Probably; they usually do." The door slid open, and some men came in. "Food," one of them called, putting down a huge kettle. "It's coffee!" Sonya exclaimed, ecstatic. "And bread," I said, pointing. Another man had two big boards nailed together; he was covering them with chunks of bread. "Oh, let's go!" Sonya cried. Everyone was on the food. The big pot had only one handle, but when we got closer, we were not so anxious to eat. There was a heavy scum on top. "Grease," Sonya said. "I bet they cooked last night's supper in it," a woman behind me grumbled. "Are those worms?" Sonya asked me in the most astonished voice I had ever heard. There were some dead worms swimming on top of the coffee. "Or lice," I said, remembering my trips to the peasants' huts. "But we'll die for sure if we don't eat; it's only a dead worm."

So we drank our coffee and ate our green bread. "The bread is *green*," Sonya whimpered while I was drinking my coffee. "Will you stop that and eat," I answered unsympathetically, "or I will go to another mattress." Sonya gobbled down her bread. "Where are we?" "Am I a map? We're far away from Vilno, that's all." "We are in Kaiserwald," a woman behind us whispered; "they divide us up here. Some go to death camps; some stay here; it's a labor camp here." We didn't even turn around to thank her.

What did she have to do with us? I could already tell Sonya was going to stick to me like skin. I took out my little pocket mirror, the sliver left over of Momma's, and began to wash off my face with the rest of my coffee. "Should I comb my hair too?" Sonya asked me. "No, yours looks fine; it will stay cleaner pinned up like that." "So what now?" she sighed. "Bored?" I asked. "Don't be mean." "I'm sorry," I said after a minute.

"Someone's coming," Sonya said, excited; the door was drawing back again. I looked up at the vaulted ceiling; it reminded me of a church. There was something else that had happened on the train; I was sure of it. I hammered at my memory; it stayed locked like a vault. Whatever was inside lived on without air. I gave up. This was shock, shock; I had only read about it. I looked around the room and at Sonya. "A good thing, an anesthetic, don't ask me how I got it." It was Doctor Yurbo's voice. I switched it off; I could do that more easily now. The barracks was huge. Hundreds of us were there, all of us smelly and messy, most of us in very good clothes, even with some jewelry; we had been the last transport, the last ones left from the big families; we had everything that was left. And still we smelled like sewers. I picked up a corner of the mattress; underneath was the rough unfinished wood. "Like a peasant's coffin," I thought to myself.

Two men in black uniforms came in. "This is Kaiserwald," one of them told us. Their backs were to the light; they were black silhouettes, paper cut-outs; we couldn't even see their faces, just the outline of their bodies, the familiar third arm, the rifle. "This is a segregation point; some of you go on from here to other camps, the rest stay here. First is a physical examination. So,"—he paused, and the sound of breathing stopped in the room—"you take off all your clothes and leave them on the side of the barracks and then come outside." Sonya looked at me in a panic. "Do what they say," I told her, beginning to unfasten the buttons of my blue dress; "do what they say." Then I took off my shoes and stockings. I was standing in my slip. "Everything off," said the second man; suddenly, his eyes were on me. I pulled the slip over my head, but I wouldn't let go of my pictures. They were fastened together, the ones Stajoe had thrown at me, with a piece of dirty thread; in between them I slipped the sliver of Momma's mirror and my comb. I closed my fist over them. "Outside," the second man commanded. So we stood there in the winter sunlight. "There are no trees here," I thought to myself in horror, "no trees. But there must be trees; why can't I see them?" A band of men in white uniforms, dressed like doctors, was coming toward us.

"What are they?" Sonya gasped, trying to grab me. "Doctors, only doctors," I told her, but I knew better; now I could recognize the face of the second man in the group. I had seen him when we walked out of the train into the building; the soldiers were wearing white uniforms over their army ones. "So," one said approaching me, "lice, eh?" He pinched my nipples. "And how is this, after the trip, all dirty, eh?" He pulled at my pubic hair. I could hear Sonya next to me breathing in terrified little gasps. My stomach was heaving and heaving. I looked down fast; the muscles were pulling the surface of my abdomen in and out. He could see it. "Gasoline for you," he said, "for the lice," and then the next man came along and it began again. My breasts were so sore I could feel the pain in my toes. But next to me Sonya was behaving. "So," one of the men said when they finished, "we will take your clothes; they're filthy—I'm surprised at you girls, your age, too— and we'll give you some of ours, but first, because of the lice—we can't have that here, in a clean camp—we take care of your hair. And stoop over when the men get to you; they have to check your rectums for ringworms and bleeding; it's for your own good, only for your own good." Sonya's hand flew to her head. With a shock, I realized mine had done the same thing. My rectum was clenching like a fist. Men began moving toward us. "Line up, please," one called; our line had become straggly again after the examination.

"Look," Sonya said to me, horror-stricken; "they have some kind of machines!" The first five men stopped, facing the first five naked women. Something silver gleamed in their hands. The silver machines moved toward the women's heads. We saw the hair falling from the heads of the women; they were standing still as statues, little piles of hair mounting around them like offerings. "This one has braids," we heard one of the men say as they got near us. He took out a big pair of scissors, cutting the braids off, then the rest of the hair off in chunks next to the scalp. "They're not professionals," I whispered to Sonya. My blond hair! My blond hair! "Look how they're taking it off in chunks, little stiff pieces all over!" Sonya was rigid with fear. "More braids," the man pretended to sigh, coming up to Sonya; the other moved in front of me. I saw the bars on his uniform move up and down under his white coat where it was open above the first button, up and down, up and down, as he raised his hand to my head again and again. I saw bits of blond hair falling from my head, catching the light as they fell over my eyes; the hairs began getting into them. "That's right," he said, mocking me, "close your eyes so the hair doesn't get in." He was finished with me. I put my hand up to my head. It was rough and prickly, like the skin of a deer, or a cactus. The other man was still in front of Sonya, "Unpin your braids," he was ordering her. She was staring in terror; her arms didn't move. "Unpin them," I ordered. She raised her arms like chicken wings and began pulling out the heavy iron pins; the thick braids tumbled down below her waist. "Should I unbraid them for you?" he asked, helpful. "Unbraid them!" I commanded again. She did so slowly; her eyes were bright as a mirror. His scissors came out; the two braids lay like drape pulls on the gritty earth. They shone there like ebony. Then he began clipping her hair. I didn't look; I knew she didn't want me to watch. "A relation of yours?" he asked solicitously. "She's nothing to me," I said without concern; "I don't care what you do with her." And then they were through.

I looked down the lines. We were all young women, eighteen, maybe twenty-four or -five at the oldest, such beautiful bodies, standing there in front of the barracks, completely naked, our heads shaven as if we were lunatics or the most dangerous murderers. I began to feel a pressure in my hand; it was the little packet of photographs, the mirror, the comb, and the lipstick. I didn't need the mirror; looking at the others, I knew what I looked like. "There are clothes inside," the man in black announced through a megaphone; the line was going back in. We were walking over hair, a carpet of hair, black braids, blond braids, little locks, curls. Stajoe had had a gold watch with a locket of my hair. Inside, our clothes were gone from the walls. "Line up," called another voice. Then a man began coming down the rows with a canister of gasoline and another clipper; he clipped the hair under our arms, then our pubic hair. "Why should it hurt so much?" I wondered, and then came the gasoline from the can, poured all over my hair, from head to toe. "Bend over," he ordered, pouring it down my back, then spreading my behind, pouring it in. It burned; I was sore from diarrhea.

I was drenched in it. Sonya was next to me, crying; I was biting my lip from the burning.

"Wipe it off, wipe it off," another man instructed coming down the line with some rags. Sonya wasn't too energetic; he scoured her himself, paying special attention to her breasts and vagina. Then, from the other door at the end of the barracks came men with huge wheelbarrows filled with clothes. They gave each of us a pair of wooden *clumpas*, peasant shoes, like Lithuanian peasant shoes, one piece of raw unfinished wood, heels, soles, backs and all. No stockings. "Let's see," one of the men said, looking at Sonya; she was very tall. "This should be fine for you," and he gave her a short dress and a couple of torn sweaters. "Let's see," he said again looking at me, five foot one, "this for you," and he handed me a huge dress, so long it trailed down to the floor, and two gigantic sweaters. "No trading!" he warned us both. We looked like madwomen. "Why are they doing it?" Sonya asked. "Look, Sonya," I said, "they are just enjoying themselves; right now, we are only flies, and they are pulling off wings." "It cannot be like that," she was crying. "It can and it is; you have to stop that complaining. You're worse than the soldiers." "Will we survive?" she asked me suddenly. "How should I know?" I took out my mirror; I had to do it. There was my face, but thinner, with big blue eyes; they couldn't bleach those; a funny-looking dress was hanging on me like a curtain from a curtain rod. It was wool. "So," I said; "do you want to look?" Her hand went up to her head again. She shook her head no. "Look," I insisted. She started to cry. "Now you have nothing else to cry about, so you're better off." It was a relief, having nothing to lose but your own life, devalued now, like the last regime's currency.

There was a commotion at the back of the barracks. Neither of us turned around. We were looking ahead; in front of us was a sliver of mirror floating with this new photograph of ourselves. "The rest of you will stay where you are," the megaphone announced. Then we turned around: half of the barracks had been emptied. "Where are the rest of them?" Sonya asked. "Other camps," a voice in back of us said; "if they come for more of us, or if the camps ask for more, or if the ghetto needs more to meet some quotas when they have actions, that's the end." "When do they come?" I asked. "Anytime; usually they don't come after they give you dinner; they don't like to waste food, so they take you out before, but sometimes they have to come back for more then too. If they counted wrong, they come back and pull you out of your bed." "How do you know?" Sonya whispered. "I escaped from Stuthoff; they caught me in a little town in Poland; I went to Rosa Field in one of those transports. The transport I came in"—she was smiling at us, but her eyes glittered; I didn't like it—"was full of dead children; they gave them the death injections. I sat with them all night. Didn't you see any? I was sitting in the middle of a whole heap of them. Children." "I saw," I said, grabbing Sonya's hand. "I did, a lot," Sonya answered. "Sonya," I said, still holding on to her; "don't talk to her; she is not right." Sonya nodded dumbly.

Another soldier came in. "He's assigning jobs," the woman behind us whispered. Neither of us looked at her. "This one for the disinfectant machine, and this one and this one," we heard as he came toward us; "and these," he said, pointing first to the other woman, and sweeping his hand past Sonya and me, "to the rail commander's." "How many to go there?" asked another soldier with him. "Forty," he answered; "count down the line starting with her." "All right, into the barracks," the man said through the megaphone when he got to the end of the line; "forty in each line; forty in each barracks." "Stick to me," I whispered to Sonya; the line went outside. The barracks were painted white. They were in a long row behind the big one-room barracks we had been in, with little spaces between each one. Each barracks had windows and little doors up and down the length of the building. "In!" the soldier commanded. Our line began with Sonya; the other women went into the barracks before ours.

Inside, the ceiling was strung with a row of naked light bulbs. There were wooden bunks, four levels high, unpainted raw wood, some thin blankets. The windows were open, and some doors. There was no stove in the barracks. "We'll have to sleep with our clothes on," Sonya whispered. "Let's take a bunk in the middle, away from the door; I don't like being near a door." I was thinking about what the other woman had said, about how they could come and get you at any time; so, I thought to myself, they would be more likely to grab someone near a door. "Oh, yes," Sonya agreed; she had no idea why I wanted that particular set of bunks. "Which one do you want?" she asked me anxiously. "The one near the top." "But you have to climb up to it! See, they have no ladders, you have to climb from bed to bed; you can break your neck." "Nevertheless," I insisted, "and you on the third level." "But I will have to climb up too!" "So you might as well start practicing now," I told her, climbing up. I was remembering one of Mischa's stories about the lice in the little village. "They don't get you if you're the highest up," he told me after Momma fell asleep. "You can shred them off and they fall on the others, but if you're lower down, the others pick them off, and they fall onto you. A man in the village died from the lice; they sucked out all his blood. You should see how big they get!" Two days later, the Gestapo surrounded our building and they took him with Verushka and the others. So if I was up high, I wouldn't have too many lice, and neither would Sonya. I could get them off before I even climbed up.

"We still smell of gasoline," Sonya whimpered from her bunk. "We're going to be smelling a lot more if that woman is right," I said without patience. "Will we survive?" she asked again. "You won't, not if you keep asking me that. Find something else to think about. How can you think about yourself anyhow, with your hair looking like that?" No sound. I was thinking of Ninka and her two thick braids, her two blond braids, the two blond baskets, holding the dry piece of bread in her hand, the man with the umbrella taking her underneath it along with his wife. "I have to escape, I have to escape," I thought, but the face of the woman who had sat among the dead children kept coming back and coming back like a circling shark. I saw the children, frozen, moon-blue. "She may die without me," I thought, "if I can, I will," I told myself, making it definite. "Think about how nice your hair will look when it grows in," I told Sonya in a softer voice. "Would you tell me a story?" "I'm going to come down there and tell you the right kind of story for such a baby," I threatened, climbing down. She reminded me of Vera. It was dangerous to let her do it.

"Give me your hand." Half-frightened, half-grinning, Sonya handed it over. "This," I said, making a fist, "is the crow, and these," I said, pointing to her fingers, "are the little birds in the nest." Automatically, Sonya curled up her hand to protect them. "This little bird got a worm," I said, bending down the first finger; "and this little bird cleaned the nest," bending down the second; "and this little bird screamed at the cat," bending down the third;

"and this little bird sat on the last egg," bending down the fourth finger; "but this little bird," I said, wiggling the pinky, "you didn't do anything! You are lazy! Go drink hot water!" and I walked my fingers up Sonya's arm to her armpit and began tickling her. She started to giggle. I had done this to Ninka and Verushka hundreds of times. "I think I'm getting a rash," she said, looking at her foot; "maybe I'm allergic to gasoline." "Will you stop looking for trouble!" I cried; "we know what to do about rashes." And I began to recite, "Rash, rash, go away from here, go disturb the pigs." "You know that, too," Sonya said, laughing; "maybe I should try it." "Go ahead, plenty of water will collect inside the windows as soon as everyone takes a few more breaths." This water was supposed to be rubbed on the rash morning and night, three times each application, and the saying repeated three times with it. I remembered the purple child, Ninka, all swollen up, the gentian violet. I started to cry. They were tears falling on a desert. They hit the sand, evaporated and sizzled; only the surface was pocked. Automatically, Sonya started up too. "I knew it," she said; "I knew it, you were engaged too." "No." We were locked together. "Married," I cried. "Is he dead?" "Oh, yes, all of them." "I am sorry," Sonya said, still crying, and we lay on her bunk, crying, until the soldiers came to line us up and explain the routines.

The sirens would wake us up at five in the morning, and our breakfast, hot coffee and some stale bread, would be brought in. At six, we would be outside, lined up, then marched off to our jobs in groups of four. Across the field in front of our barracks were more barracks, for the men but separated from ours by an electric fence. We would be counted by the soldiers before breakfast, after breakfast, when we got to work, when we came back from work, before we got our supper on the lineup, and then again when we got back to the barracks. Anyone who wanted to use the bathroom, which was like a little outhouse behind the barracks, or near the ramp, was escorted by a soldier. The whole time anyone was in the poor little place with its thin walls and no roof, the soldier would be marching around and around with his rifle. Anyone who couldn't work would be taken away in the selection. We were terrified of illness, everyone went to work sick to death; if they survived their sickness, they might still live. Usually, if they stayed behind, they were taken immediately. There was a shower in the barn in back of the third barracks; we could use it before or after work, but a soldier had to come with us there, too. "Will we get gloves and boots?" someone asked. "You have all the clothes you need," the soldier answered coldly; "we don't like complaining." He seemed to be memorizing the woman's features. "It must get awfully cold here in the winter," Sonya murmured after he left. "It does," said a German woman. I had already noticed her. Her skin was the color of fly paper. When the soldier spoke, she paid no attention, just picked white things from the front of her sweater and dropped them on the floor.

"Did you just get here?" I asked her. "No," she said bitterly; "I'm a *political* prisoner; I don't even remember what I did. I've been here a long time, so ask; you have questions." She couldn't have been more than thirty, but her hair was gray and seemed to be thinning. "You have to work no matter what," she said, looking hard at Sonya. "Is there a hospital?" "It's a piece of barracks. They let you lie there at least; it must do something for their conscience; it doesn't do anything for anyone else. But still, it's not like some of the other camps. I heard of one camp where people went for abscesses on their heads to be fixed; they were filled with worms" ("Abscesses! Worms!" Sonya exclaimed. "Malnutrition," the German woman explained impatiently); "and in the hospital they smeared on some kind of grease so the worms would grow faster." "What did they do?" Sonya asked, her blue eyes open like doors. "The ones who found out didn't go to the hospital; they washed in urine. I don't recommend the shower here much, no, I don't recommend it," she said, looking down at her wooden shoes. "But we'll have to go," I told her; "we smell all over from gasoline." "Then go now," she suggested. "Not too many people know about it yet, just the old ones. Come, I'll take you, the guard won't bother us." "What about towels?" "No towels, what do you think? Take something you don't need right away; you can let it dry later. Later, maybe, when they start to steal from the disinfectant machine, you can trade for some rags. Don't go near the fence," she warned us; "there've been plenty of accidents." "What kind of accidents?" I asked. "A woman went over yesterday looking for her husband; she got pushed or she fell. One touch, that was that. It's happened plenty, plenty." We went out with her.

It was getting dark; a cold wind was starting to blow, scuttling some pebbles and leaves; still, I couldn't see any trees. The barracks seemed built on an empty lot; the trees might have been exploded by the bombs. "Where is it?" "Here," she said, pointing at a barn. "I know it's a barn; where's the shower?" "That *is* the shower," she answered. "Come on; I'll show you." We went in. Fastened to the ceiling of the barn was one little faucet and little drops of water, dripping and dripping. "How do you turn it on?" Sonya asked. "It is on." Sonya and I stared at it. "There are no doors on the barn!" Sonya cried. "That's right, but there are some wood benches near the walls." We looked. There were two women with their dresses partly unbuttoned; their hair was longer than ours, growing back in irregular clumps. They seemed Sonya's age, and very pretty, not too thin; their bodies were still beautiful. "They're getting up their courage," the German woman said; "who starts first?" "I will," Sonya said; "the gasoline is making my stomach hurt." I saw the German woman give her a close, hard look. Maybe we were wrong to trust her; I didn't trust anyone now. Sonya took off her short skirt, her wooden shoes, her sweater, and put it with the other sweater she was using for the towel. She moved under the dripping faucet. "It's freezing," she called to me. I could hear her teeth starting to chatter; her lips were turning blue. "No soap?" I asked the German woman. She just shrugged her shoulders.

"Look," she said suddenly, pointing at Sonya's stomach below her belly button. "Maybe she's pregnant?" I whispered. "No," the German woman said in a quiet voice; "no, that's not it at all. They didn't see it on the lineup?" "No." Sonya skipped out from under the dripping faucet like a three-year-old. The German woman and I smiled at each other. "Those two are taking a long time to get their courage up," I commented to her. "Perhaps they're also ashamed," she answered, the smile leaving her face. "But of what? They've been here; they must be used to it." "You go on," she told me. Sonya was rubbing herself with the sweater from top to bottom. "Hair is less trouble this way," she called in her high chirpy voice, rubbing the towel over her prickly head. I knew her cheerfulness wouldn't last long. I was standing under the water faucet where it wept its icy tears. I remembered Momma and Anzia washing my hair, one half of the head at a time, over a great basin, and the flowered porcelain pitcher that poured great thick streams of hot water; after the third rinsing, I would look out of the water at the room, making it distort. Momma always washed my hair, and Vera's, when Anzia was baking and the Russian stove was heating the whole house. Then she would take the half of the hair that was washed and comb it and braid it, and with one hand I would hold a towel over it, and they would start on the other side. I remembered how, when I went to medical school, we had little white felt hats, with beige sun visors, and a little felt band that ran around the visor and the rest of the hat, the band the color of an American beauty rose, and how hard it was to order a hat for me because we had to find one my hair would fit under.

"Snow must blow in here in the winter," I called to the German woman. I didn't want to know her name. Once you knew a name, the person was attached in some way; I didn't know how, but attached. I didn't want it. "In drifts," she called back. I ran across to the bench and began rubbing myself all over. When I looked down at my body, I looked like an eight-year-old girl, no hair at all, so thin, only my full breasts proved all the rest of my life was not a story someone else had told me. "My name is Rosa," the woman said; my heart sank as I finished buttoning my blouse. "Put your shoes on first thing; otherwise you get so cold, you never warm up." "Ask her about that lump," she whispered to me. "Sonya," I asked, "aren't you pregnant?" "Oh, no, Anya, I lost menstruation over a year ago; I can't be pregnant." "That happens to everyone here; no one ever bleeds." "It happened to almost everyone in the ghetto," Sonya chirped up. "Not to me," I said bitterly; I still menstruated regularly. "That's too bad," Rosa said, looking at me critically; "it's better here without it. Who needs it? It gives you cramps; you can't work. It is just danger, danger, danger." "What do you do about it?" I asked her.

One of the women had gotten up and gone over to the faucet; she still had her clothes on. She began to take them off just before the circle of dampness left by the faucet and the shedding drops. I could feel Rosa's eyes on me. Then the woman took off what appeared to be a kind of nightgown she wore under her dress. Her whole body, her whole body, was covered with abscesses; one on her shoulder blade was pouring pus; there was another running on her left buttock. "What is it from?" I gasped, terrified. "Malnutrition, lice, who knows? If there's no menstruation, it all stays in, the filth." Sonya's hand traveled to the lump on her stomach. "That's not an abscess," I whispered. "Then what is it?" "A cyst, a fibroid maybe, not an abscess." "Thank God," she said sitting up so straight she seemed run through by an electric shock; "but sometimes it hurts." "Cysts do hurt," I told her. "So, as long as we're here, I might as well put my old body under," Rosa told me casually. "Why don't you two go back? We share towels, some of us with the abscesses; they'll let me use theirs." We stared at her in horror. "I'll see you at the barracks," she said; and looking at me: "Maybe you know how to lance them?" "What could I lance them with?" "There are knives," she said mysteriously; "if someone knew how to use them." "Please take your shower," I said. Sonya and I went back to the barracks. "I don't know why this cyst hurts so much sometimes," Sonya said, "and this rash on my arm, it hurts all over too." "Don't worry about it; everyone gets something or other in here." "Those bodies." I kept quiet.

At five o'clock, the siren went off. There was the same kettle of coffee covered with its layer of grease, and the same green bread shot through with worms, like the coffee we drank. We ate as if it were the world's most delicious food. Then we started outside.

"Rail commander's group here," a soldier was calling. "Disinfection, here," another called. I went to my group. Sonya straggled up. "Line up in fours," the soldier ordered, and then he began counting. I watching his lips. "Thirty-eight, thirty-nine, forty," and then, just to be sure, he started once more. There were two soldiers to escort our group. One was very tall with red hair and freckles; the other was an odd-looking thing; he slouched. When he saluted as we began to walk, he never got his hand to his head; he looked as natural with his rifle as a cow with a saddle. I wondered if he even knew how to use it. We were walking down a village street. The brick houses were few and far between; there was dense underbrush and some trees. Then the road turned into a country road, and there were no more houses, just pine trees. It was a thick forest we were entering; the air was dizzying, like the *dacha*. "At least there'll be oxygen," I thought to myself; "that will save us." We walked two miles, or three miles; I would try to keep count, but I couldn't. My mind would keep wandering; it seemed endless. Suddenly we came to a huge clearing; there was track after railway track. "This is Dundangen," Rosa told me.

"Rail commanders!" cried the red-headed soldier. On a far track, a red freight train, like the one that had brought us, was waiting. On both sides of each track was what the soldiers called the ramps, cement platforms about six inches from the ground. On each of these was a series of big gasoline pumps and wagons were already rolling up to them with empty canisters. When they reached the asphalt, the wagons made a horrible clatter, then stopped. "So," said the odd-looking soldier, "one takes turns pumping, the others carry the filled canisters to the trains; then the pumpers carry the canisters, and the carriers pump." "He is cuckoo," I heard the red-headed soldier mutter; "cuckoo." But he has nice eyes, I thought, looking at him, big dark eyes, almost like a dog's, and constantly shiny, as if there were some permanent tear stretched tight across each pupil. "What am I doing, thinking about a soldier's eyes?" I thought, shaking myself. I was getting thinner and thinner; I must weigh ninety pounds. The canisters looked as if they would be very heavy when they were filled. Rosa began the pumping and we began the carrying. The first time I tried to move a canister, I thought I would crack in half at the waist. "You have to do it," Rosa hissed at me, and I did do it. Then I came back for another. Sonya was moving canisters, too, but she was crying. "Stop it," I told her; "what's the matter with you?" "My stomach," she gasped, "it hurts." "It's your imagination," I snapped at her. She stopped crying. "I feel better already." She went back for another. But soon she was crying again. "She should go to the hospital," Rosa said. "Why?" I asked, waiting for the canister to fill up; "there's nothing wrong with her." "There is something. You'd better ask while Erdmann is here." She jerked her head in the direction of the teary-eyed soldier. "He'll do it without sending her for a selection." "I can't." "Then I will."

Meanwhile, a group of men was arriving from another camp. "Russian soldiers, prisoners of war," Rosa muttered while I was waiting for another canister to fill. I spoke to one of the Russians near me, on the other side of the ramp—"miserable day," something like that. He wanted something from me immediately. *"Golka!"* he said to me, "needle!" I had one, hidden in with my pictures and mirror. *"Zaftra,"* I told him, "tomorrow." After that, he would always leave me a little bit of his food, right from his mouth. He would push his ration plate toward me; I ate it, every bit. *"Xorosho,"* he would say, "good."

But after that first night, Sonya was put in the hospital. Every night after work, I would ask to see her; I wanted to help in the hospital. I told Erdmann; he instructed the others to let me go without interference. Sonya's pains were getting worse, but some days she was fine, and so cheerful. "Oh, Anya," she would bubble; "when we get out of here we'll have such a good time," and then, "if I only had some farina, I know I would be well; I would." "Two eggs is what I need," a woman from the next bed said weakly; "if I had two eggs, I could breathe." The Russian had little pieces of wood and paper, even some matches. I would take them from him and heat up some water to drink with a piece of my bread in it, or part of the Russian's potato and give it to them. "Oh, I feel better already," Sonya would say every time.

The work went on and on, every day the same. A train would pull up. We would carry the filled canisters from the ramp where the pumps were, up the little dirt incline to the train, and lift it into the air. Sometimes a soldier inside the train was nice and would bend down to take it from me, but usually he didn't. And the jealousy over food in the barracks was unbearable. No matter how little anyone had, no matter if it was all they had, everyone else wanted it; everyone else thought it was better than her food. One Thursday night, a woman came down from her bunk and started screaming. I couldn't understand a word. Then it turned out that someone had stolen a piece of bread hidden under her mattress. She was saving it to eat in the morning, something to have besides the coffee, which was now all we got. "That will teach you to hide it in such a stupid place!" Rosa screamed at her. "I'll ask you, you thieving bitches, you prostitutes!" the woman shrieked, bursting into tears. She climbed back into her bed, a defeated corpse. After that, the stealing got worse and worse. When I had bread left over, I kept it in my pocket, or wrapped it in the handkerchief with my pictures; anything I couldn't wrap, I ate.

With Sonya gone, I'd lost track of the days. I was a mechanical toy. I filled canisters; I handed them to the soldiers on the train; I pumped. It was getting colder and colder. Sometimes when the train left, I could see clear across the tracks to the woods on the far side, emptiness, emptiness. I worked faster and faster. Now all I thought about was Ninka, Ninka, my baby; what was happening to

291

her, how was I going to escape, how was I going to find her?

Already at night, I would trade bits of bread for whatever rags someone had gotten from the disinfectant machine in case I started bleeding; I had been there for only a half-day assignment. The machine looked like a steam engine and disinfected thousands and thousands of pounds of clothes, our clothes, to be sent to Germany. Whatever they rejected, we got. But I met Ann there. I recognized her from Vilno. She had been a prostitute, a real prostitute, and I could still see her, the most elegant lady in the city, dressed to kill, walking her two white spitzes. "Ann," I would say, "you have a hat; can I try it on just for tonight?" "Take it, take it," she said, pushing it on me. "I'll bring it back in the morning." And then I would go back to my bunk and take out my sliver of a mirror and try it on this way and that, but it was no use: it was still my face and a twenty-five-year-old face still looked exactly like itself. But then Ann got an umbrella. "Ann!" I asked; "can I have it? I'll give you anything!" "Just take it," she said, bored. She stole enough to fill a shop. This I did not give back. I pushed it between my bunk and the barracks wall.

All night and all day, I was busy with the machines. I thought about nothing else. Each day on the platform, I got farther and farther away from the ramps, and the gasoline, and the cars. "Slow down," Rosa whispered to me; "slow down; you'll wear yourself out; they'll take you." I noticed with a kind of detachment how cold it had gotten; now, when I took my hand from the iron pump, pieces of skin stuck, and my hand came back to me bleeding. A woman was coming to bring us our lunch instead of a soldier. Half of her face was covered with a wine-colored stain, and twisted, as if the muscle underneath it were permanently clenched. The other side of her face was perfectly normal. Lunch was soup, usually made from some stale bread, in the same pot as the coffee for breakfast, and the meat for dinner. She would slap the ladle onto the thin plates, and our hands, which were frozen, could not hold on to them; half went on our sweaters, scorching our breasts and bellies, then froze; half the time, we dropped the whole plate with our wooden, frozen hands. Then she would yell: "Clumsy slob! Too good for you? Too good for the food? Maybe you don't need any anymore?"

One day, after I had seen Sonya the night before, turning and turning in pain, I was waiting for my plate. I was seeing her face, and my daughter's face, Ninka's, first close up, and then rising and getting smaller and smaller, and more unapproachable than the moon. Hats! I needed a carpet that could fly. Suddenly, I felt a hard object come down on my head; a black cloth with white forkings fell over my eyes. When I got up, two women were holding me. Erdmann's angry voice was saying something to the woman. "You were slumping," Rosa told me; "she can't stand that, she's so perfect." But after that, it may have been my imagination, I was sure Erdmann was watching me especially. And there was something about him. I couldn't bring myself to hate him, or even not to trust him, and it was bitter; I was filled with bitterness like a cup. I asked Rosa who he was. "Oh, he's the Hauptmann's private secretary. He writes songs and stories. You know, Hitler this, and Hitler that." She pumped away at my canister. "They send him out here sometimes. Remember the disinfectant machine?" she asked; she talked with the pumps of the handle. "It was in front of a brick building, remember? That was the Hauptmann's house; he's really head of the whole place. There's a Gestapo officer who's supposed to run it, but he's hardly ever here, so everyone calls him the Hauptmann, the high man; he runs it. Erdmann lives in that building, too. He can do a lot." "He hardly looks like he can stand up." "He can't do a lot the rest of them do," she snapped, "but you listen to me; he can do a lot. Why do you think your Sonya is dying safely in there?" "She's not dying!" I burst out, shocked. "Come on, what is that lump; it's bigger every day," Rosa said, pumping viciously. "It's cancer, all right; you know it yourself." "No," I begged her; "it's something psychological; sometimes she's so happy and then she's so depressed. I get headaches, terrible headaches, all the time; I can hardly see. I don't have a brain tumor." "Cancer," Rosa said unimpressed. "You just got those headaches after the witch hit you on the head." She motioned me aside for the next woman with her canister; our conversation was over.

The next day it was snowing, big puffy flakes of snow. "Pretty," I murmured to Rosa as we pumped. "Snow means it's warmer, that's all." "Listen, Rosa," I told her, "I need something; I'm starting to bleed." "Ask Ann for some of her stuff. She ought to know; you should see what *she*'s got stuffed up there." "What are you talking about now?" "Remember that diadem; it was made of diamonds. Someone threw it against the wall of the barracks and no one would pick it up because we were afraid of the penalty? Not Miss Ann. She took it apart; she's got those big stones," Rosa said wisely, "in her rectum and her womb, and believe me, she's all stretched out there, inside." "I don't believe you." "So don't believe me," Rosa said, indifferent; "but you can believe me, it's hard to do something like that without anyone seeing you; we don't exactly live in privacy." "I don't believe you," I said again. "Why do you think they're threatening gynecological examinations; they're worried about our insides? I tell you, a lot of people do it."

The disinfectant machine occupied a corner of the Hauptmann's huge court; the half day I was there, a German found a pair of *tefillin* Jews wore during morning prayers, and in each was a big diamond; he put the stones in his pocket, and kicked the *tefillin* through the air like a ball. *"Juden!"* he cursed. Someone told me that in the center of the court were huge cisterns of gasoline sunk into the ground, but near the Hauptmann's was a secret point, and anyone there who wasn't in his right place had to be shot; the soldiers had their orders. I didn't even look at the cisterns, not even from the corners of my eyes. Why couldn't Rosa keep quiet? I thought to myself, angry. If I worked fast enough, I would forget what she said. But I was too fascinated for that; I was caught. Ann had a way of outsmarting them. I was still there, trying on hats.

The snow was coming down in thick puffy lines, slanting, patching on the ground until the clearing for the tracks looked like the skin of a dead animal. Occasionally, the snow would blow harder, and I could see the sun, a little ice chip. It was reaching twelve o'clock. The woman came with lunch. After I finished my soup, watching most of it freeze my stomach with a detached curiosity, I saw Erdmann watching me. He bent over and put something down on a rock to one side of the ramp, motioning to me. I came over slowly. There were three sandwiches. But the other women saw them first, and pushed me aside. I didn't get a bite. This went on for three or four days, and then Erdmann gave up. So it was true; he did notice me. I looked at my body for the first time that night. It was thinner than ever. I must weigh eighty pounds. There had been a selection that day; some of the beds were empty. I sat on my bed, eating my piece of horsemeat, and my piece of bread with its chip of margarine. I was thinking; I had no idea about what. I had one eye on the door, checking to see if it was opening, if they hadn't gotten enough for one day.

The next day at work was the same. Rosa didn't mention Sonya again. The snow was piling up and drifting over the ramp, little streams of it, curling like hair, snaking their way over to the ramp and to us. I felt my head; there was a lump, bigger than an egg, and a little crew cut, like a man's. It was getting longer, my poor hair. When we finished work, they counted us again. "Something's up," Rosa whispered. "They're always worst when they lose at the front; then they're really impossible." Two men came down the line. "Gestapo; what did I tell you?" Rosa asked, triumphant. They went up and down the line, picking out this one and that one; a long line was forming opposite ours. *"Du! Blonde!"* one shouted, pointing at me. I started to walk to the other side. Then, as if an invisible hand pushed me violently, I turned and walked back to the first line. I felt my hands pushing the women aside, pushing myself through, crouching slightly behind two tall ones. I could hear the other line crackling off through the snow.

"All right," I heard Erdmann's voice, "supper for the rest." I took my bread and meat and went back. When I passed him, he turned white as the snow on the ground. "His teeth are all yellow," I thought to myself. He never stopped smoking. Rosa told me he traded his ration of vodka to the other soldiers for more cigarettes, more cigarettes, and books. "No wonder they think he's crazy." But I was thinking: What is fate now? It was as if a hand had pushed me back. "There must be a superpower," I thought to myself; "there must be one," and I heard my Momma saying, "You will live, you have for whom to live." I was going to believe in that superpower for the rest of my life. I lay on my bed thinking about it; I believed it existed. "But it needs help," I thought to myself, getting down and going over to Ann's to see what new things she might have brought back from the disinfectant machine.

In the barracks, things were getting worse and worse. Someone was stealing food, and doing it more and more. There were more and more fights, more heads popping in the doors all night to check on us. Then, when I had just fallen asleep, there was terrible screaming. "They are coming for us!" I thought, and lay rigid. But a woman from the other end of the barracks was in the middle of the floor separating the two aisles of beds; four or five women were shaking her and someone kept hitting her and screaming, "Thief! Thief! Thief!" "She's the one who's been taking the food," the loudest one screamed. I lay in my bunk lazily, watching bodies climb down from the bunks; it was a dream. They went over to the woman and took turns beating her; then the woman was still. "That will teach her to steal," I thought to myself dreamily. Then the door swung open. It was Erdmann and another soldier. "What's going on here?" he asked in German. Then he saw the woman's bloody body; it wasn't moving. "Take her out," he said to the other one; "she's dead." And to the rest of the barracks, his voice saying, "Are you satisfied now?" It was no dream. I turned over in my bunk, pulled out the umbrella, and hugged it as if it were a doll. I couldn't stop crying. But when I woke up, it wasn't because of the siren. There was a burning smell and an odd crackling, then a hiss, an explosive sound, and more hissing. It was getting louder. I looked out of the window near my bed; the whole sky was in flames. "Fire!" I shouted at the top of my lungs. I could see others sitting up and looking out. "Fire! Fire!" the cry went up. We all climbed down and rushed to the doors. Rosa tried to open them; they would not give. She ran to a window. "The soldiers are locking us in!" she cried. "The barracks in front of us is on fire," one woman called out, and we all rushed forward, like grains of sand tilted in a glass, ants in a jar. Flames leaped from it high into the air; red shadows danced blood on the white snow. "Let us out!" someone began screaming, but through the windows were the silhouettes of the soldiers, their rifles. "It's because of a defeat at the front," Rosa shouted. "No, it started with a shot from the patrol," someone insisted. But none of us really knew. We only knew we might be burned to death. "It's because of Elsa," sobbed the woman who had started the beating; "it's because of Elsa." "This is the most terrible way to die; dear God," I prayed, "let me die any other way." And the flames came to a stop at our barracks. We didn't know how it happened—if the fire burned itself out, if the wind changed, if there wasn't enough grass between the two barracks. We were locked in. Through the windows we were ordered back to bed, and all night, the barracks were filled with sobs, getting smaller and smaller, little hisses and gasps, sounds like flames water puts out.

17

THE siren went off the next morning as if nothing had happened. When we lined up in the snow, we could see the barracks in front us, gone, the one in front of that, gone. The fire had stopped before us, and one barracks before the hospital. The smell of burned wood still hung in the air like the remains of a terrible cookout, but the snow was falling, and covering the barracks and the smell. There were two soldiers with rifles; one of them kept stamping his shiny boots in the snow to keep it off. Erdmann was not there. "How clean they always look," I thought; "they look like polished pots." The second soldier stood smoking, staring over our heads as if we were boards in a picket fence. My feet were beginning to bleed into my wooden shoes; the skin was cracking more and more in the cold. "If you get any paper, stuff it in," Rosa told me. But I couldn't get any; everyone was hoarding it. The soldier threw his cigarette in the snow; it made a tiny hole, hissed, and went out. A tiny corkscrew of smoke rose from its round grave. This endless counting! As if we were precious jewels, or the most dangerous things. The snow was a thick curtain. I was afraid I was beginning to bleed. So I had been there for almost three months. I remembered how at home in Vilno, when I came out of the bathroom, I didn't notice anything, but Momma noticed a spot of blood. All of a sudden, she came up to me and slapped me on a cheek, then on the other. "What?" I cried. "What did I do? You never hit me." "I'll tell you," she said; she was trembling. She explained there was a superstition that if you began menstruating, and got frightened, and turned pale, you stayed that way for the rest of your life. Now I wished there was a way to slap the bleeding out of me forever. I didn't like to think about her now. Instead I would think about Ninka, and even on days like this, in the snow, in front of the burned charred building, she would be like a sun on a rainy day, a cold rainy day. A third man had tramped up to the two soldiers; he began stamping his boots, imitating the first. "Frau Lavinsky!" the first one called. *"Ja,"* I answered. "If this is it, it's it; maybe it's better," I thought, coming out of the line. Just as I stepped forward I saw another line, not usually near ours, but now, because of the burned buildings, there were less lines, and we were arranged differently. It was Rachel! I waved to her, and went to the three soldiers. "Frau Lavinsky?" he asked again. *"Ja."* Rachel was alive!

At least someone was left. She would look for Ninka if she survived. "Come with me," the soldier said. I followed him, my wooden shoes sinking into the snow; it covered my ankles. I followed him for about a block; then I could see another soldier waiting. We walked toward him. The instant I saw the tilt of the rifle I knew it was Erdmann. "Here she is," the first soldier said, leaving me with Erdmann, and turning back in the snow. "Don't be afraid; don't be afraid," he said, seeing my wild face; "I'm only taking you to the Hauptmann." "What for?" I cried; "I haven't done anything, and I don't want to *do* anything," I protested. "No, no." He shook his head worriedly. "Just to clean. I came down this morning with a song; I knew he would like it." He was grinning maliciously. "And the place was a mess; he can't stand it, a real Russian gentleman of the old school. He'll never be a real German. So I said, 'Hauptmann, you need a *putzfrau* to come in and keep this place clean. Suppose the High Lieutenant should come in and see it? It's all right for you; you're in the army, he's in the secret service, but if the place is inspected, the High Lieutenant'd be blamed.'" What was he rattling on about? "He was so surprised I noticed, he thought it must look very bad, so he asked me did I know anyone? I praised you to the skies; so that's where you're going, but," Erdmann went on, "I want you to eat and rest." "Please," I cried, "are you a monster? How can you play such games? If you're going to shoot me, shoot me; never mind these crazy stories about songs and maids and rests!" Silence. "I don't blame you," Erdmann said; "you shouldn't trust me, but believe me, I'm telling you the truth. The Hauptmann, he doesn't even know you're Jewish. You're blond; you speak Russian; I told him I thought you were a political prisoner. Anyway, he doesn't care. He hates it, war; he says he got enough of it in the first one. That's why they only have him interviewing Russian soldiers, interrogating them, and running things. He's good at anything without blood."

We tramped on through the snow. I was too angry to be afraid. Why did these people have so much power over me? I was too old to be controlled this way. We were passing more and more houses; I thought of them on fire, one by one, like the barracks, the people locked in them, the doors and windows sealed. Now tales about an old-style Russian gentleman. This was not the direction of the rail commander's; this was not the forest; we really were on our way to the Hauptmann's. Our breaths went before us like little train puffs, leading the way. "Each time I breathe out in this wood," Erdmann said, half to himself, "a little of my soul goes out of my body; soon I'll have none left." "Don't bother me with your troubles!" I was too confused to know what to do. He seemed sincere. "I don't blame you," he said again; "I don't deserve anything better." "*If* I am going to be a maid," I said, suspicion finally dawning on me, "what do I have to do for it? I only clean; I don't provide other services, I told you." "Please," he said after a minute; he sounded as if he would cry; "don't you know they would kill us or send us to the front if they found us with a Jewish woman, please." "You told me they think I'm a political prisoner," I reminded him. I remembered the Germans surrounding the Gestapo block in the ghetto. "They wouldn't stop to make distinctions," he said flatly. "I'm sorry," I told him finally, "about the last thing I said."

A huge cloud of steam was beginning to rise through the trees as if someone were pressing a giant shirt for a monster. "The disinfectant machine," he said, following my eyes. "Here," he said, fumbling in his pocket, "put this on; I got it for you." Awkwardly, he handed it over; it was a little black velvet babushka. "It will cover your head," he told my shyly; "you'll look much better." "I'm not putting it on!" I cried, throwing it in the snow. He bent down and picked it up, brushing it off. "Please," he said, "put it on; it's for the best." I marched along, ignoring him. "There's a lot of food at the Hauptmann's," he coaxed; "you could smuggle some of it back to your friends at the hospital." I stomped along. The snow was halfway up my legs; I had to lift them higher and higher. I was practically goose-stepping. "I had a friend in another barracks," I said; "Rachel Ellenbogen; I would like her to be with me." "If you will just put this on," he pleaded. "All right, give it to me." I tied it under my chin sulkily. "If I could suggest that you get the bow in the middle under your chin," he said nervously. I yanked at it viciously. "Please don't tear it," he pleaded.

The trees came to an end, and we were in the big court near the disinfectant machine, facing the Hauptmann's. No one had shot me yet. I began to relax a little. It was a big square building, divided into two halves, a big wooden door in the middle. "Around the side," Erdmann told me, "is the potato cellar; also, all the laundry's down there. That's where you'll go for sheets and tablecloths," he said proudly. "I don't know about that," I grumbled. "Please." He was desperate. "Be nice." "Do we go in through the potato cellar?" "Through the front door." He was watching me as if I were going to run away or grab his rifle. "Stamp your feet on the mat," he told me, as if he were talking to a child. "Five stories," I said out loud. "One apartment on each side." He was pleased to see me taking any kind of interest. I was shivering in my two sweaters. We went in. Everything was shining; I had never seen such a clean place. It must all be a joke.

"It's a joke," I said flatly. "Please." A big man came out of a room on the left. He was in his sixties, with a small white moustache and bright blue eyes; he wore steel-rimmed spectacles. He spoke to me in Russian. "You are Frau Lavinsky?" "*Jawohl,*" I answered. He looked at Erdmann, puzzled. Erdmann was glaring at me. "The prisoner I interrogated also said she spoke Russian," he said to Erdmann in total confusion. "Can you clean this apartment?" he tried again; "it's very hard work." Erdmann was still glaring; his yellow, stained fingers were trembling. "I can," I answered in Russian. "You will have to clean the floors, and polish the furniture, and take care of the laundry, set the table, can you do all that?" "Of course," I answered in Russian. "Well," the Hauptmann said with a heavy sigh; "that's settled. Sometimes I may even come in to ask you about a Russian word; I've forgotten so much since I went to Germany. Please, sit down, Mrs. Lavinsky. Mister Erdmann tells me how hard you work, and you have nothing to eat. So we have a whole table here for you; please eat before you start."

I sat down, but I didn't look at the food; my eyes were stuck to his face. "You see," he talked, trying to make me comfortable, "my father's business failed—he made machines, a factory, you know—so he thought Germany was

300

the best place for us. Of course that was a long time ago, but that's how I know your language. But not as well as you must," he said gallantly. "Now, I interview Russian prisoners of war to find out secrets. What do I find out? Nothing. But I go, every day from two-thirty to five. Do you think you can work here?" *"Da."* *"Xorosho,"* he said, "good. The place is a terrible heap." I stared around at the gleaming surfaces. "It's a good thing Irving brought this to my attention. At my age, you know, one doesn't like to be scolded about one's room." He seemed perfectly serious. Erdmann was smiling to hear us talk. He couldn't understand a word we were saying; we could have been planning his murder, or mine. "So," the Hauptmann groaned, getting up, "I'll get back to my communications. I will feel very secure, Mrs. Lavinsky, writing them over and over, now I know there's someone trustworthy to empty the wastepaper baskets." He pretended to glower at Erdmann. "You should see his room," he laughed.

"Convinced?" Erdmann asked me. "He's too nice." "He misses his family; he has a tribe of grandchildren." "All the others have families." Erdmann didn't answer. I began to smell the food on the little table in front of me, but still, I did not look at it. Soldiers, soldiers, all over, half of them in Gestapo uniforms. "All these soldiers," I said in a small voice. "You'll get used to it. They won't bother you, not when you're working for the Hauptmann, not if they know what's good for them; it's noisier at the front. The High Lieutenant is a relative of his; all their secret service, they haven't found that out. They just know they're like this." He held up two fingers in a V and pressed them together. Finally I looked down at the table. There was everything I had not seen in such a long time. "I cannot," I said; "something is choking me." "You have to eat." Erdmann said sternly, staring at me; "please eat something." "Maybe later," I said. My stomach was rising against me. "I'll put it away, but at least drink a glass of milk." "I cannot," I begged. "You have to," he said, picking it up. I took it and choked it down. "Now some orange juice," he said, picking up another glass; "I'll bet your gums are bleeding." "Orange juice and milk; please, you'll kill me!" "Then a little bread," he argued. I chewed it as fast as I could. "I want to work," I insisted; I didn't want to sit still and look at these soldiers. "Sit, sit, rest," he begged. "Please, I can't argue with you here; I just want to work." "All right, I'll get you your sewing."

In a few minutes he came back with a man's pair of pants and twenty buttons and put them on the table. "Sew these on, please," he asked me. I took the pants, the needle and thread, with relief. Then I looked more closely: The buttons had just that minute been cut off, probably with a razor. I glared at him and began to sew. Erdmann left the room. In an hour he was back. "Finished," I said, handing him the pants. "Good, I'll bring you something else; eat some noodles," he instructed, putting some on my plate. I began picking at them. The Hauptmann came in. "Tell me, Mrs. Lavinsky, what does this mean?" "Crayfish," I said, taking a look; "what, is your code in fairy tales?" "Why not?" he asked, his red face creasing in a smile under his silver hair. "Why not?" he asked, laughing as he left. "Fairy tales, what an idea, what a *good* idea," I heard from the hall. They were all crazy here.

"There are some noodles left," Erdmann said, reappearing, holding something behind his back. "Work, please," I demanded coldly. Out from behind his back came the same pair of pants and the same twenty buttons. "How many pants without twenty buttons are there?" I asked, stitching without looking up. "Not too many more, but a lot more jackets. Listen, Mrs. Lavinsky," he spoke to me in Polish, "when you are stronger you can even wash the ceiling. Just cooperate with me for a few days. We will get your friend Sonya some food and I'll find your Rachel; am I asking too much?" I blushed the color of the trains. "How do you know their names?" "It's my business to know what's going on." "Did you tell the Hauptmann to ask me about Russian words?" "I don't think of everything," he answered, uncomfortable. "I need some rags," I muttered; "for my knee." "I understand. I'll get them," he swore, and disappeared. Even here, I was still modest. He came back with yards of white material. "How will I get *that* into the barracks?" I asked, so disappointed I was ready to cry. "I take you back in; I'll take it. Don't worry, stop worrying."

So all afternoon I sewed on buttons, on jackets, on pants, on jackets, on more pants and more pants and more pants. I began to look around the room. It was a big light room with two big windows facing the court. The white curtains were spotless; the parquet floor shone like the sun. "It could be cleaner," I thought to myself; "and the windows too, and his room, I bet it could be a lot cleaner." "No working on the floors until the end of the week," Erdmann warned me, seeing my critical eyes going over the floors like brushes. I let my eyes stray out farther. The dining room table was beautiful, twenty-four feet long at least. It ran the length of the room. There were straight high chairs with a slight curve in the center panel, and a huge embroidered white cloth. There was a big sideboard, and a little table for serving; that was where I was sitting. "A lot to polish," I thought. "He invites people for dinner a lot," Erdmann told me, seeing my eyes on it. "Look, Mister Erdmann," I said, "I'll get you into trouble if you're always talking to me. Please, do some work; write some songs; fill up a wastepaper basket. I'll try and finish these pants before you take me back to the lineup." He tapped some ashes into an ashtray and walked away; before he turned his back, I could see the beginning of a smile.

"A peasant suddenly made queen of a country couldn't be better off than this," I thought to myself. "To be out of the cold; I'd rather be out of the cold than be an ambassador!" The women would be jealous when I got back. Automatically, I shuddered. Sometimes I was more afraid of them than the soldiers. I had never gotten used to jealousy. Erdmann came back in; again he had something behind his back. "What now?" I asked; "a buttonless tuxedo?" "No," he said, producing it, "a coat for you. I have nothing to do with it. The Hauptmann doesn't want you freezing to death on the way here. Tomorrow I'm to buy you a black uniform and some black stockings and shoes." "Very appropriate," I commented, not looking at him. "He also wants to know what this word is," Erdmann said, giving me a piece of paper. "Spiderweb," I answered; "what is he reading anyway?" "Top secret, I can't give away such secrets," Erdmann answered with a grin, giving a real smile for the first time. "I think he's more miserable than I am!" I thought to myself, amazed. "What nonsense!" I reprimanded myself; "a German, miserable?" But he was miserable, I knew it.

18

WHEN I got back to the barracks, Rachel was in Sonya's old bunk. When I came in from the graying light, into the electric light that burned all night, and saw her, the whole barracks was flooded with a gold light, like the gold on the cupolas of the Russian churches, "Oh, Rachel," I sobbed, climbing into her bunk, hugging her; "where were you?" "In the barracks all the way down the line from the hospital." She was crying and laughing. "They used to line us up on the other side of them from you." "Where are you working?" I asked her. I kept stroking her face, touching her eyes, her nose, her lips. I was blind; I couldn't believe this was real, not unless I could touch it. Rachel kept holding me by the shoulders and pushing me back to get a better look. "You've gotten so *thin*," she whispered. Rachel was no thinner than she had been in our room at the ghetto. "Look at us!" Rachel laughed. I took out my mirror and we tried looking at ourselves in it together. "Two chickens!" she laughed; "two chickens, a blond chicken and a brown chicken." "You're almost a rooster," I teased, pulling at a tuft of brown hair standing almost straight up in the middle of her head. "Look," Rachel said, "I found a pair of scissors; we can fix our hair when the others go to sleep." "Put it away," I warned her; "this is a bad barracks. They killed someone in here over food, be careful." "You be careful, too," she scolded; "Erdmann told me about your new job when he brought me over. In my place it was the same thing, but she wasn't killed over food. She had something or other; maybe it was food, I'm not sure." "What else?" I asked. "Oh, it's good to be here with you," Rachel sighed. "I'm working plucking chickens and sometimes in the *kartoffel* cellar, so come down a lot for tablecloths. It's good too, there; I get something extra that way." "I can bring down things to you; they give me all kinds of food," I whispered into her ear, "but I can't eat it, I choke." "Well, you have to start," Rachel said, eyeing me critically; "I order *you*," she mimicked, "to gain forty pounds in the next two weeks." We started laughing hysterically; then we were crying. "This will go on all night," I gasped, wiping my eyes on my sleeve. "It's good to stay up for some things."

How she had changed! She was stronger than I had ever seen her; it was as if she had found a purpose. "I've been to the hospital," she whispered to me. "You too?" I asked, amazed. "Sonya didn't tell me anyone else was coming." "She's probably afraid if one of us finds out about the other, we'd stop the food," Rachel said. "But she could have told me about you!" "I didn't tell anyone my name," Rachel said; "she didn't know we even knew each other. We had some bad soldiers; I didn't want to take any chances. It was easy to get in, but I didn't want anyone to know I was going." "Are you getting interested in hospitals?" I asked, astonished. "Oh, a little, but I'm too stupid," she answered vaguely, and shy. "No, you're not, you're not. You'll see, when we're finished here, we'll both go back and be doctors and have an office together. Maybe we can even find Anzia to embroider runners for the verandah." "I couldn't do it," Rachel said, thoughtful. "You could," I insisted. "But it's silly to plan now, isn't it?" Rachel sighed, sitting back against the wall. "I *know* you will do it!" I cried. "First things first," she answered.

"Anya, look, I have an abscess on my shoulder blade; could you lance it?" I had done some of that with Doctor Yurbo; Rachel knew it. "It's been a long time." "I know, but it's hard, and it hurts. Doctor Yurbo used to say they took away your strength." "But what will I cut it with?" I was thinking out loud. "I have some material," I pointed to my side, "from Erdmann; we could make a good bandage. He might give me vodka to clean it; I could soak the rags in the hospital. But cutting it open? They won't let us have anything." "I have the scissors," Rachel answered. I stared at her; she was not the same at all. "They're not sharp." "It will hurt," she agreed, "but," she said smiling, "not very much." "Not very much," I repeated after her. "Look," she coaxed, "if I sharpen them a little on a rock?" "It will still hurt. You'd better give them to me and I'll take them to Erdmann, and when I'm in the kitchen, I'll put them in the fire, or I'll go to the hospital, and we'll put them in the fire." "Do it in the hospital," Rachel said. "They're used to your going there; it's safer." "I think we can cut it there, too. I'll slit your dress; then I'll do it, and

305

put enough over it so it drains into the bandage. We can change it back here. You can put a sweater on over the dress before we come back. We can sew the dress up here; I have plenty of needles and thread. That should look normal enough." "Good," Rachel exhaled, "you don't have any on you?" "No." "You know what your Momma would say: It's all those juices." "I'm part carrot," I agreed. "Don't go back to your bunk." "I'm not going anywhere," I whispered, snuggling up. This wasn't taking place in the camp; this was sometime in the past.

"Look how often the soldiers pop their heads in these doors to watch us," Rachel whispered; "I wonder what it would be like to sleep without all these lights on?" We were comfortable in our miseries. "Listen," Rachel whispered, "they've been mumbling about you since we got back. 'The rotten bitch, what did she ever do to deserve it; she's probably a spy; we better watch out for her; we'll freeze to death while she licks the boots of the Germans.' You can imagine." "It's what I expected; I wasn't going to talk to anyone anymore." "You could still talk to Rosa. She told them what for. She told them the Germans couldn't sleep with you unless they wanted to sleep in a grave for the rest of their lives. She told Ann to go to the bathroom and drop some diamonds into the tank; she asked Tania if she wanted to beat you to death; she asked Elsa the same thing. She asked everyone if they thought it would hurt us to have someone who might know what was happening and could tell us, and she told them they were goddamn pigs, didn't they know how you went to help at the hospital. It would serve them right if they got in and you wouldn't help them, and if they hadn't been eaten up by the lice it was because the lice didn't want them." "What did they say?" I was flabbergasted. "Well," Rachel went on, still astonished, "she was waving a knife around the whole time, God knows where she got it. They didn't say anything. I think," she searched back, "she even told them it was their filthy minds that gave Sonya cancer." "Oh, no!" I protested, horrified. "Oh, yes," Rachel said; "you could have heard a needle stitch in here. She's a good friend, that one." "She's ferocious," I said. "Why do you think she's still alive? You know how long she's been here? Two years?" Two years! I fell asleep thinking about escape: Ninka and escape.

After breakfast, Erdmann was waiting for me again. I kissed Rachel goodbye, went out, and followed him. As soon as we were out of sight of the barracks, he stopped and took something out of a bag. Heavy boots. I stared at them as if they were dragons. "Boots," he said helpfully. "Boots," he said again. "Please, you're as white as snow. Put them on; you'll only get me into trouble with the Hauptmann. He doesn't want you bleeding all over the carpets with your frozen feet, that's all." "He doesn't have any carpets," I answered sourly, "there's only linoleum on the floor." "Then he doesn't want you bleeding onto the parquet," Erdmann sighed. "None of the other women have boots," I said accusingly. "What do you want me to do?" he cried. "I'm not Hitler; I can't fix the whole world!" "I'll put them on." "You can hold my arm," he said softly. "I'll hold onto a tree, thank you." He shook his head, watching me wobbling in the snow like a sick stork, holding onto a thin branch making cracking sounds. "Finished," I said. My toes were in heaven. I wiggled them against the fur, and then wiggled them again. "My ten toes bless you," I said without thinking. "Now if you will put on the gloves," he mumbled, pulling a pair from his pocket, "the ten fingers can bless me; then the next ten, and I'll have twenty. Believe me, I need all the blessings I can get." "I thought you Germans were already blessed," I scowled, pulling on the gloves. I couldn't remember when I had last been so warm. Anzia used to pin my mittens to a string around my neck so I wouldn't lose them when I played in the court; there wasn't much danger of my losing these now. "Will I get some work today?" "What do you mean? That's why I'm taking you to the Hauptmann's." "You know what I mean. I can't keep sewing on buttons; the pants will wear out." "We'll see," he said.

The snow was even higher than yesterday. It came three-quarters up to the top of my boots; thick cottony layers covered the pine branches, bending them way down. It was quiet and beautiful. The sun sparkled blue. Our shadows went in front of us, blue. "Even our shadows are blue with cold," Erdmann commented. The snow was so high, and I couldn't feel it against my skin. I couldn't help kicking some into the air and watching the little storm settle. "Remember the little globes with tiny countries inside?" I asked him. "How you turned them over, and the snow swirled and then settled. Sometimes I think the past is like that, a little country sealed in a crystal globe; the people who are outside are outside; the ones who are in,

307

are in, trapped in the house." "Where did you go to school?" he asked me gently. "I never went to school." "Never mind, never mind." We walked on. I kept kicking up the snow, and there was a tiny smile hovering over Erdmann's lips when he wasn't puffing his cigarette. "My glass globe had a crack in it; now it's smashed." I didn't ask any questions. I looked at him sideways; there were tears in his eyes. What did he have to cry about, a German? What would they have done to him if he was a German? If he was. My mind was clicking again, like a little machine.

"Look," I said, "I don't want to ask too much, but my knee is still bleeding, and maybe infected. Do you think you could get some more cloth and maybe soak it in alcohol before I take it back?" "Why not?" he asked dully; "why not?" We passed the last trees and the court opened before us. It was under a thick blanket of snow. The cisterns of gasoline were invisible; the badly kept yard looked beautiful; even the disinfectant machine looked lovely, steam rising from it, its surface beading with drops like a horse that had run a long time. We went into the house. The first thing that struck me was the cleanliness of the room. Since yesterday someone had scrubbed the parquet floors and scrubbed the windows. They hadn't used soap; the windows were too clean for that. "What on earth happened here?" I demanded of Erdmann. It was a trick; they wanted someone else.

The Hauptmann came into the dining room where I was staring like Cinderella. Even the prisms of the great chandelier had been cleaned, probably with vodka; they gleamed like nothing on earth. For some reason it reminded me of my child. "See," Erdmann was saying, "what a good job Frau Lavinsky has done? I told you and you thought such a little thing couldn't even pick up a mop." "This is wonderful," said the Hauptmann; "I'll have to invite guests for dinner to show it off. Did you get her the uniform and the stockings?" "Of course, sir; you ordered it." "Very good, very good," he murmured, walking over to the table. "Look, the whole room is sunk in it, like a lake. It's a mirror; you can put your lipstick on just looking in it, Frau Lavinsky." Lipstick! "But what are you going to do today?" "Just what I was going to ask Mister Erdmann," I answered. "I suppose you could sweep the court; that wouldn't be too hard, would it?" he asked Erdmann anxiously. "Not if the soldiers shovel it first." "Of course, shovel first." The Hauptmann sounded indignant. "What did you think I had in mind? In the meantime, eat something, please, and if you can eat while I ask some questions, I would be very grateful." I stared at both of them. His stately head moved away slowly, and his magnificent figure came back with a long list in its hand. "What are these words, please?" he asked. "I know you're supposed to be a maid, not a dictionary," he sighed, "but mine is very inadequate and pages keep falling out of my memory. You would think a translator could requisition an adequate dictionary but I cannot; I have ten very bad ones." "Miscellaneous," I said, pointing at the first word; "tattoo," at the second; "cardiac" at the third; "femur," at the fourth; "engraver," at the fifth. "No spiders?" I asked. "I am disappointed. No toads?" "Not too disappointed to eat, I hope. I hear you're giving Erdmann trouble; eat while they shovel the snow."

"Tattoo," I heard Erdmann repeating to himself meditatively. "Your friend Rachel," he said abruptly, turning to me, "said you had some pictures of what you looked like before. I want to see them." "Why should you? She shouldn't have told you; you know we're not allowed to keep them. They're all I have!" "She said you carry them with you everywhere." I didn't answer. "I won't hurt them," he said urgently. "But the Hauptmann needs someone to wait on the table. He likes you already. If he saw the pictures, if he could only see them, he would let you do it. Then you could go down to the cellar whenever you wanted, to the kitchen, almost anywhere. Everyone would get familiar with your face, seeing you about." He was talking as if he were planning my escape. "Why do you want them?" I asked again. I couldn't believe him. "I just told you!" he said, losing his temper. "Will you bring them right back?" He promised. One of them was a picture of me in my fur-trimmed suit, the one Madame Anna Kirilova had made me. I was half-sitting on a wall, and wore a hat with a brim that half-covered my eyes. That was how I looked when the German soldier in Vilno asked me if I were a film star.

Erdmann flew back into the dining room, trailing ashes. "The Hauptmann is very impressed," he said. "I'm to get you another uniform, and a good pair of shoes, even better than the ones I got last night." "Where did you get them?" "In Riga," he said; "that's where they have the stores." "You went all the way to Riga?" "Where else could I go, Berlin?" "Was he impressed with my husband, too," I asked bitterly. "Yes, he was. He said you didn't look Jewish, either of you, now he's sure you're not." "What an achievement." "So come, I have the clothes in the kitchen. You can put them on tomorrow, or after you sweep the courtyard. Do you want to wait on the tables?" he asked nervously, needing reassurance. "Oh, yes," I said; I couldn't keep the kindness out of my voice.

"Here is the package," he said, taking a squashy bundle wrapped in shiny brown paper down from the shelf. I tore at it like a lobster. Inside was a black taffeta uniform with a little white apron with ruffled edges all around, a little white ruffled cap, a pair of black shoes, two pairs of black stockings, and underneath—a brassiere! "A brassiere!" I whispered out loud. "I hope you'll forgive me," Erdmann pleaded, "but you'll look so much better in your uniform. There is a lot of you," he said, blushing scarlet. "How did you know what to get?" I was finding it funny. The poor man shifted from foot to foot; he puffed at his cigarette, but it wasn't lit. "I told the woman you were very short, but very big on top, and she said, take this, she can always make it smaller, that's all I know." "It's very nice of you." He was looking down at his shoes. "Underneath is something else." I poked. Out came a pot of rouge and a brand-new lipstick. They were the right colors. "How did you know the right colors to get?" "I told the lady you had a little blond hair and peach-colored skin." His eyes had not moved from his shoes. "I can't think of anything else you need, but if you do, you'll tell me?" "Just the material and some alcohol." His sigh of relief filled the room. "Come eat," he commanded.

So I sat in the bright shining dining room for two hours, but always with the same miserable bit of rag in my hand. "You can get up and pretend to polish something now and then," Erdmann conceded. "The courtyard is shoveled," a soldier announced. I jumped two feet from my chair, it was so quiet. "You can sweep it now." He handed me a big straw broom, the straw tied to the old wooden handle with several whips of cowhide. "Put on your boots and gloves," Erdmann whispered, popping into the room, then disappearing into his office. So I went outside. It was like being free. While I stayed in this charmed circle, no one would notice me; no one would shoot me. I could think and look at the sky and the snow, glistening like chips of glass. I could sweep and dream about what I might find; it was always possible someone might have dropped something. And I was so warm; I breathed in breath after breath of fresh, icy air. So I swept and swept, feeling the blood move warmly through my body; the cold kept away from my hands and feet. I swept the snow into the border of trees. The wind blew a thin curtain of it back. "It's like sweeping things under the carpet," I thought to myself. I liked it. Then I heard a metallic sound as the brush moved over the stones of the court. Something had stuck in the broom; I bent down to look at it. It was a cross, a beautiful golden cross. I slipped it into my pocket and went back to sweeping. Again, a metallic sound. This time it was an old spoon, not silver, but with a little cherub floating on the handle; it went into the other pocket. I didn't want them clinking together so others could hear.

"Send her in for lunch! Can't you follow a schedule here?" Erdmann was shouting at the soldier near the door. "The Hauptmann is disgusted at how nothing is ever done on time; please, when am I supposed to write songs?" I stamped my feet, went into the kitchen, hung my coat on a hook and put my boots and gloves in front of the big Russian stove. My new clothes were still on the bench. I took them into the little room near the kitchen and put them on.

"Oh, very nice," said the Hauptmann; "very nice, I think I'll invite everyone for Friday. Do you think," he asked, "you can get used to serving?" "Will you kill me if I spill soup on someone?" I was getting too bold. "I tell you what," he answered in Russian; "I'll give you a list of whom to spill soup on, and that will take care of both our desires. You should be very grateful to Mister Erdmann, you know; very grateful." I knew what he meant. "Oh, I will be," I cried; "for the rest of my life!" No wonder he had switched to Russian with Erdmann listening. Erdmann was staring at us worried because he didn't understand a word. "Now you know how I feel when you speak Polish," the Hauptmann said to him fondly. There was affection between them. I could feel it; it was unusual to see. "It is arranged?" Erdmann asked. "Even the spilling of the soup." "What soup?" He clucked like a worried hen. "The Hauptmann says he won't mind if I spill the soup." "Oh, if that's all." "So now what?" I demanded. "Finish sweeping the courtyard; it agrees with you." And at five, he took

311

me back to the barracks with rags soaked in vodka and wrapped in thick waxy paper.

"Look," Erdmann said after we had been trudging back through the woods, which now looked like a black and white etching, "I don't like this business of smuggling food into the camp that way." I had two eggs and a little envelope of farina tied with a cotton strip under a plain babushka I had sewn before we left. "Sooner or later you'll get caught." "But the women in the hospital," I cried; "it's so pathetic, they're sure they'll be cured if they can have these special things." "It's only superstition," he said roughly. "But they believe it!" "I don't like it anyway," he said, puffing out smoke. "Their blessings, you know, I believe they keep me alive, away from the selections." "It's getting to you, too, the guilt. That's all it is, guilt. There's nothing to it. You're as crazy as they are." "You shouldn't smoke so much," I said, trying to distract him. "And I'm not even asking you what that cloth and vodka are for." He was not distracted at all. "What can they do to me?" "They can beat you, for a start." "But you take me inside," I reminded him. "That will be stopping in a day or two; then I'll be leaving you at the gate. It would look suspicious if I kept coming in. Anyway, the Hauptmann doesn't see why you can't come and go yourself."

We got to the barracks and the little gate. A group was coming in from work. "The lineup," I gasped. I had forgotten all about it, that it was real. "There's nothing I can do about that," Erdmann answered, puffing violently. I went in with the rest of the group. That night there was no selection. I took my little piece of meat, green bread, coffee, and went in. "Did you get it?" Rachel asked. I nodded. "Did you heat the scissors?" "When we heat up the eggs in the hospital," I told her. I pointed to the back of my babushka. We gobbled down our food, and went out the door to the hospital. "To the hospital," I called to the guard; "we want to light a fire for the patients." He didn't look at us. We went in. Sonya was sitting up, already waiting. "We have some farina, Sonya," I told her; she clapped her hands in joy. Her cheeks were sinking; her color wasn't good. "Some eggs for you," Rachel whispered to another patient, named Tania, wheezing on her cot. "Why don't I have any eggs?" Sonya whined. "Because you didn't ask for them; stop complaining."

We had some paper and splinters of wood; Rachel had gotten some straw from her job and I had some matches from Erdmann. We took the little pot the hospital had near its stove and put it over the fire we made. The farina went into the same pot as the eggs. "Now," Rachel said, taking the scissors from me and turning her back to the cots, "we want you to do *us* a favor and not look until we say so." I turned around. Obediently, they both covered their eyes. Rachel held the scissors in the fire. They began to glow bluish-red. She took them out. There was a little wooden table near the stove. I lay one of the vodka-soaked rags on it, putting the scissors on top. "Don't turn around yet," I warned them; "you'll spoil the food." Sonya had her pillow over her head. Tania had turned her head to the wall. Rachel took off her sweater. She had already cut a slit in her dress over her shoulder blade; there was the abscess firm and hard as a small melon. I opened the scissors. I would have to hold onto one blade and cut with the other. "Are you ready?" I whispered to her. She had the back of her hand between her teeth; she nodded. *"Bozhe moy,"* I whispered to myself and took the scissors and pressed them down: nothing. I pressed them harder—a scream was rising in my throat like a trapped bird—and harder; then I could feel it go through. Automatically I stood to one side of the abscess. I could hear Doctor Kobielski: "Always stand to one side; sometimes they spurt. You could lose an eye." It didn't spurt, but a thick yellow stream was beginning to flow from the top of the abscess. I drew the scissors down and down. "Don't put it in again and again," I could hear Doctor Kobielski; "it will be a jagged incision, and take longer to heal." I pulled the scissors down in one straight line; the room was spinning. I pulled it out and grabbed the alcohol-soaked cloth from the table, holding it against Rachel's shoulder. "It's all right, Anya," she was whispering; "it feels better now. Really it does. The pressure's gone." "There must be a gallon here," I whispered in astonishment. "Sit on the bench, this way, press against the wall. Here, I'll add another cloth. Don't press too hard. I want it to drain; then I'll put on a dressing." "It does feel better," Rachel sighed; "put the scissors in the fire again." "Don't worry," I answered, looking at them with disgust.

"Where are the eggs?" Tania whimpered. "Tania, is it my fault you wanted them hard-boiled?" There was a little water left in the pot. I took out the two eggs and began peeling them. "They're coming up; here, two eggs." I handed them to her. She couldn't stop blessing me. "And now for your farina," I told Sonya, taking a spoon from the drawer under the table, bringing it to her. "Now I will be well," Sonya whispered in relief. "Now I know it; I'm sure of it. Oh, I bless you forever, for your whole life," and she began an interminable series of blessings in Lithuanian. They cheered me up, these blessings. No matter what Erdmann said, I believed in them as Sonya believed in the farina, and Tania the eggs. They *might* save me; perhaps they had already brought me to the Hauptmann's.

"Why is Rachel sitting on the bench?" Sonya asked. "She's tired." I went back to her. There was not much more draining from the cut. It was a good clean cut, straight; I was proud of my work. "Good?" Rachel asked, grinning. "Very." "What's going on there?" Sonya whimpered. "Rachel may have an abscess. It's not good for someone sick to look at it; turn away." But they had already done it. I took one of the vodka-soaked rags and pressed it over the abscess; the skin under the cloth was almost flat. "It is a pleasure to move my arm," Rachel sighed; "you have to show me how to do it." "What should we practice on? A grapefruit?" Under the cloths was some sticky tape. Could Erdmann read my mind? I fastened it on. Rachel put on the sweater and skirt she had brought with her, stuffing the dress under her skirt, pulling it up near her neckline. "Goodbye," we called to Sonya and Tania. The sound of their blessings ran out after us onto the snow.

"Business as usual," Rachel sighed when we got back to the barracks. All the women were sitting up on their cots, shredding lice. No one was talking. When we came in, we heard someone mutter something, then Rosa's angry voice. "Can you climb up?" I asked Rachel. "Just give me a push." But she was surprisingly strong. Then I climbed up after her. "Need any thread?" "Nope," Rachel answered thickly; she must be threading the needle. "I wonder a lot what will come after this." "I wonder, too." I had the cross out and was studying it as I had never studied anything in my life. It was wonderful. If I escaped, I could wear it; it would be a wonderful disguise. I would save the spoon for Ninka; she had so few toys.

I lay on my back, studying the cross. It was a big one, four inches big, and very elaborate. Each point of the cross was not just rectangular, but shaped. The two sides which formed the points at the branch of the cross curved gently up, as if someone had cut a half-circle out of each edge. In the center was the body of Christ, so beautifully carved you could see the veins in his arms and legs, the folds in the diaper he wore. The ligaments in his body twisted as accurately as in an anatomy book. But his face was the miraculous thing. The whole face stood out in relief; the sculptured nose, the eyebrows turned slightly to one side. It was amazing; however you turned the cross, the eyes followed you. I tried it again and again; they followed. How had the man made it? Over His head, with its hair carved like delicate snakes that could not strike back, was a halo, but shaped oddly, almost three-leaved, like the outline of a clover. And around the very edges of the cross ran a design of twisted rope that looked as if it had been soldered on. But it had not; it had been carved that way. And there were strange letters on the cross; I wondered what they meant. Above Christ's halo was the capital letter *H*, and below it, in smaller gothic letters, *NR*. Near his left arm, but slightly beyond it, was the capital letter *I*; beyond his right arm, the letter *S*; some strange flowers with thorns were carved beneath his feet. "Oh, this is a magic thing," I whispered to myself, slipping it in my pocket.

I stretched luxuriously. At the Hauptmann's I could wash most of myself with a wet towel; I couldn't get undressed, but still, I felt like the cleanest thing in the world. The Hauptmann had said something about washing my hair before his guests came to dinner; it clung to my head in tight blond curls. So now I could use the sink. Some snow drifted in through the crack in the roof; an icy wind chased in after it. The wind and the snow were clean. For once, I didn't mind. I had my gloves inside my brassiere. I didn't want the other women to see them; the jealousy was bad enough because of the coat and the boots. I felt for the spoon in my pocket; the fat little cherub was floating on his wave. I put it back in my pocket. "Anya?" Rachel was calling me, but I was falling asleep.

And so the weeks began to pass at the Hauptmann's. It was disgusting to me that I couldn't work, and finally even Erdmann saw it; he also saw I was getting fatter. In the barracks, I was letting out the seams I had made in the brassiere. On some Friday nights, I waited on tables. Twenty-four soldiers would sit around the huge mahogany table, their uniforms and patent leather boots shinier than the wood. Serving them was harder than I thought. I was supposed to anticipate each of their desires. None of them ever moved to reach anything. When a glass was empty, I was to fill it; when a delicacy was finished, I was to take the tray. I had to be in sixteen places at once. But it was a chance to listen to the gossip, and on those nights, the unimaginable blessing, I missed the lineup.

"So what have you been doing?" one of the men asked Erdmann. "Oh, he smokes and goes to the library," another laughed. "Does anyone want to buy some vodka?" he asked, looking up from his plate. "Why, you want some cigarettes?" one of them jeered. "No, books, I want some books about canals." "Canals!" They all burst into laughter. I heard the whispered word "cuckoo" scurrying around the table like a mouse. The Hauptmann leaned back in his chair, pulling on his uniform as if to loosen it, and smiled. "Clear the table," he ordered me. I began taking things into the kitchen. The eyes of the soldiers followed me. I was dressed all in black except for my little white apron and my little hat, like a white cupcake. There was a table on coasters holding a huge samovar and an enormous tray of pastries. "First take in the plates and the forks," an old woman commanded me from the sink. I had never seen her before. I didn't even know who did the cooking in the kitchen. I passed around the dessert dishes, the coffee cups and saucers, thin porcelain I could see my fingers through; I was supposed to set cup and saucer down together, without making them clatter. Twenty-four of them. When dinner was over they would play cards. The Hauptmann would send me home alone. I liked the walk alone through the dark woods; for a while there was no one to watch me, and if someone was watching or waiting behind a tree, I would not worry about it. Erdmann could not come. He worried; he did not like it.

The next day, the Hauptmann left at two-thirty to examine Russian soldiers. There was nothing for me to do. Erdmann had polished the floors and the furniture during the night; he had even beaten the curtains. The place was spotless. I was standing, as usual, near a shining surface with a spotless rag. To cheer me up, he put a record on his record player; it was Tchaikovsky's *1812 Overture*. Even in his room, there wasn't a speck of dust. The bed was perfectly made; the wastepaper basket was emptied; the desk and the chair were neat as a pin, the books in the little étagère lined up like soldiers. And naturally, the doors to the rooms were open. None of the doors were ever closed, but no one stopped before Erdmann's door.

There was nothing of interest in it; a record player with some classical records and some books, cigarettes, but no vodka. Then he put on another record: Mendelssohn's *Piano Concerto*. I must have clapped my hands over my ears so hard I knocked myself out. When I woke up, Erdmann was trying to keep me from falling from the left side of his desk chair. "What is the matter with you?" he kept asking. "It's the music; I can't stand it." "No," he said, observing me; "it's something more." "No," I insisted again; "it *is* the music. It's dangerous to play Mendelssohn; he's a Jewish composer." "It's something else," he repeated again. "My sister used to play that, over and over." "What was her name?" "Vera," I answered automatically. "No, it is still something else," he mused, shaking his head. "All right," I screamed suddenly, "I'll tell you. I left my baby with a gentile family and they were thrown out of their house by the Germans and now I don't know where they are." "Tell me about the baby, tell me," he coaxed. "She's just a baby, like any three-and-a-half-year-old baby." "Are you sure you don't know where she is?" he asked; "are you sure the gentile family was thrown out of its house?" I said I was. "Perfectly sure?" "And if I did know, what should you know for? So you could tell the Gestapo and have her shooted?" "Shot," he corrected me. "Shot," I said after him.

"A baby should be with its mother," he said sadly. "That's not what the Germans think!" I screamed at him, hysterical. "Listen, Anya." He had never called me that before. "If you tell me where she is, tomorrow when the Hauptmann goes for his interviewing, I can write a letter to the people who have her and mail it in Riga. We can find out about her. I've been thinking. You have to escape anyway. You remember the Hauptmann asked you about that word 'tattoo'? There are rumors all the time now; they will be shaving your heads again soon, putting numbers on your arms, and everyone in here will have striped uniforms. Then how could you do it?" "What are you talking about, escape?" I whispered violently. "How could I do it?" "It could be done." He considered. "I think you already have a plan." "I have no such plans." I was staring at the straight grain of his desk. "Tell me where they are?" he begged. "I can't," I cried in agony; "they would shoot her. I can't send her into the fire; I can't take a chance." "You don't trust me," he said sadly. "How can I?" I cried. "You have taken away everyone from me, my mother, my father, my sister, my brothers, everyone but my child; how can I trust you?" "I don't deserve it," he said, as he had said in the forest. I was sitting on the chair crying silently. I would have liked to collapse on the desk, but I was afraid of the passing soldiers; someone might look in.

"Listen to me carefully," he said in a whisper, pretending to take a book down from the shelf. "This is something only God and I know, and now you. I am here," he said slowly, "as God is my witness, under false papers. I'm Jewish. I'm Jewish like you. I had a friend who was a writer. He knew he was dying of tuberculosis, so he went away to some ghetto to die there. He thought he could write something about it; it would be a good last thing to do. He was a noble man, a noble man. I think he was caught near Vilno. Anyway," he said, his right hand shredding a cigarette, "he took my papers and I took his. He went into a ghetto, I enlisted in the army. My whole family is dead, all of them." The rims of his eyes had turned red. "All of them, my wife, a child. But a child needs its mother, it does. You have to get out of here to find her. You don't have forever, not now, with the tattoos coming, and the shaved heads and the striped suits; you wouldn't get four inches from the barracks." I sat a long time. "I believe you," I said. "We had a writer in our room in the ghetto, a little thin man. He wouldn't go to work; he used to tell my daughter stories." "What kind of stories?" Erdmann asked suddenly. "Oh, about a man who hung his wife on hooks, and someone who was eaten by wolves because he didn't listen to his mother." Erdmann's back was turned to the window; his shoulders were shaking. "So that's that," he said. "What happened to the writer's stories?" "All burned, or thrown out, or used to line shoes; who knows?" "To line shoes, or burned, or who knows?" he repeated sadly; "who knows?" "He was killed?" he asked. "Of course!" I exclaimed, "and pretty early; he didn't work."

"Tomorrow I'll have the letter, and when you come here at two-thirty, you will give me the address?" I nodded dumbly. I didn't tell Rachel anything, nothing about our talk of escape, nothing about the letter. "If you're going to do something, don't tell anyone, not even me." So Momma had told me. Two-thirty came again, and we were in his office. "Here's the letter," Erdmann said. It was a long one, explaining that I was in the camp, that a

318

child belonged to its mother, and that the man had to come get me out, even where he should stay when he came for me in Riga after I escaped. "Now, the address," Erdmann asked, raising his pen. "I cannot," I wailed; "I cannot." "Tell me, or you'll never see her again." Could that harsh voice belong to him? "This is where they were last," I told him in a quavering voice, "Tadislaw Rutkauskus," and the address. "Settled," said Erdmann; "now we wait." "We have to have a plan," I reminded him. "Tell me your ideas."

"I've been trying on disguises. I have an umbrella from Ann, and a funny hat; it comes to a point and pulls down over the eyes. What do you think?" "I think you will need more than that," he said, chewing on his pen. "Go beat the curtains while I think." "Suppose," he thought out loud, "we dress you up as a hunchback? I could get a lot of rags and stuff one shoulder all the way up; we could smear your face. I might be able to find something else; it's the face that's the problem." He was studying me. I had a big beauty mark to one side of my chin. "Dust the bookcase; I'll think some more." I dusted. "I have it!" he shouted. "Quiet!" I scolded; "someone will come in." "No, they won't; I always shout when I write. It's good for my reputation; otherwise I would be watched more." "So what is it?" I asked, trembling. "I'll tell you when the time comes." He was trembling too, with excitement. "It will be a surprise." "Please, I can't take any more surprises," I begged him, smiling. But then I saw him put the letter to Rutkauskus in his pocket.

What if I had made a mistake? Ninka's little face was moving farther and farther away from me, down and down, until it lay in the bottom of the mahogany pool in the Hauptmann's dining room table I went back to the barracks like a dead woman. The trees were gone. I was walking through an endless muddy field. "Don't worry," Erdmann had begged; "don't worry." But I was crying. "Go in with this group." I went through the gate with them *"Du! Blonde!"* one of the soldiers called *"Stehen zie."* Another selection. But it was not a selection. Once all the groups had gone into their barracks, the soldier lifted up my kerchief; the usual two eggs were tied in place at the back of my head. "Come with me!" he ordered, dragging me by the arm. We went into the shower room. "Undress, from the waist down." I unfastened my skirt and pulled my slip over my waist. "Bend down over

319

this bench," he ordered. Turning my head, I could see him take the leather tongues, five of them knotted together at the handle, flying loose like tails; he was dipping them in the water that collected under the dripping faucet. "Now!" he began, lifting his arm. I began to scream. The pain pushed at the top of my head and my toes like something alive trying to get out. Then I stopped screaming. When I got up I could hardly walk.

"What happened?" Rachel asked, white as the lice on her sweater. "I thought they took you." "A beating," I said. "No food for the hospital tonight; they got the two eggs." "Get on my bunk," Rachel told me. I climbed on, slowly, like a crab missing a leg. Gently, she pushed up my skirt. *"Boze pomogi,"* I heard her gasp; "you're all black, Anya, black as coal." "It will get better," I whimpered, tears falling out of my eyes. "It will take a long time," she whispered in an awed voice. "Like everything else. So I will sleep on my stomach with my shell in the air like a turtle." I was already forgetting about my bottom, and thinking about the letter, the letter, the letter. Had he really sent it to Rutkauskus and Vilno?

The next day I crawled along after Erdmann. He didn't say a word, just puffed angrily on his cigarette. "Why? Why? Why?" he burst out suddenly. "Why, what?" I asked hobbling after; he had speeded up. "The telegram, I don't understand it; why such a telegram?" "What telegram?" I shouted, beside myself. "Shhhhhhhh!" he hissed at me; "what's the matter with you?" We stomped along for a few more yards. Suddenly, Erdmann stopped and turned to face me. "The one from Rutkauskus in Vilno." His eyes were shinier than usual. "What telegram?" I hissed again. "The one that said 'Be prepared to travel.' How could he do it? How? Where does he keep his brains?" Erdmann went on. "To just send it to me like that." "Did they find out about it?" "Find out about it?" he demanded bitterly. "They read every telegram that comes in here. All morning it's been 'What have you to do with Vilno?' They know all the girls here are from Vilno. When you go, it will mean the front or a bullet for me."

We crept along. I was trying to keep my back as straight as I could. Finally, I put my hand to the back of my waist like a pregnant lady with a backache. "You don't have to worry," I told him; "I'm not going." I watched my breath disappear into the trees. "What do you mean you're not going?" Erdmann demanded violently.

"You have to go now. I told you; soon it will be too late."
"I am sorry," I told him slowly, "in my whole life I have
never returned bad for good. I am not going to start now.
Whatever will happen, will happen." "That's nonsense,"
Erdmann sputtered. "Nevertheless, I am not going, and
don't try to distract me with noodles, or teddy bears, or
gloves, or whatever you think of. *I'm not going*. Don't say
it again; it's ridiculous. Even crows have ears," I said por-
tentously looking around the woods. So we stomped along.

"What did you tell them?" I asked. "What could I tell
them? That it was a trick; they knew how people here
treated me. Maybe it was someone who wanted to buy
vodka. I had no idea. How should I know what it was
about. The usual things." "Did they believe you?" "I don't
know," Erdmann said nervously, throwing a cigarette into
the snow, listening to the little hiss. "They don't think I
have any interest in women, only books. I'm so busy all
day with Heil Hitler this and Jews that, they think I hate
them. Probably they believed me." "But they'll figure it
out now if I leave," I insisted. "Yes," he agreed finally.
"So, no more discussion, and, to tell you the truth, I don't
feel like scouring the floors today." "How about peeling
potatoes?" "How about polishing the brass on the shelves;
I won't have to sit down." "Fine." We crept along to the
Hauptmann's.

There was a buzz around Erdmann all day long, but by
the end of the day it had died down. "I have to see the
High Lieutenant tonight," Erdmann told me on the way
back; "if he believes me, the trouble is over."

"He believed me," he told me the next morning. "You
know," I told him, "when we were still in the ghetto, I
heard Rutkauskus had a tendency to get drunk. Maybe he
was drunk when he sent the telegram." "That would *almost* explain it," Erdmann answered bitterly.

Five days later, Erdmann flew into the dining room. It
was a little after two-thirty. "Time to clean the Hauptmann's office," he ordered me in an unusually stern
voice. Now what was up? I followed him down the hall.
"Rutkauskus is here," he said, staring at me. I looked
wildly around the room. "No, not *here*. In Riga. He called
me this morning. I'm going to visit him this afternoon and
find out about the baby. I want you to go to Vilno with
him when he leaves." "I am not going," I repeated again.
"If anyone asks, tell them you saw me with a stack of
books so high I fell down the stairs," Erdmann suggested,

321

picking up about ten books and starting off. "How late is the library open?" I heard him call to one of the soldiers. "You're there every day; you ought to know," a voice called back, and then he was clattering down the stairs. He was back by four o'clock. "The child is fine," he told me, breathless, "but I thought you'd want to hear it from him, so he's coming here tomorrow. Also, you might go with him then." "Please don't start," I answered, irritated but excited. "How will I talk to him?" "Oh, he's coming here to arrange about buying vodka from me." "That doesn't solve anything," I pouted. "It solves everything," Erdmann answered; "you'll see."

The next morning, Erdmann decided it was time for the pots to be scoured. "Pots!" I exclaimed. "Pots!" he said severely, "and it is a very messy job. The Hauptmann does not like the whole house messed up, so you will please carry the pots out near the front steps where we can watch you, and scour them there." "There is snow all over the ground!" I protested. "You will do as you are told, Frau Lavinsky!" he shouted. A passing soldier regarded him approvingly. So I started scouring the pots in the snow.

"Ah," I heard Erdmann say from the door, "my guest; now maybe I'll sell some vodka." I looked around; I was on all fours on the court. A big man was approaching. He was tall and gangly, like a scarecrow, and carried a huge black umbrella. Even from a distance I could see the sharp, high cheekbones of a Lithuanian peasant. It was the man who had stopped for Ninka at the church! "So, Mister Rutkauskus, would you like to talk business inside or out?" Erdmann asked, pulling on his coat, and putting his rifle on over the wrong shoulder as usual. "Outside, I think. I need some fresh air after the hotel." "Do you care to walk?" Erdmann asked. "No, not just now." They had arranged themselves so I could see Rutkauskus's face; the back of Erdmann's head was to me. "I have her passport," he told Erdmann, looking around. "It's made out to Otilia Rutkauskenie, a Lithuanian. I have a lot more," he went on proudly. "I got a judge drunk in a little town and a friend and I stole all the *emblancos* and the stamps, it's legal as your rifle," he grinned. "She's not going," Erdmann said grimly. "What!" exclaimed Rutkauskus. "What! I travel over twenty hours, and she's not going? I came because the child needs its mother; what is this, she's not going?" "How many bottles

322

could you use?" Erdmann asked. The shadow of another soldier fell over the snow. "As many as you can get," Rutkauskus answered without missing a blink; "the more the merrier." "Tell her how the child is," Erdmann pleaded.

"The child," Rutkauskus sighed. "We had to change her name, you know, for safety's sake; it is Luisa Vishinskaya." He pronounced it slowly for my benefit. "Is she healthy?" Erdmann prompted him. "Scour!" he whispered ferociously in my direction. I attacked a new pot. "Very healthy, but we had a terrible time. As soon as she had enough to eat, it was Momma! Momma! Momma! What a pair of lungs. We were terrified the neighbors would hear her. We didn't take her out for a long time. Now she already goes to kindergarten in a special *drozhka* and she has a new navy sailor suit and some coral beads and a lot of medals; she likes to wear them; also some dolls, a little lamb, a room of her own, it's very nice; a painted iron bed, white walls, curtains, a little rug near her bed, very plain, very nice. Anyone would like it," he said addressing Erdmann. "I can get the bottles in a week," Erdmann said as another soldier went by. "She is used to us now," Rutkauskus went on; "she's learning Lithuanian. She goes everywhere with Onucia; that's my wife. I'm a judge," he added. "Also," he said, after thinking a minute, "we decided not to christen her. We'll wait until the war's over, Onucia said, and then if the mother doesn't come, that would be time enough. Meanwhile, we do nothing about it. Onucia says what can be better than to have two mothers?" Tears were freezing on the pot I was scouring. "What do you mean she won't come?" Rutkauskus asked suddenly. "She won't," Erdmann answered. "I won't," I whispered. "This man saved my life; I can't be responsible for taking his." "Come to your senses," Rutkauskus barked at me; "I'll be back tomorrow." For three days, it was the same thing, the scouring pots, the arguments over whether or not I was leaving.

Then Erdmann had a letter for me from Rutkauskus; it was the size of a small book. "I'll read it at home," I informed him, stuffing it in my brassiere. "Then I'll take you back into the barracks. No more beatings; my nerves can't stand anymore." It took me all night to read half the letter. "How could you fall in love with him? A German, whose hands are soaked in the blood of your nearest and dearest, perhaps even your mother's and father's?" There were comparisons made between me and every sinful character in the Bible and popular literature. The next night, I finished it. "Be warned," Rutkauskus concluded; "if I go away this time, I will not come again. You will never see your daughter. How can you do this, fall in love with a German, to give up your own daughter for a German? I warn you, I will not be back." The next day, I used the letter to set fire to the little pieces of wood in the hospital stove. Rachel and I made some farina for Sonya and Tania; Rachel had no idea what was going on.

"He's gone," Erdmann told me, as if he were pronouncing his own death sentence, not mine; "now we have to think of some other way." "Not now," I told him. "I have a feeling this isn't the right time. I'll know when it's the right time." "There is something wrong with your clock," he told me the next morning as we were trudging through the mud. "The Hauptmann is going on vacation tomorrow, and everyone says it's useless for you to be there while he's gone." His face was frozen. "So you'll work downstairs in the *kartoffel* cellar for a while, and then we'll see."

Two days later I was down in the dark, damp cellar with old German women peeling potatoes. "Eat the peel; eat it," one of them encouraged me; "they're good for you. Just gas is all you get; they give strength." Then they started talking about their dreams. I was frightened. My mind was running back and forth like a bell on a tilted board; the floor was the board. What had I done? Now how would I get out; now what would I do? "I had a dream," I said suddenly, and began telling them: "I had a dream about one shoe. I was trying to find a big enough shoe, but I couldn't get my foot in right away. It was a high shoe, with laces." "Just one shoe!" the German woman gasped, "what! You're going to escape? And alone?" "Escape?" I demanded. Was it written all over my face? "Could *you* escape? What are you talking about, escape?" "But you *will* escape, and alone," the old woman said, bending over her potato, raising her wrinkled face; "alone, the dream tells it." I didn't open my mouth the rest of the day. When I got back to the barracks, Ann took a look at me. "Escaping, eh?" "What do you mean?" I cried. "The coat; you're going to escape," she said flatly. "I've had the coat for months, months," I said, raising my voice; "all of you here are crazy." "Queen of the Hauptmann's," someone muttered. "Why are they talking about escape?" Rachel asked anxiously. "You're asking me?" But when I fell asleep, I had the dream about the shoe again; and again, it was only one shoe. The second shoe was gone. In the dream, I wasn't even looking for it.

"So," Erdmann informed me the next day with a sigh of relief, "the High Lieutenant is persuaded the Hauptmann's quarters outshine his, and he needs you there." We were marching off on another trail. Then we came to a small brick building, only two stories high. "The Lieutenant has the main floor; that's where you clean." A young man with blond hair came outside. "Frau Lavinsky?" he asked me. "*Ja.*" "Here is the closet of food," he said, taking me into the kitchen; "take whatever you want. There's a little bench if you want to rest." Then there was some kind of fuss. "You are needed in the potato cellar for one more day," he sighed; "so tomorrow, you'll start."

Our boots made sucking noises as we pulled them out of the thick slush lying like a body under the snow. Erdmann was smoking cigarette after cigarette, and throwing them into the snow. They would sink into the soft snow with a little plop, leaving exactly the same round shape as a melting icicle wider at the top, narrower at the bottom. It didn't seem to make any difference to the snow, fire or water. It was a perfect skin, I thought idly, and when it got warmer, it would turn into water, and disappear without any pain. Then the flowers would come back, and the grass, and finally the snow again. It was only human beings who were cursed this way; they were not on good terms with the earth. When they went in, they were devoured; they could not come back. Cigarettes seemed to be flicking by me like hail. "Why are you smoking like that?" I demanded. "Like what?" Erdmann asked, looking down at his hand as if it didn't belong to him. Then there was no sound.

"I don't like this," he said finally; "all this moving about. You're bound to attract attention. You're stubborn as a mule, you know. I have your papers. You are Otilia Rutkauskenie, and instead of getting out of here, you spend all your time walking back and forth between the Hauptmann's and the High Lieutenant's." I wasn't going to argue with him, but I could feel myself turning red. "You should turn purple," Erdmann commented; "you remind me of the mule in a story my father used to tell me." Another wave of scarlet swept over my face. I was painfully aware of my short hair which I wet every morning so it would curl up in corkscrews all over my head. I remembered Momma soaking it and stretching it flat on a visit to Paltava; she wanted me photographed as a Russian peasant with long straight blond hair. "A Botticelli angel!" Erdmann had once murmured to himself. But a mule! I had never been called a mule before! "Why am I stubborn as a mule?" I asked in a small voice. "Well," he said, flicking another cigarette into the patient snow, "when I was a small boy my father used to tell a story about a farmer and a mule. My father wasn't home too much; he drank a lot, so maybe it was my mother." "Please!" I interrupted, "*I* know you make perfect sense." "Do you?" He grinned at me quizzically. "It was my father. You probably guessed, didn't you?" I tramped ahead faster.

"So you wanted me to tell you why you were like a mule. Well, this mule belonged to a farmer; remember, my father told me the story; I'm not responsible for his view of mules." The snow's hand let go of our boots with a sucking sound. "And the farmer was very proud of his mule. He was a very unprepossessing mule, really, but he ate very little and he was a very well-behaved mule. The farmer used to call the mule a real gentleman among mules. So one day, the farmer decided to reward his mule, and buy him a bell; and he hung the bell around the mule's neck on a ribbon. And it was the worst thing he could have done. Do you know why?" I slushed along as fast as I could, burning red; I wouldn't look at him. "It turned out this very good mule used to sneak into the gardens of one farmer, and eat a little rye here, and into the fields of another farmer, and eat some oats there, and into the fields of another farmer and eat some hay there, but he was very quiet, so no one noticed him. But as soon as he wore the bell, everything changed. The oat farmer came out and saw him eating the oats and beat him on the back with a stick"—Erdmann looked meaningfully at my bottom—"and the rye farmer came out and saw him eating the rye, and beat him on the head with a stick"— Erdmann looked at the back of my head—"and the oat farmer came out and saw him eating the hay, and beat him with a hammer, and finally, all that was left were bones and a skull. And of course, the farmer recognized the skeleton when he found it, because of the bell. Now the point is," Erdmann continued, in his voice of exaggerated patience, "the mule had not been such an honest mule in the first place, but no one would have known if it hadn't been for the bell. But the fault was not all the mule's either, because if the farmer hadn't given him the bell, he could have gone on stealing, and no one would have noticed, and he would have lived to be a grizzled, gray-haired mule, venerated for his honesty and old age, which, as we all know, brings wisdom." A huge chunk of ice dislodged itself from a tree and was swallowed by a snow drift. "So the puzzle is, who was right and who was wrong? The mule was not so good, but he didn't deserve to die; the farmer was perhaps too proud, but should his favorite mule, his czar among mules, have been killed for his one mistake? You see, it's hard to decide these moral questions."

"Are you saying I'm dishonest?" I demanded. "I'm saying you're Jewish in the middle of a German labor camp, and I've given you a bell. And if you don't escape, you will make me your murderer." "If I had gone when Rutkauskus came, I would be *your* murderer," I answered bitterly. "My life is worth nothing," he said, starting to light a cigarette, then changing his mind. We had reached a stretch of mud near the Hauptmann's. "Why not escape in the spring?" he asked; "the flowers do." "You cannot blame yourself if anything happens to me," I insisted; hysteria was rising in my belly like a snake. "I can and I must," he answered inflexibly.

"All right," I said, defeated; "the twelfth day at the High Lieutenant's, I'll escape." I was thinking of the rain and the snow blowing in, covering me in the top bunk in the barracks as I slept, as if I were already dead. "I cannot anymore," I thought to myself; "I can't stand anymore." And the selections; how long could my strength last? I knew he was right. "How will you escape? You'll have to find some way to get back to the Hauptmann's from the Lieutenant's so we can dress you up in my office." "The twelfth day," I insisted; "I'll do it." "How?" he asked again. "I don't want you to know; I'm sorry." "Do you promise me?" "Yes." "Then I will have everything ready." "Something like a pot of acid to change my face, I hope," I muttered, fingering the birthmark on my chin. "I hardly think that will be necessary; give me some credit. Please keep walking."

We came to the Hauptmann's court. Little patches of snow lay shredded in the mud. I went in through the side door and down to the potato cellar. "Haven't run away yet, eh?" the German woman asked. "Please, don't start

327

the nonsense," I begged her; "I have cramps." I did; they were terrible cramps. I was bent over at the waist, clutching my stomach. "Here," she said, pushing over part of her pile. "I work fast, practice, always practice." "Thank you," I gasped. "The good one's here today," she whispered. She meant Kleinman, the guard. He was tall, with curly auburn hair. "*He's* no torturer," she whispered, removing the peel from a potato in one winding strip like a corkscrew. "How do you do that?" I gasped again. "Practice. You can learn when you feel better." She looked like a potato herself. "What's wrong with you?" Kleinman asked when he came in and saw me. "I have terrible cramps," I gasped at him. "Go up to my room and lie down," he suggested, taking out a key. "I couldn't inconvenience you." "It's no inconvenience. I won't be back until late tonight; stay there until you feel better." "If I can stand it, I won't bother you," I promised him. "I'll unlock the door," he said. We all knew where his room was. It was on the first floor, right opposite the potato cellar. But I could not stand it. The pain was making my legs numb below the knees; my whole back was on fire; there was a ringing in my ears. "Do you have any stuff?" the old woman asked me. I shook my head no. "Get some paper from his desk; some of those Hitler songs. They should be good for something."

I stumbled up the wooden steps, digging my nails into the rough wood. A big splinter went under my index finger nail; I was grateful to it. It took my mind off the pain in my stomach. The door was unlocked. I went in and lay down on the bed. It might have been Erdmann's room: a bed, a bookcase, a little desk. But when the pain began to clear, like snow thinning out, I could see some photographs—a blond woman and three little children. From where I was, they seemed to be two boys and a girl. The oldest, a boy, looked about eight. They were all in old fashioned oval frames, with little floral crests at the top and bottom of each oval. Silver frames, I thought, thinking of my little package under my bunk pillow: an old folded sweater, the pictures tied with string.

After fifteen minutes I felt better and went down. "Heil Hitler" was staunching the flow of blood; the old woman was right. The soldiers were afraid to throw the propaganda out. Some nights at the Hauptmann's they were expected to sing Erdmann's songs. "You are dumb," she greeted me; "you should have stayed up there more time."

"Well, I am here," I sighed, settling on the crate next to hers; "give me a potato." "Just take mine. I peel too many anyhow; why should they eat so good?" So I sat, and every hour, Erdmann was running in and looking, like a poisoned rat, eyes big and frightened. "He's afraid you'll escape, too," she whispered. "Please, stop," I whimpered; "my stomach hurts." "Ach," she muttered, presenting me with another corkscrew after she had first wiped it on her skirt; "eat it; it stops bleeding." What new crazy idea was this? Mechanically, I ate it. "What's in the rooms over there?" I asked, pointing deeper into the basement. "The laundry for all the soldiers. Here." She handed over another corkscrew peel. "You get used to it," she coaxed, giving me a third; "go on; it stops the bleeding. You even get to like it." I munched until five o'clock when Erdmann came for me. "You're pale," he said accusingly after we were halfway back. "So are mushrooms that grow in cellars." "No one wanted you in there," he reminded me bitterly. "On the twelfth day, why the twelfth day?" "I have a feeling," I said, the paper dampening between my legs.

The next day I began at the High Lieutenant's. He had one enormous light room which took up half the first floor; it was his office and apartment all in one. In a corner was a bed covered with a black spread and two pillows covered in black resting against the wall so that during the day it would look like a couch. In another corner was a tiny desk, but a fancy French one, made of inlaid wood with gold crests on each drawer, and a big crest above the center drawer. In another corner was a little table for food, and four straight chairs. A huge crystal chandelier hung in the empty room reflecting itself in the parquet floors which I was polishing with brushes on my feet; now the High Lieutenant was sure I was a *real putzfrau*.

"I need a ladder," I told him the second day; "the moldings are dirty." "How can you tell?" he asked me, puzzled. "I can't even see them, and you're so short." "If no one has seen them, they are dirty for sure, and the windows are nothing to brag about, either." He came back with a ladder and an old lady from the back yard. "I want her to hold it for you so it doesn't shake." "Fine," I answered absently. "Look." I displayed a black terry rag. "This is what you've been breathing in every night." "And to think I'm alive," he said in mock astonishment.

I had started on the big windows when the cramps came back. I went into the little kitchen and lay down on the wooden bench. It was painted white; little bits of paint were starting to chip off like the paint on our coffee kettle. Blood was streaming onto the bench, little drops splattering on the floor. I was thinking about Erdmann. "My murderer!" Where did the man get such ideas? Then I began to think about the very fine mule who politely ate, so quietly. I was smiling, looking up at the cracks of the ceiling, when I opened my eyes and saw the High Lieutenant in the doorway. My blood stopped like a clock. *"Stehen zie, stehen zie,"* he whispered, embarrassed, and went out, closing the door. Black time was chiming in my veins. When would I be able to hear those words without waiting for the leather or the stick? But the little bench was just big enough so I could turn on my side, and when Erdmann came for me, he had to shake me awake. "Wait while I clean up," I squealed, scurrying around like a mouse with a rag. "The High Lieutenant is very pleased with his acrobat," he joked at me, "but I'm afraid you're planning on breaking a leg and getting out of our little agreement." "The High Lieutenant has some old woman holding onto the ladder; just give her a net." "Are you sure you're not trying to break a leg?" He wasn't joking. "I'm finishd with the ladder, anyway," I snapped angrily. "Five days are up," he reminded me. "I can count." I went into the bathroom; when I came out, he was holding my coat.

Then ten days were up. Rachel and I had started talking more at night; I couldn't believe I was going to leave Rachel. What would happen to her without me? Now and then we even mentioned our families; it was very unusual for us. "Poor Henyk," she said one night; "he was so spoiled, he never believed they could bother him." "It's funny, Rachel," I answered her, "but I still can't believe it will happen to me, that I'll really die because of this." "Cannot, or will not?" Rachel asked. "Both. But cannot mostly." "Maybe you're right," she whispered. "And you?" "Me?" Rachel asked. "I just don't want to, that's all. You know, with these bloody feet, and the pain from them, sometimes it doesn't seem so bad; sometimes the earth seems like the best bed. But then there's the hospital. It's as if they put it in my blood that time in the ghetto; I don't know what happened. It's a miracle, medicine, I mean; it's a miracle. The same things, knives spilling blood, cutting out this and that, and instead of death you get life. At least sometimes. I just don't want to die if I could learn to do that. Even the abscess; it was so bad, now it's all better. But it's a silly straw to hold onto, because I could never read a book before in my life." "That was before." "Before, yes," Rachel said; "a long time before."

"What is the worst thing for you?" I asked. "Not the lice, or the hunger, no," Rachel thought; "no, the worst thing is my feet, how much they hurt." She laughed a little. "Ridiculous, how it's the little things. I even forget the hunger and the stealing and the work and the woman waiting to hit us if we don't stand straight, even the selections, sometimes I forget them, even that fire, but I never forget my feet. Even when I lie here with them up, they throb like two hearts looking for bodies." "If my boots don't stop hurting my feet in a few days I'm going to give them to you." "Why should you do that?" Rachel cried; "they're perfectly good boots." "Yes, but they pinch me terribly, and I have these normal shoes for the Lieutenant's." "But you still have to walk through the snow," she reminded me. "I'd rather go in the *clumpas*, believe me. I'm afraid of ingrown toenails; these press me so much. Your feet are much smaller. They'll fit you better." "I don't know why such a large body should have such small feet," Rachel mused, looking at her toes. "Your body isn't strange anymore; not really. Maybe it's the exercise." It was true; she was almost in proportion.

"Anya," she whispered after a while through a choking sound, "in the hospital"—she stopped again—"did they cut everything out? Someone told me they had orders to sterilize all pregnant women they fixed up." "Doctor Yurbo took the baby; the rest of you is just as it was." "I wanted to know," Rachel explained, "in case I should live. I wanted to know what to expect." "If you can live, you can expect everything," I promised her. "Will you come down to me?" she pleaded. I came down to her bunk. "Look at us," she laughed; "two monkeys, picking each other for lice. They didn't take anything else, just the baby?" "Just the baby," I repeated. "You know I would never lie to you about that." "You wouldn't," Rachel agreed. "You know, I'm not so jealous as I used to be. I wonder what did it?" "Probably my Momma," I sighed. "She never left anyone out; I never remember wanting anything." "Let's not talk about it anymore," Rachel said. "How's Sonya?" I asked. "Worse," Rachel said grimly; "can you get anything?" "Tomorrow" I promised. "At least now they know she's not pregnant, so they won't cut her." "Thank God for that," I sighed.

19

THE next day was to be my next to last in the camp. I polished the parquet floors three times, washed the windows all over again; the furniture was gleaming with oil. I felt feverish all over; it was as if the sun coming in through the windows was melting something, sinking in. Erdmann came for me a little before five. "I have to get back early for a dinner I'm giving at the Hauptmann's," he told the High Lieutenant. "Is she doing her work?" "Oh, she's very good; I'm afraid to sit down. Everything I touch, I leave fingerprints on." "Well, you're not here much anyway," Erdmann told him. "I'm not complaining," the Lieutenant retorted, flushing to the roots of his blond hair. "It sounded like complaining to me." "I don't care what it sounded like to you," the Lieutenant answered angrily; "it sounds like you just want to get her back there because of this dinner. She's not supposed to go back until the Hauptmann gets here." "Couldn't you spare her for a day? People are coming tomorrow, too," Erdmann said sulkily. "No," the Lieutenant barked. "I don't see what you need her for if it's so clean." "It's not so clean," the Lieutenant protested. "You just said it was," Erdmann went on like a child. "Look," the Lieutenant told him, "if you're so worried about disgracing yourself clean up with the others yourself; Frau Lavinsky comes here tomorrow." "Selfish," Erdmann muttered. "What did you say?" the Lieutenant asked, astonished. "Nothing," Erdmann shouted.

"What did you do that for?" I asked, as we turned into the lane of trees. The whole stretch of earth looked like the skin of a birch, white and black, white and black. "I had my reasons," Erdmann muttered. "You still have to think of a way to get to the Hauptmann's tomorrow," he reminded me. "You just made it a lot harder," I accused him. "Oh, no, if you think of anything reasonable that klutz will be only too happy to let you go, gloating over how you'll have to go right back, and seeing me crying

333

into my furniture polish and broom." "But basically it's the same plan? We disguise me as a hunchback, and see what we can do about my face?" "Same plan; come about three," Erdmann said. "Everyone will be finished eating; no one will notice much." "Around three," I considered. "I think I can." "I wish you would tell me how," he worried at me; "why aren't you saying anything?" "I am counting your wrinkles; when you worry, you have about two hundred. If you would stop worrying, I would have a lot less trouble. Suppose," I thought out loud, "I didn't get through the selection tonight; wouldn't that be funny?" "I'm glad you think so," Erdmann practically snarled, lighting another cigarette.

But there was no selection. There were rumors that things were going well at the front. Right after the lineup, I was going to the hospital. "Please," I told Rachel, "today I want to go over alone." She looked hurt, but she didn't say anything. In the last few weeks the commandant had installed a male nurse there. No one knew why. There were rumors that the hospital might be a nest of spies and he was there to check. Rachel settled on her bed, eating her piece of horsemeat and bread. "Here," I said, giving her some cookies and two hard-boiled eggs; "you can give these to Sonya when you go over later." It was an unwritten rule with us; we never asked each other questions.

The male nurse was there, sitting in front of the stove, blocking the heat from the patients. He was a big man, six foot five, with blond hair that stood straight up on his head, and big ropelike lips. His veins stood out on his forehead in purple twists; his cheeks were lined all over with purple veinings. His face always reminded me of some horrible fleshy flower, a mutated white carnation a florist would dye another color. So his skin looked, as if it had been yellow, but was drinking up a purple stain. "Listen, Mister Rubinsky," I said confidentially, standing just outside the circle of warmth, "I want to talk to you about something privately. You're the only one who can help me." "What do you want?" he asked suspiciously. He probably thought I was about to ask to stay in the hospital while the selections were going on. "I have decided to kill myself," I told him, "but I need a rope." "Oh, I understand," he answered, all sympathy. "There's really nothing for you here. But why hang yourself? I can make you one of the death injections, like the ones I made for the little children; you wouldn't feel anything at all." "No, no," I in-

sisted. "I want to hang; I want to hang in the forest."
"Why in the forest?" "I was always happy in the forest,
and it seems a good way to die, hanging from a tree.
Trees are so sympathetic, don't you think, like people? I
feel like it would take care of me afterward." He gave me
a queer look. "I understand," he said again, "but I don't
have a rope now. If you can come back in the morning, I can
give it to you." "Are you sure it will be a good strong
rope?" I asked. "I don't want to go around from tree to
tree, falling down all over, and just get locked up to do
cleaning again." "Don't worry," he assured me; "I'll get it
for you. But the injections are easier. Look," he said, picking up a hypodermic from the tray on the table, "I have it
right here." "I *would* take it," I said, "if you would swear
on your cross you would take my body and hang it on a
tree afterward." This time, a terrified look. "No, no, just
come for the rope in the morning." He had backed away
slightly. "You'll want to pick out your own tree; I always
did, for Christmas." "Exactly!" I rhapsodied; "exactly! I
knew you would be just the man to understand. I should
tell everyone in the barracks how wonderful you are!"
"Please," he begged, frightened; "don't tell anyone. You
have to promise or I won't get the rope." "A good strong
one," I said again. "For an elephant," he swore.

I went back to the barracks. It was almost the end of
March. There was a new season in the air. "Go over,
Rachel." When she came back, it was dark. "I'm tired," I
said. "You're acting funny; are you sick?" Rachel asked.
"No, just tired. I breathed in too much ammonia with the
window cleaning, that's all. Go to sleep." Rachel fell
sound asleep. She was still plucking chickens; the women
who watched them were worse than the soldiers. During
the day she didn't get a second's rest. When it began to
get light, I listened for the sound of her breathing. It was
deep and regular. I crept down to the floor and took my
boots, folded them, and slipped them under her pillow.
Rachel slept like the dead. She would find them when she
got up. Erdmann was waiting outside. "How are we going
to explain why I'm getting there before the lineup?" I demanded. "I'll just tell him if he needs you so badly, I
thought I'd get him up early so you could get started." "I
have to stop at the hospital first." "What for?" he asked,
frightened. "For some rope," I answered, disappearing
into the building. The man handed it to me, tilting his
335

spikey head, nodding slyly. I put it in my pocket. *"Danke shön,"* I said.

"What were you doing in there?" "I got some rope to hang myself with, in the forest; I told him trees were nice to people." He was staring at me in horror. "This way," I explained, taking pity, "they'll think I hung myself. They'll look for me all over around here, in the woods, everywhere; it will give me time." "Have you thought of a way to get to the Hauptmann's?" "Not yet, but I will." For the last twelve days, my mind had been ticking like a machine; how to do this, how to do that. I had only thought of the rope when I thought about giving Rachel my shoes and stared at the shoelaces. So I was not worried; I would think of something.

I began cleaning; it was after one, almost two. I should be at Erdmann's by three. I looked down at the white tablecloth I had just put on the table. The Lieutenant's soup was sitting in the kitchen on the table. I carried it out, and at the last minute, fell forward as if I had tripped. The soup went all over the cloth. "Oh, I have spilled it!" I cried out heartbroken, gathering up the red-stained cloth into a little bundle. "Go get another," the Lieutenant sighed; "give Erdmann my regards when you get there. Make sure you take one of their best cloths."

So I set off with the crumpled tablecloth. The trees didn't look friendly at all; they seemed like sentries, their branches, rifles. I was approaching the Hauptmann's alone; I no longer worked there. The sentries had their orders to shoot unauthorized personnel on sight. Automatically I raised my arm, holding up the tablecloth the way a waiter in the Café Europa would hold up a tray. "Hello," I called to the guards one by one, and when I got to the one in the booth near the house, the one with the orders to shoot on sight, "How long are you going to be there?" "I'm coming out soon. I just have to get some laundry." "I'll wait," he called back, joking. The blood was hammering at my cheeks as if it were not inside, but out. I went in the big front door, still carrying the tablecloth that way.

Erdmann was waiting right inside the entrance. "Give me that," he shouted, seizing the tablecloth and throwing his coat over it. "My room was left a *mess*," he thundered at me as I followed him up the stairs. He had moved his bookcase so it formed a line with his desk, and the two screened anyone behind them from the door. "Don't worry, it's been that way for twelve days," he assured me;

"hurry up." He had a little gray skirt for me, a blue silk blouse and a white sweater, new shoes and stockings. He was already stuffing something into the sleeve and back of my coat. "While I'm doing this, study the map on my desk. Look like you're dusting. The map has the directions to the Riga train station; it's a tramway, a half-hour underground to Riga. You go straight ahead down the main road. You won't have to pass any more sentries; the road's at a right angle to the one going to the barracks." I spied a little ivy plant on his desk and dug out some dirt with my fingers and began smoothing it into my cheeks.

"I'm not a praying man," Erdmann was saying, "but I'm praying now." "Please pray later," I asked him; "I'm turning green with fright." "Put on the coat," he instructed, standing back and examining me. He already had Ann's hat and umbrella. The coat was red and came down to my ankles, the hat green, the umbrella dark blue. "You look terrible, but it's your face. For the first time in my life," he said slowly, "I have stolen something." He was taking something out of his pocket. "The Hauptmann's glasses," he said, giving them to me. They were thick as my thumb, with cold steel rims. Erdmann put them on me himself. He became a blur; the room became a blur. "You'll get used to them," he promised me; "I've been trying them out. For the first time in my life, I've stolen," he whispered again.

"Are you ready?" he gasped. I started to nod my head, but the glasses nearly made me lose my balance. "Maybe you can limp?" he suggested. "I don't think I can help it," I said unsteadily. "Come down to the gate, then." There were real tears in his eyes. "Please be careful," he begged; "please let me know if you find the child." "Not by telegram," I whispered, trying to stop the room from moving. "Thank you for the mushrooms, Grandma!" he said to me loudly at the door; then we were at the gate. He walked partway down the road, in the direction of the train, with me. "About a mile, don't forget," he whispered. But the map was tattooed on my eyes. "We don't need any help now, but if we do, we'll call you," he shouted in my ear as if I were deaf; "you're sure you can sew?" I nodded my head violently. "Goodbye," he whispered. I opened the umbrella, held it over my head, and started walking. My eyes were riveted on my feet as if I were praying. I was trying to keep my balance and see the ground. "It's not raining," I thought to myself, seeing the umbrella over me like a dark blue cloud. "Close it, idiot," I whispered to myself; "close it," but it screened my face with its beauty mark. "Better to keep it open," I decided; I looked crazy enough anyway.

And so I walked along to the tramway. I was on a country path; it was gradually turning into an asphalt street. Houses began sprouting up on both sides like mushrooms, or so they looked through my glasses, and then I could see the little station, its little turnstile and sign, just as Erdmann had described it. He had sewn cheese and some bread into my pockets, a lot of both. "Only things that won't smell," he assured me. I also had money in my little purse. I had no idea how much; I hadn't had time to look. "How much?" I asked the man at the station. "Ten," he answered impatiently. "Filthy thing!" he muttered to someone in back of me as I passed. I was burning all over. I had seen my face in the little mirror while I was walking; it was mottled purple and blue. Now my whole body was on fire.

There was a seat on the train; I elbowed my way into it and collapsed. Waves of nausea were coming from some deep sea. The train was getting more and more crowded; soldiers, there were soldiers all over, the ones I had seen day after day at the Hauptmann's and the High Lieutenant's. Three of them were hanging over me, drunk. I kept my head bent, and my hands folded, pretending to pray. I was burning from head to toe. The miserable little train started with a jerk, throwing itself forward into the darkness. In the tunnel I unclenched my hands for a moment; I could see the nail marks each hand was leaving on the other. It was an eternity. There was nothing outside the windows, only darkness. It was hard to believe we were moving at all. Erdmann had stood up my collar so it covered my chin; I kept my head tilted into it to cover the mark. There was a hole of light, like a valuable coin, ahead. The train was stopping: Riga.

Now what would I do? I didn't know anything about Riga; Erdmann hadn't told me much about it. I started to walk. Away from the station and the soldiers, that was all I could think of, away from the station and the soldiers. I wove along for about five blocks, and stopped to lean against a building. I could see some of the shops; at the very end of the street was a coffee shop. "Drunk, poor thing," I heard a woman mutter. I looked in my purse; I could see into its dirty satin insides looking straight down under the glasses. One hundred zlotys. I couldn't believe it, Then I felt something warm on my legs. I bent to touch it; I was bleeding. It will stop, I thought to myself, it will stop, but it was as if the sight of money had turned the red faucet on; blood was pouring out of me like water. I could feel myself weakening already. I had to think of something. All I could think of was that Poppa had told me Riga was a beautiful city; he had been sent there once by the Russians when he worked at Panari. "An apothecary!" I thought to myself, lifting the glasses. Dimly, I could make one out near the coffee shop. I started trudging toward it, taking tiny steps; I was afraid the bleeding would get worse. It seemed miles. The cobbled streets were endless; I began counting stones. If I could pass two stones, I could get there; if I could pass two more stones, I could get there; and finally, I was there, facing the old-fashioned doors, double glass doors, "Apothecary" written in gold gothic letters on them, a gold mortar and pestle suspended by a triangular chain over the door, colored bottles of water and capsules on glass shelves lining the store-front windows.

I pushed the door open; the brass bell over it gave its familiar tinkle. "Is anyone here?" I asked faintly. An old tired man came out from the back. His suit jacket was off; a gold watch chain draped over his vest. I pulled my glasses down on my nose and tried looking at him over them. "I'm just out of the hospital," I told him. "They threw me out of bed; they needed the beds for the soldiers. And I'm bleeding; it won't stop; I can't stop it, can I lie down here somewhere?" He gave me an odd look. "Maybe until we close," he answered reluctantly. "Can you give me something?" I begged; "some calcium shots?" "How do you know about calcium?" he asked, suspicious again. "I got them in the hospital, lots," "Go lie down," he said. There was a little bed in the dark room in back. I could see the little gleam of the cot; I lay down on it. The old man came in wearing a white apron holding a huge syringe. "Up with the skirt," he commanded. The needle went in. Now he knew I wasn't old. "If that doesn't work," he said turning around to go out, "I'll give you another." I was weak; I had to trust him. The calcium had set my body on fire all over again, but the bleeding was slowing down. I pulled off my stockings, moving as little as possible. The blood had soaked into my shoes. "Don't get up to wash them yet," he said, coming back; "I'll put them in the basin for you. Has it stopped? Are you still weak?" "It's better, but I'm still bleeding, and I can't lift my head from the pillow." "Another shot," he said, reappearing with one. The bleeding stopped. I could see the front of the shop beginning to darken. I thought I heard the slap slap slap of a damp mop on the floor. "My blood," I thought to myself, "all over Riga, a trail, like in 'Hansel and Gretel.'" He came in and washed out the stockings, then put them on a towel on top of the little stove in the back. "We close in about three hours; try and sleep."

The hand on my shoulder; whose was it? Was it Rachel? Erdmann? Max? Poppa? I was looking up at a perfect stranger. I was not wet. I remembered waking up from the beating in the camp, all wet. If I had passed out, they must have thrown a pail of water over me to wake me up. The pharmacist. I recognized him with relief. "I'm closing; you have to go," he said, helping me up. I had pulled my cross out from under my blouse and put my coat over my arm. He seemed to look at it with relief. "I should have shown him my papers!" I thought, disgusted. Erdmann had given me the ones Rutkauskus had made up for me. "But where should I go?" I asked him. "I'm waiting for my husband; he thinks I'm in the hospital. I don't think he'll be here for a few days; what will I do now?" "I cannot help you," he said firmly. "Put your stockings on; they're dry." "Thank you," I answered mechanically, standing up. I was still dizzy, but better. Then I felt his arm on mine. "Eat this candy," he said, "some energy." I gobbled it down. I looked at him; he looked back at me. I was a young woman with a very dirty face, short hair, and very thin, almost normal. "You'll be all right now; it's better to start when there's light, maybe not too much?" I didn't answer, I put on my coat.

And then I was out on the sidewalk. Automatically, I was looking for soldiers. At the Hauptmann's, it was soldiers, back and forth, back and forth, from office to office, every minute. The streets looked strange to me, so wide, people walking at random, no lines marching, snatches of conversation as small groups of men and women passed in two and threes; no one stopped them, or dreamed of stopping them. But soon there would be Gestapo posters up for me. It wasn't safe for me to be on the streets; a soldier might recognize me, anyone could become suspicious and report me. I looked around from my little spot in front of the apothecary's. The baby-blue sky was giving way to gray and blue stains. In some places, the sky still blazed with light; far away, in the direction I had come from, the sky was still blue, wearing a red gold crown, the setting sun, and silhouetted against it, the beautiful cupola of a Russian church. It was a gold cupola and it gleamed at the end of the street like the cupola on the Russian woman's scarf. And suddenly, it was as if the street had turned into part of that scarf, and I was following one of its threads into the church. I felt like a needle being stitched through material to the church door, the church with the golden cupola, where I would take my place near the steps and wait. So I began my crablike crawl toward the little church.

As I got closer, I could see it more clearly. It was a little narrow white frame church. Gray slate steps led up to its unpainted wood door. I tilted my glasses farther down on my nose and peered at it. On each side of the door were two thin tall stained glass windows which arched at the top. The sun was staining the church gold and red, and then the bells began to ring, and the gold notes floated out on the blue air. I stood staring at the church as if it were the greatest marvel in the world. I had never seen anything so beautiful. "I will go in it," I thought to myself, and went in through the front door, but the priest had already finished his sermon. Mass was over. People were getting up from the dark wooden pews and beginning to walk slowly down the aisles. I stood in the shadow just inside the door in back of the last pew. The little stained glass window was casting a colored shadow like an Oriental carpet near my feet. Then the sun moved and I was standing on it.

I saw two old women begin to walk down the aisle. Their faces were pleated with wrinkles; they had pure white skin. They looked like sisters, dark eyes, sunken like prunes, but from the way they walked, from the clothes they wore, from the silver lion's head on the ebony cane one of them held, it was easy to see they had been beautiful once. They were still beautiful in the way they moved, as if the air and the sun and the moon moved for them; as if at night, they could take the stars and pin them on scarves they wore around their necks. Both of them wore little black velvet hats with brims tilting slightly over an eye, and veils of the finest black nettings. The woman with the silver-handled cane wore gray gloves embroidered with black fleur-de-lis. "At her age to be wearing high-heeled shoes!" I thought in astonishment. As they came closer, I could hear them speaking to each other in French.

"Please," I said in French (since Druzgeniekie my French had been perfect), "would you permit me to speak to you for a minute; I am quite lost in this city." I thanked God I had washed my face so carefully at the apothecary's. A woman has to look her best; it was automatic. The two old women looked at each other. "Toinette?" one of them said to the other. She nodded. "Yvonne?" the other questioned. Toinette nodded at her. "What can we do for you?" they asked, speaking almost in unison. "I am so sorry to trouble you," I began, "but I am just out of the hospital. There was a great transport of soldiers, and not enough beds, so I've been turned out, and I've been bleeding a great deal. I'm very weak, and my husband won't be here until the end of the week. I am quite at my wit's end," I finished. "Oh, my dear," Toinette said, "if Yvonne is of the same mind . . ." and she looked at her sister. Yvonne nodded. "You must come home and spend the night with us." "It is so nice of you; I cannot bless you enough," I thanked them, nervously looking down at my cross.

"I came to this church because it reminded me of an embroidery on a scarf a Russian woman, Mrs. Oblensky, gave me; I wish I had the scarf now," I said. I was having trouble taking my eyes from the cupola to watch their faces. "I always thought it was a magical scarf." "Oblensky?" asked Yvonne, looking at Toinette; "you said Oblensky?" "Yes," I said, "her husband was a colonel in the Russian army." "I believe we know her, do we not, Toinette?" asked Yvonne. "We *did*," Yyonne replied. "Phillipe will not let us know her now. You must tell us how you met her; she is a very important woman." "Also a very strange one, Toinette; you must not forget that. Phillipe always says it; she is a very strange woman." "So she is," her sister agreed; "still, Yvonne, we would like to hear about it, would we not?" "*Oui,*" Yvonne answered. "Do you know Russian?" she asked me suddenly. "*Konechino,*" I answered; "I am Russian. I was thrown out of Paltava by the Communists." "Oh, *we* are Russians!" the two old sisters cried like happy crows; "you *must* come home with us!" "How can we stand here like this, Toinette, look how weak she is. We will talk to her when we get her home."

So each of them took me under an arm, and like three octogenarians, we made our way to their house. They

342

lived on the fifth floor of a tall narrow building. "The lift is a terrible nuisance; I apologize for it," Yvonne said. Sinking toward us was a huge gilded bird cage, solid gold, covered with gold flowers and vines. "Oh, it is beautiful," I gasped; "again, it is something from Mrs. Oblensky's scarf." "It is actually a nuisance of dear Phillipe's; he insists we are made of porcelain and crack at the slightest pressure, so we must have it. He says he will not take the responsibility of a single step we make that is not thoroughly horizontal. The trouble with having a baby brother, you see how it is." Still holding me by my arms, the three of us got into the golden cage sideways, and rose slowly toward the fifth floor.

"Do sit down, my dear," Toinette said, patting the couch. "Put up your feet. Yvonne, we do not have an afghan or a blanket in this whole house?" "I cannot do everything at once," Yvonne fussed; "I am putting on the samovar, and then I will get to the blanket. There is an order to everything." Toinette had pulled a chair up to the couch and raised her eyebrows sympathetically. I began to look around the room. Beige flocked paper covered the walls; there was a perfumed smell in the air. Then I noticed the huge vase of roses on the ebony sideboard. "Yvonne's one weakness," Toinette said; "at least it is *supposed* to be Yvonne's one weakness. Poor Phillipe must come home on Fridays early to bring them from the greenhouse. Then she *will* save the petals and make rose tea, and we must drink it. It is horrible, I tell you; do not let her give you any." "Please, my dear, leave my roses alone and get some cakes," Yvonne commanded in her aristocratic quaver. "My sister orders me," Toinette said, getting up stiffly. Their furniture was all Chinese; I had never seen anything like it—low carved tables, ebony screens, jade ornaments, stone fruits in all colors. "That is jade," Yvonne said, picking up a lime, "but our best is an ivory banana; many grandchildren have broken their first tooth, and second tooth, on it." I smiled. I was beginning to relax.

I heard the crank and whine of the huge bird cage. "That will be Phillipe," Yvonne beamed; "I do wonder what he has brought us." A small elegant man with a neat French beard and mustache walked in; he had a white cone of flowers in one hand and a pastry box in another. How was it possible the fabric of the world had unraveled, leaving this small swatch intact? "You must meet our

343

guest," Toinette burbled, coming back in. "She is a Russian from Paltava, and she has a scarf from Colonel Oblensky's wife." Phillipe regarded me carefully. "You see . . ." He hesitated. "Otilia Rutkauskenie," I said quickly. "You see, Mrs. Rutkauskenie, we would love to have you here, and my dear sisters would too, but at their age they tend to be forgetful. Yvonne's daughter is coming with her three children and we will not have room." "I understand," I said; "this is war, and some people do not trust too much. I myself do not, but I have my papers here. Perhaps you would be good enough to look at them?" "No," he said, flushing scarlet under the glowering flower faces of his two wilting sisters, "but as you see, it is a small place; it is impossible. Rest a while; please do eat; but it is impossible." "I understand," I said again. A cold hand was pressing itself against my hot head. "I will see you into the street," Phillipe offered, coming down in the bird cage with me. "Please thank your sisters for me." He hesitated a minute. "You said you knew Mrs. Oblensky; she calls herself Madame Russo now. If you don't find a nice place to stay, go to see her on Five Pushkin Street. She has a camp for refugees. You come and go as you please." "Is it far away?" "On the edge of the city, as is best," Phillipe answered pompously.

After he went in, I leaned against the cold stones of the arch between their house and the next. I was trying to remember the address Rutkauskus had given me "in case you should ever change your mind, which I very much doubt, your current behavior having shown you are too far gone to save." Finally, I remembered it. I decided to put my coat back on. If I was going to explore the city, I would be safer as the hunchback. The street was crowded with soldiers, all drunk. Terrible as I looked, I was still a woman. They didn't want to let me pass. At last, I saw a young lady. "Tell me, please," I asked, "how far away is Dworkin Street?" She gave me the directions: ten blocks away. When I got there, I rang the bell of a big dark building; it was already night. A man came to the door. "A Mister Rutkauskus, my husband, stayed here, and I'm to wait for him in these rooms," I told him. "I don't know," he said, looking me over carefully. "I don't think this is the right place for you; we have too many investigations." "A Russian man suggested Madame Russo's camp on Pushkin Street," I said weakly. "Oh," he said relieved, "*that* is much better, much better." "But where is it?" I asked, "I'm a stranger here." He pointed behind me. "Almost five miles, where this street runs out. It's right on the river." "Will you do me a favor?" I asked him. "If my husband comes for me here, tell him where I've gone?" "I promise," he said. I set out.

"I'm just out of the hospital," I telegramed Rutkauskus, "and have gone to the address you told me about. If you will come for me there, you can find me by asking the janitor." I sent the telegram. And then I felt absolute panic. It shot up over my head like an umbrella gone wild. "I want to call my cousin, Irving Erdmann, in Kaiserwald," I heard myself telling the clerk. "Kaiserwald!" he murmured in astonishment. "Kaiserwald," I repeated with authority. There was a great deal of fussing; I heard his name repeated over and over. Finally, Erdmann was on the wire. "Where are you?" he was asking me faintly. "In Riga; I don't know what to do. Can you come and see me? I'm afraid." "Where can I buy it?" I heard him asking. "At Madame Russo's, on Five Pushkin Street." "It is a stupid price," I heard him say. "I'll see how much I have tomorrow, or the next day; it's not easy to carry all that." Then there was a click. But it was as if a transfusion had flowed into me. I paid the clerk for the call, tilting my chin back into my collar; then I set out on the five-mile walk to Madame Russo's.

· It was too dark to see much of the houses, but there were lighted windows. War had not touched this city. Every now and then, I could see through a window into a house. In one, a family was sitting around a large table, and a plate passed from one of them to another. On the side, a small child was in a special high wooden chair. I took special note of the curtains: There were white ruffled ones; there were flowered ones; there were velvet ones. The chandeliers were there in all their variety. Behind those dark walls with the dark court-mouths were people living their lives in silence and music, in noise and laughter, in chaos and order. A half an hour away, Rachel had found her boots, was shredding lice from her sweater and going to sleep alone in her bunk with no one to talk to. Perhaps she had gone with a selection. Erdmann was doing what? How could I have been so stupid as to have called him? A telephone call, and the last thing I said was that I would not telegram. And then as I walked I could hear him whisper, "If I'm alive, I will find you." In the telegraph office, on the phone, I couldn't hear it; I was too busy looking around me. Now I heard him. "Dear God," I prayed, "if you answer a prayer, answer this; do not let me hurt him." The world was not destroyed. It was here, in house after house. It was as if every dark house was a seed pod, every lit window a seed about to crack open. There was a world to walk in; if there was a world, there could be a child. Ninka could be alive in the world if it still existed. In the camp, I had come to believe that nothing existed outside its invisible walls.

Pushkin Street cut across my path; it was only a little street, a dead end near the river, five houses. I could see some lights glimmering on it like fish scales. I found 5 Pushkin Street and rang the doorbell. A maid answered. By habit, I had lapsed into Russian. "Who is it?" a voice asked in Russian. "A woman is asking for you," the maid called in. She would have liked to say more, but she knew I could understand. A woman came to the door. Her back was straight; her hair was parted in the middle and arranged on top of her head in two wings. It was Mrs. Oblensky. "Madame Russo?" I asked cautiously. "Yes," she answered studying me closely. "A Russian family sent me to you," and again I repeated my story about the hospital. "But you cannot stay here, my dear," she said, taking me in; "my sister is coming with her baby." Again, the same thing. "If you would just let me sit on the stairs and rest, I would leave in the morning," I gasped. "Oh," she cried, "you are so modest? There's no need for that. I have a camp. Would you like to stay there?" "I would be so grateful. My husband will be coming for me in a few days and I'm sure he'll make a generous donation to your camp." "You have papers?" she asked me. I handed them to her. "Where in Russia are you from, originally?" "Paltava." "You seem familiar to me." she said. "Perhaps I will seem more so when I get out of this outfit. You see, my husband is insanely jealous, the temper of a Cossack, and he's afraid of the soldiers, so this is how he dressed me." "I see," she said slowly, holding my elbow, and we walked the two blocks from her house to the camp.

The refugee camp faced the little river. It was a big field surrounded by trees and fenced off. "My property," Madame Russo announced. "I like having the company of my own people. We have barracks, though; I cannot do *too* much. My own house is beautiful, but of course, there's no room; and my family is always visiting, so it is no use." She took me in and introduced me to some of the

346

women. "I am Emma," one of them said, coming up to me herself; "perhaps you would like the bunk below mine?" "I would be so grateful," I said again. "Then I will leave you," Madame Russo said. I began bleeding immediately, but not too heavily. "Oh, bleeding on a Wednesday!" Emma cried; "that means you will have everything you want, and everyone you want." "I have never heard of that," I protested weakly. "Oh, it's true, it's true," came the voices of women speaking Russian from all over the barracks. "Are you going to stay here?" Emma asked me. "I don't think so," I answered; "I'm only waiting for my husband. "Most of us have decided to stay here for the whole war; it's the safest place," Emma said. She had curly black hair parted in the middle, and white skin. "You could stay, too." "Yes," I answered, "but I have a husband and child." "Oh, then that's different," Emma answered. "I think."

Two days passed. The women undressed me and bathed me and put on my clothes, washed and dry. Emma combed my tangled curls. "Is this a new style?" she asked curiously. "No, but I have been traveling so much, it seemed easiest," I lied. "I should think of it," Emma mused. "With your hair it would be a sin!" I cried. Madame Russo would come in and out, giving instructions. "See that she gets a big chunk of butter in her soup; never have I seen anything so thin walking around." I was beginning to feel much better. And then came a telegram: "Arriving soon. Rutkauskus." He must have called the man at the first address he gave me. Rutkauskus did not come until the end of the week. For most of the week I ate and slept, slept and ate; by the time he got there, I looked almost human.

"Are you going this time?" he demanded. "Of course; I couldn't go the first time with blood on my hands. Now I can." "So, tomorrow," Rutkauskus grumbled; "are you going to kiss me?" "Oh, not in front of all these women," I protested, pretending to be shy. "I travel over twenty hours, for the second time, with a hundred and five degree fever, and my own wife won't even kiss me!" he thundered. Everyone looked elsewhere; books appeared, sewing, even cards. Just then Madame Russo arrived. "You have a caller, Mrs. Rutkauskiene," she told me; Erdmann was right behind her. He was white as a sheet. The minute he saw me, he lit up like a translucent candle. "You made it!" he cried out. I was smiling too hard to tell him to keep quiet, and then I was crying. "I knew it; you're in love with him," Rutkauskus muttered in an undertone. "Oh, shut up," I said for the first time in my life. We stared at each other and stared at each other.

"You look better, so much better," he finally said slowly; "and they *are* starting with the numbers on the arms. Now I've done one thing in my life, one thing; now I can die in peace." "If you die in peace you will not let me live in peace!" I whispered to him again in anguish. "Please, don't say such things; you're my savior, nothing less than that." "I am no one's savior, not even my own," he said sadly. "You are mine," I insisted. "All right, then, yours," he said, smiling; "I'm not going to argue with a stubborn mule." I had never seen him smile like that.

"When are you going?" he asked, turning, businesslike, to Rutkauskus. "I'm taking her out of here today. We'll find a room for the night and take a train for Vilno in the morning. It's the first we can get; the partisans are doing a good job of messing up the schedules." "You can tell her all about your family history," Erdmann smiled. I looked from one to the other. "Oh, we did a lot of conferring about you the last time he was in Riga," Erdmann told me; "we know a lot about each other." "He knows a lot about me, he means," Rutkauskus said; "he knows I'm drunk so much I live most of my life in a fog of good impulses and stupid behavior. That louse doesn't drink." "Good for him," I said prudishly. Rutkauskus might be the most noble soul on earth, but I was beginning to realize that his soul was usually preserved in alcohol; when he was drunk he was impossible, and that was most of the time. I was already imagining a twenty-hour trip back with him.

"I'm so glad this is done," Erdmann said again; "but Anya, you were stupid to call me. You know who's killed? Kleinman the guard." "Why?" I cried. "For letting you lie down; that's all they needed to hear. It's a miracle they didn't find you; there are posters all over Riga, and that mark, it's not safe to take any chances." "I would like to kiss you once before I go," I gasped, flushing to my toes, refusing to look at Rutkauskus, "and if we survive the war, I will look for you, after my daughter." "After your daughter, I could not be more honored." His eyes went glassy. "Goodbye," I said as he bent down. I kissed him on the cheek. "Now, mine," I said, turning up my face to be kissed; he kissed me hard on the lips. "You have to excuse the cuckoo," he said gently; "goodbye." And he turned and walked down the street.

"So you were in love with him," Rutkauskus accused me. "I don't understand what glue sticks your mind in that groove; you're like a carriage with three wheels." I was so furious I was white. He kept quiet. "Otilia," he said, "we are leaving," and stalked off in front of me dignified as a lord.

But Madame Russo stopped us on the way out. Her maid brought us a huge pot of cereal with butter, cinnamon, and raisins. Emma and the others came out to kiss me goodbye. Affections formed and dissolved so swiftly now, hard, like sugar crystals, then impalpable, sugar in water. "It would be better to stay here," Emma pleaded; "at least until the war is over. It can't be too much longer." "No, I have to be with my child. I would *like* to stay; I really would," I said sadly. "If you cannot, you cannot," she answered, kissing me on both cheeks.

Rutkauskus was waiting in the distance. "First we have to find a room," he told me again. "I thought there might be a train late tonight, but there isn't one until tomorrow around nine." "Ninka is really all right?" I asked for the thousandth time. I felt marvelous; I was going to see my child. I could breathe. My coat was off; the stuffing was out, my roasting in it was over. "I thought of what to do with your chin," Rutkauskus said, producing something from a canvas bag; "a surgical neck support; it will cover your mark." Before I had a chance to say a word, he was fastening it behind my neck. Then he tied a wool babushka over my head. "So, very good," he said with satisfaction; "you look like a normal person with a broken neck." "I can't turn around," I complained; my neck was hot. Would it never end? "That isn't important; don't bother with nonsense," Rutkauskus said rudely. It occurred to me he was talking to me that way because he had to hurt me. I looked at him again. He was in his fifties. His hair was gray. I had never really taken a good look at him before. His face was flushed, and he had a red nose; he was a drunkard. "We have a lot to talk about," he told me. "First, Ninka is learning to read and write. She plays more. And she's a blessed child. Because we took good care of her, the priest says, Onucia is now pregnant, five months," he said proudly. "But I drink; you've guessed. So I should tell you the whole story. Onucia isn't my first wife. My first wife became a Nazi and so did my two daughters. So I thought, what kind of man raises such a family and lives with it, and I began to drink. I felt sick; I always used to drink when I was sick, so I drank. I felt sick all the time; I still do. A judge, and such a family, and what could I do about them? They could have had *me* arrested. So I drank all the time; I still do. It is not so good. But you should understand. Also, it probably isn't much to you, but I'm always awake under the vodka, somewhere. But you should understand. So Erdmann said." I was dazed. Information, ideas, were shooting into my mind like arrows. "So," Rutkauskus said briskly, "a room. Also," he added in a little aside, "I'm not always drunk when I look drunk." "How am I supposed to know when that is?" He just shrugged.

Riga was crowded. We spent the whole day looking, or Rutkauskus looked and I lurked in courtyards, near gates, and finally, when it was pitch black, he found a damp clammy flat in the bottom of a terrible building. "We have to take it," he said, seeing my face. "It's a long trip tomorrow; you'll need your strength." "It's not a hotel," I thought out loud, hesitating in front of the door in the dark place; I was trying to tilt my head back, but the collar wouldn't let me. "For the last time," Rutkauskus told me, "the hotels are full of soldiers. It would be the worst possible place." He started coughing terribly. "Smoking, always smoking," I sighed. "Not just smoking," he reminded me; "I started out with a cold." "There'll be no soldiers in the basement," I muttered in relief, ignoring him; I was tired of hearing about his one hundred and five degree temperature. "Just the kind that scamper," he grinned; "but we're big enough to fight off the Rat Reich." I was glad he could find something to be funny about; my blood ran cold. He nodded at the lady of the house who was half-in and half-out the kitchen door, an apron tied around her waist. I caught a glimpse of that apron stuck to the enormously fat woman and the upper half of her body. "It's going to be cold," I whispered to Rutkauskus. "And damp," he added, as if he were summing up the evidence.

We went down the dark hall to a little door. "In there," Rutkauskus said. "Don't break your neck; the wood steps are rickety, no handrails." "I couldn't break my neck if I wanted to," I complained. "Are you down?" he asked; "I'm shutting the light off." "It will be pitch dark!" I shrieked. "I have a candle." His voice drifted down to me, and then I saw a little flame move through the space at the top of the stairs like a shooting star, and another, bigger flame spurt to waver upward like a tulip shoot growing very fast. Then the light cast hideous shadows on his face; he looked like Frankenstein's monster. "All the poor thing needed was understanding," I remembered Vera sighing tragically. "All!" I thought to myself in desperation. "What do you think of our room?" he asked me, coming down slowly. He had a big canvas rucksack on his back, the bag he had taken my neck brace from, three quarters of it filled with vodka. It was an old unfinished cellar; the old woman had thrown some wooden planks on the ground and a big double bed with some thin, ragged blankets rested on them. There was a tiny wooden table at the head of the bed; otherwise nothing. The walls were beams of wood, packed hard with dirt in between, and the unfinished wood stairs led down; at the top was the little door. Rutkauskus had shut it.

"Ah!" he sighed with content, drinking down the contents of a big glass of vodka. "Want to drink with me?" he asked, volunteering a glass. "Where did you get the glass?" "From the rucksack, where else? What good is a bottle without a glass?" "You're very particular," I murmured. He filled another glass and drank it down, sitting on the edge of the bed, still holding the bottle, putting the empty glass covered with fingerprints down on the dirty blanket. His cheeks were flushing. He was tugging at the buttons of his coat. "Oh, Mister Rutkauskus," I cried, "you cannot get undressed here!" He stared at me blearily. "With that cough, it's so damp and cold, you could get pneumonia, no? What would I tell your wife if you came home too sick to walk? I tell you, I know what I'm talking about. You have to sleep with your clothes on, for the warmth; feel how damp it is." I pretended to splash some water from my coat. "Another drink will warm you up," I suggested helpfully. His face lit up; he filled the glass to the rim, and drank it down at once. "Conscience," he muttered. "What?" I wished he would start talking until he fell asleep. "Get undressed, Otilia," he said thickly after a few minutes. "Do you know what it's like to live with a bad conscience? Anyone can live with a bad conscience, isn't that right, Otilia? But you can't live with someone else's guilty conscience, especially if you made it, and they don't have a guilty conscience, but they should have one; isn't that right, Otilia?" "Definitely," I agreed. "So all the rest

351

of the children go to religious schools; that's the only answer." He took another drink.

"First I will put you to bed," I told him. "You just saved me from the labor camp, where they could have killed me any minute, at my age, and with a little child. It was so cold there; there were always selections"—he was beginning to nod as if he were hearing a bedtime story— "and I know you are my savior, you are, so I will take care of you. I will come to bed as soon as you are covered up and warm. Oh, it is cold here." I shivered violently for effect. "All right," he agreed reluctantly, bending down to take off his boots. The first one came off and was kicked across the mud floor in my direction; he bent over for the second and nearly fell from the bed. "Can I help you, Mister Rutkauskus?" I asked. "Think I'm too drunk to do it?" he demanded, pushing himself back onto the bed. "See?" and the triumphant second boot flew over in my direction. "I think I'll have something to drink, for my cold, you said so." He looked at me accusingly, filling another glass. The bottle was empty, but not the rucksack. There was a full bottle beside the other immediately. "Want some, Onucia?" he asked. "Otilia," I reminded him. "Otilia, that's right," he muttered stretching out. He was such a big man his feet stuck out like logs over the edge of the bed. Then came the snoring; he sounded like a train pulling into the station. I stole over from the steps and covered him with the raggedy blankets, pulling them from my side of the bed, where he slept on the other. Then I took off my coat and put it on top of him. I wanted him to be good and warm; I didn't want him to wake up. The snoring got louder and louder. The little candle flickered next to the vodka bottle; it was cold and damp.

I sat down on the third wooden step wondering if the candle would last until the morning. Sleep was out of the question. Some hours passed. Then there was rattling and scurrying; across the room, a dark shape moved, tiny, but the wavering light of the candle made it cast a deep shadow. "Rats!" I thought to myself, unfastening my neck collar as fast as I could to make it into a weapon. I thought I heard the rustlings getting closer; automatically, I knocked on the step to scare them off. Rutkauskus stirred in his sleep. "Oh, I can't do it; it will wake him up." More scurrying. I tried rapping quietly. So it went on. I was cold and clammy, my knees pulled up to my chin, arms wrapped around them; I only wanted to rap gently

352

on the steps. It was a misery. Finally, I began hearing sounds from upstairs. Rutkauskus was moving.

"How did you sleep, Otilia?" he asked me. "Oh, fine," I lied; "I'm used to getting up early. Maybe we can get the new seven o'clock train someone told us about yesterday." "We have plenty of time," Rutkauskus said. "First I need to get Ninka a present, and you have to get a manicure." "She doesn't need any presents and I don't need a manicure," I shouted. "A woman doesn't escape from a camp with manicured nails," he insisted. "Come on, let's get some food, and find a beauty salon. I'll leave you there, and come back with the present." "Please, I don't want to," I begged. "I'm afraid of the soldiers, and I'm dying to see the child; you saw the poster up about me." "Breakfast, a manicure, and a present," he repeated inflexibly.

We found a little café and I choked something down. Rutkauskus had already begun the morning's second bottle. "Now," he considered after an hour, "where to find a salon; they must have a good one on the main street." "Please," I begged again. " 'Salon de Beautee,' " he read out loud; "that one looks fine. Here," he said, giving me some money, "get yourself manicured and your hair done; I'll be right back for you." Fingers of light were beginning to creep up the sky. I felt them closing on me in my new clothes, the clothes Erdmann had bought me. "All right," I answered, zipping in the door like a rat.

"Yes, Madame?" asked a woman in a white uniform, coming up to me. "A manicure," I whispered; I could barely talk or swallow. "Right here," she said, motioning to a little table covered with a white cloth; "and your hair?" "Just a washing, please; it's so short." "But I'll have to charge the full price," she warned me. "That will be more than fine," I sighed. "Left hand, please," she commanded. "What long nails you have," she commented; "and so strong." "Yes, they've always been that way; it's the *fundament*, the base, I got from my mother. But I haven't been taking care of them, so my husband insisted I step in here right away, before we had a chance to let my mother see me. 'I'm not taking you to church with those hands,' he said." I could see her staring at my great golden cross. "Did he give you the cross?" she asked, filing at a second nail. "Oh, no, it's been handed down; it belonged to my great-grandmother." "It's a beautiful cross," she said enviously, beginning on the third nail.

"Which color polish would you prefer, Madame?" she

asked, producing a little white enamel tray of bottles. "The bright red," I answered, pointing to one. I had just noticed the little door to the second half of the salon; it was the men's section, filled with soldiers. I felt as if I were sitting on nails. "What happened to your neck?" she asked me sympathetically, putting the polish on expertly, leaving the little white moons exposed. "Oh, you know how it is," I told her. Lying was becoming second nature; it was frightening. "I was rearranging the bedroom furniture for the hundredth time, and I pulled something. It was that or lifting the baby the wrong way; or the time the train almost turned over from a mine; the doctor isn't sure. It started up almost a month ago." "Will you have to wear it very long?" "I hope not; it's already giving me a rash underneath it," I answered absently, my eyes sliding automatically to the little door and the soldiers. I was watching them through the door as if they were on a screen, but they were part of a terrible movie that could come into this ridiculous comedy at any second. "They are more vain than the women," the woman bent over to me, whispering; "massages, mud packs; you name it; they want it. I have never seen anything like them, the Germans. I don't know how they can stand to fight, it's so messy." "At least they left the city intact," I answered; "but mud packs, really?" "Really," she said; she was almost finished with my nails, drawing on their tips in a white wax pencil, so that both the moons and the tips were white crescents; my hands were in the very latest style. "I don't know how we're going to wash that hair with that neck thing," she worried. "Oh, I can't take it off!" I exclaimed. "I'll tell you what, just run a wet comb through my hair and fluff it out with your fingers and I will tell my husband you're responsible for all my natural curl." She grinned at me like a conspirator.

Then I was out on the sidewalk. But where was Rutkauskus? Soldiers were passing back and forth. I pulled on my long red coat, noticing it lapping at my ankles with satisfaction, and fastened the babushka under my chin. And there I stood for an hour. "There you are, Otilia!" he cried, lurching toward me. "I have the presents for Luisa, do you want to see them?" People were staring at us. "Not until we get to the train," I answered, grabbing his arm through his coat as hard as I could. "No, I want you to see them *here*!" he whined like a child. He pulled the paper off the two boxes and threw it on the ground. I

354

scooped it up. More people were staring. "Two Tyrolean dolls!" he announced triumphantly. "Wonderful!" I told him, "very wonderful! But we have to get to the train; you promised we could get the morning train!" "A judge always keeps his promise!" he thundered. The whole street was staring. In the middle of my panic, my mind was still working. "They must be thinking how odd we look," I thought to myself. There he was, big and weaving, and there I was, tiny, with a red coat down to my ankles, the Hauptmann's glasses, a neck brace and a flowered babushka, painted nails, a green hat and a blue umbrella. "A judge always keeps his word, Otilia," he thundered at me again; "where is the station?" "That way, Judge," a German soldier laughed and pointed; my face was on fire.

We got to the station, but there was no train. "Late," said the man in the booth, slipping the tickets under the grate to us. "Now we have to stand *here* for an hour and let people look at us!" I hissed. "A judge has nothing to hide, Otilia!" he thundered. Everyone in the station was staring at us. Finally, the train was swelling from a dot to a black shape at the end of the track. There was a huge crowd on the platform; most of them were soldiers. I kept my eyes on my shoes. "The train, Otilia!" Rutkauskus cried; he had had even more to drink. As soon as the train stopped, he pushed himself on, dragging me by my umbrella in back of him. "One seat," he thundered, pressing me into it by the shoulders. I pressed my face into the front of his coat where he stood over me.

It was a very slow train, and it was a few hours before we got a seat together. There was nothing to eat. The trains used to stop at stations and there was something to buy there, but not now. Rutkauskus wasn't hungry; he had had so much to drink. So the train went along, with almost no talking between us. Mostly, he slept or nodded. I was afraid to get up, even to use the bathroom. Finally, the train got to Vilno. It might have gone through a tunnel for all I knew. I concentrated and concentrated on the little picture of the station that occupied a blank page of my mind. I was crazy to see the child and to get into their house. Rutkauskus had just found out he was hungry. "Come, let's sit down," he said, dragging me over to a table at the café near the station. It was on an open platform covered with tables. "Please," I begged, "I cannot stay here. Stajoe used to work on this platform at the station; he had those rooms there. I was here all the time, someone will recognize me." "No, first a drink," Rutkauskus insisted, "and something to eat." "There's nothing to eat here, only drinks—beers and sodas!" "There are peasants with baskets," he whispered slyly. "You'll see. If I ask them in their own language, we won't be hungry for long." An old peasant woman passed by with a big wicker packet; Lithuanians never traveled without huge baskets of food. "What have you got there, Princess?" Rutkauskus called to her, tugging at her skirt; "what have you got there, Beauty? We're hungry; you couldn't spare something for a hungry judge?" He winked at her. The old lady blushed, and pulled out two rolls and a slice of meat. "Thank you, and God will bless you with chickens forever," Rutkauskus thundered after her. Then, whoever passed with a basket, it was the same thing. He ate chicken, beef, ham, cookies, little cakes.

"Please," I whispered, "let me save a cookie for Ninushka." "Luisa," he corrected, winking at me: "Luisa Vishinskaya, Vishinskaya, eh?" "Someone will recognize me," I pleaded again; "I don't think you want me to see the child." "All right," he said, getting up, "that is an insult I will not tolerate. Neither I nor my wife are capable of jealousy. We will go straight home; a judge is never jealous." He patted his stomach; he was full. "To the *drozhka*," he roared. "I will never live through this," I thought; I was thinking of running away and finding my way to their house myself. But the *drozhkas* were lined up, and he helped me into one. There was the familiar, familiar sound of the metal wheels clacking over the cobbled streets. We were leaving the edge of the city, going farther and farther out, in the direction of the old ghetto; the sidewalks were changing from cement to wooden ones made of planks. After a few blocks, the horse began to slow down. I could see the driver reining him in. "My house," Rutkauskus said proudly.

In the day's last light I could see a big house, one house near it, a big lot on the other side. It was a big brick house, and I thought I could see a garden in front of it. It was well tended. "Onucia's work," he said proudly; "wait until you see her vegetables in the back." I had flown up to the door and rung the bell. "Wait, wait," he was calling me, but a woman had come to the door, a large, big-boned woman with high wide cheekbones and deep-set dreamy eyes and a face that seemed to slant out straight from forehead to chin. Her cheeks were puffy, like chip-

356

munks', softening her, making her face appear as a combination of two faces, one soft sweet one from beneath the nose, a stern peasant's from above the lips. But she was beautiful. In spite of her thin brown hair parted in the middle and pulled back in a bun, she was beautiful, and she had odd gray eyes that seemed to be looking far in, or far out. She had on a gray wool dress and a fringed red shawl. Then I saw something pulling on it. A little blond head popped out from behind the gray wool skirt. It was Ninushka! There was her braid. I could only see half her head; she was fat as an apple. I stood there swaying and crying, still in my disguise. Rutkauskus was coming up. Then Ninka said something. "I can't understand her!" I screamed to myself. Onucia shrugged her shoulders and answered Ninka. I couldn't understand a word she said, either. A woman came out of the door in back of them. "The little girl says, 'Mommy, it's a beggar,' and Onucia says, 'That's all right; we have to be nice to beggars, too.'" The other woman was speaking to me in Russian. "Who are you?" I whispered back. "They call me the *Matenele*, Grandma; the Communists threw me out, so here I am for the war." Onucia said something to her sharply. Matenele caught me under the elbow. "Onucia wants you to sit down in the dining room, and then when you're rested, we'll bathe you. The trouble is, she speaks only Lithuanian, Onucia, but the child can speak some Russian and Polish, Russian from me, Polish, I don't know where."

Stunned, I let her sit me on a chair. I could see the table all set with a white cloth and covered with every kind of food: ham, beef, eggs, stews, noodles, cookies, cakes, liquors, wines. "Mommy, a beggar." I kept hearing it in Russian. "Mommy, a beggar." "She calls her Mommiti," I thought to myself, flushing all over. I wanted to get up and pull the child's hair; it wasn't my child. Then I stopped thinking. When Rutkauskus came in, I was staring straight ahead, over the table and food, out the blank window.

"Please, Matenele, ask one of the girls to get the tub," he was saying to the big woman who spoke Russian. She was dressed all in black, a black shawl wrapped around her and tied in the back. She had iron-gray hair skewered in place with large iron pins; I could see traces of rust; they left their mark on her hair. "It looks like I'm going to be your translator for good," she said grouchily. She repeated what he had said in Lithuanian. Onucia paused in the doorway, looking at me strangely. Ninka was right there, as if she were tied to her. "Onucia says we will take care of your bath and you should lie down. You know," she told me sternly, "this isn't a nice thing to do to Onucia; she thinks of the child as her own."

Onucia came out of the kitchen with a big iron washtub. "At least I will carry up the pails," Rutkauskus said in Russian. Onucia looked puzzled. "At least he will carry up the pails," Matenele repeated for her in Lithuanian. Rutkauskus asked Onucia a question when she came back with the first pail. It went into a huge kettle over the big Russian stove in their kitchen; it was even larger than I remembered ours, an odd part built under the tiles. *"Chto ete?"* I asked Matenele. "That's for the chickens. Onucia likes them fresh; they live in there. He asked Onucia if she will take care of all the introductions necessary," the Russian woman intoned flatly, "and she said yes," I nodded to her from my chair. Rutkauskus was coming in with water. "I hope he knows when to stop," I thought, seeing the kitchen fill with pails of hot water, floating us all out on the street.

Onucia talked a long time to Matenele, gesturing my way several times. "She says," Matenele began, "she told the child you are very important because you love her without even having seen her, and to prove it, she has the two dolls you brought for her, but you are so important, she must not mention that you are here to anyone because they would come to take you away." "What did the child say?" I asked in Russian. "She said we had a lot of very important people she couldn't talk about, but they didn't bring her dolls. So," Matenele asked sarcastically, "who are you?" "Thrown out of Paltava by the Russians." "I don't believe you, I know better," she said. Her face was flat, a small flat nose, with sparse eyebrows, they looked shaved and growing in, and little pale lips. "That's too bad," I answered her weakly; "who did you think I was? Stalin? You weren't the only person in Russia, you know. Anyway," I told her, "believe what you like. I don't care." "What did she ask you?" Rutkauskus asked, running over, worried. "Nothing to worry about," I told him dully. He went off down the hall.

The metal tub in the kitchen was filled with hot water. "Come on," Onucia said to me, taking me under the arm, "the water will do you good." It was her rich voice, full of feeling, without a syllable of meaning, and then came the toneless words of the Russian woman; the meaning skipped after like a little dog catching up with its owner. "Get in," came the Russian echo; "it's all right to take off your clothes in front of us." Onucia herself removed my thick glasses; the room came into sharp focus. It was a huge kitchen; there were smoked meats of every kind hanging on the wall. "There's a whole room of smoked meats," Onucia said. Through the doorway, I saw two girls going into a room. "Who are the girls?" I asked. "A nuisance," the Russian woman answered promptly without waiting for Onucia. "Who are the girls?" I said again, looking at Onucia. "They are two Jewish girls my husband took in until they're strong enough to go. They sleep on little mattresses in your room, but, because you are so important, you have the cot." "Why are you so important?" the Russian translation went on, beyond its original text.

"I would like you to go out of the kitchen," I told the old woman. Matenele said something to Onucia. "Out then," a little voice piped up in Polish; "she said 'Out then.' Daddy said," the little voice quavered on, "I should say thank you for the dolls. Thank you for the dolls, lady." Onucia looked at me with sympathy, but a gleam of triumph came through like light behind heavy closed curtains. "She has a name; it's Otilia Rutkauskenie," the Russian woman said, her back to us in the door. "Just like us," Ninka said in Polish. "Daddy said you can talk Polish or Russian, but not like us, so I shouldn't talk to you that way." "No, you can't." She babbled something about her dolls. Luisa said, 'I'm going to play with my dolls, Mommiti,'" the Russian woman translated again. Onucia patted me on the shoulder and let her hand rest there. "Everything will be all right." I didn't need the translation to tell me what she was saying. She was beginning to pour water over me from a pottery bowl; her other hand was sudsing me with a huge beige sponge foaming with soap. Then she fingered my cross, saying something in a whisper. "Thank you," I said in Polish. "She says it's beautiful," Matenele informed me. "I know," I answered, annoyed. "I thought you didn't speak the language," she said, her back still toward us.

"See how much better you look?" Onucia was asking me, holding a whole mirror up to my face. A pretty face with wet blond curls peered out at me; I wasn't even so terribly thin. "I must weigh ninety pounds," I thought to myself; "ninety pounds." I thought about Madame Russo's and the camp, the striking woman with dark hair walking in her dark elegant wool dresses, simple enough to look poor. That was over twenty hours away. "I'm in Vilno and Ninushka is here," I kept telling myself, but I couldn't believe it. "If only I could look at my old house," I thought, but I knew I wouldn't be able to go out, and again, in my ears; "A beggar, Mommiti, a beggar."

Onucia wrapped me in a big robe, "I have some clothes for you," she whispered. "I cannot take them." I was shaking my head violently. I didn't want anything of hers; I didn't want clothes. "It is only proper that the you-know-what of the you-know-what be decently dressed in her house," Matenele translated, black with anger. She didn't know what was going on. "All right," I said. Out came a beige dress with a little gold-buckled belt, the buckle in the shape of a frog. Mechanically, I began to climb into it. "Careful!" Matenele warned; "she says that material tears easily." It was thin silk. The front was cut low and ruffled; the sleeves were ruffled, too. "Look," Onucia said proudly, holding the mirror. Angry, I pushed it away from her. *I* wasn't her child! Standing still, I started to sob; I was rooted to the floor. There I was, as if nothing had happened, as if I had only cut my hair. "Enough, enough," Onucia was murmuring; "come, eat some food with us; you'll feel better right away." The little child was staring up at me, her eyes open like bird beaks. "I want my mother," I wailed in German, sobbing again. "Onucia asks that you don't speak German since none of us know a word of it," said our translator. But I couldn't move. I stood in the kitchen in the beige dress, in front of the tub, and sobbed on and on. "Leave her," Onucia told Matenele, taking Ninka's hand; "she'll come out when she's ready."

As soon as the kitchen was empty, I stopped crying. I pushed myself up on the stove from a chair and sat there on it swinging my legs. It was warm; it was Vilno. But I wouldn't stick here. The little roots starting out from my toenails were withering and dying, turning black; I could see it happening through my shoes.

I sat down at the table. The two girls were already there, both blond, both tall. "Sisters," Onucia explained; "they're leaving in a few days. There's another one here, too; Cholem, a banker, very rich. But I don't like it; he looks too good, always walking in his gray suitcoat with his hat and cane, and his silvery hair. He will bring attention to us. My husband won't send him away, and he should send him away. He should go away himself." "Why does he do it?" I whispered between gulps. I had become ravenously hungry. "He says Jesus would do the same." I was eating my third plate of food when I saw Ninka standing next to my chair watching me seriously. "Are you hungry?" she asked in Russian. *"Da,"* I said, dropping the fork with a clatter. "Very hungry?" *"Da."* She nodded her head and walked away.

"When we found her on the steps of the church," Onucia was saying with Matenele translating, "we asked her if she had eaten. She said yes. When we asked her what she'd eaten, she said challah, so we knew she was a Jewish child. For days," she said, watching my face, "it was 'Momma, I want my Momma,' until my husband thought we would have to take her back to save us all. Then she stopped." I chewed on in silence. "She looks wonderful," I said finally. "She's getting a holiday from kindergarten for three days in your honor, aren't you, Luisa?" Ninka had materialized near Onucia's elbow. "Yes, I am," she answered promptly, smiling shyly at me. "That will be nice," I answered her, a lump of bread turning to cement in my mouth. "We can play with the dolls," Ninka said. "Just what Mrs. Rutkauskenie wants to do, I'm sure," Onucia laughed. "Doesn't she?" Ninka asked, surprised. "She does," I answered her in Polish. "Time for you to go to bed, Luisa," Onucia said abruptly. "Yes, Mommiti," Ninka said, getting up from the couch and taking her two dolls.

"Do I have to translate *everything*?" Matenele asked Rutkauskus in exasperation; he, at least, knew Russian." "Everything," he answered, gnawing at a ham bone. Matenele thumped her water glass down on the table, sloshing some onto the cloth. Rutkauskus said something to her; she flushed.

"Come," Onucia told me, "let me show you your room. Listen," she said to the girls, "maybe you can teach my relative here some Lithuanian?" "We can try," one of them answered dubiously. We trooped off down the dark hall. "Luisa's room," Onucia whispered, as Rutkauskus translated, pointing to an almost closed door. "There's a light in there," I whispered. "She can't sleep in the dark. This is your room." She lit a kerosene lamp hanging from the ceiling. It had a narrow couch, a soft bench, really. "You could sleep with Luisa," she volunteered hesitantly. "No, no," I protested, flushing scarlet, "I couldn't deprive you of her." "You have the right," she said. "The right," I whispered bitterly. On the floor I could see two old-fashioned mattresses with heavy wood frames. "For the two girls," Onucia explained. "You'll get used to it," Rutkauskus said gruffly in Polish. "Who is this Matenele?" I demanded. "The mother of a prominent Communist; she takes care of the house and the child." "I don't like her," I complained. "You two should get along fine," he said; "she doesn't like anyone either." "Does she play with Ninka, I mean, Luisa, a lot?" "A lot," he answered. "I have to get along with her then; there's no choice." "I think so," he answered. "Look, on the bed, Onucia has some new nightgowns for you. In the morning, you can start to play with Luisa; we're keeping her home for three days." "Then what?" "Then she gets over her terrible cold, and goes back to kindergarten." When we came back to the kitchen, the Matenele was glowering at us across the room; Onucia was looking at her with amusement. "She deserves it," Rutkauskus said in Polish, following his wife's look.

The two girls were sitting on their mattresses chattering about something. "They've been to the market selling and buying things so they can go," Rutkauskus told me. "I think one of those girls knows German, but she won't admit it," he said in German, pointing to the first mattress; the girl looked up, embarrassed. "I thought you weren't supposed to know it, either; that's what Matenele said." "She meant she and Onucia don't know it. What do you think I was speaking to Erdmann?" The girl looked more uncomfortable. Rutkauskus raised his eyebrows and grinned. "Good night," he said, turning down the hall. Onucia was still standing in the doorway, smiling at me as if I were a small child; she looked as if she were trying to settle something in her own mind. "What a beautiful face!" I thought to myself; "what a fine smile on such a rough face." I had never seen anything like her except in paintings in museums. On an impulse, I took the big gold cross from my neck and put it over her head; all through dinner, I had seen her staring at it. "Ah!" she gasped as if she had been touched by fire. "She says," one of the girls translated in German, "she wants you to have her cross in exchange." Onucia was lifting her large iron cross over her head and over mine, where it settled, neat and warm from her body, between my breasts. "She says," the girl translated, "that when you exchange crosses you exchange

362

fates; it's a well-known Lithuanian fact." I smiled at the girl. "My name is Ruta," she said smiling back; "they say you are Anya?" "That's right; do you exchange fates if you exchange shoes?" She asked Onucia in Lithuanian. "She doesn't think so," Ruta answered grinning. Onucia came closer; we kissed each other good night. Down the hall Ninushka was sleeping. I could hear her breathing through the walls. Then I was fast asleep.

"Don't wake her up," I heard an impatient voice grumble in Russian, and then a little voice: "But it's late in the afternoon. She was going to play with my dolls," the injured voice said. I opened my eyes; sunlight was pouring into the room. "She's up, she's up!" Ninka screamed, running to my bed. "Mommiti says breakfast is all ready and you should eat it right away," she burbled. "You wouldn't be in such of a hurry because of the dolls?" I teased her. "No," she said, suddenly sullen. "Well, I am coming," I said, getting out of bed, "and I can't wait to play with your dolls. I was awake half the night looking forward to it." "Can I comb your hair?" Ninka asked suddenly. "Why do you want to do that?" I asked, astonished. "It's funny hair. When it gets dusty, I can find dust curls just like it," Ninka said. "Is it very dusty here?" I asked, laughing. "Not here!" Ninka said indignant; "Matenele cleans everything all up!" "Then where do you find the dust?" I asked her. "In the attic," she said, looking down at her shoes. "I'm not supposed to go there." "Oh, I see." "You won't tell?" "I promise," I said, giving her my comb. Ninka pulled at my hair as if I were one of her dolls; she jerked my head backward. "I think it hurts you," she said sadly; "I don't like it when they brush my hair." "Yours doesn't have curls." "But it is, what do you call it, thick?" she said, her little forehead in a frown, tugging away. "Don't take off her head!" Onucia cried, coming into the room. "Come eat breakfast."

Ninushka and I sat down at the table. "The girls are at the market; Rutkauskus is out looking for more mouths to feed," Matenele complained. "Where will he find mouths?" "Never mind, Luisa; eat," Matenele scolded her. In front of me she set down a bowl of oatmeal with raisins and nuts; the whole top of the bowl was covered with thick pieces of bacon, one layer running one way, the second, at right angles to the first, the same way logs were arranged in a stove. "She's fattening you up," Matenele mumbled, looking at Onucia. Onucia said something. "She says to tell her if I annoy you," Matenele said gruffly. "I'm sure you won't," I answered. "Humph," she snorted, a little pacified. "You eat a lot," Ninka commented. "You should, too," I told her, digging at the bottom of my bowl with my spoon. "Digging for gold?" Matenele asked me with a grin; "here." She dumped another ladle of cereal into my bowl. Onucia said something. Matenele went out and came back in with a neat plate of bacon and laid each strip down on top as if she were laying bricks. In spite of herself, she was pleased I liked the food. "Mommiti says that was very good," Ninka told me. "What was?" "The way Matenele put the bacon on." "This is like the tower of Babel," I said out loud in German. "What?" everyone said at once. "Nothing," I said in Russian; Matenele translated immediately.

Ninka and I spent the afternoon playing with her dolls. "This one goes to church," she said picking up the little one. "Why?" "Just because," she answered, putting it down. She was a solemn child. "I'm going into the kitchen," she said, getting up: "Matenele draws me pictures now." I sat on the couch, picking the dolls up and putting them down. At home, before the Germans came, I had sixty bisque dolls that sat on cushions in front of my big windows looking out on the court.

There was a commotion; the girls were back. We had dinner. Cholem was back. He was a distinguished old man, or someone who looked much older than he was, because of his snow-white hair. He spoke Russian and Polish. "Oh, you will see, Anya,"—he was talking to me as if he knew me forever—"when this is over, we will open up an office and we will let the whole world know. We will do something; you will see." "Let the world know what?" Ninka asked. Matenele translated for Onucia. "Whatever they want to," Onucia told her. "Oh," Ninka said, satisfied. But I was wondering: What would we tell the world? What had happened? Hitler, every other word was Hitler. I never thought about him, or armies, just one soldier after another, turning them like combinations in a lock.

The next morning was the same thing. "She's still asleep," Ninka was whispering. "Come away from there," Matenele hissed at her in Russian. But today I couldn't get up right away. I lay in bed watching the sun. I could see some trees through the window. There were the beginnings of buds. They bloomed even in this ice age. I lay there looking at the trees move against the sky; they were moving gently as if they were polishing the sky with thin patient hands. "An Anzia tree," I thought to myself, "a Zoshia tree, a Momma tree." I turned into my pillow and cried. Then I put on the blue chiffon dress Onucia had left at the bottom of the bed.

When I came into the kitchen, Matenele was busy drawing pictures for Ninka. "These are Jews," she was saying; "see the big horns, and the big noses? That's how you can tell them. Don't ever go near them; they eat you up." "Eat me?" Ninka asked, terrified. "All up," Matenele assured her. "What are you doing?" I asked her, horrified, in Russian; "my cousin told you she was Jewish!" I spoke too fast for Ninka to understand me. "I will tell Rutkauskus!" They had no right to have her! I would take her away from them! They were terrible people, terrible! "Go ahead," Matenele told me; "he won't do anything. He needs someone he can trust here." "I don't see why he trusts you," I answered furious; "Onucia must be an idiot." "I will tell Rutkauskus you said that," she answered quietly. "He can trust me. All he has to do is denounce me and the Germans shoot me; if I denounce him, they shoot him. So we both keep quiet. We don't want to trip over each other running to the police." "Don't do this while I'm here," I warned her. "You won't be here long," she answered casually, adding a finishing touch to her picture; "no one ever is."

I sat down to my breakfast, the same cereal, the same bacon. Ninka was sitting on a chair winding some wool into a ball. "What are you going to do with that?" "Throw it," she answered, not looking up. "Then you'll have to chase it all over," I remarked, munching. "No, I won't; Matenele showed me how to leave a tail. I hold the tail; see," she said, holding up about six inches of wool. "It won't go far with a small tail like that." "A bigger tail?" "Much bigger," I said, putting down my fork and watching her. She pulled off a long strand of wool and tied it onto the ball. "Now it goes!" she shrieked, throwing it across the room. "Is it a fish?" I asked, watching her pull it in. "No, it's not; it's a mouse. I caught it." "Good cat," I said. I finished eating while she threw the red wool ball back and forth, back and forth.

"Do you want to play with the dolls?" she asked me after I finished. "Why not?" Ninka clambered up onto the couch. She started making up stories about them: how this one ran away and then came back with a dog and a cat and an elephant. "An elephant!" I exclaimed. "They have one in kindergarten," she pouted. "In *kindergarten*?" "In a *book*. I had an aunt named Rachel," she said, not looking at me, picking up the doll's skirt. "You did?" "Yes," Ninka said. "Where is she?" "I don't know." "I think I saw your Aunt Rachel; she's fine." Ninka didn't say anything. She picked up the little doll. "I had an Aunt Vera too; Mommiti told me." "What was she like?" "I never saw her," Ninka answered angry; "how should I know?" "You couldn't know if you didn't see her." "No," Ninka said. "Are you sure you didn't see her?" "Sure," Ninka answered, pulling the little doll's hair. "But," she said, slapping one doll's face with the other doll's hand, "I have a doll named Vera Mouse." She kept on hitting the big doll with the little doll. "You do?" I asked. I was white as a shroud. "Yes, I do. Do you want to see it?" "Yes," I whispered. I could imagine what I looked like.

"Here it is," Ninka told me, slapping it into my lap. The doll had lost most of its hair and one eye. One leg was crippled by leaking stuffing. "It's a nice doll." "No," Ninka said; "the new ones are better." "What does Vera Mouse do?" "She sleeps." "Is that all?" "She plays the piano." "How do you know that?" "I heard her once," Ninka said, getting up. "I'm going into the kitchen." And so I sat there until dark with the three dolls.

The next day, Ninka didn't bring out any of the old toys, only the new dolls. But she seemed to know when Onucia was in the room, or was watching. She would stay away from me then. When Onucia went into the kitchen, she would cuddle up against me or crawl into my lap. "I like you, Auntie," she said before dinner. "That's good," I said; "I love you." "I don't like my other aunts," she said. "I thought you told me you didn't know them," I reminded her. "I don't," she said, getting down.

And then she was back at school. A special *drozhka* would come for her in the morning to take her to kindergarten. I spent the day sitting on a little bench in a window facing the street waiting for the *drozhka* to come back, thinking over and over again how grateful I was to Onucia and Rutkauskus, how grateful I was to them. And then I would find my fist clenched, so hard the nails drew blood from the palm. Rutkauskus was terrified someone might suspect the child; she was so beautiful and blond, and he and his wife were so big and rough. "It wouldn't be too bad if they thought she was left behind by the Russians," he told me in German, "but anything else . . ." He shook his big head, his voice trailing off. A bottle hung from his right hand. "You'll have one of your own soon," I reminded him. "Four months," he cried, striking the table; "maybe not even four." "Maybe you won't want her then?" I asked. "Oh, no. Onucia loves that child like her life." I turned back to the window. My fist was clenching. My mind unclenched it finger by finger.

When I wasn't looking out the window, I would go into Ninka's room and sit on her little bed or lie down on it. Her room was so nice and clean; there was everything for her. I had been right to leave her. There was the brass bed painted white I had heard about in the labor camp; the walls were hung with holy pictures; there was a little rug on the side of the bed. Onucia had said nothing could be better for a child than two mothers; when she said it, she twisted the gold cross I gave her. Was she wondering if she had really changed fates, if Ninka would really be hers? "Selfish jealous monster, to think such a thing!" I upbraided myself. I wouldn't think such things if it hadn't been for the beatings on the head in the camp. Right then I decided that no matter what happened to my life, if we all lived, I would never separate myself and my child from them. I lay on Ninka's little blue spread. There were always fresh flowers in her room. She had a little white lilac tree that grew inside, in an earthen pot, next to her bed. I was shocked to see such a thing, such an extravagance. Toys were spread out on the floor around it. "They are very wealthy," I thought dreamily, falling asleep. Every few days, a wagon of food came from Onucia's brother's farm in the provinces; I had never seen so much food.

When I slept on the bed, it was as if I were sleeping with Ninka. Then I would forget Onucia often slept with her at night. But when I got up, I would stand in the entrance to their room, taking pictures with my eyes. They had a great wooden bed, and the room was so bright. Just by looking in, I could see Onucia dressing Ninka in her blue sailor suit, fastening the medals and corals around her neck. "You brush her hair," Onucia insisted, looking stricken, and I did, every morning. "I like the way you tie bows best," Ninka announced to me one morning in Polish. I was getting used to Matenele with her kerchief always pulled three quarters down over her eyes. She drew horrible pictures for Ninka, but Ninka still ran over and kissed me whenever Onucia went out of the room. Such a small child, and she felt the terrible undertow of jealousy between all of us, tugging at her little feet. But she was not caught up; some instinct kept her, kept all of us, free. And the jealousy was terrible; we moved through it like a poisonous gas. But it was a kind of miracle, we were all thriving.

After Onucia's bedroom, I would go to the dining room and look at the big credenza, the table and chairs, the kerosene lamp. Everything was very plain. There were the familiar parquet floors, but no rugs, and no mahogany furniture, light wood, oak, as if it had been bled of its color, bleached by passing time. And Rutkauskus had his own room. That was my next stop. It had a desk and a chair and shelves of books to the ceiling. I could stand in it and Ninka's voice would come out of the walls calling him: "Daddy! Daddy!" My last stop would be the big dark kitchen. It had an electric light; Onucia never turned it off. The bathroom was the only room in the house with running water. "Why they put it here, not in the kitchen, I don't understand," Onucia sighed again and again.

And so I would go on until Ninka came home from kindergarten. Then we would play with the dolls or the ball of wool, and soon we would eat supper. "What did you do now, Daddy?" Ninka asked every day. "*Today*, what did you do *today*," Onucia corrected her. "What?" Ninka asked. "I worked very hard," Rutkauskus answered. "What?" Ninka asked, chewing steadily as a cow. "I had to find a train to take some things to Germany," he told her. "Oh," she said impressed; "where did you find it?" "At the train station, little lima bean; where else should I find it?" "Then why did it take so long?" Ninka asked. Everyone laughed. "Not all the trains want to go to Germany." "They have to if the man in front tells them to," Ninka told him. "I should have said the man in front does not always want to go to Germany; I'm sorry," Rutkauskus corrected himself. Onucia and I were beaming at each other.

Matenele rushed in and whispered something to Rutkauskus who then left the room. "We have another guest," he said, coming back in. "An important one?" Ninushka asked. "Of course," he answered her. "As soon as we're finished, Onucia, the tub." A dark girl was sitting shyly on the sofa watching us. "Fix her hair first," he told Matenele; "there's not much time. Then feed her." He got up, leaving his plate, and began carrying up water; one of the girls began carrying in full pots from the bathroom sink. "Her hair, Daddy?" Ninka asked, jumping up and down with excitement. "Her hair," he answered.

"What are they doing?" I asked Ruta. "They dye her hair with peroxide; or Matenele does it. Then she gets false papers and goes to Germany for a job. It's funny, isn't it; it's a good joke on them." I watched in astonishment while everyone got up from the table and began the fuss over the tub. "Where did he find her?" I whispered to Matenele in Russian. "He goes out looking, in the streets; we don't have enough trouble. Look, that Cholem is back in his room. He stays there if it's dark. The minute it's light, he's out trying to get caught." "You dye her hair?" I asked. "If she goes to Germany, she should be blond," Matenele answered; "so Hitler says. We've sent a lot, maybe thirty." She was mixing some smelly chemicals together. "Peroxide," she said. "They have to keep their eyes closed tight, though. I'm better now; the first one nearly left blind." Rutkauskus and Onucia shepherded the frightened girl in. "Take her clothes," Rutkauskus told Ruta, who started washing them in the smaller sink. As she washed each piece, she laid it out on the tile tunnel of the stove, Onucia was busy bathing the girl. "Finished," Matenele asked. Onucia nodded, and Matenele came closer. "Close your eyes," she commanded in Lithuanian. She began putting the peroxide on with a rag, first one strand, then another; when she got to the end, she started all over again. "It would be easier if you cut it," I suggested. "She wouldn't look so normal." Matenele said, starting a third time. "It's hard with this black hair," she sighed dramatically. They were at work as if the kitchen were a factory. "Come on, Ninka," I said; "let's play with the dolls." "Oh, no," Ninka said, not moving her head; "I want to see Matenele make her hair into gold."

In the dining room, Cholem was sitting on the couch. "You shouldn't go out so much during the day," I told him. "A person has to have exercise," he answered. "I walk; it's good for the blood." "They could follow you and find all of us," I insisted. "I'm not so noticeable as that," he protested, puffing his stomach out. "Still, think of the child, Onucia, Rutkauskus; they would be killed if anyone knew." "No one will catch me," he answered, perfectly confident. "You're taking too many chances," I cried out. "Rutkauskus won't even let me sit in the window anymore; he says a neighbor saw me. I look too good now I'm fatter, and you look good all the time." He bowed, pleased. "But a man must have his walk," he insisted.

Much later, they came out of the kitchen with the girl wrapped in a bathrobe, a towel around her head, strands of blond hair showing wetly underneath. "Matenele turned her gold," Ninushka chirped. "You're already gold." "Oh, yes," she said, pulling a braid forward to look at it; "otherwise, she'd do it to me. We tried it on Vera Mouse," she went on, "but it didn't do any good." "What happened?" "Nothing; let me get my ball," she squealed, running off.

"Mommiti wants to talk to you in the kitchen," she told me in sing-song, coming back. Onucia talked; Matenele translated. "We're keeping pots of water just inside the apartment door," she said. "If anyone knocks, you run and hide. There'll be plenty of time while Matenele pulls their boots out of the pots." "Why are you worrying about it now?" I asked her. "Now?" came the echo. "I always worry about it, but now more. One of the neighbors saw Cholem walking around the middle of town. You know, Marya, next door? She works in the pharmacy and comes up here once in a while? Anyway, she's sure some of the soldiers saw him, too." "I tried to talk to him." "But it did no good," Onucia smiled. "No," I agreed.

Almost six weeks came and went. I knew I was better and better. I never felt weak; Onucia laughed when she let out my clothes. Then she shook her head and gave some orders to Matenele; she came back some time later with three new dresses. "These are much bigger," Onucia said happily. "Oh, you should not have spent the money," I protested; "we could have sewn pieces of material into the sides." "What kind of home did *you* come from?" Matenele asked me in Russian. I blushed like fire.

When Ninka came home from kindergarten, we played with the dolls and the ball; she told me what she did in school. "I'm making a present for Mommiti," she announced importantly. "What is it?" "Oh, I can't tell *you*, but maybe I can make you something." "No, it's all right; the school just wants you to make one present." "I can make two drawings if I want to," Ninka insisted, then she covered her mouth, horrified. "See how hard it is to keep a secret?" I asked her. "I won't tell anyone, though; I promise." "She's making you a present, Onucia," I told her at dinner, "but what it is is a big secret to me." Ninka beamed at her food.

As for me, I rarely looked in the mirror. My hair was growing longer; I was back to my normal weight. I knew what I would see, the woman who had left the big house with her family but whose eyes would never reflect anyone from the family again. Except for Ninka, I thought each time with a twinge. I couldn't stop watching her. Her skin was a miracle. I wanted to touch her every minute, to be sure she was real, not a snow child, not a child with skin made of snow which covered only decay and rot and skeleton, and could melt into the earth, leaving only patches, leaving the mud with its snow-speckled hide, not alive at all. I watched her and touched her and played with her, but she was still not mine to keep.

"The Lithuanian Gestapo are the worst," Rutkauskus said that night at supper. "Who would have thought it, with their President to set them such a good example?" "It shows you the value of good examples," Onucia said in a low voice, not looking up from her plate. "But they are the worst," Rutkauskus continued, as if she hadn't spoken; "give me the Germans every time." Matenele translated on, forever. "What kind of dogs do they have?" I asked, remembering the last days of the ghetto. "The shepherds, some sheepdogs," he answered, chewing. "Sheepdogs!" I exclaimed; "how can they see anything?" "They can round up a flock in the fields; believe me, they can see well enough." "Believe him," Matenele told me; "they not only see better, they smell out things better." "But all that hair," I argued. "Just to keep the sun out of their eyes in the fields; if you pull it away, it hurts their eyes. Believe me, they're good dogs." I couldn't eat. Ninushka was cleaning her plate. "More squash and ham," she demanded. "And more stew and potatoes?" Onucia asked laughing. "More potatoes." "Give her cherries and cream for dessert," she told Matenele.

"When she first started eating, we thought she would eat a hole in the floor and start chomping on the people downstairs, but still, it was a pleasure to see her." "She still eats a lot," I wondered out loud, amazed. "Well," Onucia answered, embarrassed, "she runs around much more here—in school, especially—so she needs to eat more. Every time we asked her what she did before, it was nothing, nothing, nothing." "She was telling the truth," I said sadly. "Where could she run? There was no place for her to move.

"I cannot get over what you've done for her," I told

Onucia, picking up the little cross she gave me between my fingers. "I'll be grateful to you for the rest of my life." "So many years without a child, we would not have been bad to her." Onucia smiled her gentle smile. "But now, you see," she told me, pointing at her belly, "my husband said if we were good to the little one, God would see it, and know we deserved one of our own." "Does Ninushka know what's coming?" "Of course; we don't want to give her the big surprises she brings us from the kindergarten. She can't wait to play with it. When she finds out it's not just the same as a doll, she may have other ideas." She smiled her smile. "You are beautiful when you smile," I whispered. "Mommiti is very beautiful!" Ninka said loudly, grabbing her hand across the table. "Oh, yes, I am," Onucia grinned, gently pulling her hand loose without looking at me; "but please eat."

After dinner we sat around talking. The girls went to their room to talk separately; they were leaving in the morning. "Affairs of the heart on top of everything else," Rutkauskus commented bitterly, looking at me sideways. I ignored him. "Where do you get all the food?" I asked Onucia. "Oh, it's from my brother's farm, one of the biggest. He sends almost a quarter of his crop, and the farm's supposed to be 'taken over' for the war effort. It's amazing, such a generous soul." "It is amazing," I commented absently, "I can't believe your brother sends all this." Ninka was getting ready for bed; I couldn't see her. "I raised him, so he does it," Onucia said. "Our Momma was very young when she died. It was a cancer, a big one; it closed up her stomach." Ninushka came in wearing her white gown and holding a doll. "Ruta said to kiss everyone good night." "So she stopped talking for a minute," Rutkauskus muttered. We looked at him; he was definitely in a bad mood. "Good night, Daddy," Ninka chirped, turning up her face; "don't worry, maybe you'll find more trains tomorrow." "Of course I will," he shouted, bursting into laughter. "Good night, Mommiti," she said to Onucia, kissing her; "Auntie didn't tell you about the present?" "Definitely not; she's a good aunt." "Good night, Auntie," Ninka said, coming up to me and throwing her arms around my neck, pulling me forward. "Don't tell about the picture," she whispered into my ear. Onucia was staring, saying nothing. The little white figure wavered off down the hall. "Was it worth the trip?" Rutkauskus asked roughly.

"Come into the kitchen," Onucia said to me. "He always knows when something's going to happen," she said grimly; "every time. Now he'll be up all night drinking so he won't have to know he's waiting for it." "What's going to happen?" "I don't know; he doesn't either, but something will; it always does." "It always does," Matenele repeated a second time in Russian. The three of us sat in the kitchen for some time. "Well," Onucia said, "if something's going to happen, I had better go to sleep. You too, Anya; we can both use it." "Should I stay up all night?" Matenele asked her. "You go to sleep too," I answered in Russian. From the hall, the three of us could see Rutkauskus with his feet up at a little table, drinking glass after glass of vodka, staring at the opposite wall as if it were showing an invisible screen. The next day was my birthday: April 20. Rutkauskus emptied another glass. Only his arm and torso moved. As soon as he finished the drink, he sat still, a carved wooden man. Birthdays, there was no point in mentioning them. My birthday present had just gone to bed.

Early in the morning, there was a horrible pounding at the front door. Immediately, everyone in the house was up. Cold sweat was running in rivers down my body. "You hide," Ruta said, running into my room, pulling on her sweater. "You don't know a word of Lithuanian; we have papers, we can speak the language." "Where?" There was a strange noise coming from the back of the house. "Cholem's going up to the skylight; he'll get away over the roof." Ruta pulled me to Onucia. "Hide, right away," she ordered; then, "Luisa, get in my bed." She stood still for a minute. "Now," she told me, "get in there with her and make a line with her body. Put your head right under her feet, and make one straight line; pull the covers up to your chin. Don't either of you move, do you hear, Luisa?" A muffled *da* struggled down to me under the covers. I could feel the bare soles of Ninka's feet on the top of my head. "I am throwing covers over; remember, don't move," Onucia said, and then blanket after blanket was falling on us in a regular rhythm.

I could hear Rutkauskus thundering outside in a drunken roar: "What do you want? My wife is sick, my baby is sick, what do you want?" There was endless shouting and more thundering. I was shaking all over, but above me, Ninka was perfectly calm. Then it was quiet. "All right," Onucia said, coming into the room, Matenele right behind her. "They took the girls, no questions, no looking at papers, nothing, just grabbed them by the arm; they're in the street." She took hold of my elbow. "Move aside," she ordered. Near the door, I could hear Rutkauskus thundering and slamming locks into place. Onucia staggered into the room with one of the mattresses from the floor of my room the girls had slept on. "Out of bed, Luisa," she gasped. "You lie down," she commanded me, and then she put the heavy mattresses on top of me. Its heavy wooden frame was pressing into me like torture. "The other frame," Onucia said, and that went on top of the first. "Hide her clothes," she told Matenele.

Then the men were back. "Why should I let you in?" Rutkauskus was roaring. "Who are you to me? You take away my servants, both of them, you frighten my wife to death, I don't want to let you in." "He's drunk," one of them said in German. "Where's the man?" the soldier asked. "The white-haired one, the rich one," he asked impatiently. "No such man," Rutkauskus hiccoughed; "you're drunk; *you're* seeing things." "We will look," they answered, pushing in. I could hear them, going from room to room, the kitchen, the dining room, Ninka's room, the bathroom. Under the heavy mattresses I could hardly breathe or see. Then they came to Onucia's room where I was. "Whose little shoes are these?" "One of the girls; she was going to sell them in the market," Matenele answered promptly. "I don't believe it," the soldier shouted. "Well, they're not mine," she answered calmly; "my toe wouldn't get in them." "Your ear wouldn't get in them," the soldier said. "Maybe they would fit your dog?" she suggested nastily. From the little crack between the bed and me, I could see him raise his arm as if to hit her; then he changed his mind. "Your dog doesn't want to resign," she said sarcastically. "Look at him sniff that bed. Stupid," she said to the dog, "people were in it before. Here," she said, thrusting Ninka at the dog, "smell her." The dog started sniffing Ninka with interest and ignored the bed. But then the soldier began talking to Ninka sweetly, like a father, first in Russian, then in Yiddish, then in German. "Stop frightening my child!" Onucia screamed like a demented wolf. "Stop scaring her!" She yanked Ninka violently to her side. "I don't want you talking to her." She was afraid the child would answer in one of the languages. "I don't frighten children," the soldier sulked. "You have scared her to death, to death, get out of here," Onucia screamed, beside herself. "Out of here!" Rutkauskus thundered in Russian, "out of here!"

"Why do you speak so many languages?" the Gestapo officer asked him. "A judge should speak every language," Rutkauskus answered, drawing himself up to his six foot six. "I speak seven; what do you speak, Yiddish? I heard you," he thundered, "you speak Yiddish; the authorities will have to look into this." The soldier turned pale. I was watching from a little triangular space. "You are coming with us," another Gestapo agent said suddenly, grabbing Rutkauskus's arm. "Anyone else you want?" Rutkauskus roared; "how about the couch, the secrets it knows by now?" "Let's go," they said, marching him out of the room. There was more noise, more roaring from Rutkauskus, then silence. I couldn't breathe; my breath was coming in little gasps. I couldn't feel my arms or my legs. "I'm suffocating," I thought to myself clearly; "I'm suffocating. But they didn't get the child." The last thing I heard was my ear repeating the last words of the soldier as he took Rutkauskus: "We will be back again; do you understand?"

20

THERE was light all around me. I felt something icy cover my face, then something burning hot and clammy. Then I realized the same thing was happening to my whole body, an icy blanket, a hot one. "She's coming to herself," I heard Matenele whisper in relief. "Don't sit up," Onucia whispered, pushing me back. "We were so frightened! You came out of there blue and gray like a corpse; you weren't breathing. We couldn't call a doctor; Matenele said this would work." "She was right," I gasped weakly. "Is Auntie better?" Ninka asked, staring at me. "She'll be all better soon," Onucia promised her. "Try to take good deep breaths." I took a deep breath and choked. "Keep trying," Matenele ordered me, impatient. They kept on covering me with hot and cold blankets. I took a deep breath and let it out. Two other deep breaths escaped from Onucia and Matenele. "She's fine, Luisa," Onucia said. "You were very good in that bed," I praised her; "you didn't move at all." "Mommiti said you're a very important person and they would try to catch you," Ninka recited with her empty plate eyes. "I am very grateful to you," I told her. "You're welcome," she answered. "I mean, thank you," she corrected herself, embarrassed; "thank you." "Can you sit up?" Onucia asked me. I said I could. "She has lines all over her body!" Ninka exclaimed. There were huge black and blue lines horizontally across me, everywhere the boards of the mattress had pressed down; they were already swelling and spreading, the outer edges yellow and purple. "More wet cloths," Matenele sighed; "Luisa, get some ice."

"When will Daddy be back?" Ninka asked coming in with some ice wrapped in a towel. She missed him so soon! "As soon as the two girls are shot, that's when he'll be back." I was too shocked to move; how many times did Ninka hear things like that? "We have to do something about you," Onucia thought out loud. "They said they'll be back; they always keep their word. At the latest, they'll come back when they bring my husband." "After they shoot the girls," Ninka reminded her. "Yes, after that," Onucia repeated. "I know, Matenele; we'll put her in the stove as soon as she's better; in the pen for the chickens. If there's any danger, we'll put the chickens in with her." "Good idea," Matenele agreed. "Why can't I go in with the chickens?" Ninka asked. "Because chickens poke out the eyes of little girls," Onucia answered absently. "Is that door locked?" she asked Matenele. "Yes, and what happened to Cholem?" "I was going to ask you," Onucia said; "I was busy with the mattresses." She was such a strong, big woman. "Ruta said he went out a skylight on some roof," Ninka reported. "Oh," Onucia said slowly. "That means he'll be back," Matenele predicted in a dark voice. "You *know* this is all his fault." "There's nothing we can do about it once my husband decides, but he won't come back here for a while; he takes too good care of his skin, too good for something stupid like that." Her optimistic words came to me, after a dead space, in Russian.

"When do I have to start?" I asked Onucia, half-looking in the direction of the stove. "Right away; as soon as you can breathe. We can't take any chances. When my husband is home, and there's more going on to distract everyone, you can come out a little." "How will I go to the bathroom?" "We'll lock the door and Matenele will watch from the window and Ninka can look out the back the whole time you're out." "I'm ready to go in," I heard myself saying. Onucia nodded her head, saying something to Matenele. "We'll put in some water for you," Matenele told me, "and some bread. If you want anything else to eat, we'll come check every half hour, or you can call out if you're sure it's us in the kitchen." Onucia opened the little door. "Let me go in in a blanket; I don't want to ruin the dress," I begged. Matenele appeared with a terry cloth robe. I bent all the way down and climbed in. "In?" Matenele asked. "Yes," I answered, my voice echoing.

Then I had my choice: Either I could sit on my spine with my legs drawn up to my chin, or I could crouch on all fours like a cat with its bottom up in the air. "I'll start by sitting," I thought. "I'm closing the door," Matenele warned; "how is it?" "I can hear; some light comes in; not so bad." "It gets warm in there when we light the stove," she said. It was definitely spring now, but still there were days that blew cold like March. "Here's the water," Onucia said, putting a little brass cup with a spout and handle in with me. I held it on my lap like a doll. "Now the chickens," Matenele said; I could hear them clucking, the funny burbling noises in their throats. "Wait Mommiti!" Ninka was crying hysterically. "What is it now?" Onucia asked her, exasperated. "I have something for Auntie," she said. "She has something for you," Matenele said, opening the door again. There Ninka was standing with a branch from her tiny lilac tree. "Thank you," I said, taking it.

Matenele slammed the iron door. I could barely see the three chickens strutting in front of me, thrusting their necks forward, taking their little steps with their feet out. And the smell! I should have known! Suddenly, I felt pure hatred for the child. I pressed the lilac branch close to my nose. For a while, the perfume of the flowers would blot out the chickens. Then it would do no good. The sweet odor evaporated, like everything else. If it wasn't for that miserable child who called Onucia Mommiti, and me, beggar, I could have spent the rest of the war at Madame Russo's in complete safety. I sat there hating her. Who was she, to be so lucky, to be so spoiled, to drive me into a stove with three chickens, and for what? So I could watch her sleep with someone else and hear her call someone else Mommiti and have the honor of braiding her hair? I hated her. I wished I were back in the camp. "At least there I could have Rachel," I thought to myself bitterly. "What do I have here? A crazy Russian woman, a drunk Lithuanian judge who thinks he's Christ, and his pregnant wife whose words are translated by that troll, an old banker who's trying to get us all killed, what for?" I was crying bitterly. "What for?" I found myself asking Stajoê. "What for? *You* wanted it!" I accused him as if he were there and responsible for everything. In some way, he was.

"But she is the photograph album," I thought, seeing myself turn the pages with Momushka. What had she said, that there was no more room in their old blue one, and they would have to put our wedding pictures in between their pages. Where had my red one gone? Ninka was that living book. When I thought of her birth, Momma was there watching me polish boards and scrub floors. When I thought of working in Kaunas, I thought of calling Poppa to ask how she was. "Oh, she's fine," his voice came through the wire: "I tell her stories, and she loves them; I know she does, even though," and he would laugh, "she can't understand a word." If I thought of tickling her, there Vera stood, ready to repeat her rhyme about the crow and the four busy birds and the one lazy bird in the nest. If she was sick, I remembered everything about the purple child, and the rash, and the little carriage that looked like an auto, losing the medallion, visiting the Lavinskys, everything. She was the biggest book; every word of hers turned a page, a year, and a scene popped up entire. "So," I thought to myself, as if Momma were speaking through me, "if she brought me to this, this is where I am supposed to be." And then I heard Poppa saying, "If it weren't for the child, you'd still be in Kaiserwald, wouldn't you? It's all fate," he went on. "No, there's only responsibility," Momma shouted at him; Zoshia had just left the house. Zoshia. "It's better in here than at the window," I thought. "How warm the bodies of the chickens are. How fast they must burn up their lives." I could hear them pecking up grain on the bottom of the opening. At the window, I had three times seen women that looked just like Momushka and practically thrown myself out trying to see their faces; it was never my Momma. That was when Rutkauskus put a stop to my sitting in the window for good.

So I sat in the stove and thought, and the rhythm of the stove was the rhythm of the train taking us to Kaiserwald. In front of me, facing me where I leaned against the boards, arms folded across my chest, a woman was sitting on the floor, legs spread. With one hand she kept grabbing her breasts as if they were wild animals, with the other she was masturbating wildly. She kept talking in Polish to someone who wasn't there. "Come on, look at this, doesn't this excite you? It'll all be the same; I'll be as pretty as I was, you don't have to look for someone else; this is what you like!" Then she lifted her arms to her hair and began running her fingers through it. Her breasts lifted with the movement. "Not bad, eh?" she cooed with delight; she began writhing and gasping and calling out. I had never remembered anything about her until this minute. And I remembered saying something to Sonya about the three days and nights in the train. "Three days and nights!" she gasped; "don't you remember? It must have been at least eight!" But I let it go. Sonya always exaggerated so. Now I thought she was probably right. They were not normal trains, it had not been a normal trip; the train may have gone other places besides Riga first. But where had those

379

five days gone? I would never find out, never. If other people told me, how would I know they were telling me the truth?

It came to me suddenly: My life was not continuous; it would never be continuous again. Something, the world, or history, had intervened like a terrible editor of a movie, snatching out handfuls of characters, changing the sets wildly, changing them back again, keeping some of the actors, changing the rest, old ones reappearing with mysterious, unknown pasts trailing behind them, looking for the others, endlessly asking questions about what happened in the middle, and the rest of the group in a hurry to get on with it, and all embarrassed because no one knows the answer to the questions they ask. Life is a train constantly crossing the border from the past to the present; it moved slowly, an inch at a time, finally a car at a time. The war had transported the whole train into the future which looked the same as the past, where all the rooms were the same, and none of the people were the same and none of the people spoke the same language. And now my mind was doing it, too, cutting pieces of the film randomly with clumsy scissors, without anesthetic, and the victim never knowing anything had been taken. The jealousy, the times I had sat in the window, watching for Ninka. The valves of my heart opened; I was flesh and blood. They closed; I was stone. They opened when she left, and opened when she came in; the rest of the time I might have been a cement angel standing on a tombstone. How many things had happened in the house I couldn't remember? How many things would happen I couldn't remember because of what had gone with it? Would I ever be attached to people in the old way again? And I could see every detail in the inlay of Verushka's old piano.

I put my face in my hands and cried, the tears squeezed through my fingers. The chickens pecked. And they said this was the fault of a man named Hitler whom I was too frightened or too busy to think about. How bitter would I become when I had the time? What had I already become?

My father was twirling the globe on his desk. Then he lifted the top from the bottom and picked up his letter knife; it was exceptionally sharp. He sliced one inch from both halves of the globe, then pressed them back together. The world was no longer round, but slightly oval. He pressed it as if it were clay; it became round again. But it wasn't the same globe. It was completely solid, but not the same. There was a seam, an incision; something important had been taken out. Poppa looked at it and shook his head. He lit a match and held it to the globe. It went up like newspaper. And the flames were spreading; soon they would reach the desk and the curtains behind them, then the bookshelves. I woke up screaming. There was no one to hear me; the kitchen was empty. The chickens were scrabbling; I held onto the ladle as if it were a child.

"We can keep it open for a little while now," Ninka translated for Onucia, opening the door; "Matenele is peeling potatoes at the window." Onucia went out. "I wish I could tell you a story," Ninka said, sitting down cross-legged on the floor. "Go ahead and try; I don't mind. It doesn't have to be a good one." "But I don't remember good," Ninka complained; "the trouble is, everyone tells *me* stories." "Maybe I'll think of one to tell you in a little while," I suggested. "No, I should tell you one; how is the lilac?" "The lilac is fine." "I'll get some tulips when I go down," she promised. "Isn't it a little late for tulips?" I asked. "Not when winter wouldn't go away for so long," she answered, a little expert. "I know a story!" she exclaimed. "About two mules." She pulled on a braid and stopped to think. "Don't chew on your hair," I reminded her; "then what?" "They had to cross a bridge." "What for?" "I don't know; they didn't cross." "Why not?" "Well," she went on, picking up speed, "the first one wanted to be first, then the other wanted to be first, and they pushed each other so hard, they both fell into the water. Isn't that a good story?" she asked, bursting into laughter, pounding both fists in her lap. "Wonderful," I laughed.

"We have to close the doors again," Matenele announced coming in. Ninka went away and came back with the tulips. "Just a crack," Matenele was telling her; "we don't want the chickens out." "Thank you," I called. "You're welcome." I put them to my nose. An acrid smell. I felt the petal flesh: waxy. Like corpses. They made me shudder. Then they began to seem like presences. "They are yellow; they are lights." I hadn't seen the color when Ninka handed them in. "I have three lights like the three yellow lights of the Bedouin lamps on Poppa's desk," I thought, drifting into sleep.

In the morning, Onucia took me out. Matenele had pots and mops in front of the entrance; Ninka was watching at the back door. My legs had swollen to twice their size and I could barely stand on them. "Come," Onucia said, "we'll walk up and down from Ninka to Matenele until the blood moves again. This isn't good," she said, shaking her head. "The chickens are leaving you alone?" "Why should they bother me when you feed them so much? It's always the smell that bothers me, the smell." But she was washing me off from head to toe and wrapping me in another terry cloth robe. The first one went into a pot of boiling water on the sink. "I look like an elephant!" I cried, looking down at my legs. "There is an elephant at our school," Ninka answered without taking her eyes from the back window. "We know," Onucia said. What a tiny sentry! "All right," Onucia said to her; "get ready for school. Auntie is getting back in the stove." "First I have to get the flowers," Ninka protested. "Just hurry up," Onucia ordered her, nervous. "When do you think Rutkauskus will come back?" I asked. "Who knows how long it will take to shoot them? Maybe a couple of weeks."

Matenele helped me into the stove. Some chicken feed was poured in. They refilled my cup with water. Some bread came in, and the big pot of cereal. "I can't eat it in here," I objected. "Onucia says you must," Matenele reported. There were some whispers between Onucia and Matenele I couldn't understand. They didn't talk about me in front of Ninka; she was too likely to translate for me.

The third morning I could hardly walk at all. My legs were three times their normal size, and numb. "Can you feel that?" Matenele asked, pinching my left leg beneath the knee. "No," I answered, beginning to cry. "This can't go on," Onucia said positively; "you'll lose the use of your legs for sure. You have to stay outside; we have to take the chance." She said something to Matenele. "She's going to get a paper," Ninka explained. "Luisa, get dressed," Onucia commanded. "If you stay all the way back here," she pointed at a place near the window, "you can see her leave for school."

Ninka climbed into the *drozhka* wearing a cotton sailor suit. The *drozhka* moved slowly down the street. "He drives slowly," I said. "Orders from my husband," Onucia smiled. "Look," she said, "we found an ad. In Minsk they need someone to clean in a hospital. My husband left you a new set of papers saying you're Lithuanian, the same thing again, name Otilia Vishinskaytie. Safer. It would be best if you went in the morning. We'll get a *drozhka*; you

382

can't stay in that stove another day without becoming a cripple, and it's only a miracle Cholem isn't already back with the Gestapo." She was watching me closely. "If you leave tomorrow, you can say goodbye to Luisa first," she coaxed. Matenele translated reluctantly. "No, I have to go. Don't feel bad about it; I'll find you again." "If we all survive," she said grimly. "We will, we will," I promised her. "I don't know." She was fingering her cross.

"Take Luisa tonight," Onucia said, coming into my room. "I told her I had a cold and she shouldn't catch it." I couldn't talk at all. "She'll be all right," Onucia told me. Ninka climbed into my cot with me. "Lie against the wall so you don't fall off," I insisted. "All right," she agreed, squirming into my stomach as if she'd had years of practice. And listening to the sound of her breathing, I fell sound asleep.

In the morning Onucia had my little suitcase packed before I was up. It was yellow wicker with brown leather bands. "Here are the papers," she said, giving them to me. "Now, sit down and eat." The fourteen-inch bowl of cereal appeared, with three layers of bacon. "You must," Onucia said, without giving me a chance to say a word. Ninka was watching with big blank eyes. "Auntie has to go; someone is sick in her family," Onucia explained. Ninka just stared at me with a slightly accusing look. "Here's your coat," Onucia said when I finished; she helped me on with it. "Say goodbye to your aunt," she instructed Ninushka. "Goodbye Aunt," Ninka repeated mechanically. "Goodbye darling," I choked, grabbing and hugging her; "I'll see you soon." Ninka backed away and looked at me. "Aren't you going to say anything?" Onucia asked her. "No," Ninka said. Onucia shrugged her shoulders. "The *drozhka* is here," Matenele called from the window she was watching. "Don't you want to go down with your aunt?" Onucia asked. "No," Ninka said again. I went down alone. At the bottom of the steps I expected to find water, not solid ground. I handed the driver the suitcase and got in. "Don't I know you?" a rough voice called. It was the janitor from my parents' old building. "I don't think so; I've never been here," I answered, turning away, and, to the driver, "Please, drive fast; I don't want to miss the train." "Where are you going?" he asked. "Minsk." "Minsk, Pinsk," he said. It was an old joke; one of the cities was no better than the other. "Nevertheless," I told him, hurrying the *drozhka* along with my will; "I don't want to miss the train." "Who was that man?" he called back to me; "there are ruffians all over nowadays." Clap clap clap went the horse's heels. "A beggar," I answered.

The *drozhka* was hammering down the streets. I turned around once to look back. The street was a ribbon flapping behind us, the houses tied on for decoration. The *drozhka* held the street down, but as soon as it passed over the stones the street came loose, flapping in the air behind us, a whipping tail. We were getting to the more familiar streets. "Soon the street will swerve to the left, and there will be the railway station," I thought to myself. The driver pulled the reins; the *drozhka* swerved; we were there. "Thank you," I said automatically, paying the driver. "You have papers?" he asked. "Of course," I answered automatically. "They always check," he said apologetically. "I know," I answered, taking my little valise from him; "they checked when I came to visit." I turned and walked into the station. Out of the corner of my eye I could see the little café where Rutkauskus had sat and drunk. At a little table near the window was the *nachaynik*, the head man of the railway station Stajoe and I had both known when he worked there. "I should put on my long coat," I thought lazily to myself, looking down at the valise, but I couldn't be bothered. I went in for the ticket.

"Always checking papers!" I complained loudly, handing mine over. "Lady, I have to," the ticket man whispered, frightened; "otherwise, they shoot me. See that man with the gun? He watches, all day he watches, they shouldn't think I'm helping spies." "Every five minutes checking papers!" I said loudly again. I didn't care whose attention I attracted. "Please, lady, get on the train," he pleaded; "don't cause me any trouble." "What kind of trouble could I cause you?" I asked, refusing to move out of the line. People were muttering behind me. "I don't want any kind," he pleaded. "Please get on the train, the second platform, Minsk; you'll be there before you know it." "The trains are always late," I said loudly. "They're late, but they get there; please lady." He wrang his hands. "It will take more than overnight," I complained, finally taking back my papers and the ticket, turning away. "Your change!" he called after me. "Keep it," I said, walking off.

The train was waiting. It was only seven-thirty in the morning. There was a silver sky outside the platform; the train would be running under it, watching it turn blue, then black. I got on the first car in back of the engine and sat next to the window. I had no desire at all to look out. I don't know how long the train stayed there. Someone came through checking papers and tickets. "Again, checking?" I complained. "What do you expect, a bomb made of papers? Maybe I have a bomb in my suitcase; want to look?" "Not necessary," the man said, hurrying down the aisle.

The train was moving through fields. They were turning green. Peasants were out, loading up wagons, getting ready to bring things into the city. Little heaps of hay were beginning to dot the fields. "Very nice," I thought to myself; "very nice, another spring." It was ridiculous. I was a croquet ball being hit back and forth, back and forth, between two hammers, but there was no grass under me, no earth; no, I just flew from one sky to the other. Each sky was an elastic sheet stretched tight; each horizon bounced me back to the one in back.

"Minsk, what's in Minsk?" I could hear Momma arguing with Poppa. "Still, we haven't seen it, Rebecca; at least we should see it." "We haven't seen Africa, either," Momma retorted. "So we will go to Africa if you want it," Poppa sighed; "I think you just want to see the big furry spiders that walk on high legs. It's a historical city, Rebecca; it will be good for the children." "Then that settles it, Borya," Momma said smiling; "whenever you want to go, a place suddenly develops a history." "Everything has a history," Poppa said seriously. "Then so does the *dacha*," Momma pointed out. "You should have been a lawyer," Poppa said, smiling at her, "but since you aren't, can I throw myself on the mercy of the judge?" "Throw yourself," Momma answered him; "Anya, Vera, Mischa, we are going to Minsk." I couldn't remember anything about it, a small city, nothing interesting. "Minsk, Pinsk," Momma said coming back on the train, just like the *drozhka* driver. "But now we have seen it," Poppa pointed out. "True," Momma answered, lacing her fingers in his; "we have plenty of time. Next time, we'll all go to Dneprpetrovsk." "Why is that Rebecca?" Poppa asked, laughing. "I hear something about a big power dam on the Dnepr," Momma said. "But the dam is not historical," Poppa protested. "The river is," Momma answered, triumphant. "Don't try to argue with her," Poppa grinned at us. "Besides, it will be good for the children to go there, Borya," she mimicked. "Why?" "Because they will have to learn the name of the city before they can write to their friends." And so we returned to Vilno. What was Minsk to us? A drop of water, a drop of time, evaporated from our skins. That was before the earth had learned to reach up with its hands and pull down on our feet. I looked down at mine. They were still swollen. Why did I bother? "A woman has to look her best," Momma was saying as I took out my mirror, and then: "You will survive; you have for whom to survive." An older woman came from across the aisle and sat down next to me.

"Where are you going?" she asked. "Minsk," I answered tonelessly. "I have to look for a job; there was one mentioned in the paper." I started to pull the ad out for her. "You look so sad," she commented, observing me. "I am not sad, I am disgusted; I am disgusted with everything. It does not pay to be born." I plastered my face to the window glass. It might as well have been dark. "Why not?" the woman asked softly. "It does not pay," I repeated angrily. "I have a daughter about your age," she told me. "Good for you," I answered nastily. "Do you have children?" she asked. "Why do you want to talk to me?" I demanded; "*I* don't want to talk to anyone." "That's a dangerous state of mind, I think," the woman answered. "Do you have any children?" she asked again. "I had one; she might as well be dead," I answered bitterly. "The Russians took her; she wouldn't even recognize me anymore. Why should I even look for her?" "Have you been looking?" "Yes." "Well," the woman said, "let me tll you my name; it's Sofia Lichkov. What's yours?" I didn't answer her. "The main thing," she went on as if I had answered, "is to get through the war; when it's over, you'll find her." "I don't care if I find her," I said, staring out the window. "I have a room in my house in Minsk," Mrs. Lichkov suggested; "you could stay in it." "I don't need a room." "You have to stay somewhere," she insisted. "All right, I'll stay there," I said disagreeably.

"What kind of job were you looking for?" "Not in a hospital," I answered; "I don't want to work in hospitals." "Why not?" "I don't like them." "There are plenty of jobs," Mrs. Lichkov said. "There will come a time when the living will envy the dead," I muttered in Russian; "at least the dead are given a proper burial." "You speak Russian!" Mrs. Lichkov exclaimed in the same language. "Of course," I answered, bored. "We are Russian!" Mrs. Lichkov rejoiced; "now you *must* stay with us. I only hope

386

you won't blame us about your baby." "Why should I blame you, you're not Hitler. Did you take her?" "Are you always so miserable?" she asked me. "Always," I insisted. "We'll see," she sighed in German. "It's not safe to talk Russian while the Germans are fighting them," she pointed out. "*Konechno*, of course," I said loudly. "I think you're being impossible," she said. I ignored her and fell asleep.

Ninka was coming up to me with a little smile; she had a hand held behind her back. "I have some surprises for you, Auntie," she said holding out her hand. "What is it?" I asked. I opened her fingers one by one; there were twenty little teeth with pink spots at the top. "Are they your milk teeth?" I asked her. "Oh, no," she smiled, and I could see her mouth, all gums, and her little cheeks sucking in. She muttered something to me. "I can't understand; is it important?" She nodded her head yes. "What are you saying?" "Chinese, ha, ha for you, Auntie." She laughed and ran away; the back of her dress was cut off. Her ribs showed through her skin, and the discs of her spine.

I woke up covered with sweat. "What is it?" Mrs. Lichkov asked. "A dream," I told her, quivering. "Tell me," she coaxed. I did. "Oh, it is a good dream, very good; the little teeth means she's growing big ones and is getting ready to grow up, and the dress means she's getting more mature, you see; and the Chinese are the most rabbity people in the world; it seems she will grow up and have lots and lots of children." "It does?" "Oh, yes," she said; "oh, yes." I fell asleep again. This time Ninka was back; she had on thick glasses. "I can't see you, Mommy," she kept crying; "I can only see clouds; the clouds are coming to get me, the clouds have hands." "No, they don't have hands," I called to her. "They do, they do," she cried coming closer; "look at my hand." She held it out. "There's nothing wrong with it." "This part, I mean," she whined, thrusting out her elbow; the bone showed through. There was a huge abscess, crawling with lice. I woke up screaming. "Now what?" Mrs. Lichkov asked, putting her arm around me; "another dream?" I was sobbing violently. "Tell me," she said again. I did. A shadow went over her face. "That dream is even better than the first," she said positively. "It means all the dangers are just clouds; she's wearing glasses, which means she can see the truth, that you will come and fix her; that's what it means." "It does?" I asked again. "I'm never wrong," Mrs. Lichkov said with assurance.

"Minsk," she said, waking me up; it was early in the morning. "You can register with the police and then come home with me and then I'll take you to the Employment Office; you don't have to work at a hospital if you don't want to." "I don't," I whimpered. Mrs. Lichkov's house was five blocks from the station, in the middle of the city. It was a big brick house with a huge garden; roses were trained up one side of one brick wall. "It looks very nice," I sighed, my bones melting after the visit to register with the police. "It is very nice," she said; "but first things first; we'll go to the Employment Office." "I have something at Stub Rosenberg," the clerk told us when we got there; "but she'll have to sleep there." I looked at Mrs. Lichkov; she nodded. I had on my old clothes and old coat. "A *putzfrau*, can you do it?" "Yes." Mrs. Lichkov gave me directions; I set out. Everyone I asked knew where it was. "It's a big place, at the end of this street," one man said; "very important people there, white Russians. They work with Hitler."

I went in the front door; a man came down to see me. "Can you clean?" he asked. "Yes," I said again. In back of him was an older, yellowish woman with wrinkled skin. Her look froze me in my tracks. "Jealous!" I thought to myself. "I'll take care of her," the yellow prune announced, dismissing the man, Eric Von Hindenberg. "In the mornings, the floors and the windows, then serving for lunch," she said; "then a half hour for rest and lunch, then the second floor. Everything is cleaned up there, the floors, the windows, the silver; you take down the curtains to wash and iron. You understand me?" "Very well," I answered. The house was full of soldiers coming and going. "She's going to take the juices out of me," I thought to myself; "but I have to work."

After a week, I was lying down in the kitchen in the house when a soldier came in drunk. "How about a little kiss?" he asked, bending down. "Not now," I pleaded. "Why not now?" he whispered. I began to push him away. "Not good enough for you, eh?" he roared; he was pinning me down. "I want you to keep my things," he whispered hotly, pulling out a watch, a ring, some papers. "After my great achievement, they're sending me to the front, the first rows; what about that?" "What was your great achievement?" I asked, stalling for time. "Oh," he answered, pushing himself up and staring down at me; "I was going over a bridge in Bialistock and I saw a little gleam, probably from a candle or a match, so right away, I thought, Jews, they are hiding themselves under the bridge! I had sixteen of them shot and they send me to the front! You'll keep these things for me?" he asked, falling on me again. "You should find someone closer to you," I gasped. "Closer to *you*," he bellowed, throwing himself on me like a wet horse. "What are you doing?" roared Von Hindenberg. The soldier jumped to attention. "I'll see you in my office, go!" he ordered. The soldier saluted and fled.

"Look Mrs. Vishinskaytie," he said, "it's not safe for you here at night; we've had cases before." "What should I do?" "There's a book cellar down below the kitchen." He pointed at a little trap door. "Sleep down there. "Believe me, it's best." An hour later, I was serving at the big table. Again, it was looking this way and that, anticipating who wanted what. "Some more wine," Von Hindenberg's mistress called. "She's so slow," she complained out loud. I was dishing some potatoes into an officer's plate. They all spoke Russian. "Until all the American Jews are dead, we can't be sure we'll win," he said. I moved on. "It's dangerous, this with the American Jews," the other officer said, picking up the subject; "they have too much influence and too much money." "We should start on America right away," one of them agreed. "We must get Hitler's ear; it's too big a chance to take."

That was my first night in the cellar. It was damp, damp and cold. I climbed up on three book cartons. There was the scurrying of rats and mice; then I heard a scrabbling right under me; something was in the box I was sitting on. I jumped down, crying hysterically. "I have to leave, Captain Von Hindenberg," I told him in the morning; "the work is too much for me, but the worst is the mice." "The mice?" he asked. "In the book cellar; I'm half-dead of fright." I held out my hand. It was shaking so hard, I pulled it back and clasped it with my other hand. "I understand," he said; "there are too many rats here." "In the cellar," I said. "Of course, in the cellar. Let me pay you for the week," he said, taking out some money. "Why for the week?" came the angry voice of the yellow woman behind him. "Because I say so, you witch!" he said in Russian. I was not supposed to understand it. "You're an idiot!" she muttered going into the hall.

"We have a job in a laundry, folding linen," the man in the Employment Agency told me; "no one stays long in Stub Rosenberg. *This* job is not hard." The woman in charge looked me over, looked at my big gray cross and my papers and took me right away. "Can I start tomorrow?" I asked. I was still holding my valise. "I want to go to Mrs. Lichkov's." "Oh, a nice woman," she answered, bending her gray head; her thin gray hair was parted in the middle and thin gray braids were wound around her head like rats' tails. Her face was flushed; she had a rough frame. "Mrs. Lichkov brings her laundry here; you can bring it when you come to work." I set off down the street. Mrs. Lichkov hugged me at the door. "My daughters," she said in Russian, introducing me, "Dora and Elsa." Dora was almost eighteen; Elsa looked about sixteen. "My husband will be home later," she promised. "You'll like him; his name is Boris." "Can I go to my room?" I asked her like a robot. "Oh, yes. Here it is," she said, opening a door halfway down the hall; it was a bright white room with a brass bed and a night stand with a pitcher and water. "We'll get you a rug from the attic," Dora promised. "And some flowers," Elsa said; "I'll get some roses." I sat on the edge of the bed until they came back. Dora spread out the flowered red rug; Elsa set the roses in their vase on the table near the bed. "Leave her for a while," Mrs. Lichkov whispered. I put the valise under the bed and lay down flat, staring at the ceiling. I could not do anymore. I turned over on my side and cried myself to sleep.

"Dinnertime," Mrs. Lichkov said, waking me up. There was a big brass samovar steaming on a little table near the big oval one; I sat down on the chair she motioned at for me. "Now grace," she said with satisfaction. I folded my hands in my lap and moved my lips. They began passing around the dishes of sausages, the tray of sliced bread, the sauerkraut. Dora put a cup of hot tea down next to me. The whole family chattered happily around me. I ate mechanically. "She must have told them to act as if nothing was happening," I thought chewing a sausage; I could see pepper grains in it, but it had no taste, no taste at all. "That's funny," I thought remotely, observing myself. There were two windows in the dining room, and a long mirror between them. I stared at the mirror and stared at it. Dora must have followed my look. "Momma says it's the old Russian style, putting the mirror there." I didn't answer. Mrs. Lichkov hurriedly asked Dora something about her day at the kindergarten where she was in charge, and the chatter began automatically again. "Anya has very interesting dreams," Mrs. Lichkov said pushing back her chair; "maybe she'll tell us about them some time." "If you'll excuse me," I said in a little voice, "I will go to my room."

21

THE job at the laundry was an easy one. Some of the women were bent over the big washtubs; others were wringing out the clothes; some were around the room ironing, one ironing board after another along all four of the walls. The room was half underground; we could see shoes, feet, knees, passing endlessly. All I had to do was fold linens; I folded the days like linens, week after week. None of them belonged to me. The women talked about their families, their parents, their husbands, their children. It was soothing, very soothing. There were no men there to hide from. The bitterness was getting steamed out of me as I sat there in the moist heat of the laundry. There were lives going on around me; there were normal places. The moisture was doing wonderful things for my skin. My face had lost its white flaky layer; the cracks in the soles of my feet and my heels were filling; walking was not painful. At night, I would take off my shoes and look at my feet: a miracle. They were seamless, perfectly mended. "She has a cough," one woman was saying about her daughter; "I gave her rhubarb syrup." "Licorice is better," another woman added, not looking up from her iron. "Look at this shirt," she said, holding it up; "what do men need with so many ruffles? These Germans!" "My sister's baby is almost here," another one said. "How long now?" "A few days maybe." "Which one is it?" "Her third." "Did she hear anything about her husband?" "No, no one's gotten letters from the front, not for weeks." "He'll be a big boy when his father gets home," the woman said from her ironing board. "Oh, the war can't go on forever," the other protested. "It's trying," someone chimed in.

"Do you have any children?" one of them asked me. "Lost. By the Russians," I added automatically, folding a sheet. "Somebody probably got her; you'll get her back. The Russians love children. You know, a terrible thing, a woman got a child, and it was a Jew. She had to give it to be shot," the woman said, pressing down on a collar, pushing its nose into a corner. "That's terrible," I agreed. "Yes," the woman answered; "imagine it, taking it in, you think it's normal, you know, and it turns out to be a Jew; the war is messing everything up." I went on with my folding. I wondered about Rutkauskus. He must have been back from prison a long time now. So Ninka had her Daddy and her Mommiti. "If the war ends, and we're liberated," a voice said, coming out of the tub, "we could go wherever we want." "Where would you go?" someone else jeered; "you never went anywhere before." "It's just nice to know you could," the first woman huffed, insulted. "You know," she said, straightening her back as she got up from the tub, then holding onto it with the back of her palm, "I heard a story today. A man got sick and his mother prayed they would take her instead of him, and he got better, and she died." "Everyone knows that," one of the women said from the walls. "That's why it's dangerous to get sick if your daughter is pregnant," I put in. There was a sudden silence. "Why?" "Well, if you get sick," I repeated what Momma had told me, "it's very dangerous because whenever someone is born, someone has to die. So if you get sick, and you're the mother, you're the closest one, and usually you don't survive. It doesn't have to be the mother, just the one closest to the pregnant one who gets sick." "Is that true?" one of them asked in an awed voice. "It happened three times in my family," I said; "if I find my daughter, and she ever has children, I'm going to spend all my time praying I don't get sick." "I think *my* daughter is pregnant," one of the women whispered in a terrified voice.

They all looked at me with new respect. "We never heard of that before," the woman gasped from behind the ironing board. "No," echoed the others. "It's true," I said, folding another sheet. "Do you know any more things like that?" one of them asked me. "Well, according to the Lithuanians, if you change crosses, you change fates," I said thoughtfully. "This isn't mine," I said, picking up Onucia's big iron cross; "I gave my gold one to a woman who said she would help me look for my daughter, Luisa, and she gave me her cross." "I wonder what happened to her," one of them said in a hushed voice. "She's not in a laundry, that's for sure," I said, "although she might be if we hadn't changed crosses." "Where could she be?" one of the women asked in a hollow voice. "Your guess is as good as mine," I answered, folding a blanket. "Do you know any more of those?" another woman asked me. "I'll think about it," I promised her.

And so the weeks went by, six weeks, eight weeks. "Fat is good for the abscesses," one of the women said; "I saw it in the Russian prisoners' hospital. As long as you keep on a bandage, so the lice don't get their breakfast too." "What's that hospital like?" I asked her, not looking up. "Terrible," she answered, putting some shirts into the wringer, "people with half-faces, no arms, no legs, terrible; and the smell, it would be better to bury them, they're already half-manure; I quit right away. There's a better hospital near Mrs. Lichkov's, three blocks down from here, away from the railway station, just for the Germans. You know," she paused, "you look just like the pharmacist's wife, exactly. But," she said, putting another shirt sleeve in the wringer, "they were Jewish."

"I'm quitting the laundry," I told Mrs. Lichkov when I got home that night. "The moisture's no good for my lungs; I'm getting a cough." I gave a good imitation. "What will you do?" "They said there's a good hospital three blocks down from here." "I thought you didn't like hospitals," she reminded me. "Oh, I was mad then; I feel much better now. I'm really used to them." "As long as it's not the Russian hospital," she sighed. "Go to the Employment Agency in the morning; they always know when there's anything." "Again, Mrs. Vishinskaytie?" asked the man behind the counter; "what this time?" "I was coughing from the dampness. How about the German hospital?" "They need someone to wash bottles and test tubes," he mumbled, rummaging through his shopworn file; "you want to go? You're sure the germs aren't bad for you?" "I'm going," I said. "Try to keep this job. Three blocks past your house," he reminded me, "a big brick building. You'll recognize it; it's on a big lot, with ambulances."

"I am looking for a job in the lab," I told a nurse in the big tiled corridor. "First door to the left," she answered, squeaking off on her rubber shoes. An old gray-haired man rose up from behind a counter. "Tying my shoes," he muttered, embarrassed. "What do you want here? This is the lab." "I can wash the bottles and test tubes," I told him. "Oh," he said, relieved; "you're from the agency. I thought you were here for an abortion or something." He disappeared behind the low counter again. "Damn laces!" he exclaimed in German; "who needs such boots in the heat? So," he said, coming around the counter to me. I was dressed terribly, in an old skirt and a blouse I had gotten from the laundry for a few cents. "Let me see your hands." I stuck them out. "All right," he said; "I'll call him. Von Ehrenberg," he roared into the hall. A tall blond man with blue eyes appeared in full uniform. "He's a doctor," the old man said; "he just likes playing soldier better. Do you want her to work for you with the bottles and the test tubes?" Von Ehrenberg looked me up and down. "Fine," he said; "I'll teach her." "It shouldn't take much teaching," the old man said, leaving.

"Wouldn't you rather do blood counts?" Von Ehrenberg asked me. "I don't know how," I told him; "I'm only a *putzfrau*." "You look intelligent to me," he said; "I'll teach you." He got out the slides. "So," he began on the microscope, "first the focusing." I pretended to practice. "You learn fast," he said with admiration. "Now," he said, taking the dropper, "the stain, you smear it like this." He drew a small glass line down the slide; it was evenly covered. I imitated him easily. "You won't have any trouble," he assured me. By the end of the afternoon, I was left to myself with the blood counts. "You're very good and industrious," he said. "Thank you, Captain," I answered, my head bent over the slide. But I didn't like it. I was standing out too much here; I thought he was suspicious of how fast I was learning.

Three weeks later he came in smiling. "Would you like to go to a football game Saturday?" "Oh, I can't," I answered without thinking; "I have too much work in the lab." I knew it was a stupid answer right away. "I can excuse anyone from work in this lab," he said softly. "But the counts here aren't good; my conscience wouldn't let me," I cried. "Are you sure?" he asked. "Oh, but some other time; of course!" I said. "Look at this count; someone's very sick out there." He walked out of the room. He was as shiny as a new automobile. Then it began to happen more frequently. Did I want to go out to dinner? No, I had to babysit for a woman I met when I worked at the laundry. Did I want to go for a drive in the automobile? I had a cold. I knew I was running out of excuses. Outside, the heat was getting unbearable; the real Polish summer was here. "How about coming to a show this Saturday?" the captain asked me. "It will be nice. They're holding it near a river and lighting it up with lanterns. It will be very cool." "Oh, I cannot!" I cried. "I've just lost my child and my husband by the Russians, and I'm sore inside; I can't enjoy myself. You wouldn't have a good time; really, I can't do it." Before my eyes, his face changed. It was a round window streaked with ice. "Did you think about what you said?" he asked me. "Yes," I answerd slowly. "You're sure you thought about it?" "Yes," I answered again. "Thank you," he said, bowing, and went out.

"This is the end," I thought, getting my things together, starting to walk back to Mrs. Lichkov's house. "Something's the matter," she cried, seeing my face in the door. "I don't know yet," I told her; "maybe. I'm going to lie down." I stretched out on the bed fully dressed. Not a half hour passed before I heard a car pull up in front of the house. The engine raced, and then went dead. I knew what it was. "What do you want with her?" Mrs. Lichkov was shouting. "We have orders to pick her up," a man's voice answered, "to take her to prison." "What for?" Dora cried. "Where is she?" the man asked. The door to my room opened. A man in a Gestapo uniform was standing in the door, Mrs. Lichkov and her two daughters behind him. "What is it?" I asked without sitting up. "You are under arrest; if you want my advice, it will be better to come peacefully." I got up and walked out after him. "Take your things," he ordered me sternly. Dora ran into the room and got the little valise, stuffing the few things I had in it; she handed it to me. "We will come to see her in prison," Mrs. Lichkov warned; "you can't just yank off a citizen with no reason at all." "We have a reason; the judge will decide what to do with her. Come!" he ordered me, and I went down the long hall between them.

As soon as the front door opened, the motor of the car started up again. There were two more soldiers in the car, and three girls. "They're going to take us to a camp and finish us off," I thought. But the driver steered like crazy, swerving to avoid an ox cart on its way into the city. We were getting farther out, into the fields; the peasants' carts were on the move around us. The driver plowed through them, scattering them like weed-puffs. Suddenly the car lurched to the right and stopped in front of a dark gray stone building. There were bars all over the windows. "Out, filthy spies!" the soldier ordered us. "Tomorrow for the trial; *then* we'll get to shoot you. Everyone in a separate cell," he told the soldier coming to the door; "we don't want them sharing their lies." They took us down a flight of stairs. From the dampness, I knew it was the basement. "In here," the Gestapo officer said, pushing me in, slamming the door, ramming a bolt into place. I couldn't believe it. Spying! "Let me out! Let me out!" I started screaming. I screamed until I was hoarse. A young soldier came to the door; I was young, too. "Sorry," he said, looking in and going off.

The door was opening, shoving me farther into the cell. "Get up," the officer commanded. I must have knocked myself out. Perhaps it's better, not to know anything, I thought. "Get up," he said again; "you're going to the judge. Enjoy the trip," he mocked. "Take breaths; you know the sentence for spying." "I have not been spying!" I screamed. "No one spies," he laughed at me; "that's why we have so much disappearing from the hospital and so many trains blowing up. We know all about you Russians and the partisans." "Partisans!" I gasped; "what are you talking about? I'm not brave enough to be partisan." "The judge will tell you, I don't doubt," he said, dragging me out of the cell. I had backed against the wall. He pulled me up the steps after him. The sunlight blew up in my eyes like a mine. "Pray a partisan blows up the car," he sneered; "it's easier than a German court."

The car bumped along through the beginnings of a blue and pink day. I was squashed against the same girl who had been in the car yesterday; she had dark hair and green eyes. Her hair was very, very clean. How did she do it? "For spying also?" I whispered to her. "Yes," she whispered back, "and I did do it." "No talking!" the guard sitting on my left commanded, thrusting his rifle back in our direction. The car stopped in front of a big brick building. "Out! All out!" the same soldier commanded; "up to the second floor." We trooped into the innocent-looking house. The soldier hesitated in front of the door; there were armed guards in Gestapo uniforms on both sides of it. "In here," he said, opening the door; "in here." The three of us walked into an enormous square room; the room seemed to have backed away from us, four white horizons, set at right angles to each other, sealing us in. Facing us was a big wall with a huge blackboard; a whip lay on the shelf meant for chalk. In each corner was a little table with two wooden chairs, one for the examiner, and one for the prisoner. In one corner, a Gestapo officer was already examining a young woman.

"Straight ahead," the soldier in back of us ordered. I saw the Russian girl going to the left. "You are accused of a terrible crime," the Gestapo officer said before I even settled on the chair; "you know that? You have been accused of stealing medicine for the partisans." I didn't answer. Something was making me look into all corners of the room. *"Nicht Deutsch! Nicht Deutsch!"* I kept explaining. "You mean to tell me," he said, pounding on the table with both fists, "an intelligent woman like you, a woman with a degree, doesn't speak German?" *"Nicht Deutsch,"* I insisted again and again, and still, I was looking all around the room. The officer examining the Russian girl looked familiar to me.

I got up, knocking over my chair, and ran over to him. In back of me, the Gestapo officer was screaming and roaring, grabbing my arms, holding them behind my back. "Oh, sir," I babbled in Polish, "I've been accused falsely, just because I wouldn't go out with him; he gave me cod liver oil and a white uniform. I didn't do anything, believe me, I didn't do anything; I remember you from Warsaw, I'm Polish," I babbled; "I don't speak a word of German." The other officer was trying to drag me away. "Go back to the table," the second officer said to me urgently. "I'll come over there when I'm finished here," he told my examiner.

"What are you trying to do?" the first Gestapo officer was thundering at me. "Do you want me to take the whip to you?" He was roaring and thrashing the whip against the desk. "Answer me, tell me who gave you the medicines! You won't tell?" he snarled. "See that whip? See what's on it? Pieces of flesh!" *"Nicht Deutsch! Nicht Deutsch!"* I kept insisting. "Stop the nonsense!" he roared. "What's the trouble?" the second officer asked, coming over. "She says she doesn't speak a word of German," the first one bellowed; "I'll take the whip to her!" "What language do you speak?" he asked me in German. *"Nicht Deutsch!"* I insisted again. "Do you speak Polish?" he asked me in Polish. "Polish, yes—and Lithuanian," I added in a hurry; I knew they didn't speak a word of it. "She speaks Polish," he said to the first officer. "I'll ask her questions for you." "Yes, Lieutenant," the first one answered, the blood leaving his face; he was outranked. "Look," the new one said; "it's time for lunch; we should eat and drink a little anyway." "Yes, Lieutenant," the other said stiffly. I went to the lieutenant's table.

"I told you," I insisted; "it's only because I wouldn't go out with him. My husband was just killed by the Russians and my child is lost; how could I do it? I know you," I insisted. "What do you mean?" he asked, startled. His face was familiar. If it was familiar, and he spoke Polish, he must be from Warsaw. I was sure of it; he was sitting at a café flirting, a terrible flirt. "I saw you once at the Café Adria," I said. "You did?" he smiled, starting to preen. "Oh, yes, I remember," I went on, "such a handsome man, who could forget you? But you didn't call my telephone," I reproached him. "Perhaps I can make up for it now," he said. The first officer was staring at us; he didn't understand a word of Polish. "This is a complicated case," the lieutenant told the first officer; "I think someone is using her to cover up his own doings. It should be left until after lunch so I have a chance to think through it." "Yes, Lieutenant," the first man answered in German. "You have until lunch is over," the first one told me in German. "What did he say?" I asked in Polish, turning to the lieutenant. "He says you have until after lunch," he repeated. "Stop playing silly tricks on her," he commanded; "she doesn't understand German." "What should I do with these?" someone called from the direction of his table. He was holding up the Russian girl's boots. "How should I know?" the lieutenant asked. "Take them down to the officer in charge of transports." "What happened to her?" I asked him in Polish. "Shot," he answered, "she was spying." "She told you?" "Of course. Anyway," he said, uninterested, "we knew."

He moved aside while two guards came up and took me down a flight of steps. "Another wet cellar, another one." In the cell, I leaned against the wet wall. I was trembling all over. What had made me run to that man and not to another or another? What had made me recognize him and speak Polish to him? What had made me run from the table? Now, later, I could see the first Gestapo officer's face; he was too shocked to move. Everyone obeyed him. He could have shot me where I stood talking. I leaned back against the wet wall, exhausted.

The senator, the famous rabbi, who had married us, was standing in front of us; we were all dressed as we were during the ceremony. "You and your child are going to America," he said, just as the door swung open; he disappeared. Who had thought of it? America! It was the Gestapo lieutenant. "Look," he said, "I can't do anything right away. They'll examine you upstairs in Polish. I've already explained everything. You just tell him what you told me—how you didn't want to go out with Von Ehrenberg, and how you were accused to cover up for someone else because there was no medicine where you were; you were only in a lab. Do you understand?" I nodded. "I think I remember the beautiful girl you once were," he said flirtatiously. It occurred to me he was probably homesick. Such powerful emotions were loose in the air; they settled on your shoulder like a blessing or bullet, agreeing with history or contradicting it.

It happened as he predicted. When the man examining me had finished, the lieutenant came over. "I'll take her down," he told the other. "I can't do anything right away," he said again. "I have to talk to some people. But I can do it; don't worry. The thing is, you have to stay in the cellar for about three days. Can you do it?" "Oh, yes," I sighed, "I trust you; we're the same blood. I only thank God I'm in your hands, not that other one's." "We'll talk about the future when you're released," he told me mysteriously. A few hours later, he managed to come down with some bread and meat. "Are you all right?" he asked anxiously. I nodded over my bread.

My cell had a little window; he would come and wave to me. Occasionally he came by with more food. The morning of the third day he came back. "All right," he told a soldier with him, "let the dangerous criminal out. The commandant has decided she's innocent." He stopped me at the head of the stairs. "I'll come tonight with your papers," he told me, "but you have to leave right away, in the morning, because once Captain Von Ehrenberg finds out—he's got the blood of a count; it never cools off—he won't rest until you're accused again, and then I won't be able to do anything." I nodded my head dumbly.

When had I seen him in Warsaw? It had not been with Stajoe, I was sure of that. The only other times I'd been in Warsaw had been for my friend's wedding, and then to have my trousseau made and to meet Stajoe's parents. I was drawn into myself, marveling at my own luck. "It seems arranged," I said out loud. "What do you mean?" he asked. "Of course I arranged it." "No," I interrupted, "it seems arranged I should meet you; that's what I mean." "It does," he agreed, importantly; "I'll be there tonight." "You know where it is for sure?" I asked him. "The Lichkovs have been here a hundred times." He shook his head. "As soon as it's dark," he promised, "and don't forget my name," he warned me, presenting it to me like gold: "Joseph Jankowski."

The Lichkovs threw their arms around me, crying; I had gone through all the alleys and back streets. "I have to go," I told them; "there's a lieutenant who's coming with my papers and things. He says the other, the captain, is after me." "I understand," Mrs. Lichkov said. The bell rang; the lieutenant was standing there with my valise. "I am embarrassed," he said coming into the dining room. "The canteen is closed; I couldn't get very much, just some cheese and a little dry sausage and a loaf of bread. But here is some money; it's all I have." He gave the parcel to Mrs. Lichkov and put the money in my hand, folding my fingers over it. "I'll come get her early in the morning; she has to get the first train." "But it's a freight train!" Mrs. Lichkov protested. "There's nothing I can do about that," he said guilty; "at least it's running, which is more than you can say for most of them."

"What will you do?" Dora asked me. "Go back to Vilno," I told her. "It's my home; I have to look for my child." It had been almost three months since I'd left her. "It won't take too long; you'll surely find her," Mrs. Lichkov assured me. "And no more bad dreams." "I had a good one in the prison," I told her. "What was it?" they all asked. "The priest who married me said I would find my child; he was standing there as if it were the day of my wedding." "That really is a good dream!" Mrs. Lichkov exclaimed. "Weren't the others?" I asked mischievously. "Oh, yes," she swore; "but this is better, definitely better."

Early in the morning, the lieutenant came over and brought me the ticket, papers, and a tiny little package. "A little more cheese," he apologized; "nothing is open." I said goodbye to the family. He was dressed in civilian clothes and had borrowed a civilian car. "It's because of my fiancée I'm in the Gestapo," he swore, pulling away from the sidewalk. I was leaning out to wave to the Lichkovs. "Keep your head in," he ordered automatically. "When the war is over, you will see," he went on, "we'll get together. I think I remember how beautiful you were; you'll be beautiful with me again. When you find your child," he said, handing me a piece of paper, "I want you to go to my sister's in Lodz; she has a very big place. It will be very good for a child. And here," he said, giving me another piece of paper, "is my Field Post Number.

Please memorize it and throw it away." These numbers were kept fanatically secret, especially those of Gestapo officers. "I will," I promised him. "When the war is over, we'll marry," he said, turning his head to me. "As soon as I saw you, I fell in love with you," he insisted, "only my mother loved my fiancée," he pouted. After all this bloodshed, they still hungered for purity, especially in their women! "It's just that you are homesick," I said, flirting. "Homesick! I am not homesick!" His dignity was insulted. "No," he went on; "I want to marry you; I know what I'm talking about." "A handsome man like you, if you get married, you'll start another war in Poland." He smiled, delighted. "You'll look so much better when I'm taking care of you; I'm looking forward to it." Again I thought of Momma: "A woman must always look her best." God only knew what I looked like, all this time without sleep in the cellar, but I could look worse; I was sure of that.

We were pulling up in front of the station. The freight train was already there. "After the war," he swore, kissing my hand. "Let me help you on," he insisted. The train was crowded, filled with peasants hauling live chickens in boxes to the big city, big crockery jars of milk and buttermilk, and cheeses covered with damp cloths. "The biggest bandits, the Polish men, the gentiles," Momma was saying; "they kiss your hand after slitting your throat. They even kiss their own mothers' hands after dinner." And so they did. "What car do you want?" he asked me. "In the middle," I answered; "it's safest." "After the war," he said again, leaving the train. "You'll write to me," he called in through the window. "Of course, of course," I promised. He stood on one side watching me at the window until the train pulled out.

The train was traveling very fast. There was tremendous fear of the partisans and their mines. "They think if they go faster, they'll get there before the mines," a woman muttered, thrown against me for the hundredth time. There was the cackling of chickens and the heavy smell of curdled milk and cheeses. After one hour, I was beginning to settle in. Then, there was no warning at all, came a tremendous explosion. The front of our car rose toward me in slow motion. I saw a woman's body settling toward me like a balloon. The train had hit a mine. "Good for the partisans," I thought. The woman's body was settling on me; her dress was blue and yellow-flowered.

402

I woke up on the ground. I felt for it with my fingers; it was grass. Someone was leaning over me. He swam into focus, an old peasant man. He was pouring something into my mouth; it kept running out the side. "Drink, whiskey, drink, little one," he kept repeating. "The bottle didn't break?" I gasped, amazed. "No, only the train broke. I got your papers and your things," he said, holding them up over my face. "Rest, rest." "What happened to everyone?" I asked. I could still see the woman falling toward me. "A lot killed," he sighed; "the trains are not so good." I took my hand from my face; it was covered with blood. "A heavy shelf hit you," he apologized as if he had done it himself, "you're injured." "Oh," I said; I tried to sit up, but I was dizzy. "Wait, wait, there's no hurry," he scolded me. "It will take a long time; they have to fix the tracks." "How will they do it?" "They won't. They send a train from Vilno to get us; then they fix. So we'll be here all night. Just lie still, no moving; it's the best thing, lying still. I see stars; can you see them?" he asked as if he were talking to a child. "I must have gotten thinner again," I realized; "I must look like I'm ten years old." "They're beautiful," I murmured. "Fresh air is good, too; you'll be better in the morning, I promise." "Were a lot killed?" I asked him. "Maybe half."

I woke up covered with a light dew; it was very cool and nice. The grass was wet and sparkling, shattered chandeliers, little crystals of water. "Nice," the old man said, sitting up. "I bet you, in ten minutes, a train." "That's not fair," I complained; "I see the steam cloud already." "See, how you are better!" he said triumphant. The train backed up to us. The old man took me under the shoulders, helping me along. "You're very strong," I told him, leaning heavily. "Goat's milk," he answered; "my momma wouldn't let us drink from a cow." The train was circling in the air, then settled on the ground. "You are dizzy," he accused me. "A little," I admitted. He lowered me into a seat. "More whiskey," he ordered. I drank some down and fell asleep.

"Vilno," he whispered; "come on, little lady." We were back at the Vilno Station. No one would recognize me for a while. The sliver of mirror between my pictures showed me a face swollen and purple. I leaned heavily on his arm. A hysterical old lady in a long black coat was running up to us with crooked little chicken steps. "Roach!" she screamed at him. "You are both drunk! You are so old,

403

you old fool, to have an affair with her. At your age, don't you ever get tired?" "Please, Eva," he begged, "we're not drunk; it was an accident. You heard about the accident?" "Don't accident me," she shrieked, coming after him with an umbrella. "Please, Mrs.," I begged; "it was an accident. I was unconscious; he helped me. I could be dead. God will bless you and give you long lives together for what he did for me and everyone. He doesn't deserve such treatment." She began to calm down and look at me. "You are not drunk?" she asked. "Not at all, only dizzy," I answered; "see my head?" I pushed some of my hair back, feeling the huge swelling. Her hand flew to her mouth. "A gash," she whispered. "I *told* you," her husband said; "I had to carry her. An affair with a half-dead person, Eva, for shame." She took me under the other arm. What was I going to do? This was the city where I studied medicine, where my parents lived. When I was better, anyone could recognize me.

"I don't know what I'm going to do, Mrs. Eva," I began, starting to cry. "Your husband is not drunk but mine is, and if he sees me looking like this, he will kill me off for good. I have to find a place until I look better." "Stefan," she said in an accusing voice. "My nephew has a little hotel near the station," he told me. "Stefan, hurry up." She pulled us along. There were soldiers all over. "Something is going on with the war," I whispered. "They are back and forth, back and forth all day," Eva said. "German soldiers. But we don't know what." We came to a little brick hotel near the station. "Stefan!" she said again. "I'm going," he sulked; "first you scream on me, and now you want her in a room." He trudged off, trudged back and reported. "My nephew has a little room on the first floor you can have." "Would you do me one last favor?" I begged. "Stefan!" Eva said again. "I hear her," he whimpered. "Please ask your blessed nephew to put a big pail of cold water in my room, and a big sign saying *Do Not Disturb* on the door. My brains are all disturbed by that flying shelf. I can't take the chance my husband should see me." "Stefan, please go. Poor thing," she said, turning to me; "a bad husband, what a curse. I know, believe me," she said sympathetically. "He did not bother you too much?" "Not at all!" I cried, then pressed my head. "Funny," she mused; "what a pest he usually is."

"It is arranged," Stefan told her. "About time," she complained. "Let's take her in, look how weak she is, like a kitten." Eva put me on the bed. "God bless you and a long life," I said weakly. "God bless you, my dear, and may your husband roast in hell, drunks, God's cockroaches," she snarled. "You have some food?" she asked. "In her packages," Stefan volunteered. "You searched them?" Eva demanded suspicious. "I told him to," I piped up weakly. "Good he didn't eat it," she said sourly. "We will go. Rest and be beautiful; it's important with a drunk," she said, glowering at her husband.

When they left, I got up and locked the door. The DO NOT DISTURB sign was in place. Then I went to the window and fastened the wooden shutters; thin knives of light speared into the room. I was on the first floor. I took out my bread and cheese and cut each into fourteen identical pieces, laying them out on the little white towel covering the small table near the bed. "Enough for fourteen days," I said to myself, climbing into bed, falling asleep. "Now I'm in the scorpion's nest, but good," I thought, seeing the black uniforms with their dead faces, the skulls and crossbones. "I cannot move at all."

22

THERE was a chamber pot in my room; I did not have to go out at all. Occasionally, I could hear a woman's voice outside the door. One day it was, "But how can I clean the room? She never comes out. I don't even know if she's alive." Then a thick man's voice told the maid his uncle had instructed that the woman be left alone in there for as long as she wanted. I never went to the window. I only kept track of the days. I could do that either by counting the number of times the knives of light sliced into my room, or by counting the narrow strips of bread and cheese left on my table. There were eight pairs of bread and cheese strips left. The swelling on my head was beginning to go down. Every morning, I rationed out a cup of water for washing myself. I paid most attention to my head and eye, keeping the cut clean, and then letting the rag rest over the swelling. As the water evaporated, the rag cooled. Every day the swelling evaporated a little with it.

After eating seven of the bread and cheese strips, I was looking through my packet of pictures when I found the two pieces of paper from the Gestapo lieutenant; he had given me a little pencil and forgotten to take it back. "I will write something," I thought to myself, and on my back, began to write down all the times I had escaped from death. I did it mechanically, as if I were taking inventory. The list was very long. "I am sorry, Poppa," I said out loud when I finished it, "I believe in fate, I believe in a superpower; there is something that wants me to live."

But otherwise I did not think. My mind was a radio in a bombed house. And then I would look at the little pieces of bread and cheese and the falling level of water in the pail, leaving a little white ring from the day before. I would look at my list and wonder if I was still deceived. My bowels were cooperating with me; they had stopped working. I was shut up like a nun in the little white room with the closed shutters. I rarely got off the bed. "She's dead in there; we ought to look," the woman's voice came under the door. "I am not dead," I called out, startled at the sound of my own voice; the woman went away. The room was on the first floor, the first floor. Outside were the sound of *drozhkas*, people talking, train whistles. I never went to the window. On the fourteenth day, I looked at the last piece of bread and cheese and ate it. I felt stronger than before, much stronger. I got off the bed and looked at myself in the mirror on the door. I looked like a ten-year-old child made of white wax; huge empty blue eyes stared out at me. Then there was a commotion outside the window; many women were shouting to each other.

"They are running!" one of them shouted. "The Germans are running!" another one shouted. "The Russian tanks are on the outskirts," someone else was screaming; "the bombing is started!" "I see fire," another voice cried. I lay still and waited. The knives marched across the floor of the room. Then the women's voices were gone. "They're hiding; that's good," I thought. I went to the shutters and looked through the cracks. Germans in dirty torn uniforms, unshaven, were running down the main streets; some of them were bandaged. A Mendelssohn concerto switched itself on in my head; it was playing as loud as Beethoven's *Ninth Symphony*. "It is a pleasure to look at them," I thought to myself, not bothering to move, "a pleasure to look at them." More and more German soldiers ran down the street. "They came as if they were going to a dance or a dinner," I remembered; "now they are running like rats." There was the thunder of bombs and shelling in the background. "The city will be destroyed," I thought comfortably; "and how beautiful I look, a candle on an altar. They are burning up memories; they are burning up open graves; they are cleaning the city. It's only right, it's only right."

I stood there watching until after four o'clock, the time to get ready for supper. Then I opened the door and walked out like a wax shadow from my room. I overheard someone saying that the big canteen, with all kinds of goodies, was open; anyone could take what they wanted. Anyone! I was anyone again! "I have to get something to eat," I thought to myself suddenly; I wasn't dead. No, I looked at my arm; I wasn't dead. I took out my pictures and looked at them, then I looked at my list. I took a deep breath and went into the street.

The canteen was close to the hotel, but the locusts had already come and gone. There was a big box of cookies in a fancy tin box; I took them out and wrapped them in a cloth. "Don't touch them," I said to myself, as if I were making a vow; "these are for Ninka." They were a sacred treasure. "Now I have to find the bathroom and the janitor," I told myself, starting back to the hotel.

The janitor wasn't hard to find; she was running from room to room, pulling out fur coats, money, jewelry, anything she could find. "Listen," I said to her, "you can't stay here; they're destroying the city. We have to leave." She rushed passed me madly, burrowing into another room. "Look!" she said, coming out with a handful of rings; "gold, everything you want." "It won't do any good if a bomb hits this building," I pleaded with her; I was too weak to leave alone. "Just a little more," she called to me, plunging like a crazy fish into another room. "Look, silk robes," she called out, coming into the hall with them draped over her arm. "They will bury you in them," I answered weakly, leaning against the wall. "Why don't you look?" she coaxed me; "you can get whatever you want; you don't have much." "I hear the bombs," I argued; "what is the matter with you?" "In just a little while," she said, disappearing again. Finally she came out, red-splotched with excitement. "All right," she said; "I can come back. I have a cousin in the suburbs. We can go to him. But I don't know about you," she said, looking at me shrewdly; "I don't think you can make it." "I can make it," I whispered. "First you have to eat," she insisted; "once they get here it's not so easy to eat." She disappeared and came back in with a hen. I followed her into the kitchen. She took its head off with one swipe, plucked it, cleaned it, and threw it into a pot of boiling water. "I'll tell you one thing," she said, "I'm not going anywhere without eating. You look like a ghost," she said, looking from me to the pot and back again. "Eat," she insisted, giving me half the boiled chicken. I waved pieces in the air to cool it; I devoured it. "And the soup, it has plenty of salt," she said, shaking some more in before she handed it over. "Can we go now?" I asked, swallowing. The thunder from the tanks and bombs was getting louder and louder. "Let's go," she said, taking my arm. "What a pity to leave all this; I'll come back tomorrow." "You should

408

stay away from here," I insisted, leaning on her. We began our walk out of town.

"It's five miles to my cousin's," she warned me. "I don't think you can do it." "I'll go as fast as I can." My mind went dead; it fastened itself to my feet, making them work on strings. We were walking through the forest. "I cannot anymore," I told her; "I have to sit down and rest." "This is no place to rest," she insisted; "there are bullets all over." I listened. There were little whispering sounds, vicious insects, little pings. Something pinged into a tree. Bark splattered near our cheeks. We couldn't see a soul. "This is not good," she said again. "You'll have to go without me," I told her. She sighed and sat still. "Look," I said suddenly, pointing. She sat forward from the tree we were leaning on. There were two rows of little children with an elderly lady marching away between the trees; it looked like a vision. "Thank the Lord they're taking the children out," I said out loud. I couldn't see the faces of the children, but they were marching away through the woods, away from the flaming city.

By night time, we came to her cousin's, but the janitor woman couldn't stay still. "I'm going back to the city," she announced. "Don't," I pleaded. "Look," she told her cousin, "let her stay here; she doesn't have anyone." She handed me some slices of bread and tramped off down a little pine-needle path. The war was going on. "Hear the bullets?" he said. "You'd better dig a foxhole." I didn't know how to do it; I could barely lift a shawl. But it had to be done. I began to dig. In a few hours, I had a hole deep enough for my ankles. "You can sleep in the barn tonight," he said, "but tomorrow it better be deeper; you'll be killed by the bullets for sure." His hole was almost up to his shoulders; he didn't offer to help me. The next morning, there was more firing, more bullets. I started digging; the sun blazed down. The hole was only as deep as my waist. I kept digging; the sun was falling into a fox-hole of its own. "A few more inches," the man called to me from his hole; "your head is sticking out." Finally, I had a hole big enough to stand in. "Your head doesn't show now," the man called to me. "I'll put a pail of water near you; don't come out." I knew what was coming. I had taken off my bloomers and folded my brassiere around them; by now, my only brassiere was something made of strings and rags. It held my pictures, my little list, the mirror, the pencil, and a few crumbs of bread. "Will it be long?" I called to the man. "The Germans don't give up so fast; a week, ten days, maybe." I leaned back against the little wall of damp earth. It was dark and cool. I was starting to fall asleep.

The next morning the sounds of tanks firing woke me up; then bullets. I was very hungry. The last crumbs from my brassiere I ate last night; I wouldn't touch the cookies. I began to pull on the pieces of grass near the foxhole. "Cows eat them," I thought; "why not?" The day wore on. I ate more and more grass; the little patch of earth in front of me was bald. The next day was the same; I turned in the hole and ate another patch of grass. The third day, the same, and the fourth, and the sixth, and the seventh. The peasant never brought me anything. "He has bread," I thought bitterly, but I was afraid to complain. If he took me out of the hole, a bullet would find me right away. Then came the eighth day. I reached as far as I could for some grass: nothing, bare earth. My legs were numb. "They must be swollen," I thought; I tried to move them; they wouldn't move. I was going to starve to death in this grave. I stood there crying, patting the earth, looking for a few more shoots of green hair. There were none. On the ninth day, there still were none.

There was a rumble of a truck, then another. I heard some shouting in Russian. "Come here! Come here!" I started screaming in Russian at the top of my lungs. A truck stopped and pulled over. "Do you have any food?" I begged, crying. "I was looking for my child, and I got caught in the fire. I didn't eat; I was waiting for you." "I'm with the kitchen," a soldier said, getting out; "we have almost nothing too, just some bread." He pulled out a piece; it had his teethmarks in it. "Here, eat," he said; "I'll get you out of there soon. As soon as the rest of the equipment gets here, we'll get some more food and soldiers, I promise." I watched his green uniform with the red epaulettes retreating. "He won't come back," I thought, sobbing. Another soldier came over. *"Gde?"* he called, "where?" "Here!" I called. "Captain Ehrenberg," he said; "I have some American ham and orders to get you out." He handed me the ham first; I gobbled it down. "Now give me your arms," he ordered me. I reached up to him like a child. He pulled and pulled, but I would not move. "What is this?" he muttered to himself in astonishment. "I've been eating grass," I whimpered. *"Bozhe moy,"* he exclaimed. "Like Leningrad; you're all swollen up. We'll have to dig you out."

He came back with three soldiers and shovels. "Dig, watch out for her body, stupids!" he ordered. Carefully, they made the hole larger. "Now give me your arms," he instructed again. I reached up. "Still stuck." He shook his head in wonderment. "More," he ordered. "Hands up," he instructed again. Finally they pulled me out. My legs were swollen to four times their normal size; they were one solid column from thigh to ankle. "This is from the grass," the captain said, looking at my legs with horror; "I've seen this before. Go cut two big sticks from a tree," he ordered another soldier; "she can't walk like this." He carried me over to a tree and set me down. "Incredible!" he muttered. "I have to go find my child," I told him. "No, you can't," he said; "a child needs a mother with arms and legs. You'd be killed with her. What good would you be?" "She's near the city somewhere," I told him. "You can't go into the city," he insisted; "the whole place is filled with corpses; they're all over the street, heaps of corpses, dangling out of windows like rags. The Germans are in all the houses. They have rounds of ammunition they're using up now it's over. They know what's coming, so they think, why not get as many as they can? You know them. No, you can't go, if only because of the distance. There's disease all over. You couldn't go anyway," he said, looking at my legs; "you have to wait a few days for the water to drain out of your legs. You are an *invalid*. What good are you to her without your legs?" "I'll help you cook," I volunteered. "Fine, fine," he sighed; "just watching would be all right, too."

"At least," I insisted, "I have to call and find out about her. I know someone in the city; she could tell me something." "We can arrange that in about an hour," he said. "There's a little hotel ahead with a phone; can you call anyone?" "I want to call the neighbor who works in the pharmacy." He helped me into the truck. "Wait here," he said. I stared into the forest. I was afraid to look down at my legs. I was a monster. "All right," he said, starting up the engine.

"I got the number of the pharmacy from the switchboard," I called to him from my chair in the hotel; the hotel was still going on as if nothing had happened. "Are you Mrs. Rutkauskenie's neighbor?" I asked the crackly voice. "Yes," came the weak answer. "I am Otilia Vishin-

411

skaytie, trying to find out about Luisa Vishinskaya." There was a long silence. "Hello! Hello!" I shouted into the phone. "Rutkauskus and his wife were killed," the woman said. "They were arrested because of Cholem. Shot, Immediately shot. They arrested Luisa first." I stopped breathing. "She was Russian, they thought. They put her in a prison to be killed, but someone knew her there. Someone told me, they washed her in coffee. Maybe there were women from your ghetto whom they never got around to shooting and they knew you."

"Is she dead?" I asked loudly, holding onto the phone. "Not dead, in an orphanage." "An orphanage!" I wailed. "One of the soldiers, a Schraader, decided he wanted her. He hid her in an arch just outside the gates when they took the others in." "Where is the orphanage?" I screamed like a dying thing. "Far from the city, I think," the voice said. "What happened to Onucia's baby?" I heard myself asking. "Dead," came the voice. "How?" I asked. "They didn't know it was in the house when they arrested the parents. They locked and sealed everything; the baby starved to death, only a few weeks old." I dropped the phone. The captain picked it up, handing it to me. "Are you sure she's alive?" I asked the woman. "Yes, alive; Schraader may have taken her; he visits her all the time. Someone came in for something, a soldier; he told me. Look," she said, "I have to get out of here. There's a lot of noise; something is coming." She hung up. "Come on," the captain said, lifting me into the truck. "Come back and help us cook; then you'll tell me." "Why are the phones working?" I asked him. "It'll make less work for us later. A lot of lines are down; you were lucky." "It is horrible!" I cried, and then I couldn't say anymore. "In Leningrad, people ate rats," he said sadly, pushing down hard on the accelerator. We drove back through the forest to the Russian camp; the kitchen was set up. The captain carried me to a little bench. "Try wiggling those legs," he instructed me, "and I'll find out what you should do about the swelling." I just sat there crying. The captain was walking around, talking to everyone, everyone he talked to looked at my legs and shook their heads. I stopped watching him; I closed my eyes and listened to the sounds. There were the sounds of voices, speaking Russian. There was the smell of pine woods and birch woods; there were the sounds of footsteps on pine needles; there was the slight hissing of breezes through pine branches. The birch trees rustled like slips. "Try wiggling those legs," I would hear Captain Ehrenberg telling me in Russian; I wiggled them. I had no shoes. They had stuck in the foxhole. "It was lucky," I thought to myself, "these poor clothes didn't get pulled off like a banana skin; it wouldn't be a treat for them." A bigger breeze lifted and dropped some pine boughs; I moved a shoulder backward. Something didn't feel right. I felt with the other hand; its fingers were stiff and swollen. There was a hard sore lump under the arm. "An abscess," I sighed; "finally an abscess." And my stomach was constantly burning; I probably had an ulcer as well.

"*Zhenshina*," a male voice was saying to me, "woman, I don't know your name." "Anya Savikin," I said automatically. "I mean Anya Lavinsky." "Mine is Yakov Ehrenberg. So now we are introduced." "Drink this," he told me, handing me a cup of strong coffee. "One of the men says you should drink as much of it as you can to get the water out. Also, when we get potatoes, you should try to eat some of them raw; he says it takes the water out, too." I gulped the coffee down. "Don't drink so fast," he scolded, "you'll burn your throat." He came back with another cup. He left again, saying, "I have to start up the fires." He came back sometime later. "You can help with the dishing out."

The camp was slowly setting itself up. More and more trucks and tanks were filling the empty spaces around us. Across the little road, the peasant was staring at me in terror. Finally, he ran over like a fox. "Don't tell them you're Jewish," he begged me. "I am not Jewish." "Don't tell them," he insisted. "They think all Jews are Communists and they will start persecuting me; don't tell them." He shot back across the path, staring at me. "What did he want?" Captain Ehrenberg asked, coming back to me. He walked along slowly while I hobbled along on my two canes. "He says you're hunting Jews because they're Communists." "What does he mean?" Ehrenberg asked, puzzled; "we're all Communists now." "Maybe he means Jews are not Communists?" "An idiot," Ehrenberg muttered; "now we should start beating the trees here for enemies?" Bullets were still whistling through the branches. "While they have a gun and a bullet, they use it," he sighed. "Where do you come from?" I asked him. "I'm from Paltava." "Paltava," he smiled, "such a historical city. It breeds writers like mice; maybe I should go there when the war's over."

"Is that where you're from?" I asked, hobbling after him. "No, Leningrad," he said flatly; "the famous Leningrad." "Then I know how it is," I said. My legs were like two barrels. "You cannot," he answered me. "No one who was not there can understand what it was like." "You weren't there," I accused him. "My family was." "Did they survive?" "They say only the lowest survived; we were what you call *aristocrats*," he smiled bitterly, "so I don't expect anyone." "Still," I told him, "I have hope for my daughter, not much, but I have hope." "What can you do but have hope?" he asked; "I have hope, but I know it's hopeless; still, I hope. Soon I'll begin to hope there's an afterlife; then what will become of me, a good Communist?" We hobbled along in silence.

The noise of men was thickening. A silver mist was rising in the trees; the pine boughs near us were silvered by the moisture. "To tell you the truth," he said, "what we need more than a server is some morale. Why don't you sit in this clearing," he pointed to an overgrown field, "and pick some flowers for the tables?" I looked down at my legs. "Look at the ground," he said; "they're all over." At my feet little yellow flowers were growing, and blue ones, and some kind of purple flower that grew like a vine wound between them. "Here," he said, taking out his pocket knife and giving it to me; "call me when you fill your skirt." He lifted me up and put me down. I began slicing at the flower stems. My hands were getting sticky from sap. It was really summer. I began rubbing the yellow ones against my nose. There was a game we used to play with them. I couldn't remember it. "And there will be no one to remind me," I thought to myself. I tried to remember, but I couldn't do it. "Here," Captain Ehrenberg said, bending over me, "you take the coffee, I'll take the flowers. Pick some more; we have a lot of soldiers." "What are you doing with them?" "Putting them on a bench until you put them in pots," he said walking off. So I picked flowers until dinner was ready.

"Only a little bread with the coffee," someone warned Ehrenberg; "her stomach is shrunk. She should eat a lot in little bits." "Here," Ehrenberg said, giving me a piece of dried black bread; "dip it in the coffee." I did. "Drink some more," he urged. "Can I eat some potatoes?" I asked. A man was peeling them on the ground near the fire. "Maybe tomorrow," the soldier across from us said; "it's a miracle you can walk." "I want to start out right now, to find my baby, but Ehrenberg says no." "No is right," the second soldier said. "Look at those legs; they're all bloody. Wait until the water starts to go. It's going already. You just can't see it. These are nice flowers," he said, bending forward, sticking his nose into the middle of them. "Watch out for bees," Ehrenberg warned him; "this Poland has been no fun for us." I sighed and pulled out my mirror. My whole face was bright yellow with pollen. "Why didn't you tell me?" I complained, trying to wipe some off with the shoulder of my dress. "It looked interesting," Ehrenberg said seriously; "I thought it was the latest thing in Poland." "Very funny," I said crossly. "Too bad we don't have some leeches," someone said down the table. "They take out blood, not water," someone else answered him. It was getting dark. There were still bullets whizzing and pinging through the woods. "Let's set up her cot in the barn over there," Ehrenberg said to another soldier. An army cot materialized. They went off; I hobbled after them.

"What's this, what's this?" the peasant babbled. "A cot for me in the barn," I told him; "and if you don't keep quiet, I'm going to tell him you're a big capitalist because you have such big crops." He disappeared into the house. Ehrenberg pressed down on the little canvas cot with his spread-out palm. "She won't fall off that," he said, straightening up. "Listen," he told me, "we don't have any extra blankets; this is the best I can give you." He took out a heavy chenille German coat. "Keep it," he said, seeing my face. "The material is good; you can cut it up later." "I'm glad to have it," I assured him. "I think you're having trouble with that peasant," he said. "A little; he thinks I'm Jewish and the Russians are hunting Jews." "Aren't you Jewish?" Ehrenberg smiled; "I am."

"Chikov," he said to the soldier with him, "go get that man and drag him here." The peasant was dragged like a quaking tree. "I want you to translate into Polish for me," he told Chikov, who nodded. "We want you to be good to this woman. She's a good Russian woman living in Poland; Russia will be occupying the country now. We're leaving in a few days," he went on, "but we'll be back here in a week to check up." The peasant's head was an apple, bobbing up and down. "That should take care of him," Ehrenberg said when the Polish translation finished. "I'll be right

415

back," he told me, and came back with a pot of hot coffee and a tin cup. "Drink as much of this as you can," he instructed me, "and I am sure," he said, nodding to Chikov, who began translating again, "this man will let you use his outhouse and help you whenever he can, isn't that so?" The peasant nodded, purple.

"I wonder, Mrs. Lavinsky, how long it will take before these peasants become the salt of the earth we say they are." He was looking at my cot. "I will bet you three raw potatoes the name on your papers is not Mrs. Lavinsky," he smiled. "Of course it isn't," I answered him. "It's Otilia Vishinskaytie; I'm no idiot." "How is anyone going to find anyone else, or even themselves?" he asked himself, puffing on a cigarette. "He looks a lot like Erdmann," I thought to myself. "You're the second Ehrenberg I've met in a short time," I told him; "the other was German." "A soldier, or Gestapo?" "Gestapo," I answered. "If he's lucky, one of these bullets will get him," he said grimly; "we have no love for the Gestapo. So, good night," he said gruffly.

I lay down on the cot, and propped myself up on the pillow to drink the coffee. I drank until my stomach felt as if it would burn itself up. Then I would have to get off the cot, take the sticks, hobble out of the barn to the outhouse. Finally, I fell sound asleep. The sun was high when I woke up. "You missed a meal," Ehrenberg called to me when I hobbled up; "we saved some bread and coffee for you." "More coffee?" I asked, disgusted. "Coffee with one potato boiled in it." I looked at the chocolate potato. "Here," he said, handing me a tin spoon; "we have six or seven of those brown potatoes." "Some stew," I said, gulping it all down. "But look at the legs," he said; "you have knees again." "Maybe tomorrow I'll have ankles." "How about the flowers?" he asked, pointing at the field. "I'll go farther in; maybe I'll find different ones farther in." "No," he said. "Why not?" I asked, surprised. "More soldiers, more bullets. It will go on for weeks; they don't stop. Right here or nowhere." Again, he gave me the knife. "Two days of the same flowers; that's what I call permanence," he said, watching me try to make them stand up in the big food pots.

A truck came roaring up and skidded in the pine needles. "Chikov!" Ehrenberg thundered. "I told you! They're slippery as ice!" "Orders, Captain," he called, hopping out of the truck. "We move out tomorrow," Ehrenberg told me; "what will you do then?" "Look for my child." "But you won't go into the city?" "Why should I? She's not there." "How will you go?" "Getting rides." "Chikov," he called again; they went across to the peasant's. "Mrs. Vishinskaytie has a very important mission deeper in," he told him. "See that some friend of yours passing takes her along." "Whatever you say, sir," the man babbled. "And don't forget, we'll be back," Chikov added without any prompting. They were such big men! They towered over the little peasant. So the day passed quietly, different soldiers suggesting different remedies for my legs, everyone pointing out how much better they were getting. I ate brown potato after brown potato, drank cups of coffee after cups of coffee, and soaked piece after piece of brown bread. "I found some sugar!" Chikov said in back of me, sticking a little iceberg of it in my coffee cup. I watched it pull up the coffee. I pulled it out and ate it like a caramel. "Delicious, really delicious!" I sighed. "You will be sorry when we go?" Ehrenberg asked. "Oh, yes," I told him. I really meant it. "No one has, not for a long time," he said.

In the morning there was the noise of departure; engines starting up, cries: "Where should I put this? Should we take this? How much longer before the kitchen is ready?" I hobbled over to Ehrenberg. "You have ankles," he said, smiling and pointing. "Ankles and a flower," I answered, taking a big yellow one that looked like a daisy from the top of my dress. "Put it in your buttonhole." "Not exactly proper military dress," he laughed. "Take it out when you see a general," I suggested. "Oh, it will be black by then," he said, unbuttoning his jacket and pulling the green of the flower through. "Nothing for me?" Chikov asked in Polish, coming up behind him. I pulled out a blue flower. "I like yellow better," he complained. "Then you can take turns," I said. "Then he can pick one of his own," Ehrenberg retorted. They went back to the trucks. "Finished!" Chikov called out. One by one, the cry went up from truck to truck. "Finished! Finished! Finished!" "Let's pull out then," Ehrenberg commanded. One at a time, motors spluttered into life and roared under the pines. The first of the trucks disappeared down the road; some tanks lumbered after them, then some trucks, more trucks; there was only the kitchen division left. "Good luck," Ehrenberg called, starting up his truck. "To you, too," I called out. He nodded and waved, his truck disappearing into the pines. A little train of exhaust lingered behind like a cigarette stub still burning.

"Are they gone?" the peasant asked me hysterically; he had not been normal since they arrived. "For a week, maybe two." "He said I should get you a ride deeper in; I remember it; I do," he insisted. "Come," he said, pulling my hand; "I have a package with a little food. We stand in front of the house. Someone comes by, a farmer, I know him, he takes you off." "Why do you want to get rid of me?" I asked him bitterly. "Oh, not that, not that," he insisted; "he said it, on a wagon, you have to be put on." "He also said something about bandages for my legs," I lied. "Right this minute," he cried, running into the house and coming out with a length of cotton. "How am I supposed to cut it?" I asked. "A knife, I thought it out," he said proudly. "Two-inch strips," I told him, "and wind them around my hand like yarn so I can take them in a ball."

We stood on the little road in front of his house, waiting. A wagon passed by. "Don't know him," the peasant said; another went by. "Or him," he said. "Henyk!" he shrieked at the third wagon. "This lady, she has to go to the orphanages in the country or the Russians come after us; you take her?" Henyk nodded violently. They helped me up into the straw in back of the wagon. It jolted along for almost an hour, my stomach rising and falling with it. "Orphanage," he said, reining in his horse; immediately, it slumped down in its saddle. "It's no fatter than I am," I thought while Henyk helped me down. I leaned on my two sticks and walked to the little wooden building. A nun dressed in civilian clothes came to the door. "Because of the Russians," she explained her dress; "they hate the clergy." I explained I was looking for my child, Luisa Vishinskaya; she might have been visited in an orphanage by a Gestapo officer named Schraader. "I don't think she's here," she answered sadly, "but I will bring them out." She lined the children up in the long dark hall. "Luisa Vishinskaya?" she called. No one answered. "Do any of them look familiar to you?" she asked hopefully. "No," I said, "they do not."

"We have a fourteen-year-old boy, Vladek. He knows all the orphanages; would you like him to go with you?" "I want to go," a tall young boy said at my elbow. "He was left by his mother; she didn't want him," the nun explained. "He knows every orphanage in Poland; he could help you, and," she went on, looking at my legs, "you need help. I'll ask the priest." She came back. "The priest says you can go," she told Vladek; "it's for a good cause." "Where are you going?" she asked me. "Farther out," I told her; "I had a hint she was far from the city." "The priest is going out for services," Vladek reminded the nun; "he could take us part way." "You see what a help he is?" she said; "he's a clever boy." "What's your daughter's name?" he asked me in Polish, blushing. "I'll write it down for you," I offered, taking out my pictures with the little papers and the tiny pencil. He turned purple and faced the wall. "He can't read," the nun whispered to me. "Her name is Luisa Vishinskaya. With such a good memory, I don't need to write it down for you." He came over to me, smiling.

"I'm going," the priest called. "Wait," Vladek yelled; "the mother said you would take us part way." "Of course," he said; "climb in." Vladek climbed in the wagon and pulled me up. "The riding makes you sick?" he asked. I nodded yes. "Try to look at one piece of the wagon," he suggested. "It helps," I said after a while. "I can't understand why you do it," he said, as we passed a house. "You haven't seen her for a long time, a long time. My mother just left me there in a basket, but they found her. And then she just ran away somewhere and I came to them myself. I was," he thought, "five. No, four." "Maybe she couldn't keep you." "She didn't want to," he said bitterly. "It's hard to know." "You know, Mrs. Vishinskaytie, I want to tell you, if you find her, she won't know who you are probably: it happens a lot. But the mother at the convent always says, 'a mother is someone who comes with a suitcase.' " "I don't have one," I said dully. "Oh, I can get you one; don't worry," he said, staring at the road we were leaving behind. "We have to get off here," he said, helping me down. "It's not too far; lean on my arm." He was strong as a young horse. We came up to the next orphanage. It was the same thing. No Luisa.

We stood in the middle of the road. "I think you should try nearer the city. You never can tell; maybe she went from one to another." "No, someone told me she's far out of it," I insisted. "You never can tell," he repeated, stubborn, turning red. "Stop, Father, stop!" he shouted to a wagon. There were a man and two women in it. "They're just people!" I said to him, stunned. "No, no, a priest from an orphanage near the city. The mother told you; they wear civilian clothes. This lady is looking for her baby," he called to them; "can you take us to your orphanage?" "By all means," the priest said; "get in."

"We're going back the way we came!" I shouted. "We're going farther into the city," Vladek insisted. "I don't want to," I cried. "You're supposed to listen to me," he said; "I know about the orphanages." We were bumping along past the peasant's house; he saw me from the roadside and ran into the barn. We bumped farther and farther along. "We'll be in the city soon!" I protested at the top of my lungs. "No, we're here," Vladek said. "But the priest said they had no Luisa here," I pleaded. "You need rest," Vladek said, "and food; this is the richest orphanage." I was too tired to argue. I let him help me out of the cart; I followed him into the long red brick building.

23

I CREPT in after them. The hall was cold as an ice box after the noonday sun. The priest and nuns looked at me, then at each other. "The first thing to do is give her a bath," the shorter of the two nuns suggested. "Then she needs some sleep," the other one said; "and those legs need bandaging." "I have something," I said suddenly, pulling the cotton strips out of my brassiere. The three of them looked embarrassed. "I lived through the bombing here in a foxhole," I went on, taking a deep breath, "and I even have a poison capsule, but all I want is my child, just to find her. We have been all over, all over," I cried, motioning to Vladek, "but we can't find her." "First things first," the priest said. "Go with the sisters. You want something to eat, young man?" The kitchen was dark; one shaft of light came in from between the trees. One of the sisters took a big iron washtub from a nail on the wall and set it in the middle of the column of the pool of light. Vladek came in with a pail of water. "We want to pray for your child," the priest told me, coming in where I was sitting on a little bench. "What is her name?" "Luisa. Luisa Vishinskaya." "We will pray," he assured me, leaving. "Empty the pail," the nun told Vladek after a while; "it will be too heavy to lift. We'll start all over again." I sat there watching the little tub fill one third of the way up. "Enough water," one of the nuns said, testing it with her finger, and looked at Vladek. He went out. On my bench, I couldn't move at all. The two of them undressed me; one of them was clucking over my clothes. "You made this brassiere yourself?" she asked me, incredulous. "Of course," I answered. She started to lift off the cross; I pulled it down and pressed it against me. "I can't take it off," I apologized; "it has saved me." "We will have to get her some clothes," one of them said to the other. It was a French convent. The nuns and priest spoke only French or Lithuanian. "That would be nice," I thought to myself sleepily; "wearing these clothes is like wearing the fox-hole."

"We can lift her into the bath, Thérèse?" one of them asked. "She can't weigh more than eighty pounds," Juliette sighed; "you take her legs; I'll take her arms." They began washing me. "An abscess," Juliette said, picking up my arm; "you have to get this fixed as soon as you get into the city." I didn't have the strength to nod. "Close your eyes," Juliette told me; "Thérèse is going to scrub your head. There are lice," I heard her whisper to Thérèse. A bitter liquid went over my head, stinging my nostrils, burning my closed eyelids; my scalp burned everywhere I had scratched it. "Only once more," Thérèse told me, pouring it on again. Then there was the sweet smell of soap and something else; it was beer! I licked my lips. "She likes it," Thérèse laughed, delighted. "We make it ourselves for the nursing mothers in the village, but it's good for hair too," she told me. She wrapped a towel into a turban around my head. Juliette pulled me up and between them they put me into a robe and carried me onto the bench.

"The priest says her bed is ready," Vladek announced, coming back in. "I'll carry her," he insisted. We went off down the hall. I was dissolved in the feeling of clean skin rubbing against clean cloth. "In here," Thérèse said opening a door. A tiny room with one bed and a little table and chamber pot was waiting. I was falling asleep against Vladek's chest. "Wait while we turn down the bed," Juliette asked. "Isn't she too heavy?" "Don't be silly," Vladek answered, annoyed. "All right, put her in," Thérèse instructed. I was floating down to the bed. It was a clean bed. With the energy I had left I pushed up the arms of my bathrobe and stretched out my ankles. Real sheets! Clean sheets! "She's half dead, poor thing," Juliette murmured. "We'll comb her hair while she's in bed. You hold up her head, and I'll comb. Thérèse, you bandage those legs; look at all those scratches!" There was activity all around me, but I was sound asleep while the sun blazed into the room.

"Get up, dear," someone was saying in a very sweet voice; "get up. We're going to look for your daughter. The priest decided to go with you in the carriage; no more walking." "Oh," I sighed, sliding my feet back and forth across the sheets; "I would like to rest a little more." "No, we have breakfast ready. And some clothes," she added. "Just a plain wool skirt, not so good for summer, but a

422

good cotton blouse, and your Vladek found a little suitcase in the neighborhood. He insists you need it." "I do need it," I said, sitting up. I felt much better. "Your brassiere fell apart when we washed it," she apologized, "but maybe you'll find another in the city." She helped me on with the slip, skirt, and blouse. "I have some good bloomers," she said, embarrassed; "yours were wearing out. These are new; we made them ourselves." "Thank you," I said, looking down at the bandages on my feet. "You won't need those in a few days," she assured me; "look, the legs are even thinner than before. Come for breakfast," she begged. I was sitting on the edge of the bed; I never wanted to get up.

The priest and Juliette were standing in the dark kitchen. Vladek was sitting at the table eating. "Good cereal," he called to me, barely looking up. "Here is yours," the priest pointed; "cereal and some meat and potatoes. You need your strength. And this," he pointed at a package on the bench, "are a few pounds of meat and a loaf of bread for our trip, for the child, if we find her." "What happened to my cookies?" I demanded suddenly. "They are wrapped into the package," the priest answered quietly. "The whole time you were in the foxhole you didn't eat them?" "They were for the child; I made a vow." "We have made a vow to help you," he answered smiling.

"Are you ready?" he asked me after I finished eating. Vladek picked up the little suitcase and displayed it proudly. "What's in it?" I asked. "The German coat," he said, flushing. The wagon was waiting outside. The streets were dense with trees, but I could already make out another house; we were not too far from the city. The three of us got in the wagon; the priest turned it in the direction of Vilno. "This is nothing!" I cried to him; "she's not near the city!" "It would be silly not to try," the priest insisted in French. The cart jogged along for almost ten miles. "Almost there," Vladek announced. The cart stopped in front of a long low hut. "This is an orphanage?" I whispered in horror. "It was thrown up so fast, to take the children from the prison," the priest explained. "I am not getting out," I insisted; "there is no point. She will not be here; we're just wasing time." "My dear Mrs. Vishinskaytie," he explained, annoyance creeping like an ant into his patient voice, "if you do not look everywhere, you will always think maybe she was in the one place you did not look. Maybe this, maybe that; it will become the rosary of your life. We should just begin at the beginning." "All right," I agreed with bad grace. "It's just a waste of time," I whispered to Vladek, who ignored me.

"Take the suitcase," he reminded me at the last minute. The priest had already gone in. He came out with an old woman in a gray cotton dress tied at the waist with a rough rope; some blond strands were pulling loose from it. She looked familiar to me. She looked, I thought suddenly, like the woman I had seen leading the children away through the forest. "Naturally," I thought to myself; "those are the ones I would have seen. We were both leaving the city." "I will bring out the children," she was saying to the priest in French. She went into the long hut. "Ridiculous!" I muttered to Vladek. She came out through the door, followed by a trail of children. "Line up in the light, children," the old woman commanded; "what did you say her name was?" "Luisa, Luisa Vishinskaya," Vladek answered for me. "Is she here; is she alive?" All of a sudden the children were screaming, *"Ira! Ira! Ira!"* "What does that mean?" I asked Vladek, frightened. "It means 'She's here! She's here!' " he translated in triumph, grabbing hold of me. "Where?" I demanded in a loud voice.

"Here she is," the old woman said, bringing a tall thin child forward. Her hair was pulled back in one greasy tail; her eyes were so sunken I couldn't tell their color. "That is not my child!" I said to the mother superior; "that is not my child, I don't want her." "Listen to me," the mother superior said, "they have had two weeks with nothing to eat; they are very changed. She *is* Luisa Vishinskaya from the prison. A Gestapo officer named Schraader was visiting her here every week with a special translator; there were women who said they knew her mother and washed her with coffee." "She is not my child!" I screamed, starting to run to the wagon. "I don't want that child!" Vladek called me and dragged me back like a dog. The child was staring at me, and then at the valise in my hand. "She is the Luisa Vishinskaya who was in prison and who was visited by the Gestapo agent who brought her food," the mother superior repeated again. "She has not eaten for two weeks; her head is all abscesses. She does not look as she did. She was a beautiful child when we got her, Mrs. Vishinskaytie, that's why the Gestapo man took her out of the line of children to be shot. He hid her in an arch; she told us all about it." The child stared at me like a sick bird, saying nothing. "I have a mole on my chin; you see it?" I said. *"My* child has one on her shoulder." Suddenly I was ripping her dress; the little scarecrow didn't move. She stared. There was the mark. "It is there!" I screamed. "It is not my child, it is not her, it is not my child; I don't care about the mark!" I was completely insane. Vladek was coming toward me and grabbing my shoulders; the light was narrowing to the size of a coin. It was filled with the face of this horrible-looking child staring at me. Then the little shutter of light snapped itself closed.

I woke up lying down. I was afraid to open my eyes. The picture of the child was there like a negative: Her hair was black, her skin was black, her teeth were black, the little wrinkles or streaks of dirt were white. Her back was all black except for one white mark on her shoulder. "I have to erase it; I have to get it clean," I thought, scrubbing the parquet of her shoulder maniacally. "It's a nightmare," I told myself, pressing my eyes together tighter.

"I know you're up," Vladek said; "open your eyes." The first thing I saw was the horrible child sitting and munching steadily on a chair next to the bed. "She's eaten everything in the package, just a few cookies left; I don't know how she can eat so much," Vladek marveled. "I am your mother," I told her. "I know," she answered; "the nuns told us to pray and our mothers would come, and here you are." She finished chewing and began chomping on another cookie. "Do you want to come with me, Ninushka?" I asked her. "My name is not Ninushka," she told me, looking at me coldly; "it is Luisa." "I'm going to sleep," I told Vladek. "She'll get used to you," he swore. "You said it yourself; anyone with a suitcase!" I cried bitterly. "She'll get used to it; how should she know what's going on any more?" "Will you call me Mommy?" I asked her. "Why not?" she asked, taking another cookie out of the package. "I'm going to call you Ninushka whether you like it or not," I told her. "Will you take me into the city?" she asked. "As soon as I'm strong enough." "What's wrong with you?" she asked chewing steadily. "I hurt my legs in the forest; that's all." "How long will you keep me?" she asked "You see?" Vladek whispered to me. "Forever!" I cried; "I am your mother." "My mother's name was Onucia," she said calmly. "No, it was not," I insisted, beginning to get hysterical; "she just kept you until

425

I could escape from the camp!" "I heard something about a camp," Ninushka remembered. "And Vera Mouse, do you remember her?" "Yes," she said darkly, getting up and going to the window.

The priest came in. "How are you getting along?" he asked. "They don't like each other," Vladek answered. "How can you say such a thing?" I cried; "I love her." "You'll love her more when she thinks you're her mother; why should anyone love such a horrible-looking child?" he asked. "I am not horrible!" she screamed, turning around, stamping her foot; her blue eyes blazed out of their sockets. It was Ninushka; those eyes, it was her. "We have to take her to the city for a doctor," Vladek said, looking down at her; "look at this head; it's a bug's nest." She picked up her little fist and smacked him on the knee. "Ninushka!" I scolded. "Who is he?" she demanded. "Are you going to keep him because he doesn't have bugs; I want to know now." "He is only helping us," I pleaded with her. "We'll see," she said like a little eighty-year old. The priest was smiling. "A good sign when the fighting starts." "It doesn't look so good to me." I couldn't remember such fighting when I was a child. "It's better than the staring and staring we sometimes get," he said sadly. "Do you want to take her to the city right away, or stay over with us for the night? We can give her a bath and you can rest." "We'll go back to the orphanage we came from," Vladek announced.

Thérèse and Juliette got busy with the bathtub; Vladek carried in the water. "Oh, the head, Thérèse," Juliette sighed; "I can't touch it." "I'll do it," I said, getting up from the bench; "give me that stuff." They brought me a bottle filled with purple fluid. "Will this turn her hair purple?" "No more than yours," Thérèse answered; "like mother, like daughter." "Close your eyes, Ninushka," I ordered her. "It stings," she complained. "Close them," I commanded again. "You heard Vladek say how horrible you look; you want to go into the city with all those bugs?" She pressed her eyelids tighter, slumping down. Her shoulder bones stuck out like chicken wings. "She's very thin," Vladek whispered. "Is he in here?" Ninushka screamed at the top of her lungs without opening her eyes. "Make him go out!" Vladek went out grinning. "Now for the beer," I told her, pouring it over her head. "It tastes good," she said, lapping it up greedily. "Like mother, like daughter," Thérèse said again.

426

"We have to put you in the same bed; I hope that's all right," Juliette said. "It's fine." "You could sleep on the floor," Ninushka said, looking at me. "Ninka," I told her slowly, "you have some things to learn. A mother is more than something with a suitcase. I take care of you and love you; you do not throw me out on the floor the minute I am finished." For answer, she blinked her big blue eyes. "It is all right?" Juliette asked again. "It is," I said; "isn't it, Ninushka?" "Yes," she muttered, sulkily. "Then in the morning," the priest said coming in, "after breakfast, we'll drive you to the city." "I'm coming too," Vladek informed us; "to help." "You are going to stick to us?" I asked him, smiling. "Will you let me?" "How did I find my child? Of course, I'll let you."

So Vladek went off to sleep in the kitchen on the floor, and Ninushka and I got in the bed with sheets. They had a sheet cut in half and tied with a drawstring around her waist. Someone had stitched up the side and hemmed the bottom. This was her dress; she had on little wooden sandals. I watched her line them up neatly at the side of the bed. "Ready?" I asked her. "In the orphanage, we each had our own bed," she pouted. "What did I tell you?" I asked her. "All right," she answered, climbing in. "That stuff you put on my head makes it hurt." "Ninushka!" I explained again. "I suppose you want me near the wall?" she asked. "Yes, so you don't fall out." "I knew it," she sighed loudly. "What a hard life you have, now that you have your mommy," I mocked her. "You really are my mommy?" she said after a while. "We have the same marks; you remember," I insisted. "Yes," she answered. Her breathing was getting deeper; she was asleep. I waited a while and then went out in the hall. I leaned against the wall sobbing and sobbing, bent from the waist, clutching my stomach. This was my child; this was my life. She had prayed to God to send me here, and now here I was. She was a Catholic and her mommy was named Onucia.

"Go back to bed," Thérèse whispered; "it will come out all right. Time, it takes time. They don't trust so easily, you can understand it." "She doesn't love me, she doesn't know me," I sobbed. "You expected too much," Thérèse said gently; "but who could blame you? How could you know? We never know what they went through before they came here; they won't talk about it." "Never?" I asked. "Almost never," she answered. "Ask Vladek, almost never. They're just children. Sometimes I think they don't

427

talk because they think saying things makes them happen again." I was crying inconsolably. I didn't know my own child. But by the morning Vladek and Ninushka and I were in the wagon going to the city and I was full of hope. "We will go to the house of Rutkauskus," Ninka sang out. "He may have had to run away from the city because of the fire, like you did," I warned her. "How do you know we did?" "I saw you in the forest." "If you saw me, why didn't you get me then?" "You were too far away for me to see your face, but I was sitting against a tree, and I said, 'Thank God they are taking the children out,' I'm only glad I didn't find you then," I told her. "Why?" she asked, slightly curious. "I would have taken you and you would have been shot in the foxhole. This way the nuns took care of you and my legs got better in the meantime, while you were busy eating." "Prayers do everything," Ninushka said piously, fingering her rosary.

The city was coming into view. "Where would you like to go?" asked the priest. "Somewhere near Kafkaska Street," I said. He turned the wagon to the left. We jolted along in the silence of stopped time. Ninka had fallen asleep against Vladek. "Here we are," the priest said reining in the horse. "May God bless you forever," I said, getting down. "Thanks be to Jesus," Ninka murmured automatically, waking up. "I'll carry her," Vladek said, lifting her. "I don't want to be carried," Ninka whined. Already the wagon was starting on its way back out of the city. "Shut up, little potato head," Vladek told her. "Did you hear what he said to me?" she demanded, indignant. "If you want to be treated like a lady, you have to act like one," I told her. But really, she was too weak to walk. She wriggled in his arms. "Potato head," she muttered. He carried her along easily. "Stop it," he shouted at her. She was trying to kick him and then bite him. "Let him yell at her," I thought; "I don't want to scold her, not for a while." So we walked slowly; my legs were still painful, but I had found my child. Now all I had to do was believe it, to believe she was my child, to have her believe I was her mother. Vladek was watching me sympathetically.

"Anyushka! Anyushka!" someone shouted from across the street. I turned in terror. Germans! But it was Doctor Yurbo. "Anyushka, you survived!" he was crying; "and is that Ninushka?" "Luisa," she muttered automatically. It was pathetic; I could see it happening up and down the sidewalks on both sides of the street. Whenever two Jews met each other, they fell on each other, crying. "You have to come to my house," he was babbling; "we have food; I'll fix her head and your feet." He was already taking a medical survey. "And this young man too, of course."

"How did you do it?" I asked, amazed. "Oh, it was something," he babbled on. "We got away right before the liquidation, the whole family. Then we hid in the medical library"; he pointed to the library across the street from the school. "They walled us in with the stacks; food went in and out under the door, and everything else, and then someone died and then there was the smell and *then* there was trouble." "Who were they?" "Prominent families; especially one, we saved the life of his son, or I saved it. He paid us all back, believe me." "What did you do when the person died?" I asked amazed. Vladek and Ninka were staring, boggle-eyed. "She went out under the door, too," he said, his lips tightening. "Remember the cutting in the Prosecutorium?" he asked. "So it was done. You will tell me all about you," he insisted. "Not now," I refused; "I want to forget." "You can try," he said slowly. "I will forget," I insisted. "Of course you will." He began babbling again. "We have our own house back; two more blocks and there it is, the little palace. Oh, Dora will be so happy to see you, so happy." "And your daughters?" I asked him. "All fine, all fine," he beamed. "It was my mother who went out under the door," he explained, putting me out of my misery.

We came to his house. It was a huge two-story brick house surrounded by a huge garden. There were greenhouses on one side and a spiked iron fence ran around the grounds. "The Germans took good care of it for me," he said happily; he was so happy to see me. "What were you doing out?" I asked him. "Looking for Jews," he practically trilled; "and I find them, I find them, and bring them home and feed them. But I never expected you and Ninushka and," he hesitated, "this young man here." "This is Vladek," I told him; "he helped me find my child." "Who is he?" Ninka asked, pointing at Doctor Yurbo. "Don't point," I instructed her. "He saved your life when you had diphtheria." "More stories," she muttered. "Potato Head," Vladek hissed at her. "You have your hands full," Doctor Yurbo grinned. "We do," Vladek agreed. "Stop kicking him, Ninka, or else," I threatened. "Or else what?" she asked. "Give me a chance to think; I always

429

think of something." She stopped immediately. Doctor Yurbo was grinning like the happiest monkey in the world.

We sat at Doctor Yurbo's round mahogany table, eating. The light filtered in through the criss-crossed curtains, casting a pattern of gold mosquito netting over our skins. "How did you find her? How did you find her?" He wouldn't eat a bite until I'd answered all his questions. "It's a miracle," he sighed at the end; "maybe seven, eight, maybe ten children from the whole ghetto survived. It's nice here, isn't it?" he asked, settling back in his carved chair, resting his arms on its curving supports. The sun was turning his gray hair gold. "The Germans had to leave in such a hurry, they left food behind," he laughed. "It's not a nice thing for a doctor to say, but I hope they're all starving to death somewhere. We won't have much food though," he thought out loud, "not for long. All of Vilno is starving, such black markets, you have no idea, and the others in the house, they eat a lot. It's getting worse here every day, too." "Who are the others?" I asked. "People, just people, anyone I find on the streets. We have one woman and a child; my wife is with them. They survived in the asylum out in the country. They were there *three* years," he said in wonderment. "When the soldiers asked her for papers, she grabbed things from them and pretended to tear them up. She used to scream. 'Papers! I'll show you papers!' She has trouble with her arms, because of the strait jackets; every time there was an inspection, she was back in one.

"And my wife, Dora, is having trouble with the little one. She doesn't know how to behave; you can imagine. The worst," he said, playing with a piece of poppy seed cake, "are the two who lived in the sewer pipes; they can't walk at all. We found them sitting on the sidewalk." Ninka was listening as if he were Matenele telling a good story. "There are a lot of them?" I asked. "More every day; believe me, I love to see them. If it hadn't been for that Lithuanian family that helped us we wouldn't be here to see it. I expected to come out of the library and find Jews only things that lived in the books in the stacks." He shook his head. "So," he said, looking at me, "some pills for those legs; they must be painful?" I nodded. He got up and bent over Ninka's head. "I can't do much here," he told me; "but I'll put on some salve. It's beginning. These abscesses have deep holes underneath them; they take a long time healing up. It's the malnutrition."

430

Ninka was sitting and eating, not saying anything, her eyes scurrying back and forth to Vladek's plate. When he didn't finish a cookie, she snatched it and gobbled it down. He pretended not to notice. "I never liked poppy seed cakes," Doctor Yurbo said; "would you try it for me?" He handed it over to Ninka; she swallowed it. "Chew," he told her; "it would be a pity to choke to death after all this." He pushed the rest of the plate over to her. "Let's find some rooms," Doctor Yurbo said when we finished. "There's the little servant's house," he suggested. "It has a bathroom and two rooms, one for Vladek. Nothing in the kitchen works; you'll have to eat here." "Fine, fine," I insisted; it was a place to put our heads. We went out across the green grass. Beds of flowers were growing around the big house; the little stone house was covered with fat red roses. "This is wonderful!" I murmured; "this is like a dream!" "If your father could have lived to see this," Doctor Yurbo sighed. The two of them had passed books back and forth like plates. He took a key from his ring, gave it to me, and we went in. Everything was in order; the polished stone floors, the plain dark oak furniture; the chests at the foot of the clean beds were filled with blankets. "I wish we could stay here forever," I told Vladek. He didn't answer me.

"Why don't you go out with Vladek and pick some flowers?" I asked Ninka. "Who wants to go out?" she asked me suspiciously. "Go out; the fresh air will be good for you. In the meantime I'll make some bandages for your head from some towels." "I'm too tired to go out," she insisted. "We're going," Vladek announced, picking her up in the middle of a storm of screams and kicks. The front door opened and closed. I opened wooden chests; I pulled blinds; I made the beds. Water was running in the bathroom. "A miracle," I thought; "the house must have its own well." I looked out the window of the front room. Ninushka was sitting on a stone bench, swinging her feet and frowning. Vladek was sitting under a tree chewing on a piece of grass. I went out. The sun fell on me like a coronation. "Now what?" I asked him. "I think your daughter is pretty stupid," he said; "she doesn't know how to play hiding games." "What kind of games are those?" I asked, my back to Ninka. "One person closes his eyes, and counts to ten, and the other person hides, but your daughter doesn't know how to count to ten, and she doesn't even know to hide; *that's* why she doesn't want to play."

"*You* can't read," her voice came accusingly from the stone bench behind me. "I can't read, but I can run," Vladek answered, ignoring her. "I don't think she can run; she's too weak because of the holes in her head." I was flushing with embarrassment. Just as I was about to ask him not to be so mean, a furious stamping was taking place next to me. "I can run faster than you!" Ninushka shrieked at the top of her lungs. "You can't, and what good is it?" Vladek asked her, "when you don't know how to count." "I can count!" she shrieked, outraged. "Let's hear you," he taunted. "One two three four five six seven eight nine ten," she counted like a machine gun in Lithuanian. "See," he said, looking at me sadly, "she can't count in Polish; how can we both play with her?" "One two three four five six seven eight nine ten," she screamed in Polish. "Hmmmm," Vladek considered; "she can run and count, but she can't hide." "I can hide," Ninushka shrieked like a demented thing; "close your eyes." Vladek closed them. "You're cheating; I can see they're open." "They're closed; you just want an excuse because you don't know how to hide."

"Mother, cover his eyes!" Ninka commanded, bending so close to him her nose almost touched his. I put my hands over his eyes like a bandage. "All right, *you* count," she insisted. Vladek counted to ten. Ninushka disappeared behind the third tree of the garden. "Where can she be?" Vladek asked at the top of his lungs, peering around. A large piece of blue and white striped material was showing behind the third tree. "She's so stupid she probably hid under the bench," he boomed, bending down. A high-pitched cackle came from behind the tree. "Not there," he puzzled. More and more of Ninushka was emerging from the tree. "Maybe she climbed *this* tree," he said, turning to face the tree he had been leaning against. "I'll shake her out." He pretended to shake the trunk. A hysterical giggle came from behind the third tree. "She must have gone into the house," Vladek decided, going in. "I can't find her," he said, coming out. Hysterical laughing was rising in the far leaves. "Could she have gotten under the grass?" he asked. "I think your time is up," I said. "Did I win?" Ninushka called out, half-vicious, half-triumphant, from behind her tree. "No," Vladek said. "Yes, she did," I defended her. "I did," Ninushka shrieked, running out; now it's your turn to hide." "How do I know *you'll* cover your eyes; you're such a cheat, you'll probably watch the

432

whole time I'm hiding. Someone probably told you where to hide," he said accusingly. "I don't cheat; you just don't play good," she said. "Play *well*," I corrected. "He doesn't," she cried, looking up at me. "So, are you going to close your eyes? I'm not hiding until you close your eyes," Vladek sulked at her.

I went back into the house. From the window, I could see Ninushka running around in all directions; then there was a horrible shriek and she pulled him out from behind the fifth tree. "This is one game they should know," I thought to myself with relief, filling up the sink to wash the few things the three of us had. Then I saw the bar of soap in its wooden tray; it was a block of gold. I washed and washed while Ninka's shrieks ran in and out of the trees. Later, Vladek carried her in, sound asleep. "She fell asleep behind that damn third tree," he whispered to me, putting her into the bed, and soon we were all asleep, completely exhausted.

The next morning we went into the main house for breakfast; there was only watery oatmeal and some dried raisins. "Wait for them to puff up, Ninka," Vladek suggested. Defiantly, she gobbled one down, then watched the others. They puffed up. "Whales!" she whispered. "I'm going to catch a whale." She picked up a little fork from the table and went after one raisin. Other people were beginning to come down. Doctor Yurbo began introducing us. Then there was a noise, and some of the men at the table got up, and came in carrying two men who couldn't walk. Their skins were greenish-yellow. The men set them down on chairs. One of them gripped the edge of the table to get his balance. "The ones from the sewers," one of them smiled apologetically. Vladek and I looked at each other. "Well, I have to go out and look again," Doctor Yurbo said when he finished.

At lunch, there were two new faces. Again, we were beginning to be hungry. We would go back to our little house but now the games Ninka and Vladek played lasted less and less time; they were exhausted. On the fourth day, Vladek looked at his lunch soup. "You have to dive in like a fish to find a piece of grain," he said. Ninushka looked at the bowl with new interest. "I think on our own is better," Vladek said; "more and more are coming, and less and less food." "We could try Rutkauskus's apartment," I thought out loud. "I can say it was mine. Maybe we can get something there. Before I went away I told him where

Vera's piano was; he was going to try and get it. I can prove it's mine." "You can't eat a piano," Vladek said. "But it would mean we really belonged to the place," I insisted; "then we could have whatever else we needed." "It can't hurt to try," he agreed. "I don't want to go," Ninushka piped up. "No one asked you," he told her roughly.

"Where is it?" "On the other side of town, near the old ghetto." "That's too far," he considered. "We'd better get a ride." "With whom?" I cried. "No one around here is going near the ghetto." "We'll go to the wood market," he insisted. The wood market was an outdoor market about six long blocks away. "If we get that far, we'll find someone, I promise." We set off for the wood market, Vladek carrying Ninushka. Doctor Yurbo knew we were going to look for an apartment and Verushka's piano; he was waving to us from the front door. Then Vladek stopped. "This isn't the market yet," I complained. "It's close enough," he pointed out; "here come the carts." Some empty peasants' carts were already rolling off in the direction of the ghetto. "Hey you," Vladek called in Lithuanian; he babbled on. The cart came to a stop. Vladek motioned to the back of the cart. He climbed in. I handed Ninka up to him; then he pulled me in. He told the driver the address in Lithuanian. "What did you say to him?" "To help one orphan and a sick child in the name of Jesus." The cart bumped and jolted.

"Seasick again?" Vladek asked, shaking his head. The houses were moving away from each other; the cement sidewalks were breaking up. Slatted wooden ones were taking their place. The street came into sudden sight. There was Rutkauskus's apartment, standing as if it were outlined in fire. Vladek said something to the peasant and the cart stopped. "It looks like the house is full of soldiers," he muttered. Ninushka bent down and before we could stop her, popped something in her mouth. "What was that?" I demanded. "An old strawberry," she pouted. "Very old," Vladek said, looking worried; "let's go look."

The second-floor apartment was full of Russian soldiers. "This used to be my apartment," I said to one of them. "I want some things for my child. She has no food; she's sick." "I can't do anything about it now," he said; "you have to go to the commissar and apply for your property or we can't release it." "But my sister's piano is here," I insisted; "at least I could take that." "This one?" he asked,

434

walking into the dining room. There was the grand piano, still gleaming. "That's it," I exclaimed. "How do we know it's yours?" he asked. "Oh, under the top, in back of the little felt-covered hammers, there's a letter starting 'Dear Jakob.'" I was turning scarlet. "It's there," he said, disappearing into it like Jonah. "Don't worry, Miss," he said smiling; "we won't read it. Look, I'll sign a paper saying it's your property. The commissar will give it to you, but not right away. You can't carry it away anyhow." "But maybe you could give us some food, some towels, anything," I begged. "Look at my child. I have to rebandage her head; we have nothing to eat; we don't have a place to stay; we just got back to the city." He disappeared. "A pig's head, some bread, a few towels, that's all we can do." "That is wonderful!" I cried. "When can I have them?" "Right now," he told me; "and what is your name?" "Anya Lavinsky. And what's yours, if I may ask?" "Major Bilov, a flier," he told me. "The commissar knows where I am. He always knows where we all are," he grinned at his friend. The sound of Russian was going in my ears and down my throat like medicine.

"I don't feel well," Ninka whined; "it hurts inside my mouth." Bilov stared at her. "She looks flushed," he said, feeling her head. "She's hot." "The strawberry," Vladek reminded me. "What strawberry?" Bilov asked. "She ate a dirty one on the street." "They all get fever and trench mouth that way, or ulcers in the mouth, or something. Who knows what it comes from? You don't have any place to stay?" I was looking into Ninka's mouth; it was covered with small sores. "I could try the neighbor's next door," I gasped. "She works at a pharmacy nearby; she should be home in an hour or two." "You can stay here until then," he offered. "I don't feel good," Ninka whined again. "If I could put a towel on the piano, she could lie on it." "I'll get it," Bilov said, going out and bringing one back. We lay Ninka on the piano. "It hurts my head," she whined, moving her head back and forth against the mahogany surface. Vladek took off his coat and folded it into a little pillow. "I'm cold," she whined. I covered her with my coat. "I have some work to do," Bilov told me, going out.

So Vladek and I sat there in the window seat; he was watching for a *drozhka* near the neighbor's house. I was watching Ninushka. She had stopped moving. I remembered Zoshia dressing me up in white and lying me down in the middle of the dining room table with a flower in my folded hands. Momma had been scared to death; she thought I was really dead. "The next time she dressed me up as a bride," I remembered, "in a sheet." It was a long time since I'd thought of Zoshia. I could still hear Momma's hysterical screaming: "Get off that table; what's the matter with you? Are you trying to give her bad luck? There's nothing else you can find to do in the house? Anzia, where is Anzia? How long can it take her to do the laundry?" "I can look for Anzia," I thought to myself. "Momushka gave her so much, she must have something left. She *must* have something left," I thought, getting up to make sure Ninushka was still breathing. The breast of my coat was moving up and down; her breath had a slight whistling sound. "The neighbor," Vladek whispered. "You watch Ninka," I whispered back; "I'll go talk to her."

I flew down the stairs. "Marya Kryzpowcki," I screamed. The woman stopped in her tracks. I heard the sound of my shoes on the wooden sidewalk; I was flying through the air. "I'm Otilia Rutkauskenie. I found her," I babbled, "but she's sick. Please, can we stay with you?" "You found her?" she whispered, turning the color of the white sky. "Yes, thank you, yes," I babbled. "Yes, you told me, the orphanage, on the phone in the pharmacy, remember?" She nodded in shock. "Please, could we stay with you, just until she's better?" "Onucia would want me to do it," she whispered; "bring her over." "I also have a fourteen-year-old boy with me," I muttered, embarrassed. "Bring them over," she sighed.

"They're letting us," I told Bilov. Vladek was already picking up Ninka, tucking the coat around her. We climbed up the three flights of stairs to Marya's apartment. "You'll have to sleep in the kitchen," she told us. "It's not bad there," she said, seeing my face. "We can make a little bed for Luisa out of some chairs and pillows." Vladek carried in three plain chairs, then an armful of pillows. He lined the chairs up and tied them together with some cord Marya gave him. "She's hot," Marya whispered. "Not the same child at all, not at all." She peered down in horror. Vladek was pushing the chairs up against the wall. The wall formed one railing, the chair backs another. Then he picked Ninushka up and put her down on the chairs. "Better try to give her some water," Marya whispered, coming up with a glass. "Then we can talk." Vladek propped her up. "Ninushka! Ninushka!" I whispered. She muttered in her sleep. "You have to drink this water." I pressed the glass against her lips. She drank without opening her eyes. "Come out," Marya whispered. "I think I'll sleep here," Vladek said, spreading his coat out on the floor near the chairs. "I'm tired." He had been carrying Ninka all day.

"So, no more Onucia," Marya sighed as we settled into the stuffed chairs in her dining room. "What happened?" I asked her. "I told you; it was that Cholem. They followed him back to the house and took them all." "You said she had a baby," I prompted her. "Oh, yes, she had it at home. No trouble at all. Married twelve years without a baby and then to have it end that way. We saw them carrying out the package wrapped in canvas; it was terrible. I thought Rutkauskus was a terrible man." "How can you say that?" I cried. "He was a saint! Look at the people he saved!" "It didn't do his family any good." "Why did he drink so much?" I asked her. "I don't know; he always said it was because his first wife and daughters became Nazis, but I don't know; I think there was something more. He wanted to be Jesus; I don't think he drank when he thought he was Jesus. Of course . . ." she trailed off. "Of course he wasn't always," she finished, tightening her lips; "I never saw a man who could behave more like an animal." "How did you know where Luisa was?" I was so hungry for what had happened when I was gone. "I went to see Onucia in prison," Marya said. "She looked terrible, so thin. She never asked me about her baby; she never asked me about anything. She said there were some women there who knew you from the ghetto. It was one of those prisons where they put people until they had a chance to shoot them, and I guess they never got around to this one. Those women were washing Luisa with coffee and water. The Gestapo man named Schraader wanted her and said she would probably go to an orphanage, but not one near the city, so he could be sure she was safe from the fires."

"Women from the ghetto?" I echoed, astonished. "I thought they were killed, all of them, or sent to the camps." "I don't know," Marya said. "They used to send them to the prison while they were getting their graves ready. They just forgot about some, or maybe they needed them for something once the fighting started, I don't know. I think they must have been put in the prison before the ghetto was even liquidated." "What happened to the women?" "Oh, they're killed by now; they got around to everyone sooner or later. Onucia said she saw Schraader pull Luisa out of the line and hide her in an arch in the prison court; she didn't go back into the prison. That's it; that's how Onucia knew about the orphanage." "He was going to keep her?" "The same one who was in charge of murdering all the children," Marya said; "funny, isn't it?" "Where's your husband?" I asked her. "Riga, there's something going on in Riga. A lot of people make trips there now." Then we were quiet.

24

THERE was some noise on the street. I went to the window; trucks were passing by. In the kitchen, Vladek and Ninka were sound asleep. "I think I'll go down for some air," I told Marya. "Who is this Vladek?" she asked, her feet propped up on a tufted stool. "A boy one of the nuns gave me to look for Ninushka; he helped me to find her. He's a sweet boy." "A sweet boy!" Marya said, astonished; "he's a ferocious one. You underestimate him. If he's an orphan and alive, he has to be ferocious." "I don't know what you mean," I answered her, upset; "he's only a child, fourteen." "There are no fourteen-year-old children anymore, unless they live in America. No, no, he'd do whatever he had to for you." "Why for me?" I cried; "he hardly knows us." "You're all he has. If I were you," Marya went on, "I'd listen to him. You have no one else, either. He knows what's going on around here. Take my shawl if you're going down." She pointed at a chair, closing her eyes.

I wrapped it around me and went down, standing in the archway. It was hard to believe, that I could come in and go out of a house whenever I pleased. I looked up over my head at the little bricks forming the archway to the court. How did they get them to stay up? I had always wanted to know that; I had always meant to ask Stajoe that. Did Momma think about things like this when she went to the foot of the steps in the ghetto? Trucks were rumbling past, splattered with mud. "More and more Russians," I thought to myself, seeing the red epaulettes. The little procession began to slow down; the street was too narrow for them. One of the trucks rolled past slowly. "How much better these soldiers look than the ones in the forest," I thought; "things must be settling down." One of the men looked slightly familiar. "Doctor Ivanov," I heard myself calling; "Doctor Ivanov, stop!" I was a doctor from my cousin's private clinic in Kaunas. I raised both arms over my head again and again. He was looking around wildly; then he saw me. "Stop!" he called to the driver. "Who are you?" he asked when he got out. "You don't remember me, of course not," I went on incoherently, holding his arm. "I met you at Janek Savikin's clinic in Kaunas. I was his cousin; I worked there. You were a flirtatious man, a bachelor, I remember you, I do," I insisted, staring at him. I was afraid to blink my eyes; he might go away. "I think I remember," he said slowly; "so much has happened. What's the matter?" "It's my child; she ate a poisoned strawberry. We have no place to stay. I don't know what to do with her, the whole inside of her mouth is full of sores." "Wait!" he ordered the driver, who was not going anywhere in the jammed street. "I'll come up with you." He followed me up the stairs.

"This is Marya Kryzpowcki, Doctor Ivanov," I blithered, trying to introduce them. "Major Ivanov," he said; "where is the child?" "In here," I said, pointing to the kitchen. Ninka was muttering in her sleep. "Trench mouth and some ulcers in the mouth lining," he said. "She needs some medicine and a pacifier made of sugar. Sew some sugar into a cloth and have her suck on it." "Where will I get sugar?" I cried; "even this lady doesn't have it." "Wait here," he told me, "and I'll come back with some." "But I don't live here," I wailed. "I'm sure the lady will let you, won't you?" he asked Marya. She nodded her head. "I'll come back tonight with the medicine and the pacifier. You can stay with my wife after that until the child's better. She'll watch her while you find a place and job." "I have Vladek, too," I said, pointing to the boy on the floor. "That was fast work," he grinned; "bring him. Just wait here; I'll be back."

"You think he'll come back?" I asked Marya. "Who knows?" We went back to sitting in the dining room. The next time I looked in the kitchen, Valdek was giving Ninushka a glass of water. I sat in the window seat, and propping my head against the cool pane of glass, fell asleep. There was a knock at the door. I jumped like a grasshopper. "Ivanov," a deep voice called out. I followed him into the kitchen; he was taking out a hypodermic. I couldn't help it; since Rosa Field, they still filled me with dread. "I don't want it," Ninka was whining. "I'll sit on you," Vladek threatened. "Make him go out," Ninka insisted. "This is for the arm; the whole world can look," Major Ivanov said, smiling. "Here's the pacifier," he said, pulling a long thin bag of white muslin from his pocket and handing it to me. I handed it over to Ninka. "What is it?" she asked. "Suck on it," I told her. We were all facing her like a wall. She put it in her mouth, making a face; then she began sucking her cheeks in and out faster and faster. "You won't have trouble with that," Ivanov said grinning.

"So," he asked, "are you ready?" "Oh, yes," I answered, putting on my coat. "Vladek, where's the suitcase?" "I've got it." "Put the German coat around Ninka." "And give me a doll," she asked. He handed over a ragged one from the orphanage. "Thank you, Doctor," I called as we trooped down the stairs. "My name is Andrei," he said; "my wife's name is Olga. We got married in Russia." "How did you get to Russia?" "Oh, I was always a Communist," he said. "I joined up when the war started, almost right away." The truck jolted along. It was pitch dark. "Here we are," he said through the squeal of brakes: "Kafkaska Street. We have a little apartment on the first floor."

"How is the little child?" Olga fussed the minute we got in the door and while we settled in the second bedroom. "Still sick," her husband said. Ninushka was sucking away on her muslin bag. "One of these pills eevry six hours," he instructed, handing a flat box to me. "I don't want any pills; they poison people," Ninka whined. "No one asked you," Vladek said again. "No one asked you, either," Ninka pouted. "See, better already. In the morning, they'll be fighting. *Slushai*, Olga," Andrei said to his wife, "in the morning you go with her or the boy to register and apply for a room. And you better think about a job," he told me; "no one can have a room here without a job. You need one if you want to stay in Vilno." He finished setting up an army cot for Ninka; Vladek and I were spreading coats out on the floor. "Good night," they said, shutting the door.

The next morning Ninka was sitting up, cooler and cranky. "Will you stay with her, Vladek?" "I think I'll live," he answered. "Then Olga and I'll look for a room for us." We went out to the commissar's. We stood in a line for two hours outside the official building; there was not a soul on the line I recognized. Finally, I got an order for a room on the ground floor, 14 Freta Street. Looking at it, I murmured, "That's a good place, only four blocks from my parents' house." "Let's go look before you get your hopes up," Olga warned me. It was one huge room.

All the windows were smashed; the ground floor was built very low into the ground. The whole apartment had five rooms, a different family in each room. "The ghetto all over again," I muttered. "But you're free to come and go," Olga reminded me. "I'll take it," I decided, "but what about Vladek? He can't stay here; he's a big boy. And there's no stove. It's all right now; it's warm, but when it gets cold, we'll freeze." "I don't know why you're worrying about Vladek," Olga said, irritated, "but I'll speak to Andrei. He'll lend you the money for the stove. How can you come through such a war and still be such a prude?" "It's not that I'm a prude," I objected, my vanity wounded. "It's just that you don't trust anyone," Olga said coldly.

"Even if I get a stove," I said, nervously changing the subject, "how will I buy wood for it? It's such a big room." "That's why you have to get a job. We can get you only two mattresses; there's a shortage of everything." "What kind of job?" I was still thinking out loud. It was almost as if I had lost the ability to think about anything but practical problems of surviving. There was no electricity. I would have to have money for light. With so many people in the building, there would always be someone to watch Ninka; I could see that. "I think the First Aid Hospital needs someone; you could try there." "Can I work at night?" "I think so, why not? You can keep the baby with you at the hospital; it's not crowded at night." I was thinking I could sell in the market if I worked at night. But what would I sell? The room was so big, a big empty bag with a hole in it, heat and light pouring out. "I can't keep Vladek here," I said again. "He can live at the hospital if he wants to work there," Olga said unsympathetically; "and who knows, later you'll get a bigger place. He'll come back." "I'll take it," I said again. "Good," she said, relieved; "let's go get the others." We went back for Ninushka and Vladek.

"You found a place?" Vladek asked, overjoyed. "Yes," I answered, not wanting to see his face, "but it's only one room. I don't think you can stay there." He didn't say anything, just got busy picking Ninka up. "I'm going to work at the First Aid Hospital, in emergency at night, if I can," I told him, "and Olga says you can work there too, and sleep there, and you can stay with us whenever you want." "I'll go back to the orphanage after I take you over," he said. "No, for a while at least you can stay with

442

us," I pleaded. Even Ninka didn't say anything. "Go to the commissar's if you can't find us," Olga told us; "but Andrei said Ninka should be all better soon." "Thank you," I said, and we went off to Freta Street.

"You'll need a stove," Vladek considered, looking around, "and some wood. I'd better stay with Ninka while you go to the hospital; then I'll go over, too. Do you know where it is?" "Two blocks from Doctor Yurbo's." "I'll give her her medicine," Vladek promised. "Where are you going?" Ninka demanded. "To find a job so we can get some food." "We still have some of the pig's head left," she complained. I had cooked it at Marya's while we were waiting for Major Ivanov. "We'll need more. Just wait," I told her; "I'll be right back." In the courtyard facing the street I heard her high-pitched scream and a roar from Vladek. "Peace and quiet," I sighed, tramping off. But I was back in an hour with a job, and by supper, Vladek was back from the hospital with one, too. "When do you start?" he asked me. "Tomorrow night." "I start in the day," he said. "We won't get in each other's way," I said sadly.

But Vladek was thinking. "If I'm going to work during the day, you'll be here by yourself." His forehead was wrinkling. "Listen, I want you to do this. Tomorrow, when I go to work, you take the potato head and go into every room in the apartment. Ask everyone who they are and what they do and tell everyone who you are and what you do." "I can't, I don't know them, and what for?" I asked. "What do I have to do with them?" "What are you eating when you finish with the delicious pig's head?" Vladek asked me. "I'll buy something." "Where?" I didn't know what to say. "The stores don't have anything, if there are stores left. It's all smuggling and trading; you have to know people. You can start with the families in this apartment." "How can I just walk in?" I pleaded with him. "You knock on the door and walk in with the potato head." "He's crazy," Ninka whispered; "I told you." "I can't do it," I insisted. "I saw one of the men with a bag as big as you are," Vladek teased; "there had to be something in it." "What?" I asked. "No one knows until someone goes to the man's room." "Which room was it?" "I'm not telling. You go to *all* of them. And don't try to trade anything yourself, at least not right away. You'll go to the wrong place; it won't work." "I could go to some of the rooms tonight and leave Ninushka with you," I agreed; it was tempting. "All right, I could play hiding games with her," he thought, scratching his head. "But you know, Mrs. Lavinsky, how stupid she is; she's forgotten already." "I have not!" Ninka screamed. "Start with the first door," Vladek called after me.

I stood in the empty hall. It was cool; we were so close to the ground. I was Mrs. Lavinsky again; I was registered as Mrs. Lavinsky. How long would this last? And I was Mrs. Lavinsky knocking at strange people's doors and introducing myself, whoever heard of such a thing? I wasn't a beggar. Still, Marya had told me to listen to Vladek. I knocked at the first door. A woman popped out her head. "Oh," she sighed with relief, seeing me; "come in. You need something?" "Not exactly," I answered, feeling like an idiot. "I'm Anya Lavinsky; my daughter, Ninushka, and a young boy named Vladek are living in the room across the hall." "Oh, I'm Janina Kielwicz," she said; "inside is my little boy, Marian. But you look familiar. Don't you come from the ghetto?" I said I did. "I do, too," she sighed, motioning to some coats on the floor. "Our chairs," she explained. "Marian, he has a weak heart now. I don't know what I'm going to do; my husband hasn't come back. I can't work." So she went on. "You can't go out at all?" "Only with the boy; and then not long, because of his heart." "Marian Kielwicz sounds so familiar, the name," I puzzled. "He was the little one who hid himself in a stove when they searched for children. He thought I was dead, but now, it's no life." "Listen, Mrs. Kielwicz, I have a job at night, but a lot of times I may work during the day, too. If you could bring Marian to my room and stay with Ninushka, they could play together. I'm going to have a stove. It would be good for him; they would be warm. She wouldn't bother him, believe me, it's a trouble to get her to bother anyone." "I heard a lot of noise coming out of there," she said dubiously. "That's because she's with Vladek; he can make her play. Otherwise she just sits. What do you think? How old is Marian?" "Seven," she answered thoughtfully; "it sounds like a good idea." "He's older; maybe he'll have a good influence on her," I thought hopefully. "It *is* a good idea; this way everyone will have more food," I insisted. "Will this Vladek make a lot of noise?" "He wants to learn to read," I told her. "Maybe I could start him out now, and you could help him along?" "Where will you find books?" "I'll look around," I promised. "Marian can read already; he can help Vladek, too. He hates it, locked up in here." "Why don't you come over tomorrow?" I asked, getting up; "we'll all meet each other." "Good," she answered, seeing me to the door.

Again, the hall. "One is enough for one night," I thought to myself, but my door was open a crack. "Go on," Vladek hissed; Ninushka's head was peering out from his knees. I knocked at the next door. "I am Anya Lavinsky," I told them. "Come in, come in," said a woman, practically dragging me in after her. "You speak Russian?" she asked. "I am Russian." "I'm Lisa; this is my husband, Sergei, and this is my little boy, Sashenka. We work in the Post Office," she chattered on. "Sashenka doesn't look right to me," I observed automatically. "We think he's coming down with something," Lisa worried out loud. "You should bring him to the First Aid Hospital tomorrow night when I'm there; there are a lot of empty beds at night. I can talk to the doctors with you. I'll find out just what to do, and help you later." "That would be wonderful. Did you hear that, Sergei?" she asked.

"Maybe you need help trying to write some letters?" "I want to write to Kaunas," I told her, "but I don't know about the mails. I had a friend named Julia; I'd like to find her." "Kaunas," Lisa said thoughtfully; "the Russians have that pretty well in one piece. I tell you what. You write the letter and I'll send it with my brother; he's going there. He can take it to Kaunas himself. He's in the Russian N.K.V.D. If she's there, he'll find her, or where she's gone." "Her name is Julia Doroshnik; I stayed with her when I worked at a clinic there." "So, write the letter, it can't hurt," she went on. "Julia Doroshnik, a nice name, isn't it, Sergei, a very nice name. No, the mails are not so good," she continued as if answering a new question. "You have a child?" "Ninka, she's five." "Sasha is five, too; they can play together," she beamed happily. "Isn't that nice, Sergei?" He never said a word. We were all so lonely now. But still, I was nervous after the mention of the Russian N.K.V.D., the Russian secret police. "I'll bring you the letter," I promised her, "by lunch tomorrow." "No point in putting it off, is there, Sergei?" He smiled at me. I wondered if anything had happened to his vocal cords. It was possible. People were shy about their injuries, embarrassed about them, as if they had been their own fault. And again the cold hall. Without looking at my door, I knocked on a third.

"Come in," called a weak male voice. "I am Anya Lavinsky," I repeated again; it was getting easier. "I am Dobrowslaw Frost," he answered, hiding something with his body. "Do you have this room to yourself?" "Yes, I do," he answered coughing, "but I have an order for it. It's no use reporting me." "Reporting you, what am I, the Gestapo?" I asked, shocked. But I was disappointed; this was no baby sitter. "So *what* are you here for?" he asked, planting his body more firmly in front of something in the corner. "Look, Mister Frost," I said, blushing to the ears, "I'm sorry to bother you; it's just that I don't have anyone, only a sick child and a young boy. I was just visiting." "Visiting?" he asked, astounded. "Visiting," I repeated, as if it were a foreign word. "Can I visit back?" he asked coughing. "Of course," I told him. "What's that cough?" "Don't worry," he answered bitterly, "it's not TB. It's from smoking too much."

"Smoking!" I burst out; "but where do you get cigarettes to kill yourself with?" "From good relatives in America," he said smiling. "I would ask you to sit down, but there is only the windowsill." He pointed at it; I slid on. From my seat, I could see the big bag in back of him. "You want some matches?" he asked after a while. "You will have to forgive me; I have forgotten how to talk." "Matches?" "You'll need them for the winter. For wood." "Yes, thank you," I answered automatically. "You see that big bag?" he asked. "All matches. It's a joke here already," he went on unsteadily. "Where the Russians are, the jail is like a turnstile; the beer man who is arrested for stealing bread meets the bread men arrested for stealing beer who is coming out." "Aren't there things in the shops?" "There are things, but no one can afford them. Like museums. In the winter," Mr. Frost said, "the matches will be worth a lot. Would you know how to sell them? I don't like to bother with people anymore." "Oh, yes," I promised; "I like to sell things." "Then we'll share the money," he said, coughing. "Please come visit," I begged him; "all I have is a little water. I'm getting a stove, though." "It's two blocks down the street, in front of the university, to the well for water; you better get a pot. Where are you working?" "In the hospital." "Oh, the hospital will have many pots; that's a good place to steal. They feed you while you work." "What?" "Thick soup and bread for you." "I have to take my child with me," I thought out loud. "Probably she gets bread and salt."

"Thank you, Mister Frost. Please come visit." "You don't want me around children," he answered, coughing.

There was one more door. I knocked at it. "Empty, thank God," I thought to myself. On the way back, I stopped at Lisa's door. I noticed how she was dressed, in a heavy winter dress and heavy Russian boots; the little boy wore the same kind of boots. "You said you had a brother in the N.K.V.D.?" I asked her. "I'm looking all over for a friend, Rachel Ellenbogen, do you think he could help me?" "Oh, yes," she cried; "and do you have any material, anything? I'm a very good sewer; I can make things out of towels and sheets; I can even dye things." "I have some towels, but I need them for bandaging my child's head. But maybe later." "Maybe later," she said, all excited.

"Can I come in now?" I demanded of my door. Vladek opened it up. "So, what did you find out? You look all excited," he told me. "I do not," I protested. "She does not," Ninushka echoed. "I found someone from the Post Office who sews, and someone who can baby sit, and someone who will sell matches in the winter, or he wants me to sell them; that's not so bad, is it?" "What happened to the fifth room?" "The fifth room is *empty*," I said in triumph; "maybe you can stay in it until someone comes?" "No, better to stay at the hospital." "Why?" I asked. "I'll find out more there." So we went to sleep on the floor.

Vladek was up early in the morning to leave for the hospital; he ate a tiny slice of pig's meat and a crumb of bread. Ninushka sat up, swallowed some meat, and fell back asleep. I sat near the window, the sun pouring over my head like beer. I had to get some fat for the abscesses on Ninka's head, and some food, and save up some money. It was wonderful now with the wind blowing in through the open windows. I was watching Ninka breathe in and out. A poem popped into my head. Momma's voice was reciting: "The double windows are taken down; the street noises make their merry rounds; the bells of the church come in the room, the voices of people float in, too. There is the hammering of wagon wheels; in my soul, the wind blows free. A new life grows under the skies, endless blue. I want to go to the fields, the huge green fields of butterflies; there, spring displays its endless wares." I watched Ninushka breathing in and out; I was getting groggy. Suddenly, I saw Momma sealing a little box in the tiles over the stove in our old apartment. "The rings!" I thought. "And the pictures!" I could steal the rings for food I went out into the hall. "Mrs. Kielwicz," I said, knocking at the door, "could you watch Ninushka for an hour? I'll be right back." Then I went into my room. "Ninushka," I said, shaking her; "this lady is going to look in on you, from the room across the hall, go back to sleep." "Across the hall," she muttered, falling back asleep.

I marched along the four blocks to my parents' old apartment and began touring around. There were people living in it. "I'll come back until I think they're gone," I decided. "I'll come back here all the time; they have to leave sooner or later." I cam back every two hours; each time I could see the shadows of people moving. "The windows are all smashed," I noticed; "otherwise, it's just the same." The sun was beginning to slide down the sky when I started back from my last tour around the block. But something was happening. Suddenly, I was walking through empty streets. The people were not people. They were funny kinds of plants stuck against buildings or in the sidewalks in odd places. They were things to walk around. "Why are the streets empty, and at this time of day?" I thought. "Why are they empty, and so quiet?" I couldn't hear a sound. "If I could only see one face, if I could just see my face," but I had forgotten my mirror. There were no faces; there were just these empty streets. I stumbled back to the apartment. "Lie down," Mrs. Kielwicz commanded me; "you go to sleep before work."

For the first time, I woke up screaming. Soldiers were coming to pull me from a stove. "Where has she been? What has she been doing?" Vladek demanded. "I don't know," poor Mrs. Kielwicz was pleading. "Looking around," I whispered, sitting up, fastening my eyes on his like leeches. "No more looking around for a while," he said, taking a jar out of his pocket, then pressing me down. "Some tea from the hospital." "No, first for Ninushka." "She had hers, drink," he insisted. I drank it; it was bitter. "Go to sleep," he repeated; "you have only an hour until you leave for work. Are you taking Ninushka?" "Of course," I whispered.

Vladek woke us up. "Come on, I'll carry Ninka," he said; "then I'll get some sleep. She'll keep the whole hospital up," he said, glaring at her. "What's the matter now?" I asked. "She bit me when I gave her a pill." "He wanted me to swallow it without water," Ninka complained. "She swallowed it fast enough when I hit her on the back."

"She could choke that way!" I scolded him. "I could have choked," Ninka repeated in an insufferable voice. "You didn't; too bad. Let's go," he told her, fastening her shoes. "Up, Potato Head," he said, throwing her up into the air and catching her. There was the hint of a smile on her gray face. "Are you sure you're not up to anything?" he asked me. "What could I be up to?" I answered innocently; "you told me to look around yourself." "But I want to know where," he protested. "Don't worry," I said wearily.

The hospital was a big brick apartment building. "First Aid is this way," Vladek said, marching off down the corridor on the first floor. "I'm Mrs. Lavinsky," I said to the doctor who came to the door. "I am Doctor Dudek," the man answered me in Russian. "Can I keep my child here?" "Oh, yes," he said, peering at her. "Just put her in an empty cubicle and get a uniform; it's a busy night, a lot of drunks." "Drunks?" Vladek echoed. "Vladek, go home and sleep," I ordered. "Doctor Dudek," Vladek began, "Mrs. Lavinsky is only big as a mouse." Vladek, go home," I insisted. "He likes you," Doctor Dudek said, watching Vladek stomp off in a fit. "He works here in the day," I told him, avoiding conversation. "What can you do besides carry bedpans?" he asked me coldly. "I finished three years of medical school, three and three-quarters; I can do a lot," I promised. "Inject me," he said, handing me a hypodermic. "What's in it?" "Salt water." I injected him. "You don't have to worry about drunks," he said. "You come with me on rounds and give injections and change dressings. Is that all right with you?" "Oh, yes," I sighed with relief. "We'll have to change your classification, so you get more money."

We went from bed to bed. In one, a woman was lying unconscious. She looked familiar. "Who is that?" I asked the doctor. "Rachel Ellenbogen, a concussion. She went back to her old house, part of it fell on her; that's what the neighbors said." I felt Doctor Dudek's hands on me. The room was spinning again; it had no center, a record without a spindle, the way it had spun since the day Warsaw was bombed. "She's my best friend," I whispered. "Then you're lucky; she'll be all right. She comes in and out of it." "There's an empty room in our apartment; I have to get it for her," I insisted. "The commissar's office is closed at night," he reminded me. "Oh, closed," I repeated; "she knows a lot about medicine and hospitals, too." "Go first thing tomorrow morning."

A bell tinkled from the emergency entrance. It was Lisa with her boy, Sasha. "They're Russian," I whispered; "I think the boy has the measles." "Stay where you are!" he ordered them in Russian. Their faces froze. "Masks," he told me, tying one around his face, then checking mine. "All we need is an epidemic here," he muttered. "Take him to Isolation, fourth floor," Doctor Dudek ordered, writing a prescription and admittance form. "Thanks, Anya," Lisa whispered, leaving. "You know her, too?" he asked, amazed. "She lives in my building. I told her to come; the little boy didn't look right." "You didn't go too close?" "With my daughter? I stayed across the room." "That's something, anyway," he sighed. "Do you have a husband, Mrs. Lavinsky." "Killed." "I would like to visit you sometime." "I would like to have you, but to be honest with you, I don't really want anything to do with men. I'm going to be satisfied with having my child; she's all I have left; she's all I want." "Whan an idea," he muttered, annoyed; "will you have room for friends?" "Of course," I answered, insulted. "I will be glad to help you any way I can," he said. "Why are you so helpful?" I asked, suspicious. I was getting very bold, now that the Gestapo was gone. "I have no one; it's very simple. Just these in the beds." He motioned at the sleeping heaps. "It's like being back on the battlefield in the middle of the night." "Where are you from?" "Leningrad. I'm not going back." "I met someone from Leningrad, a Captain Ehrenberg. He helped me. He won't go back, either." "He'll go back and check; then he won't stay," Doctor Dudek predicted grimly. "Come on," he ordered, looking at his watch, "antibiotics and insulin shots." We began the rounds.

So the days passed. I spent time touring the block where my parents had lived; at night, I worked. When I wasn't busy I slept in the cubicle at the hospital with Ninushka. "You know," I told Doctor Dudek, "I would like to get my sister's piano. Bilov, a flier from the Russian air force, said I could get an order for it." "Get an order and we'll help you," he promised. A week later, Doctor Dudek, Vladek, and two young boys from the hospital took apart the piano, carried it downstairs from Rutkauskus's apartment, carried it to a cart Vladek had coaxed out of a peasant, and set it up in my room. "So now you have a piano and three coats," Doctor Dudek said; "congratulations." "The stove is coming next week!" I was annoyed. "The complete home." He smiled bitterly. "A drink all around, to celebrate the arrival of this untuned piano." The bottle passed around. Vladek took a long drink, I looked worried. "I've been drinking since I was a baby," he assured me. "He has, too," Doctor Dudek said; "probably potato whiskey, right?" "That's right," he answered, blushing like fire. They started singing some Russian songs. "Do you know the one about the butterfly whose life is so short?" I asked him. He began to sing it; the others joined in. Lisa and Sergei knocked and came in; they had a bottle of lemonade. We passed it around. I recited my poem in perfect silence. There was thunderous clapping. "Do you want to recite, Ninushka?" asked Doctor Dudek; "like your mommy?" "Oh, yes," she said, and began reciting the Lord's Prayer. "That is very good," he said clapping. Vladek was laughing hysterically.

"So a night off isn't so bad," Doctor Dudek said; "what do you know about that? Before you came, I was thinking of taking my own life. Who else wanted it?" "What does it mean, Momma, 'taking your own life'?" Ninushka asked. "I never knew," I said sadly; "it would have been so much easier than going on, but I never thought of it." "You don't think about it much when others are trying to take it away from you," Doctor Dudek said thoughtfully, "only when they get everyone else's." The room was quiet. I had a vision of the empty streets without sound.

"Sing the butterfly song again," I pleaded. The singing started up again, but Doctor Dudek wasn't singing; he was staring at his hands. "By the way," he said as he was leaving, "my name is Mischa." "And mine is Anya." "A funny name for a nun," he said with an odd smile. "You know I'm Jewish?" I asked suddenly. "Of course; the little one was in a convent, wasn't she?" I nodded. "Good night," he said; the others straggled out. "Oh," he said, turning back, "Rachel is starting to wake up. You might stop by tomorrow, or better, I'll send Vladek to get you if she does." I had been spending hours watching Ninka breathe; now I was doing the same with Rachel. What did Rachel think about behind those closed eyes? If she wanted to scream, no one could ever hear her. "She may not be quite right when she comes out of it," he said. "They're usually a little off; it's the coma." "Good night," I said again. He went out. I watched him go down the courtyard into the street.

"You should marry him," Vladek announced. "I'm not even sure I'm staying in this country," I said. "And besides," he finished for me, "you don't care about anything but the child." "I know you don't like it," I answered him. "Two dedicated people are better than one, that's all." "That's something to think about," I agreed. "I think I'll sleep on top of the piano," I said, spreading out my coat on its closed top. "You like it there," he said, puzzled. "You and Ninka on the floor," I ordered. "And there aren't even mice," Vladek wondered on out loud. "Good night," Ninka piped up, and then came the sound of her little voice, praying.

A few days later, the huge stove came. Vladek promised to find someone who could cut the pipes to order. "It will take me forever to pay Doctor Ivanov back," I moaned. "As long as you have the stove," Vladek said, leaving for work. I had been three weeks in Vilno. Ninushka was eating my food at the hospital, but her abscesses were not much better. I needed more bandages and fat at home for the day. "Tomorrow I'll tour the block again," I promised myself, falling asleep on the piano. It was getting colder. A chilly breeze was definitely blowing through the apartment. "Money," I thought, falling asleep for good.

"Mrs. Kielwicz," I asked, knocking at her door after Vladek left, "could you watch Ninushka for a minute?" "Bring her in," she answered. I set off for my parents' apartment. There was no sign of life. I marched up to the door; it was open and I went in. A little boy, three at the oldest, wandered down the parquet hall at me. "Where is Mother?" I asked him. "Working," the little boy said. "And Daddy?" I asked him. "Working also." "What are you doing, are you being good?" I chattered at him, going into the kitchen. "Your mommy wants me to get something." I began pulling chairs up to the table in the kitchen. I stood on the first chair; I was far away from the tiles. I still had a hammer in my pocketbook; it was there every day. I put the chair up on the table; I still couldn't reach the tiles. Then I noticed little wooden boxes in the corner. "Would you hand me the boxes?" I asked the little boy; "I'm building something." I climbed down onto the table and put the boxes on top of the chair. Then I climbed on top. I was like a figure on a church steeple; the whole tower was swaying. "I am going to break my neck," I thought distantly to myself, pulling out the hammer. Then I began pounding away at the tile. It would not come loose. The little boy was sitting on the floor, looking up fascinated. Momma had sealed the tiles up like a safe. I pounded and pounded. Finally, the tile began to work itself loose. I dug in my fingers. I could see a knuckle starting to bleed. I didn't feel anything. I wanted it: the box. Finally, I felt my fingers on it. I was pulling on it; I had it in my hand. I jumped down to the table, climbed down to the floor, and ran out of the house. I was on fire from head to toe. I fell back into my apartment gasping for breath. Ninushka was still with Mrs. Kielwicz. Then I opened the box: There was Momma's big diamond ring, and Poppa's diamond ring, and her pin, my diploma, my index from medical school, the pictures of Stajoe and me near the rock at Druzgeniekie. "Now I will have bandages and food for a while," I thought to myself. But something had escaped from the box like a dangerous gas. It was time, old time. I had to take care not to breathe it in.

For the next few days I was afraid to go out. Vladek was suspicious. "You don't look sick to me," he kept saying. "I'm telling that to Doctor Dudek so he doesn't worry." "And Rachel?" I asked him. "She wakes up and talks about someone named Jakob Katzenellenbogen, and whether it's a boy or a girl, over and over. You might as well wait. She's getting better, the doctor says." I stayed home; I was afraid someone from the old neighborhood would recognize me and accuse me of stealing. The fourth day I did go out. I walked and walked; the streets were turning to slats. I exchanged my father's diamond ring for two eggs. The peasant was looking at me expectantly. The whole field was filled with wagons. "I need a lot of meat," I told him; "a lot." He pointed at a kiosk across the field. Meat was hanging from hooks. "I want a lot of meat," I repeated. "Can you pay?" the peasant demanded. He was wrapped in rags; there must have been three layers of them on his feet. "It depends on what you have." "I have half a pig and four kilos of pig fat," he said, looking at me, smirking. I took out my mother's big diamond ring. "Is that enough?" "I don't know about the fat," he said dubiously. "Then give me back the ring." "All right," he growled; "you drive a hard bargain." Then I went back, carrying the heavy packages.

"Where did you get that?" Vladek demanded the instant he saw what I had. I told him about breaking into the stove. "How much did you pay? You paid too much," he shouted when I told him; "they cheated you. I told you not to trade without me." I felt as guilty as Ninushka with her strawberry. "And where are you going to cook that?" he asked in a rage, pointing at the pig fat. All we had was a box of candles and some matches from Mr. Frost. We had some pots smuggled out of the hospital, but no wood for the stove. Vladek stormed out muttering. "Doctor Dudek says you can cook the fat in the lab tonight, *if* you're feeling well enough," he added sarcastically. "I suppose you thought about what you're going to put on her head after you put on the fat," he asked me; "or are you just feeding the lice?" "I didn't." "Look, cook the fat tonight. Lisa knows some soldiers who are selling material, sheets, everything. What have you got left?" I showed him my mother's garnet pin. "Give it to me and I'll come back with *money*." In a few hours, he was back. "Give half of this money to Lisa," he told me. "She'll get a lot of sheets to dye for clothes, and plenty left over for the Potato Head's bandages." I nodded.

"So," Doctor Dudek said, "would it be too much trouble to give some shots before you get too busy in the kitchen?" I trudged guiltily after him. I bent over Rachel's bed. "Rachel?" I called. "Anya?" she asked, opening her eyes, then closing them again. "I told you she's getting better." "But now we have to get her a place," I insisted. "Vladek already has the order; I sent him." I floated after him. "Inject the arms. At least aim for them," he scolded; "you nearly got the bed." "The wood for the stove is coming tomorrow. It will be all set up, will you come?" "I'll come and bring something too, don't worry. Will you hurry up with the insulin before we have everyone in a coma?" "How's Sashenka?" I asked him. "He goes home tomorrow; it looks like a good day for you." "Oh, yes," I babbled on, starting to tell him about the sheets Vladek wanted me to buy. "Don't tell anyone about that," he warned me; "it's illegal, absolutely illegal. You could be arrested. I'm not going to tell anyone; don't worry," he assured me, seeing my face. "Go cook the fat," he sighed. "I hope no one with a good nose comes by to inspect tonight." There was a drunken roar from the emergency entrance. "Fun and games," he said, turning around; "this one probably turned over a truck."

By lunchtime the next day the stove was working. Then Lisa burst in, weighed down by sheets. "Bandages," she cried out, handing me strip after strip, laughing as if they were ribbons for decorating a dance hall. "Come over her, Ninushka," I ordered. Under the abscesses, we could see the deep holes. I picked out the lice; they were white and squashy, slimy. Then I covered her scalp with the fat. Lisa and I tied the bandages around her head. "Come in my apartment and we'll dye these sheets. Sergei got me a sewing machine. And you can use my stove to cook the meat." "What meat?" "Oh, Vladek told me; come on." I followed her in with Ninushka. "She looks like a war casualty," Lisa laughed. She had two big tubs out, one filled with red dye and one with blue. There was a big pot with a cover on the stove. "Put the meat in there," she said, bending over the tub, already dipping in a sheet; "then we can get busy with this."

By the time Vladek got back we had five red sheets and five blue sheets hanging from ropes across the room. "What are you going to do with those?" "Make peasant dresses," Lisa said. "We can sell them in the market for much more than we paid for sheets." "Mrs. Kielwicz can sew, too," he said. "You can get her to do alterations in your room when you go to the market. I heard women in the hospital complaining about how they can't get alterations." "How do you know she can sew?" I demanded. "I found out; no one has windows," he pouted. "So it looks like we are set," Lisa said, standing back with satisfaction, listening to the dye dripping from the sheets into the pails and tubs and onto the floor. "I have to get home," I told her; "Doctor Dudek is coming for dinner." "The stove is working fine," Vladek put in. "The man really fixed the pipes up while you were over here." "Who paid him?" "I did," Vladek said; "with some money left over from the pin." "You're a genius!" I whispered. "You should hear me read!" he announced. "I'll read for you later when the doctor goes home." "Get Ninushka to help you," I suggested. "She does."

Doctor Dudek arrived with a box of chocolates and nuts, a bottle of vodka, and a box of noodles. "Where did you get the candy?" "Where should I get it?" he asked me. "A present from a grateful patient." But he had bought it in the store; it was as expensive as gold. "Here," he said, handing the whole box over to Ninka. She began eating. "Aren't you going to share with Vladek?" he asked her. "Here," she said grumpily, thrusting a piece of nut in his direction. "I didn't know you were so generous," I said, my eyes on her. "Here," she said, handing him a tiny piece of chocolate. "Do you want me to give him all of it?" she screamed, seeing me looking at her. "A whole piece might be nice," I commented. "Here," she said. "Thank you," Vladek answered. Ninushka smiled. We played the untuned piano and ate pig's meat and boiled noodles and candy and vodka. "This is like heaven," I sighed. "It is," Doctor Dudek agreed. "He wants you to call him Mischa," Ninka said. "How do you know?" I asked her, blushing. "He said so," she answered, going back to munching her candy.

The next morning, I woke up to a knock at the door. "Who is that pest?" I heard Ninushka muttering from her coat. "Such language, Ninushka!" I scolded her. "Vladek says it," she complained. "That's no excuse, and besides, Vladek is a boy." I climbed down from the piano and went to the door. "Who is it?" I asked, opening the door the tiny crack it would open now it had the chain Vladek had put on. "Anyushka?" a voice was calling; "Anya Lavinsky? It's me, Stanislaw Worcik, you remember me, a friend of your late father's?" I threw open the door. How many times he had eaten at our house and come home from the bank with my father! There he stood, looking just as always, neat in a striped suit and gray hat, polished boots, a walking stick, everything. It was as if nothing had ever happened. "How did you find me?" I cried, hurrying him in. "I thought I saw you near Doctor Yurbo's, so I went to the commissar's and checked the room orders, and here you are." "Oh, come in, come in!" I kept crying, getting out a candle and a match and a little pot. "I'll make you a glass of tea." "Oh," he said, looking around, "you have nothing here; you don't have any beds." "No, I don't," I said blushing. For the first time, I felt ashamed. "You don't have any beds," he marveled, looking around, "and it will be winter soon. Listen, Anyushka," he went on in a concerned voice. "I know a way for you to make a lot of money, but you would have to go to Riga for a few days. Could you do it?" Ninushka was sitting up on her coat, peering at him from under her bandages. "I don't like him," she pronounced. "Is that Ninushka?" he asked. "She's gotten so big." "Big, but not too much to eat. I'm trying to save up some money for the winter, wood, the stove is going to use up a lot." "Then this job might be just the right thing for you," he said.

"What kind of job is it?" "Oh, nothing hard; but you know how it is. I don't have time, and the mails are just no good. The bank has important documents that have to go to Riga and come back from there. We just need someone to go in a little plane and bring them and take them back. It pays a lot, believe me, a lot." "When would I have to go?" "Tomorrow would be the best. I can come for you in the morning and bring the valise with the papers. The only thing is—I have to warn you, I have to be honest, the soldiers are terrible, terrible—you have to watch the valise every minute." "I have to ask Lisa first," I said, going out of the room.

"Lisa," I began, "I have to go away for a few days to see a friend, but I can't go unless someone will watch Ninka. Could you do it?" "I'll take care of her as if she's mine," she swore; "I'll bandage the head and put the fat on and everything." "Just don't tell Vladek," I made her promise; "he worries too much." "I can go," I told Mr. Worcik, coming back into the room. "So I'll come in the morning with the tickets and valise. It's a little plane. I don't even know what kind it is; all the markings are painted out."

Mr. Worcik was back early the next morning. Lisa was going to send a message to the hospital that I was sick and couldn't come for a day or two. We drove along in a little car to a tiny airport on the outskirts of Vilno. "You get seasick, I remember; your father told me," he said. "I do." "Don't look down," he advised. But it did no good. I watched the plane race past the little trees and start lifting over them. Below were the tops of houses, some of them built in triangular patterns that formed the intersections in the city; I could see fields of rubble. My stomach was heaving horribly. I was rigid with fear. Every now and then the plane would drop straight down, as if it were falling out of the air. I thought the pilot was doing a trick. "Air pockets," he explained, shouting over the noise of the engine. "Don't look down; it won't take long," he shouted. There was another man on the other side of me. It was my first time in a plane. It didn't seem strange. The sensation was almost familiar. It was familiar; my feet had lost contact with the earth. I closed my eyes and started praying, always the same thing: "God, God, bring me back to my child." "We're landing," the pilot called out; the little plane was coming down. The wing on my side tilted toward the ground; then the other tilted. Then we were heading straight for a strip of gray cement. The little plane hit, bounced, and bounced, and bounced to a stop.

"Here we are!" cried the pilot, jumping down and running around to my side. I was positively green, but still, I held on to the valise for dear life. Soldiers were all around, and hungry people who had lost their flesh; everyone was staring at the valise. I staggered out to the front of the airport; Mr. Worcik had given me sixty rubles for my trip.

"Sixty Trotska Street," I told the driver. I couldn't open my eyes: we might have been traveling through a tunnel. My stomach was jumping up and down like a frog, my forehead was sweaty and cold. "We're here, Miss," he called, the *drozhka* stopping. He helped me out. I wove up to the door of the brick house and twisted the bell. A man dressed in a perfect business suit appeared. "I am from Mister Worcik," I said weakly. "Have you got the valise?" he asked me. I handed it over. He took it into his office; I followed him. He had a little key that opened it up. It was full of money, just money. "I'm supposed to give you dollars in exchange," the man said; "yes, it's all here." He prepared another, identical valise. "When does your plane go back?" I was staring at him, speechless. "When does your plane go back?" he asked again. "In four hours," I gasped. "Well, don't miss it," he told me, handing me the second valise; "Mister Worcik wouldn't like it." "Call me a *drozhka*," I told him. "It's here," he said, coming back a few minutes later. I had fallen into a chair, rigid as iron. "Where are you going?" he asked me, suspicious. "None of your business," I answered, walking out and slamming the door.

"I want to go to the camp in Kaiserwald," I told the driver. "You mean the camp for the German prisoners?" "That's it," I answered, settling back. I could not believe it, that a friend of my father's should do this. But it was happening; it was still happening. The *drozhka* jolted and jolted along. In twenty minutes, we had left the city behind and were going down a path through the woods. The road began to look familiar. "Here it is," the driver called.

It was the same camp, but the barracks were full of German soldiers. "Except their conditions are normal," I thought. And all over the ground, flowers were growing. They knew they would get out. I picked a daisy and held it to my nose. Its acrid smell filled my head like a cloud; I began to sob. Clouds were passing overhead in a fast breeze; there was a chill wind in the air. They would heat the barracks for winter. These men just had to wait until the war ended and preparations were finished; they would

458

go home. I could come and go as I pleased, but never back to the same place. I could see Rachel; I could see the showers; I could see myself, bent over a bench, naked from the waist; I could see the guard dipping his leather tongs in water before beating me across the bottom; I could see the barracks flaming against the sky, the sharp smell of smoke, the crackling of paint, the guards at the door with the machine guns so we couldn't get out. I would be forever attached to this camp by an invisible umbilical cord, infinitely elastic and infinitely strong, one that could never be cut; I would forever be one of its inmates. I don't have to believe that, I told myself, shaking violently, but already I did believe it. Bright clouds were sailing down a beautiful sky; flowers were growing all over in neat lovely beds. "The earth is swallowing all those things," I thought, and envied it. What it took in, it broke down and used; what I took in stayed as it was; I broke down. What I took in built great walls, like the Great Wall of China in paths of my mind; I was losing so much everyday. "Wait for me," I told the driver. "I want to go to the office and see if someone's here."

A soldier was propped against the flagpole; the Russian flag was flying overhead. The flagpole was white and clean, like a new bone a body would grow and cover, a healthy body. "Who knows which prisoners are here?" I asked him in Russian. He pointed to the little wooden building in front of our old barracks. "Ask anyone in there," he told me. I walked in. "Do you have an Irving Erdmann here?" I asked. The man behind the desk checked his list. "No, we don't. Is he a relative?" "Not a relative," I said, turning like a zombie, getting back in the *drozhka*. "To the airport, please," I told the driver. Again, soldiers were all over, every eye on the valise. One of them almost snatched it out from under me; I was sitting on it. "Excuse me," I said, "you made a mistake. This is not Russia; what is the matter with you?" People turned around and looked at us; he disappeared into the crowd. So I sat on the valise like a hen hatching a crocodile. And my eyes were all over. "If they catch me," I thought in horror, "I can never go back; this is smuggling. How could he do it, how could he do it?" But the pilot was standing over me. "Ready?" he asked. I nodded my head like a chicken off to the slaughter. We went out on to the airfield. The plane lifted into the air. I kept my eyes closed. "I'm glad Poppa is not here to see this," I cried silently. Finally, the little insect landed with the two of us outside of Vilno.

Mr. Worcik was waiting with a *drozhka*. "How could you do it?" I cried to him. "How could you! You ate with us so many times! If they had caught me, I could never have come back here; it was worse than the Germans!" "Oh," he insisted, "I did it for you, just for you, you had so little." "Oh, no," I shrieked, "you did it for the dollar, just for the dollar." "Please calm down," he begged. "I have news for you. I know that's your plane. I don't care how you got it. I asked the pilot; he told me it was yours. I want to go to Warsaw." "To Warsaw?" he screamed; "are you crazy? There is nothing there, ruins, just ruins; they haven't even cleared out the mines." "I want to go," I insisted. I had to find someone from my family, or Stajoe's family, someone, someone I could trust. "If you don't take me next week, next week at the latest, I will denounce you. My neighbor Lisa and the others already know where I went. Her brother is in the N.K.V.D." He turned the color of a dissolving cloud, blue underneath. "Look," he argued, "it can't be done. There's no transportation; just a few paths for pedestrians." "You'd better do it," I insisted. "The most I could do would be to fly you in near the edge of the city," he pleaded. "How would you get the rest of the way?" "I'm sure you know an airfield." "An airfield! It's rubble for miles, it's all flat, a pilot could land anywhere." "Then he can take me." "What for? It's a tomb, that's all it is." He tore his hat from his head and threw it on the ground.

"Nevertheless, I want to go," I insisted, "and without any valises. And you'd better have a lot of money for me after this," I threatened. "To do such a thing to me, and after living through a whole year, a friend of my father's, you should be ashamed." "I only did it for you," he pleaded again. "If you say that once more," I said cold as snow, "I'll go straight to the police right now. Take me home," I demanded; "I want to ask Lisa what the penalty is for smuggling." "You're an accomplice," he shouted, hysterical. "An *ignorant* accomplice who tells the truth voluntarily; a very little accomplice who looks twelve years old. They'll believe me." "Please forget about Warsaw," he begged; "it's more dangerous than any smuggling. There are mines all over the city, I know there are." "Just take me home," I said. He kept looking at me sideways. "When will you come to arrange about the trip?" I asked getting down. "If you come later than Wednesday, I'll arrange about you; I mean it. The plane will have to wait for me all day, too; I can't stay longer than a day." "Think about the child," he begged. "How dare you mention the child?" I screamed at him. "Who else do you think I'm thinking about? I have to find family. I can't trust anyone anymore."

"Where were you?" Vladek demanded. "Oh, I tried to find our old maid, you know, Anzia. But look," I showed him, "how much money I have." "We have to find a place to hide it," Vladek told me, busy looking around, "and now's the time to buy wood; much cheaper than later. We'll pile it up in a corner of the room." Ninushka was clinging to my knees. "Come lie down with me," I asked her; my feet were turning into water, soaking into the ground.

"Here," Doctor Dudek said, handing me a brown bottle when I came out of the white cubicle in my uniform. "What is it?" "Cod liver oil." He had given me a bottle for Ninushka when I began work. "There's still some left," I said, trying to hand it back. "No, that bottle is for *you*," he insisted; "you've been sick too much lately. You have to take some before you go on rounds." We went into the little office for the charts and the tray, and he filled a huge spoon. "Swallow it," he commanded. "It smells," I complained, pushing his hand away. "I don't have time to mix it in orange juice; just swallow," he ordered. I swallowed. "So now you know how your daughter feels," he prescribed. Once in the morning and once at night," he prescribed. Tonight, most of the beds were empty. I bent over Rachel's. "Anya?" she asked again. "Yes, Rachel," I said, pulling up a chair. "I went back to the old house." "You did?" I never knew where in time she was living. "I wanted to see my room, but a plank was left in the ceiling and it came down and hit me." "When was that?" I asked her. "I don't know. When I got here," she said; "not long ago." Doctor Dudek was standing in back of me. "You've been here five weeks," he told her; "it was a concussion." Rachel felt for the top of her head. "Bandages?" she asked, letting her hand rest on top of the sheet. "Yes," I answered. "Did they shave my head?" she asked, her eyes filling with tears. I looked at Doctor Dudek. He shook his head no. "They just washed it, your hair," I told her. "That's good." She sighed deeply with relief; she was tired. "You got away, Anya?" she asked. "Did you find Ninushka?" "I found her; she's sleeping in another cubicle. Should I get her?" "Yes," she whispered. Doctor Dudek came back carrying Ninka. She was still sleeping against him. "What's wrong with her head?" Rachel asked, seeing the bandages. "Abscesses from malnutrition." "We all have something wrong with our heads," Rachel said weakly. "I wanted to get into a hospital, but not this way. How long before I can get out?" "About four weeks," Doctor Dudek said; "we have to be safe." "Where will I go?" she asked, closing her eyes. "We have a room for you in my apartment, on Freta Street." "I had to go back and see myself no one was left; stupid, wasn't it?" She was crying quietly. "I am the same way." "You didn't find anyone, only Ninushka?" "That's all." "But there's Stajoe's family in Warsaw," she reminded me. "Ninushka is all I want," I said, cutting her off. "How did you get out?" "They took us to Stuthoff after the defeats. I pretended to be dead in a big field. There was someone, I don't know who it was. I remember grabbing onto his ankle so I wouldn't cry out when they kicked me. Then the Americans came." "How did you get back?" "Rides, with soldiers, mostly." "Look, Rachel, I should tell you I may be gone for a few days to look for Anzia, but just this week." "Anzia," Rachel sighed; "I forgot. She would be alive." "She is," I assured her. "I just have to find out where." "The others, Onucia, Rutkauskus?" "They aren't," I answered her. "Please, go to sleep; the longer you sleep, the more we can talk." Rachel closed her eyes.

"I have an abscess," I said, trying to distract Doctor Dudek. "Fine, fine," he said; "but what's this about looking for Anzia?" "I have to, this week," I lied. "I'll work some day shifts and make up for it. I promise." "And who will take care of Ninka?" he asked, looking at me strangely. "I'll ask Lisa. If she says no, I won't go," I assured him. "You're sure that's where you're going?" "Of course." "I'll cut the abscess when you get back," he told me. "I don't know why you didn't mention it before." "I wanted the job." "She was afraid," Ninka informed him from the entrance to her cubicle.

25

WHEN I got home I went into Lisa. Ninushka had fallen asleep again on the floor. "Lisa, listen, I want to tell you something, but you can't tell anyone. Will you promise?" "I promise." "I'm going to Warsaw." Warsaw!" She choked on her cold tea. It was very early in the morning; Sergei stirred in his sleep. "I have to find out if anyone from Stajoe's family is alive. Every time I see a tall man here I think it's him; if I see a Chasid, I think it's his father. It would stop if I knew for sure. I'm tired of walking up to packages of clothes and finding the wrong face on the top; believe me, I have to go." "No," Lisa argued. "I've heard only the most terrible things; it's worse than a death camp. How would you even get there?" "I have a plane." "It's not for smuggling?" she cried; "the Russians would send you to Siberia for life without even a question." "No, I just want to look, no smuggling," I promised her. "But you may not come back. There are still buildings blowing up," she went on; "in the letters I read all about it." "You're not supposed to do that," I reminded her, smiling. "This isn't a joke," she said, gray; "what would happen to Ninushka if something happened to you there?" "She'd have her Aunt Rachel; Rachel will be out of the hospital in a month." "The poor child will feel like a croquet ball for the rest of her life," Lisa cried. "This is madness, believe me." "Will you watch her?" I begged. "I'm going anyway." "If you're going anyway, what can I do but say yes? But it's stupid, believe me, it's stupid. We still have to sell the dresses in the market; why don't you wait for that?" "No, I'm going now," I told her. "I can't take anymore." I kept seeing myself breaking into my parents' kitchen, wobbling on the little tower of boxes; then it was my mother, packing mortar around the tile; then I was hammering at it again. I had opened all the graves. Now they were all walking around. I had to get them back in. "All right," Lisa agreed, resigned; "I will pray. And wear a cross," she warned me," "and take your Polish papers. They may still not like Jews so much there."

"I'm going to Warsaw with you," Vladek announced when I got back to my room. "What are you talking about?" I demanded; "I'm not going anywhere but the hospital!" "Never mind all that," he said, trembling with fury. "I heard you and Lisa at the window." "Remind me to rent my next room in a church steeple," I snapped at him. "I am going," he insisted; "you won't know what to do with yourself. You said something about a plane. Is it landing in the middle of the city, did you think about that?" "On the outskirts," I admitted. "Then I'm going," he said. "You need a friend to watch the pilot; I can imagine who owns a private plane after a war. You'd never get to the city yourself." "I can take care of myself," I said, flushing. "Good," he repeated, "then you can take care of me, too. Either I go, or you don't." I kept quiet. "When are we going?" he asked. "Wednesday, if it's a nice day," I sighed. "Don't tell him about me," Vladek warned; "just tell him to be sure to have extra fuel and no one but the pilot. I'm bringing a friend, too," he finished severely. "I'll go out and call him," I said defeated, putting on my coat.

"Are we going Wednesday?" he asked, seeing my face when I came back in. "Wednesday," I answered. "If we get back alive, I'm going to read that letter of Vera's in the piano." Wednesday Vladek was at the apartment at four o'clock in the morning. "I didn't see a cloud on the way here," he muttered, disappointed. The day began to creep out of its box. It was bright silvery blue; there wasn't even a streak of cloud. "It doesn't look like rain," I remarked. "No, but I'm hoping for a mudstorm, or locusts, or even a rain of blood." "Stop being so dramatic; it's just a plane." "Let's go," Vladek ordered; we went out and stood in the court. At six, Mr. Worcik drove up in his car. "Who's this?" he demanded. "My ward," I answered; "he's going, too. He's never been in a plane. And follow his directions; we have to pick up his cousin." We picked up another young man near Rutkauskus's house. "Now for the airport," I sighed. "What are these, your body guards?" Mr. Worcik demanded. "Exactly," I told him. "And don't forget it," Vladek said roughly; "I even have this." He took out a Russian army gun. "Where did you get that?" I asked, horrified. "I have drug duty during the day; I have a permit," he explained, pouting, "and," he said, turning to Mr. Worcik, "my friend has a knife, so the plane will want to wait for us; it will definitely want to do that." "What did you think it was going to do?" Mr. Worcik grumbled. "Planes fly; they don't decide when by themselves."

We drove on in silence. The little airfield came into view. It was a cleared circle in the middle of rubble on one side, and trees on another, grass on another. "That's the plane," I said, pointing. Vladek looked as if he had just seen a vampire. "You don't have to go," I told him. "It's not from the movies; it really goes through the air." "Hurry up," Vladek said. "We're not afraid, are we, Stefan?" Stefan shook his head, quaking. "Just don't look down," I suggested helpfully. "Do you have the extra fuel?" Vladek demanded. Mr. Worcik nodded furiously.

We got into the plane. The last thing I saw was Mr. Worcik kicking the side of his car with his shoe, then bending down to polish the car with his hand. The plane began lifting from the ground. "It goes so fast," Vladek marveled, "just like in the movies you took me to. This is wonderful, eh, Stefan? Look," he said suddenly, "the Botanical Gardens, the center of the city, you can see it all at once; look at the streets, they look like lines of chalk." "Please sit still, before you fall out," I begged. "I'm strapped in," he answered, straining to look. "See those burned places on the ground; what are they?" I looked down; my stomach went up. "It's a shadow from a cloud," the pilot explained, softening. "A shadow from a cloud," Vladek marveled; "impossible; we could see it down there." "You would be *in* it down there," the pilot corrected him. "Look at the forests," Vladek laughed; "they look like messy heads; look at that scrawny forest; it looks like the Potato Head before her bandaging." "Will you be quiet?" I whispered greenly. "Water!" he shrieked. "That blue button down there; no, it's more like a spilled egg," he said, pointing it out to Stefan. "Look how it changes color." He went on and on.

The little propellers droned through the air. The plane bounded up and down on sheets of air I could not see, then fell vertically through holes. Finally, I fell asleep against Vladek. "We're going down, Mrs. Lavinsky; look," he pleaded. "I prefer not to." "No, look," he insisted. He was pointing at mile after mile of chunky-looking earth. "What is it?" I asked. I couldn't see a house or a tree for miles. "Rubble," the pilot said; "bombing. There's a little strip near here," he said, beginning to circle. "Oh," I moaned, clutching at my stomach. "How far from the city is it?" Vladek asked. "About eight miles," the pilot said, making a larger circle. "There it is!" he shouted, pointing to a thick chalk line on the ground. "We're going to land on that?" I cried. "I'm not going to look." "It was your idea, lady," the pilot said, sitting forward in his leather jacket and goggles; mine were pressing over and under my eyes painfully. "He probably got me the wrong size deliberately," I thought to myself. The plane bounced and bounced again; then it rolled to a stop. "We're here," the pilot said. "Mister Worcik said I can't wait later than six o'clock." "You'll wait until we get back," Vladek warned him. "Stefan will keep you company. Here's the gun," he said, handing it over to Stefan; "don't let him get too close to it." "You probably don't know how to use it," the pilot sneered. "He was with the partisans for years; he can shoot the propeller off with that thing." The pilot kept quiet.

"Now, remember," Vladek scolded, as we started out, "we have to be back by six; five would be better." "Why five?" "It's even lighter." "You just want to look out again," I complained. "How many planes do I go in?" he asked me; "it's unusual. This way," he said, pointing to the left of the plane; "there's a road here somewhere." We were going through some grassy fields. They were buzzing with mosquitos and bees and flies. To the right were acres of rubble. "How do you know there's a road?" "I saw it coming down." There was a little dirt road on the other side of the field. "Now what?" I asked. "We wait for a cart?" "No such luck," he said. "We walk and hope one comes along while we're walking." We walked along fast. There was a rattling noise in back of us. "Take us to our homes in the city," Vladek cried; "take us home." The cart went by without pausing. Vladek cursed. "How far have we gone?" I asked. "About two miles; we may have to walk all the way." I plodded along in back of him at the edge of the field. There was another rumble. "Take two orphans home to Warsaw," Vladek called; "we'll pay you." The cart stopped suddenly in a neighing of horses. "Should have thought of that before," Vladek muttered, disgusted. "Where are you going?" the driver asked us. "Near the Krasinsky Gardens," I told him.

I sat in back, watching the road go away without any trouble; the plane was out of sight. Vladek was up on his

466

knees peering over the horse's head. "I can see some buildings," he called out, excited. I turned around. There were three tall buildings. We could see right through them, as if they were invisible, or we were; they were just the outlines of buildings, walls, with holes for windows, beams dividing apartment from apartment, all the ceilings and floors gone, empty beehives, the bees gone or dead. "Marszalkowska Street," the driver said. The little street was getting wider. Up ahead, some cars were moving. "Trucks," the driver said. We jolted past them. There were two trucks, then a truck filled with men under a canvas awning, then a cannon on four wheels. We were beginning to pass people in the road. They were walking along in ragged coats, carrying packages, large pots; someone had a white chamber pot and rifle. Almost everyone wore a dirty rucksack. The women had on kerchiefs and heavy boots. "Everyone going home," the peasant muttered.

Then I saw the cart was going over tramway rails in the street. The electric lines overhead were gone, erased. "No public transportation at all," the driver said, answering Vladek. Everywhere we looked, ruins. "We're in the city," the man said. "Oh, no," I argued, "there are no buildings." "We are in the city," he insisted, "just ten blocks to the gardens." Fronts of brick houses were standing up erratically. Through some of the blasted windows the sky showed through clearly. Through others, only hills of dirt and stone slid down from the tops of the crumbling buildings. At the corners, bricks were blasted out in irregular patterns so that it looked as if two jigsaw puzzles only needed to be pushed together. Piles of bricks and dust were heaped up against the brick buildings like snow drifts. Here and there the pole of a street lamp curled over the brick streets like an iron flower; all the bulbs in them were smashed. The day had turned gray.

"Krasinsky Gardens," the driver said, stopping the cart. "But where are the trees?" I asked him. "The Germans killed the trees," he answered. "Killed the trees?" I echoed. "They had orders to blow them all up, but there's still some water in there." He pointed to the center of the gardens. "But a lot of mines, a lot, I wouldn't go in." "Kill the trees," I repeated again. "They weren't supposed to leave anything alive," the driver explained as if it made some kind of sense to him. "Trees?" I asked again. "Kill the trees; they went around blowing them up. And the furniture; they were supposed to kill all the furniture." "Kill

467

all the furniture?" I echoed helplessly. "You know, couches, chairs, credenzas, kill them. There should be nothing left for anyone to come back to." "Kill a credenza?" I repeated. "Don't worry about the mines in the gardens," Vladek told the driver, paying him, helping me down, watching my face; "we're not going in there." "Kill a credenza?" I repeated again, incredulous. They didn't know the difference between what was living and what was dead. Now I had caught it, the disease. The dead were more real to me than the living.

"So where is this house you are looking for?" Vladek asked, ignoring my mumbling. Across what was left of the street, a woman in a thick gray skirt, a heavy sweater, and a wool babushka was making a neat pile of bricks. She had about eighteen rows already four feet high; on each she was spreading out fabrics for sale. At the foot of her pile was an iron pot, resting on some hot bricks. We could see the steam coming up; she was washing something in it. She bent over, pulled out the fabric, and hung it to dry on the bricks. A little stool with one leg broken was upended in back of the pot. "Firewood," I thought. It was a children's stool.

"This way," I told Vladek, picking my way over some bricks; we turned the corner to the Lavinsky house. Suddenly it was as if we were walking through ancient Egypt, drained of color. Every house on the block had been demolished. From where we stood, we could only see the white back wall of one brick building. Wall after wall came down the left side of the street in triangles, like the pyramids; triangular heaps of rubble came up to the walls to meet them. The triangles were scored with horizontal lines which must have once been floors. We could see square shapes which must have once been doors at the bottoms of most of the triangles. Some of the triangles were still covered with plaster. Others had peeled down to the brick. We started walking by the pyramids; the fronts of the houses were blasted away. I stopped at the first building. Four chimneys were standing up, unharmed; below them, three stories of windows were set into the back wall of a house. The spaces for the windows looked unnaturally deep, as if they were vertical coffins. There was one tree on the street. It was black and blasted, forking at the top like a divining rod. It looked normal for a tree in winter, but it was full summer. Ahead of us, a man in a peasant's cap and jacket was walking propped on a crutch; he had only one leg. About a hundred feet in front of him another woman was walking; she looked identical to the one selling fabrics on the bricks. There was a constant scurrying among the rubble. "Rats," Vladek said. "What does that sign say?" Vladek asked, pointing to a chalked square on one building that was still mostly in one piece. Bricks and stones were vomiting out of its windows. "*Sprawdzono Min Niema* 522," he read out loud; "Checked. No mines." "You're not going in any buildings," he told me.

"We just turn this corner," I told him. But we didn't have to. The corner building was gone. Piles of brick led up and up to the Lavinsky's old building. I could see it through the empty space on the corner. The peaked roof was left, and one of the chimneys. The little dormer windows jutting out from the roof of the attic apartments were left entire; they stood there, as always, like little dolls' houses, five of them facing us, but the rest of the building was entirely transparent. I could see through it to the next street. "So," Vladek asked. Then I saw a little old man sitting on a piece of a barrel. He had a long uneven beard and looked like a Chasid. "Excuse me," I said, bending over him, "do you know the Lavinskys?" "All killed," he said."How do you know?" I asked. "They tell me everything," he said, turning his dirty yellow beard up to me; "they wanted someone to tell everything; they picked me. The Germans started. First they cut off my beard; then they shot people in the street. I kept getting in line; they kept pulling me out. They even fed me. My hand doesn't even shake so much," he said, putting out a claw hand with nails that curled around his fingers like roots.

"Did they take the Lavinskys to the ghetto?" "No," he said, "there were public executions. They took them to Wolska Street and shot two thousand at once; that's when they went. Almost right away." "How do you know they didn't get to the ghetto?" I begged him. "I said they told me everything. Now everyone comes to ask me about the corpses. What a fate," he sighed. "Why did they leave you alive?" I demanded, suspicious. "Did you inform?" "They just wanted to tell someone. No one was too happy to hear about it. They picked me." His face was so wrinkled it looked like a rotted potato. "I am going to look at the ghetto," I cried. "I wouldn't do it," he said. "Why?" Vladek asked. "It's only rubble, two hundred million cubic meters. They told me, they were very proud; two hundred million cubic meters, rubble. It is a desert, with some sewer pipes maybe, and some children, and a big church in the center." "A church?" I echoed. "A church," he went on tonelessly, "on Nowolipki Street; they decided to save it. Its steeple was for observation and firing points. They were the gods sending down bolts. That was for the uprising. You think it was only the Jews they wanted?" "I don't believe you," I whispered. "Who does?" he sighed. "Want to see a newspaper? It's about the first. I have some interesting places marked; maybe you remember how people used to advertise if you lived here. So," he began reading from a yellowish sheet, smearing the print with his fingers, "let me read to you. I have so many stories: 'All soccer players of Warsaw are requested to report at the Sports Section, Headquarters of Civic Militia, Twenty-three Osnuabsja Street, Warsaw-Targowek.' Do you play soccer by any chance?" he asked me. " 'Will buy any book, also in foreign language, fairy tales. Also shoe polish, shoe laces.' Such a cultured city," he went on.

" 'This is to inform our parents, Stanislaw and Anna Orlikowski, Twenty-one Sienkiewicza Street, that we are Alive. Waiting for you to come and take us. Six Bialastocka Street, Apartment Twenty-eight. Warsaw-Praga.' Here's a good one: 'Am searching for my son Wieslaw Grott who was one year five months old on August Seventh, Nineteen Forty-four, in Chlodna Street; a German took him away from his father and gave him to some unknown woman. The boy had fair hair, dark eyes. He was wearing two shirts, a blouse with blue and white stripes, dark blue sweater. Please inform Wladyslaw Grott, Fifty-one Grojecka Street, Warsaw-Praga.' 'Will sell white and red fabric suitable for national flags. Inquiries: Eighteen Chlodna Street, Apartment Ten.' Nothing yet?" he asked, looking up. " 'Ladies' hairdresser open: first-class staff, permanent wave, iron-curling, manicure, eye-brow and eyelash dying. Reasonable prices. Six Kowelska Street.' Oh, here's one for you," he said, looking at Vladek: " 'Lawyer will buy gown, Civil Code. Will rent typewriter three to five P.M. Twenty-seven Wilenska Street, Apartment Six.' No good?" he asked sadly, shaking his head. "Here's a long story: 'Am searching for two girls, seven years old, Jolanta and Krysyna Zielinski. Address before uprising: Forty-four Grojecka Street, Apartment Twelve, Warsaw. They were later in Pruszkow Transition Camp, after which no trace was left of them. Please inform at Forty-four Grojecka Street, Apartment Twelve, Warsaw.'

See how the birds go back to their old nests?" he asked us, smiling bitterly. "And there," he went on: " 'Will clear of rubble a lot or backyard in the Stalowa Radzyminska area: inquiries Thirty-four Radzyminska Street, Apartment Seventeen.' Also, 'Newsboys wanted immediately. Newspaper distribution office, *Czytelnik*, Seven Srodkowa Street, corner Stalowa.' So," he said, "very nice, the news. You can imagine what the industrious rubble-clearer will find in that rubble," he said, grinning horribly. His teeth were rotted yellow stumps. "He's crazy," Vladek said, unable to move.

"Of course I'm crazy," the old man said, shifting slightly, loosing the stench of a dead body on the air, "but you are too if you insist on touring Warsaw while there are still two hundred thousand unexploded mines in the city; oh, yes there are," he assured Vladek; "the Germans are still killing everyone after they've gone. I suggest Saint John's Cathedral for you; really, it's more interesting than the ghetto." "Let's get out of here," Vladek said, pulling me away. "The madonna there has a lot to recommend it," he called after us.

"This way to the cathedral," I told Vladek. We passed skeleton after skeleton of building. We would get up to one that looked untouched and then the side wall would be missing; or we would turn a corner and see one saved, a miracle, and looking through the windows, we could see the street in back of the one we were on. "Why are you listening to that crazy idiot?" Vladek complained; "there are plenty of churches in Vilno." I didn't answer him. "Is it far?" he asked. I nodded my head. He managed to stop a cart full of bricks; we climbed on top of the stones.

"The cathedral," the driver said, stopping. I opened my eyes. We were facing the church; there was the madonna, her head bent on her hand, on a pedestal under an arch of light, but the arch spread in all directions, jagged. To her left, one arch still stood with its leaded windows; on the right, the window was completely destroyed. In front of her, one nave stood complete. The ceiling was only a crazy pile of black wooden rafters. And standing in the middle of the church was a long flat cart made of wood with four huge wheels with rubber tires around them, a white horse in front harnessed to it. A peasant loading bricks into the cart. The poor horse had his head down. "A horse in the middle of a church," Vladek whispered, astonished. In back of the horse was a pyramid of loose stones; another pyramid rose up from the base of the madonna to empty space behind her. The buildings on both sides of the church were blasted entirely; we couldn't even tell their shape. "Now where?" Vladek asked. "The ghetto."

He stopped four carts before we found one that would take us. "I'm going there for bricks anyway," the driver said. The cart jolted along. "It never was a good section," he continued, "but now it's no section at all. I used to be a lawyer, you know; but we have to eat." "Where do you live?" I asked him. "In my old house." "Did they check it for mines?" "No; we decided to take a chance; even an animal needs a home. Our neighbors weren't so lucky. Their little daughter found a shell and played with it. That was the end of her and two rooms." We jolted along some more. "This is it," he sighed. We were looking at a vast plain of broken bricks, stones, white dust. "Do you want to get out?" he asked. "No," I said, staring at a field. Near us, two children were sitting on a sewer pipe. "Do you want us, lady?" the big one called out. He was a boy; I could see that under his long hair. I didn't answer. I was staring at the church. It dominated the whole world. It was untouched, except for some kind of annex to the right of the big steeple. "They used it to shoot from," the man explained. "I know." "This must be what we saw from the plane," Vladek said excitedly; "remember, all those criss-crossed white lines?" "I wasn't looking," I answered dully. "Listen," I said to the driver, "could you come back for the bricks later if we pay you ten American dollars to take us back to our plane?" "Why not?" he said; "I never though tourists would start so early." We jolted back.

I was remembering the cupolas of the churches, the endless domes, the beautiful statues on their pedestals in the formal gardens, the statue of Copernicus. I asked the driver about it. "He's not sitting pretty anymore, blasted like everything else, even a piece of his pedestal; it looks like a grave now." I thought about Mrs. Lavinsky complaining about the Chasids coming for dinner Saturday night. There was no one left, no one. We went by building after building, or wall after wall. It was as if the city had fallen into some solution of time that was dissolving it. The buildings looked as if they were under construction, just the frames, the openings for the windows, the lines marked out for the floors, but then, if you looked more clearly, there were the jagged lines, the iron railings

472

guarding nothing, the white dust over everything. Little steeples stood in the middle of pyramids of bricks; curved balustrades stood with pink marble pillars holding up nothing. Three houses would pass whole, connected houses, the last ones a crazy design of bricks and shapes, things thrown down in a fit. Every building looked like a dying patient, or a terribly sick one, waiting for help. They stared at us, one after another, with their square eyes or arched eyes. "We are rebuilding," the man in the cart said proudly. "Are you?" I asked. I heard my voice coming to me through an empty window, catching on a black tree, running over some rubble, stopping by an old man, going down my throat like a rat. "The plane," Vladek shook me; "the plane." He paid the man and we got down.

Stefan was sitting next to a dead sparrow. "What's that?" I asked him. "He wanted to prove he could shoot, he proved it," the pilot answered grumpily; "are you ready?" "Why did you do it? Why did you have to do it?" I was screaming at Stefan, crying hysterically. He looked at Vladek, amazed. Vladek shook his head, picked me up, and put me in the plane. "Why did he do it?" I kept repeating all the way home. I wouldn't look down, or back, but sometimes I could feel Vladek shaking his head.

26

MR. WORCIK'S car drove us back to Freta Street. "Did she find what she wanted?" he asked Vladek. They carried on their conversation as if I weren't there. "I think so," Vladek said doubtfully. "What an idea—Warsaw!" Mr. Worcik spluttered. "Yours about Riga was even better," Vladek snarled. The car was pulling up to the sidewalk. "Don't come here again," I heard Vladek saying. "Look, Mrs. Lavinsky," Vladek said, taking my arm, "I think the Potato Head should stay with Lisa tonight." I nodded numbly. He took Ninka to Lisa's. "She's staying," he said, getting on his coat; he had spread mine out on the piano. "Don't stay," I told him. "I don't mind someone crying all night," Vladek answered, stubborn. "Good night," he said and turned over on his side facing the window. On top of the piano, I began crying softly. I would not read Vera's letter taped inside the lid. "Let the coffins stay locked," I thought to myself. "Let them stay closed." The moon was making a path from the sky to my mahogany perch. "Maybe I will read it later," I thought to myself; "maybe." I cried on and on. If Vladek heard me, he didn't give any sign. The sky was brightening.

"I am going to Palestine, or America," I decided. "As soon as I have some money, I am going." My eyes were swollen shut; I had to breathe through my mouth. The whole front of my face was shiny with tears and phlegm. I couldn't move my arms and I couldn't stop crying. "So now it is only Ninushka and me," I thought, starting all over again. Light was beginning to fill the room. "Vladek," I called. I was sure he was awake; he didn't answer me. The whole room was getting bright. I heard him move. He came over with a rag dipped in water. "Wash up and I'll get the Potato Head," he told me. Ninushka came into the room with Lisa. "Your Mommy has a cold; do you know what that is?" he asked her. "I know," she pouted; "everyone's always sick around here." "That means you can't scream and shout all the time, or jump up and down," he told her. "I never do those things!" She stamped her foot, beside herself. I smiled and took a deep breath, choking on the air. "Thank God you're back," Lisa sighed. Her eyes were bright as glass. "Now we can get busy with the dresses." "And the matches," I added in a hoarse voice; "I have to make a lot of money." "Wood can't cost so much," Lisa protested. "I have to make a lot of money, a lot," I said again.

"Are you going to work today?" Lisa asked me. "Oh, yes, but from now on," I said, climbing down, "it's days at the markets and nights at the hospital." "And when will you sleep?" Vladek asked, staring at me. "I can sleep with Ninushka when it's quiet; I don't need much sleep." "One thing after another," he mumbled, looking down at his shoes. "Do you want to start with the dresses today?" I asked Lisa. "Oh, yes," she burbled. "I have three done, and a little one for Ninushka; we can take her and Sashenka, too. I made him a Russian shirt, with some buttons down the side, and some baggy pants; they won't have to die in this heat." "You know where the market is?" Vladek asked. "I can't go; I have to work. Try not to let her give everything away," he warned Lisa. "Don't worry," I told him grimly.

We dressed the children and started out. "Oh," Lisa told me as we went along to the wood market, "I found some nurses from the military hospital who need washing done. I said we could do it. And Mrs. Kielwicz will make alterations. She'll stay in our rooms with Marian. She said we won't have to worry about going to the market and leaving the children alone with the stove." It was getting cold at night; it was the beginning of September. "That's good."

"You're not saying much today," Lisa observed. "There's the library," I said, pointing. The library formed one boundary of the market. Lisa was flushed with excitement. "Vladek said to go to the last part of the market," she said. "Do you know what this is?" "No, but we'll find out," she promised me. We walked down the street, and we were in it. The market occupied a field in the middle of the city streets; it was one city street wide. The first thing we saw were the fish stands. Everything was open. There was a little roof over it, and benches in front of it. On the benches were huge tubs; fish were swimming in them. Immediately, Ninka and Sashenka were in up to their noses. "Come on," I told Ninka; "this is not an aquarium." She started to complain. "We'll stop on the way back," I promised. "The fish look good," Lisa whispered, frenzied. "I don't know when I last saw a fish," I agreed. "Oh, I meant to tell you," she interrupted herself, "while you were gone a nun from the orphanage came to visit Ninushka. She said she was coming back with some fish and bread for Vladek and the little one; she was happy he was learning to read. 'Now he can become something,' she said." I saw Ninushka staring at the fish hanging from hooks on the back wall of the stand. "Come on," I said, pulling her along.

Then we were passing wagon after wagon filled with wood. "This is what we do with our money when we get some," Lisa sighed; "burn it all up." "Nice horse," Sasha said, reaching out to one. Ninka yanked him away from it. "They bite," she told him severely. Then we came to a place where everything was spread out on the ground: all kinds of berries, pottery jars full of milk, boards with slabs of cottage cheese, and endless muslin bags. "What's in those?" Ninka asked. "Cheese, little girl," one of the women answered her. "How do you take away the milk?" I asked. Only our maids had gone to the market. "You have to bring your own pitcher," the woman said; "or your own bag for the cheese; we don't have much." There were bags of mushrooms and baskets of eggs; little boards on benches were covered with wet towels covering little lumps. "Oh, that's butter," Lisa said, relieved; "butter is always covered with a wet towel." "Why?" asked Ninushka. "It cools off when it dries and makes the butter stay cold," Lisa explained. It was obvious Ninka didn't believe a word of it. "Why does it do that?" Sasha asked. "I don't know; it just does." "I want a mushroom," Lisa said suddenly, going over to one of the stands. The woman opened up the little sewed bag. "That one," Lisa said, pointing to a small mushroom. "Two kopecks," the woman said. "One," Lisa offered her. The woman handed over the dried mushroom; with a grin, Lisa slipped it into her pocket.

Farther on, we could see the last part of the market. People were just standing in place with both hands over their heads as if they were being arrested. As we got closer, we could see a woman holding a pin in one hand and a pair of shoes tied together by their laces in the other. "This must be what Vladek meant," I said. After this, we could see only the street with its neat row of houses. "It's only a little lot," Lisa said dubiously. "Vladek said this is where the most intelligent ones come. If a peasant needs a pair of shoes, and she has something good, then she doesn't display it on her linen runner; he says she brings it here and trades." "We don't need a stand?" Lisa asked. "We are the stands," I told her. Ninushka cackled. "Look at that pin," I muttered, seeing a woman holding up a pin. It was made of three interlocked circles, one circle on top. "I want the pin," I told Lisa. "How much is the pin?" Lisa asked. "Four rubles," the woman told her. "Ten kopecks," Lisa said. "You are starving my children," the woman mumbled, handing over the pin. "Put it on, Anya," Lisa whispered. I fastened it to the front of my blouse. It was still the same blouse and skirt Erdmann had bought me.

We found an empty place and held up the three dresses; Ninushka and Sasha sat in front of us in our shadows. An hour passed; nothing happened. Then it was one, two; still nothing happened. Suddenly women began swarming all over. "How much for the dress?" one of them demanded. "Make an offer," Lisa told her. "One hundred kopecks," the woman said, looking at the dress with longing. "Oh, I don't know," Lisa said, "I think that other woman wants one." "One hundred and fifty," the woman offered. "Two hundred, no less," Lisa insisted. The woman paid us. "Two fifty for the next one," Lisa whispered. We sold them all. "We have a fortune," I whispered, half dead with excitement; "let's go get something." We flew over to the wood market. "How much is thirty bundles?" "One hundred kopecks," the man told me. "We'll take the wagon load for thirty kopecks if you'll ride us home on it," Lisa told him, "but first you have to let us get some food." "You mean thirty for the whole wagon?" he asked her. "That's right," she said. I held my breath. 'Hmmmmph!" he snorted like a horse, but didn't contradict her. He nodded at us. "Let's leave them as deposits," I whispered to Lisa; we put Ninka and Sashenka up on top of the wood. "Sit still," I warned them.

"Oh, butter," Lisa whispered; "I want a little butter." "I want a fish," I cried. "You watch me buy it," Lisa said, running over. "How much is this half-dead fish?" she asked, pointing to a big one swimming happily around. "That's a good fish," the woman shouted at her. "A good fish?" Lisa said at the top of her lungs; "what's that mold all over it?" People were stopping to look. "I don't see any mold!" the woman cried, looking this way and that. "I'll let it die in peace in my kitchen for ten kopecks." "Ten kopecks!" the woman screamed, as if she had been stabbed in the heart. "The worms we catch it with cost more, the hooks cost more." "The worms and the hooks are better for the health; look at that moldy fish," Lisa addressed a passerby. The passerby stopped, coming over, curious. "All right, fifteen kopecks," said the woman scooping it out with a net, slitting its throat, and wrapping it in paper. "And don't come back," she shouted at us as we went off. "Now for the butter," Lisa announced. "How much is that melted butter?" she demanded of the man selling. "It's not melted," he said picking up the cloth. There it was, a solid whitish-yellow lump, beaded with cold water. "It sits in the sun a whole day and it's not melted, so tomorrow you'll sell rancid butter, I see your game," Lisa scolded him. "A piece this big"—she spread her hands six inches apart—"ten kopecks." He shook his head no. "I won't pay you anything for it tomorrow when it smells to high heaven," Lisa threatened at the top of her lungs. "Look," he said, "I recognize your accent. I see you don't have anything. This time you can have it for ten kopecks, but no more of these tricks. I have a family to feed too. And what are you going to take it in; you don't have anything." Lisa tore a piece of paper from the fish. "Just put it here," she said, ashamed. "No, it'll smell; wrap it in this." He gave her a piece of newspaper. "You have the same germs on it already," he assured her. "It's quite a haul," she said, laughing like a child as we went back to the wagon. "We can fry fish in the butter. Also, I heard the soldiers are selling all kinds of things, shoes, dresses, on some streets. I need some, let's buy." "Tomorrow," I promised. "And more sheets," Lisa reminded me. We rode home with the children on top of the wagon like conquerors of Rome. Lisa put the food away while Ninushka and I went to sleep on the floor; then she woke me up, and I left for the hospital.

I sat next to Rachel's bed thinking out how much money I would have at the end of the week. Ninushka needed new clothes, at least some boots for the winter. I needed something for myself. We needed more cod liver oil. It was starting to get dark early. I would have to get some *karbit*. I wondered if Ninushka had ever seen it in the orphanage. It was a little piece of stone you put in a can and filled with water. It let out a little gas, and you lit it with a match. When you were finished, you blew it out, and emptied out the water, or covered the can, if it came in one, to keep the gas from evaporating. Usually, we just put in a little piece, what we thought we would need. It didn't give much light, but it was something. "At this rate," I decided, "it will take me years to get out of the country. I have to think of another way to make money. I will sell Vera's piano," I decided. If I was leaving, I couldn't take it with me anyway. "I'll sell that last," I decided, thinking it over. Then I remembered the day they had taken us to the ghetto—these pictures kept coming back to me like horrible photographs, and Doctor Yurbo's voice behind them, mocking: "Forget? Forget? You can try to forget; you can try to forget." The woman next door had rushed in with the peasants, snatching everything she could get from my parents' apartment. Someone had come into Emergency with a bloody arm and told me that this woman, Mrs. Fedro, had our furniture. So the gossip went. I would ask her for some things; then I wouldn't have to pay to buy them. If Mrs. Fedro didn't give them to me, I would go to the commissar and have her arrested. "It is a miracle," I thought, "to have police to go to." But then I remembered Lisa telling me they could send me to Siberia without asking anyone any questions. "No, I have to leave," I said to myself again; "I have to leave Poland." I would go to the neighbor's house tomorrow, before the market. There might be things to sell. And I would really have to find Anzia; she must have some jewelry left. And I would get a good dress made from a sheet and better things to sell, and the matches. It was possible to work out.

Rachel opened her eyes. "How are you?" she asked. "I'm fine," I laughed; "I'm thinking of going to Berlin." "So am I," Rachel said; "what else do I have to do here but think? The only times I've ever been happy were in hospitals; they have a good medical school there. I think I could stand the Germans until I came back. I'd probably have to start over from the beginning, with the gymnasium." "No," I told her, "I want to go there so I can leave for Palestine or America; I don't want to be here anymore." "We can go that far together, then," Rachel said. "I'm much better." Her voice was stronger. "Yesterday I sat up; today I walked around a little. It gives me a headache, but I don't get dizzy anymore. Where were you?" "Warsaw," I said. "Oh." Rachel was looking at me as if I were a page in a book. "And now you're leaving? You shouldn't have gone there." "That's right." "A whole city fell on your head," she said. "I'm lucky, I think; I wasn't attached too much. Sometimes, the times in the ghetto seem the best to me. What a horrible thing to have to say about your own life," she murmured, looking down at her blanket. It had just recently appeared. "It's getting colder," Rachel said. "I wonder if there's any money left in your yard," she thought out loud. "I could tell the police about it, and ask them to dig. I'm sure they would if I told them they could have a part, whatever they thought was fair, if they found something." "That's a good idea," Rachel agreed; "how is Ninushka?" "Sleeping in the cubicle." "You ought to join her," Rachel said; "you look exhausted. That young man who calls her the potato head visits me every day. You'll break his heart when you leave." "I can't take him; it's too much. I can barely feed myself and Ninushka." "Well, he's getting attached to me," Rachel thought out loud; "he reads me stories," "I can imagine," I laughed. " 'The Fox and the Crow' is very good, what do you mean?" Rachel teased. "Go to sleep," she said again; "look, I'm shutting my eyes."

The next morning, a scurrying sound woke me up in the apartment. I stiffened on the piano, forcing myself to open my eyes. Three dried leaves were chasing each other in circles, curled up like mummy-bodies. I was shivering. Ninka was still asleep on the floor. I put the blanket we had traded for in the wood market on top of her. "Lisa," I whispered, going to her door, "I'm not going to the market today; can you go?" "I'll have to leave the children with Mrs. Kielwicz then," she whispered back. Sergei was still asleep. "Two of them are too much around here." "Fine," I answered; "it's getting cold." "We have to do something about these windows," she sighed, watching the gray and white cat Vladek had brought to catch bugs jump out of her room through the window into the court. The children were forbidden to play with the cat. I was sure they did anyway. "Maybe tomorrow we'll have something to sell," I said, pulling on my long red coat, setting off for my parents' block. I got to the neighbor's house and twisted the bell. Mrs. Fedro came to the door. "It is Anya Savikin," I called in through the crack. "What do you want here?" she demanded. "Mrs. Fedro," I began, "I know you didn't expect us to come back, so you didn't think there was any harm in it; I'm sure that's how it was." The clawing hands of the peasants were all around her head, suspended claws. "But I am back with my little baby and we don't have anything." "You can't have anything," she shouted, starting to push the door shut. I pushed back. "I'm not asking for much," I told her. "You keep the furniture, but I want some of the blankets back, and some towels and pots and dishes; I'll come for them tonight." "I'm not giving you anything," she shouted again, slamming the door.

"We'll see about that," I thought to myself, walking off to the market. "Who do you see about someone stealing from you?" I asked the butter man. "The commissar's office; they usually come to you." "Which way?" I asked. "Two miles that way," he said pointing to the right; "the egg lady's going that way." I got in with the boxes of chickens and baskets of eggs. "There it is," she said with a shudder as I climbed down; the new cold wind was whipping my hair around my face. A soldier was sitting at a desk inside the entrance. "I want to report some stealing," I told him. "Third office on the left," he pointed. I opened the big oak door. The building was only a big house. I wondered who had lived here before. "I want to report some stealing," I said again. "Yes," the man said, looking up.

"When we were taken to the ghetto," I explained, "my neighbor, Mrs. Fedro, took furniture and crystal and sheets, blankets, and clothes. We have nothing; I'm working day and night," I told him. "Did you speak to her?" "She slammed the door. She said I can't have anything. A Major Bilov, a pilot, said I could ask for him here; he knows I have a piano, a mahogany one. He told me I could come here for justice." "Bilov is around somewhere," he mumbled. "So," he said, "her full name," beginning to fill out a form. "Masha Fedro," and I gave him the address. "Also," I added, "my husband buried a lot of gold in our back yard. I can't dig it up myself, but if you could lend me three soldiers, you could keep whatever you think is fair, and," I saw the light in his eyes, "one night he and my brother buried a lot of jewelry in Mrs. Fedro's flower gardens; we didn't think anyone would look there. But of course, I can't look now myself. We never thought of that," I added sadly. "Oh, Bilov and I would like to do that," he said. "We can get a third; that doesn't even have

481

to be official. In the meantime, we arrest Mrs. Fedro. Bilov!" he shouted down the hall, getting up. "Oh, hello," Bilov said smiling under his blond hair; "did you get your piano?" "We're going to arrest a Mrs. Fedro; want to go?" "Sure, I'm sick of it here," he answered. "Rosinski!" the first man whose name was Sergeant Yablonsky, shouted down the hall; "take over for a while." The three of us drove off down the street in a truck, chattering in Russian.

"Mrs. Fedro," the man from the desk called, hammering at the door. "Yes," she quavered. "Under arrest," he announced in Polish. "This lady has accused you of stealing; you will show us her things." The whole dining room was filled with our furniture. Our crystal chandelier hung over the table. Across the hall, I could see the gleam of our dark oak dining room furniture, the big credenza Momma used to lock. "She has *all* our furniture," I wailed. "Do you want your furniture back?" Sergeant Yablonsky asked, taking out his pencil. "No, just the kitchen things, blankets, sheets, things like that." "You took all those things?" Bilov asked in an astonished voice, looking at her. "Yes," she answered, like a guilty child; "but we never expected them back. She thought so herself." "You didn't have to rob the dead while they were still living," I screamed at her suddenly. "Take what belongs to you," Bilov said. "It is disgusting, this pillaging." "I don't even know what that means," Mrs. Fedro wailed. "The commissar will explain," he promised. "For one thing, it means all the stolen articles will be taken from you for the state." We went through the rooms. "Get the sheets first," Bilov advised me; "then you can wrap all the other things in it. All day, this goes on. You wouldn't believe it. You'd think the furniture had real legs and ran from house to house at night." "Carrying pots and blankets," I reminded him. "They fly," he sighed. "There are no windows to keep them out," I said, thinking of our apartment. "Someone told me you were working at the hospital," Bilov said, folding two sheets inside the one I had just spread out; "I heard they have good thick glazed paper there. You'd just need some wood for the cross-bars; it would even let in some light." "I'll ask; thank you."

"That Mischa Dudek is a good doctor," he said; "I'm standing on one of his legs now. "It's good they got him off the field. Finished in here?" he asked, looking around. I had six sheets and a tower of blankets stacked on the sheet spread out on the bed. "Finished," I said sighing, "but I want to check the closet for sweaters." I opened the doors: There they all were, my beautiful dresses, and Vera's purple suit with the gold epaulettes. I pulled out the figured sweaters from Zakopanie. "And this," I said suddenly, pulling out the purple velvet suit. "Is that yours?" he asked dubiously. "My sister's," I answered. "No furniture?" Yablonsky asked again, still writing in the dining room when we came back with our pots and sheet bag. "I bet she doesn't want to stay in Poland," Bilov guessed. "You can always claim it later," Yablonsky told me, glaring at Mrs. Fedro and adding some items to his list. "So we'll drop you off," he told me, "on the way to the prison, and then we'll come back for her flower beds and your back yard." "Flower beds?" Mrs. Fedro wailed in panic; no one answered her. "You may be in a lot if trouble," Yablonsky told her threateningly; "not even giving this lady a sweater for her baby."

"I'm back," I called to Lisa. Yablonsky thumped the tied-up sheet and the pots down on her floor, waved and went out. Ninka and Sasha were reading to each other in a corner. "What have they got there?" "Some books on planes Vladek got," she said. "Last week they had one on first aid; Sasha practically killed me in my sleep with a tube or something." "Tourniquet," Sasha volunteered without looking up. "Can't Vladek find some stories?" I asked her. "They say they're tired of the fairy tales," she answered, tilting her head in the direction of the children. "Now he has to read them to himself; they get annoyed if he even comes over with a word." "Incredible," I mumbled. "I'm going back to my piano; wake me up in time for work." "How many sheets?" Lisa called as I was leaving. "Seven, and five blankets; don't cut up the blankets." "Seven," Lisa was exclaiming, transported to heaven.

"Up, Anya." Lisa was shaking me. Vladek was already there; the smell of fish soup filled the room. "Don't let them choke on the bones." I began getting dressed. I always ate at the hospital to save food. "You can have some of this," Lisa insisted. "It's mostly water and bones; it just tastes good." "Delicious," I said, drinking it down. "We sold another dress and some kerchiefs," Lisa told me; "Janina made a lot of money on alterations." "Good for her," I said, putting on my coat. Ninushka was putting hers on, too. The routine was settling in. "Let's go," I said, taking her hand; "you know how to fly a plane yet?" "It's not so hard," she answered. "You have to read that book to me; you promised," Vladek pouted. "You can't have this one if you don't." "What's that one?" I asked, shaking my head awake. *"The Campaigns of Peter the Terrible."* "Peter the Terrible," Ninka echoed, impressed. "Good grief," Lisa sighed. "Don't worry," I told her; "I'm going to talk to Mischa Dudek; he knows all the fliers. We can get them some stories." "You'll come back with something about the stomach lining; I can't stand it; it's like living in a hospital." "Don't worry," I said again, suddenly remembering; "I'll get some of my father's books from Mrs. Fedro. They're digging up her flower garden tomorrow." "What?" Ninka asked. "Never mind, I'll explain later." Ninka and I set off, her little hand in mine. The top of her head was still bandaged. "I'm going to get the doctor to look at that head tonight," I said. *"You're* supposed to get your abscess cut," she taunted; "he told me to remind you. Can I see Aunt Rachel?" "In the morning; you know that."

Ninushka went to sleep in a tiny cubicle. A little *karbit* lit the tiny room. She still hated sleeping in the dark. I put on my uniform and went out into the ward. Doctor Dudek was sitting next to Rachel's bed. "Tibia," he said, fingering the bone in one of her fingers. "Tibia," she repeated after him, obedient. "Spleen," he said suddenly, pressing his hand into the lower part of her stomach. "Spleen," she repeated smiling, covering his hand with hers. "Heart," he said, lifting his hand. "Oh no," laughed Rachel, pushing his hand aside; "I know where that is." "Toe?" he asked, his eyes fixed on hers, bending to the foot of the bed. Rachel was laughing a deep laugh. Doctor Dudek caught sight of me. "Oh, Anya," he said guiltily; "I'm teaching Rachel anatomy." "So I see." "She learns fast," he told me, blushing. "I'm sure she does." "I'm coming home at the end of the week," Rachel cried, "and you know what—Mischa says you can wash my hair tonight." Her dark hair was well below her shoulders. "That's wonderful, it is wonderful," I said bending over, hugging her. She reached up, hugging me. On the other side of the bed, Mischa Dudek was looking at us enviously. "Now you will have to come over all the time," I told him; "we want you to. The children are reading all about tourniquets and pressure points. You'll be our most valuable guest, won't he, Rachel?" "Oh, yes," Rachel cried.

It was impossible not to smile at her, she was so happy. "You can wash her hair, and I can cut your abscess," he

484

told me; Ninushka reminded me." "You *told* her to do the reminding." "What difference does it make; it's there," he pouted. "Oh, go on, Anya!" Rachel cried; "you know all about it. He can give you a shot." "How am I going to work without lifting an arm?" I asked him. "I'll wash Rachel's hair if it takes two arms," he promised; "and you should be able to handle a hypodermic with one good arm and one that raises as high as your shoulder." "Why not tomorrow?" "You know, I think she is a coward, isn't she, Rachel?" "She is, she is!" Rachel cried. "Come on, then," he said, "and try not to make so much noise you wake up Ninushka." "Oh, stop it already," I complained, following him to the little white emergency room.

"Peel the uniform to the waist, take off the brassiere." He took out a syringe. "You're not so little after all," he said, smiling. "Stop it!" I cried, turning purple. I remembered Momma telling me how she and a friend had once locked themselves in an outhouse to cut pieces out of their breasts; they thought they were too large on top for the fashion, but they lost their nerve the minute their clothes came off. "So that's done," Doctor Dudek said, pressing a huge gauze pad up under my arm. "I didn't feel anything." "Complaining?" he asked; "I'll cut under the other arm. It was the shot. It never hurts when you have a shot; you know that." "Rachel didn't have a shot when I cut hers." "Rachel is something," he agreed. "She is," I said in intense confusion; "she really is." "I think she may get to medical school yet. We are so short here, you know, and we want more women doctors; there aren't enough men to go round the professions." "If she stays here," I reminded him. "Don't you think she will?" he asked, worried. "I think she will," he answered himself, his face clearing. "And when she's really better, she can start working here, too."

27

"ARE you going to the market today?" Lisa asked me when I got up; it was a little after ten. "No, I'm going to look for Anzia." It was happening more and more, plans forming themselves in my mind without my knowing about them until they were ready for me. "How will you find her?" "Someone in the market said she lived in a small town about thirty miles out; I have a little map." I showed her the charcoal drawing on back of the paper we had wrapped the fish in. "Why don't you just go to the market with me?" Lisa pleaded. "I have another dress ready, and some children's things. It's a nice day, not too cold, we could take them with us, the children." "No, leave them with Janina; I have to see Anzia; I have to get things done." "Your idea of getting things done is wearing me out," she sighed. "What's that?" she asked, pointing to a heap covered by a sheet in front of the pyramid of wood that filled one corner of the room. "Waxed sheets of paper for the windows. Doctor Dudek gave them to me, enough for us, and Rachel's room, too. Vladek will nail on crosspieces from the wood pile. Doctor Dudek will explain it to him at work." "So it's Doctor Dudek again, is it?" Lisa asked, frowning. "He's Mischa to Rachel," I told her. "Look, it's a long trip; I have to get going." "I don't see why you need to," Lisa complained. I was already buttoning my coat. "It's getting cold; we'll need a lot of money if we're going to live and I'm going to save up money to go, too."

"How are you going to get there?" she asked, resigned. "There's someone sick out there who needs a shot and some bandages; the peasant's cart is coming. He'll take me the rest of the way later." "Ninushka looks better without her bandages," Lisa said. "Better, but the doctor says she'll have to wear a hat in the house all the time as soon as it gets cold, and the fat has to keep going on her head every day. But all she needs on top now is a kerchief." "The holes are filling up," Lisa said, bending over to look at Ninka. "Hardly any," Ninka said without looking up. "Mommy was a big baby at the hospital last night. Doctor Dudek told me. He said to watch her and see she doesn't get hot." "A fever," I corrected her. "Hot's just as good," Ninka answered, turning a page. "What *is* that?" I asked her, annoyed, getting ready to leave. Outside, there was the sound of metal wheels and horses' hooves. *"Campaigns of Peter the Terrible*; he lived in Paltava," Ninka answered, glued to the page. "He didn't live there; he fought there," I said. "Same thing," Ninushka answered again. I went out, shaking my head.

The cold wind was winding itself around my ankles and legs like rope. "Stocking and boots," I thought to myself; "we have to get them. I have to tell Bilov to get some books from Mrs. Fedro." "Mrs. Lavinsky?" called the peasant from the wagon. "That's me," I said, climbing into the back, swallowing hard. "You don't look like no doctor," he grumbled. "Funny, you don't look like a peasant," I grumbled back, seeing the apartment running backward. "What then?" "What then what?" "What do I look like?" "Peter the Terrible," I answered. There was a horrible chuckle from up front. "Did Doctor Dudek tell you you have to take me to Zelazna Village?" "After you fix," he answered. "How is the baby?" "Hot like a stove." "What have you been doing to him?" "Putting covers on." "Are you trying to cook him?" "Stove is on also," he muttered. "Well, hurry up this horse or we'll have to throw him in a river to cool him off. After we go to Zelazna, I'll come back to check. If he's not better, we go back to the hospital." "No hospital," he said positively. "Why not?" "People die there." "People die in huts more," I answered; "God will never forgive you if He sends me to take the baby to the hospital and you do not obey His will." He mumbled something. "What?" I asked, watching the stones give way to dirt. "I see about it!" he screamed roughly. "God sees everything," I repeated mechanically, breathing in the pines.

My stomach was doing its usual grasshopper dance. "He don't die?" the peasant asked suddenly. "I don't know; I haven't seen him." We joggled along for over an hour and a half. "House!" he announced proudly. A little hut, shaped like a kiosk with a thatched roof, stood in front of us; chickens were chasing each other around the yard. Some birds swooped out of the trees and ate some seed. "Damn bird!" he shouted, waving his arms. There was a big pole in front of the house with a pot hung from the top; a face was drawn on it with charcoal. "The baby did that?" I asked. "The birds," he said. "The birds did it?" "Frightens them," he grumped. Inside, the hut was like an oven. An old stove made of bricks held together with mud was roaring with wood; there was more green wood drying out in a corner. Somewhere the baby was screaming. "Where is the baby?" I asked. The peasant pointed at a cot. The child was buried under blankets and coats; I fished him out. "What is this?" I asked; "a boy or a girl or a bundle of clothes?" The baby was giving ear-splitting squalls. "Boy," he said. I carried the baby outside. The mother followed me out; she was wearing at least three skirts and two shawls, the usual babushka tied under her chin.

"Help me get him out of this stuff," I told her, holding the baby. She began pulling things off him; the mound of clothing got higher and higher. "He must be the size of a nut," I muttered. More and more clothes were peeled off; a tiny baby emerged. "So," I said, putting him down on one of the coats he'd been wearing; "let's see what's what. One hundred and three degree temperature; he has an infection." I turned him over: no rash. From the way he was screaming, he sounded as if he had swallowed a hatchet. "Open your mouth," I said, prying his mouth open. One little tooth stared up at me like a tombstone. "Nothing there," I said. The parents sighed with relief. "Does he move his bowels?" I asked. "What?" the woman said. "Does he fill up his diaper?" I asked again. "Oh, yes, he does." "Throws up?" "No, no." His right ear looked fine. I started to put my little flashlight against his left ear and he shrieked so loudly I almost jumped. "Ear infection," I said with relief; "nothing to worry about." I took out the hypodermic, filled it, and gave the baby a shot. His mother was starting to pick up the clothes to put them back on.

"No clothes *at all*," I ordered. She looked at me as if I had gone mad. "He is too hot, much too hot," I explained; "he needs to get cooler, do you understand?" They nodded solemnly. "But not to freeze, do you understand? So," I went on, "keep him out here, in the shade, under this flannel blanket. Then when the house cools off, you can take him in. He has to have these pills every four hours." They looked at each other, stricken. "No clock," the man said. "In the morning when you get up," I said;

"when the sun is straight up in the sky; when it gets dark, and in the middle of the night. Can you do that?" The woman nodded violently, starting to cry. "Baby live?" the man asked me; "no hospital?" "I don't think so," I told him, "but I want to look at him again when we come back from Zelazna." "Let's go fast," he said in a hurry. "Don't rush; we have to wait for the medicine to work anyway. Just don't make him hot," I said to the woman. "Don't make him hot, you understand? He'll cry more and be sick more if he's hot." "Yes, yes, yes," she said, pulling on the tails of her shawls with every word.

"Let's go," I said, getting in the cart; "you're sure there's an Anzia in that village?" "The cucumber man's lady," he answered. We rattled along. "Here," he said finally, stopping in front of a big brick house. "Where is it?" "Second floor," he told me; "hurry please." "There's *no* hurry," I said again; "the medicine takes a long time to work." He nodded sagely. I climbed up to the second floor. "Kobielski," I remembered, knocking at one door. Anzia answered; it was Anzia. Nothing about her had changed. I was turned to stone. "Anyushka!" she screamed, grabbing me; "you are not alive?" "Yes, I am," I said. "You are not alive!" she screamed again. "Yes, I am," I insisted, as if I had to persuade her, "and Ninushka, too." She was pushing me into the dining room, running into the kitchen, making some tea. "I have some honey cake," she babbled, slicing a piece and putting it on my skirt. "Eat." She was staring at me as if I were a magic mirror. I couldn't stop looking at her. Her life had continued; the earth had opened its alligator jaws and eaten whole chunks of mine, flesh, blood, everything. Perhaps she was right; perhaps I wasn't alive, or the same person wasn't. I was sitting in my chair, resenting her, the uninterruptedness of her life.

"I cannot believe it," she said finally; "eat, eat." "And Ninushka, too!" she said finally. "No one else?" "No one else. I am leaving Poland, Anzia; I'm going out of the country." "Oh, no!" Anzia cried. "Too much is different," I said. "Not so different," she coaxed. "How is your husband?" I asked. "Drunk, always drunk," she sighed; "we make a lot, but he drinks it all up. I even get beatings." "See, everything is different," I whispered; maybe I had been hoping to come here with Ninushka and live with her. She was quiet. "I came to ask you," I said, taking a deep breath, "if you had anything left from Momushka; I

489

know she gave you a lot." "She gave me everything she could! And not just things, either," Anzia cried. "But he has swallowed most of it." "You don't have anything?" I asked in disbelief. "Oh, I didn't say that; did you hear me say that?" Anzia asked in her old sly, conspiratorial voice; it choked my throat to hear it. "I have some jewelry," she whispered; "it's hidden; come."

I followed her down the dark hall. "In the eggs," Anzia laughed; "he never looks there. This was a sacred trust; what did you think?" she asked me, insulted. At the bottom of the egg basket were four or five yellowish eggs. Anzia pulled them out. She cracked one smartly against the table. Momma's garnet bracelet fell out. "I wasn't going to let him get it," she said, victorious. "It took me a long time to think up this glue; it was worse than making fancy Easter eggs." She cracked another egg. Out came Mother's diamond and pearl ring and a little gold watch. The third egg hatched out a pair of diamond earrings and a sapphire. "That's all I have," Anzia whispered, stuffing them in my pocket, filling up the egg basket again, "except for the silver basket."

"I want you to keep that, Anzia." Tears were streaming down my face. I wanted to thank her for having stayed alive. She was a cord, a thread, a telephone wire going back into the old rooms where the old voices still spoke; her memory went back further than mine. "How can I keep it?" she asked; "he doesn't even know I have it. It will be my present for Ninushka, when she gets married." Ninushka married! "Where do you keep that?" I asked her, starting to smile. The corners of my mouth went up; my face cracked like porcelain. "We have a lot of preserves," she said, taking down an enormous crockery jar, breaking the wax seal. Apricot jam flowed into the skin; the little silver handle of the basket began to emerge. "Got it!" Anzia exclaimed, dragging it out; the whole inside was filled with leaking apricots and syrup. "We will wash it off," Anzia said busily, rinsing it. "Here," she said to me, wrapping it in a towel and handing it to me, the whole little ark with its paired animals, Noah and his wife leading, or following, it was hard to tell. "Don't forget, when Ninushka gets married, and don't lose it," she scolded. "I won't lose it," I said, crying again.

There was a drunken husband; I had to go. "You will visit us? My address is Fourteen Freta Street; Rachel's there, too." But it wouldn't be the same; it would never be

490

the same again. She knew that, too; she wouldn't want to go back. "Rachel!" she exclaimed loudly. "Don't worry, I'll come," she swore. "I'll see that Ninushka. And Rachel," she added. But we both knew she never would. "Goodbye, Anzia," I said kissing her. We were both crying.

"We can go?" the peasant asked, softened. "Go on." The horse started off. The old apartment was a bombed building; then it was dissolving to mist. Was that really all she had? Maybe her husband hadn't drunk everything up; maybe she had sold things, who knew? People changed so. "How can I be asking myself such things?" I thought, horrified. "I am becoming a monster. Not to trust Anzia!" The peasant's cart was stopping in front of his house. "One hundred degrees," I told his parents; "much better. Give him the medicine. Don't cover him up too much, put a little hat on his head, one that goes over his ears, and if he's not better in a week, send someone back to the hospital for me." "Yes, lady," the peasant said loudly; they were overjoyed. "We go back now?" It was almost three in the afternoon. I would barely get back in time for work. "Now," I answered, climbing back in the cart.

After the visit to Anzia, life changed. Something had stiffened inside me, an old exoskeleton like the ones in the labs we studied before anatomy: prehuman. I sold Momma's garnet bracelet, the band made up of garnets shaped like flowers, one huge flower bursting its petals apart in the center. People from the village began coming up to me with expensive things to sell for them. I kept a quarter of what I was paid. "They trust you," Lisa marvelled. I had given Doctor Dudek the silver basket to lock up in the hospital safe with the drugs; it was the only thing I wanted to keep besides the pictures. We were making more and more money. In the safe, the little basket was filling with bigger and bigger bills. But it was also getting colder and colder. Snow streamed against Vladek's waxed windows, feeling for the cracks with fingers like an experienced safecracker's. It piled up against them in thick drifts.

It was too cold for the children to go out. Ninushka and Sasha got along well, reading, reading, but after a day in the house, there would be fighting, pulling books away from each other, shrieks, accusations. "He kicked me." "She threw the book at me first!" Mrs. Kielwicz took Marian back to their room. "His heart can't stand it," she apologized, blushing. "It's a good thing we have Janina here doing the alterations," Lisa sighed. Going the three blocks for water was getting to be more and more of a problem. Lisa usually went because she had boots. Rachel wasn't strong enough to go. She was beginning work at the hospital and was busy studying medical books flat on her back. The stove was blazing constantly; it ate wood like a forest fire. The room was so big and the windows so bad, we were constantly feeding it just to keep from freezing. In the apartment, Ninushka had to wear a thick quilted hat lined with cotton. Lisa had made it for Ninka because the cold hurt the sores on her head. Her fingers and toes were always wrapped in cotton; we couldn't find any gloves.

"I wish you wouldn't go to the market so much," Lisa insisted; "you're wearing yourself out. Look how thin you're getting again." "I have to," I answered, leaving with two sweaters buttoned under my coat. I had no boots. I would stand there all day holding up the jewelry and scarves the people from the city gave me. At the end of the day, my legs were so numb I couldn't feel them. I would have to watch where I put each one down. "A wagonful of wood," I told the woodman every day, and then I would throw myself over the wood like a long rag, and so he would bring me home, my legs dangling from the back like dead flags. Lisa unloaded me with the wood. After she and Rachel carried me in, they showed the woodman where the bundles went. "I know already," he complained.

"This wood is wet!" Lisa shouted one day. "So is snow," he shouted back at her. "I can't help the skies; you stop the snow, the wood dries out," he roared, throwing the wet bundles down. "It's going to take hours to start this fire," Lisa complained. "I have some old newspapers here," Rachel said, going back to her room. "I saved them; I thought this might happen." Still, it took the three of us an hour and a half to light the fire. "I think the wood should be spread out," Lisa considered; "it would dry faster that way." Rachel and I began spreading out the logs and sticks; the whole apartment looked like a raft. "Wonderful," Lisa said, "the children can't play in here. Sashenka, did you hear that?" she demanded. "You and Ninka can only sit and read." "On different sides of the room, I hope," Valdek chimed in. He was living at the hospital. He and Rachel seemed to be studying together;

492

Doctor Dudek was instructing them both. "They're both good," Doctor Dudek had said. "I know how to sit," Ninka protested. "Let's see you practice first," Vladek growled at her.

Our teeth were chattering; it sounded as if typewriters were loose in the room. No one's disposition was getting any better. Lisa was afraid to leave the fire for a second; if she stopped fanning it, it would go out. "I think one's catching," she called back to us. A hissing steam cloud was coming from the stove. "Ninushka, eat your meat," I ordered her; "we have to go to the hospital." I was picking up a blanket to wrap her in. "I'll carry her," Vladek said. "I want to walk," Ninushka protested. "No one asked you, Potato Head," Vladek answered, throwing her up into the air. She squealed with delight.

We set off for the hospital. Three little jets of air preceded us. The night was blue-black and starless. "Freezing," Vladek said, stopping to stamp his feet and warm up his toes. The snow shone blue under the huge white moon. Long blue shadows of light floated before us like mysterious fish. "Are you going to be a doctor, too?" I asked. "Vladek can't be a doctor; he's too dumb," Ninka chimed in. "Don't be nasty," I scolded her. "Not so dumb as you are," he answered. "I want to, but you know what I am," he said slowly; "my parents had no teeth. No one can read in my village . . ." His voice trailed off. "So you could be the first; you could go back there and fix them all up." "Ha!" Ninka said loudly. "I don't want to go back there," Vladek told me. "No one wanted me there. Why should I go back?" "I don't know." "No wonder no one wanted you," Ninka complained; "you're squeezing me." "Will you shut up?" he said to the top of her head. "Maybe she wanted you, but she couldn't keep you. Maybe she was too sick." "Sick of him," Ninushka added. "Shut up," he said again. "She wasn't sick," he told me; "she just didn't want me; she told everyone." "Then you could stay here; then you don't owe them anything." "I probably would go back now and then, just to see the others, if they were all right." "There were others who were good to you; there must have been." "No one would be good to him," Ninka announced positively. "Ninushka!" I ordered; "keep completely quiet! You are really horrible tonight! I don't want to hear another word from you." "Glllllllblllle glurb," Ninka said. "What?" I asked. She repeated the noises. "You said you didn't want to hear another word so now she's making noises," Vladek explained in a tired voice. "Silence altogether!" I commanded. She kept quiet.

"There were people," Vladek said finally. "Well, you have plenty of time to decide," I finished; we were standing outside the hospital. "We'd better take the Potato Head in," Vladek said, still embarrassed.

"It's too quiet in here," Doctor Dudek said, looking around the ward; eight patients were sleeping peacefully. There was a five-year-old with swollen glands in one of the cubicles. "What do you think it is?" I asked him, straightening up. "We'll wait for the blood tests." "He keeps coming down with everything, doesn't he?" I said, thinking out loud. "And he has a lot of bone breaks. I saw the pictures." "We'll wait for the counts," Doctor Dudek said roughly; "it's nothing good." "I can do the counts." "Please, stay where you are; it's too quiet already," he complained again. "I could go out and find you some patients," I volunteered, "but I think you're just missing your night school." Doctor Dudek blushed. "Vladek says something about becoming a doctor." "I don't see why not; it's one of the virtues of Communism," he answered pompously. "How true," I answered him. "And what does Communism do about quiet nights in the hospital? Shouldn't people take turns getting sick? This isn't right, all these empty beds. I think it's poor planning." "Oh, Anya," he interrupted, irritated, "sometimes you're just like your daughter." "It's the first time I've ever heard the comparison made just that way," I told him, pleased.

"If I leave," I persisted, "who will Vladek stay with? Or does Communism share friendship, too?" Doctor Dudek was getting angry. "He'll probably stay with Rachel," he told me. "They got very close when she was sick, and now they study together all the time." "But is it quite proper? He's such a big boy and Rachel had gotten to be such a big girl." "Anya!" he warned me, raising his voice slightly. "It is a problem," I went on sweetly. "Rachel may find an even bigger boy to watch her; that will settle that." "Will you please go to the cubicle and go to sleep with Ninushka? And don't bother Rachel with repeating our conversations." "Oh, no," I swore, "she still gets headaches easily, and also," I paused, "there are some things you should talk to her about yourself." "That abscess of yours," he said with a light in his eyes; "I forgot to check it." "Somehow I think it will wait for a while," I answered, scurrying into my cubicle. "How warm it is in here," I thought, stretching out next to Ninushka. I could hear her breathing through her mouth. "A cold," I thought; "now we'll all have them." I started counting her breaths; I was up to seven when I was sound asleep.

I woke up to a horrible clatter. There was some kind of incredible screaming in Russian coming from the emergency entrance. "I'd better get up and help Doctor Dudek," I thought, putting my feet on the floor. As usual, my feet hurt from the cold. During the days at the market, they would split and bleed. The screaming was still going on as I turned the corner. "Some crazy Russian woman," I thought to myself; "all this sharing of happiness is driving them out of their minds." Then I saw Lisa. She was frantically waving something, and Doctor Dudek was trying to grab her arms and force them to her sides. "Be quiet!" he was pleading; "this is a hospital. I'll get her." "Something happened to Ninushka!" I shouted from where I was. "She's in the cubicle; what's the matter with you?" he asked, turning around to me. "To Rachel, something happened to Rachel!" "Nothing happened to anyone," he said grumpily; "she just wants to tell you something. I can't stand it," he muttered, walking off; "all of you have gone crazy."

"I've got it," Lisa shouted, falling on me; "I've got it. I told you he would get it!" "Do you have the measles?" I asked. There was a little girl upstairs with a case. It was the worst thing I could think of, except for a fire, at the moment. "No, the letter!" she shrieked, beside herself. "From my brother in Kaunas; he found your Julia Doroshnik!" "No, he didn't," I answered. "He did, look, here's her picture." She held out a picture; it was Julia, a man and a little boy. "Who are those other people?" I asked confused. "She's married to the man, Frederich Zamenhoff, and that's his nephew. They're adopting him, I think. Anyway, the thing is, that is a letter from her, with her address, and you can write tonight, and my brother, he'll take it right back; that's why I came over." "Who's with the children?" I asked automatically. "Rachel's with Sergei. Are you awake?" she demanded suspiciously. "I don't know. I'm sorry, can I see the letter?" Lisa produced it. "Julia says they're leaving the country, too; they're leaving Kaunas in a few months," I read out to Lisa; "and she's married, you know that. She married someone who got tired of fighting with his mother and sister in the ghetto, he decided to move in with her, and she said, if he didn't

495

marry her, he'd have to go back. That sounds like Julia," I sighed. "It *is* Julia," Lisa insisted. "She says I should write her and tell her when I want to go and we can meet in Lodz or Szczecin and go to Berlin together. She says it's not easy; it's dangerous, that's what she says. What a handwriting!" "My brother made her write it in a hurry," Lisa apologized. "I have to give you my letter back tonight?" "So my brother can take it back with him," Lisa explained with the patience of a saint. "And he says not to tell too many people you want to get out of Poland. The Russians don't want workers leaving when everything needs rebuilding. Don't forget that; it's important." "Understood," I answered, my head already bent over a sheet of paper. Doctor Dudek walked into the room, flushed, started to say something, and walked out.

"Dear Julia, dear Julka," I wrote, "I found my child, Ninushka; everyone else is gone. In two months I should have the money to meet you. That will be in the middle of January. I'll go to Lodz first, and then Szczecin. You can find out where I am, or I can find out where you are, by checking the orders for rooms. If you can, write in care of Lisa's brother again; I would write more, but he's waiting somewhere. You can trust him. Don't worry. It's a miracle you're alive," I wrote; my hand was trembling. "Thank God. I love you, Anya." "Julka alive!" I exclaimed to Lisa, handing the letter over. "I told you we'd find her," Lisa said triumphantly. "How did she do it?" I wondered out loud. "My brother said she told him something about living in a haystack. She'll tell you herself; he must have got it wrong." "A haystack!" I exclaimed; "why not? Sewers, haystacks, under bridges, why not? There's nothing I wouldn't believe anymore."

"Hello, Aunt Lisa," Ninka said from behind us; "is Vladek sick?" "No, no one's sick; your mother just got a letter from a friend." "Oh," Ninushka said, turning around and going back to the cubicle. "All news is bad news," Lisa said, repeating the proverb of our apartment, and then our private joke: "You have to learn to take the good with the bad." None of us were very good at that anymore. "Are you going to the market tomorrow?" Lisa asked. "I am; I have to sell some of Frost's matches for him." "No," I said, "I think I'm going out to look for Bilov and ask him how to sell Vera's piano." "What will you sleep on?" Lisa asked, astonished. "Other people sleep on coats and mattresses; why can't I?"

"Satisfied now?" Doctor Dudek interrupted; "you've woken up the diabetics." "Don't worry," I told him. "Rachel isn't leaving Vilno with me." "She said she was." "That was a long time ago, and besides, I wouldn't take her." "Why?" he asked suspiciously. "She doesn't want to go; that's why."

Three days later Bilov and some soldiers came for the piano; a rich old lady in the center of the city wanted it for piano lessons. "Already, piano lessons," Mrs. Keilwicz marveled. Rachel didn't say anything; she sat watching my face. I sat still for an hour. "The room looks much bigger," Rachel volunteered in a small voice. I was sitting on the window seat, looking out. I turned into the room. Ninka was staring at me like a little bird. "I forgot the letter," I shrieked, staring at her. "What letter?" Rachel asked. "There was one of Vera's taped inside," I cried. "I'll get it," Rachel said, putting on her coat. "How will you find it?" "Don't worry," she said, leaving.

Two hours later there was the sound of an auto. Doctor Dudek came in with Rachel; both of them were flushed with the cold. "Freezing," Doctor Dudek said, stamping his feet, standing in front of the stove; "freezing." "Take off your coat; you'll get warmer faster," I ordered automatically. "Have you got any books for us, Uncle Dudek?" Ninushka asked. "It just so happen I have," he answered, pulling a fat square one out of his pocket; "but I think it's too hard for you." "It sure is," Vladek said from his corner without looking up. *The Three Musketeers,*" Ninushka read out loud. "What's a musketeer?" she asked him. "I told you it was too hard for her," Vladek said; "give it to me." "A kind of soldier," Doctor Dudek said, ignoring him.

Rachel was standing in front of me; she handed me the letter. I took it and put it in my pocket. "Aren't you going to read it?" she whispered. "No, I only want to have it," I whispered back. I was starting to cry again. "Oh, Anya," she said, sitting down next to me, rocking me back and forth, "are you sure you want to go?" "Absolutely," I answered, crying. Ninushka was staring at us. "It's nothing," Rachel assured her; "nothing. Grown-ups act like this sometimes." "I'm not going to grow up," Ninka answered. "It doesn't look like it," Vladek said, tugging at her book. "Let it alone!" she complained, getting up and running across the room. "At *least,*" Vladek said sarcastically, "you could read it to me, if you still remember how to read." "I'll read," Ninka said happily. "Once upon a time," she began and stopped, giggling like a mad creature. "That's not how it begins," Vladek said, blushing. "No," Ninushka answered, and began reading seriously. "What a monotone," Rachel sighed. "She'll never sing on the stage," I agreed.

28

IT WAS the beginning of January. During the day, Lisa and I still sold in the market. At night, I came home on the wood wagon, feet dangling. Rachel studied and watched the children. They played hiding games with each other and with Vladek, in the hall. The snow drifted down steadily. Before the little mountains against the buildings had time to get slushy or gray, or fill with holes left by melting icicles, a new dusting came down. "I'm going soon," I told Rachel; "in about ten days. I'll have to get the money and things out of the safe." Rachel said nothing. "You'll have to hide the money somehow, and the basket," she finally answered. "You can help me sew most of it into my coat." "I wish you wouldn't go," Lisa repeated for the hundredth time. "It is better that she does," Rachel spoke up. "Rachel!" Lisa gasped, scandalized. "She has to," Rachel tried to explain. "You don't know her, once she makes up her mind." "But she could finish medical school here," Lisa protested. "No, she couldn't," Rachel contradicted her; "not here."

"Where are we going, Mommy?" Ninka appeared. "To Szczecin, we have friends there." "We have friends here," Ninka complained. "You'll understand later," I promised her. "I'll understand *everything* later," she said bitterly; "you always say that." Suddenly I had no strength at all. "Suppose I don't want to?" Ninka asked. "You'll go anyway," Vladek informed her. "Are you coming, too?" she asked hopefully. "I'm staying with Rachel," he answered. "But you'll like it better when you get where you're going; you will. You'll see; you're going to be in one of the places we read about in books." "What place?" "It's a surprise," Vladek assured her. "I read about it in a book?" Ninka asked him. "You did." "What book?" she asked, trying to trap him. "You'll know when you get there," he told her, "and then you can write me a letter and tell me if it's really like what the book said it was; that is," he peered at her, "if you can still remember to write. I wish *I* were going," he sighed dramatically. "It's supposed to be the most wonderful place in the world; it even has elephants and zebras." "Is it Africa?" Ninka asked, puzzled. A month ago, they had been reading *Flora and Fauna of Africa*; Rachel and I could hardly understand a word ourselves. "Not Africa," Vladek told her; "you've used up your one guess." "You didn't say how many guesses I could have," Ninushka pouted. "I know," Vladek thought, "I'll go with your mother, and *you* stay here with Rachel; it's such a wonderful place." "*I'm* the one who's going," Ninka insisted. "If you say so, but I want to go. I think I'll ask your mother." "Mommy, don't let him!" Ninka screamed; "I want to go and see the elephants!" "You can go," I promised her. "See?" she shouted, sticking her tongue out at Vladek. "Don't do that, Ninushka," I said in a flat voice. "Why not?" she asked; "he's not so nice." "It doesn't matter; ladies don't do things like that." She made a face at him. "They don't do that, either," I told her. Over the top of her book, she crossed her eyes at him. "I saw that, Ninushka," I warned her. "I'm going to see Marian," she pouted. "Be sure and behave," Rachel called after her; "he's sick." "He'll be a lot sicker when she gets in," Vladek shouted. "No, he won't, you big germ," Ninka shouted back. "Where does she think of things like that?" I asked Rachel. "She uses her imagination," Rachel sighed; "her head is really better. It is all settled then?" "Absolutely settled."

That Monday, Ninka and I were taking the train to Lodz. We were all there an hour early. "The train will be late," Doctor Dudek assured us grumpily. "Good!" Rachel said vehemently. "You promise to write to all of us?" Lisa asked crying. "Since we met, I've never been happier, not in all twenty-four years of my life." "I promise, if the Communists fix the mails." Doctor Dudek snorted. "Mrs. Keilwicz had to stay with Marian," Lisa added irrelevantly. Mr. Frost was watching in the background. Vladek was carrying Ninka; he had her tucked under his chenille coat. She was wearing a dress made out of the heavy German coat. Her woolen coat came from the market. "I wonder how many matches that cost?" I thought, looking at her. "I wonder if she'll really miss Vladek." "Do you think you'll learn to write to me, Potato Head?" Vladek was asking her. "I *can* write!" she pouted, starting to smile right away. "I have something for you," she said, sticking her little bare hand into her pocket. "Here." She pulled out her copy of *The Three Musketeers*. "You don't have any more story books," Vladek reminded her. "I was almost finished anyway. You can write me the ending, *if* you know how to write," she grinned. It was the first time I had even seen her give anyone something. "Monkey," he said, throwing her up and down, the book still in her hand. "I'll put it in your pocket," Ninushka said, beginning to poke around at Vladek inside his coat.

"She's growing up," Doctor Dudek said. "She's only six!" I protested. "Still," he said. She tickled Vladek for a while, cackling her high loud cackle, then slid the book into his pocket. "When the train comes, you can kiss me goodbye," she announced importantly. "Suppose I don't want to?" he asked. "Then *I'll* kiss *you* goodbye." "You win again," he sniffed: "the fair thing is, we'll kiss each other." Ninushka cackled again.

The little steam cloud on the horizon was growing, pure white. "Rachel," I said. Her face had changed so. She was twenty-five. The bones in her face had come out. She had high, pronounced cheekbones and dark skin; her almond eyes had darkened and widened. "She looks like an American Indian," I thought; "she looks interesting." "You look wonderful, Rachel," I told her. "I feel wonderful; it is all your fault," she said laughing, starting to cry. We fell into each other's arms. I could feel her body sobbing, the rough wooden texture of her coat, the wet smell of the wool from the melted snow. Doctor Dudek walked away embarrassed. "Grown-ups act that way sometimes," I could hear Ninka informing him didactically.

The train was pulling up, stopping. I put Ninka on the iron step above me; then I got on. "Goodbye, Rachel," I said, bending over to kiss her. "Goodbye, Anya," she said, kissing me. Her face was so shiny with tears it looked as if it had been covered by a thin, shiny membrane. "Goodbye, Potato Head," Vladek called. "Goodbye, Germ," Ninka called back, hysterical; "I'll write about the elephants." "And the zebra," he called to her at the top of his lungs. "Lisa, goodbye." I bent to kiss her. "Goodbye, Mischa," I said, kissing Doctor Dudek; he turned away abruptly. "Here," Rachel said suddenly, taking something from him; "he nearly forgot the basket." "There's a hook inside your coat for carrying it," Lisa reminded me. "She was a shoplifter in another life," Mr. Frost mumbled softly. "Take good care of the stove and Sashenka," I told her. "I will," she promised. "Goodbye, goodbye, goodbye," we all began again, and then the train blew its first whistle. "Goodbye, Vladek," Ninushka was screaming like a fury, and we were inside.

The train was crowded. Ninka was climbing over two perfect strangers to reach the window and wave. "Excuse me," I said to the two, pressing my face to the window. I waved to them until they were only dots on a long black line against the white snow. We were on our way to Lodz, and then Szczecin, and then Berlin, and then Palestine or America. "Mommy, I have a seat," Ninushka shrieked; "sit down; I'll sit on you." And so the train picked up speed. The war had been over for some time.

"I have to go to the bathroom," Ninka whined five minutes after the train began moving. "No, you don't; you went to the bathroom before we left." "I want to go," she insisted. "The train doesn't have a bathroom; you'll have to wait." "I'll go look for one," Ninka said, scrambling off my knees. "There's a bathroom three cars back," the man sitting near us said. "I'll come right back," Ninka promised. "You're not going anywhere," I threatened, pulling her back onto my lap. "I've never been on a train; I want to look," she cried, squirming from under my arms and starting to climb across the old man's knees. "I'm sorry," I apologized in a hurry. "Ninushka, get back here!" "Look how fast things go by," she marveled. "It's all right, Miss," the old man said, sliding as far away from the window as he could get. "At least don't jump around and bother the man," I begged her. She didn't answer; she was staring out in fascination. "The trees are running away from us," she shouted. Some people turned around. "Quiet!" I hissed. "Oh, you should look, Mommy!" she insisted. "I don't think we would both fit there," I answered. "No," she agreed, pressing her nose against the glass. There was already a family of smudges around it.

The old man sitting next to me shrugged his shoulders and smiled. "Going far?" he asked. "Lodz," I told him. "You'll have trouble," he whispered; "no houses, the N.K.V.D. is all over." "Thank you," I said, "but I don't want to know yet." I closed my eyes. Sometime later, I could find Ninushka climbing back into my lap. "The houses run away, too," she was whispering to herself. There were the two of us and two valises.

I was in Saint John's cathedral. "Who are you?" the white horse asked me. "Never mind who I am," I told it;

"what are you doing in the church?" "What everyone else does in church," the horse said; "I came here to pray." "But this isn't a good place," I said; "the roof could fall on you. And horses don't go to church," I reminded him. "Of course, I'm not really a horse," he said, tossing his mane. "But you are fastened to a cart; people aren't fastened to a cart." "I'm not really a horse," the animal said again; "look." He reared up. There was a neat seam under his stomach; some tiny things were climbing out. "Oh, you're a circus horse, I mean a horse suit with people in it." "Exactly," the horse said; "something like the Trojan horse, but I've already conquered everything, or swallowed it, and the people are a little funny." One finally came out. It was only part of a body; the rest was all bones. "I play the piano," it said; "you should see me do it." Another skeleton was climbing out. "I am really a building," it said; "look, there are bricks in my eyes." I was trying to back away, but I tripped over some rubble. "If you won't look at that," the skeleton said, "look at this." He turned around; his back was made up of naked bricks held together by plaster. "You shouldn't do that," I whispered. "I can play the piano, too," it said, but the horse was rearing up and its hooves were about to come down on it.

"Aaaaah! Aaaaah! Aaaaaah!" I woke up to the sound of my voice screaming as if in labor. "Mommy! Mommy!" Ninushka was crying. "What's the matter, Mommy?" She was the color of a boiled chicken. She was sitting up on her knees, facing me, and shaking me by the shoulders. I stared into her big blue eyes; her thick braids were showing from beneath her quilted hat. The old man next to me was patting my arm. "I think your mommy had a bad dream," he said, patting Ninushka next. "Was it about soldiers, Mommy?" Ninushka was terrified. "Are you sick, are you hot?" she asked, putting her little hand on my head. "No, no, it was just a bad dream, about a horse," I murmured. "Go to sleep," Ninushka pleaded. I moved slightly in my seat. The silver basket pressed against my right side. "I'm coming with you to Lodz," the horse said from the aisle. I woke up shivering from head to toe. Ninka had fallen asleep. "Traveling is not good for everyone," the old man said, shaking his head.

"Lodz!" the conductor called. It was night. "Where can we find a room?" I asked the station master. "Not until the morning," he answered. "I don't think there are rooms. People are pouring in here like sand. The city's buried in people. You can go to the Office for Apartment Orders and ask about a permit; you won't get anything." "What are we going to do?" I wailed. "There are some benches with roofs over them, down the street," he said; "a lot of people live there." "They live there?" I asked. "There's nowhere else; go try it." "Come on, Ninushka," I said, taking her by one hand, the valise by the other. Ninka carried the little one. Somewhere inside it, I could hear Vera's letter throbbing and the pictures breathing. "Maybe I was wrong to leave," I thought; "maybe I'm really crazy."

"Here are the benches," Ninushka shrieked, hopping up and down. Some bundles of clothes raised themeslves up from the benches, looked at us, and settled down. "Put the valises here, Momushka!" Ninka cried. "You sleep under the coat," I told her, taking out the extra one Vladek had gotten for me. She got on the bench as if it were the most normal thing in the world. "Do I know what I'm doing?" I asked myself again, curling up in back of her heels. The next day it was snowing. "Ninushka," I said, "let's use the bathroom near the station and buy some food." There was a man selling bread and another cooking coffee on an outside stove made of bricks. I counted out the money and paid for it. Then we went back to the benches. Ninka was buried in a magazine she found on the train. "What's that about?" I asked her. "Collective farming," she read out slowly; "it has nice pictures of cows." "I'd better get some books," I thought; "otherwise she'll go crazy, too."

Everytime someone passed I jumped up, asking them the same thing: Did they know a place to live? Finally, I got directions to the Office for Apartment Orders. "Sorry," the man said, "but there's nothing now; everything's taken." "But my child and I are sleeping on benches outside," I cried; "and it's snowing." "No one asked you to travel. Next!" "It's stopped snowing" Ninushka pointed out. "That means it will be colder," I said bitterly. "Let's go to sleep."

"I can't stand it," I said the next morning; "this sitting around doing nothing." We were on our way back from the bathrooms to buy some bread and coffee for lunch. "Anyushka!" someone called. "Aunt Dora!" I shouted. It was a friend of my mother's from Vilno; I had given her daughter French lessons and they had given me all the sodas I could drink. "Aunt Dora!" I cried, hugging her.

"What are you doing here?" "Oh, I live here," she said; "but you, what are you doing on these benches?" "I'm trying to get out of the country," I wailed; "there are no rooms." "You have to stay with us," she said decisively, picking up our valises. "But I've got to warn you; I've married again. This one isn't so nice. He thinks you have to beat a wife to keep her good. Do you think you can stand him? I can't stand him," she added. "Anything! Anything!" I cried. "Have you got any books there?" Ninka asked, putting down her magazine, and grabbing her hand. "Oh, yes," Dora said, "even a little boy, a little bigger than you, who reads them. Your mother warned me about it, Anya, but I never listened. Another baby at that age. Well," she sighed and laughed at once, "it will give your daughter someone to play with."

"There's not so much damage here," I said, looking around for the first time. "No," Dora said, "not too bad. About every fourth house is all walls and no floors, or all floors and no walls, but not too bad. Still, the bombs took the rooms with them." "Here it is," she said, pointing to a narrow brick house with a peaked roof and little peaked dormer windows growing out of it. "We have some rooms on the first floor, but you'll have to sleep with Ninushka in the hall. We have a kitchen, a bedroom, and the hall; that's it. We didn't get along too well in a whole apartment; you will see how it is in a small one. The only thing is," she thought, looking at me, "I forgot to tell you about the bedbugs. Bedbugs all over; that's how we got the place. The other people ran out scratching." Ninka cackled. "I'll help you get rid of them," I promised. "Oh, you can't," Dora insisted. "Yes, you can," I told her. "You throw pots of boiling water against the walls and get the wallpaper off; the bugs live underneath." *"Bozhe moy,"* Dora gasped; "this is going to be something. The water's two blocks away." "As usual," I said.

The next few days Dora and I walked back and forth with her son, Andrei, and Ninushka with pots of water in both hands. The pots went on to the stove; then the water was thrown boiling against the walls. Ninushka and Andrei had to stay in the bedroom. They were both reading. "Bookworms," Dora muttered, throwing another pail of water against the wall; "the place is full of bugs." "What has she got to read?" I asked, carrying a big kettle to the stove. *"The Three Musketeers.* She told Andrei she wanted to finish; he had it. Next, she has a book about rabbits."

505

"That's more like it," I said, going down the hall with an empty pail to fill it with boiling water. On the third day, there was a knock at the door. "A letter for you," Dora told me, coming in; "it arrived by messenger, someone rich." "It must be Julka," I thought out loud. "Dora dear," I asked, "could they please stay with us? Just for a few days? Then we'll all leave. They'll only have a little with them. We can sleep in the hall, all of us." "I'll ask Grigory," she said.

"He doesn't like it," she told me, "but he thinks they'll help with the bedbugs." Grigory had yet to lift a finger. I was remembering Julia and the house in Kaunas. "Don't count on her helping," I warned her. Finally, the house was bugless. I went to bed on the floor. Grigory even gave poor Ninushka looks that made me jumpy.

The next morning, the bell rang. There was Julia, breathless. "Frederich is coming up with the things, and with Jerzy," she gasped. "Oh, he went to get three suitcases," I said, thinking of the three people in the picture Lisa had shown me in the hospital. "Three suitcases?" Julia asked, puzzled. "One for each of you," I said impatiently. There was an enormous noise behind her. Frederich staggered in under an enormous packing crate. "Only nine more to go," he gasped, starting down the stairs. A thin yellowish boy, younger than Ninka, stood on the balcony like a dying plant. "Bring him in," I told Julia. "In," Julia commanded remotely. The little boy moved in hesitantly. "Julka," I asked in a panic, "what did that man say about nine more boxes?" "Oh, you know how it is," Julka said. She looked even more Oriental than ever; she was thinner. No matter where she was, she looked as if she were smoking a cigarette in a holder. "He was so rich. He still is, you see. So it was, 'It is a pity to leave this, and a pity to leave that,' so we have it all with us." "But Julka," I pleaded, "we have only this poor hall to sleep in, all of us; where are the boxes going?" "Frederich will think of something," she answered indifferently; "he always does." "Has the little boy eaten?" I asked her. "I don't know," she said, puzzled; "have you eaten, Jerzy?" "No," he said in a quaver. "Ninushka!" I called, "take this little boy in with you and Andrei and get him something to eat." Ninka led him off like a trained nurse. "Probably practiced in the orphanage," I thought.

Frederich was appearing on the landing with another crate. "Oh, no, Julka," I said, losing my temper. "You move these things in here and we have to sleep on the streets; get them out!" "Be reasonable, dear Anya," she said in her cool voice. "I told you, Frederich will think of something." "The ceilings," he gasped, carefully lowering the second crate on top of the first. "What?" I shouted. "The ceilings, hooks," he gasped, going back down the stairs. "Julka, I didn't take *anything*!" I pleaded. "A shame," she said, "but he is really so attached to his things." "I think we'd better go into the room with the children," I told her. "I'll go crazy out here." "So," Julka said, settling herself on the bed so that the three children had to move down. Ninushka got tired of balancing herself at the foot of the bed and took her book onto the floor. "When I last saw you, I was going out with that Max Katzenellenbogen you met in Zakopanie, you remember? Well, Frederich, Mister Zamenhoff, he's a friend of Max's; another millionaire. They tend to swim in schools, don't you think?" Julka laughed, opening her embroidered velvet bag. "He's ten years younger than I am," she said, crossing her legs. "I have to be very careful of my looks; that goes without saying." From the floor, Ninushka was staring up at her, hypnotized. "But he has so much money, Anya; you would not believe it. He's from one of those families who buried their money and dug it up again. Remarkable," she considered. "I'm sure Frederich wasn't responsible for hiding it. He's very handsome, as you see, but between the two of us, no genius, no genius at all. Still, he manages everyone. Perhaps it's his eyelashes," Julka considered again.

"Who is this Jerzy?" I asked. I was already spinning out of my world, hypnotically into hers. "His nephew," she answered carelessly; "I think I wrote you something about it. He was in the ghetto with me, in Kaunas. He comes from a family of cats, real cats, I tell you. The room was like a cuckoo clock. Every hour on the hour, they came out and fought with each other. There wasn't enough food; this one had done this; that one hadn't done that. It's amazing how some animals revert to type, isn't it? And he, with his five maids, he couldn't stand it, the racket, so," Julka continued, "he moved in with me. Very simple. I was very quiet, I can tell you," she laughed again; "especially in the dark. I've had so much practice. And I thought," she paused, lighting a cigarette, and putting it into the holder resting on her long skirt, "we *might* survive, and I'd rather survive rich than poor."

507

"How *did* you survive?" I asked, wide-eyed as Ninushka. "I'd rather not talk about it, how we got out," Julka said. "It's slightly embarrassing. But we did get out before the liquidation, and all over, first bombing, then stealing. It was dreadful, but we found a field full of haystacks. I wrote you about this?" she asked irritably, puffing on her cigarette. "Is she a queen, Mommy?" Ninka whispered. "Sometimes I think so." "What a nice child," Julka beamed. "I didn't understand about the haystacks; tell me," I prodded. "Well, we had no money, and we were miserable, so I thought, well, the haystacks looked like little buildings, and we dug out the center of one, and I put a sheet over the opening. I drew pictures on it, and we lived inside. A house to ourselves, as usual. It was rather fun," Julka laughed, "but of course we got very cold begging. It was nice to get back to the little haystack; it even had a stove." She laughed again. "You should have seen it." "A stove in the haystack?" Ninushka gasped. "Children should be seen and not heard," Julka told her. "I think I hear Frederich."

Frederich and a workman were standing in the hall. "Right up there," Frederich was saying, pointing to the ceiling. The workman's ladder was propped against the hall. "Hooks for the boxes," Frederich told us. "Be sure they're good and strong," he told the man, "or you don't get paid." "I told you he'd figure something out," Julka grinned. "He always does, or someone else does. He's so used to it; it just takes place." "Julka," I said, trying to talk to her seriously, "it's dangerous traveling around here. We're going to be sleeping on the floor like sardines; I don't want to sleep with those icebergs over my head. We should be getting ready to leave, not screwing hooks in the ceiling over this poor family." "In whose name is the Apartment Order?" Frederich asked suddenly. "In my name," I answered flushing. It was true. Dora and Grigory had just moved in. Before Dora met me, the two of them had spent all their time arguing over who was to go register; until I came no one had gone at all. I had gone to the office and spoken Russian and gotten the order right away. "Then there's no hurry," Frederich said calmly, "I have some things to do."

That night we were all lined up against each other in the hall, sleeping like train cars. Ninushka was treating Jerzy as he own private doll. Every time I looked up and thought of the boxes on the ceiling, I turned on my stomach and wept in terror. Grigory muttered all the way to the bathroom, stepping over us. "We have to get out of here," I pleaded in the morning. "As soon as I finish my business," Frederich whispered soothingly and went out. When he came back, he had baskets of meat, fish, cheese, milk, and bread. "Excellent meal, I congratulate you," he said to Julka when we finished. I had prepared everything. "Thank you, my dear," she answered, smiling. "Julka," I said to her the next day, "what is his business?" "I find it better not to ask, Anyushka," she warned. "We *have* to get out of here; I feel like chunks of the sky are about to fall down." "You worry too much, Anya," she said, and then Frederich's feet were on the steps.

"Some boots," he said, giving them to me. He took another basket of food into the kitchen. Grigory was somewhat resigned, but not much. Two hours later there was a pounding at the door. "*Do* open it, Ninushka,'" Julka asked. "N.K.V.D.," one of the men said. "We are searching the premises," and they got busy turning everything over. "The boxes, take them down," they ordered Frederich. "Teacups and comforters, sirs," he assured them; "you'll just waste your time." "We decide for ourselves," one of them answered gruffly. Ninushka and Jerzy were clinging to me, terrified. "Nothing here," one of the men decided. "We're leaving," he told Frederich, "but we'll be back."

"Julka," I demanded, pulling her into the bathroom, "either you tell me what's going on, or all of you go, at once. I'm not joking." "It's nothing so serious," Julka said solemnly. "All he does is buy gold with the paper money. There's a money exchange or something; I don't think there's much to it." "Then why were the N.K.V.D. here?" "Well, it's illegal, of course," she answered, as if she were talking to an idiot.

Two more days went by; the children were visibly fattening. Jerzy clung to Ninka, who read with an arm around him, smiling slyly to herself. It had been days since I had thought about the white horse. "So maybe it is worthwhile to wait," I thought. There was a pounding at the door. "N.K.V.D.!" a man's voice called; "take down the boxes."

"Julka," I insisted, "I cannot stand these endless searchings. Sooner or later, they're going to find something. I didn't go through everything to live in a Siberian ice pack. Either we go tomorrow together, or you go alone." Julka stared at me, inhaling her cigarette. "I'll be right back," she said.

"Frederich says we can leave in the morning, but he doesn't understand the hurry. Why can't you relax?" she asked me. "Relax!" I shouted. "With tons of teacups hanging over our heads and soldiers here every minute waiting to send us to the coal mines. You are crazy!" "Well, we are going in the morning," she said calmly; "there's no need to be so upset. It will be your fault if we have to go to Szczecin any old way at all. If we had time, Frederich could make *good* arrangements." "Never mind the arrangements!" I screamed, beside myself. "I want to get somewhere. We are getting nothing done here, nothing, nothing, nothing! I don't believe he can make arrangements!" "I heard that," Frederich said in a hurt voice. "In the morning, we're going," Julka repeated, bored; "really, you are being unreasonable." Dora and Grigory were hovering in the background, too speechless with rage to talk.

"Get up," I said to Ninushka the next morning; "we're finally leaving." Frederich had begun to take a box down from its hook. "I don't feel good, Mommy," Ninka whispered; "my head hurts." "Frederich, please, bring the lamp over here." Ninushka was covered from head to toe with a red rash. "Oh, no," I wailed. "I don't feel good, either," Andrei complained. "Or me," Jerzy piped up. Andrei was also covered with a rash. Measles. There was nothing the matter with Jerzy. "Julka," I called, "the children have the measles. We will be here for ten days at least. Frederich can make his arrangements." "Measles?" Julka asked as if she had never heard the word. "Doesn't that mean they have to stay in a dark place?" "It does," I said firmly. "How will I read?" she pouted. "I'll have to read in the kitchen." "Oh, Julka, don't worry," Frederich said; "I'll get you some fashion magazines and make arrangements about a special train. I already know almost enough families to fill it up." "Can he do that?" I asked Julka. "Of course," she said pouting, retreating to the kitchen. "It's damp in here," she complained. I didn't answer. "It is not fair," she called out. "Jerzy already had the measles. Now we have to wait for you."

So we had two weeks of constantly patrolling the children to be certain they didn't read or scratch. One day, I went down for water, and Ninka was reading over Julka's shoulder in the kitchen. "Frederich," I screamed, "you have to do something about her; she is entirely irresponsi-

510

ble. I cannot do anything." "Oh, I'll help you," he said; "I love children." And he did help, and the children did listen to him. And almost four weeks after their arrival, we were on Frederich's specially commissioned train to Szczecin.

29

"I SUPPOSE we have to go," Julka said, settling in. She had seen to it that we were the first ones on the train. "It was comfortable there." I didn't say a word. "Wait till *you* get the measles!" Ninka threatened her. "Ninushka!" I said. "No matter what you think of a grown-up, you should be polite." Julka gave me an odd, amused look as the train began pulling out of the Lodz Station. Each of the children had a window seat to himself. "Szczecin," Julka said, stroking Frederich's knee, "it should be interesting, shouldn't it."

"Wake up, Ninushka," I said, shaking her; "we are in Szczecin." "Szezecin," Ninka repeated; "what a funny name. Are there places to live there?" "I don't know," I answered, tying her hat on tighter and inspecting her from head to toe. Snow was hitting the windows of the train in little puffs and sticking in shapes of small cotton balls. We got off. The station was gone; only the platform was left.

"A ghost city," Julka whispered, turning pale. We looked around. Everywhere were skeletons of buildings; rubble slid into the streets leaving a path big enough for two people, sometimes only for one. "Frederich, I told you," Julka whispered to him urgently. "They told us it was just like Mexico; they undress you and take everything you have. It's complete anarchy. I don't see why we had to come here." "You know why we had to come here," he whispered to her as if she were a child, "it is the border city. It is the only place that will take us to Berlin." "There has to be somewhere else," she insisted, looking around frantically; her hand holding her cigarette was shaking. "Put on your gloves," Frederich coaxed. "Give me your cigarette and put on your gloves." Julia pulled on her gloves. "Sit down on the bench," he coaxed again. "We are all going to sit on the bench, aren't we, Anya?" I nodded. The children were crying. "It's cold," Ninushka was whining; "Jerzy is hungry." "Are you hungry?" I asked her. "He's more hungry," she answered, starting to cry.

"Look, Frederich," I told him, "we have to do something. Julka is just no use. She's sitting there crying with the children. We'll freeze to death. We have to do something." "Julka," he turned to her, "we are going to look for a place to stay." "Julia," I added, "I will not go unless you promise to watch the children. Ninushka is my whole life. Do you promise? Promise me, or I'm not going." "I promise, I'll be good," she answered in a quavering voice.

Frederich and I set off down the street. I had on my big iron cross. I opened the lambskin collar to display it prominently. "Let me do the talking," I begged Frederich. "It is my pleasure," he assured me, stamping along through the powdery snow. It dusted the streets like the confectioner's sugar Anzia shook over her cakes. "That's an ordinary idea," I thought, "or it ought to be." "What is the matter with Julka?" I asked him. "She's falling apart like a cookie." "Oh, she's not very good at all at this," he answered; "she's always terrified something will happen to me." We were approaching the center of the city. I had a babushka tied over my head, the heavy Russian boots, like the ones Lisa wore, and the cross, resting on the frozen triangle of my breast.

"All the houses are bombed," Frederich said in an awed voice. "That's what Julka said," I answered him. "That means there's no place to stay," he concluded. "That's exactly what it means," I told him. "You can see right through the buildings," he marveled, stopping to stare through one. "You look through the building, and I'll get busy," I said, crossing the street to stop a woman. "In the name of Jesus," I began; "please give us a tiny place to stay. We have little children. The whole family is on the streets." I stopped everyone who came by, and to everyone, I said the same thing: "In the name of Jesus." Finally, one old woman with snow-white hair showing under her hat answered me: "I'll tell you, darling; I could give you a key to an apartment, but half of the steps are destroyed by shrapnel. It's a big apartment, but you understand, there's no glass at all in the windows. You might find some blankets and things in the closets there to cover yourself with, but it's dangerous, it is dangerous. The other side of the building is just gone. You could fall off the steps and be killed. Are you sure you want it?" "Give me the key!" I cried, hugging and kissing her. "God will

513

reward you. We are only orphans; anything is better than the streets. I thought," I babbled, "I saw something move under that rubble." I pointed to a tower of it across the street. Some sheets of concrete were lying at angles on top of each other. "They hide in there," the woman said, "especially after dark. They usually don't kill you, but they knock you down and take everything. You have to be careful. The address is Forty-five Bracka Street. Please be careful; I'm not trying to kill you." "Oh, I am so thankful!" I kept crying. "Wait until you see it first," she said, "and please, the stairs, watch out for them; I've never gone back. I'm too frightened." She tapped her walking stick nervously. She didn't like being out in the open. "Thank you!" I cried again, running off to get Frederich. "We have a place; let's get the others!"

The apartment was seven blocks from the railway station. I was carrying Ninushka, and Frederich had Jerzy. Julka complained every inch of the way. "You can kill yourself," she complained, half-twisting a stockinged ankle. "It is simply impossible to see the stones under all this snow." "Will you try and control yourself?" I hissed at her. "It is not really far, Julia dear," Frederich assured her. "Seven blocks is seven blocks; couldn't you find someplace nearer?" I stopped dead in my tracks. "We will stay here while you look," I threatened. "Oh, now that we have started, we might as well finish," she grumbled, trudging along again. "She complains a lot, doesn't she, Mommy?" Ninushka asked in a loud whisper. "Yes," I answered noisily. "Aunt Rachel *never* complained," Ninushka remembered. "Julia is not Rachel," I said, picking my way over some stones. "Ninushka, try not to kick me with the backs of your shoes." Her feet went rigid. "You don't have to hold them like boards, either," I sighed.

"This is the house!" Frederich cried from up ahead. "It's only half a house," Julia wailed in a wounded voice. Half of the house had been blown away. Only the framework was left, and on the fourth floor, where our apartment was, one or two rooms of the apartment across the hall from us remained intact. "Let's go," said Frederich, enthused; "it's getting dark." We had a few candles; he lit one in the street. "I'll go first," he volunteered. "Do you have to?" Julka asked him. "Do *you* want to?" I demanded. We went up the steps. Half of them were torn away by bombs. It was a straight drop down to the ground floor. "It is making me dizzy," Julka complained.

"Please keep quiet," I snapped at her. "Listen, Ninushka, Jerzy, you can't go near these stairs; press yourselves against the wall when we're going up." All of us were pressed against those walls like wallpaper. "Here it is," Frederich announced, turning the key. The whole apartment was untouched. Only the windows were smashed, but there was no electricity or water. In the dining room, the table was half set. The silver candles were out on the embroidered white tablecloth. Places were set. Little towers of china sat on the buffet as expectantly as eyes. "I'll get some water," Frederich volunteered, finding a pail in the kitchen and going down. "Be careful," Julka called, hanging over the railing like an Oriental carpet waiting to be beaten.

I was already looking through the whole apartment for something to eat, a little flour, anything. There was nothing. "Now, Frederich," I told him, when he came back with the water, "you do the rest; go find a little food and wood somewhere. There's no heat in here; there'll be crying all night. I know you're not used to hard labor, but it's only fair; I found the place." He started down.

"I have some flour and some ham," he called, coming back up in an hour, "but no wood. I can get some across the way, I think." "What do you mean?" Julka was screaming hysterically. "Julka," I said, "please come help me look for blankets. The lady who gave us the key said there was a closet full of them somewhere." "Where should I look?" "In the *closets*," I answered impatiently. Then I went onto the shattered landing to watch Frederich. He was picking his way across the beams like a tightrope walker to the next apartment. It was terribly dangerous. "He has the balance of a cat," I thought, watching him; "and how handsome he is. Julka is right. He looks like a movie star." He came back, balancing on the beams with a load of shattered wooden beams. "So much more of the wall demolished," he said cheerfully; "I'll start the fire in the stove."

Downstairs there was a knock on the door. I was frightened to death. "It is the N.K.V.D., already, the N.K.V.D., they followed Frederich," I thought. "I'll go down," I told Frederich, creeping by inches down the wall. A man was standing in the doorway. "Don't be scared. This house belongs to me. You're welcome to use everything in it. My sister told me you're here. I used to live here, too. I'll come back with a little sugar. Did you find the closet in the bedroom, and the chest at the foot of the big bed? They're filled with blankets." "Oh, thank you, thank you," I answered. "But when you come in, could you just knock and come up yourself? I'm terribly afraid of these stairs." He was back in half an hour with the sugar and some jars of strawberry jam.

"I just don't like it," I told Frederich: "why should he be interested?" "Probably because we're living in his house." "Look, Frederich, I can't stay here doing nothing. Tomorrow you have to go to that Zionist organization we heard about in Lodz. We don't know anyone else who knows how to get us to Palestine. I have the address. We'll never get out of the country sitting here and eating ham." "Why always in such a hurry?" he asked me. "Because the children will freeze, and we'll get killed on the stairs." "I'll go tomorrow," he promised, just to shut me up. "Go where?" Julka demanded in a terrified voice. "And be careful," I whispered to him. "The N.K.V.D. are looking for people like us; they don't want any strong bodies getting out of here." "I'll be careful," he sighed. "What are you talking about?" Julka demanded. "I'll go," I said resigned.

The next morning I was up at six o'clock. Momma's gold watch was still keeping perfect time. "Where are *you* going, Frederich?" I demanded. He seemed to be edging out of the apartment. "Oh, I have some business," he answered cheerfully. "The first business is to put some of the blankets over the windows," I told him. "The quilts would be better. They're thicker." "But they are such beautiful quilts," Julka objected; "I'd like to take some of them." "Frederich," I said, threateningly. "Right away," he promised. "And another thing," I went on; "if the children are going to stay her with Julia, she has to watch them. I'm not going anywhere otherwise." "She'll do it," Frederich promised. "That means keeping the stove going, and feeding them," I instructed her. "I'll feed them now," he said. "Julka will give them lunch. It won't take you long, anyway."

I sat down at the kitchen table and wrote out the address of an apartment near us: 48 Bracka Street. Then I folded it up and put it in my pocket. "She's just sitting there," I warned Frederich, starting to button my heavy coat. Julka had pulled a chair up to the stove and was reading a French fashion magazine. "Don't worry, don't worry," he pleaded. I started down the steps, clinging to the walls. Outside, the snow was piling up and up. The thick flakes softened the scene, like a misty photograph. "We'll be getting out of here soon," I thought, stamping through the snow; "maybe any minute." "Which way to Plocka Street?" I asked a woman at the corner. "Twelve blocks that way." She pointed straight ahead. "Then it's one way to the left. A lot of bombed buildings there," she warned me. "Thank you," I answered, starting off. The snow was covering up the hills of rubble and drifting through the ruined houses. It clung to some of the blasted walls in patches, like moss. "A pretty day," I thought to myself. In back of the snow, the blue sky pushed through, and the tiny eye of the sun, all white.

"Plocka Street," I read through the snow, turning left. "One Hundred Two Plocka Street," I sighed in relief. It was a small brick building, two stories high. The left side was bombed. On the first floor, I could see men moving inside; they were dressed like me, in odds and ends. I went in the door. "So you want to go to Palestine?" one of them said, getting up and coming up to me. "You want to leave this poor, bombed country?" "Palestine!" I shouted. "Are you crazy? I'm not going anywhere; I am looking for an apartment. Look, I have the address; I'm just lost." I took out the little piece of paper with the Bracka Street address. "That's not near here," he said, reading the address. "I understand; you want to go to Palestine." "Palestine! Who wants Palestine!" I screamed. "I only want to be free of you! Someone told me this was a better section to look for an apartment," I insisted. "Look," said another, "I know you are Jewish; I know you want to go to Palestine." "I am not Jewish!" I insisted, unbuttoning my coat, and showing the cross. "A Jewish woman would not wear a cross!" "They'll do anything," the man said; "don't tell me. My wife is Jewish." "I don't care if your wife is Turkish!" I shrieked, beside myself. "I am a Catholic, a Catholic!" "No, you are not," he said calmly. "I bet I know prayers even *you* don't," I told him. "You'll need them," he told me; "you are under arrest." "You cannot arrest me," I shouted; "I left my baby with a crazy woman at the train station." "Come on," he answered, pulling me out onto the street.

Inside, I had turned to stone. My skin was about to slide off. "We'll sit in the back," he told the other man who was starting up the truck. "Listen," he told me in Polish, "I'll give you good advice. I *know* you are Jewish." "I

517

am not Jewish," I repeated mechanically. "I know a nice judge," he went on, ignoring me. "The only thing is, you're better off waiting for him; he doesn't come in until later." "Waiting for him where?" I asked. "In the court," he said; "that's where we're going." "What are you?" "Russian N.K.V.D.," he answered. "We dress up this way to catch people trying to get out." "I am not Jewish," I said once more; "I was just looking for an apartment." "Here's the court," he answered, ignoring me. The truck was stopping in front of a wooden building on a cleared lot. Inside, was one big room, with two huge stoves in the two front corners. "Sit here," he motioned to the back bench. "I'll call your case when the judge comes; he has a Jewish wife, too." "I am not Jewish," I said again, dully.

Hours began to pass. I looked at my watch; it was a little gold sun. Eight o'clock. Nine o'clock. The blind watch face stared up at me. I turned it over and stared into its round gold back; my face stared back at me, made fatter in its curved surface. "I wonder what it would be like to turn gold in Palestine," I thought. "I wonder what it would be like not to be cold and hungry. What will happen to Ninushka now?" I thought again, again, again. But then I would look at myself in the gold watch, and once, Momma's face was in it. "You will live," she was saying; "you have for whom to live." "But I have messed it all up, Momma," I cried. "You never know how a story ends until you read the last page," Momma told me; "remember, Poppa always used to say that." "This one is over," I told her. "Oh, no," she said, surprised; "you haven't read Vera's letter; you haven't answered your father's riddle. You have to tell me what's in the letter first, and you have to answer the riddle." "What riddle?" I asked her. "Oh, you will find out," she said, laughing; "you're always so impatient. I'm very impatient to hear the letter," she said. "I always wondered what they said to each other." "Your turn," the soldier said, shaking me by the shoulder.

"You were arrested at the Zionist organization," the judge read out. "That organization is completely illegal." "I was looking for an apartment. Here," I said, producing the little piece of paper again. "I am not even Jewish. I don't understand this. I walk into a house with an empty floor and they drag me off in a truck." I was sleepy and talking through glue. "What religion *are* you?" the judge asked cynically. "Catholic," I answered. "I came from an orphanage near Vilno." I mentioned the name of a priest there. "It's a French orphanage," I added for no reason. "Say something in French," the judge demanded. "I am not Jewish," I said in French; "I was looking for an apartment." "This is an obvious mistake," the judge told the soldier; "release this Catholic woman." "Thank you," I said dully. I could say thank you in every language in Europe. "Thank you," I told the soldier. I turned by watch dial side up in the street. It was still snowing. It was one o'clock.

"Have the children eaten?" I asked Julka, climbing back in. "Not just yet," she said, turning the page of a magazine. I started mixing some flour and sugar and slicing the ham. "Give me some water, Ninushka," I asked her. "It's freezing in here," she whimpered, climbing down and coming over. Frederich had put some quilts on the windows, but the fire in the stove had gone out. "Julka," I told her, "tomorrow Frederich goes. I'm not taking any more chances." "Does he have to?" she asked, turning another page.

"I am sorry," I told Frederich the next morning. We could see our breaths in the apartment. "Absolutely no more. You have to go. They may not be watching today. And take Jerzy with you. I want Ninushka to get some rest; she's still weak." A warm peach light was starting to come in through the down quilt nailed over the kitchen window. "All right," Frederich answered, fastening Jerzy's hat and buttoning his coat; it was obvious he loved the child. "We'll take the bus," Frederich told Jerzy cheerfully. "Oh, buses," Jerzy said. "*I* like buses," Ninushka piped up. "You're not going anywhere; read your book and stay under the covers." From the dining room window I watched the two of them set off down the street as if they were going on a promenade.

One hour passed, then two, then three. I knew what had happened. Four hours passed. "They were arrested," Julka began screaming. "Will you keep quiet?" I demanded; "you'll wake up Ninushka." "Anya!" she grabbed my arm. "You have to look for them; you have to go." "If they're arrested, there's nothing I can do." "You could bring Jerzy back," she said shrewdly. She knew how I loved the children. "Julka," I warned her, "if you do not take care of Ninka, I am not leaving this room." "I will, I will," she promised feverishly. "Give me some money for a bus," I demanded. She pressed a big bill into my hand. "Some change, that's all I need; what would a driver do with this?" I handed it back. She poured a handful of change into my glove. "I am not going to Palestine now," I sighed, buttoning my coat. "Don't wake her up," I warned Julka. "And when she gets up, make sure she eats something, some hot water at least, and some flour and water mixed with sugar; bake it in the stove." "I will, go look for then," Julka pleaded; her eyes were completely wild.

The bus let me off on the corner of Plocka Street. Through the window of the Zionist organization, I could see Frederich sitting with Jerzy. Some of the same men who had questioned me were standing over him. I was back and forth, back and forth in front of the building like a demented fly. How could I get the poor baby? But I was afraid to go too close again. I hid in an archway across the street and watched. A truck came up, and Frederich marched out with Jerzy; a long line of people came out behind them.

"Where are they taking those people?" I whispered to a woman who had stopped next to me to watch. "To the prison." "Where is the prison?" "On Karowa Street; I wouldn't go near it." "Is there a bus?" "That one, two blocks down, where the wall with one window is." I went off to the bus stop.

"Tell me," I said, stopping a soldier near the prison; "what can I do? A man was arrested taking my child for a walk. It isn't his child; it's mine. He's been trying to get him for a long time. I don't have to tell you, you understand, don't you?" I said mysteriously. "Who is the man?" the soldier asked. "Frederich Zamenhoff; I curse the day I met him. I was so little, and my little baby is Jerzy Lavinsky." "Is your name Lavinsky?" the man asked. "Yes," I answered, blushing. "I see," he smiled; "I'll get the brat for you." He came out carrying Jerzy and handed him to me. "What will happen to those people?" I asked him. "They go to trial." "When?" "Who knows," he answered; "it's a nuisance, all these people trying to leave the country." "I wish him the most terrible fate," I swore righteously. "It is hard to have a baby with no father," the soldier said. "You have no idea," I agreed. "Still, men will be men," he said, smiling at me. "You still see him?" "Sometimes," I admitted. "Don't give up hope; he may darken your door again," he joked, "if he's not sent to hard labor." "Will he earn money if he is?" I asked hopefully. "Certainly not," the soldier answered, indignant, "for crimes against the state, one works for the state to repay it." "I see," I said, pretending to think. "Then we'll probably starve," I concluded mournfully. I was carrying Jerzy; he was staring back and forth at us as if we were completely crazy. "I doubt it," the soldier answered. "The judges have sympathy for family men." "Well, thank you," I said, carrying Jerzy back to the bus stop. "He doesn't look like you," the soldier called after us.

The stove was working. Ninka was munching on a piece of burned bread. "You should take it out before it turns to ashes," I scolded Julka. Ninushka got up and took Jerzy into the bed Frederich had put near the stove. "Get under the covers," she told him; "it's better." "Where is Frederich?" Julia asked, looking wildly around. "He is arrested." "Arrested!" she screamed, bursting into tears before she finished the word. "He cannot be arrested. I am nothing without him, nothing. You have to get him out, you have to get him out; I am nothing; get him out," she was screaming. "Julka, I cannot do anything today," I insisted. She kept screaming in Polish; she seemed to be talking to other people. "Get a hold of yourself," I shouted at her. "These men are not Nazis; they're not going to shoot him. They'll let him go, what is wrong with you?" Julka stopped screaming and sat down rigidly on a chair. "In the morning," I promised her, "I'll go and see what I can find out." "All right," she whispered. While going through a drawer for some silverware, I had found a diamond bracelet; I wrapped it in the silver basket and hid it in the lining of my coat. Maybe it would do some good.

"Julia," I said, beginning the same lecture, "I want you to understand I am not going to get Frederich if you will not watch the children." She was sitting near the stove in a trance. "It's freezing out," I warned her; "you can't let the fire go out anymore." Last night, the owner of the apartment had brought us some more wood. "I'll be good," she promised in a metallic voice. "Otherwise I will not go; he can stay there forever," I threatened again. "I promise, I'll do everything," she swore.

At the prison, I saw the same soldier again. "They're not out yet?" I demanded, incredulous. "Why should that lazy bum be in there where it's warm?" "It's going to take a long time, maybe more than a week," the poor soldier apologized. "He gets to sleep in there for a week!" I shouted. Frederich must have recognized my voice; his face appeared at the window. "There he is," I shouted; "let him out. I will take care of him worse than the judge." "I can't do that," the soldier said, grinning. "You'd better go home and wait; it's very cold out here. Why stand out here and look at that old dog?" "You're right," I sighed, turning around for the bus.

From the foot of the stairs, I could hear the children crying; mixed with the cries were all kinds of strange clattering noises. I flew up the four flights of stairs. Julka had out every pot and pan in the apartment. They were spread out all over the kitchen floor. She was down on her hands and knees, scouring them. "What are you doing?" I shouted. The fire in the stove was out. The children were screaming in terror. I began stuffing some wood into the stove. "I'll light it, I'll light it," Julka said, getting up. Her hands were trembling so hard she couldn't hold a match; she nearly set her skirt on fire. I slapped the match out of her hand and stamped it out. She was completely uncoordinated. I understood. "Go back to the pots," I ordered her. I was lighting the wood.

"You have to understand, Stanislaw," I heard her voice coming from behind me, "it is not that I have anything against you; it is just that I like Max so much better. But it would not hurt if you gave me some money." I turned around to look at her. She was addressing the thin air. "Julka," I said, helping her up, "come sit near the stove." The instant she sat down, she started screaming. "I am nothing without him. I gave up my life for him; I lived in a haystack. I am nothing. He is younger than I am, he ran away from me; he won't come back." She was completely hysterical. "Listen, Julka," I said, shaking her violently; "listen to me. He will leave you if he comes back and finds you like this. You look like a ninety-year-old woman. You are an old hag; he is a young man." Slowly, Julka raised a trembling hand to her cheek. "You are a brown prune," I insisted; "who would want you? You have to fix yourself up." Julka pushed back her hair with one hand. "You look like a witch on a stick. You should see your hair; it is such a haystack, Frederich could live in your head. God forbid he should see you like this." "God forbid," she whispered after me. "That's right," I hissed; "look at your nails. You look like you've been digging a hole for the winter. What would Frederich say?" "Frederich?" she whispered, confused, focusing on me. "Frederich," I said; "he's arrested, but he's coming back; the soldier told me. We just have to wait, but when he sees you,

he'll fall right off those stairs and kill himself from fright.'
"I have to get dressed then," Julka said, getting up shakily.

"That's right," I said, following her into the bathroom.
Her coffee cup was filled with water for mixing makeup.
"Let's start with your hair," I suggested, beginning to
brush it. Her hand took the brush from me. "You don't
know the first thing about makeup," she insisted; "I'll do
it." She stared into the mirror with her shiny look. "Come
into the kitchen when you're through." She didn't answer
me. I began pulling a mattress out of the bedroom in front
of the stove. "Julka will have to sleep here," I told
Ninushka; "she's going to need a lot of sleep, too." "Is she
sick?" Ninushka asked groggily. "Yes, very."

Gradually, Julka began to calm down a little; her hands
were still shaking and sometimes, when she stared into
space, her lips began to move. "Julka," I told her after
four days, "it's your turn to go down and get some food.
Frederich will not even recognize the skeleton you have
become." She got up like a mummy. "What's the matter
with her, Momushka?" Ninushka asked. "Don't ask," I
told her. She and Jerzy were spending all their time in the
bed in front of the stove. Ninushka read to him, or to herself, and slept; she was getting sadder and sadder. "We
have to get out of here," I thought desperately.

"I'm back." Frederich was standing in the doorway; he
was completely unshaven, hollow-eyed, ten pounds thinner.
"Where is Julia?" "She's out getting food." "Food," he
sighed. Julia came back with a huge basket almost an hour
later. "Cheese, eggs, meat, and bread," she said dully. I
grabbed it out of her hand. "Frederich!" she screamed,
seeing him. She looked wonderful. Every hair was in
place; all her makeup was on. They grabbed each other.
"You look nervous," Frederich said, looking worried. "She
is nervous," I told him; "worse than nervous." Frederich
stared from her to me. "I understand; I'll take care of it.
She'll be better as soon as we get out of here." "What
happened to you?" Julka cried piteously. "The usual," he
said cheerfully. "A few beatings; they took my rings.
Jerzy!" he boomed, swooping down on the little boy and
swinging him up. Jerzy wrapped his arms around Frederich's neck and began wetly kissing him all over. "Better
than a shaving lotion," Frederich sighed. "Have you forgotten me?" Julia pouted.

"Listen," Frederich said, shaving in the bathroom, the
two of us behind him; "I know how to get out of here.

We buy a lot of vodka and some Russians who have trucks will take us to the Russian zone in Berlin." "How did you find out?" I asked him. "You find out a lot in prison." "Is it dangerous?" "The worst they can do is send us to prison, so what choice do we have? We try, go back, or stay here." "We'll go," I insisted. "I have a list of families," he said, producing it, "but we need about five more. It costs a fortune. We'll get two trucks." "Trucks," Julka pouted; "no trains?" "There are no trains," Frederich told her impatiently; "they're all bombed. I'm going out to finish with this," he said, getting up. He hadn't taken off his coat; outside the kitchen, it was colder than the street. "I'm going with you," Julka announced. "No, you're not," Frederich answered, picking her up and putting her down in the bed in the kitchen; "you're staying here. I want you fatter." Julka beamed up at him.

Frederich was back before dark. We were always back before dark because of the stairs. "All done," he announced cheerfully; "we have the trucks. We leave the day after tomorrow." "Ninushka," I said turning around with a piece of bread, cheese, and bacon; "I want you to eat and sleep as much as you can in the next day and a half." Ninushka made a face. "Don't waste time making faces," I ordered her; "eat. How far is it?" it finally occurred to me to ask. "About one hundred and twenty miles," he said sweetly; "not so far away." "Not so far!" Julka exclaimed. "This was *your* idea, my dear," he answered, turning to her with something like annoyance.

Two days later, we were all waiting on a corner near the train station for the trucks. Julka looked elegant as ever; Frederich, standing next to his ten packing crates, the newest filled with quilts, teacups, and crystal from the apartment, was showing signs of wear and tear. I had both my coats on. Ninushka was wearing three sweaters under her coat and a towel was wrapped around her head under her hat. I had stuffed woolens into her boots and gloves. She looked like a fat grocery bag. I thought about my valises. One had the silver basket, the diamond bracelet, a few more clothes for the two of us, two handmade bloomers, a handmade brassiere, a pair of normal shoes for me. In the other, I carried some extra blankets and towels and a few pair of wool stockings I'd found in the apartment. Vera's letter and the pictures were tucked between my breasts. "This is all of Poland I'm taking," I thought to myself; "this is all." From the corner of my eye, I could see the white horse; he seemed to know he was being left behind, but there was still hope in his eyes. It frightened me he still had hope.

One of the trucks pulled up. It filled without us. "Why aren't we going in the first truck?" Julia sulked; "are all those people going first because they're doctors?" "Maybe it's better," I told her; "maybe it's fate. It's probably better." We climbed into the truck under the flapping awning that covered it. "Who's driving?" I asked Frederich, settling Ninushka on my lap. "A drunken Russian soldier," he answered laughing. "This is their part-time job; real capitalists, aren't they?"

The truck began rumbling along. Ninushka's weight was helping to settle my stomach. It was inconceivable to think that we were leaving Poland. Once, in Druzgeniekie, a French doctor had gotten my Momma to promise she would send me to medical school in Nancy. She had promised. But then I had found out that with my father's kind of papers, I would never be allowed to return. To be separated from my parents! It was a horror I couldn't imagine. Now, each street we passed seemed to be one of them, a flat tombstone for them. "I don't even know where their graves are!" I thought, agonized. We passed one street: Momushka. Another: Poppa. Another: Vera. Another: Mischa. Another: Emmanuel. Another: Anzia. Another: Zoshia. Another: Rachel, Vladek, Doctor Dudek. Now they were going by faster and faster. "But I have Ninushka," I thought, "and now I will forget. I have Ninushka; I have all of them." Her little head was nodding in rhythm with the wheels. I was falling asleep.

There was a sudden squeal of brakes. "A lot of noise up ahead," Frederich whispered; "that's why we stopped." After an hour and a half, the driver walked back. "They stopped the truck up ahead," he told us; "we'd better wait." We sat in the car. Hail was bouncing off the canvas top over us like machine gun fire. "All right," the driver called back to us; starting up the engine. From between the rails of the car, we could see the other truck. Soldiers at the checkpoint were marching people out and taking them to a little sentry post. "We're going through!" the driver called out exultantly; "They're busy with the others!" We saw the border sign; the truck was rolling along like a comet. "We're in Germany!" Frederich howled like a wolf. "You can do anything!" Julka crowed. "Where did you get the vodka?" I asked suddenly. "Not all of it was real vodka," Frederich roared; "some of it was straight alcohol!" "Are you trying to get us killed?" I giggled loudly; "where did you get that?" "Oh, the hospital workers get it," he grinned; "money stretches out like gum." "It's Berlin," someone was crying. We could see the buildings up ahead of us. "We're going into the Russian zone," someone said. The trucked braked in front of a big building. "This is where you get out," the driver said, letting down the gate. Frederich jumped down first; I handed down the children. I sat on the edge and dangled my legs. "Come on, jump!" he dared me. I slid off. Behind me, Julka was jumping down. It was almost dark.

30

IT WAS completely dark outside, but we could make out the lines of the big rectangular building. Frederich had taken the driver aside. I heard some laughing. The Russian soldier began unpacking the crates, setting them down in front of the building. "I'll stay out here with them until it gets light," he called to us: "you go inside." From the sidewalk, we could hear the muffled roar of voices. "There must be a thousand people in there," Julka whispered. We opened the door and pushed in; the building was packed with people like smoked cigarette stubs. "I have to go to the bathroom," Ninushka wailed, waking up. "In a minute," I told her; I was frantically looking all over the place to put her down. Finally, I saw a little table. I began elbowing through. When people didn't move, I jabbed them or kicked them. "Now," I said, putting Ninushka on the table, "let's see what's what." "I want to go to the bathroom," she said again. "And me," Jerzy wailed. "Julka," I called her. She was plowing through after us. "Sit on this table while I find the bathroom."

"Where is the bathroom?" I asked an old man sitting near us. He pointed toward the right corner of the room. "Come on," I ordered, picking up Ninushka, and motioning to Jerzy with my head. "I don't like it here," Ninushka wailed. "We won't be here forever," I answered, pushing someone else out of the way. The place had the horrible smell of unwashed bodies. The people in the room smelled like the water dead flowers were left in too long. "Here it is," I said, pushing open the door. "Ich!" Ninushka cried, clapping her hand over her nose. The room was filled with urine up over our ankles; feces were swimming all over. "We're not going in there," I said, turning around; "it will have to wait until morning." "It smells, Momushka," Ninka complained. "You're telling me," I answered. "The minute it gets light, we're getting out of here."

"I smell something good," Ninka announced when we
527

got back to the table and I put her down on it. I looked around. Some man had a big kettle of coffee and a basket of rolls. "I'll get something," I told her. "Don't let her get off this table, Julka," I said; "don't let her get off this table. Ninka, watch Jerzy." I came back with four rolls and a huge tin cup of coffee. "Hold the handle," I told Ninushka; "the cup's hot." We passed it around. "Finished?" Everyone nodded. I gave the cup back to the man. "Thanks, lady," he said, wiping the rim with his dirty apron. "Go to sleep, Ninushka," I told her, coming back and wedging my body in front of her table like a wall. Jerzy was squeezed between me and Julka. "What do we do now?" Julka asked. "We wait for morning," I told her.

Finally, light began to come in through the dirty windows. "Frederich," I told him, "it's impossible in that bathroom; we'll get a disease. Julka is no use. You have to get her to watch the children and to wait for us somewhere. We have to look for a place; it's the same thing all over again." More and more, that was how it was; people in Szczecin had thought we were the married ones. "She can sit on the boxes with Jerzy," he agreed. We went off to find bathrooms. A storekeeper let us in. "Julka," Frederich told her, coming back, "we have to walk all over; I don't think you'll want to go. Why not sit on the boxes with Jerzy and Ninka—the boxes are so valuable—and we'll come for you as soon as we have something." "It's cold out," she reminded him. "If you don't stay, you have to come with us," *I* reminded her. "Go to the bathroom with Jerzy, and then we'll go." "All right," she agreed reluctantly, setting off. "Here she comes," Frederich sighed. She was holding something. "I have some new magazines," she announced, smiling from ear to ear.

"I want to go to the French zone," I told Frederich, leaving. "Why the French zone?" "I'm tired of the Russian madness for law and order," I sighed, plodding after him; "and we can't speak English." "What about the German zone?" he asked; "I can speak German." "I can't stand the sight of it," I answered him. "You mean the sound of it," he smiled, correcting me. "You can take the tramway across the street to the French zone," a woman told us, "but it's just as crowded there." We climbed onto the first car that came. It was strange to be on a trolley again. I was trying to remember when I had last seen one. "It must have been in Warsaw," I thought with surprise, "when we lived on Marszalkowska Street." Frederich

528

jumped off, and handed me down. "Such a gentleman," I mocked. "When I am with such a lady," he teased; "come on, why be such a lemon?" "This is not exactly heaven," I answered him. "I spend all my time thinking what next? What next? And all I see is a blank window; I'm looking out of a window, and nothing's there. Maybe it's because the window is on a very high floor," I said, trying to turn the conversation into a joke.

"You don't know what's coming next," he said seriously; "we have some idea. I've written my sister in Salt Lake City, and she'll probably get us papers, so we'll go there." "Salt Lake City," I repeated; "it might as well be China." "What will you do?" he asked with interest. "First, I'll try to get out of the country while we still have our bladders left; after that, I just don't know." "You don't want to stay and finish your education?" he asked. "Julka told me how much you wanted to be a doctor." "I want to finish, but not here, not here. I can't You know, sometimes when I look around, I don't see people at all; I see soldiers, Gestapo soldiers, with those terrible dead heads on their caps." I didn't know why I was talking to him like this. "Well, I am stupid," Frederich sighed; "when there are people, I see people; when there are soldiers, I see soldiers," "I've been lucky in everything but my mind," I said. He didn't answer. I wondered if he understood me at all. In my old age, I was beginning to resemble Vera more and more. "Old age," I thought to myself astonished; "I'm only twenty-seven."

"What's going on there?" Frederich asked, pointing. Some soldiers were shouting at an old man who was holding out a package of cigarettes. He turned it this way and that way. "Please," he kept pleading in Polish, "don't take me away; don't arrest me. I don't understand you." "What's the matter?" I asked him in French, stepping forward. Twenty-seven and still a busybody. "This man is selling cigarettes; we think he stole them," the policeman explained. I translated that to the old man. "Oh, no, Miss," he said, grabbing my hand with his wrinkled, freckled one; "these are from my American family. Look, I still have the letter." He dug in his pocket and thrust it toward me. "I'm just selling so my family will eat something; they're mine to sell, please tell them." I translated his explanation to the soldiers. "How do we know to believe him?" one of them asked me. "Look at the old toad," I went on in French. "Where would he get money to trade on the black market, or the nerve to steal anything? No, I'm telling you, you're making a mistake." "Miss, Miss," the old man was jabbering to me in Polish, "please take care of this. I will do anything for you, anything in the world." Frederich was standing by, amused. "All I need is a place to live," I told the old man. "I have a little baby, and this man and his wife have a little boy." "You can stay with us, believe me; it's a U.N.R.R.A. building. You get registered; they even get you food. Just make them let me go." "He wants me to make you let him go," I told the soldier. "You see how innocent he is? He thinks you're Nazis and you're just pulling him off the streets because he's Jewish." "God forbid," the soldier whispered under his breath, "we should ever become like them." "Look," I told him, "I have the letter he was trying to tell you about; it's in English. Can anyone read English?" "We'll get someone. A Nazi, God forbid!" Another soldier arrived. "Do you speak English?" the first one asked. "Ah, oui!" he said. "Who wants to speak it here?" "Just read this letter to us," the soldier asked. "It says they're looking forward to seeing him in Canada or Detroit." The soldier looked up, puzzled, "and they hope he can use the cigarettes because they read in the papers there are none here. Also, they're sending candy bars because they read in the papers there are none of those, either. What's this all about?"

"Well, now you see," I pleaded, "you have grabbed him for no reason, and look how you've frightened him. He's older than your father. You'll make him sick; he's been through enough already." "Let him go," the soldier said. "Oh, thank you, thank you," the old man cried, kissing my hand when he understood what had happened. "I thought they were taking me away forever." "You said we could stay with you," I reminded him. "I've only got a kitchen," he apologized, "but you're welcome to it. I'll get you registered so you can get the food ration. There's no food in the whole city. Believe me," he swore, "it's worse than during the war." "Tell him we have plenty of money," Frederich instructed. "He says it makes no difference; there's nothing to buy. Tell me," I asked the old man, "what is your address?" "Ninety-eight Steinhauser Alley; we'll wait for you. You have a little baby? My wife will make you something." "She's really six and a half," I told him; "I just can't stop calling her that. But the boy is only three and a half." "We'll have something," he swore. "I can trade for these cigarettes now; right here," he said looking around, "where that man can see me." "We'll be there soon," I promised. "This man," I pointed to Frederich, "has a lot of boxes." "Boxes?" the old man echoed. "He hangs them from the ceiling on hooks," I told him, hoping he would forbid Frederich to bring them. "Oh, from the ceiling is all right," the man sighed; "I guess it's all right."

"Julka, we have a place in the French zone," Frederich told her when we got back. "I'm going to get a wagon for us and the boxes." "The French zone!" Julka exclaimed. "How wonderful! It is my favorite language." "You'll be speaking it in a kitchen," I warned her. "All five of us are going to live in that kitchen." "What?" Julka asked, freezing. "It's that or the streets." A wagon was already pulling up; the driver began loading the boxes into it. Julka and Frederich sat with Jerzy on one side; Ninushka and I sat on top of the boxes on the other. I felt safer that way; they couldn't fall on us.

"You will be a translator; we need one here," the old man told me. "Look, I have a bed for your baby." He had two chairs tied together, pressed against the wall. "The other little one will have to sleep on the chairs." Julka glowered at me. "I can speak French," she said loudly. "Good," the old man said, turning away without interest. "I am Joshua Levin," he told us. We began introducing ourselves. "I don't know," Frederich said, looking around; "the boxes can go on the ceiling, of course, but three of us can't fit on that floor with Jerzy." "I'll sleep on the stove top," I said in a voice that grated on my own ears. But Jerzy was beginning to cough terribly. "I don't want to interfere," Mr. Levin said, "but that child should see a doctor." Jerzy was coughing gently. "In the morning," I promised. "Right away," he insisted. "If it's TB he has to be isolated, and another couple in the apartment is going into the American zone; the other two will have to stay in that room with him." Julka looked at me triumphantly. "Where is the doctor?" Frederich asked, frantic. "In the U.N.R.R.A. building, six blocks straight down." Frederich picked Jerzy up and marched off. "We may have our own room yet," Julka said, perching herself on the edge of the stove, lighting one of her endless cigarettes. "Doesn't that bag have a bottom?" I asked.

"It is TB," Frederich said; "the beginning of it. We have to isolate him, and I have some medicine, but not

531

much. He needs rest, only rest." "Does that mean we get the room?" Julka asked. "You get in right away," Mr. Levin fussed like a sick hen, "right away; we all have children here. Some people!" he said to me as they went out. "The people who left gave me a folding cot to sell. Would you like it for your Ninushka?" "Oh, how much is it?" I cried. "I can't take money from you," he answered, "not this one time. I didn't want to say anything while the others were here," he whispered, "but how can you sleep on the floor? All night it's people coming and going to the bathroom, you know how it is. No one's plumbing is so good anymore, and even the stove, sometimes people get up to use it." "I'll sleep on the stove; I was going to, anyway." "*On* it?" He measured me with his eyes. "Oh, yes," I said, trying to reassure him; "on the little metal part in back of the burners. I can curl around." "If you think you can," he worried, "but tomorrow, we register you for food, and you can put your little girl in school. They are even organizing nice little plays for the children. A Doctor Heinz does it; it's very nice. Then you'll get your food, too." "I'm really so thankful," I told him. "And while Ninka is at school, you can sleep on the cot," he smiled. "I had thought about it," I admitted, smiling.

The next day, Frederich and I went with Mr. Levin to register. I had my *matritza*, my birth certificate, and my medical index, but Frederich had nothing. He was from Kaunas, a Lithuanian, and Lithuanians were not allowed out of Poland at all. "You will need someone to sign for you before a notary public, that you aren't Polish, or we can't register you." "I'll do it," I spoke up; "he's my cousin." We went off to the notary's; then we came home, registered. "Ninushka," I told her when she woke up, giving her one of Mr. Levin's cookies, "tomorrow you start school. They have good soups there for lunch." "That's nice," she said, falling back asleep. "That child is positively green," I thought to myself frantically. If anything happened to her, I didn't want to live. Frederich and Mr. Levin would come back with pitiful rations. When we got to Berlin, I had stopped eating; everything I had, I gave to her, to her. But she was fattening up at the school. "Now *you* have to eat," Mr. Levin insisted.

"Momushka! Momushka!" Ninka screamed flying up the stairs after two weeks at school; "we're going to be in a play. You have to teach me to recite something." "Why a play?" I asked dully. Every morning when I got up from the stove, my legs were swollen and sore. Every five minutes, someone was tramping through to the bathroom, and at least twice a night someone wanted to use the stove; why shouldn't they? And then it was too hot to lie down. I would fall asleep, waiting for it to cool, standing against the wall. Once I fell asleep in the toilet and the furious pounding of another occupant tore open my eyes to the sight of a German soldier vanishing into the tiles. "They want to show us off. Doctor Heinz said so, so they might get more food and things from U.N.R.R.A. We need more crayons and paper," she announced importantly, "especially red crayons; we have none of them left. We have a lot of black ones, though," she said thoughtfully; "no one likes them." "And white ones probably," I added. "Oh, a lot of white ones," Ninka sniffed. "You can't draw anything with white, unless," she mused, "you draw dead people, but you have to have black paper, and we don't have black paper."

"So what do you want to do?" I asked in the same listless voice. "I *told* you," Ninka answered impatiently; "I have to recite anything. But I don't know anything, not to recite." "I'll teach you something in French!" "Not in *French!*" she stamped her foot. "I don't know French." "The people in the audience don't know anything else. I'll tell it to you in Polish and Russian, and then you can memorize it in French." "Do I have to?" she asked. "You have to. 'The Fox and the Crow,'" I began in Polish. Before I was halfway through, Ninushka was giggling. "Now in French," I said; "'*Le Renard et le Corbeau.*'" "'*Le Renard et le Corbeau,*'" Ninushka repeated after me in a horrendous accent. "Very good," I told her. "Now let's start on the next line." And so we spent the next week practicing. It kept my mind off Jerzy and his coughing. When Frederich wasn't out, he and Julka stayed in there with him. Once in a while, Julka would wander out. "Do you want a magazine?" she would ask lazily. "No, thank you." I was afraid of the germs. Then she would wander back. She and Frederich had bought a real bed; Jerzy had another. "Is he coughing less?" I asked her. "Thank God," she said; "I'm finally getting some sleep. Look at these black circles." Dramatically, she pointed to her eyes. "Too bad for you," Ninushka said from her fable; I didn't bother correcting her.

"Where is the play?" I asked Ninushka the night before. "In a *big* room," she said dramatically; "they rented it specially for this." "Are you nervous?" I asked her. "Oh, yes," she swore, "but I have to do it, or we won't get our crayons."

The big room was packed with the children's parents or relatives and officials from U.N.R.R.A. A little boy went up first. He recited some kind of poem about springtime in a quavering voice, making a hundred mistakes. "Look at those Americans," I whispered to Julka in Polish. "How do they know what the little children are feeling? The children pour their guts out for crayons and all they care about is filling themselves up." "How do you know?" one of the men said, turning around and speaking to me in my own language; "how do you know what every American man feels?" If the ground had opened up and swallowed me, I couldn't have been more happy. "I'm sorry," I mumbled to him. "Why don't you let me take you home after the show?" he asked. "We'll see," I said.

Then Ninushka appeared on the stage in a little sailor suit looking like a bean sprout. " '*Le Renard et le Corbeau*.' Once upon a time a fox seed a crow with a big piece of cheese. The fox wanted the cheese, but the crow was too high up in the tree." She was improving as she went along. "So, the fox decided, I will compliment the crow. '*Oh, Monsieur le Corbeau, bonjour*,' said the fox; 'you have such a beautiful beak.' " Ninushka stopped and peered into the audience. I waved back. She quavered on. " 'You have such beautiful feathers; everyone says you are the most beautiful bird in the wood.' The silly crow began preening herself. 'I heard that you have the most beautiful voice; I would give anything if you would sing.' The silly crow was so excited by the compliments. 'You are the queen of the forest, of the world, of the whole universe; won't you please sing for me,' said the fox. 'And besides your beautiful looks you have such a voice, won't you please sing for me!' The crow was so thrilled she got dizzy, opened her big beak, and let the cheese fall right into the mouth of the fox. So we learn," Ninushka finished, "not always to open our mouths when we get lots of compliments." She had added the moral herself in Polish. All over, people were laughing and clapping.

From the corner of the stage a man came over and bent down to talk to her. "Erdmann!" I thought, getting up and running to him. But then I recognized him immediately; it was Mr. Joseph Brodsky. He was in charge of U.N.R.R.A., of all of us. "Do you have a mother?" he was asking her. "Are you an orphan?" "This is my Mommy!" Ninushka cried, catching sight of me, starting to hide herself behind me. I knew what he wanted; he wanted to adopt her. Everyone in the zone knew all there was to know about him. He had been married for years and had no children. "Oh, I'm glad to meet you," he said. "I thought perhaps your daughter had no one." "She has me," I answered, picking her up, almost squashing her. "Why didn't you think so, because she looks so terrible? It's because she has no food; she's really a beautiful child." I was furious. "Please," he pleaded; "we are having a little dinner after the play. Won't you let me put the child to sleep in there until it's over? I'll take you home. There's no harm in it." "*If* there's no harm in it," I answered. "I assure you, she's a very bright child; I'm interested in her." "You won't try to take her away." "What do you think I am?" he demanded, hurt. "Other people have tried," I said in a hard voice. "I understand. I won't even try. Please come."

He picked Ninka up and carried her next door. I could feel everyone's eyes sticking in my skin like pins. Here, he was a king. He could give you everything; if you would take it. "Let me put her to bed," he pleaded again. I followed him into a room and he tucked her into a big bed under some quilts. "Oh, it's nice here, Mommy," she said, lying on her back, putting one arm over her head and falling sound asleep. "Come eat," he said to me, smiling. The table had every kind of food I had ever seen. I ate and ate. Each time a plate came by, I took a little, but plate after plate was coming by. Soon I felt I was going to burst; I was groggy with exhaustion. "You are more tired than your daughter," Mr. Brodsky laughed; "let me take you home," "Oh, no," I insisted, sitting up straighter. "I'll carry her home. We're used to it; I don't want to change her routine." I didn't want him to see where we lived. But he insisted.

"So where do *you* sleep?" he asked, putting Ninushka, sound asleep, down on her cot when we got home. I didn't say anything. "Why are you smiling?" he asked. "I am not smiling," I insisted, pulling down the corners of my mouth. "You cannot tell me you leave the child here alone with the stove," he persisted. "You're smiling again," he said irritably. "Thank you for a wonderful evening, Mister Brodsky," I told him; "it was so nice of you." "You have not told me where you sleep," he repeated. "On the stove," I answered, blushing scarlet. "On the stove?" he echoed, incredulous. "There, in back of the burners." He stared at me. "Probably you think I'm crazy," I suggested, "or you pity me; which is it?" "Neither, believe me," he swore. "I wish I had someone to sleep on a stove for. Mrs. Lavinsky," he said, "this isn't charity, or even a special favor. U.N.R.R.A. has a clothing supply for refugees. I want you to come down tomorrow and get some things; I want to try and find you another room. This is ridiculous." "I like it where I am," I told him. I was afraid of what he wanted. "At least let me send some food for the child." "Maybe a little," I agreed. "Good night," he said; "tomorrow will you come for the clothes?" "If I get some sleep tonight," I answered, smiling at him involuntarily. His eyes were abnormally bright as he left the room. "But he must be used to this," I thought; "he must know what goes on." "You *do* have luck," Julka said, coming in. "I'm glad you know him; now Frederich can go visit him. He wants to be in charge of administering the building; he says we can get more food that way." "Good night, Julka; out," I ordered her. Frederich was already occupied with his business, and while he was gone, I had to watch Jerzy.

A few weeks later, Frederich and Julka were sitting on Ninushka's bed; she was on Frederich's lap, and I was on the stove. We were eating our usual ration of herring and bread. For supper, we usually had macaroni or potatoes. "Frederich," I began, "what kind of business are you doing now?" "More or less the same thing," he answered, swallowing a piece of herring. He and Ninka had a game. Before they ate the fish, they had to pretend to catch and spear it. "More gold money?" I asked. "Oh, no," he said; "this is simple, and not so heavy to carry. I trade one kind of franc for another; one is worth much more." "Then what do you do with it?" "Then I put it in that special closet I bought for the hall." A tall closet now filled half of the narrow passageway. "Is it legal?" I asked. "No, of course not," Frederich answered, "but I have to do something; as you are always saying, Anya. A man can't afford to sit around doing nothing all the time." "I can't stand any more inspections," I warned him. "Don't worry, don't worry," he assured me, beginning to chase another piece of herring around the sea of his plate. Ninushka had yet to catch her first one. She grabbed it, and gobbled down her bread. "Frederich," I began again. "I want to settle this. Someone will follow you home. We will all be in trouble." "No one will follow me," he insisted.

" 'Oh no,' cried Athos, smiting his chest. D'Artagnan will never suffer for me,' " Ninushka was screaming at the top of her lungs down the hall. "What are you doing?" I demanded, grabbing her; "other people are still asleep." She was standing just outside the doorway of Jerzy's room. "I'm reading him a story," she complained. "You said I couldn't go in." "You're not reading this way," I told her. "Just give me the book and Julka will read to him. I promise you, she'll read." "I've got a copy of *The Scarlet Pimpernel* from Mister Levin," she added. "She'll read that, too," I sighed, dragging Ninushka back to the kitchen.

"Julka," I began, but there was a knock at the door. Mr. Levin's head popped in like a fat white cloud. "The police—" he started to say. "Frederich!" I screamed. "Let him finish," Frederich said calmly, eating another small piece of bread. "The police, Mrs. Lavinsky," Mr. Levin explained, "have cheese from U.N.R.R.A." "What are they doing with cheese?" "I don't know; maybe they don't want a riot over the food, but they need someone to translate for them and to cut it." "I would be more than happy," I answered jumping up. "Do they only need one?" Frederich asked, "No, two." "How about me?" "Fine, you come too."

Downstairs, a little car was unloading block after block of cheese. A big table made from boards and sawhorses was set up in the hall. "What kind of cheese is it?" I whispered, amazed. "Swiss," said Mr. Levin, shrugging his shoulders. "Now," said the policeman; "who speaks French?" "So," he addressed me, "you have to divide the cheese between the people in the building. We're getting so much stuff lately. Maybe the Americans finally heard there was a war. This is going to happen a lot. You don't mind?" "Mind?" I gasped kissing him on both cheeks; "I am so happy to do it!" "Well," he blushed, "if you do the work, you get an extra pound, maybe two," he said, looking me over. "One for each kiss?" I laughed. "Maybe even something for the little girl," he suggested, grinning at Ninushka, who was staring at the table like a fox. "Let's get started," he told the other man. "Every family gets a slice this big for every three people, this big for four, this big for five, and so on. You understand." "Oh, perfectly!"

I cried out again. People were beginning to come down and line up.

Slice, slice, slice. Two hours passed. "My arm is beginning to hurt," I told Frederich. "How many people are there in this building?" "Almost five hundred," he answered, cutting faster and faster. More cheeses were coming in from the street. "I don't think I'll be able to eat it when we're done," I said, looking greenly at another slab. Finally, we were finished. The policeman came in with half a slab. "Here's your share for the work," he said, giving Frederich a quarter of it. "If you will excuse me, I want to talk to Mrs. Lavinsky about something. The rest is for you," he told me, "but take this, and give it to the little girl to take up in her sweater." Ninushka was already unbuttoning it. "Oh, thank you," I cried, half out of my mind. "The next time I think it's meat," he grinned.

No sooner had we hidden the cheese than Mr. Levin was back. "This time they're looking for someone to run the building," he sighed. "The rabbi is sick. I thought Mister Zamenhoff might want to do it." "I want to," Frederich answered behind me, chomping on a huge chunk of Swiss cheese. "You'll be in charge of rations, rooms, everything. But the rabbi is still in command," Mr. Levin told Frederich; "he's just sick." "Now we'll really have things," Frederich gloated. There was a knock at the door. "What now?" I groaned. I wanted to get out and trade the cheese for some things; Ninushka already had a piece she was ordered to eat, and was gobbling it down. "See," I told her, "the good luck your fable brought us?" She grinned and took a big bite.

A man was standing in the door with a big basket. "Is there a Ninushka Lavinsky here?" the man asked. "She is my daughter," I answered. "Ninka, go into the hall." She climbed down from the stove and scrambled off. "This basket is for her," the man said. "Can I put it down, please? It's very heavy." "Who sent it?" I asked suspiciously. "Mister Joseph Brodsky; it's food for the little girl. She's very sick, he told me." "All right," I answered. "I have to bring back the basket, so if you would unpack it," he apologized. Out came jar after jar of preserves, a can of caviar, a big piece of smoked bacon, some smoked ham, two loaves of bread. "Thank you," the man told me, picking up the basket and leaving. I took the jar of caviar and a bigger piece of cheese; now we could really trade. From down the hall came the bored sound of Julka's voice reading, probably *The Scarlet Pimpernel*. I peeled Ninushka from the wall just outside the doorway. "We're going shopping," she began chanting, dancing up and down like a maniac. " '*Le Renard et le Corbeau*,' " she began to recite. "Very good, oh, very good," I said, laughing uncontrollably. The food from the basket was hidden behind the stove and under the clothes on her cot.

"Mommy, there's a woman with a cart!" Ninka shouted, pulling loose of my hand and running over. "Nothing," she called back; "paper and pencils and cigarettes." She ran over to another. "Here, Momushka!" She shrieked, jumping into the air. "Clothes!" "Don't be so excited," I said, coming up slowly; "we really don't need too much." She understood right away. "This pillow doesn't look too bad," I said, thumping it in the middle. "I see some feathers come out." "You don't see any such thing," the woman answered. I put it back. Ninushka was pointing furtively at some shoes. "Do you have little sizes?" "Here," the woman said, pulling some to the top. "I can try them on?" "Try them on. She's not going to buy anything," she whispered loudly to her husband. The shoes fit. "Boots, Momushka!" Ninka whispered. "I have boots." "You don't have bloomers," she said loudly. I turned purple. "Here are bloomers," the woman pointed. "How much cheese for the pillow, two pairs of bloomers, and the shoes?" I asked her. It was already sliced. In Germany, food was gold. "Three pieces." "Two." Then in back of her, I saw a little boy crying. His whole head was covered with a rash. "All right, three." I handed them over. "Momma," Ninushka pleaded in a new voice, "could I buy one piece of paper and one real pencil?" "What for?" "I want to write to Vladek." I broke off a little piece of cheese and wrapped it up. "Try this." She flew off and came back with two pieces of paper and a pencil. "You did a good job," I admired. "I told her she looked hungry standing in the cold," Ninka beamed. She was hugging the paper as if it were a baby. "You'll crumple it," I warned her; "roll it up." "You hold the pencil," she begged me; "I might lose it." I put the fat blue pencil in my bag.

The next morning there was another knock at the door. "Miss Ninushka Lavinsky," the man said, bringing in the same basket, ready to unpack it. "Take it back!" I ordered. "I am sorry. Take it back. Back!" I ordered again, seeing him ready to argue with me. The third morning it was the same thing. "Back," I said again. Ninushka was pouting. "I could get more paper and write Aunt Rachel and Aunt Lisa, too." "Why don't you write them all a letter on one piece?" "It's not the same." The fourth morning it was Mr. Brodsky himself. "I'm here inspecting the building," he said, not looking at me. "I hear Mister Zamenhoff is in charge of the building committee. Too bad," he hurried on; "we usually like to have a rabbi." "Mister Brodsky, please," I pleaded; "the others will see you here. You don't know what kind of an element lives in this building; they're all so jealous." There was a long silence. "You said your daughter needed air." I didn't answer him. "We could go for a ride in the country. Why not?" "Why not?" I cried. "If you picked us up here, we wouldn't be safe from the others at night!" "I don't have to pick you up here," he answered. "You can take the bus to the American zone, where the play was." "All right," I said, surprising myself. "In two days?" "All right," I said again.

31

"MOMMY! Mommy!" Ninushka was waking me up; "we have to get the bus." "At five in the morning?" I grumbled, looking at my watch. "Go back to sleep." "Momushka," she cried again, "we could go look around the American zone; you said you wanted to." "And we could buy some paper, is that it?" "We could do that, too," Ninushka agreed. "All right." I climbed off the stove. Last night had been a good night. People had used the stove only once. "Let's go." As usual, we were completely dressed except for our bloomers. "Put on your warm coat and let's go." We got on the bus. "Do you know what time it is?" I asked her. "A quarter of seven," she answered, looking at my watch; "it pays to get a good start," she mimicked. I was half asleep. "We're here," Ninka shouted, dragging me off.

We were on a good street, wealthy buildings; there was very little bombing. "What do you want to do? Knock on doors?" "Let's look and think who lives in them," Ninka suggested. So we walked around. "I'm finished thinking," she finally said. "Good," I said, seeing a little park and a bench; "let's eat some of the jam and cheese sandwiches." We each ate two. "Let's take another bus," Ninka pleaded, seeing one coming up; "we can run; we'll get it." We got on. "Nine o'clock," I complained; "we don't meet Mister Brodsky until twelve; you're driving me crazy."

"Oh, look, Momushka, at that funny lady," Ninka whispered; "she looks just like Aunt Rachel." "Rachel is much younger," I said, dismissing it, but opening my eyes a little wider. She did look just like her. I opened my eyes again. Rachel and I were sitting in her bedroom on the peach-colored quilt; sun was coming through the leaded windows and peach curtains. We were inside a flower in her room when the sun shone. "Look at this one," Rachel was saying, turning the page of the rust-colored album. We looked at the picture a long time. "Doesn't she look like an Indian?" Rachel asked. "That's my Aunt Tania; she lives in Germany." "Pardon me," I said, jumping out of my seat; "aren't you a member of the Krasinsky family?" "Yes, I am," the woman answered, startled; "who are you?" "I'm a friend of your niece, Rachel. More than a friend; we were neighbors, and we were just living in the same apartment." "What happened to my family?" she asked, grabbing my hand. Now I was sorry I had gone over to her. I knew what had happened. "They're all dead, except Rachel." "Rachel is alive!" she marveled. "Oh, I will have to send her money, clothes; everything; you have to tell me where she lives." I gave her our old address on Freta Street. "In Vilno," Ninka added helpfully. "You have to come home with me," the woman said, grabbing my hand again. "I am Tania Krasinsky. I have a wonderful place nearby; I'd like you to see it." "Are you the Tania who got the yellow rose for an anniversary?" I blurted out like a child. "The very one," she answered; "but the story had a happy ending. I live with a general now. First, it was a General Oblensky. He's gone, but first he rebuilt my whole house after the bombing. I tell you, it's a better life than I had before. I don't even know what to do with half my things." "You could give some to us," Ninka suggested. I glowered at her. "Oblensky?" I thought out loud; "didn't he have a wife?" "Oh, he still does," Tania said, laughing. "She's still helping Russian refugees somewhere in Poland. She won't have a thing to do with the Communists, which made it nice for me until the Russians had to leave the city, I can tell you that. We get off here" she said, getting up, and taking Ninushka's hand. Ninka was looking up at her, mesmerized.

The house was a little palace. "We can't stay long," I told Tania; "we have to meet someone at twelve in the American zone." We were in the Russian one. "A jeep will take you over," she promised; "sit down." The dining room was furnished in the French style: gold chairs with tufted velvet, glass surfaces, mirrored walls, the ceiling reflecting the whole room upside down. Ninushka lay down on her back. "What are you doing?" I demanded. "Look up there," she shouted; "I'm stuck to the ceiling." She propped herself up a little. "I'm going to fall off!" Tania was grinning at her. A maid wearing a little gray uniform came in. Tania whispered something to her. She came back with a silver tea tray, two silver teapots, and a tray of iced cakes. There was a large glass pitcher. "What's

542

that?" Ninka asked, her mouth already full. "Lemonade," Tania said, pouring some out for her, then pouring two demitasses for us. I was eating cake after cake. "Could I take a bite of some cakes to see what's in them and put them back?" Ninka asked. "No, you cannot," I said, scandalized. "Why not?" Tania asked, pushing the plate toward Ninka and ringing a small glass bell. The maid went out and came back with another plate. The first one was filling up with cakes wearing the prints of Ninka's teeth.

"Oh, I must tell *you*," Tania said; "I knew your mother, and *you* have a cousin somewhere in America, a Regina Metterman; she lives someplace in New York." "That means you have an aunt, Ninushka." "I have lots of aunts," she answered, unimpressed. "This is a real one, a relative; relatives take care of each other." "No difference," Ninka said. "I'm beginning to get tired of that expression," I told Tania. "But you are sure?" I was so excited I was shaking the demitasse cup against its little saucer. A member of the same family, the same blood. She would help us. "Oh, very sure," Tania told me. "After my divorce, I was going over there, and I would have visited her for your Momma. I even had her address for years, but it's lost now, of course. Come," she said, getting up, brushing crumbs from her embroidered skirt.

We followed her down the gleaming hall. Ninushka kept dancing up to the faceted mirrors. "It's a fairy palace, Momushka!" she kept whispering. "Why can't we stay here?" "Because this is not our place. Keep quiet." "You could stay here," Tania suggested; "it gets lonely sometimes." "No, thank you," I said firmly. "Oh, Momma!" Ninka wailed. "My bedroom," Tania announced, going to a closet. "Please, take some things; I have too much." "I don't need anything," I insisted. "You need brassieres!" Ninka shouted. Tania opened a drawer and took out five. "You might have to sew some material in front," she thought, looking at me. "I'll give you a sheet. What else?" "She doesn't have a nice dress," Ninushka added. "What kind does she like?" I was green with shame. "Velvet, like yours," Ninka instructed. "I saw a picture; she had on a green velvet suit; and she has a purple suit with gold on it that belonged to someone." "I see," Tania answered, rummaging in the closet; "here." She took out a cut-velvet suit, a jacket and skirt. "The only thing is," Ninka mused, "she doesn't have a blouse, either." "Oh," Tania said, diving in again, coming out with a pale yellow blouse. "It

543

shines!" Ninka screamed. "It's satin," Tania explained. "I can't take it," I said flatly, sitting on the bed. "Don't listen to her," Ninka pleaded.

"Look, Anya," Tania told me, taking my hand, "I would give you the whole house for telling me about Rachel; well, let's be honest, *almost* the whole house." "She saved Rachel's life; they told me," Ninka piped up. "Will you keep quiet!" I hissed at her. "Rachel would have died twice, or maybe three times," Ninka ignored me. "Mommy took out her dead baby, and fixed a sore, and then a building fell on her, and Momushka fixed her head." "Is that all true?" Tania asked, astonished. "Hardly," I whispered. "Well, you're taking those things if I have to call the soldiers to dress you myself. And you," she said, looking at Ninushka, "which of these do you want?" She opened a large china cabinet filled with dolls from all over the world. Ninka's mouth fell open. "You are taking *only* one," I reminded her. She glared at me, edging closer to the cabinet. "This one." She pointed to a fat baby doll dressed in a satin Chinese suit. "Are you sure?" Tania asked. "Oh, yes," Ninka breathed. "There's a problem here," Tania said, turning to me; "I don't like giving away only one at a time. They get too lonely. You'd better pick another to keep it company." "Can I, Momushka?" Ninka asked. I nodded dumbly. "This one," she said, pointing to a bisque doll wearing an old-fashioned satin wedding dress, a small satin rose over each ear. "That one breaks," I warned her. "Oh, they all break," Tania said. "Let me wrap them in some towels so they don't break when you go."

"We have to go!" I exclaimed, looking at my watch. "I have to go to the bathroom," Ninushka said slyly. "That way," Tania pointed. "She only wants to see it," I sighed. "It's all green, Mommy; the stone is cold. It shines!" Shrieks were coming out of the room one after another. "Never mind the tour," I called; "hurry up!" "Can we come back?" she asked. "I am expecting you," Tania shouted down the hall in a very undignified way. "Good, when?" Ninka shouted back. "Tomorrow," Tania screamed at the top of her lungs. Finally, we heard the toilet flush. "Oh, you're smiling," Tania beamed at me; "good. Listen, why not put on the suit for the day, and come back here and change; it can't hurt. Use this mirror; I'll get the car." I took off my gray skirt and blue blouse, the same ones Erdmann had gotten me, and put the clothes on. A miracle looked at me out of the mirror. "A little big and a little long," Tania pronounced coming in; "we'll fix it tomorrow. I'll ride over with you. Who are you meeting?" I told her about Mr. Brodsky. "Does he speak English?" Tania asked. "I do, perfectly. I would love to meet him." "Maybe tomorrow he'll come, too, bet he's a very busy man; I don't know why he has time for us." "Not so busy, and he has some reason," she grinned. "It's not like that," I assured her. "Too bad," she sighed.

Mr. Brodsky was waiting patiently at the corner in his car. "Are we going on a picnic?" Ninka asked as we climbed in. "A *ride*, Ninka," I reminded her; "you need the air." "A picnic," Mr. Brodsky said. "Is it really in the country?" Ninushka asked. "In the country, on a farm." "I hope there are some blankets," Ninka said, looking around. "I hope Momushka won't lie on the grass in that suit." "Ninushka," I whispered fiercely, "are you going to spend the rest of the day embarrassing me to death?" "Plenty of blankets in the back," he assured her, steering us out of the city. "What kind of animals?" Ninka asked. I gave up. "Some sheep, some cows, and a goat; I think a goat." "A goat!" Ninka marveled. "Why don't you go to sleep?" Mr. Brodsky asked her. "Then you'll have the energy to chase them around. I have to talk to your mother." Ninka promptly squeezed her eyes shut. "She's not sleeping," I warned him.

"It's only about the visa," he began; "I've been trying to get you one. I don't think it will take too long, but Palestine is out." "Why out?" I asked in a thin voice. The windows immediately flew open in Ninka's eyes. "They're only letting out parents to children, or children to parents. I'm having plenty of trouble with you, because you need someone to guarantee you in America. Of course," he turned a corner, "I'm doing that myself." "Why?" I cried. "Because he wants to," Ninka said through closed eyes. "And that's all I want to do," he said, sliding his eyes from the road to me; "that and go for some drives. It's not so pleasant here for me, either, with my whole family in New York." I was quiet. "And stop sending back the baskets for the child," he scolded. "It's ridiculous; you can tell she's anemic by looking at her. You don't want the consulate doctor giving you trouble about *her* papers?" I turned to ice. "I'll take them," I promised.

We were joggling along through pleasant green hills, one rolling after another; little farm houses nestled here and there. "Can I wake up now?" Ninushka asked. "By all means." "Oh, it's pretty!" she said, clapping her hands; "my dolls will like it here." "What dolls?" Mr. Brodsky asked. "I'll explain later," I answered weakly, but Ninka was already babbling out the whole story.

"Here we are," Mr. Brodsky announced, turning in through a little gate onto a dirt road. "The farm," Ninka shouted, standing up in the car; he reached over automatically and pushed her down. "We get out here," he said, pulling over into a clearing in the woods. Ninushka had already clambered out and was running into the field. "Flowers!" she was shouting; "flowers! Come look!" She was running around like a demented butterfly, picking them by the armful. "Help me spread out the blanket," Mr. Brodsky asked. Out came hamper after hamper. "No herring for me, please," Ninka called, dancing back. "We have other things," Mr. Brodsky said, pointing; there were noodle puddings and beef slices and boiled vegetables. "Eat," he said, watching her take a huge portion of the noodles. "Sometimes she reminds me of the story my father used to tell about a toad," I sighed. "I am not a toad," Ninka objected. "Don't talk when your mouth is full," Mr. Brodsky and I said together. "A meal is always better with a story," he said, watching me eat carefully so no drop would touch the suit or the blouse. He was filling our two glasses with wine and had a thermos of orange juice for Ninka. "Why can't I have that?" Ninka pouted. "Because," I answered. "That's right," Mr. Brodsky agreed. "Try a little bit of everything," I advised her; her fork was an invading army. "So, about the toad," Mr. Brodsky said, settling back comfortably.

"Once," I began, looking at Ninka, who was freezing in her place, the fork halfway to her lips; she loved stories, "there was a toad who was jealous of an ox. 'Why can't I be the same size?' he asked himself. 'All I have to do is puff myself up.' So he puffed and puffed and puffed. 'Am I bigger?' he asked his friend the bear. 'Exactly the same size as you were,' came the answer. He puffed and puffed again. 'Now am I as big as the ox?' the toad asked. 'Not nearly as big,' said his friend. So the frog puffed and puffed and puffed and blew himself up like a balloon, and he blew himself up so much, he popped like a balloon and that was the end of him. The moral of the story is," I finished, "jealousy will get you nowhere, and neither will stuffing yourself like a toad," I said, glowering at Ninka.

"That subject seems to be on your mind lately; jealousy," Mr. Brodsky observed. "You're not living in my building." "You could live in the servants' quarters of our building," he suggested; "I told you I could get you a room." "No."

He changed the subject. Ninka was off to look at the animals. "How long would it take to get a visa?" I asked, my voice trembling. "Well," he thought out loud. "I have to handle it, and I'm all over the place. I hope three weeks, no more." "You really think you can get it?" "I am sure I can. But are you sure you want to leave? That man you said had no heart, the American at Ninka's play, he has his eyes on you; he's been asking me all kinds of questions about you. You could stay here and be a very rich woman." "I've already been through that, or something like that." I began fishing furtively in the front of my blouse. "Here," I said, thrusting the pictures at him. "Oh, this is you," he said laughing and pointing at the picture of me in my suit with my huge silver fox collar that came down to the waist; "you haven't changed at all." "Oh, I'm not such a monkey as to believe that," I laughed back. He held the picture and kept looking at it. "A monkey?" he asked. "Another of my father's stories," I sighed. "Tell me the story," he asked, stretching himself out on the blanket. "You don't want to hear silly stories." "I do," he insisted, covering his eyes with his arm.

" 'The Monkey and the Mirror,' " I began, imitating Ninushka. "I see where your daughter gets her talents from," he said from under his arm. The sun was blazing down. We were in the fringe of a shadow cast by the pines at the edge of the meadow. "If you're going to tease me," I pouted, "I'm not going to recite." "Recite, recite." "Once upon a time—you understand this?" I asked him. "So far, continue." "Once upon a time there was a monkey who found a mirror. 'Oh,' she said very quietly to her dear friend; 'what a horrible face. Her grimaces! Her wrinkles! I would die of misery if I looked even a *little* bit like that! But I have to admit I have some friends, I can count them on my fingers, they *do* look like her.' Then her friend the bear answered, 'Instead of looking at others, look at yourself.' Such is human nature," I finished up with a sigh; "they hate to recognize themselves." "What other stories do you know?" "Oh, no," I protested; "you tell *me* a story."

"I'll tell you about me," he said; "that's a short story. You know what I do; it's because I know so many languages." "And you like to help people," I put in. "I like to help people," he agreed. "Here," he said, rummaging in his pocket without getting up; "in the wallet there's a picture of my wife. Twenty-two years and no child. I thought," he went on, "if I took this job I wouldn't be so lonely, but when you're in charge, it's like being all alone. I can't just come over and visit you, can I?" he asked, looking up at the sky. "That's my worst fault, loneliness, I'm always lonely. So when I saw your child, I thought she had no one, and I thought, 'Why not?' She looked like a lonely child." "I suppose she is," I murmured. "Why doesn't your wife adopt one?" I asked; "there must be other children?" "Maybe when I go back," he mused; "maybe then. If you go to America," he said suddenly, "you have to meet her, and my mother. She's from Poland, too. She'd love to talk to someone who's just been there." "Where does she live?" "Brooklyn?" "Brooklyn?" I repeated. "That's right," he said, laughing. "You're laughing at my accent," I said, smiling at him. "It's warm here; lie down," he coaxed. "As far away from me as you can get." I lowered myself onto the blanket, taking care not to wrinkle the suit.

A butterfly fluttered past my face, almost touching my nose. Ninka's little shrieks were floating back to us. "It's always hot here," he said; "even in the winter." "Do you come here a lot?" "Whenever I can." "Look," I told him, "I just met a nice woman, Tania; she speaks English. If I do get the visa"—"you'll get it," he interrupted—"if I do get it," I continued, "she'll be here after I leave. I know she would like to meet you. Will you be in the city tomorrow?" "Just tomorrow," he answered, resigned. "Then you're invited," I cried. A white cloud puffed across the blue sky like snow. "The sky must be blue ice," I said without thinking; "look how fast the little cloud skates. It must be going home." "Tell me another story," he said after a while.

"Oh, please, you and my daughter; you'll drive me crazy with those stories." The butterfly was back, circling. "It's orange with black circles," I told him. His eyes were still covered. "What, the story?" "No, the butterfly; there's a butterfly here." "I'll look later," he said, tired. There was the sound of a bird singing, high and insistent, as if it were calling for help. "Do you know any story about birds?" "Birds." I thought. "About a cat and a night-ingale," I said finally. "Let's hear it." "No laughing," I ordered. "Once upon a time, a cat pounced on a nightingale

548

with its claws. 'I heard,' said the cat, 'that the whole forest envies you for your beautiful voice. The whole world compares you with the most famous of singers; your voice is so marvelous that all the shepherds are crazy about it. I myself would love to listen to it. You see, I am a very cultured cat. Don't shiver; don't be stubborn, my friend the nightingale; you have nothing whatever to fear from me. I am only a devoted admirer. If you will only sing something to me in your beautiful voice, I will set you free in the forest and the beautiful fields. When it comes to music, I love it as much as you do. Very often humming to myself, I have fallen asleep.' Meanwhile the poor nightingale was being crushed by the strong claws of the cat and was completely out of breath. 'So,' said the cat, 'these gasps are what everyone in the forest is talking about?' and she squeezed the bird harder. 'Sing just a little, at least a little,' the cat pleaded. But our poor nightingale could not sing, only squeak. 'Oh,' said the cat, disgusted, 'I have heard better singing from my kittens. With this singing you charm the forest and make everyone talk about your wonderful voice? Your singing is nothing to envy,' said the annoyed cat. 'We will see; maybe you will taste better on my tongue than you do in my ears,' and with that, he ate the bird all up. Isn't it funny?" I asked.

"Not very," Mr. Brodsky answered. I could hear the voices rising in the trees, the song about the wounded man, the song about the daughter who died of love and was buried in the middle of the road. "I told you it wasn't very funny," Mr. Brodsky said, bending over me with a handkerchief. Without knowing it, I was sobbing. "I understand," he said. "My brother was killed on a medical ship. Every time I saw a child's toy boat, I was dissolved like a cloud." "I don't even know what I'm crying about," I sobbed, burying my face in the rough texture of the blanket. "Well, maybe you'll find out later. Come on, Mrs. Lavinsky, blow your nose. Turn up your face." I turned it up. "Blow your nose," he insisted. "Now what's the matter?" Ninushka asked coming back. "Your mother told me a sad story; she always cries at her sad stories." "Oh," Ninka said; "I found a pig; I'm going to look at it." She marched off. "She's getting tired," I told him through gasps.

"I know some of these stories, too," Mr. Brodsky said; "from my grandmother. I want to tell you one. It's called 'The Unthankful Pig.' " " 'The Thankless Pig,' " I corrected. "My grandmother always called it 'The Unthankful Pig,' " he insisted. "So, there was this very hungry pig who sat under a tree eating acorns and she got nice and fat. Not being satisfied, she started eating the roots. Then the tree got very upset and spoke to the pig. 'Unthankful pig,' said the tree, 'don't you see these acorns are growing on me?' " "Wonderful," I gasped. "Mrs. Lavinsky, God knows I wanted a child. But I wanted to enjoy it, to take care of it, to watch it grow up. Face it, it might not have liked me when it wasn't a child anymore. But I wanted one because I liked them, nothing else. But really, children are unthankful little pigs. You have to have your own roots; you can't wrap them around her. I hope when you go away, you'll find someone just for you." "Never," I insisted. "At least someone who could help you with your daughter; that's only fair to her. It's hard alone. You'll count on her too much." "Never," I repeated; "I won't do anything to hurt her." "I should make that man who saw you at the children's show stay here and marry you," he sighed. "Ninushka is tired; it's time to go," I said, getting up exhausted. "When should I come for you tomorrow?" "I'll meet you at the corner two blocks away at eleven," I told him.

When we got home, I checked Frederich's closet; he had two and a half stacks of money climbing to the top of the closet. "Something is fishy," I thought. Ninushka had crawled onto her cot and gone to sleep. "You missed the meat ration," Frederich said, coming over with a few pieces of ham and one piece of cheese. "I can see through this ham," I complained. "Come on, Frederich; how many times have I done things for you? You could give me more." "I have to be fair," he insisted. "I will go to the rabbi; I have to feed my child," I warned him, near tears.

In back of us, someone shouting was getting closer. "All right, you bastard," a man roared, "I want my share of the food; *I* have a little boy, too. What happened to our almonds?" "Almonds?" I echoed. "Almonds, and eggs, lady," he boomed. "I warn you," the man shouted, "I know what you're up to; I know why you're cheating on the food. From now on, I'm going to watch every step you make." "There *was* no more," Frederich insisted. "Let's go to the rabbi," I said to the man.

"Rabbi," I begged, "we have little children. Look what Mister Zamenhoff gave us, and he's supposed to be a friend!" "You ought to have more than that," the rabbi answered, coughing; "here." He went over to a barrel and scooped out a full ladle of almonds. "For you," the rabbi told the man, pouring them straight into his pocket. "Put out your hands." He gave the man four eggs. He did the same with me. I was too shocked to talk. That Frederich should cheat me! "Have you noticed the way Mrs. Zamenhoff is dressing?" the man asked me slyly. "I got this suit from a friend in the American zone," I pleaded frantically. "Not you," the man said irritably; "you usually look terrible, like everyone. Her, Mrs. Zamenhoff; ask her about her clothes."

"Julka," I said, going in, "I want to talk to you." "Oh, what a beautiful suit, Anya!" she cried, seeing the eggs in my hands. "I *must* have one like it." For the first time, I noticed what she was wearing. Her head was wrapped in a black velvet turban with a huge rhinestone pin set to one side of it in the latest style; she wore a matching black dress, shoes, bag, and beautiful stockings. "That's a nice dress, too," I said innocently; "what store does it come from?" "Store!" Julka exclaimed, insulted; "it's not from a store! It is from a salon! I go only to the very best ones in Berlin. And you should, too," she added, eyeing me critically; "that suit doesn't fit you just right." "Never mind the suit. Are you buying clothes while the children are starving?" She didn't answer me. "It was bad enough you packed up all the teacups and quilts in Szczecin, but this is terrible. I don't even know if you're giving Jerzy his share; he doesn't sound better to me." "He's better," Julka said nervously, going back into the room. Later, I could hear her voice, talking on and on to Frederich. "In a few weeks," I heard him promise her. "Why are we listening?" Ninka whispered in back of me. I turned her around by the shoulders and marched her down the hall.

"Where is he?" Ninushka was dancing up and down in the corner; "I bet he forgot." "I'm sure he did not forget," I said, craning my neck; "anyway, he'll want to meet Tania. And Ninka," I warned her, "I want you to behave. Don't lie on the floor and don't ask for any more dolls." "I wasn't going to do any of those things," she complained. "Good, I'm glad to hear it." "There he is!" she shouted. Mr. Brodsky's car was coming up. "How are my two favorite ladies?" he asked, handing Ninushka into the car. "Fine," Ninka answered sweetly; "how are you?" "Fine," he answered.

"This is Tania's," I said pointing. We pulled up in front.

Ninka was ringing the bell before we got out. "Here we are, Aunt Tania!" she was shrieking; "do we get any cakes?" "All kinds," Tania assured her. "It's nice here," Ninushka whispered to Mr. Brodsky. "I am relieved to hear it," he answered, smiling to her. Tania had the whole table set with caviar and cream cheese, sliced roast beef, turkey, and plates and plates of cakes. "That plate is for Ninka," she said, pointing. "I'll start right away," Ninka promised. "No, you don't," Mr. Brodsky said, catching her; "eat some food first." We sat down. "How much more do I have to eat?" Ninushka asked, looking up at him. "Just more vegetables." Ninka made a face, but kept eating.

"So," Tania said, "I have some American records; let me put them on." "They're not much," Ninka said. "Momushka used to have louder ones." "These are for dancing," Tania informed the music critic. "Can I dance with you, Mister Brodsky?" Ninka asked. "Please do," he said, picking her up and dancing around. "What's that dance called?" I asked, curious. "The fox trot." "The fox trot!" Ninka shrilled. "That's a good joke!" she kept repeating over and over. Her high cackling laugh filled the room. "You are very funny," she told Mr. Brodsky. "I can't take the credit; someone else told me the joke first," he grinned, putting her down.

"Tania has a lot of dolls; do you want to see them?" Ninka asked him, not looking at me. "I would love to see them." "Tania, I am sorry," I pleaded. "Oh, I love it," she said. "Here they are!" Ninka called, running up to the cabinet. "Did you ever see *so many* dolls *all* in one place?" "It just so happens," Tania told her, "that I fell across a young man doll all dressed up for a wedding; he would go perfectly with the bride. In fact, I think he's been crying all night missing her, and if he goes, then the baby doll has to go; it's a shame, but that's the way it is." "Tania, you are spoiling her!" I protested. "I am not spoiled," Ninka objected; "do you think I am, Mister Brodsky?" "She learns fast," he said to me; "you're going to have trouble there. She knows all about divide and conquer." Ninka was cradling the dolls and drifting back to the living room with them. "At least she won't lie on the floor," I sighed.

"I have a box of things for our hostess, from the canteen," Mr. Brodsky said, going out the door. "Oh, you should catch him!" Tania advised. "He's married." "That

552

doesn't make any difference. Look at me; I'm on my second married general," Tania instructed. "Even if he wasn't, I wouldn't want to marry anyone, and if I did, what makes you think he would want to marry me?" "I think it," Tania answered, positive. "But first, I have another dress for you. Don't worry, don't worry," she hurried on, "I'm too fat to fit into it, but you should take it to a seamstress. I know one who's not expensive at all, and she can fix the coat that matches the dress, too." "I'll drop her there when we leave," Mr. Brodsky said, coming back in. "I'm going to the bathroom," I moaned. I pressed by cheek against the green marble; I could hear Tania talking to Mr. Brodsky. "If that little widow wasn't so against it, I would try to marry her myself." "Aren't you married?" Tania asked. "That could always be fixed," he answered calmly. Their voices drifted off. There was a little knock at the door. "Momushka, I heard—" I yanked Ninka in by the arm. "Don't say a word," I warned her; "not one word, if you know what's good for you." "He said he wanted to marry you!" she hissed at me. "I said not one word!" She was getting ready to object. Then I remembered Vladek. "It's a secret," I whispered to her, "but you probably don't know how to keep secrets." "I know how to keep secrets!" she exclaimed. "Then let's see you do it. Mister Brodsky will get into trouble if you can't keep this secret. Do you want that?" She shook her head.

"Do you want to take some cakes with you?" Tania asked, seeing us. "No," I answered. Ninka was nodding her head violently yes. "Do you want to see the dolls again?" Tania asked. Ninka practically dislocated her neck. "You can talk and keep a secret at the same time." I hissed at her. "Yes, Aunt Tania," Ninka said in a little voice.

"It is so nice here," Mr. Brodsky sighed, sitting on the gold leaf love seat; "it's a pity to go." The music was still playing in the background. "Your friend Tania is a very interesting woman; she reads a great deal in English. She told me a lot about you, too." "What did she tell you?" "About your marriage, medical school," he answered. "Shouldn't you stay here and finish? Then you could leave." "I can't stand it here; I have to leave as soon as I can." "Do you know why?" he asked, looking at me oddly. "No, I just know I need to do it." "I hope you won't be sorry." "What is more than one thing to be sorry for?" I asked him. "War," he sighed to himself, his eyes turning inward. "Come, we'll get the child and the dolls and the clothes," he grinned, "and I'll drop you at Tania's seamstress." "Maybe it is you who are making the mistake by not going home?" "No, I am not," he said; "I know I'm not, but I'll have to, sooner or later." "At least you have the choice," I said bitterly. "Don't you?" "The whole world made my choices for me," I snapped; "how am I ever supposed to know what *I* would have done? My own failures, they don't even belong to me; they won't even belong to me later. Don't talk to me about going back!" "Let's change the subject," he said, sadly.

"This dressmaker is in a bad section," he fussed; "be sure to leave before dark." Ninka was already scurrying up the stairs. "She's a fast anemic mouse," he laughed. "Goodbye," I said; "come visit us when you come back." "Don't worry," he answered, starting up the car. Ninushka was already pounding on the third-floor apartment. "Seamstress?" Ninushka asked a woman. "Across the hall," she said, slamming the door. "Ninka, knock, don't break the door down." She tapped softly. I knocked over her head. "Some clothes to be altered," I told the woman who came to the door. She was busy with her pins in a moment. "Now they just need sewing," she said, sitting back; "I'll fix the suit first. My husband," she talked while she worked, "is trapped in Poland. It's such a tragedy the war ended so fast; he was going to come back with a pretty little baby. We don't have any children," she went on, her needle stitching in and out.

"Momushka!" Ninka screamed from the other room; "come look. It's the man, it's the man they told you about." "Ninka, come out of there; you're not supposed to wander around other people's apartments." "No, no," she shrieked, "come here; it is the man, the same man." "Excuse me, please," I said, getting up. Ninka was dancing up and down in front of a photograph on the mantelpiece. "It's him, Mommy!" she kept screaming. "Who?" I asked, grabbing her. "The man, the one from the prison, the Schraader, the one who brought me food at the orphanage!" "Keep quiet!" I ordered her. She fell into a frightened silence. I grabbed her hand. "The suit is done," the woman called back cheerfully. "So, as I was saying, it's a pity the war ended so fast. Now I don't know what happened to him or the child." "What was your husband's name?" I asked her. "Anton Schraader." She picked up the cut-velvet suit; the room was starting to spin. There were soldiers walking out of the seams of the four walls.

"Momushka! Momushka!" Ninka was calling; something cold was on my head. I was lying in a tangle of clothing and sparkling silver pins like splinters from a shattered window. "You fainted," the woman told me. "Your husband was the man who almost murdered my child!" I screamed; "*this* is the child he was bringing home!" "Please, please, go away," she begged, trying to push us out. "I won't charge you anything; you can have anything you want. Take my ring; just go away." "You're afraid someone will find out you're married to a Nazi!" I screamed. "Momushka, let's go," Ninka pleaded. She was pulling me to the door. "Take your clothes, Momushka," she whispered; "take them!" The woman was frantically wrapping them into a bundle. "Take it away from her, Momma!" Ninka pleaded. I grabbed the bundle as if it were a child. A pin pricked my skin. "Let's go, Momma," Ninka begged again.

"Now you are going to cry," she sighed while we waited on the corner for a bus; tears were pouring down my face like a hemorrhage. "Will you tell the police?" Ninka asked; "or is it a secret?" "It's a secret," I gasped. The man had saved her life. "He was a nice man, Momma; he was; I don't understand it." "No one does," I answered, stroking her hand with my salty one; the bus came, and we took our seats.

32

"THE police were here," Frederich shouted the minute he saw us; "did you tell them anything?" "I should talk to the police?" I gasped. "They searched the place!" "Did they find anything?" "No, thank God," Frederich sighed. "Julka and I are going for a walk, we're so nervous." Julka appeared behind him fully dressed. "Why are you taking that valise?" I demanded. "I need to get some things cleaned," she answered. "Would you mind giving Jerzy supper?" "No, but something has to be done about that closet." "I'll move it out," Frederich promised. But by late night, they still were not back. "They've been arrested," I thought, terrified. A week passed; then another. They still were not back. Jerzy no longer had to be in isolation; we all stayed in his room. He was fatter and happier than ever. Ninushka read to him so much I had to stop her before she was completely hoarse. "Are they dead?" Jerzy asked one day. "No, but I'll find them," I promised. "Mister Levin," I asked, "could I leave the children with you?" I left to the sound of *The Scarlet Pimpernel*.

"Almost eleven," I thought, looking at my watch; "I'll go look in the American zone. If I can't find them there, I'll go to the consulate." I hadn't walked three blocks in the American zone before I saw them, the two birds in all their feathers. Julka tried to pull Frederich away, but they realized I had seen them. "How could you do it?" I shouted. "Not even to leave me a note, or to send someone? I've been worried to death thinking you were killed, or in prison, and the little boy," I said, fixing on Frederich, "has been crying his eyes out." "We're not going back," Frederich said guiltily; "it's too dangerous. That man has been watching us." "If you'd fed his child you never would have had this trouble," I shouted at him, turning around. "Where are you going?" he called after me, but I didn't answer.

"Mister Brodsky, please," I said into the phone. There

was some static and mumbling at the other end of the line. "Mister Brodsky, yes," came his voice. "It is Anya Lavinsky. My friends left me alone with their little baby; they're in the American zone. I want to be there, too," I cried. "Go back home," he insisted; "I'll come get you and put you and the children in the U.N.R.R.A. barracks." I got back on the bus like a machine.

"Pack up, Ninushka," I ordered her; "Mister Brodsky is taking all of us to the American zone." "Be careful with my dolls," Ninka warned. "Go help Jerzy," I told her.

All three of us got in the car with Mr. Brodsky. "They are no friends of yours," he said, when I had finished crying out part of the story. "What do you mean?" I demanded. He wouldn't answer. "What do you mean?" I asked again. "He's keeping a secret, Momma," Ninka piped up. "Tell me; I have a right to know," I insisted. "When the consulate interviewed them for their papers, my assistant asked Mister Zamenhoff about the little blond widow with the child. Do you know what he said? 'What about her? We have nothing to do with her.' So you see who your friends are," he concluded. "Who?" Ninka asked. The car stopped. "Barracks again," I sighed. "You won't be here long, I promise you," he said, driving off.

"Don't unpack everything," I told Ninushka when we settled on our bunks; "just a few things you need." "I need my dolls," Ninka insisted; "and my sailor dress and my bloomers." "All right, your dolls." "And my books." "And your books." "Why shouldn't we unpack everything?" she asked. "Because I have a feeling we won't be here too long." "Why do you have that feeling?" I ignored her. "Are you going to marry Mister Brodsky?" "Are you going to keep a secret?" I demanded. "Oh, I didn't mean it," Ninushka gasped, covering her mouth. "Too late, the bird's already flown out of the cage. Just don't say it again, especially here." "Can I say it at Tania's?" "Ninka," I warned her; "do you know what a secret is?" "I know," she pouted; "I won't tell anyone. I don't like secrets," she announced. "Why don't you just read to Jerzy? I have a feeling your Aunt Julka will be here for him soon." Julka appeared an hour or so later. I was staring off into space. "You see who your friends are." I couldn't see anyone. "Did you forget something?" I asked the transparent woman. "A small boy named Jerzy perhaps?" "Anya," she started to say. "I do not want to speak to you at all; take him. That's it." "He'll want to visit you," she insisted.

557

"Send him with someone else," I answered, lying down on my bunk. She left, tugging Jerzy after her like a bundle of bricks.

"Momushka," Ninka snuggled up to me, "why don't you want to talk to Aunt Julka?" "Listen, Ninushka, I don't want you to learn the wrong things from this. You shouldn't stop talking to friends when they're bad to you, but I don't want to talk to anyone who would leave a little sick boy all alone and forget about him." "We had him," Ninka said; "I was reading to him." "It doesn't make any difference who had him; they didn't have to leave him."

"You left me," Ninka said, peering; "maybe I shouldn't talk to you." "I had to leave you," I told her. "Why?" she asked, staring at me like a judge. "Because where we lived, there were bad people who wanted to kill all the little children." "I am not little," Ninka argued. "You were then; that was a long time ago." "Why didn't they kill you?" she asked. "They wanted to." "Why didn't they?" she insisted. "I ran away; I was lucky. I don't know why they killed everyone else and not me." I could feel the blood again; I could see the soldiers at the sentry points; I could see the pharmacy, the train, the little golden cupola of the church. "Where did you run away from?" "A bad place, worse than a prison." "Oh," Ninka mused, "is that where Aunt Rachel was, too?" "Yes." "Did you leave her there?" "Yes." "Why?" "Someone wanted to help me run away, but he could only help one person. He dressed me up like an old woman, to look funny." "Why did he help you?" "I don't know," I said; "I think I was lucky." "Rachel wasn't lucky?" Ninka asked, puzzled. "Only time will tell." "I don't know what that means," Ninka complained. "It's not important," I said; tears were starting to roll down my cheeks. "You left me and Aunt Rachel," Ninka said accusingly. "I had to," I answered, still crying. I remembered Vera going with Jakob. "I don't understand what it means," Ninka said again. "If you did it, why is Julka so bad?" "Don't bother about it; we'll figure it out some other time," I said, turning on my side. "Momushka," Ninka whispered, "are you crying?" I didn't answer. "Did I make you cry? I won't anymore; I'll be good." "You didn't," I answered in a muffled voice. "Oh," she exhaled with relief; "you just cry a lot," she said positively. "I think we should talk to Julka," she said later. "Why?" I asked her. "She has Jerzy and we don't have friends, not a lot." "Maybe you're right," I said; "let's go to sleep."

In the morning, a woman came over and woke me up. "Telephone call for you in the next building." "Come on, Ninushka," I called, the two of us pulling up our bloomers. "It's Mister Brodsky," the voice said; "I'm going to pick you up." "Two blocks from the barracks," I pleaded. We got in the front seat of the car. We drove and drove. The road was turning into a country road. "Funny," he said finally, "you don't even ask me where we're going." I was wearing a white dress made from a sheet; it was one of Lisa's dresses. I had been saving it; I didn't want it to get dirty. "Why should I be worried?" I asked. "You're not German; you're not the Gestapo. There's nothing for me to be afraid of." He looked at me sideways. "You have a funny momma," he told Ninka. "She cries a lot," Ninka agreed. "We're going to fix that right now." "Can you fix her?" Ninka asked, her eyes popping open. "I think so," Mr. Brodsky grinned. "I am not a faucet, Ninka," I said, insulted. "A faucet," she cackled, "a faucet, that's a good joke, too." "She's just discovered jokes," I warned him. "I remember," he answered, steering the car along.

I kept raising my hand to push the hair out of my eyes. "You should wear a hat or close the window," she suggested. "No, I like this." Sheet after sheet of blond hair was blown in front of me; I was seeing the world through a curtain of my own gold hair. "Where are we going?" I asked finally. "To the consulate!" he said, grinning. "Really!" I gasped, "to the consulate!" "To the consulate!" he repeated, stepping on the accelerator. "Are there cakes there?" Ninka asked, puzzled. "No, but there are tickets to the country Vladek told you about, with the elephants and the tigers." "Oh." She slid down in the seat, disappointed.

"Here we are," he said, pointing to a big building. "Mrs. Kramer," he said to the woman at the desk, "would you watch this big girl until we come out?" I left Ninushka with her. In the big curtainless room, seven men were sitting around a big wooden table, their faces reflected in it like distorted flowers. The conversation began quietly enough, then suddenly one of the men was shouting, "*Frau* Lavinsky, that's what she is; she is not Polish, just look at her. She is German." I sat there in my white dress with my blond hair, crying. "Ask her some questions about Germany!" Mr. Brodsky roared. They asked me something about streets, history, schools. "I don't know," I kept pleading; "I am not German. I have my Polish *matritza*, even an index from the medical school in Vilno," I cried, taking them out. "Probably taken from a dead body or bought on the black market," the same man said cynically. Someone asked me another question. It must have gone on for hours. Finally, Mr. Brodsky got up and smashed his fist onto the table: "Either Frau Lavinsky leaves for America on the first boat, first-class, or I resign my post!" There was total silence in the room. "I am not German," I whispered once again. "You heard me!" Mr. Brodsky roared. There were whispers back and forth, up and down the table. He was a very important man. "All right," one of them said finally; "we'll sign the papers." "And I want the papers for her child and the medical exam done today," he bellowed at the top of his lungs. The door opened and Ninushka's head peeped in. "Go away!" I whispered to her. "That child looks German, too," the man muttered. "Where are the papers?" Mr. Brodsky insisted; "you are all so slow. I don't know how anyone gets out of this country. *And* the ones for the child," he said looking at the papers someone gave him. "Just a minute, for Christ's sake," someone muttered. They passed the papers down the table in a hurry.

"Come on," Mr. Brodsky told me, "let's get Ninka through the doctor's; you, too." "All in one day?" I asked, amazed. "I have to leave again in a week," he told me, "and the first boat leaves in two days." The three of us walked as fast as we could. Finally, Mr. Brodsky picked Ninka up and we ran up to the third floor and down the hall. "Medical certificates," Mr. Brodsky announced, walking in; "we need them in a hurry."

"The woman is all right," the doctor said—I was sitting rigid on a painted white metal chair— "she has the beginning of an ulcer, I think; that's all. But the child can't go. She has only a fifty percent hemoglobin count; I don't know why she's still alive." He was picking up a large stamp that read *Unsuitable for Immigration*. "Please," I begged, going over to him, "she's my whole life. I can't leave her. If you make her stay, you're sentencing her to death. You should have seen her when I got her," I babbled on; "she was much worse. She will be better; I know it." "Against the rules," the doctor mumbled. "Doctor, please; I'm almost a doctor myself. I appeal to you professionally; I know how to take care of her. I *will* take care of her. You will kill me if you don't let us go." I heard a tearing sound. "You will kill us both." I felt my hands pinned behind my back. Mr. Brodsky let me go. I had torn the front of my dress wide open. *"Bozhe moy!"* I gasped, pulling it closed. The pictures of my family lay all over the floor. "Here," said the old doctor, bending to pick them up, handing them over. "I want them to go," Brodsky insisted. "I want to see the elephants," Ninka said. "Elephants?" the doctor asked. "Doctor, she is a very bright child. Please, what do you care where she dies? If she's going to die, let her die with me." "All right," he said slowly, signing the papers. "I hope this isn't a death certificate. Please don't mention this; I am breaking the rules." "Oh, thank you, thank you," I cried, hugging and kissing him, half out of my mind. "Anya, Anya, come on, come on," Mr. Brodsky called, pulling on me gently. "Come on, Mommy," Ninka pleaded. I walked out of the room between them. I couldn't feel the floor or see the ceiling; I was floating through empty air, a senseless cloud.

"You go to sleep," Mr. Brodsky ordered me when we got to the barracks; "it's all settled now. On Friday, you leave on the *Marine Perch,* nothing fancy, a military ship." "Will you come with us?" Ninka asked. "I can't," he said sadly. "You won't see the elephants," Ninka warned him. "Maybe I'll see them when I come visit later." "Good!" she shrieked. "We can fox trot, what a funny joke!" and she burst out laughing again. How much did she understand of what went on around her? I never knew.

The days crawled by. Ninushka was under orders to get as much sleep as she could. When she was awake, she packed and unpacked her dolls. "Now you try it," she glowered, taking them all out again; "I don't want to break them." "Are you taking Vera Mouse?" I asked her. "Oh, yes," she said, frowning at the others. "Look how wrinkly they get." "Where will you pack Vera Mouse?" I asked. "Nowhere," she said; "I'll carry her." "Oh." I closed the suitcase like the lid of a coffin. "We have two small suitcases again," I said to the air. "And the silver basket, and the diamond bracelet, they count like a whole suitcase, right?" "Right," I said.

Early Friday morning Julka came over. "Anya, I want to apologize before I go," she insisted. "It's all right," I said, embarrassed. "We're going on the *Marine Perch* today, to New York," she bragged. "So are we." "We will see you then," Julka smiled. She looked as if she had walked out of one of her fashion magazines. "I don't know if we'll see you," I answered her; "we're going first-class." First-class was reserved for Americans who had been trapped in Europe by the war. "First-class?" Julka asked. "First-class," I repeated venomously. Julka turned completely white, turned on her heel and walked away. "So much for her apology," I muttered to myself.

This time Mr. Brodsky came to the barracks for us. "I'm taking you to the ship myself," he announced. "Oh, boy," Ninka said. "Where did she pick that up?" Mr. Brodsky laughed. "God knows," I answered. We drove in silence. Ninka was jumping up and down, pointing up every piece of grass on the road. "Water!" she screamed. "Boats!" We walked down streets to the dock. "Bremen-hoff," I thought, making a mental note. There was the little gray ship. "That's it?" I asked. "That's it," Mr. Brodsky answered; "want to change your mind? There's still time." "Never," I answered. "Very flattering," he said gloomily. A whistle was hooting. Far out in the harbor another ship was lowering itself into the seagull-colored water, like a top, deeper and deeper into invisibility. "I will be sick all the way," I predicted. "I've asked some people to look after you," he warned. "Let them take care of you; let them take Ninushka to eat if you get seasick." "I will," I promised. I was hot and cold by turns. "You'd better go on," he said gently.

The minute I stepped on the boat, my stomach heaved. "Everyone to their cabins," someone was instructing. I lingered, watching the skyline. "Will the elephants be right there?" Ninka cried. "Oh, no, we have to look for them." "What is this boat *on?*" Ninka demanded; she was almost seven. "Water," I answered. "Water," she whispered; "will we sink?" "Of course not; American boats never sink." "Good," she squealed, running this way and that. "To your cabin, Miss," a man in a white uniform said in German; "down one flight and to the right." We went down. It was a clean little room with two bunks. From the porthole, I could see Mr. Brodsky watching the ship. I stared out at him, waving. "He can't see me," I thought; "already I am only a ghost to him." After another ten minutes, he turned and walked slowly away. "Well, Ninushka," I said, "we're going to New York." "You said America," she scolded me. "Same thing," I mocked her.

33

WHY can't we go on the deck?" Ninushka insisted after we had been in the cabin two minutes. "These are not bunks," she said; "look, nothing holds them up. I'm not going to sleep on them," she announced. "They're screwed into the wall," I said wearily. "Will water get in through the screws?" "No; please sit still. You're making me seasick." Ninushka was jumping around, taking out her dolls and laying them across the pillow of the bunk. "Ooooooh, the sheets, Momushka," she gasped; "they are smooth!" She stroked them again. "They feel like your skin. They're the same color." "Don't get carried away; I know how bad I look." "When are you going to turn green?" she asked me. "What?" "You told Mister Brodsky you turn green on boats." "In a little while," I promised her. I was sitting at the foot of the bed, my feet dangling in space. The ship was moving.

A thin, dark-haired girl came in. She said something to us in English. "We don't speak English," Ninka said; she was a monkey when it came to words. The English words she learned she spoke with a perfect American accent. "We speak French." "Oh," the girl answered, relieved. "I'm Anita. I won't be here too much," she announced; "I stay with a friend a lot." "She could stay with us, too." "Never mind, Ninushka," I warned her; "let Anita do what she wants. Why were you in Germany?" I asked her. "Giving ballet lessons when the war broke out. But I couldn't keep step with the goosesteppers," she laughed; "it's good to be going home." She had on an expensive wool dress and matching blue cashmere sweater. "Can I feel your sweater?" Ninka asked. "I thought you wanted to go out on the deck," I reminded her. "I do," she said, dancing up and down; "can we go?" "We'd better," I said, climbing down; "I don't know how much longer I'm going to last."

There was a knock on the door. "Hello, I'm Sonia

Dorfman," a woman with black hair said. "I'm a friend of Mister Brodsky's. He said you would be dying of seasickness in five minutes, and I know just what to do about it." "I have about three minutes left," I answered her; "I have to take this one up to the deck." "Oh, a good idea," Mrs. Dorfman said; she was at least fifty. "Remember, Sonia Dorfman, if you need anything. And there's something going on up there I think she would like."

We climbed back up the iron flight of stairs. "Not exactly the *Queen Mary*," Mrs. Dorfman observed. She wore such beautiful shoes, with such high heels; even on the boat, she balanced on them perfectly. "Believe me," I told her, "I would like to kiss every inch of this ark." "It does look like an ark," Mrs. Dorfman agreed, looking around; "it looks hand-made, anyhow." The skyline was gone. We were surrounded by a slate-gray sea; seagulls were diving and screaming around us. "Momushka, I got a feather!" Ninka shouted. "Are those cats?" she asked, pointing up to the sky. "Birds," I said; "you know cats can't fly." "They sound like cats," she said, staring up at them; "maybe they are cats inside, wearing feathers." "That's a nice idea," Mrs. Dorfman said, pointing. "Look," A black man in a white uniform was throwing oranges to a crowd of passengers. "Oh, I'm getting one, Momushka," Ninka cried, spinning off. "It's not a ball at all," she pouted, coming back; "it doesn't jump back up." The whole orange was squashed. "It doesn't bounce, you mean," I corrected her. "It doesn't." "It's a food, a fruit, you're supposed to eat it, not throw it," Promptly she took a bite, peel and all, and spit it out. "Ugh!" she choked. "I don't like oranges." "You're supposed to peel them first," I said, picking it up; "like this." She watched while I took off the orange skin. "Now try it." "It's better," she agreed, unenthusiastically.

"Momushka," she went on in her loud voice, "why doesn't that man with the oranges wash his face? Look how it's all smeared." "His face is always like that; people with dark skin are called 'colored.'" "You call them 'dirty,'" she glared at me. "No," I said. "You know how Rachel is yellower than I am? Well, some people are born that dark color." "It doesn't come off?" Ninka asked. "Not even if they wash all the time?" "Never, that's just how they look." "Well," Ninka thought it over; "it's not so bad. No one can tell when they should wash their face." "You need to wash yours," I pointed out; "you're sticky as flypaper." "I want to stay up here and look at the water. Look, things are floating in it." "Go get it over with," I told her; "my stomach is telling me to get back to the cabin." "I heard a man say it was going to rain," Ninka said; "why should it rain? There's enough water here." "Did he say rain or storm?" I asked, terrified. "Storm," she told me. "Oh, God," I thought. "Ninushka, I'm going downstairs; do you remember how we got there?" "Yes, yes," she answered, peering into the water. "These waves aren't so big," she complained; "the whole thing looks just like a quilt." "Well, it isn't; there are fish in it. I want you to come back down soon." "Mrs. Dorfman will take me," Ninka said, without bothering to ask her first.

Anita had already left the cabin; the little room was white and tiny and clean. I lay down on the bed, my stomach rising and falling out of rhythm with the waves. When I woke up, Ninushka was on the other bunk reading *The Scarlet Pimpernel*. "That's Anita's bed," I told her. "She said I could use it," she answered, flat on her back, turning a page. "How many times have you read that?" "Three times." She turned another page. Outside there was a clap of thunder. Ninka ran to the porthole. "I bet the waves are bigger now," I whispered. "Oh, good, they are." "Good," I gasped; "I'll never live to get there." "Momushka," Ninka said later, "it's time to go eat." Mr. Brodsky had arranged for us to eat at the captain's table. "I can't go," I moaned. "I'll take her," Anita volunteered. "Fine," I agreed, not turning over. "We'll bring you back something," Anita promised. "Please don't," I said, turning greener at the thought of food. They went off. Rain was pouring out of the sky onto the sides of the boat. The porthole was covered with water streaming icicle-thick. "Just my luck," I thought, not daring to move. Ninka came back in. "I have a bag of food for you and a bottle of tea." "I don't want it." "You didn't see the captain in his costume," she scolded; "you're going to miss everything." "I'll see it tomorrow." "You didn't meet the Max Man, either," she said; "he's taking people out of their rooms and throwing them on the floor." "What?" I said, raising myself up on one arm. "There's a man from downstairs," she explained. "He takes everyone sick and throws them out on the deck. I told him to get you." "Thank you very much," I said, falling back down again.

There was a knock at the door. "The Max Man!" Ninka cried. I sat up in terror. "Please!" I cried, "I don't want to be thrown out on the deck." "I'm afraid your daughter has it wrong, just a little," he smiled. "There are so many people seasick, I'm helping them out into the air; then they feel better." "What's your name?" I asked weakly. "Max Meyers," he said. "Oh, the Max Man. Ninushka," I told her, "this is Mister Meyers; please don't call him silly names. Mister Meyers," I said, trying to get up, "I really don't want to go out, or even get up." "This man also hanged someone," Ninka announced. Mr. Meyers blushed. "What are you talking about now?" I demanded weakly. "She's heard some gossip," Mr. Meyers said. "My brothers and I caught the head of our company from Auschwitz; the one who murdered our father; we took him to prison. He hanged himself before the trial, that was all." "That is something," I said with as much admiration as I could muster; "would you please talk to me about it more some other time, when I feel better?" "I'd be delighted," he said; "but it's nothing to talk about at dinner," he sighed. "It's all the Americans want to hear. I never want to talk about it again." "But you will," I answered, "because you won't forget. But it's no wonder you don't want to talk about it," I commiserated nauseously.

"There's a Russian lady doctor coming to see you, Sonia Dorfman; I think you've already met her." "Oh, yes, I did; that must be who Mister Brodsky had her hunt me up." "Well," Mr. Meyers said, "she's very nice, and she has a bottle of something for you. You'll feel much better, not perfect, but better, so drink it. Will you watch her, young lady?" he asked Ninka. "Oh, certainly," she said importantly. "I would like to talk to you about things some time," Mr. Meyers said seriously. "You've been through it; you don't seem like a ghoul. Maybe one last time, I'll talk about it one last time." "It's definite," I promised him. Another knock. "Come in," I called. It was Sonia Dorfman. "Here's the doctor," Mr. Meyers announced.

"No wonder Mister Brodsky was so anxious for me to keep an eye on you," she said in Russian. "Here," she said, handing me a big bottle of yellow liquid; "it tastes poisonous, but it works well enough to make you walk around." "Well enough to eat?" "There you'll have to force yourself," she laughed. "See to it," she told Ninushka. Ninka was puffed up like a frog. I had managed to prop myself up against the wall of the cot. "Drink some now," Mrs. Dorfman coaxed. "I don't have a spoon," I grumbled, pushing it away. "Just two swallows from the bottle will be fine." "Come on, Momushka," Ninka pleaded. I drank it down. "I feel better," I admitted. "Right now it's your imagination," Mrs. Dorfman said, "but you'll see. It will work. Every two hours," she warned. "Thank you Doctor Dorfman," I said, as politely as I could. "Please call me Sonia," she grinned mischievously. "How long is this storm supposed to last?" I asked them. "As long as five days," Mr. Meyers said in broken Russian. I unscrewed the bottle cap and took another swallow. "Don't drink it all at once," Sonia cautioned; I only have a few more bottles." "Five days," I moaned.

The next day water was still coming down in sheets; the little ship pitched this way and that. "It's lying down on its side!" Ninka cried with delight. "Stop exaggerating," I whimpered. "Come on," she insisted, "it's lunchtime;" she used the American word. I went with her to the table. The food was marvelous; I couldn't eat a thing. Ninka attacked everything in front of her. "Eat bread," a woman sitting next to me coaxed: "you'll feel better." I choked down two pieces. "Momma?" Ninushka asked, looking up at me. I flew away from the table back to my cabin. I was vomiting as if I were vomiting up a whole life. "Anyone would think you had morning sickness," Anita sighed. "Here," she said, bringing the yellow bottle, "drink this."

The next day was the same, but I could eat a little and keep a little more down. The fourth day, I could watch everyone eat and even eat a piece of bread myself without fleeing from the room. But when we got back to the cabin and the bunk, I would have to lie perfectly still, or I would be at the sink, vomiting. Ninka came back and began to read on Anita's bunk. "Why don't you ever come over here?" I asked. "No," she said, "I can see better over here. That Mister Max is funny; he knows a lot of stories. He was telling someone a fairy tale about cooking people in ovens." "Ninushka," I said, "don't talk to strangers. Leave that poor man alone." "Everyone asks him questions," she pouted. "All the more reason," I said.

The next day the sky was filled with clouds rolling by sweel after swell, but no rain. Ninka and I went up on the deck. "Here's a chair, Momma," Ninka cried, sitting on it until I could get there. I stared at the sea. "There really are no buildings on it anywhere," I thought, amazed. "But they say whole cities have sunk under it, and they never find them. I wonder if they still look?" "That woman looks familiar," I said out loud to Ninka, seeing someone a distance from us. "Is she another aunt?" Ninka asked, standing up. "I don't think so. No, her name is Mrs. Cibiki." It came back to me like a wave capsizing the boat; she was the wife of the Nazi officer I had been sent to massage when I was in the ghetto. "Ninka," I whispered, "you sit here and guard the chair." I crept up farther. It was Mrs. Cibiki. She was chattering happily to a group of men and women; a cluster of little children was swarming around them. Suddenly she caught sight of me. There was some hurried whispering; they vanished. "Is anything the matter?" Sonia Dorfman asked, appearing at my elbow.

"Nazis," I babbled, hysterical; "I saw them. They're on this boat. I massaged her; I know every inch of her body. It is her. I have to tell the captain." I ran away from Sonia down a flight of stairs and pounded on the captain's door. "It can't be true," he said, when he understood what I meant; "this boat is for people getting away from the Nazis." "It *is* true. I swear it. I'll find them; they're hiding," I shouted, beside myself. "Captain." It was Mr. Meyers' voice behind me. Ninushka was holding his hand, frightened. "A lot of Germans," he explained patiently, "threw out their own papers and claimed to be German prisoners, or Polish, or whatever. There are a lot of Nazis coming to America this way; we all know it. It is *not* impossible," he answered the captain's objections; "I'm going to help this lady look. If we find them, you have to lock them up. It's the rule." "You can look," the captain said, puzzled, "but I don't think you'll find anything. Probably," he said, "the lady is just upset; the weather's upsetting everyone." "You don't understand," Mr. Meyers answered; "you weren't there. She's locked on this ship with those people. You can't understand what that means."

The two of us were up and down, in and out; we asked everyone. It went on for three days. They had just vanished under the horizon. "I didn't think you would find them; not once they saw you," Mr. Meyers admitted. "How about calling me Max, anyway?" "Max," I said in a flat voice. "You need sleep," he insisted, leading me down to my cabin. "Did you find the bandits?" Ninka asked. "No," I answered, climbing onto the bunk. Where had she learned that word? "I want to talk to Max," I told her; "why don't you go look for Sonia?" "All right," she agreed, going out. "Why can't I find them?" I cried; "you said you found your father's killer?" "That was different," Max sighed, sagging on Ninka's bunk. "Why?" I demanded; "why can't I do it?" "Look, it's a long story. We
568

came from a little village in the country and we were very rich. The peasants showed the Germans where we were. Jealousy. You know, we had the kind of family that had two orchestras for dances every Saturday," he explained. "And the Germans grabbed us all one Saturday at the dance. So someone grabbed by mother, and one of the Nazis hit him across the chest. Then Momma went over to my father, and one of the Nazis shot her. The rest of us wound up in Auschwitz, the long-time survivors. There were supposed to be none; you're looking at one," he said bitterly.

"Poppa wasn't strong. The bandit in charge of us had us running to work over railroad ties; no matter how fast we went, he wanted us going faster. If someone had diarrhea, he ran with it running down his legs. After two days of this running, they began watching Poppa. Then three weeks later, he was behind the rest of us, and the officer shot him. Just shot him. And I couldn't stop running to go back. And my brothers couldn't. So we swore to get him after the war. The Americans freed us all in Germany; all the Germans were trapped there. But someone from the camp saw the murderer, and my brothers, there were two, they stayed behind. We got together a whole group from the camp, and we searched the city. We got him, the murderer of my father; we got him arrested. But before that we sat on the benches waiting for the trial. It was the only happiness of my life, waiting for him to get up there in front of the judge. We had enough witnesses for an army. But he hanged himself in his cell; Ninka told you that. I know what they look like, the hanged ones," he said slowly. "I picture him like that every night before I fall asleep; it works like a sleeping pill. We got him, the murderer of my father."

"Auschwitz?" I asked. "The death camp, the worst of them." "I'd like to know about it." "I can't talk about it," Max said; his eyes were spilling out water. "Just let me tell you one thing. When we had sores on our faces, my brothers and I, we had to wash in urine; there wasn't enough water; and if we went to the hospital, we got poison; so we washed in urine. And my job," he sobbed, "was to take the dead bodies and shovel them into the ovens." He stopped. "I have a picture," he went on gruffly, "after liberation, right after, of all the dead bodies." He handed it to me. There was a huge pyramid of bodies, heads and arms emerging at the most unlikely places. "The bodies are all black!" I said without thinking. "Burned, or dead for a long time," he said. "And here I am in my striped suit." He handed me a picture of a skeleton. "What's in back of you?" I asked, studying the striped suit he wore. It reminded me of the striped dress Ninka was wearing the day we left her at the church. "The gates to Buchenwald; I took a tour," he said bitterly.

"You know," I said slowly, "I could talk to you about anything without being ashamed." "There's nothing I haven't heard about, nothing; you can talk about anything, but not me. I want to forget." "Forget," I echoed; "the word doesn't exist." We sat still, not saying a word. "You found your daughter," he said; "that's better than finding someone's killer. It doesn't really make the dead walk. Maybe I thought it would. I'll never forgive my brothers for staying in Germany," he added; "never. They always were stupid; they would have died a hundred times in that camp if it weren't for me." "Don't you get lonely?" "*Get* lonely? Is there some other way to feel?" Ninka popped back in. "Why don't you come with me?" Max asked her; "there's a little show for the children in third-class." "Can I, Momma?" "Please," I said, turning to the wall. "If I see Jerzy, can I speak to him?" "Of course." "And Aunt Julka?" "That's up to you." My lids were turning to iron; I was half asleep before they were out the door.

Momushka was talking to me. "You will always be young," she said approvingly; "it's the structure of your bones. Why don't you wear your blue coat? Only shorten it; it is again in style. I don't understand why you don't wear it. I don't understand why you won't go to France," she continued. "I'm sure we'll find a way for you to come back. We hoped your father would have the good papers by now, but Anya, he's sure to get them, even if it's too late for this year. It's not really such a chance." Poppa was standing in back of her, smiling and nodding. "You see I was right," she said; "looking one's best is the thing. Of course, you always did a lot better than that," she said proudly. "It's a good boat, Anya," Poppa said, "not a hole in it; which reminds me of a story." "Borya," Momma said, interrupting him, "there's no time for stories. Anya, how do you know you can never come back? Something will change, and meanwhile, you promised." "A promise is a serious thing," Poppa added, beginning to whistle an aria from *Tosca*. "Well, never mind," Momma sighed. "How is your health? That's the important thing. Your health and your looks, what else do you need? I think you need to gain some weight; here, I have a list." She took it out and handed it to me. "Come with us," she pleaded, starting down the hall, and I started after her, but when I got into the long dark hall, it was empty.

"They didn't wait for me," I thought, and then I was staring back into the cabin. They still filled the room. Momma was smiling. Poppa was still whistling. Then I looked out the porthole, the little window, the eye on the sea, and when I saw nothing on the other side, I knew it was a dream. That was the first time I had dreamed about them, but I was sure it would happen again and again, just as I knew every time I looked in a window when I woke up, I would know I was dreaming and they could vanish. I took out the pictures of myself, Stajoe, Ninka, and Vera. In one, a picture of the whole family, Momma and Poppa stood happily behind us. "Well, then," I thought to myself, "I don't need pictures of them." And then I thought of my cousin in America, Regina Metterman; she might have more pictures. I remembered, they had sent her some. I fell back asleep. "This seasickness cannot last forever," Momma was saying; "it is perfectly normal. In ten days, you will be there." So they were coming with me.

Sonia Dorfman came in early in the morning. "No more fever or chills?" she asked me. "I feel much better; I'm even coming to breakfast." "There's not a wave to be seen," she promised me. "Your hair hardly even blows. What are *you* doing here?" she asked, turning to Ninushka. "Mister Meyers has been looking all over for you; he was looking outside where it's so nice. He has a book of pictures of New York for you." Ninushka folded up her book and sat up, looking interested. "Are you going to teach Momushka?" she asked. "Teach me what?" I asked. "Well," Sonia said, smiling, "Mister Meyers and Ninushka decided you should try to learn a little English before you get there. We only have time for a few words, but I have this Russian-English dictionary; it should help."

"Oh, they're not like each other at all," I cried, taking a look. "No, very few words sound the same; you're going to have a lot of trouble." "How do you say that?" I asked, pointing up to the ceiling. "Sighing?" "No," Sonia said, correcting me. I tried again. "Let's try the floor." "Flour," I said happily. "No," Sonia said. "I cannot do it!" I cried. "I'll help you, Mommy," Ninka said, scrabbling over. "*Patalok,*" she said, pointing at the ceiling, "*seeling,*"

571

drawing it out. "That's right," Sonia said. "Look, why don't I teach Ninka the words first, and then she can teach them to you?" "Momma's stupid, I guess," Ninka mused. "Your Russian is nothing to brag about," I told her, blushing scarlet. "Some people think Russian is the hardest language in the world," Sonia told her sternly. "What is this word?" She pointed at *stol*: table. "I can't read those funny letters," Ninka cried. "But your Mommy can. She even knew how to speak Russian when she was *two years old*, didn't you, Anya?" Sonia asked impressively. "I did," I answered, depressed I hadn't thought much about these complications. "What's this word?" she asked me, pointing at the Russian side, first whispering the answer to Ninka. "Automobile." "Oh," Ninka sighed, astonished; "that one has a lot of those letters." "Your Mommy's not so stupid," Sonia told her; "you just have to help her. Some people have trouble with English. No one knows why." "Will she get better?" Ninka asked, as if it were a disease. "Certainly, especially if you help her." "Go out and play with Mister Meyers," I said suddenly; "I want to talk to Sonia. We'll have a lesson later." "I'll get someone to tell me some words," she promised, flying out of the cabin.

"What is it like when we get there?" I asked her. "A lot of big buildings," she said. "I know that," I answered impatiently. "Where do we go when we get there? Do we have to find places ourselves?" "No," Sonia said, shocked; "they have the whole Hotel Marseilles for us, and food; there's a dollar fifty allowance per person from the Joint Distribution Committee, and I think even something extra for clothes." "That sounds wonderful," I sighed; "no more sleeping on benches." "Oh, Anya," she protested, "it's not like that at all. There wasn't a war there." "No war there," I repeated. "Of course I know there was no war there." "Knowing is not believing," Sonia said sternly. "Listen, Sonia," I said energetically, "war or no war, they won't give us money forever. We have to find some jobs. Maybe if we went together somewhere, like the Ministry of Health, you could do something about being an American doctor, and I could even finish medical school." "We'll go," she promised. "It is exciting, isn't it?" I asked her. I couldn't stop smiling.

We went to the table and ate for almost an hour. For the next two days, I ate as I had never eaten before. "We're almost there," everyone was whispering. Then we began looking out of the portholes and watching from the deck. The children were betting each other books, toys, games; the winner would be the first to see a building. "I see it," someone screamed. "That's not a building," another child shouted; "that's a lady." A huge green woman was standing in the harbor. "That's the Statue of Liberty!" I gasped in disbelief. Sonia and I began laughing and crying and hugging each other wildly. All over the boat the same hysteria was spreading. "There's a building," all the children were screaming. Some low brick buildings with dormer windows were coming into view, and in back of them, enormous jagged ones. "It's the New York skyline," I gasped, hugging Sonia; "we are here!"

The little transport boat pulled into the dock escorted by two tugboats. "I don't know what we need them for," Max grumbled; "they're not much bigger than our boat." "Tugboats," Ninka repeated in English. "Tugboats," I tried to repeat after her. "Not now, Momushka," she cried, practically falling into the water. Max grabbed her and picked her up. "Oh," she gasped, "look at those buildings, Momushka; none of them have holes in them. Look how big they are. Why don't they fall down?" "They're called skyscrapers," Sonia told her. "Skyscrapers," Ninka repeated perfectly as a record, marveling. "Look at that one," she said, squirming in Max's arms; "it's biggest, isn't it, a skyscraper? I like it here, Momushka," she decided. "We're not even off the boat yet," I told her, but I couldn't stop smiling.

"We're at the pier," Sonia cried. Suddenly people were pouring on and off, grabbing each other and questioning each other; it was absolute bedlam. "Come on," Sonia said, pushing us ahead of her, "let's get off this boat!" "Aunt Evelyn!" one of the passengers was screaming. In the mass of people, thickening and thinning like a wave, I could see Julka hugging a sunburnt woman with dark hair. "Her sister," I thought. Jerzy was hidden by the clustering bodies; then I saw Frederich hoisting him up on his shoulders. "There's Jerzy!" Ninka screamed. "Who are these people?" she asked, pointing to the Americans swarming all over. "Oh, they are aunts coming to meet relatives from our country." "Where is our aunt?" Ninka asked, looking up at me. She kept looking around. Everywhere, people were falling into each other, crying and screaming. "We don't have any aunts." "I'll be your aunt," Sonia promised; "aunts come with candy and baby sit and help out, things like that." "Aunts come from America; these do," Ninka insisted. "Rachel didn't come from America," I reminded her. "It's not the same." She started to cry.

"Come on, Ninushka," Max shouted, picking her up and throwing her on his shoulders; "we're going to a hotel." "A hotel?" Ninka asked. "Oh, yes, you go to the dining room and tell them what you want and they bring it to you. They can even make your beds while you're eating." "Oh," Ninka mused; "do they have children's shows?" "No, but they have movies, your Momma told you all about those, and cartoons all over the city." "Movies and cartoons?" Ninka asked, fascinated. "He's a nice man," Sonia said, watching him. "Good for him," I answered, grinning; "believe me, I'm not in such a hurry to get married at all; she's the only thing I care about." "You should be careful," Sonia warned me seriously; "they grow up so fast, and then it's goodbye, Mommy." "No," I insisted. "You'll see," Sonia predicted; "and then you'll be left alone. Don't be a fool." I was too angry to answer, but then the sight of the big buildings wiped everything out of my mind; they were so many gray erasers. I had a sudden vision of Anzia curling the ruffles on the big pillows in my room with the curling iron, and then I walked out into the street, breathing its fish smell, my mind empty as a slate.

34

"I LOVE it here," I told Sonia a few weeks after we had settled in. The food was marvelous. The Joint Destribution Committee had given me five dollars for new shoes, and three dollars for Ninka; she hád arrived with her broken wood sandals. All over, people were laughing and joking. It was as if we were on the longest holiday of our lives. Everything else was over, finally over. Ninka was teaching me words, but she had certain favorites: witch, fairy godmother, wicked stepmother, frog, dog and cat, lion and tiger. Sonia had become her aunt and bought her books of fairy tales and even a book from the zoo. After lunch, she was going to see it herself with Max; she was so excited, she could barely sit still. Down the table, someone was telling a joke: "A mother was nursing her baby on the bus, the the baby just cried. So the conductor came over and said, 'Listen, lady, if she doesn't want it, I'll take it myself.'" Ninka gave her high-pitched cackle. Everyone turned to look at her. "Good heavens," I said to Sonia. "They grow up fast," Sonia answered with a grin.

At night, there were dances. Then the hotel was like a slave market. We went every night. Men whose whole families had been killed in Europe were trying to find someone who spoke their own language and came from their own country; they had spent the war years trapped in America. "Trapped," Sonia sighed; "they don't know what they missed." "Are you married?" one of them said, coming up to me. He was the fifth that evening. "No," I answered, "and I don't want to be." "At least let me take you out," he pleaded. Max was upstairs reading to Ninushka. "All right," I agreed. The next night the man and I went to a fancy restaurant on 34th Street; the menu was in French. I relaxed. But he was determined to show off his English. "If you please, if you please," he kept saying to the waiter in a horrid pompous way, and then it was: "Trout for me, and for the lady, dog." The waiter stared at him. "For the lady, dog!" he repeated again loudly. That was one word Ninushka had taught me. I covered my mouth with my napkin, but the next thing I knew, I was shrieking with laughter. "What's so funny about ordering dog?" he asked me, just as I stopped laughing. "It's delicious with orange sauce." I had just taken a sip of water, and little drops flew through the air when I started in again. "I do not know what's the matter with you," he said, sulking. "Trout, sir," said the waiter; "and here is the dog." I began laughing helplessly at the sight of the poor duck. I picked up my fork and dropped it. Every time I looked at my plate, I was off again. "Please eat the dog. Stop it," he pleaded; "everyone is looking at us." The evening was a complete success for me; he couldn't wait to get out of there.

"There's no need for a cab," I told him, as we climbed into one. "Hmmmmph," he snorted, looking at me, puzzled. "For the lady, dog," I told Sonia, knocking on her door, screaming with laughter. It became our password for the courting dance in the hotel. People were snatched up right and left. A yellowish, older woman named Dora came in one night to complain: "I don't know what will be here," she moaned; "it's so hard to get married," and two nights later, she was back with the news. She was marrying a young man, fifteen years younger than she was. "And my teeth are just stumps," she marveled; "but, of course, on the boat, I filled out the rest of me," she preened. "And," she added, "he says I look just like his mother." His mother was dead. So it went on. "Max," I kept pleading, "go down; meet someone. I have no desires." "I'm happy to stay here," he insisted, telling Ninushka another story. When I came back late, he would return to his room.

A Mr. Bibilov knocked at my door one morning. He was in charge of us, and took Ninka to children's shows, movies, the top of the Empire State Building. "I wonder if I could ask you a favor?" "Certainly," I said in English; it was the one word I uttered in that language of which Ninka approved. ("What is that word in French?" she had asked suspiciously. "Certainment," I told her. "Doesn't count," she answered, biting into another cookie from her huge bag. The bag had enormous butter stains all over it, like a secret map. "You just left off the last part.") "I have to send this letter to Brooklyn," he said, producing it. "Do you think you could possibly take it for me?" "Why

576

not?" I hadn't been on the trains enough; this would be a chance to learn. "How do I get there?" "You change for the local at Atlantic," he told me. Then he saw my face. "Don't worry," he said, writing the address down; "just show this to anyone. They'll point you in the right direction." "I'm going," I called to Sonia who was across the hall with her door open. Mr. Bibilov was taking Ninka off somewhere. "Not the zoo, I hope; you came back half dead last time." "We saw every inch of it," he laughed. "I want to see the elephants," Ninka insisted. "Good luck," I sighed, waiting for the elevator, watching the little arrow move up to the number of our floor.

I couldn't get over these trains, these deep gray and black echoing chambers. It was as if the city were built on a world that had once sunk, and these were the old sea chambers, and now the trains, like worms the color of sharks, ran through on motors instead of swimming through. "Atlantic Avenue," I thought with relief, rushing off. "They slam the doors on you so fast," I thought. I was always standing up two or three stops in advance whenever I went anywhere with Ninka. There were signs pointing in all directions, trains rushing after them. I had to ask someone. "Church Avenue?" I said. The woman stared at me and shook her head. Finally, I saw a Chasid. "Church Avenue," I gasped in relief; "I don't know how to get there." But instead of answering me, he grabbed me. I jumped backward, and into the next train, almost getting caught between the doors. "I don't believe it," I marveled. "New Lots Avenue," the sign read. "Oh, I am lost," I cried to myself. Finally, I found a lady who spoke French. I staggered up the steps to the brownstone on Church Avenue, delivered the letter, and started home. The woman who took it spoke Russian and gave me return directions five times. It was dark when I started walking back. For the first time, I felt the weight of my feet on the pavement. I looked down at the cement sidewalk; there were no cracks in it, no splits, no ravines. Bushes and trees were set neatly into the street, up and down its length. It was solid. The ground did not open up here. "I love it here," I sighed to myself again. Ninushka popped out of the lobby at me.

"I found something new," she screamed at me. "Step on a crack, break your mother's back," she translated. Then she began leaping from crack to crack in the sidewalk. "Oh," I moaned, clutching the base of my spine. "It works!" Ninka screamed with delight, running back in. Max was there, waiting for her. "Some poem," I told him. He shrugged his shoulders. Ninushka was looking around the carpeted floors for more cracks to leap on. "It looks as if you'll have to wait until you go out again," I told her. She kept looking. "Stubborn little thing," I thought to myself.

"Anya," Sonia cried the next day, "they're liquidating the kitchen; a new transport is coming." I turned white and cold. "Oh, it's good," Sonia said; "we get tickets to a good Jewish restaurant instead. Let's go." And so we went. Basket after basket of bread disappeared before the main course materialized; the waiter stared at all of us in amazement. "We'll probably have to look for rooms soon," I told Sonia. "Yes, they're already putting up notices; we should get started early." "Oh, I would like to," I cried; "It's nice, this eating in the restaurants, but a little degrading too, you know?"

So we started looking at notices. Ninka and I trailed from place to place. One street had too many cars; another had too many people. That made me nervous. Finally we rented two rooms at a Mrs. Green's on 102nd Street and West End Avenue. "Such big buildings." Ninka gasped. "And with a park in front of them." I pointed it out to her. She had a room at one end of the apartment; mine was at the other. No sooner did we move in than Ninka came down with a terrible cold. "I knew it," I sighed; "it was too good to be true." All night I was up with her. During the day Max came and read to her. After three days, Mr. Green came in. "We were thinking," he said in German, "you should take your child to the hospital." "To the hospital?" I cried, outraged. "Do you take your boy to the hospital for a cold?" "You're making a lot of noise in the kitchen at night," he complained. "I doubt if you even heard me, tiptoeing around," I answered in a cold voice; "I didn't make a sound." "With all this going on," Mr. Green said, "it is only right that you should also clean house if you're going to rent the rooms with food."

"I think you should get out of here," Max told me when we went back to my room. "How can I?" I cried; "I don't have any money." "You said you had a cousin, a Regina something. She might be able to help you out." "What can I do?" I cried out; "stand on the corner and call her?" "You can use the phone; don't be ridiculous." He marched down the hall and came back with the phone book. "Look up her name; it's alphabetical." "Here's a Metterman," I said pressing my finger down so hard its tip turned white; "but there are two!" "Call both," he said calmly; "I'll go ask Mister Green if you can use the phone." "Is there a Regina Metterman?" I asked the first voice. Someone hung up. "Is there a Regina Metterman?" I asked again. "Speaking." "I am your cousin, Anya Lavinsky; I'm from Poland, but I just got here from Germany. I would so like to meet you," I babbled in French. "Where are you?" Regina asked. I gave her the address. "I'll be right over," she said, hanging up. We went and watched from the kitchen window.

"See?" Max said; "Jewish families. I told you you had nothing to worry about. You're a cousin." A big yellow cab pulled up at the curb. A beautiful dark-haired woman with piled-up hair, wearing a dark mink coat, stepped out, and looked around. I began knocking on our window. She looked up, smiled and waved. "Don't break it," Mr. Green warned me.

"So," Regina said, sitting down on the bed as if she had lived in the room all her life; "you have some family after all. We've been giving money and reading papers, but we can't guess how it was. I'm just sorry there aren't more," she said sadly. "She has to get out of this place," Max said. "Her daughter is sick and the man here wants to work her to death." "Anya," she said, "you find a place. Saul and I'll take care of everything until you get on your feet." "I can't take anything," I insisted. "This is what families are for. Believe me, you won't make a hole in our pockets," I smiled at the strange new phrases. "Let's see Ninka," she said, getting up.

"Oh, a cold," she sympathized, bending over her. "I brought a book," she said, handing her *Heidi;* "I'm your Aunt Regina," she said. "I told you we had an aunt," Ninka snorted through her stuffed nose. "She should see a doctor," Regina said, pressing something into Max's hands; "promise me she will." I promised. "And as soon as you find anything, you call me." "I'm going to start looking right away," Max swore. Regina looked at him, then at me, and smiled. "It is nothing," I whispered to her as we went to the door. "He seems to be a good man," she whispered back; "that's the important thing, not looks. Call me," she insisted. "I will." "There are phones even on the street," she reminded me; "I'll be waiting." "In the booths?" I asked her, amazed; "I thought they were bathrooms," "Bathrooms you can see through?" Regina asked, laughing.

"Anya," Max began, "Ninushka is almost better; you and Sonia should start seeing about school. I'll call her and look for another apartment." "I'll take Ninka to the doctor to be sure." "Where will you take her?" "There's something called the Brooklyn Jewish Hospital; I saw it on a map when I went with the letter." "Fine," Max answered impatiently. "I want to talk to you about something." I didn't open my mouth. "An apartment is expensive," he began awkwardly. "If you go to school, you won't have anyone to leave Ninka with, but if we were both there, one of us could get a night job and one a day job; it could be done." "No," I answered automatically. "It wouldn't be much of a wedding," he coaxed; "you'd hardly even notice it. You don't even have to love me." "I don't," I said bluntly. "You just think you don't; it will be best for the child," he insisted. "Would you be good to my daughter?" I asked, thinking. "You know I wore a cross after the war?" "So what?" Max asked; "you're worrying about nonsense like that?"

The month before at the hotel, a man had come over and started talking to me in Yiddish and English; I didn't understand a word. Then he came back with boxes of shoes and slippers; some had animals on them, kittens, all kinds of toys. Finally, I found someone to translate. "He wants to adopt your daughter," an old man said, translating for me; "he'll set you up in an expensive cosmetic shop in return." It seemed to me as if black armies were marching on the hotel, pounding on the doors. They were in my ears. "I should give her up, after I went through the war, now I have a chance to bring her up the way I want, now that I have all the possibilities?" I screamed, grabbing her. The old man translated. The man left his box of shoes and fled. He never came back.

"I *am* good to your daughter," Max insisted. "I even take care of her when you go out with other men." "You wouldn't mind my being a doctor," I asked; "if I could?" "Every Jewish boy wants to grow up to marry a doctor," he joked. "I'm serious," I complained. "I would be proud." I blushed like fire. "I did a lot of things to be ashamed of in the war," I whispered. "Did you inform?" Max asked. "No!" I exclaimed, shocked. "Then you didn't do anything," he said, dismissing it. "The only one I heard called an angel during the war was the Death Angel of Auschwitz." I felt something soothe, as if it had been covered with syrup.

"All right," I said after a little while. "All right what?" "All right, I'll marry you." "What are you crying about?" "Angels," I gasped. "I'll start looking for an apartment tomorrow," Max began planning, "and someone told me there's a G.I. Bill, not a G.I. Bill but something like it, that will give me a loan for carpentry or upholstery school. There's a shortage of those things around. People always need something to sit on. If you're at a hospital, maybe you could go at night." "We'll see," I said cautiously. "I'll find the apartment first, of course," Max reassured me. "No, we'll see about the hospital first," I answered; "I don't know if it will work out." "It can't hurt to try," he insisted.

The next day I took Ninka to the Brooklyn Jewish Hospital. "We want a doctor speaking German," Ninka sniffled. Somehow the nurse at the desk managed to produce one. "Doctor Klugman," he said, introducing himself; "what's the trouble with the little child?" "She has a cold and she's anemic." He examined her. "Nothing serious," he told me. "These pills will clear up her nose and you should bring her here every week for iron shots; she'll shoot up like a tree." Ninushka pinched her nose; she was reading *Pinocchio*.

"Excuse me, Doctor Klugman, but there is something I want to ask you," I said, pulling out my medical school index. "I finished over three years of medical school in Poland; I would like to finish here." He took the sheets and shook his head at them sadly. "These wouldn't count here," he said. "You'd have to start all over, and then there's an endless waiting list. But," he went on, "a registered nurse is a good profession. We could probably waive some courses for you if you could take the others. You'd make a lot of money." "I can't, I have a little child," I wailed. "One of the professors might be willing to give private lessons," he thought, "and then you would have to come to the hospital for only half a day to learn our system; it's different from Europe, the beds and everything." "I know a woman who's a full doctor, from Russia; maybe we could share the lessons?" "It could probably be arranged," he agreed, "and then you could share the costs. We might even be able to do something about her later; if she finished. But it will be hard for you. Everything you learned was in Latin, and you don't even know English."

"I'm teaching her," Ninka volunteered. "That should speed things up," he smiled. "How long do you think it will take?" I asked, worried. "At least a year, and you'll have to study hard. Come back tomorrow," he said. I left Ninushka with Max the next day and went back. "I didn't forget you," Doctor Klugman said. "I'm glad," I answered, the trains still roaring in my ears. "It is all arranged. You can start next week: lessons and work."

Sonia and I managed to schedule the lessons at night; immediately we were studying. She knew much more than I did and helped me out. Max was searching for an apartment we could afford. In three months, he began his classes. "I found one!" he shouted, coming into the Green's one night. "It's on Ninety-second and Amsterdam; five rooms. The rent is seventy-five dollars." "How can we manage it?" I was already planning. "We can take in boarders," I said finally, "from the hotel. I can do the cooking and cleaning; we'll even make money." "It will be hard," Max warned. "Here nothing is too hard," I swore; "when can we move in?" "As soon as we give them the three-hundred-dollar deposit." "Three hundred dollars!" I choked. "Are you crazy?" "Call Regina," he told me.

"Oh, no problem," she said. "You found a place; that's wonderful. Come tonight when Saul is home." We had been going on Friday nights for dinner. They were millionaires with a factory that made rubber soles for shoes. "Look at the maid," Ninka whispered every time. The maid was all dressed in white. Ninushka was sure she was a nurse. They lived on the East Side in a huge townhouse with beautiful mahogany furnishings, inlaid wood, crystal, and big silver candlesticks, but they had Chinese furniture, too—carved screens with jade designs, tall tables shaped like flowers, and carved all over with flowers, carved coffee tables with people carrying food to markets carved out of red wood. "It's cinnabar," Regina told me, seeing me scrape at it furtively; "that's not paint. That's the color of the wood. Here's a little candy box, cinnabar, too." "It smells good," I told her. The next thing I knew, she had one for me for a present. It was a cinnabar cigar box sitting next to my plate Friday night.

"Why does Uncle Saul get his own food?" Ninka asked. "Because I'm a diabetic," Saul answered her. "What's that?" she asked cheerfully, eating some apricot meringue. "That means some foods, like candy, make me sick." "That's a catastrophe!" Ninka exclaimed; that was her latest word, and chocolate was her favorite food. "No, it's not so bad," he answered, chewing on some dry roast beef; "you don't like candy much when you get older." "Oh, that is a lie," Ninka cried; "everyone likes candy!" "It's not polite to tell someone they're lying," I warned her sharply. "But he *is*," Ninushka insisted. "Maybe some people always like it," Saul added; "but I don't." She stared at him, outraged. "He said it again!" she whispered to me. "Eat," I ordered. "I'm watching; he'll take some," she whispered positively.

That night we arrived early. "Here's the money," Saul said, handing me three bills as if they were three pennies. "So you two are getting married? Regina told me; it's the best thing." "No, it's not," Ninka said. I turned to her, shocked. "Why not?" I asked. "He is not a doctor, or an engineer," she said; "he is nothing. *My* father was an engineer," she bragged. "I saw pictures of him too; he was much better-looking." We were embarrassed to death. "The most important thing," I told Ninka, "is a good heart; there were *plenty* of rich men I could have married." "You should've," she said through a piece of chocolate she had gotten from the coffee table. "Max took you to the zoo and the movies," I reminded her. "So would a doctor," she answered, unimpressed. "You'll get used to it," I assured her. "I won't," she promised, getting another nut cluster and devouring it. "What do we need him for anyway?" "What do you think?" I asked Max later. "She'll get used to it." But he didn't sound happy. We started planning the little wedding.

First I moved into the apartment; Sonia rented the first room. She had found the cousin of a cousin who gave us some broken-down chairs and a table, and then we discovered the Salvation Army. "What a *wonderful* place!" Sonia kept marveling, but I was too busy burrowing and tunneling to make a sound. Max came over one night and found us painting the table and chairs green and red; the horizontal bars were red, the rest green. He set to work making curtains for the windows in blue and red flowers. Old lamps came out of Regina's basement, and an old braided rug, one Oriental one. The place was so cozy, no one wanted to leave. Everyone who came to look at a room took one. When the sun shone in through the red and blue curtains, the whole apartment looked like it was alive, burning with blooms. And so we began, like ants, hand over foot, foot by foot.

"Anya," Max said coming in, "I was talking to a man at the store. He says it's illegal for the landlord to charge us seventy-five dollars. He wrote out this letter to the Rent Control Office." "Maybe he'll take it away altogether;" I pushed it away, frightened. "He can't; the man told me." The landlord came up a few days later. He was a Lithuanian peasant and spoke German. "I have a letter," he told me; "I have to give you back some money. Your rent is forty-five dollars now." Oh, it was a holiday, a feast. But the landlord stayed friends with us. He came and ate the thick old-country soups I was always making; we were all living on them. "Now we can get married," Max announced. "All right," I said.

We went to the courthouse and came back to the table covered with cookies and candies and cakes. There were crowds in the apartment—everyone who rented a room, friends from the hotel, mostly men—and almost all looking for wives and husbands. Some of them were such pests Max and I had tried thinking of how to pair them off. And two couples did get paired off. Now here we were, getting married ourselves. "Didn't you remember I'm a diabetic?" Saul asked. I turned red as fire. If I could have pulled the tablecloth from beneath everything and covered myself with it, I would have been happy, I was so ashamed. "I am going right out," Max cried, and came back with pounds of roast beef and turkey. "Only one of us is diabetic," Saul grinned; "come on Anya, where is your smile?" I hadn't stopped smiling since the boat reached the dock. There were so many possibilities! The whole air was filled with door after door. Anything could happen. And Ninushka, Ninushka was safe. Now it was up to us. I always trusted myself.

On Friday nights all our friends came over. On Wednesday, I began preparing, going down to Orchard Street to buy lamb shanks for fourteen cents a pound. Then everyone came and brought records for the phonograph, and danced and there was no one to bother us; it was our own place. Even the landlord would fix anything so he could come. So the night went on in singing and dancing; some men had brought wine and vodka. Everyone was happy. Faces were burning in the heat of so many bodies. Regina was beaming like a queen.

After that, the months went by quickly, perfectly. Regina insisted on putting Ninushka in a special yeshiva and paying three quarters of the cost. I was free to study;

Ninka was learning and learning. She was speaking perfect English. Every day she was getting healthier. There she was, blond and strong, the life seed. And when I got pregnant again, I spoiled it; I would not go through with it. "Only one," I thought. She would be next; now it was her turn. "You're still a young woman," Max insisted; "you're only twenty-seven." "No," I insisted, "you said it yourself; after what we've been through, we should not be parents. How many times at night do we wake up screaming, thinking it's the Gestapo, or worse?" But Ninushka was growing and growing, and I was working as a nurse at night, and Max working during the day. We found a larger apartment. One of the old women I had taken care of on the wards came up to me one day on the street and asked, *"Now* is there anything I can do for you?" And I told her yes, we were being chased out of our old building; they were tearing it down; and she gave me the key to hers. "I was going to liquidate mine," she said; "it's beautiful, only eighty-five dollars. I was hoping to see you about it." "Let's go," I begged; "is it in the East Zone?" "East Side," she laughed; "East Side. No, it's not. It's on Eighty-sixth and Central Park West. Believe me, you'll never find anything like it again." And so we advertised the contents of the apartment for sale.

A man came and paid us $350 for everything in the apartment, all the furniture and the drapes, and all it was was the red and green chairs, Max's drapes, a table and a few beds, the walls painted in their bright colors. So we did move, and the new apartment was beautiful. The little lake in the park twinkled back up at us through the windows. But the old landlord called us. "He isn't moving in; he hasn't taken anything," he wailed. "I'll call him," I promised. "This is Anya Meyers," I said; "our old landlord tells me you haven't taken the things or moved in." All I had taken were our personal possessions and an upright piano I had gotten for Ninushka; those and some pictures from the walls, maybe two. "Oh," he said sadly, "when you left, all the personality left too; all the warmth is gone; nothing is left." He never moved in. It was so cozy, no one ever wanted to leave. "You went away," he said, "and with you the niceness of the apartment. It is really a shabby place," he finished. So he lost $350. And he never moved in. And it was, it was so cozy, no one ever wanted to leave. And now the new one we had was warming itself, too.

EPILOGUE:
And Then There Were None

✺

I shall not murder
The mankind of her going with a grave truth
Nor blaspheme down the stations of the breath
With any further
Elegy of innocence and youth.

> Dylan Thomas, *A Refusal to Mourn*
> *the Death, by Fire, of a*
> *Child in London*

Rich Man, Poor Man

On a bench in a shack, a poor man lay.
Does it pay to be rich, he used to say?

Never good food or drink to taste?
Only to save for a rainy day?

We leave so much behind when we die,
But if I were rich, I would take it and fly.

Give parties and balls in a home so nice,
The whole world would say, he lives just right.

And I would never forget all others in sight.
The life of the rich who fear to pay

Is just like a hell on a very hot day.
So he thought to himself again this way.

Just then a wizard was passing by;
His voice buzzed into the shack like a fly;

Would you like to be rich? the wizard asked.
You said you'd be good just as I passed.

Here is a purse I give to you
And if you want money, this you should do:

Pull out each time a ten ruble coin.
As soon as you have it, another is born.

You can take as many as you want away.
When you have enough, throw it away.

Just one thing I must warn you about.
Not one coin must leave your house

Until the purse goes into the sea.
Now you may say goodbye to me.

The peasant lost his mind with joy;
Then he thought, it is only a toy.

I am not awake, it is only a dream.
So he pulled a coin from the bottom seam.

Only until morning will I take them out.
Then the purse goes out of the house.

I am rich, he said to the morning sun.
But fortune's are nice; why have only one?

A lazy man I have never been,
Money for a dacha, a drozhka, three trees,

A village would be a nice thing to see.

But still it is only a little bit;
My purse and I will stay and sit.

And so the days walked with the weeks,
Time counts wrinkles in the old man's cheeks;

Now he even forgets to eat.
A long time ago, he lost his count

And so he dies in the shabby house.
The moral of this is plain enough.

As soon as he went to the sea with the purse
The poor old man felt worse and worse;

His heart would jump, he could not see,
Throwing it out is the death of me.

It really is like a faithful friend,
If I drowned it now, how to make amends?

For all his endless time and trouble,
He dies as yellow as his rubles.

Russian fable as told by Anya Meyers.

590

35

WHEN I weigh the good days of my life against the bad, except for my childhood, I don't know if I could select more than one year that was really happy. To live more than half a century, to push away the years, for what? What have I accomplished in my life? I ask myself this more and more, now that I have started opening the rooms to the house in the past which were kept locked so long. I don't know what I was afraid of finding there. I have never had the graves of my family; perhaps I was afraid those rooms were where they had come to rest, and if I opened them there would be the terrible smell, the dead arms reaching up or not reaching up; I don't know which would have been worse. But I'm happy in those rooms now. And now that I am fifty-two, I spend more and more time in them, so that sometimes, when I come back to the rooms of this world, it is like swimming up from under water and finding a white locked door at the place of entrance. And then the rooms I live in now seem to have filled with the artificial snow of sealed globes and thickened; moving into them is like moving into an ice cube.

I spend more and more time talking to my mother. Whenever I have a problem, I ask her, "Momushka, what should I do." And I try to imagine what she would answer me. I know I am not the same person I was, that I am absolutely changed. But when my parents come to me in dreams, they never notice how worried I am, how I am obsessed with my grandchildren and my daughter; my parents never mention the children at all. So there are times when someone who has accomplished everything in life dies—our President, a king—I ask myself, "What for? What is it for?" To do so much and have it all taken away, to be taken away from everything, and yet, I do not want to die; I want to live. I remember Momma saying that in the ghetto: Everyone wants to live, no matter what the price. It is impossible for me to believe that I cannot accomplish anything; that the film which has recorded the story of my life was spliced one third through to an irrelevant reel by a maniac, that what began in the past will never continue in the future. I still have hope. I would still like to be elegant, to be admired. I would like to do something to help people, especially children. I would like to work with them in a hospital. But it all depends on my nerves. When I first came here, I thought there was nothing I could not do; I still thought I would forget.

In our first apartment, I studied during the day and cooked and washed clothes at night. I used to squeeze orange bits through a rag for Ninushka's eyes, and then I would be ready to walk to Orchard Street to buy lambshanks for our parties. And for a while, it did seem as if I would have everything I wanted. During the fall and winter, I worked as a registered nurse. During the summer I had a concession at the Catskills, at a resort, selling jewelry and running a health salon. Ninka and I lived in a little cabin at the edge of the woods, and Max came upon weekends to visit us. Ninka had the best air. And she was so affectionate. Until she was sixteen, she would come into bed and cuddle up to me. Now it is all gone.

I worked in the operating room in the winter, and the more I worked, the more I cried. Every time Doctor Klugman saw me in the hall, I was leaning against the wall, crying. When I put on my coat to go home, I was crying. Finally, he told me this was not the job for my nerves. He told Max that after what I had been through, this was the worst possible thing for me. I kept trying to tell them that it started when they operated on a little child, maybe three and a half, and they found her whole stomach filled with cancer, but every time I tried to explain, I began crying again. The two of them shook their heads and my nursing career was over. My hopes that when I made enough money, when Max was finished with his carpentry school, I could go back to medical school. That was over, too. I used to tell myself, "You'll get used to it." But I didn't realize. A man I met when I first came here begged me to write out my story. I told him I was no writer; he said his sister could transcribe it for me. But I said, "Oh, no, I am going to forget." And I thought I would forget.

I have not forgotten anything. If I am alone for even five minutes, whole sections of my life unfold in front of me. They are so vivid, they are like scenes from a movie, except the scenes are three-dimensional, and immediately the director with the small mustache casts me as the main character.

So for a while, Max and I did other things. When he had time off, he used to peddle the shoes Regina's husband, Saul, gave us. We took them to the Russian farmers in New Jersey. I remember Max asking not "kakoi size," but "khaki size," which means something else in Russian: bowel movements. And we were hysterical with laughter for weeks. Even then, it seemed there were no problems that could not be solved. And then I began to have the dream that he and I could become a cook and a chauffeur; Ninushka would have a wonderful place to live and good food to eat, good surroundings. But time has a way of passing. Max's store began to do well; customers would give him old furniture when he upholstered something of theirs. I began selling; I was good at it. So I took a little store on the corner, but it was always closed because I was always home watching Ninka, or, finally, watching her children. Now I have moved into another part of Max's store; I sell old furniture and antiques. Strange, because my grandfather was a famous antique dealer in Paltava, how things turn out. The store is so tiny sometimes I feel as if we are living in a coffin.

And still, there are times I do not want to complain. All kinds of people come into the store. There is still so much I want to know, and they tell me. But I cannot fool myself: I am only hearing about their lives, not living them. And they cannot distract me for long. From the minute, I found Ninushka, she was all I worried about: her health, her health. I was a madwoman about food. If my Momma hadn't fed me so well, squeezing juices with her own hands, for four children, twice a day, would I have survived? I am sure it is the *fundament* my mother gave me that protected me. So I tried with Ninka, and she grew into the most beautiful girl. It was a miracle to see. I was never so beautiful. It was like watching a rare flower grow. Sometimes, I think, if I were to tell the truth, I would have liked it like that, Ninushka staying with me as my plants stay in the house. But I could never have permitted it; I wanted a normal life for her. And she has it: a husband and two children. But things have changed so. Everyone wants to be independent now and she is no exception. She keeps telling me, the best thing is to be free, to work and travel. It breaks my heart. I must have made a mistake. Her favorite sentence is, "Mother, it is nineteen seventy-three."

Things have changed so much. Perhaps it is my fault I cannot accept them. I would like Ninka to raise her children as I raised her and as my mother raised me. But her childhood was not like mine. I think I remember her asking me if what I went through for her was worth it. How could I answer such a question? Sometimes I think she is all that kept me alive; and really, in the beginning, I did not want her. I do not believe life is up to us, that we can make all the choices. Hitler chose for us. There was someone above him. I had no choice but to go through those things. In ordinary affairs one has more choice; you can accept more responsibility. I accepted mine for her; I grew to love her. That was the natural way. If it had been a normal life, if we had lived in Warsaw, if there had been no war, if I had finished medical school, then I would have gone through a life like everyone's life. I do not know how that story would have ended. But being so helpless like that, we have come to feed on our bitterness, become suspicious, lose even more what we love. And even that was not our choice.

And it is odd, even when I am alone in the store, even when I sit here with the antiques gathering dust. I remember things: the night at the resort I decided to sleep in the hotel instead of our cabin and the woods took fire from the storm, and all the guests thought we were dead. Ninka's screams came from our window: "Come look, Momushka!" And the cries of the women as we came down: "Anya! Anya!" or the time a man held up our store last year and shot Max in the arm and I went after him, thinking there were no more bullets in the gun, but when the police came, they found two. Even when I sit here thinking of these things, I believe there is something that intended all this: I believe in a superpower. I believe in fate. I believe there was something that wanted to keep me alive. Perhaps it was my mother protecting me, she was so good. Or the blessings of the women in the hospital at the camp. How many times have I asked myself: Why Verushka? Why Vera? She was such a good girl. Why Poppa? Why such a father? He was a saintly man. My Momma, such a mother. She was human, she had her faults; but she loved to live. She would have given everything in the world just to have stayed with me. But I was

594

chosen to live, or doomed to live, depending on my mood for the day.

I believe God wanted someone to live to become more experienced, to live longer, to have certain influences. There are many of us. I don't know what the influences are. I just don't know. I am not intelligent enough to know. I am intelligent enough to know that my belief makes it easier for me to live; I feel warm with it, like a blanket. And then I wonder, what are my influences, my experiences? What have I learned? I do not understand today, any more than I did thirty years ago, why all that had to happen to us. It is as inexplicable as an earthquake. I think humans are just combinations of all the natural things: animals, stones, earthquakes, storms, and, sometimes, the eruptions, the cruelty. And then I rebel; I remember what my father was, and I cannot believe it. I sit in the store, day after day, hour after hour, pulling troubles from the magic purse of my past. I am obsessed about my little grandson's head. The maid who takes care of him is not careful enough; I am sure of it. I can see it as clearly as if it were happening in front of me, his falling against the stove and splitting his head wide open. The first time I saw it I believed it was a vision; I called my daughter immediately. She thought I was crazy. Probably I am driving her crazy with these worries. But I cannot stop myself. And she does not like it when I come over with juices or chickens for the little ones; I can't get over my fear they eat too little. But she was so undernourished, and she survived. Perhaps she thinks, if she went through so much, and she is still string, she does not have to be as careful as I was. I don't know.

So what are my experiences?

Sometimes I think the whole war was a punishment of some kind. When it began, I remember thinking the war was a punishment for all the intermarriages. My father thought it was ridiculous to think such a thing. And then I was confused. Events were so ridiculous no explanation could be ridiculous enough. Sometimes I think it is a payment for our new country, for Israel. Maybe it was to warn people, to show them what could happen. Could you live in a family like mine and go out and kill and kill and kill? I could never do it. I remember during the war thinking, "Oh, when it is over, I will get even; I will do to them what they have done to us." And there is this picture I will never forget, when they were taking the children. A

595

Gestapo officer picked up a litle boy and swung him by the feet into a tree. His skull shattered like an egg; his brains shone down the tree and dripped onto the sidewalk. It was so terrible it took me ten years to remember seeing it. But such things happened, and they were the rule. They did happen. I do not believe that anyone is as happy about the human animal as they were before.

But is that enough? I cannot believe that is enough. I am the biggest pacifist. When the television shows the Is-raelis taking cabs into Arab countries for retribution, I am so excited and overjoyed I can barely sit still. I have such palpitations I am afraid of a heart attack. Which of us went through that without an undying desire for revenge? And my own marriage? How much of it had to do with Max's revenging his father? When he told me about it, I felt as if I had been able to do it myself. But then I think of the Six Days' War. There must have been children killed. I cannot believe it is worth killing even one child to carry on a war.

I have not tried to find out what other, wiser people think the war meant. Who can know what it meant? I don't believe anyone can. So I satisfy myself with simple answers that suit the weather of the day. But I believe it had a purpose. I believe there was a hand over my head, shielding me. I even remember the day the belief began. It was the day at the university when the boys with iron nails went aftet the girls and my Poppa called from work and would not let us go out. I remember sitting with Momma thinking, "What for, the chosen people, what for? Chosen for what? For this, to be endlessly persecuted, just because we are Jewish?" And it was then I began to believe. Even the endless persecution was a form of being chosen. But then, as I said, I remember our President's death, and I think, what for? What is any life for? But these are questions I cannot answer.

So what have I learned from the war? I spend hours, days, trying to decide how I am different from others my age because of the war, and how I am just the same because of time. "Mother," Ninka says, "it is nineteen seventy-three." I am flying, high with hopes—perhaps I may get to do something yet, be listened to again, be admired again—and my daughter says this one sentence and I am not twenty anymore, I am fifty-two. I am shot down. But surely any old person feels this. Sometimes I think the biggest tragedy is not to feel your years, to be young inside.

You go along, feeling like a young girl, with wide open blue eyes, and then you see a picture of yourself: wrinkles are closing your eyes; your skin is whiter than ever, but not the nice kind of whiteness; your light blond hair is white. And the children you hoped for so much are leading their lives without you. I had a grandmother; my mother used to tell me she always said, "Eh, children, they are a treasure, but a false treasure." Momma told me that many times. My grandmother, an uneducated woman, a plain woman said, "false treasure." I don't know where she got that from, but I believe her now. These are not things I have learned from the war. Women come into the store and sit in the chair across from me and complain by the hour, and always, it's the same thing, the children, children. But still, I love to live.

I am living through everything. I am not only interested from a corner. I thing I'm up to date, but my convictions, the environment in which you grow up, it stays with you. I like everything decent; I like everything nice. I like to know what other people think. One woman who comes in is a Communist. She told me, "Even you, Anya, if a person has money, you think they're all right." "Where did you get that idea?" I asked her. "I, who left everything behind, I'm interested only in money? You told me your own daughter said this time she would marry only a rich man, so who is interested in money?" Then the mother complained that her daughter had become so bourgeois. I asked what was wrong with that. "Listen, Edna," I said, "how can you discuss Communism, not being there? Why don't you go see how it looks? There is the worst fascism there. I don't give a damn for money; it's only bitter if you don't have money for food, but you don't eat up all you have, anyway." So, I wanted to give my money to the children for a house, but they said no. So it will be left to them when I die, and why should it be a festival when a mother dies? It would be so much better to see my work. So again, I am back to the children. I remember a family: Emma's. She was marvelous. The father adored his daughter, and he bought her a mink coat. Emma said, "You are demoralizing her," he was like all fathers in this country, and the coat went back. It was hard on Emma because the father adored the daughter and then the hostility between mother and daughter was unbearable. Now the daughter lives in California with her four children, and the mother is absolutely dead, forgotten. But the father had heart disease, and he had to live with a housekeeper; finally, he left his housekeeper all his money. And these people led normal lives.

So what have I learned? I have learned not to believe in suffering. It is a form of death. If it is severe enough it is a poison; it kills the emotions. Sometimes I think I died when my Poppa died; since then I've been one of the walking dead. There are days when I think my flesh is made of rubber, and underneath, only a demonstration skeleton of plastic. It is amazing to me that I gave rise to life; but that was before the war. Things have to be exaggerated, so exaggerated, for me to feel them. Before, I was so sensitive. And then there are days when it all evaporates and anything, a glimpse of a face on a train, a child falling on the street, makes me cry. Suffering has absolutely no purpose; normal suffering, yes, but suffering like ours, perversion, no. All of life is a war. How well I see it. The television warns about cancer; immediately, everyone has it. And some people will have it. Poor Sonya in the camp. I never asked Rachel about her. Of course Sonya died there. I didn't want to hear about it. And I never, never read Vera's letter. Maybe the man she married was already married. I don't think so, but it's possible. I don't want to know. Every day is a movement in the war; every day you lose and get older. I just have to look in the mirror. I used to say, "I never had a toothache before Hitler; I never had a sick day in my life before Hitler; neither did my father or mother, none of us." Someone laughed at me. It is hard not to think like that; if he hadn't come, we would have lived on and on, just as we were. But we are all ruled by death. It is always coming. I remember playing cards with my cousin Regina. A woman bent over to pick up a card; she never got up. And before we could call the police, her son was rummaging through her safe before the authorities could get there. We were straightening up his mother and he was rummaging through the safe. Hitler is a mystery to me, to want to be king of it all, the king of death. Why? I believe in a superpower, but I don't believe in anything after this life. But I am in no hurry to die; there is no rush. Tomorrow may always bring something.

Suffering is the best teacher; I have learned that. Everything I learned during the war I have never forgotten. How to survive. I could do it again, I think, even at my age. I need to believe that. But with that, I learned to worry about what might happen to make me need to survive. I never stop worrying, I'm so good at it. And the lessons I learned were drawn into my brain like hieroglyphics pressed in by a stick. I am used to danger. I can't understand a life without it. That was one of the hieroglyphics of suffering, the nonsense syllables. If suffering isn't there, I have to find it. So our store is on one of the most dangerous streets in the city, and so it is next door to a man who came from our ghetto and fought in the resistance. And in our building there are more people from the camps. Suffering teaches you you can never forget; you can only repeat and repeat—unless you are one of the miraculous, lucky ones. But I haven't met any.

My husband says it's important to have these people around because only people who were there with us can understand what it was like. But sometimes I think only people who were there with us are the only people we think we can trust. If we moved, we would be in a richer neighborhood; we would attract attention. Still, it is silly. In this neighborhood, we are the richest and attract attention. But this neighborhood is not like the rich ones we used to know. It is more like the neighborhoods that haunted us after the war in Europe. We are reliving it all again.

And my daughter: How much of her trouble comes from the suffering I went through to save myself, then her? I couldn't trust anyone; it was a plot or plan every minute. Lies flew out of my mouth like moths. I had to be so careful that her head was bandaged, that she ate, that she got the vaccine for typhoid; I would not trust her with herself. I would never let her wash a dish. I was wrong. My parents always trusted me, and being trusted, it creates a kind of obligation to deserve it. But I never did trust her. And sometimes I wonder. There was never any safety for so long.

And we were never free from dreams; we still wake up screaming the soldiers are after us, the Gestapo is after us. Once Max woke up standing on his bed. We had another friend who used to wake up so soaking wet we had to cover everything he slept in with rubber beneath the cotton; he would not marry. He kept saying it wouldn't be fair. Perhaps it wouldn't have been. Certainly, he is strange now. So there was always this dangerous situation. It made such an impression, now it always exists. And I wonder if we make ourselves safe by causing the danger ourselves, and then escaping from it, if we are condemned to spend our lives on this street, just so that at the end of every day we can go to bed having spent the day making faces at the dreams, laughing in their faces. But who is really laughing? And what do we really accomplish?

I remember my daughter's first real romance. Ninka came home with a Greek boy named Aristotle. Oh, he's a Jewish Greek, she insisted, and he insisted, too. How many times in the past had she refused to go out with someone because he wasn't Jewish? I don't know how often we told her the story of the girl who married a boy from the Index in Vilno, and then, when the Germans came, he threw her right out onto the street, and she was killed before everyone else. We told her this again and again, describing the girl, Irna; she had a heart-shaped face and olive skin. She was one of the best students in the university, a psychologist before she was even twenty. And a figure like a statue—she could not go down the street without men turning around to look at her—and big blue eyes. Everyone in Vilno knew her, she was so beautiful. And there she stood in front of her expensive house, with her husband, the doctor, not even coming to the window to see her, and the Germans saw her looking around in bewilderment and shot her down. She fell, like a beautiful willow tree, her hair streaming almost the length of her body. He had thrown her out in her bathrobe.

But this one, she insisted, was Jewish. And by this time, Ninka could have anyone she wanted. By now, she was so beautiful it tore the heart. People used to come up to us when we walked on the street. One man once came up to us with a rose. "Allow me," he said. Aristotle was very nice and very polite. If I had to go to the grocery, he would offer to go in my place; of course, I would not let him. But who ever heard of a Jewish Greek?

Then, one morning, he came by early, on Sunday. He asked me if I would mind if he took Ninka to a concert in honor of Mendelssohn to be held in a big church. "Oh, Mendelssohn," I said, "if she wants it, why not? But be sure to be home for lunch," I insisted; "she is not very strong." He promised. Then it was one, two, three o'clock; they still were not back. So I went into Ninka's room and looked for the little black book she had; there was his number. I called. "Excuse me," I said, "I am Ninka's mother. She and Aristotle went to a concert; they're not back; I'm worried." "I don't know where they are," she answered in a crabby voice; "I'm just back from church."

I still don't know how I got onto the chair. All my life centered on her, I thought to myself; I don't care about myself. Finally, they came in. I asked where they had been. They said they had gone to a poetry reading. Ninka was blushing. My temper was rising like steam. As soon as he left the house, I asked Ninka if she was sure Aristotle was a Jew. She said he was. I told her he was not, and she demanded what I meant, outraged. Then I told her I had called his mother, and she was just coming back from church when she answered the phone. Ninka was infuriated I had called. So I could see how it was. She liked him already; it was too late.

I lay on the bed like a dead doll. "Mother, get up," Ninka ordered; "there's nothing wrong with you." I told her I would appreciate it if she would go into the kitchen and get some more ice for the pack I had pressed over my heart. It took her half an hour to make the trip. "Any better?" she asked sarcastically. "There's nothing wrong with you." I didn't ask for anything else. She came back again in an hour. "I will never be better," I told her. And it was true. Whether I was sick or not, I looked sick, and still, she would not stop seeing that good for nothing. I stayed in bed for two weeks. It did not help. She was still seeing him.

I told Ninka he was forbidden to come to the house; if she wanted to see him, she would have to see him somewhere else. "You know what I went through," I reminded her. And it would have been better if I had stopped there, but I couldn't. I insisted everyone who went through what Max and I had would act this way toward their only child, a child who had been saved by a miracle. Ninka said miracles had nothing to do with it. "Just think!" I ordered her. "I don't want to think," she answered. I told Max I was going to bed; he told me I wasn't doing anyone any good in bed. And the next thing I knew, Max was bringing Aristotle into my room; he had called the boy. Max told Aristotle he was not wanted. He asked Aristotle what his father had been; he had been a tailor. Max said calmly he meant what *nationality* had Aristotle's father been. When Aristotle said his father was a Ukrainian, Max told him the Ukrainians were the worst anit-Semites, and if his father were alive and found out he was dating a Jewish girl, he would kill him himself. Aristotle became very righteous. He said *then* he would have nothing to do with

601

his father. He added he was not religious in any case. Max asked him why he couldn't convert to the Jewish religion if religion meant so little to him and so much to us and he became very indignant. Why should he change his religion, he asked us, he liked his religion. Then we both knew. And I started in. I told him he was a good and handsome boy and brilliant; anyone would want him. I asked him why he wanted to come where he was not wanted. Then Max lost his temper. Ever since the war, he hasn't been able to tolerate even the smallest lie. He roared at Aristotle that he told us he was Jewish! He called the boy a liar. Aristotle said that maybe we would get used to him. Max threw him out.

Then, when Max and I would be walking on Broadway, we would see the two of them with their arms around each other's waist. "It may not be love, but it looks like it," Max said. "I have to do something," I insisted. But Max said there was nothing I could do. Meanwhile, a lawyer Ninka used to go out with kept calling all the time. He asked me what had happened to her. He said she used to feel like a queen when he took her out; everything that was on the menu was on the table. Now, he said, she would only see him on week nights. "Mrs. Meyers," he pleaded, "I'm not used to being the second dish." I promised him I would see what I could do. I talked to Ninka. I told her that Fred had called and how important it was to him that she see him. She told me she was busy and went into her room, closing the door. When Fred called back I told him I couldn't do anything. I complained to Max that she used to tell me everything about her dates. "It was just like with me and Momma." Fred stopped calling her, and she and Aristotle were wound like two strings in a rope. I told Max I was going to hang myself by it; I told him I wanted to jump out of the window. He begged me to calm down; I was not normal. I couldn't talk, only cry. I asked him if we raised her for this, that she should be killed by a Ukrainian. "A Greek," he reminded me.

Then it was summer, and we went to the hotel where I had my concession. "Inhale," Max joked; "he's not here." I was even looking suspiciously at the trees. Such letters! "What do you want to do? Get married? Change diapers, cook meals, become a slave?" I was half dead after each one. Then one day she ran out suddenly. I was not so stupid; I followed her. Of course, he was there at the hotel. We went to Florida; we only went by car. There he was

602

standing on a corner as we drove by. She must have told him where to come. "Max," I sobbed at night," there is more than one of him; he is a whole army." Max tried to calm me down. The war was starting over; buildings were shattering. "You cannot tell me there is only one," I insisted; "he is all over the world." It was impossible to talk to me. No wonder I look so much older than I am. Finally, I decided that when we got back, I would do something. I could start appearing on corners, too.

One day I asked Ninka what church Aristotle's mother went to. She told me. It was a church on 96th Street. Then she asked me if I was going to convert. I put down my spoon and shouted at her. And to think that before the war, I never raised my voice. She ran out of the room with her hands over her ears. I remembered that she used to do that when we talked about the war. When we first moved into the second apartment, I began to talk about it. I couldn't stop. I talked like a machine. Ninushka used to run through the house, slamming every door, and I would find her sitting under the covers with her hands over her ears. Then one day I was telling an American woman my story; I wanted everyone to know. I told her about my first husband and how he died. "And how is Stajoe?" she asked me. She hadn't been listening at all. A switch moved in my head. I stopped talking about the past.

The next day, I took the rings and jewelry I still had left from Anzia's hoard and Momma's stove, and went to the pawnshop. I came home with $1500. I waited until Ninushka had eaten her dinner, and then I told her I had a wonderful surprise. She wanted to travel so badly, and I had tickets for her from a Jewish agency; she was going to Israel. She said she was not going. For three days she did not talk; she did not eat. Then the night before the trip she came into my room. I lived under my ice pack; I took it from my eyes. "Mother," Ninka said, "I had a dream. The plane, you know, the one I'm supposed to take tomorrow? It crashed." "You know what it is?" I asked her in a poisonous voice; "it means you will not want to come back. And don't tell me these crazy stories. You'll be overwhelmed by what you see." She asked what she could see in a little piece of sand. I told her that remained to be seen, I just wanted her to enjoy herself. I told her I only wished I were in her place and she offered to give me the ticket. "Enough," I yelled; "you are going."

"Children are the biggest sadists," I told Max. He asked

me if I wasn't glad now we hadn't had any more. I said I didn't know; it might have been better for her if she hadn't been the only one. Max answered it would be better for me if I didn't think about her so much. He was upset. I remembered, for two days after our wedding, she wouldn't talk or eat.

But we stuffed her onto the plane at Idlewild and she left. Every hour on the hour I was calling the airline until they told me the plane had landed. She was staying with Doctor Yurbo's family, and finally her time there was almost up. I told Max I was going to cable her and wire her money. I wanted her to stay longer; I didn't want to take any chances. "It's already eight weeks," he reminded me. "We redid her whole room; don't you want to see her face when she sees the wallpaper and furniture?" I didn't want to see her face for another four weeks. I went out, to the bank and then Western Union. I would tell her I might be able to make arrangements and come over myself. But she had already left Doctor Yurbo's for the airport when the telegram came. So she arrived. "What am I doing here?" she asked, looking around. "I should have stayed." She was overwhelmed when she saw her room, and for two months she did not see him.

Finally, a friend invited her to lunch. Friend! There are no such things as friends anymore. Aristotle was there; along with the shrimp salad. It began again. My headaches began tearing my skull apart with their crab claws. Max swore she would get tired of Aristotle. But I knew her; she was as stubborn as I was. She might not. I have to do something, I thought to myself, and all night, I lay awake, plotting. Then in the middle of the night I woke up suddenly from a catnap. I felt a sensation, like snow, drifting across my cheek. I had an idea. I was going to the church on 96th Street.

The next morning, I dressed myself like the plainest Christian woman I could imagine, in a long skirt I took from the store, and fastened a babushka under my chin, and a big gold cross from the safe went around my neck. It was freezing cold. Hailstones were driving at me like bullets as I plodded along toward 96th Street. Now I will talk to the Greek priest, I decided. The wind changed its mind, and pushed me along. And not as a Jewish woman, I thought triumphantly, but a Christian one. The church was very gloomy inside, almost dark. I knocked on the secretary's door. A man about fifty came out; he was very polite. "I would like to speak to the priest himself," I said; "can it be arranged? I don't speak Greek," I warned him, "only Russian." "But first," he answered, "tell me, are you married? Do you live alone?" "I am not married; I live alone." "Oh," he told me, "we should go out sometime." "Oh, gladly, gladly," I answered; "I will prepare Greek food. But first, I have a very urgent problem. And I have to satisfy my goal; it is to save a Greek boy from Jewish hands." Inside, I was doubled over with laughter. This was the story of my life. "I'll help you," he promised, "and later, we'll go out for dinner." "Oh, no" I cried; "you'll come to me for dinner!" So he arranged the meeting with the old priest.

"You baptized him," I pleaded with the priest; "now a Jewish girl wants to make him marry her. It is very hard for him to get away; they all want him." "I know," he quavered in a weak voice, as if he had swallowed a record, and someone was already slowing him down with their finger; "his mother called about that already." "Father," I said, "we have to do everything. I am a Christian woman; I will do more than I can. It cannot be allowed that such a brilliant boy, such an educated boy, should fall into Jewish hands, and the mother, she is so miserable, she does not eat." Already I was starting in on her. "But I am old," he croaked, lifting his eyes to heaven; "it is cold out, hail, how can I go?" "You don't have to walk, I will pay for the cab," I promised him, running around to the other side of his desk; "they live on Jane Street. But what will you accomplish if you go? I am not alone; I am delegated by a group of women. We all know his mother; she is heartbroken. The best thing," I swore, "is to send him to Greece where his heritage is." "But our church has no money," the old priest whispered in his slow voice. "You just don't worry about the money," I assured him; "we will sell our rings, only to save this one Christian soul. We will even sell our crosses!" He raised his eyes to heaven.

I came back three times, three times the same thing. In the meantime, I sent a donation of $25. They didn't take a penny, but they sent Aristotle to Greece for a whole year. Oh, I was beside myself! But I forgot the mails. Still, he wrote. Would she send him some old coats for some old men, this, that. "I am sure," I told Ninushka, "he has met someone there." She didn't answer. "When you were gone," I continued, "he didn't stop calling me, inviting me out to talk to him, only for spite; he is no good." No answer.

Then I was playing cards with Pauline when an acquaintance asked how my beautiful daughter was. I said she was fine; there was no point in telling the whole world. Then the woman said she had a friend who had just moved from Israel whose son was a brilliant boy and she asked me if I would mind if she gave this boy my daughter's number. "Why not?" I asked, trying to sound bored. But there was no one home to answer the phone and speak to him. She was never there. He kept calling and calling. Finally, he stopped. Then the next time he called he told me he thought I was not letting him talk to her because he had an accent. "Listen, young man," I told him, "this isn't her routine, but you keep calling; if you give me your number, I'll see she calls."

I told Ninushka she had to do this one thing for me; she had to call him. She grumped. Another evening wasted. Then she asked me what I had found now: a rabbi? When he came, she had on her school clothes. Max and I disappeared into our room like mice; the two of them went into her room. At twelve o'clock they were still talking. "This is something," Max marveled. I begged him not to get my hopes up.

A week later when Max came in I was sobbing. I told him he shouldn't have gotten my hopes up; I asked him if he knew what Ninka was going to do now. She was going to introduce the new boy to Aristotle! Max wouldn't believe it. "Oh, yes," I went on bitterly. "She told him, 'Come out with all of us; you can meet everybody. Aristotle will be there, and I will; you come, too.'" Max wanted to know what she was thinking of, how she could do such a thing. He asked me if Ninka thought this was a new way to keep him. "Maybe she doesn't want to lose him, but she doesn't want to keep him either; maybe she wants to find out if he'll kill her because she's Jewish. We shouldn't have talked about Irna so much. Oh, she is terrible to the boys!" "Let's wait and see," Max suggested, resigned; "let's watch the news." "From one disaster to another," I muttered, slumping down next to him. "You always said how nice it was to have a group," Max muttered. "Not this way," I said, getting up, starting to dust.

But slowly she started seeing more of the new one, Michael, and less of Aristotle. I told Max I thought something was not right between them now. Maybe he *had* found someone else in Greece; he was so stupid, with all his honesty and more honesty, he probably told her. Max thought the change was probably just that she had met Michael; he said I always made things more complicated than they were. He thought Michael wasn't doing badly with Ninka. I complained that he kept her out too late. Max reminded me that I wanted them together and they had to have time to get to know each other.

Six months went by; they were always together. Then one morning, Ninka came into my room looking as if she had a stomach ache. "I think I'm going to get married," she said. "I thought you wanted to work and travel." "I'll probably get married," she said with the same long face. "I'll call the rabbi right away," I promised her. I flew to the phone like a bat. I hadn't even checked to make sure Michael had asked her to marry him. I called out the question; she said he had. "Monday? That will be fine," I told the rabbi; "that will be perfect." I told Ninushka she was getting married Monday night. "This Monday," I added. "All right," she answered.

I had her come with me to the bank. She didn't want a real wedding; instead, I was giving her money to travel. When I asked her why she didn't want a big wedding, she said there was no point in doing anything at home for strangers; we had no relatives. I begged her to let Max take us to the store and get a hat for her head. It was a mistake. All the way to Macy's she was crying; her eyes were swelling shut. I wanted to jump out of the car. But finally we came back with it; a little band, a piece of veil, and a shop-worn flower. "I'm not forcing you," I reminded her in the elevator; "I have nothing to do with this." She didn't answer me, only cried. The next morning was Saturday; she didn't get out of bed. I called her, begging her to eat something. She didn't answer. Finally I called a psychiatrist who always came into the store. "Ignore her," he said; "that's the only thing to do. Don't even go near her. Just ignore it. It used to happen to men all the time. Now it happens to women, too; they're more independent." Meantime, Michael kept calling. He knew, he said, I had told him they were getting married on Monday, but he wouldn't believe me until he actually saw us at the synagogue. I assured him she would be there, crossing my fingers, knocking on wood.

Finally, Monday, the day of the wedding, came. As if the psychiatrist had been a prophet, Ninka got up. "I want a glass of orange juice," she said, standing in the doorway. A vivid picture of Vladek shot through my eyes like a comet. I rushed to the icebox and got it for her. She drank it down. Then she told me we had a couple of hours; she would put on a dress and be ready on time. I asked her to brush her hair; it was her wedding. I asked her what she was going to wear for a coat. "Something," she answered through the toothpaste. I brought her my white one. She put it on in the bathroom and stared into the mirror. The minute she was dressed, Max and I flew to the synagogue with her. Max had already called Michael's parents. Max told me Michael's father said it was the first shotgun wedding he had ever heard of with the rifle pointed at the bride. He wanted to know what was the matter with Ninka. Max ignored the question. But he repeated it to me. I told him we'd figure it out later, and threw on my coat, hurrying him up, too.

We were there before everyone else. I wanted to know where Michael was. He was supposed to be in his apartment, changing clothes. "He'll be here," Ninka said, a condemned prisoner. There was still a cold spot on my heart from the compress I had had pressed on me all day waiting to see if she would come out of her room. I honestly believed I would die before the day was over. Max whispered to me that he thought Ninka had made Michael agree to all kinds of conditions before she said yes. We were staring around, our heads turning like weathervanes in a wind. Finally we saw his parents coming in; Michael arrived on time. The whole ceremony took ten minutes. The whole time my eyes were glued to her. I don't know what I thought, that she might run out, that she would say no when the rabbi asked for her consent. I remembered Momma telling me of the endless preparations for her wedding, how it had gone on and on and on. She was the most beautiful thing I had ever seen, but paler than a ghost. "I wonder," I thought to myself; "I shouldn't have told her about how I stayed behind to be with my mother and father so Stajoe had to come to the ghetto too. Maybe she thinks as soon as you have children, you can't get rid of them; you can't move. Or they can't move without you. Or you have to choose between people. Maybe she doesn't want the responsibility because of me." There was something missing, something important, in what I was thinking, but I was not used to thinking; I had forgotten how to concentrate on anything but Ninka twenty years ago. But I forgot about everything when I saw them kissing.

I asked Max what we were going to do next. All we had in the house was an ice pack and some orange juice. Ninka informed us we were all going to a café, and we went to one on 72nd Street. Michael pointed out the booth with the rabbi who had just married them. "Poor thing," I whispered into Max's ear; "I think we shortened his life." Max asked Michael where he was taking his bride. There was some mumbling between the two of them. "Look," Max said, "you'll be on the plane tomorrow; here's some money. Go to the airport and stay overnight." They smiled at each other.

The next morning we were all there to see them off. "Ninka," I whispered urgently to her, "you don't have anything to wear, please buy something in Europe." "Oh, I won't need anything," she said, smiling; "we're camping in a truck."

"Thank God," I whispered to Max as the two of them went up the ramp toward the plane; the four of us watched until the plane took off. And of course, they wired us for more money so they could stay longer. They were eating and sleeping in the car. I had saved her again, and of course, I thought it was settled.

36

STILL, when I talk to her, she says the best thing in life is to be free. "You wouldn't have married Max if it hadn't been for me," she argues. "And I am glad I did," I answer; "now I love him. Where would I be without him? Absolutely lonely, waiting for you to call." But then she tells me, "This is no world for children, Mother." And the truth is, this is a rotten world. The first Yom Kippur we celebrated in our new apartment, someone came in and stole most of my pictures of my family, of Stajoe and me, sitting in front of the Café Europa, and I was wearing my big panama hat. It was a tragedy for me, a real tragedy. I had so little of them left. And they left some of the jewelry behind. But of course no one can take the memories that stick; my mother's face in the morning when we got up from the mud of Rosa Field, my father's face in the Botanical Gardens, Stajoe walking away from the ghetto like a tall, tall tree, Vera's whole stubborn body refusing to come with us when the Gestapo surrounded our block.

During the war, I never believed I was going to die. Not once did I believe it would happen to me. Sometimes I think it was because of that, and because I never thought about myself, always others, others, that I did survive. Now, I do not want to think so much about others. When I was young, I always felt safe. Now that I am old, I don't have that feeling. Sometimes, I think it was that I was so young, so attractive, so I was saved. Now I am not so attractive. No one can be attractive at fifty-two. It is dangerous to be old; it is dangerous to care about other people so much. For a long long time, I thought about going to a hypnotist. I knew others would laugh at me, but I thought, why not? Strange enough things have happened to me in my dreams, in the predictions of the Cabalist. Then I sat down to think about what I wanted him to erase. First, I thought I would want him to take away my obsession with the children. I would have peace. Then I thought no, that would not help. I wanted him to make me forget Stajoe. But would that be enough? No, I wanted him to make me forget the whole war; that terrible thing that killed everyone, that changed me so terribly. I began to get more enthusiastic. If I was really going to do it, I would have him make me forget everything up to the minute I came to this country. Everything. My parents, Rachel, my sister, Stajoe, the war, my parents' apartment. My first memory would be the feel of the concrete against my feet in front of the dock where the *Marine Perch* came to rest. I would not even remember the ship, or how I had gotten there. And since I pray in my own words, I prayed the hypnosis would work.

One day, without telling Max, I went to a man a customer had told me about. "He's a real doctor," she assured me; "he's even done experiments. You don't have to worry about him." So I went early one spring morning when the buds on the trees were still chartreuse and people were coming in and out of Central Park in shorts and halters, browning and beading with sweat. A little breeze stirred my hair, and I noticed how it didn't blow in the wind the way it used to, but lifted more heavily, because now, of course, it is bleached, and that has its effect, too. I sat in his elegant Chinese office for an hour. "I can't do it," he told me bluntly. "And I don't see why you want me to. This life is trouble," he said in a German accent, and I saw the blue numbers running down the inside of his forearm. "You'll just collect more and more of them." He was as old as I was. "The Jews get fewer, at least so I think, and what will you have left? At least now you have your memories." "My memories!" I cried. "But they are so terrible, and the good ones, there are so few of them for all the years." "Make more of them," he told me. I thought he was a cruel man; the war scarred so many people. Afterward they could not even feel at all, not even some of the time. "I won't be responsible for taking those away from you; even," he finished, "if it could be done. And," he said, "to be so beautiful, even at your age, I don't know what you're complaining about. *I* should be in such good shape." I asked him if he had the same kind of bad dreams, and he said naturally he did. I asked him if he had children, and he told me, no, he was afraid to have them. He had two before the war, he said, as though admitting it. So that was what the psychiatrist-hypnotist said. And he was probably right.

Then I decided I wanted to go to see two women in California who had been in my camp: Emma Spitzer and Annabella Lehmann. They hid when the Gestapo officers came down the line holding their children and looking for the mothers. They were saved and the children were killed. Someone came back and told me Emma had married a very rich man and gotten so fat no one would know she was the same person. She and her husband travel all the time; she has never had more children. I wish I could go talk to them about it. How could they leave their children? How do they live with themselves afterward? I cannot even leave my living child alone for one second. I would like to talk to them. I know I wouldn't judge them; I wouldn't ask the questions obvious enough to hurt them, I've come through too much for that. There were no normal lives during the war, no ethical lives. If there were ethical lives, and I believe mine was one, it was a matter of fate. It was my character: I had to stay with my Momma. It was Vera's character: she had to stay with Jakob. It was my mother's: she hid herself from me. And it was Stajoe's fate: he had to come after us. He could have taken the visa and left. But that was not his fate. And still, I wish the hypnotist would make me forget him.

Even Rachel is painful to remember. Every so often I used to get a letter from her. She stayed in Vilno and became a doctor; now she is married to Mischa Dudek. I am always happy for her, and then sorry for myself. In her last letter, she told me Vladek was still staying with them, but soon Vladek and his wife were moving out because they were about to have a third child. Rachel and Mischa have three of their own. "It was too crowded for him to live anywhere else all these years," she apologized, but I knew the truth. Poor Rachel, she still hasn't gotten used to her good nature. And I remember running back from medical school as if it were yesterday and calling her: "Rachel, come out, Rachel," and she would come out on the balcony in her nightgown. "You should be ashamed," I would call back to her, and dance back into the house. And who would have thought it? Rachel, who could not get out of bed? And Vladek is a doctor, too. So, if it is not a rotten world, it is a strange one. Now that Vilno is part of Lithuania, I only get letters when somebody goes into the country and brings them out. So it seems reasonable to me that Rachel should have survived. Her life means something, she is doing something with it. And she has two boys and one girl. The girl is as ugly and hopeless-looking as she once was, but Rachel is beautiful now with a wild kind of beauty. The older she gets the better she looks. Two gray wings of her hair sweep back from her cheeks. She wears her hair in an old-fashioned chignon; when it's loose it must cover her whole body, and even from the picture, I can feel her beaming.

So then, why was I saved? Always I felt this hand over me. Always, I was the lucky one. And to be chosen out of my whole family; I don't understand it. To spend all my time alone, or in the store, remembering tragedies. If I had had the second child, it might have been better. It might have started the normal parts of me up again, the way they inject medicine into a stopped heart to make it beat. Then I think, no, I am too attached. I would have been a slave to her, too. Yet, I have been a favorite all of my life. I was my father's favorite. Maybe that's why it's so hard for me now. For a long time, I thought all the old women who used to come to the store to talk and sell me things were just moving out of the city—it was so dangerous—that was why I never saw them. Now I realize they have died. Almost all of them have died. And sooner or later it will be my turn. I would like to do something, to understand, but I know I will not. Now it is my husband, Max, who is my biggest happiness; Max, and my dreams. The children are so cold; to think about them at all makes me cry. I love Ninushka more than anything in life, and it does no good. But more and more I review the past, the earlier days, and I think, comparing our days, and the days of young women today, positively I prefer my times. We were so happy; we dreamed. Everything was precious. My daughter does not have that. Few people have that.

I wish I could be more self-centered.

One day a friend came into the store and wanted to buy six stamps. She wanted to pay me for them; the letters were important to her. But I didn't want to take the money. So I said I only had two and I would give them to her. But I think she saw the roll in my desk drawer, and I wonder what she thinks of me? I'm so afraid of being cheated. And last night, Max finished eating, and before he was half through, I was trying to yank the dish from the table. It's not cleanliness, not that at all. The sight of empty dishes with eaten food, leftover food, frightens me to death. I don't know why; someone said it's a phobia.

And then after that, I had a dream about going to my cousin Regina's before she died. She didn't know me and I didn't know her. I ran into the kitchen and the maid was cooking some meat on the stove. I pulled out a bone with some meat on it and began running down the street; then I hid in an alley and ate it. I felt like a thief. And I would never learn to speak English properly. I speak like a Russian trying out a new language. If anyone asks me, I tell them I am Russian. Ninka has never understood why I want to sound and write like an illiterate. I can't tell her. And for a long time she was ashamed of me for it.

This month, we get our reparation money from the German goverment again. It pays our rent. Reparation money! What a concept! To pay for a whole world, nothing less than the globe my father's hand rested on, a whole world they destroyed. To pay for our dreams, the people we lost, our lives, like plants with roots dangling clotted with earth, walking, walking, walking from place to place. To pay for amputating lives. Oh, I am not the same person. I was a person who loved, who trusted, who never accepted defeat. And now I am not whole. There are chunks of flesh the war bit from me; my clothes cover them. And that, with all my vanity, is how I visualize myself. A monster. Not like others. And the guilt. If I had been able to save the others! But I was good for none of them in the end. Our whole world was destroyed, erased, as if it were less than a spelling lesson on the blackboard. We take the money. At least they don't have it. This is what we have come to. This.

Sometimes it seems as if it was only yesterday that I came running like crazy to the bank to tell my father about the medical school. I can still see the tears in his eyes. I can still feel the door in back of me opening and the people running in. People! There were so many! And I can still see myself sitting on the edge of Momma's bed; it is four o'clock in the morning and I am talking to her. No matter where I was, I used to bring her some candy. And how I told the boys, "I have to have something for Momma, or she would never fall asleep." But she would never fall asleep until I told her the whole story. It goes so fast, so fast. For one minute of pleasure, years of misery and pain.

And my daughter's children, why do I worry about them so? They are not mine; they are hers. I have had my time of suffering and paying and trying to survive. They

614

have their own parents. They are lucky with each other, but they are my obsession. The best part of life is childhood; I began it in a tissue, a caul. The doctor told my Momma that made me a lucky person. Ninushka was born with a tissue covering her head. And in the beginning, she did have less luck than I did. But perhaps she will catch up. The worst part of my life is over. I should enjoy the rest. So Max says. "Why torture yourself?" he asks me. And my only answer is that I cannot help it; it is my miserable, miserable disposition. I am absolutely changed. "Where is my smile?" So he asks me.

So it seem like yesterday I am running to my father. And now I am having more and more dreams, strange dreams. Two nights ago, I dreamed a great orange flood came out of my body smelling like oranges, but when I looked down, there was no cut, no opening, nothing. I was frightened, but I was not frightened. "What is it?" I kept asking myself. "It smells so nice; almost like perfume." And the night before, I dreamed I saw Ninushka sitting in the front seat of her car with a tiny little baby, a newborn baby. It must mean something; dreams always do.

And last night, I had a very nice dream, a very long dream. It has been a long time since Stajoe came to me in them, so I am not so afraid to sleep. I was in the big apartment of my parents, and they had decided to move. "Where are you moving?" I asked Poppa. "Oh, you will love it, Anyushka," he told me. "The house has a big garden, with nice flowers, and one tree which grows expecially big cherries, I never saw such big cherries. Oh, your mother will have so much to do; she will make a lot of cherry wine." He was so joyful, and so pleased; his smile never left his face. Momma was busy packing the household. "We will take *everything*, Anzia," she insisted. "We've had these things so long it would be a sin to leave them; they're like family." And Anzia flew about smiling, and running to the wood market to hire workmen to build the special crates. Momma was singing the song about the butterfly, and from the back, Vera's music poured into the house with the sunlight.

Then we were in the new house; it was in the country, like the *dacha*, but it was a mansion. There was a huge, curving staircase going to the second floor and parquet floors and stained glass windows and everything had been painted before we came. Drapes were already hung up by the superintendent. And then I dreamed a very very long table, all with goodies that Momma baked, poppy seeds, full of everything. "What is it, Poppa," I asked, "a party?" "Certainly, a party," he said; "a new house, there is always a party." Then Mischa and Emmanuel were fighting over where the furniture in their room should go. "It reminds me of a story," Poppa said, "about three friends who decided to pull a wagon. One was a swan, and one was a fish, and one was a crayfish. The swan wanted to fly in the air, and the fish wanted to swim in the water, and the crayfish wanted to go backward, and" Poppa said, pausing, "the wagon is still there, to this very day, but it has turned to stone." Then I went into Vera's room. She was in bed, and the bed was all white and clean; she was a very immaculate girl. "What are you reading?" I asked her. "I'm waiting for Jakob to come," she answered. I understood. She didn't want me to stay because she would be shy; she had such respect and love for me. "Is he coming soon?" I asked. "In about ten minutes." So I stayed another two minutes, and kissed her and went out.

It was such a wonderful dream, I didn't want it to end. But automatically when I woke up, I looked in the window, and they all vanished. And then I fell back asleep and had another dream. I was climbing very high on a ladder to reach my little brother. He had climbed to the top, but I knew it wasn't safe, because there was no wall for the ladder to rest against. I grabbed him, but then, at the last minute, he disappeared from my hands. And when I looked in the window, this vanished, too. But now I can picture the new house as clearly as the camps, or the ghetto, or the apartment we live in now where I sell everything we get that is valuable because I don't like valuable things in the house, or the old apartment where everyone came for the wonderful, wonderful parties. Orchard Street, fourteen cents a pound.

And when I am in the store, I am very lonely, in spite of Max, in spite of the children, in spite of the dreams, and so I am putting my feelings on paper. Paper has patience; therefore I am putting my feelings on paper. And more and more I have this feeling I cannot get rid of, that I will dream about the house, and when I turn to the window, they will not vanish; they will be there.